the Fallen Nightingale

a novel

John W. Milton

Swan Books
Beaver's Pond Press, Inc.
Edina, Minnesota

Photo of Enrique Granados, from the Ernest Schelling Collection, International Piano Archives, University of Maryland

Photo of John W. Milton by Sandi of Afton Woods

Photo of Douglas Riva, from the pianist's files

ISBN 1-59298-071-6

Library of Congress Catalog Number: 2004107767

Book design and typesetting: Mori Studio
Cover design: Mori Studio

Printed in the United States of America

First Printing: December 2004

07 06 05 04 6 5 4 3 2 1

Swan Books is an imprint of Beaver's Pond Press, Inc.

Beaver's Pond Press, Inc.

7104 Ohms Lane, Suite 216
Edina, MN 55439
(952) 829-8818
www.BeaversPondPress.com

To order, visit www.BookHouseFulfillment.com or call 1-800-901-3480. Reseller and special sales discounts available.

To my wife, Maureen Angélica Acosta,
who believed in this journey as much as I

Enrique Granados i Campiña
(1867–1916)

Table of

Contents

Catalunya Map

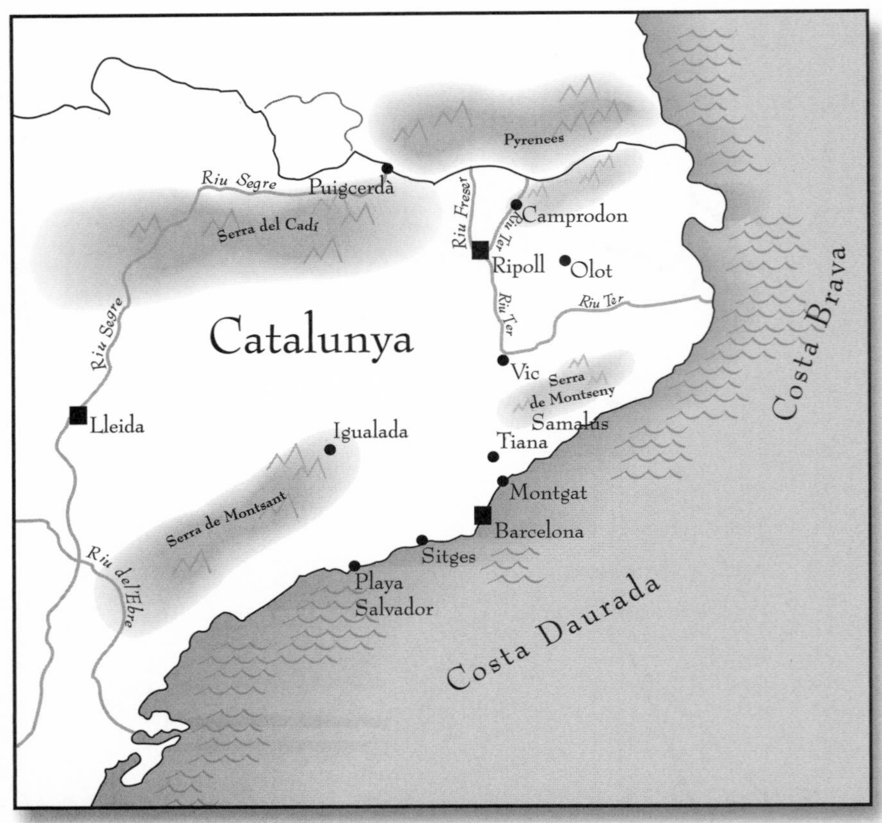

Barcelona–capital city where Granados lived from 1874 to 1915

Camprodon–Pyrenees village where Albéniz was born in 1860

Costa Brava–Mediterranean coast from Montgat to French border

Costa Daurada–Mediterranean coast from Ebre delta to Montgat

Igualada–textile center NW of Barcelona, hometown of Godó family

Lleida–small city NW of Barcelona, Granados' birthplace in 1867

Montgat–seacoast village east of Barcelona on rail line to France

Olot–rural Catalan town in foothills of the Pyrenees

Playa Salvador–beach west of Barcelona, Casals' vacation home

Puigcerdà–vacation place on French border in the Pyrenees

Ripoll–industrial city at end of rail line from Barcelona to Puigcerdà

Samalús–hamlet NE of Barcelona, S. Salvador de Terrades hermitage

Sitges–seacoast village west of Barcelona where Rusiñol had retreat

Tiana–village NE of Barcelona where Clotilde Godó lived

Vic–village on rail line from Barcelona to Puigcerdà

Rivers (rius):

Riu del'Ebre
Riu Freser
Riu Segre
Riu Ter

Mountain ranges (serras):

Pyrenees
Serra del Cadí
Serra de Montsant
Serra de Montseny

Barcelona Map

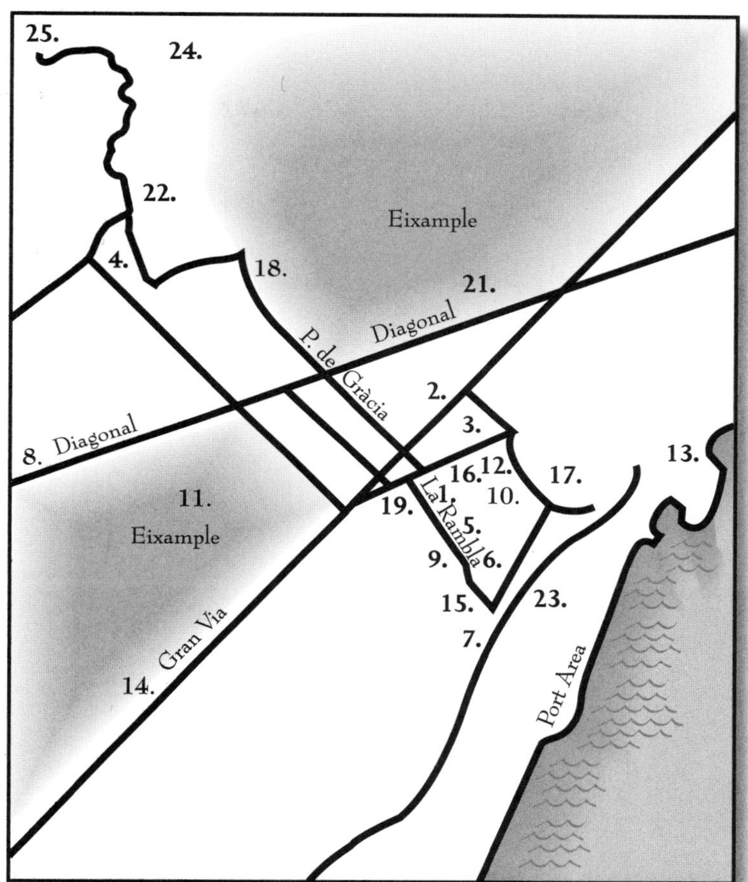

1. Granados music academy and family residence, first location
2. music academy and residence, second location
3. Girona, 20—academy and residence, third location
4. Andreu residence, Sant Gervasi
5. Café de l'Ópera—gathering place for opera people
6. Can Culleretes—restaurant favored by Albéniz and Granados
7. Christófer Colom—statue of the "discoverer" of the Americas
8. Diagonal—a principal avenue, running SE to NW
9. El Liceu—principal opera house, built in 1856
10. Quatre Gats—gathering place for young bohemians
11. Eixample—where Barcelona expanded in late 19th century
12. Church of Sant Pere—where Granados was married in 1892
13. Estació França—embarkation for train travelers to Europe
14. Gran Via—a principal avenue, running SW to NE
15. La Rambla—boulevard connecting waterfront and l'Eixample
16. Palau de la Música—concert hall, orchestral and choral music
17. Parc de la Ciutadella and Zoo—site of Exposition of 1889
18. Passeig de Gràcia—major avenue in l'Eixample
19. Plaça de Catalunya—main public square, transportation hub
21. Sagrada Familia—Gaudí's cathedral
22. Sala Granados—recital hall and classrooms
23. Set Portes—restaurant near the port area
24. Tibidabo—mountain overlooking Barcelona
25. Vallvidrera—village on the northern edge of Barcelona

Author's Foreword

This is the story of pianist and composer Enrique Granados (1867–1916) during the last seventeen years of his life. In my six years of research, many previously unknown facts relating to Granados' life have been unearthed. I've concluded that his story is most faithfully told in the form of a novel, rather than in a conventional biography.

The characters, based on persons who lived during his time, are portrayed through the eyes of Granados. Some of them–Pablo Picasso, Enrico Caruso, and U.S. President Woodrow Wilson–still enjoy widespread recognition. Others–notably Pablo Casals, Isaac Albéniz, Manuel de Falla, Jan Paderewski, Fritz Kreisler, Anais Nin, and Joaquin Sorolla–were known best in the late 19th and 20th centuries. Still others, including several who were most important in Granados' life, are now mostly unknown and forgotten. With such a rich and varied cast of real characters, it was necessary to introduce only four fictional ones, all of them minor, to fill gaps in the narrative.

Most events in this novel take place in Catalunya, a region that includes northeastern Spain and southwestern France. Its largest urban center is Barcelona, where Granados lived and worked most of his life. Catalan, the region's language, is of the Romance family, similar to but distinctly different than both French and Castilian (Spanish). The origins of both Catalan and Castilian are rooted in Latin, but in different Roman settlements, the blending of Latin with disparate indigenous languages resulted in two distinct modern languages.

Catalunya existed as an independent kingdom, aligned with the region of Aragon, as early as the 9th century. Catalan autonomy declined sharply in the

15th century: through a process that has been widely disparaged, the Anti-Pope Benedict XIII selected a Castilian prince, Fernando, to be king of Aragon and Catalunya. Shortly thereafter, the marriage of Fernando and Isabella of Castile consolidated the area that is now known as Spain. Since then, Catalans have been part of this larger nation whose capital is Madrid, enjoying varying degrees of autonomy. The relationship between Barcelona and Madrid has often been characterized by rivalry, interdependence, and resentment.

After the War of the Spanish Succession in the early 18th century in which most Catalans backed the losing side, much of their political autonomy was revoked by the Bourbon dynasty, and political power was further centralized in Madrid. Castilian was installed as the official language and Catalan universities were closed. But the language survived in its daily, vernacular form.

Catalunya has prospered economically, accounting for a large proportion of Spain's industry, agriculture, and trade. Its energy, entrepreneurship, and orientation to the larger economy of the Mediterranean were recognized from the late 17th century on, providing a sharp contrast with the class-stratified quiescence and isolation that often prevailed in much of the remainder of Spain. By the 19th century, Barcelona had become one of the major economic centers of Mediterranean Europe.

From the period 1808–14, when Napoleon Bonaparte ruled Spain, through the early 20th century, Catalans resisted control by the central government and the Roman Catholic Church with which it was aligned. Outbreaks of violence against these powers were common. With the emergence of syndicalism and anarchism in the late 19th century, Barcelona was a site of frequent bombings, burning of churches and convents, and assassinations–followed by harsh repression.

Emboldened by Catalunya's 19th century economic success, a growing interest in Catalanism was expressed in the evolution of its politics as well as in renewal of Catalan literature. As in Ireland–also controlled by a larger empire–this took the form of poetry, often blended with the performing arts. If Catalunya could not win political independence from Madrid, at least it could create its own cultural autonomy.

What followed, in the late 19th and early 20th centuries, was an explosion of cultural expression known as "la renaixença." Though Barcelona remained in the second echelon of cultural centers, its artistic, business, and political leaders envisioned that some day it would rival Paris, Vienna, and London. But once again, during the dictatorship of Primo de Rivera in the 1920s, political autonomy and artistic freedom were suppressed. Both the Catalan flag and the national dance, the sardana, were outlawed, though they were again restored under the short-lived Spanish Republic of the early 1930s.

When the forces of General Francisco Franco won the Civil War in 1939, drastic measures were taken to bring Catalunya–which had largely sided with the Republicans–back into the fold. Thousands of Catalans were shot without trial; tens of thousands were deported, or fled into exile. Catalunya lost its status as an autonomous region and was broken into four smaller provinces. Publications in the Catalan language were forbidden, and it could not be taught or used in schools (though this was relaxed in the 1960s when it was allowed to be taught as a "foreign" language). Artists such as Picasso, Miró, and Dalí were anathema. Some music teachers were jailed simply because they assigned their students the music of composers who were influenced by folk songs of Catalunya, including Granados and Isaac Albéniz.

When Franco died on November 20, 1975, Catalunya celebrated. Catalan flags came out of hiding, streets and plazas were filled with sardana dancers, and the language–which had survived once again through daily conversation–soon appeared in newspapers, radio, television, and books.

Enrique Granados, the consummate artist, was not politically inclined; in fact, he abhorred mixing art and politics. He considered himself as Catalan as anyone, but resisted pressure to glorify Catalunya in his compositions. Because much of his music was inspired by people and locations in other parts of Spain, Granados has never been widely revered in Catalunya, where he was born and spent most of his life.

The fate of Granados' musical legacy may be better understood by comparing the rivalry between Barcelona and Madrid with that of two other pairs of cities: Dublin and London, and Quebec City and Toronto. Their differences are not merely linguistic, rather they reflect the larger political and cultural differences between very distinct peoples.

Throughout his life, Granados experienced the alienation of an outsider–in Paris, in New York, in Madrid, and even in the place he called home: Barcelona.

Principal

Barcelona and Madrid.

Enrique Granados i Campiña (Enric, 'Ric)
Clotilde Godó Pelegrí—student of Granados
Pablo Casals (Pau)—cellist and friend of Granados from adolescence
Amparo Gal de Granados (Titín)—Granados' València-born wife
Carmen Miralles de Andreu—friend and confidante
Dr. Salvador Andreu i Grau—Carmen's husband, pharmacist, patron
Isaac Albéniz ('Saco, 'Saquito)—composer, colleague, close friend
Enric Morera—composer and rival
Frank Marshall—Granados' assistant, later his successor
María Oliveró—student of Granados
María Ojeda—student of Granados
Fernando Periquet—writer, Goya enthusiast, opera librettist
Paquita Madriguera—one of Granados' most talented students
Francisca Rodón—Paquita's mother
Antonia Mercé—ballet, flamenco, and interpretive dancer

Paris and Céligny (Switzerland)

Joaquim Malats ('Quinito)—pianist from Barcelona, close friend
Fritz Kreisler—popular violinist, composer
Tórtola València—celebrated interpretive dancer
Ernest Schelling (Henry, Henri)—American pianist, composer
Jan Paderewski—world famous pianist, later President of Poland
Robert and Mildred Bliss—U.S. diplomat and wife, assigned to Paris
Jacques Rouché—general director, Paris Opera

New York

Giulio Gatti-Casazza—impresario, Metropolitan Opera
Malvina Hoffman—sculptress, student of Auguste Rodin
Enrico Caruso—world-famous operatic tenor
Archer Huntington—founder of the Hispanic Institute of America

Washington, D.C.

Juan Riaño y Gayangos—ambassador of Spain to the U.S.A.
President Woodrow Wilson—28th President of the U.S.A.

England and English Channel

Ismael Smith—Catalan sculptor and friend
Henri Mouffet—captain of SS *Sussex*
Wilder Penfield—Rhodes Scholar and medical student at Oxford
James Mark Baldwin—world-renowned professor of psychology

PART I

Chapter One

Tiana, July 1977

The piano student looks through a black iron gate at a small chapel, its umber walls weathered and bold against the sky; she pushes the gate, which creaks as it swings open. How unusual: a private chapel for this villa, a curious token from the past. For Núria Planas, about to celebrate her nineteenth birthday, it's a souvenir of a time that she knows only from history books and her family gatherings. Old men cursing the dictator Franco, and recounting the barbarities of the Spanish Civil War. In Núria's family, only the old women go to church.

Núria looks back at the woman who sat next to her on the bus from Barcelona, who told her of a notable pianist living in this village of Tiana, who showed her the way to this ivory villa, anchored to the uphill side of the village and overlooking the waters where the Costa Daurada and the Costa Brava overlap far below.* A pianist with a grand piano, said the woman on the bus, a patroness who brings in the finest musicians from Barcelona, a very old woman who'd been alone as long as anyone could remember.

Looking back through the gate, Núria sees the woman waving her forward. "No need to be afraid," the woman said, "Doña Cloti loves to talk about music. She's delighted with visitors." Núria tightens the band securing her waist-length russet hair and bites her lower lip. She's inside the gate and it's too late to turn back. She creeps toward the villa's portico.

After two tentative rounds of knocking, an ancient man opens the massive front door; the jacket of his black suit is buttoned. He listens without expression as Núria explains why she's come to Tiana, nods when she tells him she's a student at the Conservatory of Barcelona. A pianist.

---

* See Map 1: Catalunya

His face brightens. "Ah, sí. Una pianista." She cannot discern from his shrug whether there's been an endless parade of pianists knocking on that enormous door. Or–her worst fear–that she's the first.

"I'm writing a paper about the composer Isaac Albéniz," she explains. "They say he once lived here in Tiana. Long ago. He was also a famous–"

"Sí, sí. A fine pianist. And of course a famous composer. Doña Cloti knew him personally. She speaks very highly of Albéniz. Though he died many, many years ago."

Núria nods, holding her breath. Albéniz died sixty-eight years ago. This old woman knew him. Perhaps coming here was not such a foolish idea, as her friends tried to portray it.

"I will tell her you are here," the old man says. "Please be seated."

Núria stands by a massive wooden chair in the entryway, looking around in a space that is larger than the entire apartment where she lives with her father and two younger brothers in the modest Esquerra section of Barcelona. And larger by far than the flat in the seedy Barrí Xinès district where her fiancé, violin student Carles Pujol, lives. With a scholarship and her job in a café near the Plaça* Catalunya, Núria can afford to study at the conservatory. Her father is a professor at the university, but the Planas family lives in a different realm than this.

There's a marble-topped table next to the front door. A tall wooden cross stands on the table, and a newspaper lies next to the cross. Even from across the tiled floor, she recognizes the Barcelona daily *La Vanguardia*. To Núria, it's the newspaper of the Franco regime and the Spanish monarchy, printed in Castilian, known for its editorials against greater autonomy for Catalunya, and rarely seen at the university.

In contrast to morning traffic in Barcelona, the laboring engine of the bus climbing out of the city, and the buzzing of people on the narrow streets of Tiana, this place is utterly silent. Núria's still perspiring from the round-about route taken by the woman from the bus: up the avenue named for Isaac Albéniz, past the restaurant where he once gave a recital. Cooling off in the entryway, Núria straightens her sleeveless blouse and adjusts her bra, touching the fabric where it's soaked with sweat from climbing the hot cobblestone streets of Tiana in mid-summer. She blows her finger tips dry.

The silence is broken only by a sporadic clatter of pans in the kitchen and a radio broadcast of today's game of fútbol. Still, so peaceful here, compared with life back in the city. What a fine place to practice the piano! The old

---

* For this and other Catalan and Castilian words, see Glossary.

man descends the grand staircase, escorting a short gray-haired woman, whose bright eyes scrutinize Núria as she crosses the entryway.

"Buenos días, and welcome. I am Clotilde Godó Pelegrí. And who are you, my dear, come to visit me this fine day?" She comes closer, with a smiling show of fine white teeth. The woman's voice is crisp with a lofty Castilian austerity. The language of the empire, Núria's father would call it. The language of Franco. And the only language she was permitted to learn in school–until Franco died two years ago.

"I am Núria Planas, senyora. I study piano at the Conservatori. I was told you might not be offended if I came to your home."

"Offended? No, not offended, my dear. I am purely delighted you've come! Vicente tells me you're interested in Albéniz," Clotilde says, gesturing toward the ancient man, who's now retreating toward the kitchen and the fútbol broadcast.

"Yes. You see, I'm working on a paper about Albéniz–his contribution to Catalan music, and my professor thought it a good idea to come to Tiana."

Clotilde frowns. "Did you say, Catalan music?"

Núria is startled, but recovers. "Oh, senyora, I mean the music of Barcelona and Catalunya–and the music of all of España."

Clotilde lets the young student stumble, having intended to startle her. To Clotilde, there seem to be Catalan flags everywhere since the death of Franco, whom she supported. Everyone's speaking Catalan again, every utterance has to be pure, one hundred percent Catalan. Apparently this young student is swept up in the fervor. But Clotilde believes it's wrong to put the music of Albéniz in that category, wrong to say he was a Catalan composer. "Do you know we have an Avenida Isaac Albéniz in Tiana?" she asks her visitor.

"Yes, senyora. I met a woman on the bus, and she took me there. She showed me the restaurant where Albéniz played. L'avi Mingo."

"It's now called L'avi Mingo, but it *was* the Café Giral when Albéniz was here to play with Joaquín Malats. On the last day of the village festival, in 1906. When Albéniz told me he was working on a piano suite which he called *Iberia*. Or was it *Azulejos*? No, that was later–when he was dying."

"Did you say, *Azulejos*?" asks Núria. "That's the very piece I've been learning!"

"Then you must play it for me."

Núria shakes her head. "No, senyora. I'm not ready to play it publicly."

Clotilde shrugs. "Of course. I know the piece is difficult. But I'm only asking you to play a little bit of it. For me, privately. And, my dear, you don't have to speak so loudly–my ears are very old, to be sure, but they still work well enough. Not perfect pitch, no, but I never had that. Now come with me–would you like café?"

They are seated at one end of a large oval table in the dining room, waiting for the ancient maid, Matilde, to bring café. Núria describes how she came to be interested in Isaac Albéniz. Her mother's family came from the mountain village of Camprodon, where Albéniz was born; Núria's maternal grandfather, Antoni Jardí, played cello in Camprodon's chamber group and once met Albéniz himself; and Grandfather Jardí regaled Núria with stories about Camprodon and its most famous progeny. So when she was assigned to write a paper about a Catalan composer, she was predisposed toward the one who came from her mother's village. "That wasn't such a foolish reason, was it?" she asks.

Clotilde watches her closely. At this age, she too was a piano student–until succumbing to her mother's exhortations to marry the young banker, Lluís Marsans. To relinquish any ambition for a musical career and become a wife in a loveless marriage and a mother whose only children, a boy and girl, both died in infancy. Clotilde reaches over and touches Núria's hand. "No, my dear. Your grandfather was of Camprodon, as was Albéniz, and that's not foolish at all."

Núria is touched. "Thank you, senyora."

Clotilde hopes the young woman can relax and feel welcome. A fresh pair of ears, someone who hasn't heard all the stories. But the differences between them are striking. This girl is careful and withdrawn, while according to her own father, Clotilde was "the most exhuberant girl in the world." Between them there's an interval of seven decades: from the culture and politics of Barcelona when Clotilde was young, through the deep, bitter divisions of the war years, and now–with the death of Franco–to a newly reborn Catalunya. So many differences. Yet, do they really matter? Just now, at this moment, aren't they simply two women who love music, waiting for their café? "That's a wedding ring?" she asks.

Núria hesitates. It was her late mother's wedding ring, and she put it on her ring finger when she agreed to Carles' proposal. "No. I'm not married, senyora, but I have un promès."

"Ah, sí. You have un novio," Clotilde replies, offering a gentle correction to the young woman's use of Catalan.

Núria bristles, hearing an implicit critique. She wonders if this old woman understands what it's like to be forbidden to speak one's own language on the street, not being able to learn how to read and write it in school, what it's like to have a father who is a language teacher but could not teach Catalan here in Catalunya, who had to go to Saskatchewan in Canada to teach it, had to leave his family here for two years. "Yes, I have un novio," she says.

Clotilde sweetens her tone, sensing the young woman's discomfort. "And who is this young man?"

"He's–he's a violinist. His name is Carles Pujol."

"And is he a good violinist?"

"Well, not yet. But I believe he will be. Some day."

Clotilde hears romantic pride in Núria's wavering voice. These young men and women today, they fall in love and if they stay together perhaps then they'll marry! In Tiana only a few of them say their vows at the church, the rest go off to the town hall and get themselves married by a judge. Yet, there's a note of tenderness in Núria's voice for the young violinist. After a moment Clotilde asks, "And where does your father's family come from?"

At first, Núria senses a challenge, but Clotilde's eyes seem only curious. She's amazed that the old woman remembers so much, even things that happened in 1906–the year Núria's grandfather was born. Clotilde is a marvel, a true discovery. Núria raises her demitasse and replies that her father's family, the Planases, are from Igualada.

Clotilde leans across the table. "Igualada!"

"Yes, senyora. Do you know where it is?"

"My dear, I was born there! My father was born there. All the Godós come from Igualada. Oh! And *your* father's family is from Igualada?"

"Yes, and I remember going there many times to visit my grandmother. You see, my grandfather was killed in the Guerra Civil. But before the war he worked for the textile factory in Igualada. I think it was the 'Igualadina Cotonera.'"

Clotilde's eyes open wide. "What wonders! That textile factory belonged to my father. My father was Ramón Godó."

"I do not know, senyora. I never knew my grandfather. I simply know he worked for that textile factory, and then he joined the Republican army. That was the end of his story."

"Oh. I am sorry! I imagine your grandfather was a fine man, and believed in what he was fighting for. War is so horrible–for everyone! For three years when the war was here, I had to leave my home. The Republicans wanted it, and my family was sympathetic with the monarchy, so they came here and told me to leave. They didn't harm me, but they killed several of the monks and nuns–right here in Tiana! And when I came back after the war, they'd taken some of my most precious things. No matter what you believe in, war is a waste. A dreadful waste of lives! It was such a destructive time for all of us in España. For your family, as surely as for mine."

Núria cannot think of anything to add. She takes a deep breath and changes the subject: "Senyora, would you tell me more about Isaac Albéniz? Who he was, what kind of man. What it was like to be with him. I've never known people like Albéniz, famous people, people with his creative genius. As you have. How did he compose so much beautiful music when he spent so much time performing? With a family too. And I've been told he was seriously ill for most of his last years. How could he have the energy and inspiration to write a masterpiece such as *Iberia*? I'd be very grateful if you could help me understand these things."

Clotilde is touched by Núria's modesty and sincerity. "My dear, I'll try to help you understand so you can write your paper. So you'll begin to know what kind of time that was. For Albéniz, and for the others. We had a special kind of renaissance here at that time, and though there were so many fine musicians in Barcelona, there were just a few of authentic genius."

"Oh, yes. On the way the woman from the bus showed me a plaque in the restaurant that tells about a concert of Albéniz and Joaquim Malats. Did you also know Malats?"

"My dear, I knew all of them: Albéniz, Malats, Falla–though he was from Cádiz. And Pablo Casals. And of course my own maestro, Enrique Granados."

Núria imagines them from photos she's seen in the national library. Dark suits, dark hats, dark beards or bushy dark moustaches, dark eyes. Photos full of shadows dark as slate. She hears shadows in the old woman's voice, and wonders how this can be. How, on this bright summer day? Núria says, "I've heard of them, all of them. But not so very much about Granados."

"No, you wouldn't have heard as much about him," Clotilde replies. "Not about Granados. Well, come with me."

They walk through a parlor that extends deep inside the villa. It reminds Núria of a school tour of the royal palace at Pedralbes, built for the last king before the Civil War, Alfonso XIII. The high-ceilinged room is full of mammoth, dark credenzas, chairs and tables, gilt-framed mirrors, religious paintings, and tapestries. All dust covered, signifying this part of the villa is seldom, perhaps never used. Every fine piece is of epic scale, shrinking the solitary matriarch walking by her side. There were no fine pieces where Núria grew up, yet she enjoys wandering through the shops along Carrer de Montcada. She loves to fancy what it would be like, sitting in majestic chairs down the street from the Picasso museum, with images of nearby Cubist and Blue Period women etched in her memory, and wafts of old leather and dust in her nose.

"This is such a big place," Clotilde explains, "and I'm the only one left to enjoy it. Of course, Matilde is still with me, though she's so very old, and her arthritis is so very painful. She can hardly get around. And her husband Vicente, whom I rarely need to drive me any more, he does the errands, and listens to fútbol on the radio. The young girl Conchita comes over from the village of Alella to cook. And Elena, the darling granddaughter of my brother Pompeyo comes to visit with her husband Àngel. But mostly it's just me and the Virgin."

Núria turns her head. "The Virgin?"

"Yes, the Dark Virgin of Montserrat. I have a statue of her, a copy of the original, right here in my own little chapel. She watches over me."

"Yes, senyora." The little chapel that caught her eye as she opened the gate.

"You see," Clotilde says with a sweeping gesture toward the room full of treasures, "there are so many, many antiques in this place." She stops and points to a gold cross around her neck and the wrinkled skin visible above her pale green dress. "I don't suppose you like antiques."

"Oh, yes, I do," Núria answers.

"Splendid. Then you'll surely like me!" Clotilde has the tinkling laugh of a young woman.

Beyond the double doors of the parlor is a room bathed in midday light. It is bare except for a grand piano, directly ahead, and a chair between the piano and a tall, louvered window that allows a pattern of striped sunlight to fall onto the tiled floor. Clotilde asks Núria to raise the cover of the piano, and the young woman notices the instrument is cracked from exposure to the sun. "Would you honor me by playing a piece?" asks Clotilde. "It may be slightly out of tune, especially since Flavio died. He was my tuner for many years."

Núria's mind is circling. What can she play? Dare she play the piece by Albéniz? The very difficult one, *Azulejos*? She could just play the opening. But does she know it well enough? She walks around to the keyboard.

"It's a Pleyel," Clotilde says. "Selected personally by Maestro Granados, in Paris. There, you see his signature?"

There are two signatures. The more legible one is by Juli Pons. Núria asks who that is.

"Juli? Oh, a friend of mine. A fine pianist. Also a student of Granados. He was the last one to play on this piano, and he's been dead three years. No, look over here," she says, pointing to a larger, less distinct autograph.

The old woman's finger points to the right of the word "Pleyel." Núria deciphers the large gold "E" and the down-and-up tails of the "q" and the "d." She notices the lower stroke of the "E" is extended all the way under the signature to the final "s" and she presumes he fashioned that "E" at the end of his signature. After seeing that name, heard only in the most cursory way during her course in music history, hearing the faint tremolo in Clotilde's voice when she says "Maestro Granados," and remembering her muted promise, Núria feels compelled to play the opening of Albéniz' piece *Azulejos*.

She waits for Clotilde to be seated in the chair and begins: the slow opening with the right hand, now softer with the left, leading to the initial theme, which climbs to the top octave and teases its way up and down before the theme rises with the left hand, now with more pedal, then fading away before rising to a rhythmic incantation, and then the theme again, and now the sweet lyricism of the theme again, as if reminding the listener of hope yielding to melancholy, then achingly slow, dancing to resolution. Núria stops. The next part is more difficult; she's not ready. She shakes her head and looks toward the old woman.

Clotilde's eyes are closed over a pair of tears. With the first notes of *Azulejos*, she experiences a torrent of memories. Music so familiar, like the beating of her heart, though she only heard Granados play it a few times, early that summer of 1910. She's impressed by the young woman's earnest effort, and proud of her own restraint when Núria does not use the pedal properly. That brings more tears, as she remembers the time she first played for the maestro at his Acadèmia Granados. One of the preludes of Chopin, the piece she'd played to win the prize competition at the Colegio de las Damas Negras, the one she played with such confidence. But the maestro reached down with his amazingly large hands and stopped her. He told her bluntly, "That is all very bad–you have to change everything." He told her the position of her hands was all wrong; he told her if she was going to play a pianoforte–not an organ–then she'd better learn to use the pedal. His words stung, burning and engraved forever in her heart, and though the audition erased her pride from becoming the best pianist at the colegio, she accepted the critique without letting him see a single tear, though later there were many, and she resolved to change everything–if that was what the maestro wanted from her.

"That is truly an elegant piece," Clotilde says to Núria, "and I know it's very difficult. But you are brave, and I feel your passion for music. I know you'll work hard. Some day you'll play it with great distinction. To get there, I'd start with the pedal."

Núria smiles. "Thank you–for letting me play this piano."

"Did you know that Albéniz died before he finished that piece, and before dying he asked Granados to finish it? That was in 1909, and when he finished,

Granados offered Joaquim Malats the first chance to play it, but then, soon after, Malats also died. If you'd look at the cover page of your score for *Azulejos*, you'll see the note in French: 'Oeuvre posthume terminé par E. Granados.'"

Núria has enough French to understand. "Granados? He and Albéniz and Malats were friends?"

"Oh, mercy yes!"

"And Granados was your maestro?" Núria asks.

"He was. Until the day he left."

"He left?"

"Yes. He went to New York for the world premiere of his opera." Clotilde's voice fades.

"He was an excellent maestro?"

"Not simply that. He founded an academy of music–the most celebrated in all of España. He was the only one–of Albéniz, Falla, Viñes, Malats–who was truly devoted to teaching others how to play properly. He was–" Clotilde leaves the sentence unfinished.

Núria musters the courage to say, "There's so much I don't know about that time. So much, and it was so long ago. And, senyora, it was not easy to get my professor's approval to do a paper on Albéniz. He did not think Albéniz was truly Catalan. Oh, Enric Morera, yes. And Pau Casals, of course, the world's greatest cellist. 'But why Albéniz?' he asked me. He stared at me, making me feel bad and fearful of asking him a second time: could I please do a paper on Albéniz? But I asked him anyway, and I changed the idea behind it–I said I'd study the impact of Albéniz on Catalan music. By then, I'd fallen in love with his music, with *Rumores de la Caleta*, with *Iberia*, and I didn't want to give up my idea. My professor kept saying Albéniz wasn't truly Catalan. I persisted, and finally he agreed."

"Oh, that's nonsense! Albéniz simply fell out of favor during the war. How dreadful–the Republicans renamed the street with his name, right here in Tiana, right here where Albéniz came for the summers, where his daughter Laura was born! They changed it to Avinguda Francesc Macià, after a Republican politician. How absurd! I was at mass praying for the soul of Maestro Granados on his birthday, July twenty-seventh in 1936, when they arrived in their military trucks. I came out and saw the church was surrounded by the men of Tiana, who kept the militia from burning it down. So those devils went up to the monastery on the hill and killed three monks. What criminals! Yes, and that day was *this* day, July twenty-seventh. His birthday."

"That seems so very cruel!" Núria replies, "There are some things, like art and music, which perhaps should not be mixed with politics. I consider myself as Catalan as anyone–my grandfather was killed fighting for the República–but for me music comes from deeper within us than politics. It comes from the heart and soul!"

Clotilde steps forward, leans over, and embraces the young woman–a warm abraçada. "Yes. You're right. Your words could have come from the very mouth of Granados."

Núria is surprised by the old woman's sentimentality. She looks down at the sheet music above the keyboard of the piano, and alongside it a black-and-white sketch, depicting a man kneeling before a woman. The music belongs to this cracked piano and this deteriorating villa. The music is ancient yet somehow still pristine, without any of the telltale creases and rips and stains so characteristic of sheet music that has been played over and over again. Núria stares at it, wanting to graze it with her finger tips as she reads the printed words on the front cover: "E. Granados *GOYESCAS* 1a. Parte de Los Majos Enamorados 1911."

"This *Goyescas* is the masterpiece of Maestro Granados," Clotilde says, sitting beside Núria on the piano bench. "What you see is a copy. The original was taken by the Republicans when they occupied my house! But I had this copy made as a precaution, and thank God for that. You may look at it," she adds.

Núria reaches up and lifts the sheet music from the piano. She opens it very carefully, fearful of staining or tearing it. There's an inscription inside the front cover: "To Clotilde Godó. Greetings from your maestro. Enrique Granados. In Barcelona, June of the year 1911." She smiles, recognizing the signature. There is also the number "2" above the inscription. She asks what that signifies.

Clotilde answers in a low voice. "In those days, composers would issue special editions, to people they wanted to honor. Such as family members, close friends, patrons, or others of importance. They would have fifty copies made and no more."

"So this was copy Number Two? This one he signed for you? This was Number Two?" Núria is self conscious about her repetition.

Clotilde hesitates. "Yes. I suppose it was because I was one of his favorite students. Or at least then, at the time of this composition."

Sensing a fragile moment, Núria waits before asking, "Would you tell me what kind of teacher he was, this Maestro Granados?"

"Ooooh, he was very strict! Everything had to be just right, or he'd send you back to work. You would work, work, work on it until everything was just right. He didn't care how long that took, just so you finally mastered it. Sometimes when he played a piece–to show me what he meant by 'just right'–I'd notice he didn't play it the same as he had the time before. Of course, I didn't dare ask him why it was always different. Ah, he was very demanding, but also so very gentle! And generous, and forgiving. I'd do anything to see his eyes open wide and see his smile when I played it just right. I'd do anything for that!"

"And would you know who received copy Number One?"

"Oh, yes. That was Alfonso."

"Alfonso?"

"Forgive me, my dear. His Royal Majesty, King Alfonso XIII of España."

Núria is stunned. Once again, she hears the dusky rasp in Clotilde's voice, and thinks, what a romantic time it must have been! The music of romance, of Albéniz and *Azulejos*–the piece she'd been playing without knowing that Granados finished it for his dying friend. And a special edition: copy Number One for the king, copy Number Two for his student. How different life must have been in that time for her father's father, who worked for the father of Clotilde. And she senses the shadow, resonant in Clotilde's voice and lurking just behind her eyes, and wonders: was there more about this Granados than just music? Who was he? A dear friend of Albéniz. A very exacting teacher. Would my professor care if I wrote my paper about all of these famous composers who once came to little Tiana?

Núria looks down at the sketch of the kneeling man and the aristocratic woman, propped on the piano's music stand. She recognizes the work of Goya, and gently touches the corner of the sketch. "And this, senyora? This is related to his music?"

Clotilde smiles. "Yes, of course. This is one of the *Caprichos* by Goya."

"I adore Goya! I've seen his works on a visit to El Prado. There are so many there."

Clotilde laughs. "The answer is, yes, Granados was inspired by the *Caprichos*, and wrote this piece to translate the spirit of Goya's art into music."

Núria feels her brain about to burst. She looks at Clotilde's small hands with trimmed nails, wondering how she'd ever play a tenth. "Senyora, do you still enjoy playing the piano?"

"Oh, no, I haven't played in many, many years."

It is late afternoon when Núria leaves the villa. Her writing hand aches from filling a notebook with Clotilde's memories of Albéniz and Malats and Granados.

Standing under the portico, Clotilde sees that the sun lies low over the garden, its light gilding the stucco wall of her chapel and vaulting over the diagonal cut of the ravine that is always dry except during the occasional deluge in springtime. The sun is descending to the spot where it will disappear behind the ridge running down to the seaside town of Montgat. These last few moments of direct sunlight–still a source of delight. Unfailingly they evoke the summer of 1910. Waiting for him in the garden. Clotilde watches as Núria reaches the gate, turns and waves. Clotilde returns the wave and watches the gate as it's opened and closed, watches as the young woman disappears down Carrer Edith Llaurador.

How fond she was then of Rubén Darío's poetry! Sitting here, reciting her favorites. Especially this one:

> I know there are those who ask:
> why do you not still sing
> those same wild songs of yesteryear?
> They do not see the work of just an hour,
> the work of a minute, and the wonders of a year.
> I, now an aging tree, used to moan so sweetly
> from the breezes when I began to grow.
> But the time has passed for youthful smiles:
> so let the hurricane move my heart to song!

Oh, the wild songs of yesteryear! That day when she left her family's Barcelona home on Rambla de Catalunya, strolling lightly with the sun hovering over Montjuic and the sea beyond. Circling the Plaça Catalunya and turning left at Carrer Fontanella, dodging through the busy intersection at Portal del'Angel, watching the street numbers for the first time, walking toward her audition with the maestro. Finally, seeing the number "14" on the building, and the sign: Acadèmia Granados. From her home to the audition, as if she were growing up at last, finished with the colegio and with the nuns who watched her like hawks, ready for this new adventure at the place where she could learn to play the hallowed music of Mozart as it should be played, and the music of Chopin and Schubert and Beethoven. Would that first time have been less memorable if the maestro didn't bluntly tell her, "That is all very bad–you have to change everything?"

All of that so long ago. How can she recall what happened that one afternoon so very long ago? What spirit guides her through the labyrinths of her mind, guides her to places where the garden still flowers and music still resounds and the nightingale still pours out his song in the gloom of night?

Chapter Two

It seems, from how she approaches the piano, that Adela Montserrat Ferrer Girona has not prepared for her lesson today. Mincing steps, turning to smile at her maestro, holding the smile a bit too long. But it's her dainty trek across a priceless Persian rug that is most incongruous for this tall and handsome princess of the ruling class in Barcelona. Not her lack of devotion to the Chopin prelude that was assigned at her last lesson.

"You found the piece difficult?" Enrique Granados asks, anticipating the answer.

"Ah, yes, Maestro Granados. Very difficult." She rolls her eyes.

He dismisses the familiarity in her gesture. "Well, we'll begin with the scales. And the arpeggios. Then the Chopin."

"Oh, maestro. If only mine were as large as yours!" She raises her hands–they fit her angular body. Fingers strong and tapering, longer than those of most students. There's no reason she can't learn to play the easy Chopin preludes, perhaps some of the easier Mozart. And for what Adela wants from playing the piano, that's sufficient. "Your hands are more than large enough," says Granados. "If you practice, you'll be able to play this."

"Ah, sí. I do need to practice more. Much more. But even then, I'd never be able to play this piece–as you do." She flutters her eyelashes.

Granados is used to Adela's coquetry, and ignores it. "I don't want you to play it as I do, I want you to play it your own way. Mine's not the only way–to be followed slavishly. It's simply my way. And you can have yours. But first you must absorb the music until it becomes as familiar as the tip of your nose. Then you can perfect your own way."

"Yes, maestro." She sits on the bench, stretching her arms and fingers above her, while the afternoon light from the louvered twin windows creates a beguiling profile of her face and the stream of black hair pulled across the tops of her ears, fastened with a silver barrette behind her long neck. The outline of her breasts is also visible through the lace-trimmed blouse, unbuttoned at the neck. She lifts her pleated skirt, exposing her knees, then turns and asks, "May I begin?"

Granados is bemused; the question is gratuitous. "Yes, Adela, you may begin. With the scales."

After two years of giving her private lessons, Granados knows that Adela cannot fit enough piano practice into her daily life. Learning to play is merely one of the social graces presumed essential for young women of Barcelona's alta burguesa to prepare them for marriage. A smattering of Chopin, a bit of Mozart, perhaps even a taste of Beethoven. Sonic ornaments for their ornamental lives. Yet he's grateful for the steady flow of students that this custom provides to musicians who must teach in order to support themselves and their families, as he must. And as Adela begins the scales, Granados' mind drifts away.

He has a number of talented students: Mercè Moner, Ferran Via, Emilia Ycart. Pepita, daughter of Eduardo Conde–whose patronage allowed Granados to study in Paris–she's a good pianist. And Francisca, daughter of Carmen Miralles and Salvador Andreu, also shows promise.

The piano salon is on the second floor of the baronial Ferrer Girona residence on Rambla de Catalunya. Granados hears the chattering of birds in the trees along the boulevard that runs down the middle of the street, and the intermittent clip-clopping of horses as they draw carriages and vans up and down the pavement on each side of the boulevard. Nearby, the sound of Adela Ferrer playing scales on the Cusso y Ortiz concert grand piano, a recent gift on her eighteenth birthday.

With students who have innate talent and work hard, there's no need to stoke the passion. With those who are learning piano because it's expected, he doesn't count on their ever catching fire. For their fathers and grandfathers, there was ample passion in pursuit of their dreams: sugar plantations in Cuba and the Philippines, textile plants, paper mills and foundries, shipyards and fishing fleets, olive orchards and vineyards, trading and merchandising, banking and finance. Catalan passion for building things and making money and pushing the boundaries of Barcelona outside the old city walls.

But Adela Ferrer and the late 19th century generation, beneficiaries of that passion, have missed the taste and thrill of initiative, its double edges of risk and reward. Their choices: to follow the tracks of the pioneers, or lay back and enjoy the fruits of their inheritance, or rebel against it. And these require different forms of passion. Only a few, seeking the exhilaration of new discovery, are engaged in reviving the ancient language, art, and culture of Catalunya.

Adela stops and turns toward Granados. "With your permission, maestro, I'd like some fresh air. It's difficult to concentrate with perspiration in my eyes." She unhooks two more buttons at the top of her blouse and pulls out a pink handkerchief to dry her forehead.

"Of course."

She goes to the louvered twin windows and pulls them open. "Ah, there's a breeze. That will be much better." She turns, her blouse revealing the vale between her breasts, and sits on the piano bench, pulling her skirt up to the middle of her thighs. "That's much, much better," she says, enjoying the cool air flowing across her skin. "Oh, maestro, you must be roasting in this heat! Don't you want to remove your jacket?"

Granados has perspired most of this hot early summer afternoon in the dark suit that his wife Amparo laid out this morning. A woolen suit, since this spring has been unseasonably cool in Barcelona. Adela's comment seems patronizing. "Ah, but I've been sitting while you've been working," he replies.

"Are you not roasting?"

"Yes, I'm roasting." He removes his jacket and unbuttons his vest.

"Can I hang your jacket, maestro?"

He shakes his head. "No, thank you. I'll just put it on this chair."

She bows her head slightly and offers a wide smile. "As you wish."

"Thank you."

"Do you wear that when you play?" she asks, pointing to a leather band with a bronze medallion on his right wrist.

"Always," he replies, raising his wrist. "It's my good luck charm."

"Isn't that the head of Beethoven?"

He nods, and Adela goes back to the scales.

This student has flirted before. Her languorous moves, her deepened tone of voice, her fluttering of eyelashes. But he's no longer young and careless. This is not Paris, where he did all the wild things young men do. Nor the same as going to the Barrí Xinès with Pablo Casals, drinking in the bars with Italian and Turkish sailors, laughing while the bar-girls rubbed their breasts across their faces. Nor like the escapades when he and Casals and Mathieu Crickboom performed in San

Sebastian, and French girls walked with them from the concert to their rooms near the beach.

Granados is nearly thirty-two and father of three children, with one more expected this summer. If it's a boy, he'll be named Victor. And Granados' life is already complicated: teaching nearly two dozen piano students, preparing for the Barcelona opening of his new opera *María del Carmen* later this month, practicing the pieces he'll play with Joaquim Malats in June, finishing works for piano and orchestra and for a Catalan lyric theatre, spending time with Amparo and the children, and developing the idea of converting the *Caprichos* sketches of Francisco Goya to music. All the while praying that the savage fevers and blinding headaches and wrenching abdominal pains–which have disabled him for weeks on three separate occasions since his childhood–will not return.

That is his life, and there's no time or appetite for dalliance with this seductive princess barely half his age. Even while admitting Adela is unusually attractive. When she opened her blouse and lifted her skirt above her knees, his was a predictable male reaction, quickly suppressed by the awareness that this heiress of the alta burguesia belongs to an alien world. He'll never belong to it, though he needs to exist on its periphery, tasting it, occasionally reveling in it, living off its endowment, and all the while being patronized by it. He's not tempted by Adela, who'd take him only as an ephemeral lover, offering herself in that special way of young princesses who allow eager men to blow off their sexual energy, yet preserve the sacred portals for their marriage beds.

"May I play the opening of the Chopin, maestro?"

Granados nods and folds his arms across his chest. When Adela begins, he's stunned. Nothing in her desultory scales prepared him for this. She begins Chopin's first prelude with astonishing authority and tenderness. He leans forward, scrutinizing the long fingers of her right hand through the rolling chords of the middle section. And even when she plays the ending too loudly, using the pedal as if she's just remembered it's there, he's moved by what clearly seems the result of devoted practice by a student who appeared to have no deep motivation for such an effort. Is this the same Adela who's shown so little interest in excelling at the piano? Has this short piece of music somehow inspired her to reach beyond? Otherwise, how could she have played this so well?

"Have I displeased you, maestro?"

He shakes his head. "No, no."

"I worked very hard on this piece. For you."

"No, I'm *very* pleased with what you've done."

"I ask because you're frowning."

He smiles. "No. I'm sorry. That's not it. Would you play it again? And this time, try to keep it soft at the end."

"Soft at the end."

"And less pedal. Adela, please understand–I'm very pleasantly surprised."

"You're surprised because–?"

"As you said, it's a difficult piece. And–"

"And you think I'm just one of the foolish young women who have useless lives and care not a bit about the essence of life. Maestro, I could forgive you for thinking of me that way. But I do want you to think better!" Her face is flushed.

When the lesson ends, Granados puts on his jacket. Still mystified by Adela's performance. "I'd like to give you more of the preludes," he says, "but I didn't bring them today."

"No," she says, "you didn't expect me to be ready." She takes two steps toward him.

He shrugs. "Yes, that's right, Adela. I'd like you to have them before the next lesson. Could you pick them up?"

She shakes her head. "I cannot have a lesson next week. I'll be at our summer home. In Puigcerdà."

He conceals his disappointment. "It's a wonderful place, Puigcerdà. A peaceful place. So close to the mountains."

"You know Puigcerdà?" she asks.

"Yes, I go there often, as a guest of Dr. Andreu."

"Oh? The famous doctor of the pills? His home is right next to ours. On the pond."

"Yes? Well, you'll have a fine time up there with your family. We can have our next lesson when you return."

She looks down. "No, that's not possible, maestro. Because after Puigcerdà I'll be getting ready for my marriage. The wedding is in July."

"Oh, then you have my warmest congratulations! That's good news, isn't it?" He knows the answer from her lowered eyes. "Not good?"

Adela shakes her head. "My mother decided it's time for me to marry–she picked my husband. And it's someone I don't love, could never love. Never!" Her voice breaks. "But my mother persisted–for months and months, and ignored all of my protests. I have no more energy to resist."

"Is there another whom you'd prefer?" he asks.

She hesitates. "No. And that's part of the problem. This one she picked for me is from the family of one of my grandfather's partners at the bank. So everyone thinks he's a fine match. But if I can speak personally, maestro, I must say this one is not a man I could ever respect. He knows nothing of life. He wants to know nothing. He's sliding along without a single idea of what it means to be alive. Oh, he has such tiny eyes! So close together–not like yours. He tries to grow his moustache–it's not like yours, more like a pair of anchovies! His lips are so thin and inexpressive. He laughs nervously at everything, so I'm not sure if he's mocking me or just doesn't understand. His hands are small and moist. Not like yours. And when I think of being with him–which of course I have not been–it chokes me."

"And your mother knows how you feel?"

"Of course. And it makes no difference. She says my father was chosen for her, and they've had a good life. Why wouldn't I want that too?"

"Well, I'm sorry, Adela."

"I shouldn't trouble you, maestro." Her voice trails off.

Granados shakes his head. "No, truly I am sorry. And sorry you won't be able to continue. You played this Chopin so well." Granados picks up his hat and the notepad that contains his early sketches of the new piece of chamber music. He nods. "I wish you good luck, Adela, I do. And I hope you'll be back after the wedding."

Adela watches Granados as he steps back toward the door to the music salon. She knows that when he's gone, more than this door will close. "Oh, maestro! Forgive me for what I must say! Forgive me for asking: why do I have to be so young and you so old? And married–with all of those children!"

Twilight slides onto the streets of Barcelona as Granados walks down the gradual slope of Rambla de Catalunya, heading for Carrer de Montsió and a gathering of his friends at the bistro called Els Quatre Gats–The Four Cats.* He remains perplexed by the lesson with Adela Ferrer.

She didn't stumble. Not at all. Jarred me she played so well. Showed me strength. And took a risk. Shame she can't continue!

Granados knows how much he needs the income from piano lessons, but it leaves so little time to perform and compose, and he struggles to contain his resentment. Yet he's thankful that the wealthy merchant Eduardo Condé hired

---

* See Map 2: Barcelona

him to teach his children, paying him so generously–one hundred pesetas a month–that Granados no longer had to play in places like Café de las Delicias. Teaching, despite its drawbacks, is far better than catering to a café manager's banal musical taste.

Unlike those young "bohemians" who were born wealthy, Granados and his friend Pablo Casals are always concerned about money. Lacking Casals' frugality and the discipline needed to save up for such major events as moving to Paris, Granados–under pressure from Amparo–has saved some money, but invariably he squanders it. On musical ventures, or on some tempting luxury, like buying two parrots for his daughter, Solita–to the dismay of Amparo, who found a new home for them within a week.

Casals leaves for Paris tomorrow. He's on the brink of recognition, and knows it won't come if he stays in Barcelona. Ten years ago, with funds provided by Eduardo Condé, Granados was able to spend two years studying in Paris–before marriage and a growing family. He'd like to go back, but Amparo implacably opposes moving the family from Barcelona. Instead, he'll see Casals board a train to France tomorrow morning.

Granados hoped his opera *María del Carmen* would appeal to a larger audience and enjoy a wider commercial success than had his early piano compositions. To infuse it with authenticity, he and the librettist, Josep Feliu, visited the orchards in the east central province of Murcia, the setting for the opera. The fragrance of apricots, peaches, oranges, and lemons stirred treasured memories of citrus blossoms in Santa Cruz de Tenerife when he was a little boy. He was stunned when Feliu died shortly after finishing the libretto, and several months before the premiere in Madrid.

After its opening last November, *María del Carmen* received eighteen more performances and Granados was decorated with the Cross of Carlos III by María Cristina, Queen Regent of Spain–thanks to Casals' cultivation of Her Royal Highness. But critics in Madrid said Feliu's libretto was weak. They criticized the work for deviating from the standard formula for light Spanish operas–known as zarzuelas–yet they praised the music.

Granados believes *María del Carmen* is his best work to date, deeper and more complex than the early successes: *Danzas Españolas* for solo piano, composed nearly a decade earlier, and *Valses Poéticos*, also for solo piano. The musical stage seems his best opportunity for recognition in the wider world of music. And after opening *María del Carmen* in Barcelona, he plans to complete a lyric drama, *Petrarca*, based on a poem by the highly respected Apel.les Mestres. It will be exciting to work with Mestres. Catching the wave of modernism–just what people want. He's confident they'd love *Petrarca*.

But failure in January of Granados' collaboration with Adrià Gual on another theatrical piece, *Blancaflor*, has left a lingering, bitter taste. He was brought in late to provide the score after Isaac Albéniz bowed out, with little hope of salvaging it. On opening night, three of the orchestral players failed to show up, and the intermission was too long. Still, the critics should have loved *Blancaflor*. Based on Catalan folk legends–and they invariably praise anything Catalan–good or bad. Instead, they were unusually harsh.

Granados crosses the boulevard Rambla de Catalunya as shopkeepers begin to shut their doors and hang "Closed" signs in the windows.

So many projects! So little time! How to find time? Easy with no sleep. No students no concerts. No wife no children. Sleep under the piano. Easy–if everything were different. And the world upside down. And fates were kinder!

Close to the surface, and always dancing in Granados' imagination, is the art of the Spanish master Francisco Goya, seen last summer in Madrid. He's captivated by Goya and how he depicted the soul of Spain. Especially Goya's portraits of royalty in his time. The white rose of their cheeks. Glistening hair against black and red velvet. Hands of mother-of-pearl and creamy jasmine, covered with gems. He's captivated by Goya's portrait of the 13th Duquesa de Alba–María del Pilar Teresa Cayetana de Silva Alvarez de Toledo. Dressed in white with a scarlet waistband as a platform for her breasts, a matching red bow above it, a cascade of dark hair reaching down to her elbows, a mouth that seems about to open, eyes that reach out to pierce and mesmerize.

He wonders how Goya's images of majos and majas, the flashy street people of Castile, can be transcribed to the medium of music. And will he be the one to achieve this? He dreams of Goya and the rumored love affair with La Duquesa de Alba, delights in the sound of her name–Goya called her "María Teresa." The image of Goya living on the outer edge of the aristocracy in Madrid one hundred years ago, yet always serving it, mirrors his own relationship with the alta burguesa of Barcelona. Serving his patrons and teaching the young women who seek to learn only what they need from the piano to adorn their opulent lives. Artists and aristocrats, ever separated by an enormous chasm, reaching out but scarcely touching. Trying to defy the disparity between their realms.

Students like Adela Ferrer come from a long progression of women betrothed for some external convenience, including La Duquesa de Alba–married off at fourteen to the Marques de Villafranca, himself barely twenty. An unending sacrificial file of nubile women, parading to a refrain that emerges again and again in Goya's satiric sketches known as the *Caprichos*. It's not so much that

Granados romanticizes the aristocratic life of Goya's Castile; rather he enjoys the snarl and bite of satire in the sketches, recognizes the artist's obvious alienation from his patrons, and his bitterness at being rejected by La Duquesa for a coterie of new lovers. What a recipe for lyric theatre! But Granados' first effort to convert Goya's art to music was a failure; he confided to Casals that it left him broken-hearted.

So try again some day. At the right time. When angels say it's time.

Granados approaches the intersection of Carrer València, where a group of schoolgirls is singing at the entrance of a school. He watches as one of them darts across the street. Younger than Adela. Laughing, effervescent, and intrepid as she cuts in front of a horse and carriage. As he looks her way, she stops on the sidewalk, waves and darts into the doorway of a large brownstone mansion. He smiles and moves on.

Granados passes *El Siglo* department store, owned by his first patron, Condé. Who heard him play a Schumann sonata, then hired him to teach his children; whose generosity enabled him to study in Paris. Condé took the place of the young pianist's own father when, after suffering for many months with injuries sustained in a horseback riding accident, Calixto Granados finally expired in the family's flat.

Thank God Condé liked that Schumann! Imagine still playing Café Delicias! Like a slow death.

At the corner of Carrer Aragó, he passes the pharmacy that purveys his headache medicine, and this evokes a constant fear of losing his health again, as he did in Paris when typhoid fever prevented his entering the Conservatoire. Weeks of lying in that foreign city with burning fever, searing headaches, wearying malaise, aching constipation, and raspy coughing–with doctors saying he'd always carry the typhoid germ, it could come back any time. Which it did eight years later, costing him a chance to become professor of piano studies at the Conservatorio in Madrid.

At the busy intersection of La Gran Via, Granados looks off to his right where the last of the sunlight strikes the high clouds drifting down the coast. Heading westward toward the Strait of Gibraltar and beyond it beloved Tenerife in the Islas Canarias–where he enjoyed his boyhood "four years of paradise." Beyond Tenerife, an enormous world waiting for his music. The United States of America, where his friends Albéniz and Casals have toured. Granados admires the Americans, would like to go there someday–if only he didn't have to cross the ocean. His worst nightmare. What if railroad trains could just fly over the ocean? No, that won't happen, someday he'll have to get on a ship. Find a way to push through the fear.

Granados crosses the broad, circular Plaça Catalunya, which separates the old sector of Barcelona–a walled, medieval city rising from the harbor–from l'Eixample, where the city expands at a boomtown pace. He prefers this route, though it's not the shortest. It takes him down the city's main artery, La Rambla, where he's surrounded by surging crowds; past the bird sellers and the shrill cacophany of song from cages full of canaries and parrots. These birds in cages, but not the nightingale. Not he who sings his melancholy song in the darkened trees. The trilling of that lone nightingale, heard first eleven years ago in Paris, lives on indelibly.

How it echoes! So young then. Before suffering from those who envy–who lack compassion. A laurel leaf for every thorn in the artist's crown. Tears falling at his feet giving birth to flowers of consolation.

Granados dodges the stream of carriages and horse-drawn trams, and slices through the exodus of people heading for the bars and cafés at the end of their workday. He slows in approaching the flower stalls, unhurried, confident his friends will be waiting, that they'll be lost in conversation about war and politics, love and death, art and beauty, and local gossip. It's nearly nine o'clock, dark overhead except for a thin crescent of pink clouds high in the west. Electrification has come to the streets of Barcelona, so evenings are brighter than during his boyhood when he lived in the labyrinth behind the sprawling La Boquería market just down La Rambla.

Progress? Electricity in the streets and homes. Soon, the horseless carriages. Students barely know how to use the simple pedal of a piano!

When he first catches sight of her, the woman is at a flower stall, dressed in the style of Barcelona's most affluent. She's hatless, hair glistening in the light of the lamps, she's unescorted at this hour of the evening, she's nearly as tall as he. She picks up one bouquet after another, seeking the most ravishing bouquet, holding each one up to the light as she shifts her weight from foot to foot with the grace of a ballet dancer. Granados stops and lets the swarm of pedestrians flow past. He hears the shrill chatter of the caged birds on sale and the snorting of horses hitched to delivery wagons leaving La Boquería market.

The woman chooses her bouquet, pays for it, pirouettes, and glides up La Rambla toward Granados. As they pass, her face reflects light from the streetlamps. Her mouth is a magenta rose. Their eyes meet. Her face glows with the colors of assorted cut flowers. He cannot remember a woman of such stunning beauty and grace. Not here, not in Madrid, nor Paris.

With a name derived from a Catalan term for "only a few people," and an ambience patterned after the bistros of Montmartre, Els Quatre Gats is a gathering place for artists and intellectuals in Barcelona. Located on the narrow Carrer Montsió a short distance from La Rambla, Quatre Gats occupies the first floor of a building that was the first important work of the young modernist architect, Josep Puig i Catafalch. It was opened two years ago by painters Miquel Utrillo, Ramón Casas, and Santiago Rusiñol as a gathering place for their "tertulia"–a circle of friends discussing art and politics, arguing, and exchanging jokes and gossip. They recruited a friend of Rusiñol's and a would-be painter, Pere Romeu, to be their tavernkeeper.

The three owners, bearded and dressed in tailored suits and wide-brimmed hats, are sitting at a long mahogany table in the bar of Els Quatre Gats, smoking cigars and sipping from steins of beer. A colossal chandelier hangs above the table, and on the wall behind them is a large painting by Casas, depicting his unnerving tandem bicycle ride with Romeu, an exercise fanatic; it shows two men in white slacks, shirts, and caps, pedaling in unison, Casas in front with a pipe in his mouth–into which a cigar has been inserted. He seems to be pushing hard to keep up with the tall, lean Romeu, whose upright position and thin smile suggest demonic amusement.

But on this day, barging out of the kitchen, Romeu is not amused. "They have no right to speak such slander!" he exclaims, waving both hands and splashing red wine on the tile floor. "It's an outrage, and I refuse to listen to it." He slips on a blotch of wine, and recovers.

"Calm down, my friend," Rusiñol says, his long, unkempt hair contained by a black felt sombrero. "What's the problem?"

"They say I've been serving seagulls!" cries Romeu, whose greasy hair laid back over the top of his large head, protruding teeth, untrimmed beard, and ingrained frown don't endear him to customers of Els Quatre Gats. He leans over the table and scans the faces.

"Seagulls?" Rusiñol asks.

"They say the pigeons I serve are not pigeons–they're seagulls!"

The three painters explode in laughter. Utrillo falls off his chair.

"You think it's funny? What's funny, this kind of slander?"

Casas is first to respond. He pulls his portly body up to the table, adjusts his rimless glasses, and tries to mollify. "No, it's not right to make fun of you, Pere, but everyone knows you go to swim in the sea every day–even in winter, and everyone knows there are many seagulls where you swim. Can you blame people for coming to that conclusion?"

Romeu's eyes are bulging. "Do *you* believe I serve seagulls here?"

"No," says Casas, glaring at Utrillo, who is holding both hands over his mouth. "I enjoy the pigeons. You could offer more Catalan food."

Utrillo, older than his partners, has an angular face, indented cheeks, heavy lids over his eyes and bags under them–souvenirs of years of debauchery in Paris. He tries to counsel Romeu. "If you didn't insist on going to the sea every day, even in winter, perhaps the rumors would cease."

Romeu sneers, searching for a final insult, and finding none he stuffs his hands into the pockets of a wine-stained, double-breasted gray vest and returns to the kitchen.

Lluisa Vidal, a painting student of Casas, is greeted by the trio as she arrives at the long table. She wears a billowing, dark green skirt and long-sleeved white blouse. Her hair sweeps up like an inverted mushroom, exposing her neck and ears. Vidal is the only woman invited to sit with the tertulia.

"You've been away." Casas says, sounding peeved. "I was hoping we could talk about *Pèl & Ploma*."

She disregards his annoyance. "Oh, the new magazine. The one we talked about? I'm interested, Ramón. Tell me more."

Casas reaches into a portfolio and places a sketching pad in front of her. "Here's my idea for the first cover." It depicts the smiling face of a young woman against a black background. Her chin is outlined against bare shoulders. She wears a large white hat with rising birdwings.

"Oh my!" At first glance, Vidal imagines a white chicken on a platter, with drumsticks rising. She chooses her words. "The hat is really quite–fantastic."

He searches her oval face for hidden barbs. "I swear it's not a fantasy. I saw such a hat, just the other day, on a woman coming out of El Liceu. I swear! It's not my idea of a hat, but it's got–"

"Hair and feathers," Vidal says. "I get it–*Pèl & Ploma*."

"You like it?" asks Casas.

"Well, it's quite a striking first cover! When will it appear?

"Next month. I wonder if you'd be interested in doing some work."

"Yes, of course. I've just returned from Puigcerdà, so I need to get settled in my new studio. How about coffee next week?"

"Puigcerdà?" Casas asks.

"Yes, with my family, at Doctor Andreu's chalet–"

"The famous doctor of the pills? Rusiñol knows him."

"We've been going there for years," Vidal explains. "Since he married Carme Miralles. Granados was there too."

"Not with his wife."

"No, alone. He and Carmen have been dear friends since–forever!"

"Oh, I imagine they're *very* dear friends," Casas says.

"Don't be rude! Friends–and no more! Granados says the doctor's chalet is a place to get away from the complications of life. Told me that ten years ago he composed *Valses Poéticos* in just a few days at Puigcerdà."

Casas shrugs. "Yes, some of my best work is done in isolation, but I think his best work is still *Danzas Españolas*."

Joaquín Nin, a young pianist from Cuba, arrives while the group is retelling stories of anarchist bombings in Barcelona, the public garroting that Casas condemned with his painting, *Garrotte Vil*, and the return of the Spanish army from a shattering defeat by the Americans.

"That war was the inevitable result of the greed of our alta burguesa," Utrillo says. "They profited for years on the suffering of others. Fortunes made on their plantations of sugar and tobacco, and built on slavery. Disgusting–time to end that!"

Casas, whose father amassed most of his wealth on just such ventures in Cuba, nods in agreement.

"Ah sí, but those men also took advantage of the central government in Madrid," Rusiñol argues. "It's plain to see the industrialists have made their–shall we say?–arrangements with the crown. Pledging their loyalty, hoping for royal titles. Will the streets of Barcelona be overrun with new marqueses and counts? Of course, I don't sympathize with the anarchists either."

"A stupid war," Casas says. "All wars are stupid, but this one was so horribly botched by Madrid. They just stumbled into total disaster! And it will hurt us all in Catalunya, not just the industrialists. They'll find ways to recoup their losses. How about the unemployed?"

"How about the ones returning from the war?" Vidal asks. "It's shameful to see survivors coming off the boats. Emaciated, crippled, like a procession of walking ghosts, barely alive. And for what? To join the swelling ranks of unemployed. Those poor men–how will they ever recover?"

Rusiñol lifts the brim of his hat. "You mean those who went to fight in place of the rich sons of the alta burguesa? Oh, friends, I'm sick of people who claim our country is martyred–for stupidly picking a fight against one of the most powerful nations!"

"But what can be done to restore the place of España among nations?" asks Nin, who at twenty is grateful he wasn't caught in the war back in Cuba.

Rusiñol pounds on the table. "Not España–Catalunya! May I quote our illustrious friend, Maragall? 'Listen, España, to the voice of a son who speaks to you in a language that is not Castilian!'"

"It is not unlike the time of Goya," Casas says, "when España was fighting for its freedom from the Bonapartes."

"No, it's worse–our country has finally hit rock bottom," says Rusiñol. "It's just as well. The old empire is finished, just as the rest of Europe is rising."

Rusiñol turns to Nin. "By the way, Joaquinito, will you be prepared for the recital at my festival? Just two more months."

"What are you playing?" Vidal asks.

Nin turns to Vidal. "I'm playing *L'Alegría que passa*, by our esteemed Don Santiago."

Rusiñol holds up his hands. "Ah, but I just wrote the words. The music is by Morera."

"Well, if it's Morera's, it must be *very* Catalan," Vidal says.

"Ah, Lluisa," Rusiñol protests. "You don't think I'd let our young friend play music that sounds Castilian, do you?"

"You mean like our friend Granados?" asks Utrillo.

Rusiñol shakes his head. "No, he's different. Granados is a genius, our finest pianist. Better than Albéniz and Falla. When he comes to Sitges, he sits at the piano for hours, improvising and never playing the same passage twice, entirely lost in the music. What a genius we have among us! He's Catalan enough for me."

"I agree," Nin says. "Granados is our greatest virtuoso! And does anyone know how hard that man works? Has to teach–more than he'd like–to support his family. With what time's left over for composing–so many new works, such magnificent music! All the while fighting tooth and nail to make a living. I say his effort is nothing short of heroic!"

"It's remarkable–he does so many things, so well," Vidal says. "And he doesn't deserve criticism he's not Catalan enough! Art shouldn't be subservient to politics!"

Rusiñol raises his stein of beer. "Absolutely. Art must stand apart from the confusion of politics and war. Otherwise, we become propagandists."

A short man with close-cropped dark hair and an oversized moustache enters quietly and is hailed by the group. His squinting eyes dart from face to face. It's the young cellist, Pablo Casals, back in Barcelona for a few days before moving to Paris. In a reedy, excited voice, he tells them he has a letter of introduction to Charles Lamoureux. "The best orchestral conductor in France," he explains. By playing with Lamoureux, Casals hopes to realize his dream: a career as a cello soloist.

"But tell me, Pau, aren't you already the world's best?" Casas asks.

Casals laughs. "That's flattering, but I must convince others. And Paris, not Barcelona, is the place to launch a career."

Utrillo is skeptical. "But isn't Barcelona at the very center of modernism?"

"Yes, but still too limiting. Paris is the place!"

"You're right, Pau," Utrillo replies, "as much as we love Catalunya, there's a gigantic world out there."

"Barcelona's much too provincial," Casas says. "If something's not purely Catalan, it's discounted. We were talking about Granados. How was his opening? Weren't you with him in Madrid?"

Casals' eyes brighten. "You would not believe how well it went!"

"Truly?"

"Yes. *María del Carmen* was premiered in November. Granados personally conducted the orchestra and the critics were very impressed. By the music more than the libretto. I helped a bit with rehearsals."

"I had no idea," Vidal says. "I've seen him several times since then–just last weekend in Puigcerdà, he didn't utter a single word about any success in Madrid. I just assumed it hadn't gone well."

"That's typical," Casals replies. "He's very shy about his work–until he's at the piano. No, this opera was an enormous effort for him, with all his distractions–performing, teaching, and of course his four children."

"There are four?" Vidal asks.

"Well, three. And another this summer. My little godchildren. He's so joyful when he plays with them–he too becomes a child. To prepare for *María del Carmen*, he spent several weeks in the orchards of Murcia, to better understand the setting."

"My God, several weeks in the orchards of Murcia!" exclaims Utrillo. "He's not just a virtuoso, he's a saint!"

"Well, it sounds marvelous," Rusiñol says, "but our critics were unhappy because it opened in Madrid, not here. And they weren't impressed by his decoration by the royal Castilian family–our oppressors, if you will. Here they'd prefer music that's more Catalan."

Casals' face reddens. "That's not fair!"

"I'm just repeating what I hear," Rusiñol insists.

"That's stupid talk. He's the very first composer to write music with a real Catalan flavor–without mere borrowings from our traditional folklore. That's true genius! For me, Granados is the greatest, most original, and most poetical of our composers. I'm proud to be like a brother to him. We should all be proud. This man is truly our Chopin, our Schubert."

"Bravo, Pau," Vidal says. "Thank you for saying that. You also speak for me."

The door opens and the sound of boots on the tile floor heralds another arrival. There's silence in the small front room of Quatre Gats, then a slender man's silhouette appears in the neo-Gothic arch of the bistro. He takes two confident steps forward into the light of the barroom, then stops to unfasten his cloak. He stares at the group, which now occupies every chair around the long table. The arched eyebrows, mouth turned down at its corners, hair falling over the left eye, and face bereft of the commonplace moustache are familiar to regular patrons of Quatre Gats.

His mercurial charm, physical magnetism, brilliance, vitality, Andaluz jauntiness–and willingness to learn the Catalan language–have earned a place in the tertulia for this intense young man from Málaga, a diminutive painter of seventeen who's defying the limits of classic art training. He never lets Rusiñol and Casas forget his desire to exhibit here, where his sketches and paintings can hang next to theirs. So far his pleadings have been in vain. Having interrupted the conversation, the young painter–Pablo Ruiz Picasso–grabs a chair and swaggers over to the long table where he's greeted by a blend of amusement, derision, and grudging respect.

Granados enters Quatre Gats, circling the long table, greeting each of his friends, and exchanging warm, double-cheek abraçadas with Lluisa Vidal and Casals. When he's introduced to Ruiz, Granados is hailed as "one of the marvels of Barcelona." Granados raises his head in feigned hauteur and exclaims, "Yes, young man, I am Pantaleón Enrique Joaquín Granados y Campiña. But you may call me Enric."

Ruiz is unimpressed. "Oh? Well, I am Pablo Diego José Francisco de Paula Juan Nepomuceno María de los Remedios Alarcón Herrera Crispín Crispiniano Santísima Trinidad Ruiz Picasso. You may call me Pau."

"A large name for such a small person," Rusiñol says.

"And a small talent," adds Utrillo.

Ruiz responds with a sneer and lifts his stein of beer. "Touché!"

A slender girl with wavy fair hair, who's passing through the bar with her family, stops at the long table to greet Granados. He rises and gives her an avuncular hug. "Maestro," she declares, "I think I'm finally learning the piece you gave me–the Mozart."

"That's good news, María. If you're learning the Mozart, you must be practicing."

"Yes, I am. Every day."

"Marvelous. I look forward to your next lesson."

She smiles and returns to her family as Romeu arrives with a goblet of red wine for Granados. "Ah, maestro, such a sweet, lovely young thing! I see why you're so devoted to teaching."

Granados expects no better from Romeu. "Oh? Why, my dear Pere, I believe you're confused," says Granados. "Aren't you the one named Rome-u? Where are all your Juliets?"

The group enjoys the pun. His levity is welcome when the group begins to take itself too seriously.

"She is comely, but very young," Casas says.

"Come now, Ramón, if you're suggesting there's something between that girl and me, forget it! And be assured that Amparo would cut off my extremities if she found me with a student."

"All your extremities, Enric?" Rusiñol asks.

Granados laughs. "Except for my hands. She's a very practical woman, and those bring food to the table."

"Enric, you're just bubbling tonight," Vidal says, recalling the shadow of melancholy on his face when she saw him in Puigcerdà. "Do you bring us good news?"

"Yes, you do seem bursting with something," Casals adds.

Granados grins and looks around the table. "It's the power of beauty." He shakes his head and turns his palms up. "I just passed the most stunningly beautiful woman in the world." The group leans forward. He pauses, then laughs. "That's it."

"Who is she?" Casas asks. "Someone we know?"

"Dark or fair?" asks Rusiñol.

"Rubenesque?" Utrillo asks. "Please say she's not from Barrí Xinès–not one of Ruiz' girls."

Granados waves off their speculation. "No, she was a complete stranger. I saw her buying flowers on La Rambla, and–"

"And?"

"Nothing. Wait–just a minute." Granados walks over to the upright piano in the corner, uncovers the keyboard, adjusts the stool, and begins a meandering improvisation. His eyes are closed as he recalls the radiance, grace, and colors of the stunning woman and her flowers, and he's immersed as he describes her with his fingers.

As he plays, Rusiñol turns to Casas and whispers, "If he plays with this much passion after seeing a mere stranger on the street, just imagine how glorious his music would be if he were deeply in love!"

Pablo Casals waits at the entrance of l'Estació França, where trains depart for France and the rest of Europe. He's musing about his first, unsuccessful trip to Paris three years ago when he sees Granados step down from a cab on Avinguda de L'Argentera.

"The train is late," Casals says, "so we have more than an hour. Let's walk over to the park." Parc de la Ciutadella, site of the Universal Exposition of 1888, affords a quiet respite from the heavy morning traffic.

"I bring fond greetings from La Argentina," says Casals, smirking.

Granados laughs. "What? That skinny little devil in the operetta?"

"Yes. With the big green eyes."

"Whose father was going to put her in the conservatorí?"

"Yes, that one. Every time I see her, she asks: 'when will Maestro Granados return to Madrid?' Entirely love-sick."

Granados rolls his eyes. "Love-sick? She's only ten years old! And why should she have asked about me, Pau, with you in Madrid?"

"Nonsense! She's waiting for you, Enric."

"Then she'll have a long wait. She's quite nervy–even asked me to compose a piece for her to dance. Don't I have enough on my mind?"

They approach l'Hivernacle, a tropical greenhouse with a small café. "Not easy to leave all this," Casals says.

"This?"

"This town. This land. Family. Friends. So many good times, my brother. Barrí Xinès. Quatre Gats. Remember San Sebastian–playing the Gran Casino?"

"Yes, with Crickboom."

"What a grand time!"

"And ruining your reputation with the royal family," says Granados.

"Not quite. If that were true, the Queen Regent would have slammed the door on me. And also on you. Of course she didn't."

"And hearing the great Sarasate. Extraordinari!"

"What's extraordinary is, that man never practices!" Casals replies. "I can't imagine playing the violin so well without practice."

"Well, I confess–I'd sell my soul for more time to practice."

"You? But you're just like Sarasate. Geniuses–with the gift of improvisation. For me it's always hard work, every single day–just to live up to my instrument."

"You're much too humble," Granados says.

"No. Just realistic. Practical, Enric. Català. That's all."

"I was just your age on my first trip to Paris," Granados recalls. Struck down by typhoid, so instead of the Conservatoire, he had to settle for private lessions.

Casals recounts spending most of his own first stay in Paris bedridden. Doctors said he had dysentery, then changed their opinion to enteritis, without explaining either of these maladies. "What saved me," Casals says, "was coming home and sunning on the beach at Sant Salvador."

"Are the fates conspiring against us?" Granados asks. "Is it predestined?"

Casals looks up, as if that had never occurred to him. "Of course not! Everyone has a disastrous first trip to Paris. But this time I'm going alone–without my mother and younger brothers. I guess that means I'm growing up." He shakes his head. "What a horrible thought!"

Granados laughs. "This time you'll succeed, Pau."

"Yes, because this time I know exactly what I must do."

"It's the opportunity you've worked for. I have no doubt–you're on your way! Not staying here to suffocate."

"Yes. No matter what happens, better than spending my life teaching the untalented."

"Oh, so right! Between us, I'm going to establish my own academy. To teach piano properly."

"Excellent," Casals says. "Tell me, how's that work on Goya?"

Granados shakes his head. "Not going well. *Los Ovillejos*–my first effort–was a complete failure. The idea was there, but I just couldn't find the way."

"Don't be discouraged. It's not easy to convert the art of Goya to music."

"No, but I still have it–down here." Granados points to his heart.

"Of course. You won't give it up."

"Someday I'll find a way to make Goya's work come alive!"

Casals claps him on the shoulder. "If anyone can, it's you, brother."

"I need to get away from the complications of my life. Paris could do it, but that's not possible. Amparo would never move."

Casals nods. Barcelona is on the outer edge of European culture. There's a yearning here to become another Paris or Vienna or London, but that will take a long time. If it ever happens. So Casals tries to rally his friend, telling him he needn't suffocate in Barcelona. He too is on his way, with *María del Carmen* and his new work with the poet Apel.les Mestres. Casals says Granados can be the one to lift the music of Barcelona to new heights. And someday this may become another Paris.

Granados smiles. "Yes, perhaps–if my work is better received. If I'm considered sufficiently Català."

"Ayy, don't say that! Foolish to say that!"

"Well, Morera says–"

"Enric Morera? Don't pay any attention to him! You have more important things than worrying about Morera."

"But haven't you noticed, he's become the favorite son of Catalunya? We did a concert together for Catalunya Nova and the critic for *Diario* raved and raved about Morera–and damned me with faint praise. Morera's the 'moderniste'–whatever that is, as if I'm merely a purveyor of ancient music! He's everywhere! Collaborating with Rusiñol on a piece for the festival in Sitges. Involved with Vives and Millet at the Orfeó–"

"Forget all that," Casals urges. "And, my brother, be careful not to trust Morera."

Granados cocks his head. "No? Why do you say that?"

"Well, you're generous and trusting, and I love you for that. But Enric Morera? After shaking his hand, I'd want to count my fingers. Morera will take whatever he wants and leave you flat as he moves on. Listen–if you never take any advice from me–work with him when you must, if it helps *you*. But do not trust him!"

"Pau, I only mention him because he's *here*."

Casals bristles. "And how does that matter?"

"He's here and I'm here and everyone else is leaving. Performing all over Europe. You and Malats and Albéniz. I'll be the last one left behind."

Annoyed, Casals replies, "You can be the romantic–that's who you are. But don't romanticize the life of traveling from place to place! Hardly romantic! Long train rides from city to city, bad food, hotels that should be condemned, performing for rude audiences, then on to the next. I hunger for that life, but I know from Malats and others it's far from romantic."

"Easy for you to say," insists Granados.

"No, it's not! It's a practical view of what my life will be if I'm fortunate to emerge from the hundreds of cello players in Paris, if Maestro Lamoureux understands me–as those fools in Brussels did not! If luck is with me, then I'll have a life of the solo performer–my greatest dream. But romance? That's only in the soul of my cello."

Granados smiles. "I'll miss you, Pau. You're indeed a brother. It'll be difficult with you so far away."

"Then come to Paris. Stay with me. Any time."

"Thank you, I'll try. I will. Someday you and I will celebrate the opening of my opera in Paris."

"Opera? Which one?"

"Be assured, there will be operas," Granados says, seeming to have recovered his confidence. "Operas far too grand for Barcelona."

Casals looks up at his friend. So mercurial, down and up and down, purely a poet, fragile like a child. Though nine years younger, it's as if Casals is the older brother. "Then it's settled," he says. "You promise to let me know when you're coming to Paris."

"Of course."

"And, my brother–be careful with Morera."

There's loud scuffling on the steps leading up to the third-floor apartment on Carrer Tallers, a narrow street of small shops and residences west of La Rambla. Amparo Gal de Granados greets her husband and three of their four children as the front door is flung open, banging against the wall, and the entryway is filled with youthful cavorting and excited voices. Granados enters, crosses the hall, and kisses his wife lightly on the forehead.

Seven-year-old Eduardo is the first to insist on being heard. "Mamí, we went to the park! We went to the zoo!" As he begins to recount the afternoon's outing in copious detail, Solita, five, and four-year-old Enrique also clamor for their mother's attention.

"One at a time," she commands. Turning to her bemused and exhausted husband, she says, "I was wondering what became of you!"

"Ah, we lost track of time," Granados replies, ignoring the irritation in her voice. "Too much fun. And we waited a long time for a cab. Near the Arc de Triomf."

"Just the same, I was beginning to worry," Amparo says.

Granados turns to the children. "All right, tell Mamí what was the best thing today."

"The zoo, Papà!" says Solita.

"The lake!" says Enrique. "Can we go in a rowboat? Please!"

"Perhaps," Granados concedes. "But what if it tips over? Who would save us?"

"I'll learn to swim!" Enrique says.

Granados laughs. "Fine. Now tell your mother which of the flowers you liked best."

Tossing her head, Solita takes the lead. "The bougainvillea! I like the way they climb."

"No. The hydrangeas were better!" Eduardo says.

"Eduardo," Granados admonishes, "that may be your choice, but don't say 'no.' There is no right or wrong answer."

"Yes, Papà."

"I like the purple ones," says Enrique, who watches his older brother carefully and avoids pitfalls.

"Papà, what's your favorite?" asks Eduardo.

Granados ponders. "Well, your choices are splendid. For me? The passion flower." He recites from Tennyson:

> There has fallen a splendid tear
> from the passion flower at the gate.

and raises his hands to subdue a ripple of childish impatience. "Calm down, everyone. We haven't asked your mother which she likes best."

Amparo shakes her head and turns toward the children. "I'm not surprised your father likes passion flowers. But my favorites are roses."

"They're pretty, Mamí, but such sharp thorns!" Solita replies.

"Solita, please show more respect," says Granados. "A choice is a choice. There's nothing right or wrong with any of them."

"Yes, Papà."

"When can we go again, Papà?"

"Well, Eduardo, shall we take a walk after dark? We could catch the tram to Tibidabo and look down at the lights of l'Eixample and look up at the stars and–if we're lucky–hear the sound of the nightingale singing and–you'll like this, Enrique–look for the snails that come out of the ground at night and take over the rocks."

Enrique is ready to go. "Now, Papà? Now?"

"Soon. Perhaps next week."

Amparo motions to a uniformed girl who enters carrying the toddler, Victor, from the parlor. "Matilde, take these big ones and get them cleaned up before dinner."

"But Mamí, I have to practice," says Eduardo.

"You may practice–after you're cleaned up."

"And Papà promised he'd play Parcheesi with us," Solita says.

"Yes, I'll play with you," Granados says. "After dinner."

"Go, now. Your father and I have matters to discuss."

As they leave the parlor, Granados wonders what "matters" Amparo has saved for him. Probably money, always in short supply; always sets her off. He follows her into the sitting room; through the open window shades he hears the sound of horses pulling a wagon over the cobblestone street below.

She stops and turns to face him, arms folded across her swollen belly. "First of all, Enrique–my love–I don't like this new girl, not a bit. This Matilde–I don't like her at all!" A full head shorter than Granados, she glares upward, her lips pursed in the shape of a tulip blossom.

"Oh?" When her arms are folded, he knows she has more than trifles on her mind.

"She lied, Enrique. Said she was fourteen, but in truth she's closer to ten or eleven."

"Yes. Well, does she do a good job with the children?"

"That's not it–she's too close to Eduardo's age."

"Mi amor, he's just seven. Surely, at that age–"

"Ah–easy for you to say! At Eduardo's age, boys begin to learn bad habits. From whom? From their fathers, of course!" Her eyes open wide. "Am I wrong? Eh?"

Granados shrugs. "Perhaps not–but small boys learn mostly from their mothers. They're just curious about things. But saying Eduardo's going to be interested in this young girl, isn't that going a bit too far?"

"I think not! You're not listening to me. With this one coming soon," she adds, pointing to her enlarged waistline, "I won't be able to keep an eye on all of them–not all the time."

"Well, I agree, and having another will make it harder for me to support everyone. So, Titín," he answers, using her nickname, "after this one we shouldn't have any more." Bearing children nearly every year has drained the vitality of the effervescent young woman he courted just nine years ago.

Amparo glares at him. "So now you think we have too many children? Well, these aren't miracles." She points again. "Not exactly miracles. You're the one–not me, who comes home late from evenings with the men, smelling of cigars and licor de Marivaux. You're the one who climbs on top of me!"

He shakes his head. She's not being fair. It's been weeks since his last evening out. Pau's gone, as well as Malats and Albéniz. When she's upset, it's best to stay calm.

"Answer me! Am I wrong? Is this a miracle?" Her index finger arcs from her abdomen to his face. "Is it?"

He shakes his head. "I haven't been out with the men. Not lately. I've been working with Mestres–"

"And you expect El Liceu to be any more interested in this one?"

"Yes, of course!" He hears Eduardo practicing, playing scales.

"And you seriously believe those music snobs at El Liceu will accept anything besides Italian operas?"

"Yes, when they've heard *Follet*. Yes! And when Albéniz comes back next month, we'll be working with Morera on a new season for Teatre Líric Català, and you'll see–*Follet* will be a sensation."

"Well, I do hope you're right this time. At least you'll get your own music played! Suppose it's bound to be more successful than last year's concert series. Don't forget, I was against your investing so much of *our money* in that, and of course everyone gained from it except you. Including your fine partner Morera! If he's such a good socialist, why does he always have his hand in someone else's pocket? This time–I warn you–don't spend our household money on any deal with Morera!"

From down the hall, Eduardo's arpeggios sound better. He needs to spend more time with the scales. "That's not fair," Granados replies. "I did recover our money."

"Yes, but you could have made more just teaching."

"You don't understand. If concerts are more successful, we'll have better orchestral music here."

"So what? Barcelona's not your responsibility–your family is! And there you were–in a position to have your music played, and didn't! You always step back and play everyone's music but your own."

"You make it sound so simple. It's not. How much respect would I have if I were impresario and conductor and composer of the music?"

"I'm not an expert on respect, but I know this: if you get your music played, we'll have enough food to put on the table."

Granados raises his voice. "Don't you think I know that? Listen, if we're going to stay and live our lives here, I want to make this a better place, so some day it could become another Paris."

She snickers. "Well, that's pretty ambitious for someone who can barely support his family. You're a maestro of pretty words! Just like Don Quijote, seeing everything through a rose-tinted imagination. Everything idealized. Thinking we have more money than we have, thinking you're spending less than you are. And, when you're home, spending most of the time with your nose in a book–Unamuno, and poets with unpronounceable French names!"

He shakes his head. "That's not fair." His voice is sullen.

"And now, this thing called Societat Wagneriana? What's this? Another windmill?"

Granados explains that he and Joaquim Pena are interested in the music of Wagner, and the connection between his music and the myths of Catalunya. His voice is measured. "It's going to be–"

"Another romantic venture. Meanwhile, this baby I'm carrying is going to be real–not an illusion. I'm convinced it's a girl. And you know with a girl it's not just one more mouth to feed. Girls are more expensive."

"Yes, I know that, Titín. Girls and their mothers."

"Don't be rude! I'm not the one spending our money foolishly. Like buying those parrots for Solita. And that absurd cage. Not I buying the fine suits and shirts and hats to look like English royalty strolling up and down La Rambla."

Her words sting. "But I need to be well dressed! I need to look successful. My clothes are not a luxury. When I went to play for the Queen Regent, I had to buy a whole new outfit to be presented to her. Did you expect me to receive medals from the royal family dressed like a cab driver? That was *not* foolish spending!"

Amparo shrugs. "All right, you had to dress up for royalty. Enough of that. I have one more thing. The most upsetting!"

He braces for the new subject. "More than money?"

"I'm done with that–for now. It's about your idea to start an academy of music. Just like Don Quijote to start your own academy. And what happens if you can't earn enough to support us?"

"You make it sound like such a gigantic risk, Titín. Surely you know it's Salvador Andreu who would provide the investment. He would take the financial risk."

"Ah sí, the rich and famous Doctor Andreu! And his lovely wife Carmen. How fortunate your old sweetheart married so well!"

Carmen? Old sweetheart? Dalliances once in a while–but never with Carmen. She's a sister. Never more.

"She was never my sweetheart," he counters. "Simply a dear friend."

Amparo bores in. "Yes, but just how *dear*? I see the way she looks at you. She worships you."

"That's foolish."

"Not as foolish as saying I'd move to Madrid–when you were trying to get that job at the Conservatorio. Have you forgetten that?"

"I haven't. I appreciate your being willing to move."

"Shall we talk about all the times you go up to your dear friend Carmen's place in Puigcerdà? And stay most of the summer. Do you go there to see the charming Doctor Andreu–twice the age of his pretty wife?"

"You exaggerate, Titín. I've been going there for years, when my work requires peace and quiet. For instance, *Valses Poéticos*, which I could never have composed here, not between lessons. It's one of my best works. Do you begrudge me *that* time in Puigcerdà?"

"That's not the point. Tell me, then, when you go to Puigcerdà, is the good doctor there with his shapely wife? Or is she alone? Does she still play her harp? Do you still play sweet music together?"

Granados shakes his head, closes his eyes, and counts to five. "You're being totally unfair! Last time I was there, Carmen was visiting her brother Francisco. Who's dying! Only Salvador was there, and the children, and the family of Lluisa Vidal. I spent nearly all my time sleeping and working on *Follet*. You call that a sin?"

"No, not that," she concedes. "But don't let me find out there's more going on between you and Carmen. Or one of your infatuated students."

"Oh?"

"For instance, that bewitching María."

"María Oliveró? She's a child! Thirteen years old. That María?"

"I don't know which María. There's a tall one who looks more like twenty-five. Besides, La Duquesa de Alba was married at thirteen, and she was surely no saint!"

"That's entirely unfair! Every music teacher in Barcelona is accused by his wife of carrying on with students. And mostly it's untrue." His head is pounding, as if a migraine is about to return.

Amparo rises to her tiptoes, both arms outstretched and hands clenched in tiny, plump balls. "That's different. Look at the others—Casals, Albéniz, Morera—not a handsome one in the lot. In fact ugly, compared with you. Look at you! God gave you too much beauty to go with your genius. I know what Carles Vidiella said: if only he'd been born a woman! So don't play the innocent with me. Not with me. It's not very becoming. And just so you don't forget, I've seen that tall María look at you with her cat's eyes. I'm no fool!"

He holds his breath and closes his eyes. Dizzy with so many things to keep in place. Pain in his head and whirlpools in his heart. She can rant and rave. How can she harm him?

Chapter Three

Planet Earth 1901

Nineteen hundred and one. The planet is more crowded: one billion six hundred million inhabitants, and getting smaller, thanks to the inventors of wireless radio, horseless carriages, and aircraft. As forewarned by Aesop, familiarity is breeding contempt. Action engenders reaction, as human beings are caught in the laws of physics. And hope–born in this dawning by an ideal of greater commonality–is wavering as clouds whirl on the horizon, gathering force and violence like a tropical storm in the Cape Verde Islands before it crosses the South Atlantic.

It promises to be a century of industrial and economic progress. The Eastman Kodak Company is incorporated in Trenton, New Jersey; the Flatiron Building is added to the New York's growing forest of skyscrapers; and Michigan farm boy Henry Ford's employer, the Detroit Automobile Company, goes into bankruptcy, leaving Ford unemployed for most of the year–until victories on the racetrack enable him to attract investors for his new motor car company.

The pace quickens in science and technology. Electric tram systems are installed in London and Paris; Guglielmo Marconi receives and sends the first radio signals across the Atlantic; and patents are filed on items that will become household staples: Gillette's disposable razor blade, and the vacuum cleaner. The Wright brothers of Ohio build a wind tunnel and test their theories of flight with a series of gliders on the coast of North Carolina, but by year's end they're discouraged and Wilbur says to Orville, "Not within a thousand years would man ever fly!" He will be proved wrong next year. German high school dropout Albert Einstein, whose theory of relativity will turn the world of physics upside down, becomes a Swiss citizen, tries to get a teaching job, but confesses he's "given up ambition to get to a university." And Viennese physician Sigmund Freud–arguably the father of psychology–whose first book was considered a failure, writes *Psychopathology of Everyday Life*, which is notably more successful.

Most of the industrialized countries prepare for war. England and Germany discuss an alliance, but failing to achieve it, they embark on separate routes that will pit them against each other in 1914. Russia and Japan jockey for position in Korea and Manchuria, and will be at war by 1904. Parallel to the European arms competition, Germany launches SS *Kronprinz Wilhelm*, second in a series of "four-stacker" luxury liners, and England's White Star Line launches the SS *Celtic*, to be followed in ten years by the larger SS *Titanic*. German Kaiser Wilhelm brags about achieving a place in the sun for his empire's naval armada, which he predicts will soon rival the British Royal Navy, long dominant on the high seas.

The Royal Navy launches its first submarine, *Holland I*, equipped to fire one torpedo. (The original inventor of the underwater ship was Narcís Monturiol i Estarriol, a Catalan who tested a prototype, *El Ictíneo*, in the port of Barcelona in 1859.) Controversy surrounds the use of these ships, since they're considered only suitable for the weaker powers in an arms race. Despite widespread opinion that submarine service isn't worthy of a gentleman sailor, Britain continues to build subs. Germany follows suit, and will have a rival force of *Unterseeboots* (U-boats) ready for action by 1914.

Peacemakers are rare. Jean Henri Dumant, Swiss founder of the International Red Cross and originator of the Geneva convention that prescribes conduct between combatants, is rescued from bankruptcy and his life as a roaming derelict, and is awarded the first Nobel Prize for Peace.

Barcelona

The city's population has doubled in the past thirteen years, and now exceeds one half million. Much of this is due to poverty in the countryside after the disastrous war against the United States of America three years ago, and to the destruction of the vineyards of Catalunya by an insect-borne disease with a lilting Greek name: phylloxera. Barcelona is now expanding into the foothills north of l'Eixample, and railroads link the city to the rest of the Iberian peninsula and northward to France. The electric Tramvia Blau carries passengers to the Mount Tibidabo area being developed by Dr. Salvador Andreu, an entrepreneurial pharmacist who has built a large pharmaceutical company and is now a major real estate developer. Other tramvias link the coastal main line to hilltop cities such as Tiana and Alella. And automobiles and motorcycles will soon arrive.

In Barcelona, resentment of the central government in Madrid and its military forces has grown since the ill-considered war against the U.S.A., and this year's regional elections are won by Lliga Regionalista, a new conservative Catholic party that favors more autonomy for Catalunya—or at least less interference from Madrid. Lliga Regionalista is headed by political activist Enric Prat de la Riba i Sarrà and the young lawyer and financier Francesc Cambó i Batlle, whose extraordinary capacity to organize and inspire give the new party its margin of victory.

Prat and Cambó, trusted by the alta burguesa of Barcelona to provide a favorable political climate for their industrial ambitions, are allied with the right-wing cleric, Fr. Josep Torras i Bagès, whose influence extends into many corners of Catalan life, including art, architecture, theatre, music, literature, finance and politics. Fr. Torras, for whom the Catholic Church is the foundation of Catalan heritage, is also sought for guidance by Antoni Gaudí, who's been ever critical of apostles of modernism such as Ramón Casas and Santiago Rusiñol. Along with the Llimona brothers, sculptor Josep and painter Joan, Gaudí helps establish the culturally conservative society known as the Artistic Circle of Saint Luke, which opposes the freewheeling, anticlerical, bohemian life style of those who frequent such cabarets as Els Quatre Gats.

Another prominent political figure is Dr. Bartolomeu Robert i Yarzábal, who entered the political arena after an illustrious career in medicine and became mayor of Barcelona two years ago. As mayor, he sanctioned a strike that was aimed at relieving Catalan bankers of a tax imposed by the Madrid government to help pay for the war of 1898. In the showdown, Madrid declared war on Catalunya, and Mayor Robert backed down only to save the city from invasion by the Spanish Army. For this gesture of defiance, he's been lionized by the region's industrialists, including Dr. Salvador Andreu.

Aspirations for Catalunya's autonomy are also reflected in the proliferation of its language in literature; an epic poem, "L'Atlàntida," by Father Jacint Verdaguer i Santaló, appeared in the late 1870s as if to demonstrate its potential. Later, when Verdaguer's "Canigó"—extolling Catalan identity—was published, the poet-priest was welcomed into Barcelona's innermost circles.

As the Catalan language is uplifted, a rediscovery of ancient Catalan monuments spurs the so-called "excursionism," which taps into a deep vein of patriotic feeling. Every ruin becomes a shrine to be restored, the holiest of which is in the northern Catalan city of Ripoll, renowned as "the cradle of Catalunya." The movement achieves a cultlike status among some Barcelona artists, naturalists, and hikers, including Rusiñol.

Adding to the momentum for "catalanism" is the first celebration this year of the historic battle of 11 September 1714 in which Rafael Casanova i Comes, then

Barcelona's city council leader, led the city's militia against the forces of Philip V in the War of Spanish Succession. The red and yellow Catalan flag waves in profusion throughout the region, and the sardana, a dance with mediaeval origins in rural Catalunya, becomes a favored way of expressing Catalan identity.

Modernisme originally referred to the architectural style of Gaudi and his colleagues, most notably Josep Puig i Catafalch, designer of the building where Els Quatre Gats is located, and Lluís Domènech i Montaner. A style in which the curve is predominant over the straight line, decorative richness prevails, and there's a strong bias against symmetry. Now Modernisme has become a blanket term applied as well to the literary, musical, and visual arts in Barcelona. Implying a new opening to Europe and cities such as Paris, Berlin, Rome, Milano, Vienna, and London, and suggesting a turning away from Madrid and the heartland of Spain.

Parisian influence is strongest, with widespread use of French phrases among artists aligned with Rusiñol, Casas, and Utrillo, who studied and worked in the French capital and brought home the techniques of French Impressionists such as Degas and Manet. Their works are regularly displayed in a series of shows at the new Sala Parés on Carrer Petritxol.

Modernistes are eager to show their sensitivity to art, and to explore new ways to shock the alta burguesa families from whence they mostly come. They disparage the realism of Zola and Flaubert, preferring the current flavors of idealism and symbolism. Choral music is popular, with a proliferation of groups in Barcelona and the surrounding cities of Catalunya. Belgian playwright Maurice Maeterlinck is idolized, as is the Norwegian Henrik Ibsen. The writings of Friedrich Nietzsche are revered, as is the work of such American transcendentalists as Ralph Waldo Emerson. Walt Whitman's poems are translated into Catalan and widely read. But above all, the cultural trendsetters of Modernisme adore the operas of Richard Wagner, based on epic themes that serve to evoke the grandeur of Catalunya's distant past.

Nineteen hundred and one. Granados pushes ahead with his idea for an academy of music for advanced students of piano and voice. "Acadèmia Granados"–its sound is lyrical, played over and over in his reveries. Someday to be engraved on a brass plaque. After nurturing the idea for a decade, describing the uniqueness of his academy to anyone who'd listen, Granados fears his drumbeating will come back to haunt him. He must not wait too long. What if he dies without taking the first giant step? Not preposterous, since his father died in his late fifties and his brother Calixto died at forty. Granados is just turning thirty-four. Ample time if he doesn't squander the next decade.

This summer isn't the most convenient time for him to realize the dream. He's fallen behind in composing *Follet*, which must be finished for the new season of the Teatre Líric Català. His life is full of interruptions, and with each passing day he longs for a quiet time and a remote place to devote his energy and inspiration to finishing *Follet*. If it's received well, the recognition that he craves in his own city may follow. If not, another missed opportunity. And he'll remain "nostre Granados"–our hometown musician. So he must make time for *Follet*.

Meanwhile, the fifth Granados child has arrived. Natalia, with wisps of brown hair, her mother's round face, and her father's large, charcoal brown eyes. When students come to his home for lessons, as they often do, there's a perpetual cacophony of earnest but uneven piano music, interrupted by the maestro's corrections, bickering among his rambunctious older children, Amparo's quarrels with the nanny, Matilde, and periodic crying from the newborn Natalia. Always a perfect B-flat, occasionally followed by a G-flat, lower on the scale. An interesting sonic blend, but even between lessons not an ambiance for composing new works.

Acadèmia Granados. He doesn't doubt its ultimate success, but knows that the journey from raw concept to offering classes will require many decisions. Inevitably, not everyone will embrace them. He braces himself for the challenges.

Amparo is his first concern. She won't let him forget that his classical concert series failed to ease their financial problems last year, and their initial investment was lost. Her lashing words–"I'd like to believe this is different, but you haven't convinced me"–are a common refrain. And how will Mathieu Crickboom react when Granados says he's leaving his friend's school, where he's been teaching for years? He expects an explosion. He hasn't convinced Amparo, and he dreads walking into Crickboom's office with his resignation. Yet, while conceding these are real concerns, he assures himself they're not insurmountable.

On a positive note, he's being encouraged by some of his closest friends and colleagues. Isaac Albéniz agrees that offering advanced training to the most promising students will allow more of them to stay in Barcelona, rewarding the city with their talent. Domènec Mas i Serracant, a former student and now music director of the church where Granados and Amparo were married, is eager to become Granados' assistant at the new academy. And his close friend and neighbor, Dr. August Pi i Sunyer, has agreed to be a member of Acadèmia Granados' board of trustees.

"Of course your friends are with you on this," is Amparo's refrain. "You stick together like pigeons in the rain. But where will you get the money? Isn't that the first step? And if your famous academy falls flat, how will you feed us? We can't eat piano music! You won't have Crickboom to work for and there are already too many pianists out there trying to book concerts. So tell me: where will you get the money?"

After a week of nightly tirades, Granados resolves to find the money. Now, with no further delay, it's time to see Dr. Salvador Andreu's wife, Carmen Miralles. The last time they met, she said, "When you decide to do this, I insist you talk to Salvador. He's a good man, and very generous. Could be an enormous help."

Now Granados and Carmen are sitting at a small table in front of an ice cream parlour on Rambla de Gràcia. She leans forward onto her elbows as he asks once again, "How can you be sure your husband wants to help?"

She raises her wide-brimmed white hat, and laughs. "Dearest Enrique, you're so bright about some things–so dense about others! Can you doubt that I know what Salvador wants? Don't you know, when it comes to my passion–my music–dear Salvador is willing to do anything I ask? You're so amusing!"

Granados pushes back. "How, when he's so busy with all of his businesses? How could he find time for my idea?"

She lifts her hands, palms up. "Your idea is an investment, is it not?"

"Yes, but not like pharmacies and drug companies and real estate. All those things, those are real investments."

She laughs again and runs her gloved finger along the lace trim at the top of her blouse. "I don't expect you, o maestro, to recognize an investment, but you're looking at Salvador's favorite one."

"Of course," he says, smiling at last. "How stupid of me."

"Precisely. Now, my dear, you must come up to Puigcerdà. Next week. We'll all be there–Salvador will be back from France–and you can have the same guest room. Your favorite–overlooking the pond."

"Where I woke up with the opening notes of *Valses Poéticos* ringing in my ears. Yes, I could bring my notes on *Follet*."

"Of course you'll bring them. I've just had the Ortiz tuned. And you must stay on. But beware, dearest one, if you don't talk to Salvador about your idea by the second day, I'll have the children throw you in the lake."

"I don't swim."

"That's the point, estúpido. What do we need with a man whose heart is full of dreams and not willing to make them come true?"

"All right, then. All I have to do is convince Amparo it's a good idea for me to go to Puigcerdà."

Carmen rolls her eyes. "You can manage that."

"She's always so jealous–"

"Stop it! I hate it when you're helpless."

He glares at her. "You don't know how Titín–"

"Shall I talk to her?" She stands up.

"No. I'll take care of it."

"That's a brave boy!"

Puigcerdà

Dr. Salvador Andreu i Grau sits in the garden of his xalet–his vacation home on the edge of the pond. Behind him the Pyrenees rise high above the tiled gables of the chalet. It's a breezy afternoon in late summer, and he pulls his wicker chair from a favored spot that is now shaded. The sun begins to warm his face, and as he loosens his tie and starched collar he closes his eyes, enjoying a restful interlude. He arrived late last night, after a long train trip from Paris to Prades, and a rocking ride on the narrow-gauge "Little Yellow Train" that winds up through the Pyrenees region of Cerdanya to Puigcerdà. To his sanctuary.

Andreu welcomes these days away from the fast pace of his life–exporting the cough drops and chest salve to France, Germany, and Latin America; developing new products for the Spanish and export markets; expanding the country's pharmaceutical association; and carving out the new housing developments of Sant Gervasi and Tibidabo on the high ground above l'Eixample. He runs his fingers back through the crests of gray hair bridging his ears.

"How well you look, Salvador," his French associate said the day before yesterday, seeing him off at Paris' Gare d'Austerlitz. "Do you have a secret elixir?" Andreu told him the secret was being married to a younger woman. That kept him young, that and having six children to ensure he won't fall into indolence. "Ah, so that's the secret," replied the Frenchman, "of course, to be married to a younger woman."

When they met, Andreu was more than twice her age; it was Carmen's utter zest for life and brightness that captivated him. And after thirteen years, captivated he remains. Her enthusiasm for music is boundless, but she doesn't hesitate to offer ideas on any subject, even his business ventures. She can bore through the outer crust of details and ask him the very question he isn't prepared to answer. He's in awe of this. And Carmen manages their households without apparent effort, keeping a step or two ahead of the children. He wonders, what's *her* elixir? And now, as he watches her glide across the balcony, he feels a deep gratitude that the fates that spin the threads of life have brought him together with this graceful, ravishing woman.

She leans over, kisses his angular cheek, and sits on his lap. "It's about Enrique," she whispers in her preferred language, Castilian.

"You invited him to come up?" asks Andreu in his, Catalan. Their family and friends are used to this ongoing duet of languages.

"Yes. I told you, last night. You were exhausted."

"Well, a pleasant surprise. And Francesc is coming up with Lluisa."

"Yes. And we'll dine at ten."

"Molt bé, my precious one. And what exactly is it–about Enric?"

She laughs softly. "He wants to ask you a question."

Andreu leans back. "Aren't you the mystery woman. A question?"

"Mi amor, I'm going to take the children out to gather herbs and mushrooms, so you men will have all the time in the world for questions."

He laughs loudly. "Am I detecting the fine hands of the beautiful harpist? So deftly plucking my strings?"

"Ah, you've been in Paris far too long, darling Badó," she says, using the Catalan diminutive for Salvador. "You're just imagining things."

Andreu puts his arms around her waist and squeezes hard.

Granados, dressed in a dark blue double-breasted suit and light blue ascot, is pacing in his room; it's nearly time to ask Andreu for help with the academy. His room at Xalet Andreu provides a view across the pond and over the wide valley that separates the Sierra del Cadí from the higher peaks of the Pyrenees along the border with France. On the southern entrance to the valley is a high pass near the village of Quexans that Granados crossed over last evening, where the road, after more than sixty kilometers of switching back and forth through forests and rocky escarpments, finally straightens out and descends to Puigcerdà.

The initial portion of his now familiar journey from Barcelona, starting at the Plaça de Catalunya train station, runs north through the most mountainous of Catalan regions, following the ravines carved by winding rivers, passing through small cities, skirting rocky slopes where sheep graze on the hills, where castles oversee small villages–some merely collections of brown stone dwellings, and monasteries are nestled high above.

Granollers, whose vines and olive groves date back to Roman times, is the first city on this rail line; then Vic, a pre-Roman community dominated by the Montcada Castle, where the train runs parallel to the River Ter; then the grazing lands of a broad plain, followed by rolling grain fields surrounding Manlleu, and sheep ranching in the countryside outside of Torelló. Ripoll, the next major stop, is one of Catalunya's most important monastic centers; here the Ter converges with the River Freser winding down from the French border; it's the last stop for passengers bound for Puigcerdà, where during the Carlist war of the 1830s the Monastery of Ripoll–one of Catalunya's most revered places–was sacked and its monks murdered by a roaming army of volunteers. Ripoll is also one of Europe's most important producers of firearms.

The rest of the journey continues northward by horse-drawn coach, from Ripoll to Ribes de Freser–on the eastern edge of Granados' home province of Lleida, where people suffering from chronic indigestion seek the curative powers of its baths. From Ribes, the road runs westward through countless switchbacks north of the Serra de Mogrony, with the often snow-topped peaks of La Pleta Roja and Puigilançada in the southern sky, and finally drops into the wide valley of Puigcerdà.

A long trip up to be sure, but leaving the rush and clamor of Barcelona and passing through the heart of the Catalan countryside to these splendid mountains always brings Granados a surge of bright energy and inspiration for the work he loves best. And even in the short time since arriving, working as always at the piano, he's finished two full pages of orchestration for *Follet*. With Carmen's prompting, however, his chief aim in Puigcerdà is to ask for her husband's patronage.

At five o'clock, with the sunlight softening, Granados walks to the place in the garden where Andreu is waiting. They greet each other and sit down. "Pleasant trip up?"

"Oh, yes," Granados replies. "I always enjoy it."

"Splendid time of the year. The best. Grapes ready for picking and harvest time in the grain fields. Olive pickers reaching up. Leaves starting to turn."

"Yes. Quite a splendid time."

"Cigarette?" Andreu's hand reaches out of the vested, ivory-white, and cuff-linked shirt, extending an opened silver case of Gauloise. His hair has turned silvery white and receded to the back of his head, leaving a high forehead at the top of a narrow face; at the bottom are a narrow moustache and goatee, both peppered with a few darker hairs of his youth. At sixty he's nearly twice Granados' age, yet of the two men Andreu seems more animated, at least more driven.

"No, thank you," Granados says. "Never been much of a smoker."

"D'acord! Probably not good for one's health. All right now, Carmen says you have a question."

"Well, not merely a question, Salvador. You've heard about my idea for an academy. For the best of our students, so they don't have to leave town. I've been thinking about it for years."

"Yes indeed. Sounds like an excellent idea. And, to get to the point, my friend, you're looking for money to start this academy, and you have reason to believe I'd be interested."

"Of course you'll have many questions, and I'll try my best to answer all of them."

Andreu shifts into his role of skeptical investor. He wants to know how much initial investment is needed; what it will cost to operate such an academy; who will be the day-to-day administrator; how many students are needed to support it; who'll teach classes besides Granados; what other investors have been approached; and where it will be located.

Granados tells him of a location on Carrer Fontanella, between La Rambla and Portal de l'Àngel. He and his family could live in the back and reserve the front rooms for lessons. Granados will teach piano and develop a curriculum for basic techniques such as the use of the pedal. Other maestros are interesting in joining him and bringing their students; they'll be paid only for the lessons they give. No salaries. And several of his best students–he mentions Emilia Ycart, Pepita Virella, Baltasar Samper, Mercè Moner, and Antoni Massana–are eager to follow him to the new academy.

"Those are your students? Or Crickboom's?" Andreu asks.

"They are mine. I am their maestro."

"But when you leave Crickboom, you'll take these students with you?" Andreu is testing Granados' willingness to compete against a friend. "Aren't you afraid he'll be unhappy with this?"

Granados hesitates, then nods. "Crickboom's school isn't offering what my academy will offer these students. Eventually they'll leave and go to Madrid or Paris."

Andreu strokes his beard. "So it's not your problem if Crickboom's unhappy. Right?"

"Right."

"All's fair in love and war."

"I suppose so. Two more things: I expect this academy to be my primary source of income, and I will be the administrator–you won't have to wonder who's in charge."

Andreu smiles. "It sounds like a promising idea. Have you talked with any other investors?"

"Not yet. You're the first."

"Hmm. Well, I suggest you see Eduard Condé. He helped you before. Make sure to ask him to be on the board of trustees–you'll need a strong board."

"I've thought of that too. My friend Dr. August Pi i Sunyer–a great music lover–has agreed to serve."

"August? Bright young fellow. Father was a great physician. 'Course he's got a couple of uncles who're Republican rabble-rousers, but shouldn't hold that against him, should we? Still, you'll need people with more stature in town–how about the ex-mayor, Doctor Robert? Not a man in town who's better regarded. And he's got connections everywhere."

Granados shrugs. "I barely know him."

"Oh, I'd talk to Robert. He owes me a thing or two. Don't worry–he'll serve. And he'll give you credibility with the Llimona brothers and the Saint Lukers. Good people to have on your side."

Granados understands. Having Robert involved will help him reach the more conservative elements of the alta burguesa. And having Robert as a trustee might even help Amparo see this isn't just another risky venture. He recognizes the value of prominent members on the board, and thanks his host for the suggestions. He savors the words "I'd talk to Robert" as a sign Andreu's predisposed to be a patron of the acadèmia, but realizes that doesn't ensure a commitment.

Andreu stands up and clasps his hands behind his back. He needs time to think through the request, he tells Granados.

After dinner and alone in their bedroom suite overlooking the pond, it's Carmen facing questions. "My principal concern," Andreu says, "is that our young maestro has no experience in administration, none at all. No denying he's brilliant as a pianist. His reputation as a composer seems to be growing, and his students are apparently devoted. But none of these prepared him for starting this new academy. It's like starting a new business. Right?"

Carmen waits for him to finish. "What you've said is indisputable."

"So you agree?"

"Yes, I agree that you should have this concern. As with any investment. But it's not the entire picture."

Andreu smiles, recognizing her intention to convince him to help Granados. "And the rest of the picture?"

"Enrique was the chief organizer of the Societat de Concerts Clàssics last year, and it finished the season without any debt. The last of the concerts was extraordinary–Granados, Malats, and Vidiella. Despite having the wrong pianos."

"If it was so successful, why did it fold?"

Carmen takes a step toward her husband. "Truthfully? It folded for two reasons: first, the audience in Barcelona isn't ready for orchestral music, and second, Enrique was carrying the whole venture on top of everything else. A solitary and exhausting experience."

"Ah, but won't starting this academy be solitary and exhausting?"

"Somewhat, mi amor, but he'll not be alone. He'll have excellent instructors. And, as you've suggested, a strong board of trustees. And since you're wise and shrewd, you'll put me on the board."

Andreu laughs in appreciation.

Carmen has momentum. "Hear me out. Enrique is very bright and as you've said so many times, brains are essential. And he knows how to work–passionately–to achieve his goals. And he's absolutely honest. You know, my most beloved, this is a most important thing. So the idea of starting an academy is a very good one indeed. There's obviously a need for it, and as you've said so often: where there's a need, there's money to be made."

Andreu listens, enjoying her fervent response to his concerns. He tries another thrust. "But you agree he lacks any kind of experience in business administration?"

She laughs. "Badó, my love, of course he does. But I know of a certain pharmacist who decided to develop housing, and people said he had no experience in architecture or in construction, and yet–"

Andreu laughs, knowing she's taken the straight line to the heart of the matter. "All right, all right. My basic question is how is Enric going to keep everything going? Bringing in the students. Supervising instructors. Getting the bills paid. Watching the expenses–he doesn't seem the type to be able to live like an artist, when he's just exactly that."

Carmen smiles, as if he's taken the bait. "Well, it's your decision whether to invest in this or not, but I'm not going to tell you there aren't any risks. However, if *you'd* never taken risks, mi amor, would you be anything more than a nice neighborhood pharmacist who mixes powders in the back room and smiles when he sells a bottle full of who knows what? Would you have invented a medicine for coughs? The little 'Joanolas'? Or a chest cream for South America? If you wanted to avoid risks, would you have courted a harp player who was young enough to be your daughter? No, I rather think not!"

Andreu rolls his eyes. She is his match.

Granados is in the salon, seated at the Ortiz & Cussó. A piano made in Barcelona, and though not as prestigious as the French Pleyel, well suited for his work on Act II of *Follet*. He reaches up and fills four measures with notes on a composition pad placed above the keyboard between a pair of double candelabras. Act II begins with a storm scene, followed by a love duet between Nadala and the poet Follet in his cave. Too Wagnerian? Too much like *Tristan and Isolde?*

He plays the notes again, imagining a soprano singing them. His lips purse as he hums the line, then he erases the last measure and pauses, remembering this old friend, Carmen's piano, from earlier visits to the Andreu chalet, thinking this time it's in an acceptable state of tune, a little off in the lower octaves but quite satisfactory. Considering how far the tuner had to travel, taking the train up to Ripoll and the bumpy coach through the mountains, and carrying a heavy tuning kit up the arduous stairs from the Puigcerdà station. Quite satisfactory, much more in tune than when he composed *Valses* in this same room eight years ago. As he reaches up to put the next measure on the pad, he drifts back to the conversation with Andreu.

Will he be my patrón? Dream for me–for him another business venture. Another skin cream. Without a patrón–impossible. My only venue–my only stage. He'd talk to Doctor Robert–means he'll say yes?

Granados looks out the window, across the pond and eastward where the late afternoon sun lights the rolling hills of the valley. Turning to the left, he sees the shining snow-capped peaks of the Pyrenees across the French border. He leans back on the piano bench, letting reverie interrupt his work again.

So many late nights spent at Xalet Andreu, retelling stories of Paris with Carmen's brother Francisco Miralles, who moved back to Catalunya eight years ago after thirty years in France and was staying here while Granados composed *Valses Poéticos*. Francisco, his sketching mentor in Paris, who showered him with praise and asked Granados to sit for an oil portrait that four years later arrived as a wedding gift. Depicting the twenty-two year old pianist in white tie and black jacket, hair and moustache trimmed short. Francisco, whose soirees with an older bohemian crowd mesmerized Granados, whose lurid women enthralled and baffled him, whose favorite model Gabrielle–rumored to have died of poison the year before Granados arrived in Paris–lingered ethereally in the atelier. Francisco, whose life of "montmartrisme" tantalized the young pianist so that he moved to a small room on the Rue Fontaine, nearer the atelier, only realizing after eight months that he couldn't keep pace with the nocturnal, absinthe-swilling crowd and still remain devoted to his music, that it was time to go back to the place he'd been sharing with Nano Viñes on the Rue Trèvise. Francisco, who died earlier this summer, only fifty-three.

Francisco gone forever. Another gone too soon!

During Granados' first months studying in Paris, Carmen came to see her brother only once, while Granados was recuperating from his illness. Then she went home to Barcelona and married Andreu, leaving her harp at Francisco's atelier. One day after she'd gone, Francisco showed him a painting in progress–of a smiling Carmen holding a parasol and glancing obliquely toward the viewer as she walks across a bright meadow. Granados asked, what news of her? Not much. What does an older brother know of a young woman's life? Later, hearing that she was promised to Andreu, Granados was overcome by sadness, even though there'd been no romance and he knew they weren't meant to be promised to each other. Didn't belong together.

"Dreaming?" Carmen's voice drifts into his reverie.

Granados hears her voice and the rustle of her skirt as she slides onto the piano bench next to him, and feels her hip nudge his own. She's redolent of wild herbs. "Yes. Una fantasía."

She smiles. "Was I in your dream?"

He takes a deep breath. "Yes. You and Francisco."

She closes her eyes, filled with tears.

"So many good times," Granados says. "Here, and in Paris. I miss him so much!"

She nods and wipes her eyes. "He was so very ill. So much pain. At the end, I was grateful he didn't have to go on with it."

"It's very, very sad."

Carmen looks up, over the piano, through the wide bay window in the music salon. "He always loved it when you came up. Said there was nothing finer than sitting in this room, hearing you play. Especially the improvisations. Said he loved it more than painting." She runs the tips of her fingers along the side of his head and down to his neck. "Is the piano satisfactory?"

Her touch is like a soft zephyr. "It's in very good tune. Thank you." He asks about the scent of wild herbs. "Is it thyme? Rosemary?"

Carmen rubs the fingers of her right hand together and the scent intensifies. "Both. Gathered up in those hills. My favorites. I rub them all over."

He looks at her heart-shaped face and long tapering neck, and stops there. "Are the children practicing every single day?"

She giggles at the non sequitur. "Truthfully? Nearly every day. Especially Paquita. Of course, not as much as their maestro demands." Carmen points to the composition pad. "And your work?"

He gives her the long answer. "I've finished another piece for solo piano, *Rapsodia Aragonesa*, and just sent it to Madrid. You know Goya was from Aragon. I've done some more work on *Rosamor*, but it's a big lyric opera like *Follet*, and right now there's a deadline on that one, so I've put *Rosamor* aside. Again. Also I've started a series of piano solos which I'll dedicate to Eduardo: *Cuentos de la Juventud*. And there's the orchestral piece, *La Nit del Mort*, which is partly finished, but considering that Barcelona isn't quite ready for orchestral work I've got ample time to finish it later. Above all, there's *Follet*," he says, pointing to the composition pad.

"This *Follet*. What's it about?"

"Idealized love. Follet's an itinerant poet who's courting Nadala, the daughter of the Count Martí. She's enchanted by him and finds her way to the cave where Follet lives. They sing their duet and of course they consummate their love amidst a violent storm and the light of dawn finds them together. Sworn to secrecy, Follet sings of his love for her to the trees and to a nightingale."

"Oh my! Idealized love, a big storm, a love scene, and a nightingale. How operatic!"

He laughs. "Yes, but listen–the storm is a forecast of the tragedy to come, not just a storm of the elements–it's also about the temperament of the heart. And instead of being followed by a gentle calm, as in nature, it's followed by a poignant sadness in the poet Follet."

The wind chases them as Granados and Carmen walk around the pond, past the slate roof and brown fieldstone vacation chalets of the alta burguesa whose gardens are separated by walls of cut stone, two meters high. There is constant scrawking from shore birds as they scoot on the sand, and creaking from the oarlocks of small, white rowboats leaving and returning to a stone pier with ponderous columns on the north side of the pond. Overhead, pine trees wheeze and moan as they bow in the wind. Granados removes his jacket and puts it around her shoulders.

They stop and sit side by side on a stone bench, with a view of the widest, sunniest valley in the Pyrenees, the only one that runs east and west. Steep pastureland rises above the town, flanked to the north and south by snow-covered peaks. This luminous valley is the core of the region of La Cerdanya, where Spain and France merge at the trout-filled Riu Rahur, where the border separating them is treated on both sides with humorous disdain. It is only one country: La Cerdanya.

Now the sun has dropped behind the array of snowy rock walls of the Serra de Cadí, rising from the Riu Segre and its river villages of Bellver and Martinet, whose peaks connect La Cerdanya with the principality of Andorra. The light, striking only the tops of the tallest pines, is bleached and fading as pointed shadows from the trees reach out over the wind-whipped pond.

Carmen breaks the halcyon silence. "Salvador is somewhat interested in your academy. You are not to know this." She raises her finger to her puckered lips.

"Yes? He told you?"

She laughs. "There are no secrets between me and Salvador–except those we choose." She laughs again. "I know that's very enigmatic. What I mean is, you may have convinced my dear husband to be your patrón. You may have, provided there's a way to keep track of his investment. Salvador is perfectly brilliant when it comes to pharmaceuticals, but music is not his business, nor his passion. It's yours. So you'll need a way to let him know how your academy is progressing. Not just the names of instructors and students, whom he barely recognizes. He'll want to know about things like income and expenses. That's the crux of it for Salvador. And there is indeed a way to accomplish this."

"And it is?"

She smiles and raises her hand to his cheek. "Dearest Enrique, I'm the person who can translate what's happening in your world for my Salvador. He trusts me, and I believe you do as well."

"Of course. I'd trust you with my life."

Carmen frowns. "Ah, we don't have to go that far. If Salvador puts money into your idea, you and I will have to work closely. As if we were partners. You will be the heart and soul of it. You can be Apollo with the golden lyre. And I will be the messenger."

"Artemis? My twin sister?"

"No, I'll be Hermes."

"How can I refuse such a blessing?"

"Oh, my dear, it'll not all be sweetness and light. There will be times when you'll rebel against this arrangement. For you, o poet, let me recite from Coleridge:

> Alas! They had been friends in youth;
> But whispering tongues can poison truth;
> And constancy lies in realms above;
> And life is thorny; and youth is vain;
> And to be wroth with one we love
> Doth work like madness in the brain.

He nods. "From 'The Ancient Mariner?'"

"Yes. Now, listen well. Salvador Andreu needs to feel he's in control of his investments. He'll want all the bills paid promptly, and all the collections deposited promptly, and good records kept at all times. At all times."

"That's not impossible," Granados replies. "Do you think me so impractical?"

She laughs. "Dear Enrique, you have so many extraordinary gifts and talents. You are such a wonderful friend. Even, I suspect, a kindred spirit. Just the same, you can't be gifted in everything. That wouldn't be fair to the rest of us! So, if Salvador decides to gamble on you, please let *me* provide a few ordinary little pieces in the puzzle."

At dinner, Granados sits across the table from Lluisa Vidal and her father, Francesc, the furniture designer and decorator who works with Gaudí and other notable Catalan architects. Vidal's talents as an art dealer and designer of glass and metal works have earned him a favored position with the alta burguesa, who've commissioned him for their homes and their offices. As a result of this notable success, Vidal has become a patrón for Pablo Casals, Isaac Albéniz, and several other musicians.

Vidal rises and lifts his glass to Granados for reorchestrating the "deficient original" of Chopin's *Concerto in F Minor* and receiving uncommon praise from the Barcelona critics. "Brindis, Enric! To even greater success!"

Granados rises, bows and raises his glass to Lluisa Vidal. "Brindis to you, Lluisa! Soon you'll go to Paris to study and paint at the center of the art world. Brindis to you, who've given me so much encouragement, who've braved the crude banter at Quatre Gats and given our group of scoundrels a glimpse of a time when men and women will sit together and work together and respect each other for their merits. Dear Lluisa, may you go with God, may your talent and work be blessed, and…may you return to us who will miss you while you're away!"

Andreu is the next to rise. He toasts his wife, his family, his friends. He gives a brief elegy for Francisco Miralles. He remains standing and lifts his glass to Granados.

"This brindis is for you, Enric, an old and dear friend of my beloved Carmen. This is for you, for your incredible talent, and for your constant devotion to music in Catalunya. For your commitment to bringing fine music to our mercantile town. For your patience in giving lessons to our children, regardless of their talent. And most especially for your passionate dream of creating a place for talented young musicians of Barcelona to help them rise above the ordinary–and shower the rest of us with their gifts. My brindis to you, my friend. And to the new Acadèmia Granados!"

In the excitement, the clinking of glasses of cava, and the bubbling acclaim, Granados does not fail to note that the calmest eyes and the steadiest hand around the table belong to his new partner, Carmen Miralles de Andreu.

Chapter Four

Barcelona, June 1901

Granados looks ahead as he threads his way through evening foot traffic on narrow Carrer Montsió, and sees the elaborate stone carvings and iron grillwork of Casa Martí. The building's moderniste curves seem to undulate as they reflect light from the streetlamps. Els Quatre Gats is on the building's ground floor.

For some time, Granados hasn't stopped at the cabaret. Only a pair of meetings here with the music critic Joaquim Pena, to discuss forming a group to promote the music of Wagner. As he enters the bistro area of Quatre Gats, scene of so many raucous gatherings, Granados sees Isaac Albéniz sitting alone on the far side of the long table, under Casas' painting of the tandem bicycle. Albéniz wears the familiar dark suit with vest, white shirt, and red bow tie. A gold watch-chain, strung through a button hole of his vest, encircles a corpulent midsection. The room is nearly deserted, with only one other table of diners, and it's quiet except for a clatter of pans from the kitchen and piano music coming from the large cabaret behind the bistro. Someone struggling to play a Mozart sonata. Granados walks around the table and receives a bearlike hug from his short, portly colleague, whose dark thatch of hair nestles under Granados' chin.

"You'll forgive me for starting without you," says Albéniz, returning to a large earthenware casserole. "I was famished!" He wipes a napkin across the wide mouth in the middle of his curly black beard, empties a beer stein, and holds it up to read an inscription: "He who lives a good, simple life needs good food and much laughter. Couldn't have said it better myself."

Granados hangs his black derby on the back of a chair and sits across from Albéniz. "What're you having?"

"Oh, this is today's special, the ragout of rabbit. And mussels," he adds, reaching into the casserole and sucking the meat out of a dark shell. "And some pork, and also some fish. It's food from the mountains where I grew up. Bon profit! Would you like a taste?"

Instinctively, Granados shakes his head. After ridding himself of the digestive agonies that plagued him while he was working on *María del Carmen*, he's avoided the rich foods that so delight his friend. The doctor warned he may have an ulcer. Ever since, he imagines something with sharp teeth gnawing its way through the wall of his stomach.

Pere Romeu comes out of the kitchen, wearing an apron that carries the marks of many sloshed glasses of wine. As if it hasn't been laundered for years. "Ah, Enric. Haven't seen *you* in ages. Can I get you a cava?" Romeu's lost some of the panache and incivility of the years when Quatre Gats was a thriving rendezvous.

"That'll be fine. And some bread." Should be bland enough to satisfy his annoying doctor.

"Say, Pere," says Albéniz, spraying broth across the table, "where is everybody?"

Romeu frowns. "Well, some of the regulars left town. Casals and Malats are in France. Ruiz and Casagemas and Pallarès and the Sotos–that crowd of young rowdies!–they used to fill this place, you remember. Now they've mostly gone away."

"Yes. I've seen them in Paris," says Albéniz. "As for Ruiz, he's changed his name to 'Picasso.' Some sort of revenge on his father. But what about Casas? Utrillo? And Rusiñol?"

Romeu shakes his head, and returns to the kitchen.

Granados leans toward his friend, who is draining the casserole. "Rusiñol and his coterie have moved to the Café Vienna. On the Plaça."

"But isn't he one of the owners here?" Albéniz asks.

"Well, I don't come here much any more, 'Saco, but I hear he and Pere aren't getting along so well, and you know 'Tiago–he's always looking for something new, something different."

"Hmm. Well, it's not easy establishing a bistro outside of France. Not the same cuisine, not the same wines. And Pere's food has never been first rate," says Albéniz. "Remember how we used to joke about his seagulls? Though I must say, this ragout is quite acceptable."

Granados laughs. "My dear 'Saquito, how would you know? You throw everything together in a mishmash. And you eat so fast, how would you know what it tastes like?"

"You sound like my doctor! Now he says I have 'entero-colitis membranosa'–sounds absolutely terrifying–so he's ordering me to give up the puro cigars and the cognac and spicy foods like botifarra. Of course–all of them favorites! He says I'll die too young, and I say it's too late for that. It's already been a long, long life."

"But we all die too young. Is it ever time?"

"Suppose it depends. Mostly we die too young. I'm not ready, I'll tell you that. But worry? My dear wife's the worrier, she never gives me a moment's peace. 'Don't do that, don't eat this.'"

"And of course you don't pay any attention to her, or the doctor."

"Surely not!" He blows a ring of blue smoke over Granados' head.

Granados laughs. "Is it really true you're moving back? How wonderful!"

"Yes, it's true. I've purchased land and we'll soon be building. Not a shovel stuck in the ground yet, but I'm in love with it!" Romeu scrambles across the tile floor with a glass of cava and basket of bread for Granados, and a plate of botifarra for Albéniz, who slides them into his casserole. "As I was saying, our home will look out over l'Eixample. And Sagrada Familia."

"Gaudí's obsession," Granados observes.

"Yes, his great fantasy. What a crazy man! At any rate, we'll be up where Bonanova meets the new funicular, the one going to Vallvidrera. On high ground, just as my doctor ordered. That should silence him–for now."

"Not far from Tibidabo. Where Andreu's building."

"Andreu? The famous Doctor Salvador Andreu? Who married your old sweetheart?"

Granados rolls his eyes. "Carmen–my sweetheart? Have you been talking to Doña Titín?"

"Not at all. Why?"

"She's convinced that Carmen Miralles and I are lovers. That I go up to Puigcerdà when the good doctor is away. And my dearest Titín can be merciless!"

Albéniz takes a slice of bread from Granados' plate and pushes it around his casserole, soaking up traces of broth. "My dear 'Ric, do you know any married man who doesn't have a few escapades? Harmless little dalliances? It's not about fidelity. Not to excuse what my father did, going off and abandoning us!"

"'Saco, you're much too persuasive. But I tell you there's nothing going on between me and Carmen."

Albéniz laughs. He's known Granados for more than twenty years, since Granados was a scrawny teenaged prodigy with close-cropped hair and enormous café noir eyes, who won the Concurs Pujol. Now he's a young maestro dressed in the fashionable English cut, with a green tie bursting out of a starched collar, his pale face framed by thick swept back hair and festooned by a much emulated handlebar moustache. Albéniz is amused. "Oh, you are so 'Ric-issimo! Why, Carmen is a delicious woman. I've always loved her name: song of the mirrors. She sparkles, does she not? And molta exquisida–so exquisite! Who'd suspect she's had six children?"

Granados waves off the frivolity. "Yes, she's exquisite, she's a dear friend, and I enjoy seeing her. But there's no dalliance! That would never happen."

Not after she met Salvador. Confessed she once dreamed of us together. Hah! That was later–easy to tease me later. Easy in Puigcerdà after two or three glasses. She did well finding Salvador so rich and famous and unmarried. Far better than a composer scrambling for every peseta.

Albéniz reaches for another slice of bread. "Okay. But it wouldn't matter to me if she were your lover. As long as you don't leave Doña Titín and the children."

Granados sighs, leaning back in his chair, and changes the subject. "What news do you have of Pau? I haven't seen him since last September."

"I think he's doing fine, though the last time I saw him he was leaving for another tour. Said he was relieved to be off again–he'd been playing at the Café Suez to make ends meet."

Granados is dismayed. "Pau–playing in cafés again?"

"Yes. And Malats."

"But Pau told me he'd played for Queen Victoria–two years ago, just after leaving here. Sent me a telegram! So excited about gold cufflinks from the queen. And I heard his touring was a great success. Lamoureux said he was 'predestiné.' And he met Jan Paderewski, who used the same word: predestiné. I thought surely Pau was on his way."

"Yes, but everyone died."

Granados winces. "You mean Morphy?" he asks, referring to Casal's benefactor Count de Morphy, secretary to the Queen Regent of Spain, who'd introduced the young cellist to the court in Madrid, and secured funds for him to live comfortably while he studied with Tomás Bretón at the Conservatorio.

"Yes, he was the first to go. But then Lamoureux died soon after offering Pau a position with the opera."

"What a tragedy!"

"That's one way of looking at it, my friend. Yet wasn't it splendidly fortunate that Morphy wrote the letter to Lamoureux before he died, and also introduced him to the singer Emma Nevada, who promised to take Pau to Amèrica on her next tour? And how fortunate for Pau that Lamoureux gave him a position with the opera before *he* died!"

Granados resists. "Would you say the same thing about the Queen Victoria dying just a year after Pau played for her?"

Albéniz sends Romeu back with another order, for a bowl of tripa catalana, a stew made with the stomach and intestine of a cow. "Forgive me, you must be starving! Pere will bring you some more bread. And I promise not to snatch it away."

Granados isn't moved by this gesture.

"So you think me crass to look at Pau's career that way?" asks Albéniz. "Death strikes us all randomly. Look what happened to Ernest Chausson, that freak bicycle crash. Such a young man. Such immense talent. What a loss! Then Morphy, also my benefactor and a dear friend. I still grieve for him. As you'd grieve for the good Doctor Andreu."

Granados shakes his head. "So you're saying if Morphy and Lamoureux died sooner, our Pau–the greatest cellist in the world–might still be playing in the Café Suez?"

"What I'm saying is, life is like roulette." Albéniz pulls another puro out of his jacket and bites off the tip.

"Then if Pau and Malats were having to play in cafés to support themselves, what does that say about Paris?" asks Granados. "Isn't it the musical mecca?"

Albéniz lights up and expels a long stream of smoke toward the chandelier. "Yes, it's the mecca," he concedes, "especially compared with the others. London? Not just a rotten climate, no, it's not even close. Vienna? No longer. Rome is too Italian and Berlin too German. Florence? Fabulous painting and sculpture but not music. So that leaves Paris. That's why every one wants to go there. So it's full of talented people who are sent there by their mentors. Full of hopefuls who've outgrown their home towns and want a chance at the big prize. I went there, you went there, Pau went there. You know what I mean. Then comes the day of reckoning. There are only so many recital halls, only so many days in the year. And you can be the best violinist in Madrid or Milano, but there are thousands of violinists in Paris who may be just as talented, and if the difference is slight, how does one get selected?"

"It's that way everywhere," Granados replies. "What's different about Paris?"

"What's different, brother, is that musicians from Spain never quite get through the front door. Know what I mean? Oh, they think we're odd sorts of celebrities. Sometimes they make a fuss over us, they invite us to their soirées, sometimes they recognize us with prizes and medals. The French are terrific with honneurs. We get baubles and benificence."

Granados challenges him. "But you were the center of attention when I came to Paris, everyone was at your place on the Rue d'Erlanger–Sarasate, Casals, Arbós, Rusiñol, Casas, Zuloaga. And you seemed to have Parisians eating out of your hand."

"Don't get me wrong, the French like us to be there, we add spice and color to the scene. Some of them, like Fauré and Saint-Saens, do appreciate what we have to offer, but mainly we're placed on the fringe, and they'll use our music to fill in the programs–as long as we ration it. But if we cross the line, like Malats did, the French will shout obscenities during a concert and tell us foreigners to take our Spanish music back home. No, senyor, their attitude is, we're not quite up to their level, not in anything. It's not just about music, where the heroes are Debussy and Ravel and Massenet, but also in painting–that's owned by Degas and Renoir, and food, wine, fashion. Can't think of anything Spanish that is considered the equal of the French version." Albéniz laughs. "Ah, well. The exception is the puros from Cuba. They're smoked in the best salons. But Cuba's no longer part of Spain, thanks to the stupidity of our government. What I'm saying, 'Ric, is that Spaniards in Paris are never going to get inside the front door unless they become Francofied."

Paris–so many things. Didn't know about a front door. First time away from home. Wild nights at Francisco's atelier. Wonderful nights with Vives and Malats. Poor and always dreaming. Joyful to be there.

Granados asks, "You're suggesting success comes easy here?"

"Mierda! The problem here is that the audience is mesmerized by the Italians. I like Verdi well enough, and I learned from him. But a taste of Puccini goes a long way, far's I'm concerned. Donizetti is so predictable. And Mascagni? Overrated. Though you wouldn't hear that in the luxury boxes at El Liceu. No senyor, it's like an addiction, it excludes everything else. The only recourse you and I have is to show the Italians how to do it properly. And only then will the crowd in this town be ours. So it's just the two of us, two sons of the Catalan countryside, of the same mind and spirit, going forward into the lair of the Italians. But you can have the crowd, 'Ric. It's not for me. The crowd here, or anywhere, is capricious! Only thing I want is to leave something for posterity. That's all that matters."

"Yes," Granados replies, "that is all that matters."

"Now, enough of this talk about Paris," Albéniz says, "tell me what's happening in our own city of wonders and madness, where I'm back to build a home for my family. Is it safe for my children?"

Granados says Barcelona is more peaceful than in a decade earlier, when bombings were common, and police violence against the radicals, anticlericals, and anarchists; when the notorious Captain General Valerià Weyler i Nicolau—the same Weyler whose later brutality in Cuba provoked the United States to stop Spain's oppression of the rebels—was brought in to stifle the unrest; when workers and students were plucked out of cafés and sent to the prison on Montjuic, and many were garroted or sent off forever to the penal colony at Rio de Oro. Compared to then, Granados says, Barcelona is quiet. Of course, there was a general strike on May Day, when police used machine guns against the workers, but that occurred mostly out toward Badalona. In the main, things have calmed down.

"I'm relieved to hear that," says Albéniz. "Didn't intend to bring my family into a battle zone."

"You haven't."

"And where are all bright lights of the new century who used to gather at this very table? All gone?"

"Well, you know Rusiñol moved his coterie. Utrillo and Casas went with him. You know Ruiz and his chiquillos are to Paris. And Lluisa Vidal has also gone there. María Barrientos is in Milano, hoping to debut at La Scala. Nin is back in Havana. Old Mestre Pujol has been dead more than two years, rest his soul. Some of the others come and go. The Orfeó is tremendously successful. Crickboom has his school, where I worked, and his concerts. Still Crickboom."

"And you, 'Ric?" Albéniz asks.

"Well, last year it was the Societat de Concert Clàssics, which I expected to be successful—I'm afraid this town isn't ready for orchestral music. I've written a piece for orchestra, *La Nit del Mort*, but I'm not sure where to take it. And of course *Follet*."

"Yes, *Follet*—more on that later. 'Ric, I couldn't find anyone here to take my *Catalunya*—even with such a popular name. So I had the Société Nationale premiere it in Paris." Albéniz sighs. "In this town, we're up against raging Italianophilia. Hail to Verdi and Puccini, and the rest of us are a bunch of nobodies. But I heard your concert season was a great success."

"We had good audiences. Good reception from most of the critics. And for the last concert, excellent reviews. Not a financial failure."

"So what was it?"

Granados is pensive. "Honestly? It was sheer exhaustion." He pokes a finger at his shirt. "This master juggler had too many balls in the air."

"Sounds familiar."

"There's a lot happening here. I'm not going to claim it's another Paris, but some day–perhaps. Some day."

Albéniz sips his cognac and sways his head from side to side, obviously skeptical of Granados' eager effort to convince him things are fine here. He finishes the last of his tripa catalana, and plucks another slice of bread from Granados' plate. Romeu takes his order for another cognac. "Now about Morera and this lyric theatre," says Albéniz. "I said I'd be willing to help keep it alive, and offered him *Merlin* for next season. And I won't even offer it to El Liceu. That place! Such smugness. Arrogance. If I were Italian, Don Isaaco Albenizco, they'd accept any old obscenity. Anyway, the deal with Morera is that we'll present *Merlin* and Morera's *Emporium* and your *Follet*. Twelve performances, four of each–that should make everyone happy. Musical drama. Glory to Catalunya! Three local composers at their very best. Sound pretty good?"

"Yes, sounds stupendous."

"And–between you and me–we've tried everything else! So we'll finally discover whether we have any talent at all, right?"

"We have talent, 'Saco. It's for the world to find out."

"Well said! And we need to live a while to make sure it happens. Now, tell me–and don't be polite–how much do you trust Morera?" Albéniz is swirling his cognac, holding eye contact.

Should he know about Pau's warning? Yes he deserves to know.

"'Saco, I've worked with Morera several times, and I've no reason personally not to trust him. I should ask you–he was your student."

"Oh, yes, but many years ago. You've been working with him just this year."

"Well, I find him difficult," Granados admits.

"Difficult? You mean, caustic?"

"Yes. And bitter. Sarcastic. He wants everything to go his way. And sometimes his intense politics gets in the way. He started a new choral group, Catalunya Nova, because he thought l'Orfeó had lost its socialistic mission! What does that mean? So without him l'Orfeó has become even more successful."

"I hate to see people mix politics and art," Albéniz replies. "Morphy used to worry about my getting too close to the Wagnerians. Warned me not to become a disciple of Morera. Me? A disciple of Morera?"

"That's absurd. But you ask about trust. Before he left, Pau warned me to be careful with Morera. Gave no particular reason. Count your fingers, he said, after you shake hands with him."

Albéniz nods, dipping the tip of a new cigar into his snifter of cognac. "Then we'll have to go into this with our eyes open. And keep track of our fingers." He laughs. "No problem for you, 'Ric, you're a virtuoso–but I need every last one of mine."

Granados walks down La Rambla toward the sprawling port area, Barcelona's gateway to the world since Roman times. The sky is leaden; incessant rain has fallen all night and through the morning. Tiny needled droplets sting his hands and gusts of wind surge up the promenade, rustling the leaves overhead and spraying his face. He tightens his grip on a black umbrella and dodges a large puddle.

Thank God! Demon migraine gone. Time off from searing every fiber in my head. Coffee and bread aren't roaring up my throat. Pelted by rain–far better than those needles of pain.

Opposite El Liceu, he looks up at the large Longines clock just below the peaked roof of the opera house. Reliably, the clock runs twenty minutes behind. After estimating he'll be late for the meeting with Albéniz and Morera, but only by a few minutes, he relaxes and cuts behind a trolley car, crossing a busy sidewalk onto a quieter street with slower paced pedestrian and horse-drawn traffic. The echoed clipclopping of their hooves is muted by the rain and the dancing puddles. Now he's entering La Mercè sector of the Old City, which extends from this street, Carrer de la Boquería, down to the Passeig Colom, named for the presumed discoverer of the Americas. Cristòfol Colom–a hero to some, but a killer of indigenous people to the city's young intellectuals.

La Mercè was once the neigborhood chosen by Barcelona's most prosperous merchants to site their colossal mansions, built side by side along its narrow streets with elaborate high porticos proclaiming their owners' commercial success. With expansion of the city into the new area of l'Eixample, La Mercé has become less fashionable. Now the mansions stand as evidence of former glories: many are divided up into apartments and offices, and on some streets nearer the port, into bars and cafés and transitory lodging–catering to sailors on shore leave, recent immigrants, and job seekers drawn to Catalunya's throbbing economy.

Granados turns off Boquería and walks down the narrow Carrer d'en Quintana, where on a sunny day the laundry hangs from balconies of the apartments high above shades the sidewalk below. He moves past Can Culleretes, the oldest restaurant in the city, where the food is predictably good and the waiters amiable, where he plans a celebratory lunch after this morning's meeting with his new partners, Albéniz and Morera.

Celebrate if all goes well–if 'Saco's not too playful and Morera's temper's under control. Too much to hope for? A lyric theatre. Perfect venue for Follet. *Should be financial success! Titín won't be so critical.*

Now he crosses Carrer Ferran onto Vidre, which runs through Plaça Real. The rectangular space is surrounded by one-story arches and ringed by sidewalk cafes, all deserted today. The plaça's flocks of pigeons are in their lodgings, somewhere in the walls and arches that comprise the Gothic quarter. Gone also are the songbirds, so the prevailing sound is of raindrops pelting the awnings and stacks of tables and chairs in front of the cafés. And as he passes under the palm trees, taller than the street lamps, Granados thinks of the palm groves of Tenerife in the Canary Islands and how he used to enjoy walking through them, hop-skipping through them–wondering if coconuts would fall–and plodding, marching through the sand, holding hands with his older brother Calixto and sister Zoe. Those palm trees of his boyhood were perfectly in their place, yet are somehow out of place in the center of this bustling city.

Granados walks around the fountain that anchors the plaça, avoiding windborne spray, walks between two iron sculptured posts topped with eight lamps, an early design of Gaudí, then darts out of the open space to resume winding through cobblestone streets. He recognizes his destination, an office building where the new venture, Teatre Líric Català, will be launched today. He enters the lobby, shakes off his umbrella, and walks up a flight of stairs.

Albéniz waits for him in the breezeless, sticky office of the attorney who drafted the partnership agreement. Albéniz is dressed in a pearl white suit and crimson tie; the gold watch-chain hangs over his groin; the arched frame of his glasses, propped on the tip of his nose, rises above a thick, unbroken line of eyebrow. As Granados is escorted into the room, Albéniz mutters "Bon dia" while he cuts the tip off a coffee-brown cigar. He finishes the task and looks up. "Ah, Enric, so it's you and I arriving first, waiting for Morera. And the others."

"Others?"

"Yes. Morera said Miquel Utrillo will be here to serve as secretary. He's been designing sets for Morera. And Antoni Niubó. He's going to invest in our little enterprise."

"Niubó? I know that name. Isn't he the one called 'The Mattress Maker of Gràcia'?"

"You've met him?" asks Albéniz.

"At Sitges–last year, maybe two years ago. A friend of Rusiñol. I got the impression he helped finance the Festes Modernistes. Looks and sounds like a financier."

"So he's part of Rusiñol's entourage. And, of course, so is Miquel. And Morera."

"Precisely."

Albéniz lights his cigar and laughs. "I hope you and I are sufficiently *modern-iste* for these people."

Granados snorts. "That's probably too much to hope for, 'Saco."

"Well, I surely don't hope for it. I'd just as soon not be another rose in Rusiñol's garden."

The door opens and three men enter. Utrillo comes around the table and greets Granados and Albéniz with a cordial abraçada, then presents Niubó, who rocks side to side on his stocky frame as he shuffles forward. Morera moves quickly to a place at the table, and reaches across to shake hands with Albéniz and Granados. He clips off the end of his greeting. Albéniz, in a sly but matter of fact tone, asks why they are late, and Granados holds his breath.

Morera seems surprised and grabs the bait. Tilting his head back, staring through his rimless glasses, down a long hawk's nose. "Well, I can assure you, Albéniz," he replies, "if the rain hadn't slowed us down we'd have been here right on time."

Albéniz laughs. "And was it not the same rain that fell on Granados and me?" Niubó and Utrillo also laugh.

"It doesn't matter, Albéniz!" Morera's ears, shaped like mussel shells and placed near the back of his head, have reddened. Seems unnerved by the mocking tone.

"Or did you think we paddled here? Like ducks?" Albéniz asks.

Utrillo intervenes, injecting a familiar air of Parisian sophistication as he leans onto the table and lowers his head. The overhead light shines on his small patch of hair. "Senyores, we could converse about the weather for the rest of the day, but if we do there will be no agreement."

Albéniz bows his head. "Yes. Of course, Miquel. As always, your logic is unassailable. Pay no attention to my abruptness. But if we are to conclude this before lunch–as would be my very, very strong desire–please tell us what we've come here to agree to."

As Utrillo fingers his long, thin moustache and begins to answer, Morera interrupts him. It's very simple, he asserts, unless someone chooses to make it complicated. The Teatre Líric Català will present a new season, going beyond his own "pioneering" work the previous year. It will run from August to the early part of next year. There will be twelve performances of the new works, and there will be others, as yet unnamed. "To be determined by us," Morera adds. He barks the last word, shifting his closely spaced eyes to Albéniz and Granados. Both are talented pianists, he's willing to concede, whose forte is to compose for their instrument, yet compared to him, he suggests, neophytes in the realm of musical drama.

Albéniz, aroused by the invidious comparison, holds back. "You're saying, twelve performances of my *Merlin*, twelve of your *Emporium*, and twelve of Granados' *Follet?*"

"No, I'm saying, four of each. A grand total of twelve."

"And the other composers?" Granados asks.

"There is nothing firm, but I believe Lapeyra and Bartolí will be interested. We presented their works earlier this year at the Tívoli, and both have new ones in progress. And perhaps also Joan Gay." Morera pushes his wavy long auburn hair back from his high forehead.

"And these would be presented at the Tívoli?"

"No," says Niubó. "The Tívoli is too expensive. And the Líric is nice, but too small. We'd have to fill every seat, and raise ticket prices just to recover our investment. I'm hoping for much better than that!" He looks around the table for signs of dissent.

Granados returns his gaze. Of course, Niubó's business sense is why he's renowned as the "Mattress Maker of Gràcia."

Niubó stands and places his hands on the edge of the table. "I've concluded that the Dorado is the best venue," he says, looking down at the others. "First, it's less expensive. But large enough for your productions. And second, it's available. So I've asked the management to hold some dates for us."

Granados shrugs. "I haven't been in the Dorado for some time" he says. "Has anyone?" He turns to Albéniz, who's relighting his cigar.

"I think it will be suitable," says Utrillo.

Morera lights a pipe, hunched over and frowning as he sucks on it. "I agree. It's suitable."

Albéniz asks how much investment is needed, and when. "I'm a little short, senyores, since I'm building a new home," he explains. With minimal prompting he describes the view he'll have of the entire city. "How much must we invest now?" he asks.

Niubó sits down. "To hold the Dorado for August and September, we need one thousand five hundred pesetas. Five hundred from each of you." Niubó says he's willing to advance money for the sets and for recruiting the cast and orchestra.

"Five hundred apiece will get it launched?" Granados asks. He can sign a bank draft, and the bank will accept it, but then he'll have to explain all of this to Amparo. For her, some carefully chosen words.

"Yes, that will get it launched," replies Niubó.

Granados seeks affirmation. "Tell me, Morera, this agreement is binding on all three of us? You and Albéniz and me?"

"Yes," Morera replies, barely opening his mouth. Granados watches him, thinking of Casal's warning. There's nothing on the surface to distrust. Morera sits stiffly, his jacket buttoned up to a high, starched collar and a yellow ascot, his eyebrows bisected by a deep crease that runs to the hairline. He simply looks like Morera.

"Then tell me," Albéniz says, waving his cigar, "what happens if one of us takes his work to another venue?"

Morera pulls the pipe from his mouth. "What do you mean?"

"Just what I said. We're signing an agreement that binds us to offer these works for this new season. So I assume we're agreeing not to offer them to anyone, anywhere else. Not in Madrid or Paris or London. Am I correct, Morera?"

"That's correct," says Utrillo.

"Morera?" Albéniz asks.

"Yes, that's correct," Morera replies. "You have my word."

Albéniz continues. "Well, then, I said I wanted to help you with your Teatre Líric Català. That's why I'm here. You remember that, don't you?"

"Of course."

"And I said, even though Catalunya is my homeland, as well as yours and Granados', that I'm not doing it simply to promote Catalan culture, I'm doing it to give the three of us a venue for our work. To advance our art. And I'm willing to offer *Merlin* to make it a success. I'm content to be part of this–as long as *you* don't ask me to turn the magician Merlin and the Knights of the Round Table into Catalan heroes!"

Now flustered by Albéniz' ironic puckishness, Morera's eyes open wide and he shakes his head. "Oh, surely I wouldn't do that, Albéniz. But you do see, I presume, that these works of ours exemplify the best of the culture of Catalunya. That is what this is all about. Of course you see that."

Albéniz is offended by the condescension in Morera's voice. "Ah, yes, how could I not see that? Everything will be most correctly in accordance with the culture of our beloved homeland. Otherwise, I'd have no interest in having an opera about King Arthur and his English knights performed here. And your work, *Emporium*, surely it's based on folk tales of Catalunya?"

"It's based on mythology. The libretto is by Eduard Marquina. He's one of us. So the spirit of the music and the libretto are authentically Catalan. Just as is *Follet*–with Mestres' libretto."

"Is it possible your work's derived from Wagner?" Albéniz asks.

The room is silent. Granados, unsettled by the political overtones, avoids eye contact. Utrillo laughs, and observes that all of the librettos will be in Catalan.

It's time to sign the agreement. Albéniz, Granados, then Morera. Utrillo signs and writes "secretary" under his name. Finally, it's signed by Niubó.

"Well, all of this leaves me famished," says Albéniz. "Let's go over to Can Culleretes."

"Please accept our apologies," says Utrillo. "We must meet Rusiñol at the Inglaterra. But surely, some other time?" Morera gets up and walks to the corner where the umbrellas have been drying.

The restaurant Can Culleretes has been serving traditional Catalan food since 1786. Though it's the busiest time of the day, the waiter finds Granados and Albéniz a good table in the side room, away from the kitchen. They settle into comfortable chairs, surrounded by candles and paintings. A basket of fresh bread is quickly served, and a pitcher of vi negre, the red house wine from Penedés.

"Here's to our venture," says Albéniz, lifting his glass. "May it be an enormous success!"

"And may there be many more."

Albéniz orders the Culleretes specialty, peix variat–a seafood stew–and Granados orders the pasta with a light clam sauce.

"So how did it go, partner?" asks Albéniz.

"You were there, 'Saco. What do *you* think?"

A cigar needs clipping. "Morera's an odd chap, is he not?"

Granados laughs. "You kept him on the edge of his chair."

"Oh, that's where he'd be anyway. He'll spend his life on the edge of chairs. I thought he'd choke when I suggested his new work wasn't more Catalan than ours. Catalanisme! Modernisme! Arghh! Either too much this, or not enough that! Why this lionization of our smallest talents in this little dot on the world map?"

"I prefer not to know. But, 'Saco, what could Morera say? When we're all devoted to Wagner, all influenced by him? Keep in mind, people loved *Tristan and Isolde* when it came to El Liceu two years ago, so we should also be successful. I got a standing ovation at the opening of *Picarol*. And you'll see, *Follet* will be much better!"

"Yes, it should succeed," Albéniz concedes, "if it were simply up to you and me."

"Agreed. I don't like Morera any more than you do, and I'm going to watch him closely, but he's part of the musical scene here, and we're better off with him than without. Let's not create any more obstacles for the two of us. I'm sure this is a great opportunity, and it's well worth having even a humorless partner if it helps us become properly recognized here."

"Yes, you're right." Albéniz dives into his seafood stew.

"There's no denying you and I've had success," Granados continues, "but has that brought recognition? Not really. For the alta burguesa of our beloved city, it's enough to enjoy discussing operas in the splendor of their Club del Liceu. At least to talk glibly about them. Especially the Italians." His voice is shaded with irony. "Endless conversations about Donizetti and Verdi and Rossini. After all, don't all the great operas of the world come from Italia? And the great symphonies, aren't they all from Germany and Austria? No, at El Liceu it's really social prestige that counts. Men arriving in their fracs and white ties, women lacing up in their gowns, putting on their ornate hats. How splendid to be driven to the porte cochere at El Liceu, to greet the others crossing La Rambla. And to watch the less privileged pedestrians coursing up and down the promenade through a window of the club. Those pedestrians out there? Ah, sated by lesser forms of music! Like the canço popular, the folk music of Catalunya, the choral music by Clavé–who naively hoped to create an educated working class. And who really cares what music those people out there like? If it's not the cultivated music of the inner circle, if it's not the music of patróns who built their opulent mansions in La Mercè and now are moving up to l'Eixample, always breaking new ground–except in their reverence for the Italians. What do they care?"

Albéniz raises his head from the bowl of stew. "And you think us two country boys from Camprodon and Lleida are going to loosen those stuffed shirts at El Liceu?"

"Yes!" Granados affirms. "We can reach them. All we need is a chance. And this lyric theatre is the way for us to cross over!"

Albéniz smiles as if slightly infected by his friend's enthusiasm. "Somehow you always manage to see the sun shining through the clouds, don't you, 'Ric? Always. But hear me, that is truly a gift. Hold onto that. And never lose it! And truly, I'd give anything for you to be right."

"I am right, 'Saquito."

"I love it when you sit up and sing like a bird. The kind of bird I hate in the morning when my head is pounding and I'm trying to put little black dots on my composition pad. The kind I'd kill for having that kind of cheerfulness!"

"Not the song of a nightingale."

"Mercy, no! El rossinyol? With that mournful song, singing to lost lovers and shattered dreams. Singing in the darkness. Mercy, not him!"

Granados' voice is higher pitched. "You remember when we stayed up all night in Paris, transposing Beriot's music? And walked out into the early faint beginnings of sunrise to hear that nightingale?"

"Yes, surely it was mournful! Alien and chilling."

"You could say that, but perhaps he sings to greet the new day. Perhaps he's just early in his celebration, while the other birds are nesting."

"And perhaps you're *the* most romantic one ever, to see it that way," Albéniz says. "But don't let me discourage you. Hearing beauty in that sound in the darkness–that's to be revered. Blessed. And as you know, I'm not a spiritual man."

Autumn, 1901

They're sitting around the table in the same room where they signed the agreement in June. Their placement–with Granados and Albéniz on one side of the table and Morera, Utrillo, and Niubó on the other–suggests a polarization among the partners of the Teatre Líric Català. As Albéniz trims the tip of his cigar, Morera turns to Granados.

"Congratulations on your new academy, Enric. Felicitats!"

Granados is surprised at the affability and warmth of the compliment. Have he and Albéniz been too critical of their partner? Perhaps Casals, as shrewd as he is about such matters, was too suspicious. Perhaps Morera can be trusted.

"That's wonderful news, for you of course, but not only for you, Enric–also for the cultural life of our beloved Catalunya." Morera is smiling, bobbing and dipping his elongated head, reaching up over his prominent forehead to resettle his auburn mane, licking his thin lips as he extols the promise of Granados' new academy, as if it were his own idea. "Yes, I have always thought that's exactly what this city needs, a place where our finest musicians can continue to study without being forced to leave our homeland." He leans back in his chair, nodding to affirm his generosity. "Of course, I trust you'll not try to lure my best students to your new academy, my friend."

Granados laughs. "Lure your students?" Morera, in a matter of seconds, has switched from affability to suspicion.

Morera leans forward, his eyes probing alongside a deep cleavage. "Jaume Pahissa? He'd stick with me no matter what. So would Lambert and Sancho.

Of course, I don't begrudge you Domènech Mas, he's been on his own for a while. He'll do well."

Granados resists. "But we're going to concentrate on piano and voice, and those students–your students–are only interested in becoming great composers. There's really not a problem."

"You mean, not problem for me–like for Crickboom?"

Granados feels the barb. "No. You're mistaken. Crickboom was very gracious when I told him I was leaving. He couldn't have been more gracious."

Morera shrugs. "Ah, well, I didn't mean any offense. As I said before, and I said it from my heart, felicitats on opening your new academy."

Albéniz has been filling the room with clouds of blue smoke from his puro. "Well, senyores, can we discuss business? Before it's time for lunch?"

Niubó opens by contending that Morera made an earlier investment in the lyric theatre, so he deserves a larger share of the profits. "In business terms, senyores, he comes to the table with some existing equity. Surely you must see that."

Albéniz snarls. "I would concede your point if last season had been successful. It wasn't. Not to be argumentative, but since it wasn't, there's really *negative* equity. Not to be crass, but Morera should get less."

Utrillo jumps into the debate. "That's unfair, Isaac. The season was not a failure. And Morera should be credited with launching a theatre devoted to Catalan lyric music."

Albéniz waves this off as if it were a fruit fly. "If it were such a magnificent season, why did our friend Morera ask me to premier *Merlin* to make this new season a success? Isn't it true, Morera, you asked me not to offer *Merlin* to any one else? That first meeting, back in April. Isn't that true?"

Granados watches the three men on the other side of the table, amused by their resemblance to the cuadrilla that he saw three years ago at work in the plaza de toros in Madrid–the only corrida he's ever attended, and only after strong pressure from Fernando Periquet. Having walked the Prado Museum with Periquet until his feet swelled and ached, having been inspired by the paintings and sketches of Goya, Granados was susceptible to the argument that watching toreros in action would enhance his understanding of Goya. After all, hadn't Goya produced a series of bullfight prints during his last years in Bordeaux? Capricious logic, but for Granados that one late afternoon in the plaza de toros was sufficient. He was stirred by the pageantry and music and costumes that heralded the killing, dazzled by the elegant bejeweled women in the shaded boxes several rows below where he sat with Periquet and a friend, the bullfight reporter for *El Pais*. Women with dark eyes in the shaded boxes, like modern majas, sleek and gleaming and watchful between painted eyelids. But then the first toro thundered out of the gate and the fierce work began in earnest. Pageantry forsaken as the picador thrust a lance into the shoulders to weaken the toro and force his head to drop. Then sharp-pointed banderillas were placed on the crest of hemorrhaging wounds. And finally the torero, after dedicating the beast to an enraptured young woman whose breasts glowed in the afternoon sun, strutted with his cape and sword to the center of the arena to finish the work. Four thrusts and the toro stopped charging. Spraying gore as he shook his head from side to side, the toro slid onto his haunches and stared with dying eyes toward the royal box, as if catching a last glimpse of the sunlit breasts, refusing to die until the torero plunged a dagger into his neck and severed his spinal cord. By this time the catcalls and jeers of the audience were augmented by a torrent of seat cushions hurled at the once-strutting torero, who now slid back into the protective custody of his cuadrilla.

As Granados watches the others, now it's Morera and his cuadrilla pitted against the snorting toro, Albéniz.

Morera turns to Granados. "What do you think is fair?"

Granados looks around the table. "Well, it seems a bit ridiculous to be having such an argument about sharing the profits, when artistic and financial success are never easy to achieve. I'd rather talk about how to find the best players and singers for our works. That's what's important–having popular and critical success, and if I get my money back, it's an extra blessing."

"In other words, you agree I should get forty percent," says Morera.

Granados shakes his head. "No, that's not what I said! But if we spend the next six months arguing about these kinds of matters, the season will come and go and we'll all be losers."

"Exactly!" says Albéniz, plunging back into the arena. "We all put in our money, and we're offering our best new operas for the season, so the rewards should be identical. And I'm not willing to concede on this!"

Morera folds his arms, staring at the table. He looks to Niubó, whose main interest is in getting paid for the money he's going to advance for booking the theatre and hiring the orchestra and singers. He looks to Utrillo, who wants to be guaranteed that the money he spends for the sets will be reimbursed. "So you two don't even care how we split the profits?" asks Morera.

Albéniz interrupts. "Are you trying to get them to side with you?" He wants the three partners to settle the issue, with Niubó and Utrillo as witnesses. He shifts his eyes from one to the next, and back to Morera.

Finally, Morera concedes. He's disappointed that Albéniz could not understand his point of view, but he's willing to move on to other matters. He lowers his voice and asks if there's an objection to presenting his *Emporium* for the opening performance of the season.

"Yes," answers Albéniz, no more provocation required.

"You object?"

"Yes, Morera, I do object."

"Would you be willing to state your objection?"

Albéniz gives a long audible sigh. "Very simply, having *Merlin* for the grand opening will attract a wider audience. With *Merlin* there's a chance to present serious Catalan opera and to receive more publicity in the local press. A chance to make this city appreciate something other than Rossini and the Italians."

Morera raises his voice. "Because it's yours? Not mine? Is that what you're saying?"

"I wouldn't be so sure, Isaac," says Utrillo. "Morera has an incomparable reputation in this town. You haven't been around all these years."

"You're right," Albéniz replies, seizing the bait. "I haven't been stuck here all these years, but that's not the point. I'm simply convinced that opening with *Merlin* will make the season more successful. So everyone will get his investment back. Isn't that what we were arguing about a minute ago?"

Morera turns to Granados. "Would you prefer to have *Follet* presented first?"

Granados shakes his head, saying he needs more time to finish his work. Having it presented last is perfectly acceptable.

Albéniz rushes forward. "And that's the second reason for opening with *Merlin*–it's finished! It's ready to cast." He points his cigar at Morera. "You need time to finish *Emporium* and 'Ric needs more time for *Follet*, so there shouldn't be any argument."

Morera's eyes smolder as he looks to Niubó and Utrillo for support.

After the meeting, Granados and Albéniz retreat to the side room at Can Culleretes, away from the noise and heat of the kitchen. As the waiter delivers bread and a pitcher of red wine, Albéniz blows the first jet of puro smoke over Granados' head. "Well, now what do you think of our partner Morera?"

Granados shakes his head. "A strange experience. Since all of us should be equal partners."

Albéniz releases a sinister laugh. "It's not funny, but Morera is as changeable as weather in the mountains. He's with you, then he's not, then he's with you again. How do we keep track?"

"You think he really expected to get the lion's share of the profits?" Granados asks. "And let *Emporium* be presented first?"

Albéniz shakes his head. "I'm not sure. It's as if there's never enough of anything for him. He always wants something fixed, some issue resolved. As if he's looking for things to go wrong. I couldn't live my life that way, could you?" He motions for the waiter, and is delighted that one of his favorites, escudella i carn d'olla, is back on Can Culleretes' menu.

"This will embellish what began as an arduous day!" Albéniz exclaims at the thought of diving into his favorite dish.

Escudella–a broth with a pasta of thin noodles known as "fideu," stewed meats, and assorted vegetables–is the oldest and most revered dish in Catalunya. It's a mark of culinary distinction in a society with few pretensions, with a similar place at the Catalan table that "pot au feu" occupies in France, and "cocido" in Castilian Spain. Escudella, described as a blending of a thousand essences, is especially beloved in the mountainous counties of El Ripollès and La Garrotxa, where Albéniz was born. In that area, it's not uncommon for families to sit down to escudella more than once a week, provided there are meats available.

As they wait for their food, Albéniz describes in detail those special places where he's found the best escudella: the tiny place on the edge of the Old Jewish Quarter in Girona, the restaurant below the castle in La Seu d'Urgell, the bar on the plaça in Vic, the hotel in Martinet, and the place on the edge of the village of Vernet in the French Conflent. Those were "splendiferous" occasions, he recalls. Each a feast worthy of three Cuban puros. Each an occasion to comfort and restore, to salve wounds and revive troubled spirits. Albéniz closes his eyes and inhales deeply, then releases a smoker's rattle. "But the most remarkable time was in Prades in the Roussillon, and how well I remember it. I made the innocent mistake of calling it 'pot au feu' and was instantly corrected. 'No, senyor,' said the maitre d', 'this is escudella–far superior to that French concoction!' I never made that mistake again."

Granados is puzzled. "But you were in Prades–in France."

Albéniz laughs. "No, senyor, I was in Catalunya. It's only the French government that is confused about the Roussillon. In Paris they say, of course it's French, or how can it be the birthplace of General Joffre, who stood with his army and defended Paris in 1870?"

"You're saying General Joffre's Catalan?"

"To be sure. Born in a small village near Perpignan. I used to see him from time to time in Paris. Later he was posted in the Conflent and once we met quite by chance in that divine place in Vernet. I looked up and there was Joffre with his escudella. He recognized me and asked if my opera had been successful–the one that died horribly in Bilbao. Amazing he'd remember that! So, I thought, he's not just a warrior. I'd presumed he was of an entirely different world. Soldiers fight the wars while painters, poets, and musicians create art–but their worlds never meet. I was wrong."

Granados' father, grandfather, and brother were officers in the Spanish Army; his brother Calixto died two years ago from a tropical disease acquired while serving in Cuba. But as a second-born son, Granados was not pressured to uphold the family tradition. In fact his father, who once played trumpet in the military band, encouraged his younger son to develop his musical talent. "I come from a military family," Granados says, "but I'm still opposed to wars. We need the army to protect the country, not to pick fights on others."

"Of course. But you see how wrong I was about Joffre? He's not just a warrior. In Paris, he'd come to our soirees and listen to chamber music. For hours! I once met Joffre at the home of a Polish countess, quite a stunning woman with an unpronounceable name who played the flute quite admirably. But somewhat bizarre: she wanted to have a recital featuring Franz Liszt and me. Imagine–Liszt and me! Though it never happened–Liszt was too busy, he was hardly ever in Paris, and then he died."

The escudella is served by two waiters and Albéniz, after sniffing it approvingly, begins to scoop it into his mouth. Granados raises his glass above his bowl of suquet, the simple Catalan fisherman's soup of scorpion-fish and sea bass, potatoes, onions, and tomatoes. "Bon profit, 'Saco. Here's to our splendid new venture."

Albéniz lifts his face from the bowl and snarls. "More splendid indeed, were we not locking horns with Morera and his retinue."

Granados laughs, recalling the image of a torero and his cuadrilla. "But you make such a fine toro! Toro bravo, charging straight ahead."

"You laugh, but would you rather I let him get his way? Morera tries to play the torero but he'd make a better wasp!"

"I like that image," Granados replies. "Still, he did back down. Let's look on the bright side–this will be a splendid success and we'll be appreciated here at home–at long last!"

"I hate to be skeptical, but with Morera I'm never sure what's going on behind those pince-nez glasses."

Albéniz' attention has been drawn to the platter of meats and vegetables that are served on the side of the broth. "I'm trying to find the peu de porc," he explains.

"A pig's foot–that's important?"

"Absolutely! It's not a proper escudella without one." Albéniz motions for the waiter.

Granados watches as the two men cock their heads and scan the platter of meats. The waiter is sent to the kitchen to fetch the chef.

"This is what you represent as escudella?" Albéniz asks.

The chef, as wide as he stands tall, with a splattered apron stopping at the toes of his shoes, looks down at the platter and affirms that it is just that.

"If so," Albéniz says, "there should be at least one peu de porc. At least one!"

"Senyor, there were several peus de porc in the cauldron. I selected them myself at the market. Perhaps you didn't receive one."

Albéniz is resolute. "That's what you say, but I doubt you had any in there at all. There's a certain something missing in the taste of the broth."

Now the chef is obliged to defend the honor of his kitchen. "With deepest respect for your fine sense of taste, I'm offended at the inference."

"I've seen no peu de porc. Can you prove there were any?"

It's the last harsh cut for the chef, who steps to the edge of the table and recites the ingredients of his escudella: cabbage, potatoes, celery, turnips, carrots, parsley, garlic, chickpeas, chicken, meatballs, two types of sausage, mushrooms, bacon, ham, chunks of stewing veal, beef bones, ground pork, and veal. And peus de porc. "Does Senyor Albéniz believe that is sufficient?"

Albéniz glares back. "No," he replies, biting off the tip of another puro, "not if I don't see any peus de porc!"

An envelope is waiting from Albéniz. Inside, a succinct message: "Critical meeting. Café l'Opera. Five o'clock."

The café is a short stroll downhill on La Rambla from Carrer Fontanella, but this afternoon the autumn wind slashes up from the harbor and it feels like a long walk uphill. Granados pulls the brim of his hat down over his brow and stands his jacket collar up to protect his neck. It seems that just the other day he was passing through crowds of people coming and going from La Boquería market, that the birds were in full song, and the flower stalls brimming with cut peonies and roses. Stylish women sitting in their broad skirts and thin blouses at the sidewalk café tables, hatless, their hair glowing in the sunlight. Less than a month ago. Now it's late October–the tables are stored for the winter, the flowers are gone, and this broad main artery of Barcelona is nearly deserted. There will be three months of chilling weather and stiff winds.

Granados, though he knows this stretch of La Rambla intimately, remains intrigued by the visages and past-life echoes of its history. On his left and behind the shuttered flower stalls is El Palau Mojà, which belongs to the descendents of Antoni López i López, founder of a commercial empire in Cuba–including a large slave trade, and later a transatlantic steamship company. López, who was made the first Marquès de Comillas by King Alfonso XII, was also the original patron of the poet-priest Jacint Verdaguer, whom he appointed chaplain of his steamship company. For more than two decades, Verdaguer–popularly known as "Mossen 'Cinto"–has lived in El Palau Mojà, serving as the López family's official dispenser of alms to the poor.

There's been ongoing tension between Verdaguer and his benefactors. It began when the priest distributed alms more generously than the López family intended. A later excursion into mysticism and exorcism resulted in Verdaguer losing his preferred status with the family, then headed by the eldest son, Claudi López i Bru, second Marquès de Comillas. Since things were patched up three years ago, Verdaquer's spiritual and physical health seem to be on the wane. Other than daily crossings of La Rambla to say mass at the church of Betlem–on the family's short leash, where he can't cause trouble–Mossen 'Cinto is rarely seen.

Poor Verdaguer! Servant of God or servant of López? How can he live in this palace? Doesn't belong here. Where does anyone belong?

Now Granados passes El Palau de la Virreina. He's walked past this palace countless times, always imagining the presence of ghosts from the time of its builder, Manuel d'Amat i de Junyent–a ruthless and effective Spanish military governor in South America, and subsequently the Viceroy of Perú. D'Amat's liaison with the Peruvian actress "Perricholi" was the inspiration for Jules Offenbach's opera, *La Perichole*. The affair also resulted in a son, abandoned by his father, who later got even by joining the army of José de San Martin in the successful fight to liberate Perú from Spanish rule. Retiring to Barcelona, Viceroy d'Amat built this palace in the 1770s and moved into it with a new and more carefully selected wife. He died three years later, leaving a young widow; the building has since been known as "the palace of the viceroy's wife."

It's quiet on La Rambla. The chattering caged birds are gone and the pigeons, fond of poking their heads through the bars to swipe the food of their caged brethren, are now wintering in the crevasses of the Gothic Quarter. After passing La Boquería market, Granados stops at the corner of Carrer de l'Hospital and looks down the street where he played in another cabaret, Café Filipino, just prior to leaving for Paris. Where he was expected to accompany a wide range of untalented amateurs. Singers and dancers, flautists and bassoon players.

What a nightmare! Playing with them desperate to preserve my sanity. Two interminable months!

He crosses the wide promenade that runs up the spine of La Rambla, dodging behind a horse and carriage, and now he's across the street from El Liceu, where composers of operas in Catalunya aspire to have their works premiered, and vocalists dream of lifting their voices in its many-tiered, resplendent space. More than an opera house, it's also a private club for the alta burguesa, whose musical taste is as solid and predictable as the industrial base of Catalunya. The odds of getting an opera produced in this majestic venue, dating back to 1847, are enormously better if the composer is named Rossini, Verdi, or, more recently, Wagner.

Across from El Liceu is the Café l'Opera, where vocalists go to be cheered or consoled after their auditions, where established celebrities gather to relive their moments of glory. One of these, Wagnerian tenor Francesc Viñas, is sitting this afternoon with Albert Bernis, impresario of El Liceu, and Amparo Alabau, a soprano whose debut took place earlier this year as Micaela in *Carmen*. Viñas is rolling his balding ellipsoid head from side to side as he regales the ingénue from València with stories of his early days at El Liceu, punctuated by a few bars of an aria, while Bernis offers less pretentious versions of the anecdotes. Both vying for her. In passing, Granados greets Bernis and Viñas, and they chat about the Wagnerian Society. Bernis introduces him to Senyoreta Alabau, noting that she shares both birthplace and given name with Granados' wife.

Granados walks farther into the café and sees Albéniz, scowling and staring into his cup of coffee. "Good afternoon to you too," Albéniz says. "And, if you please, what's so goddamned good about it?" At their last meeting with Morera, Granados imagined his friend to be a toro bravo, but this afternoon Albéniz seems more like a bear. "My stomach is killing me, 'Ric. The pills are useless. All the idiotic doctor says is, 'stop smoking, stop drinking, stop eating too much.' Stop doing anything! Do I need a doctor of medicine to give me that worthless advice? Would he rather I died of starvation?"

The improbability of his friend expiring from lack of food brings a smile to the corners of Granados' mouth. "I'm sorry. I shouldn't be amused by your stomach pain. I've had my share."

Albéniz jabs both thumbs into his prominent belly. "Have you had the shooting pains down here? Both sides?"

Granados shakes his head. "Mine are mostly right down the middle. But 'Saco, you didn't send for me to give medical advice."

"No. It's about Morera."

"There's a new problem?" Granados asks.

"Yes."

"What now?"

"He's gone."

Granados is stunned. "He's gone? Gone?"

"Yes, gone. To Madrid."

"You mean, he's no longer here, he's moved to Madrid? Not just gone there to perform?"

Albéniz shakes his head. "No, my message came back with a note that Morera is no longer here, so I went to see Utrillo, knowing I'd find him with Rusiñol and his entourage at the new place on the Plaça. Sure enough, he was there. I took him outside and asked where Morera had gone. He said he didn't know, he'd heard about a trip to Madrid, and I could tell Miquel was trying to avoid telling me what he did know, so I pressed him for more, and he said Morera went to Madrid see Ruperto Chapí–the zarzuelist."

"Chapí? I know Chapí. He was here earlier this year, with *El rey*–"

"Yes, *El rey que rabió*. The angry king. I wasn't impressed."

"What business would Morera have with Chapí?"

"After I pressed Miquel harder, he said Chapí was planning a season of lyric drama in Madrid and invited Morera to participate. With *Empòrium*."

"*Empòrium*? But we have an agreement!"

"Yes! So I asked Miquel to meet us here. He couldn't come, so I invited Niubó. It's time you and I get some answers."

When he arrives, Niubó doesn't seem to have any. Yes, Morera went to Madrid to meet with Chapí. It was Chapí who contacted Morera, not the other way around. Yes, the discussion includes a premiere of *Emporium* in Madrid early next year. No, he doesn't know when Morera will return to Barcelona. No, he doesn't know what this means for the Teatre Líric Català, but obviously if *Emporium* is presented in Madrid, it won't be premiered here. No, he doesn't know what Morera's motives are. It's only speculation, Niubó says, but Morera may think he'll be more successful in Madrid.

Granados is angry. "But we have an agreement!"

Niubó shrugs, as if the theatre business is the same as making mattresses. Agreements are made to be broken.

Furious now, Albéniz raises his voice. "Listen, Niubó–Morera wanted me to help him keep this Teatre alive, so I said I'd offer him *Merlin* and not offer it to anyone else. Then I moved my family back here and began building a house. These are real commitments, you understand? Not empty gestures. Morera said he was grateful to have *Merlin* and wanted Granados to offer his newest work. That's why the three of us got together and signed the agreement. In writing. With witnesses–you were one of them! And we put in our money to hold the theatre. Now explain to me how Morera can simply ignore the agreement and make a deal with Chapí. Explain this to me!"

Niubó, the successful industrialist, knows when not to expose himself to further liability. He shrugs, offers a lame apology, and leaves the café.

Albéniz and Granados sit silently, with their coffee cooling on the table between them. The chatter and laughter and arias around them seem as loud as bombs, as sharp as swords. They look past each other, each in a private grief, reeling from thoughts of revenge, wondering how they'll explain this to Rosina and Amparo.

Albéniz breaks the spell. "I'm hungry. No, famished!"

"I can't believe Morera would do this."

"But he did. Pau was right–we never should have trusted him. I never imagined it ending this way. Never thought our Catalan brother would go to Madrid–to feast in the land of the tyrants!"

"Pau was right–and we were foolish," Granados says.

"Yes. So much for Morera the Catalan patriot!" Albéniz drips in bitterness. "Breaking with l'Orfeó because they weren't true to the ideal of a Catalan worker's chorale. What a joke! Morera isn't Catalan, he's a chameleon, he doesn't belong anywhere. He'd do anything for fame and fortune. I want to kill him!" cries Albéniz. "How dare he do this!"

Granados shakes his head. "He sent his picador to do the dirty work."

"You mean Niubó?"

Granados recalls the last meeting with Morera; the bullfight analogy is no longer amusing. "Yes, the torero has fled the plaza."

"Exactly! And the torero–he's the one I want to kill. Grab him by the throat and squeeze until his shifty eyes are still."

"That would suit me fine. But you won't."

"Of course not," Albéniz concedes. "We're men of the arts, not warriors. We can't cross over the line like Joffre. We're expected to be refined and sensitive. Can't strangle people. We sit and take the slings and arrows."

"There must be another way to get our work presented."

"Damn it! I'm sure there's a way to stop Morera!" Albéniz is still seething.

"There may be. But if we stop him so his work isn't presented in Madrid, we lose our partner and there's no Teatre Català, so we lose anyway."

Albéniz stares at Granados. "You're right–damn it! It was a foolish dream. We were foolish to dream it, foolish to trust Morera. It was foolish for me to move my family here and start building a house." He pounds his fist on the table so loudly that diners all over the room stop talking and waiters halt in mid-stride.

"All is not lost," says Granados with fading conviction. "We'll think of something."

Albéniz, trying to recover from the betrayal, has done just that. He points over Granados' shoulder at the front window of l'Opera, over the promenade, at the façade of El Liceu. "That's where I'm going with *Merlin*. That's the next stop. And you see who's sitting across the room? The distinguished impresario, Albert Bernis. Over there, trying to look down the dress of that new soprano. Albert, shame on you! But he produced *Clifford* and *Pepita* for me just a few years ago. He made me translate the librettos into Italian so people would think they were written by Rossini–I'm damned if I'll Italianize *Merlin*–though this isn't the time to take a stand on that. Damn it, 'Ric, I'm going to get Bernis to present *Merlin* at El Liceu–or there's no reason for me to be in this town."

"Surely you won't move again," Granados says, with dread in his voice.

"I'd rather not. Imagine how it would upset Rosina and the children." He crimps another puro. "But there's no time to waste. Bernis is sitting there and I'm sitting here and *Merlin* is suddenly without a venue. Time for me to be charming. Perhaps he'll accept an invitation for dinner."

"Good luck," says Granados.

Spring, 1902

From the terrace of the Hotel Jordi in Vallvidrera, on the upper slope of the coastal range Serra de Collserola, the metropolitan area of Barcelona falls away toward the sea and spreads along the Mediterranean shore, interrupted only by a craggy, pyramidal mound of Montjuic. Where the first Barcelonans settled in pre-Roman times, though noted today mostly for its military castle–a prison with torture chamber for rebels and radicals, stone quarries that have supplied much of the city's construction, citrus orchards, and the city's new cemetery.

On a clear day, the view from Hotel Jordi encompasses the old port of Barceloneta; the Gothic quarter and Cathedral, preserved from an era when the city was surrounded by stone walls built by Romans, Visigoths, Moors, and mediaeval barons; La Rambla and Plaça Catalunya; the quadrangular blocks of l'Eixample and the early towers of Gaudi's master work, Temple Expiatori de la Sagrada Família; and further up the incline, the growing housing developments of Sant Gervasi, Gràcia, Sants, Pedralbes, and Bonanova.

By night, sheer density of light defines the promenade up the middle of La Rambla and the other principal streets that have been electrified, and blurred patches of glowing light indicate where the city continues to expand. In contrast, Montjuic seems a darkened hulk crouching on the edge of the sea, between the harbor and the delta of the River Llobregat.

A narrow road leads northeast from Vallvidrera to the highest peak of the Collserola, El Tibidabo, bare on top except for a wooden platform still standing from the visit of Queen Regent María Cristina fourteen years ago. However, El Tibidabo is directly in the path of Barcelona's dynamic expansion and it will soon be transformed. Giovanni Bosc has acquired a large parcel for construction of a temple to be dedicated to the Sacred Heart of Jesus. Last year, Camil Fabra–Marquès d'Alella–began to build an observatory on the peak, and a funicular railway has been completed, ascending from the area of Avinguda Tibidabo. And a company belonging to Salvador Andreu is building an amusement park and restaurants near the top of the funicular on El Tibidabo.

To reach Vallvidrera, there is coach service from several points in Barcelona, and from the north end of the Barcelona-Sarrià rail line; pressure is mounting for construction of a tramway or extension of rail service. Yet Vallvidrera still looks and retains characteristics of a rural Catalan village. To the north of the village center is the baronial Vil.la Joana, built in a woodsy area on the site of the original parish church, where tonight the poet and priest Jacint Verdaguer is dying in a second story bedroom.

On this clear night in April, blessed with a canopy of stars overhead, the departing Isaac Albéniz is being honored by a "despedida" dinner at Hotel Jordi. A gathering of old friends: Granados; writer Àngel Guimerà; violinist Mathieu Crickboom; the young pianist Josep Barberà–one of many protégées of Felip Pedrell; pianist Carles Vidiella–along with Granados and Malats a disciple of the late Joan Baptista Pujol; librettist Apel.les Mestres; guitarist Francesc Tárrega and his student, Miquel Llobet; tenor Frances Viñas; singer and playwright Francesc Casanovas, who is now art critic for a Barcelona daily; the founders of the Orfeó Català–Lluis Millet and Amadeu Vives; and music critics such as Joaquim Pena and Suarez Bravo. Santiago Rusiñol and Ramón Casas are here to swap memories from Quatre Gats, but Miquel Utrillo–one of Morera's "cuadrilla"–is not. Telegrams are read from Pedrell, now in Madrid, encouraging Albéniz to seek a venue for *Merlin* in the capital city; from Malats in a German town on the Rhine with a long name; and from Paul Dukas, Vincent d'Indy, Gabriel Fauré, and Claude Debussy in Paris.

Even with attendance by nearly four dozen admirers–each resolved to offer a farewell brindis, Albéniz manages to consume three helpings of the rabbit stew, washed down by a rare "cava reserva" contributed by Casas. After the last of the toasts, he stands with a full glass of brandy and a fresh puro, and motions to Granados to follow him.

Albéniz is at the outer wall of the terrace with his eyes raised to the stars. "I'm touched by all of you coming up here," he says with uncharacteristic softness. "But surely you know–so I don't have to repeat it, I'm fed up with this town and I'm obliged to leave. It's more difficult, seeing everyone tonight. This could have been my home. I'm going to miss you, 'Ric."

"And how *you'll* be missed!" Granados replies. Now this, after the departures of Casals and Malats. Now Albéniz going away, and once again it's Granados' fate to remain.

"Por dios, I'm not going to China! We'll come back to Tiana every summer. You must stay with us. And wherever we are living, you're also welcome."

Granados smiles, recalling the same words from Casals three years ago. "Thank you. That's very sweet."

Albéniz brushes it off. "Mierda! I did everything in my power to get *Merlin* presented here–so I could finish building my house and stay here." He points to a patch of lights below them and off to the right. "There it is! There's my 'torre.' Where we were going to live. Do you see it?"

Granados peers down, trying to following the line of Albéniz' index finger. "Hmmn. I think so."

"Well, there's Bonanova, and you see where it intersects with the funicular? That's it! Nice and high–lots of fresh air."

"Yes. I see it now, 'Saco." He's still not sure.

Albéniz shrugs and laments, "I loved my house. I wanted to live there." He raises his voice in anger. "Can you imagine those imbeciles at El Liceu?"

Granados braces for another recounting of the *Merlin* rejection.

"Such a suspicious bunch. Such deep hostility. And the last straw–insisting that I submit it to a group of so-called experts! Experts? At what? Italian operas? If only my name was Albenizzi, they would have loved it!"

"You didn't deserve that." As if it's their mantra.

"It's no different than the way they treat you," Albéniz says.

Granados nods. "What if I changed my name to Granadini?" He laughs, wanting to change the subject. "Well, 'Saco, this place will not be the same without you."

"Not the same? But don't you see, this place *will* be the same–with me or without me. There's no changing this place. Barcelona's determined to remain a large, provincial city no matter how many romantics want it to become more. No matter how many operas you and I create. It will cherish the works from Italy and France and Germany and take its native sons for granted. Let's face it, to El Liceu we're just a couple of country boys. Country boys from northern Catalunya. Camprodon. Lleida. Country boys. What's ever come from those remote places? Lumber and textiles? No, I've got to move away, got to find a venue for *Merlin*." He suddenly clutches his chest.

Granados sees Albéniz' eyes are closed and his face contorted in pain. "'Saco! Are you all right?"

"It's been worse than ever. And the hideous diarrhea–I've memorized each tile in the bathroom! And the doctor? Nothing but lectures about eating and drinking and smoking. And the places he suggests for taking the waters–they're all too expensive."

"Well, you're not going to listen to the doctor and you're not going to listen to me, right?"

"That's right."

"So I'll be a friend, and be silent."

"Silent or not, you're a wonderful friend. And the business with Morera, I know that leaves you without a venue for *Follet*. And here I am, selfishly crying about *Merlin* when you're in the same boat."

Granados has wrapped the betrayal in gossamer of spun sugar. "Yes, but I have so much more work to do. Not having to rush it for the season gives me more time. I welcome that. And Amparo, she was very understanding–a pleasant surprise. She didn't turn the loss against me."

"Your work–*Follet* and the rest–will find an audience, don't worry. You have too much talent," Albéniz says.

"You're right. My time will come."

"And meanwhile, you've created the finest academy for music in all of Europe."

The next morning, Granados and Albéniz walk arm in arm to the train platform of l'Estació de França, followed by Albéniz' wife, Rosina, and their children. Albéniz leaves for Madrid today, where he'll ask Ruperto Chapí about presenting *Merlin*.

"It wasn't Chapí's fault Morera betrayed us," he reasons, "he didn't know of our agreement until I wrote him. That was after Morera disappeared."

Granados waves him off. "Look, 'Saco, you don't have to explain. I don't blame you for going to see Chapí."

They reach the train and the porter begins to load the baggage.

Granados leans toward Albéniz, so the children can't hear. "I just heard something this morning about Verdaguer. Wanted you to know."

"Mossen 'Cinto? I heard he was reinstated by López, but imprisoned in that awful palace on La Rambla."

"He's very close to death," Granados reveals.

"No! Poor Mossen 'Cinto."

"He's not in the palace. Last night, when you and I were at the hotel, he was on the other side of Vallvidrera–at Vil.la Joana. Barring a miracle, that's where he'll die."

Albéniz shakes his head. "So we could have worse to complain about. We're still young, we're still alive, we're still creating music. Poor 'Cinto!"

"Yes, poor 'Cinto. So ahead of his time. Or behind it. Never easy being an artist and a priest and a mystic. If he were just one of those, he might belong somewhere. But being all of them, where? There are no venues for his kind of magic."

Granados walks slowly away from the train station, along Marquès de l'Argentera, the broad avenue that runs parallel to the harbor. At the restaurant Set Portes, he cuts between wagons bringing fish from the piers of Barceloneta, and crosses over to La Llotja–a massive neoclassical building from the 14th century that over the years has housed an opera hall, military barracks, a ballroom for the aristocracy at the time of Goya, offices of the chamber of commerce and industry, the Barcelona stock exchange, and the La Llotja school of fine arts. Granados heads west again, toward the statue of Cristòfol Colom at the base of La Rambla.

Now 'Saco's gone too! So familiar–leaving the train station alone. Expert at wishing friends luck on their new adventures. Expert at walking away smiling. No smiling music in my head today–it's a funeral march.

Granados turns right on Carrer Avinyó, passing behind the church of La Mercè, walking more briskly now, trying to remember an appointment made for him later this morning. The details escape him. At Carrer de Ferran he takes a detour that finds him passing Can Culleretes, where he and Albéniz dined to celebrate their agreement with Morera–now just a sweet, impossible fantasy–and turns onto Carrer de la Boquería, conscious that will bring him to La Rambla above El Liceu. Why walk past it, and be reminded he doesn't belong there?

Entering the broad space of La Rambla, he looks up toward the flower stalls and the bird shops, remembering the time he'd seen the woman of stupefying beauty buying flowers, then converted the light and mystery of her face and figure to twelve tones on a piano, how his spirit was moved, how the woman and her flowers leapt into his finger tips at Quatre Gats. Strangely, still remembering that woman. He turns at Carrer de Fontanella and walks toward Number 14. One flight of stairs up from the street is the Acadèmia Granados, and behind it on the same floor is his family's apartment.

The academy has expanded even more rapidly than Granados dreamed. He's pleased that his assistant director, Domènech Mas, shares a devotion to the intense course of study, requiring students to meet high standards. Two of the best, Emilia Ycart and Ferran Via, performed last month at the Salle Chassaigne and are now giving lessons to some younger students. Granados' design for the academy includes ascending layers of expectation. For admission, students are required to take an exam that shows their current level of performance, then are divided into three categories: elementary, intermediate, and advanced. During the nine-month school year, students take two exams each month to ensure they are indeed progressing in their category. At the end of the year, prizes are awarded to students with the highest marks on the exams. The academy arranges musical concerts for its patrons in which elementary and intermediate students perform, and public concerts featuring advanced students and faculty members, including Granados.

When a new student arrives, Granados asks for a scale, an arpeggio, and a few bars from a piece of music of the student's choice. This allows him to make his own "diagnosis"–not unlike the manner in which a doctor would assess a new patient. The student is then required to undergo several weeks of "corrective treatment," and to abstain from piano playing–which tends to reinforce the student's bad habits–except for a fixed-hand exercise, and the scale and arpeggio of C minor. These are repeated endlessly, until the student shows a complete understanding of positions for hand, wrist, and forearm, and proper flexing of the thumb. Granados also requires the student to master his techniques for using the pedal. How can even the most talented of them play well without correct pedal technique?

"There's a young lady waiting for you," says Mas, greeting Granados at the entrance and following him into the large corner practice room that serves as Granados' office.

"What's her name? Who recommended her?"

"Her name is Clotilde Godó Pelegrí. She has a letter from her teacher at the colegio."

"So she's sixteen or older. I'd rather get them younger. And serious, not just preparing for marriage."

Mas shrugs. "This one seems pretty serious, maestro. I think she'd be disappointed if you sent her away without an audition."

"Oh, I'll see her." And as Mas turns and heads for the door, Granados asks, "Should I know who the Godós are?"

Mas' eyes dance. "Molta alta burguesia. They're from Igualada, the owners of textile mills and paper mills, and here in Barcelona, *La Vanguardia*."

"Ah, we surely don't want those people coming after us, do we? No more bad reviews!"

"No, senyor."

Another princesa in love with the piano? Rich family. Another Adela? Wrong to let my mood get in the way. Carmen would say give her a chance.

The young woman enters his office with no hint of apprehension. Her alto voice is clear and unwavering, respectful but confident. "Buenos días, maestro," she says. "I have a letter of introduction from my teacher."

He takes the letter, noticing her wide mouth, prominent cheekbones, and attentive eyes, and motions her to sit down at the piano.

"So you won a prize?" Granados asks.

"Yes, maestro. It was the final competition. I played the Chopin *Prelude Number 15 in D flat*. I'd like to play it for you."

He's not used to such assertiveness from a sixteen-year-old. "Yes, well, we have a standard way of judging applicants. I'd like you to play a scale and then an arpeggio and then you can play a bit of the Chopin."

"Of course, maestro. And I hope you'll allow me to play more than just a tiny bit." Her voice exudes confidence.

"You may proceed."

He listens as she plays the scale and the arpeggio, seeing that her hands are positioned incorrectly. His comments can wait. But after she plays a few bars of the Chopin, he steps up to the keyboard and places his large hands onto hers, producing a discordant jumble of notes. "No, no, no. That is very bad. You have to change everything."

She seems stunned, and visibly holding back the tears. "Change everything? I don't understand."

"To begin with, the position of your hands–all wrong. You must learn the proper positions for hands and wrists and arms. And if you want to play the pianoforte–not the pipe organ–you'll have to learn the proper use of the pedal. The pianoforte is not a plaything. It's not a toy. It's not something for exercising your fingers. It's not a diversion for social gatherings."

Her voice has lost its confidence. "In other words, learn the piano all over again?"

"You could put it that way, Señorita Godó."

She responds quickly. "I'm putting it that way, maestro, because that's what you're saying. You're telling me to start over again and learn to play it your way."

"No, no. You're mistaken–not my way. The proper way to bring music out of the instrument. If you choose to."

"Of course I choose to. That's why I'm here. I could have gone to one of the other music schools or I could have gone to Madrid. I could have gone to Paris and found someone who would help me become a better pianist. But I didn't. I came here because I was told this is the finest music school in Europe. That's why I'm here!"

Granados is amused and flattered. "Told this is the finest school in Europe? Who told you that?"

She smiles. "To tell the truth, maestro, I made that up."

He closes his eyes, knowing he's been outflanked by a sixteen-year-old. He turns to hide his smile from her, to regain his composure. "All right, you may come next week. Please see Maestro Mas–he'll get you started. You have a lot of work to do, Señorita Godó. I promise only that you will work. No more than that."

PART II

Chapter Five

Barcelona, Summer 1902

"I'll get right to the point," says Carmen Miralles, squinting at Granados and tilting her head. "Your affair with the student is becoming a scandal."

Granados stiffens. "The student?"

"Don't play with me, Enrique. You know which one!"

Carmen's brown hair is gathered at the top of her head, accentuating the cameo shape of her face, and tied with a magenta ribbon. A scoop-necked white blouse hangs from her shoulders, accentuating her long neck. The sleeves, trimmed in lace, end just below her elbows. Today she's using a darker red lip rouge, which emphasizes the fullness of her lips. A matching magenta sash is tied around her waist, drawing attention to how well she's retained the shape of a younger woman. She looks splendid to Granados, as always, but now as he looks across the table he sees a withering flare of contempt in her dark eyes.

He tries to deflect it. "If we both know which one, there's no need for guessing games."

"All right, then, what's going on with María Oliveró?" She holds her lips pursed with the last syllable.

The sound of the student's name is jarring. "Oliveró? There's nothing much. Just a bad case of infatuation–on her part."

"Ah, she's infatuated? That's all? And you're simply an innocent victim?"

"No. That's not the entire story."

Carmen pursues him like a hunter knowing where the prey will go to ground. "Do you plan to tell the *entire* story to Amparo?"

Granados shakes his head. "Of course not. It's too complicated." He leans forward. "It's no longer a secret? Someone must have told you."

"My dear, I'm at your academy quite often and I've seen this one come for her lessons. She's nice looking, not as pretty as the other María, but very comely. And it's hard to miss her infatuation."

"Are you the only one to suspect?"

"I can't swear to it, but Mas and the others seem oblivious. They don't know you as I do. And I have pretty good intuition. And you're a dangerously attractive man, obviously. And this isn't the first time."

"You're right. Flirtations–they're not so rare. Many students become infatuated with their maestros. It's nothing new, and nothing to get excited about." Waltzing away from Carmen's challenge.

"Then you're willing to stop encouraging her?" she asks.

"Oh, you think I've encouraged her? Taken advantage–that's what you're saying?"

His air of offended dignity only confirms her intuition. Carmen closes her eyes in frustration. "I don't have to–it's written all over your face."

"What are you asking me to do?" he asks.

"End it!" Carmen snaps, leaning forward. "You have a lot to lose if you can't keep your pants buttoned. You're a musical genius, but that won't help you. Students depend on you for their future. Your staff adores working for you. You have many, many friends, and some who love you from the bottom of their hearts. You have financial backing for your dreams. You have music in your heart and a soul that is overflowing–and a world out there that is poorer for not hearing it. And, not incidentally, you have a good woman who's given birth to five lovely children and cared for them while you pursue your passions."

"Yes–and I'm grateful for all of my blessings!"

"They are not worth risking for a dalliance," Carmen says, rising to signal the end of their lunch. "End it now!"

Even Carmen's fine intuition missed the fact that Granados is involved with two of his students–with fatefully similar names: María Oliveró and María Ojeda. Her suspicion is drawn to the younger woman, Oliveró, whose guileless adoration of her maestro is plainly evident, not to the more cosmopolitan

Ojeda, who's learned the art of subterfuge. It's not surprising that Carmen is confused, nor that Granados' evasive response serves to blur their identities, nor that his evasion is a by-product of juggling both María O's in the same melodrama, as if they were two dimensions of the same person, as if they were identical balls of different colors tossed aloft by the master juggler.

Just as red is rarely confused with blue, the María O's are a study in contrast. Oliveró is sixteen, shorter, more serious, with light-brown curly hair, more handsome than beautiful. Her interest in studying piano is heartfelt, her efforts driven by devotion to music. For Oliveró, music isn't mere training for marriage, nor a strategy for proximity to Granados. Her infatuation is throbbing, feverish, adolescent. Her blue eyes more adoring than coquettish. She daydreams of being held in his arms and wonders how that might happen. When it does occur, it's a congratulatory abraçada by her maestro after she passes the exam for a higher level at the academy. Her legs fold as if they were sails on a becalmed ketch, but she wonders no more. She writes the first of several letters to him, infused with poetry written by others, as if words of strangers could carry her across the huge gap between maestro and student. After four years of study, Oliveró has become a nubile young woman. It's no longer unthinkable to touch him in private and feel the magic of his oversized hands. Hers is a secret love, shared only with Father Trias, the young priest of Sant Pere de les Puelles, where Granados and Amparo were married ten years ago. The priest hears her confessions and asks her to pray the Rosary every day to give her strength to resist.

Ojeda's passion for Granados, on the other hand, is that of a twenty-two-year-old who no longer wonders how to find herself in Granados' arms, who's already found intimacy with two other men, both fiancés. Ojeda has been studying piano since a violin-playing uncle concluded she was unusually talented. As a student of Granados for seven years, her inherent talent falls short of her bright perseverance–with which she's risen from elementary to intermediate to the brink of advanced level; at the end of each year she joins other students in recitals for their families and friends. But Ojeda's real excitement, judiciously concealed, occurs when she enters Granados' office for a lesson. She passes through the academy without fanfare, and might have escaped any notice except for an attribute that sets her apart from the other students–her remarkable beauty.

Ojeda's long legs and slender body are better suited to ballroom dancing than to ballet, though she's accomplished in both. Her large green eyes could scan men of above-average height and meet theirs head on. A narrow waist accentuates her breasts, and she enhances this with corsets that raise and thrust them forward. She wears her thick black hair long, so it flows down her neck and onto her collar bones, except for formal occasions when it's pulled up and tied behind her head. She has wide shoulders, slim arms, and long fingers that allow her to reach a tenth chord without straining. Measuring with Granados, whose hands are reputedly the largest in Barcelona, her fingers extend up to his last set of knuckles. Ojeda's face is elongated, with a strong chin, high forehead and cheekbones that create a delicate shadow from her elegant nose and wide mouth back to the rising curve of her jaw. Her upper lip forms a parabola over its partner, displaying her fine teeth. At fourteen, her radiance attracted a swarm of boys and men; at nineteen, after a broken engagement, her parents anxiously tried to find her an older, well-established man of the alta burguesia. They are grateful she's not sufficiently talented to seek the peripatetic life of a concert pianist.

Granados hasn't been impervious to her allure, but he's accustomed to harmless flirtations that arise from the imbalance in power between maestros and their young students. Slips and brief transitions–they are commonplace and unremarkable. And he's slipped once or twice, falling into dalliances that led to brief and inconclusive affection, assuaging the curiosity of the students and admonishing the maestro to regain control. But so far, not once with Ojeda. While he looks forward to lessons with her, and in idle moments lets his mind drift into fantasies of being with her–once envisioning her lying on his couch, naked under his wool topcoat, waiting for him–Granados' life is already too complicated, he's too busy balancing all of his projects and his children and trying to follow his doctor's advice.

From the first time she saw Granados, Ojeda was mesmerized. He was the quintessence of what she'd dreamed of. Not only the most dashingly handsome man she'd ever known–a view widely shared in Barcelona–but also the most accomplished. Virtuosity. Genius. More than those–sheer competence. That was the most attractive thing. Along with his astonishing knowledge of literature and poetry; his romantic nature, always envisioning the life ahead; and his talent for sketching. He'd done one of her, showing a lithe, catlike woman with dark flowing hair and strings of jewels around her neck–and she treasured it, guarding it between unread pages of the Holy Bible in a drawer next to her bed.

Once, as he demonstrated how to play a few measures, she watched his outsized hands with a quickened pulse and later imagined them placed on her bare hips, lowering her onto him. Another time, his long fingers sliding between her legs. Ojeda has no illusions of becoming a concert pianist, but music is not merely a social grace for her; she'll do anything to remain a student of Granados. To see him at least weekly, she'll practice all night to show she deserves to be his student. She knows she'll never go with him on those romantic journeys to Madrid and Paris, places she's only visited with her parents, nor does she expect him to leave his wife and children–it would be foolish to let that creep into her mind–but it doesn't prevent her from adoring him, idolizing him, wanting him in whatever ways fall within her grasp.

It's Ojeda's habit, after entering Granados' practice room in the corner, to take off her jacket. She lays it carefully on the overstuffed couch covered in pink chintz and embroidered in gold fleur-de-lis, rolls up her sleeves, and unfastens the top two buttons of a starched white blouse. Then she sits down, moves the piano bench to a distance that accommodates her long legs, pulls the hem of her skirt up over her knees, stretches her fingers in an exercise that resembles a pair of butterflies rising, and strikes a pose like a bird about to leap into flight until she sees that her maestro's eyes are watching her, until he's ready to hear her play. Then she begins to play.

When it began, last winter, it began with the third button from the top of her blouse. Later, he would obsess on that button–the precise point where the unraveling began. On that day, Ojeda came into his office, placed her jacket on the couch, and rolled up her sleeves. And she unfastened not two but three buttons of her blouse. One, two, three. She did not look his way nor signal that anything unusual had occurred. She did not need to.

He noticed, fond as he was of watching her, and later recalled this was the same day she asked to change the time for her lessons. She wanted to have the last lesson before the mid-day break. Not difficult to arrange. Later he realized this facilitated their becoming lovers.

One, two, three. So that her blouse was opened down to the top of her corset. She gleamed in the sunlight on that balmy day. While he watched, the light kissed the tops of her breasts.

Other than this one small deviation, María adhered to her regimen. She moved the piano bench away to give her long legs and arms a more relaxed reach for the pedals and the keyboard. The lesson began and continued, and after the allotted time she left with the habitual curtsy. With her back turned to him, she buttoned up her blouse.

Two weeks later, in addition to the third button, she unfastened the top hook of her corset, exposing the place where her breasts converged.

Teetering on the edge of indecision, Granados asked, "Is it too hot? Sun's bright. We could go across the hall."

"Oh, I don't want to bother you. Yes, it's hot. Not just the sun."

"No? I'm not sure–"

She closed her eyes, wondering only if this was the time. She turned away from the keyboard. "I need to tell you some things, maestro, having nothing to do with the piano."

She told him she was engaged again. Her fiancé was from a fine family, she said, but hadn't been ready to settle into the family business, so he took a commission in the army at a most unfortunate time–a few months before the war against America. He was assigned to a Spanish infantry batallion in Santiago in Cuba, one that was savagely attacked at the San Juan and Kettle hills. Most of his comrades were killed or wounded and he had a leg wound, but he and other survivors regrouped and were prepared to fight on. Instead, the generals decided to surrender; all of their resolute men became prisoners. They were shipped back home in disgrace.

"He came back very bitter," said Ojeda. "Very disillusioned. After the war in Cuba, going to work for his father seemed trivial and pointless. He'd sit with friends from the army and drink himself into a stupor and read passages from Nietzsche and curse the government in Madrid for starting a war against the Americans and curse the generals for betraying their troops."

Granados' brother Calixto had not been bitter. He returned from an assignment in the Philippines, sick with a tropical fever from which he died the following year after long months of suffering. But Calixto had not been bitter. "War is horrendous," said Granados. "Your fiancé could have died."

Ojeda stood up and walked to the window. "I didn't know him before he left for Cuba, but his sister says he was an optimist. I can't imagine, he's so cynical now. She said he was fond of adventure, that's what attracted him to the army. An excellent student, talked of becoming an attorney. A fine athlete. And the center of attention anywhere. He must have left those things in Cuba," said Ojeda.

Granados was puzzled. "You say you're engaged to this man?"

"Yes, but I'm not ready to take that final step. Not yet. You see, I was engaged once before. Someone my parents selected for me. After a few months of getting to know him I broke it off. My parents were upset but I gave them good reasons. So there I was, three years older and ten years wiser, when I met this man who'd been in Cuba."

"Do you love him?"

She laughed. "Love him? You mean, courtly love from afar? Across the ballroom, across the parlor?" She laughed again. "No, not that way. Far from afar. We've been brash, close and intimate."

He held up his hand. "Should I know this?"

"I need to tell you," she countered. "It's not as if you're a stranger. My greatest confusion is about my love for *you*–so different from my love for this man or any of the men who've been my suitors. Sad to say, I've been spoiled by you. That's not fair to you, I know, not at all fair. You and I are maestro and disciple. That shouldn't stand in the way of my finding another man to love–but it has." She paused, but Granados had turned away, shaken by her candor and sensing he'd have to offend her to end the conversation.

She caught her breath and continued. After the horrors of the war in Cuba, anyone would have problems coming back to resume a normal life. So she forgave him when he lost his temper, when he passed out from drinking. And he could be very affectionate and very exciting to be with. But did she love him? Romantically? That could never be. Has this engagement been good for her? "It helped me understand the world isn't perfectly ordered, perfectly rational, perfectly controllable–as my parents and so many of the alta burguesia want us to believe," Ojeda said. "As if there were no savagery, no gypsy passion, no lust that beats like a second heart deep within us. They're afraid of those things. So was I. But the taste of the untamed, the scent of the loam that is mother to us all, they've moved me. To shaking at my core!"

He wanted to summarize; perhaps that would restore some distance between them. "Sounds as if he's touched something you're unwilling to give up. So you won't–until you find someone you can truly love."

Ojeda shook her head. "No. I *have* found someone I can love." She took a step toward him.

"Yes, but that person's already married, with five children."

"Yes, but he loves me." Now there was urgency in her voice.

"Yes, but not the way you say you love him."

Tears were running down her cheeks. She fell onto the couch, covering her head with her jacket. He waited until her sobbing subsided, walked over, and reached down to comfort her. Ojeda turned over and took his hand. She raised it to her mouth and held it there as she slowly parted her lips and flicked him lightly with the tip of her tongue. He felt her breath and her tears. She released his hand as he sat down next to her, and unfastened her blouse down to the waist, then released the hooks of her corset, slowly one by one, never setting his eyes free. Then she pulled her long skirt up to her hips.

Several weeks have passed since Granados and Ojeda first became lovers. No surprise that his life's more complicated. He caroms between dizziness and shame, unable to escape it by rationalizing the affair as ordinary, as commonplace. That isn't sufficient; he had higher expectations for himself. He fears discovery by one of his staff or a student barging into his room, so he's asked them not to disturb him after the twelve-thirty lesson, explaining that his doctor ordered him to nap in the early afternoon, hoping nobody's keeping track of Ojeda's late departures. He asks himself, should he be surprised? And in moments of calm reflection, he knows that when she comes through the door for her lesson a swirl of lust will course through him. After each interlude, Carmen's words echo in what he's telling himself.

This must end! The sweetest birdsong the loveliest flower of spring—rapture beyond imagination. But it must end! Don't want to give it up but it must end. Will grieve for her smell and taste but it must end! Today!

Granados waits for the conclusion of her lesson, and when she is rising from the piano stool, stretching her sinuous body in the sunlight, he tells her. It's his maestro's voice, flat and soothing, so useful when telling students they've failed. "What I'm going to say may sound harsh, María. Perhaps arbitrary. Even cruel. But I've thought about it, and it's my only choice. You see—"

She interrupts, as if she knows what he's going to say. "You want to end it. How do I know? Your eyes." Her voice breaks, but she pushes ahead. "You cannot hide anything, not from me. I've been seeing it in your eyes the last few times, not just today. Your eyes tell me everything. They're like a pair of stages and I'm the audience and I can see what's playing. Comic scenes, tragic scenes, romantic scenes." Her voice breaks again, and her tears are unrestrained.

"I'd like to explain."

Now she's sobbing, now she laughs and steps forward. "You don't need to, dear maestro. Please don't try. Please, mi amor. You're breaking my heart, that's enough. I know what you'll say. Every last word. Please don't—it's not necessary."

"But I am sorry."

"Don't be! I'm not sorry, not a bit. While it lasted it was splendid. My fault for thinking there was a chance. For being too romantic."

"I've failed you."

"Don't think that. Romance can't last forever." She looks down.

He scrutinizes her, relieved to see her eyes are drying. "Just the same, I'm sorry for causing you pain. And taking advantage of you—"

She glares at him. "Taking advantage of *me*? No, maestro, we seduced each other! It was mutual. Better we celebrate—I chose you and you chose me. You weren't coerced, nor was I. We chose. Now you have the choice of ending it. And I'll abide by your choice. So this is goodbye, isn't it?"

"How long have you had these headaches, Maestro Granados?" The doctor's voice is practiced and authoritative, and Granados hears a note of condescension.

No surprise. The doctor might be treating someone with a serious illness. That's the time to see a doctor–not to appease Titín.

"I've had them for years, doctor," Granados replies.

"And precisely where is the pain? Could you point to it?"

Granados raises his long index finger to the right temple, midway between the eye and the ear. "Right here."

The doctor wants to know if Granados is experiencing other symptoms. Pain? Yes, it's insufferable. There's nausea and sometimes Granados has difficulty seeing notes on the page. Before the pain, flashing lights and a kind of numbness in his hands.

The doctor scribbles on a notepad. "How often?"

Granados cocks his head from side to side. "Three, four weeks."

"And what do you do when the headache begins?"

"I look for the closest dark room and lie down and wait for the pain to go away. My wife takes care of me."

Doctor Iglesias scrutinizes his notes, and renders his conclusion. He tells Granados he apparently is suffering from migraine headaches. "We're not sure what causes them," the doctor says. "Poor sleeping habits perhaps. Unusual stress. And too much of the good things–coffee, wine, cheese, fruit–not easy for Catalans to give up." He prescribes some pills that will relax Granados when he feels the pain coming, and suggests he drink chamomile tea. "Some patients," adds the doctor, "have experienced relief when their forehead and temple are rubbed with oils like rosemary, mint, or lavender. But I have to tell you, maestro, there's no easy cure for migraines."

Granados thanks him. "I don't expect an easy cure," he says. "But I promised my wife I'd see you–instead of complaining."

The doctor laughs. "And the other problem? You've had trouble digesting your food?"

"There's pain down here," he says, pointing to the lower right portion of his abdomen.

"Only on that side?"

Granados nods. "And sometimes up here," he adds, pointing to the area just below his sternum.

The doctor motions him to the exam table. Granados tells him the pains seem to come and go in random fashion. He describes where–specifically, and how often. The doctor looks at the top sheet of paper in Granados' file. "Your weight seems to fluctuate. Quite a bit since your last visit. Have you had nausea or vomiting with these abdominal pains?"

Granados nods.

The doctor leans forward. "You've had fever? Diarrhea? Rectal bleeding?"

Granados' anxiety rises. "Not always."

The doctor nods. "You have inflammation in the small intestine–the ileum."

"Is there a cure?" Granados asks.

Doctor Iglesias frowns. "It's not easily treated. For some patients, long periods occur between episodes, continuing for years. Then it comes back. There's no permanent cure. As for the pain in the upper abdomen, it's probably an ulcer. I'm curious–did your father die of digestive problems?" asks the doctor.

"No."

Died slowly horribly. Injuries from the riding accident. Years of suffering.

"Well," concedes the doctor, "there are some things we can do about this. To alleviate–not cure. Less coffee, less wine, no smoking. And some patients get relief from drinking a glass of milk before a meal. It coats the digestive system."

"And this ulcer, it's not curable either?" Granados asks.

The doctor shakes his head. "I'm afraid not." He returns to his notes. "Tell me, maestro, are you eating and sleeping regularly and giving yourself a chance to relax a little each day?"

"Yes, why?"

"Because you have the symptoms of a man driving himself too hard."

Granados walks through the Café l'Opera, scanning the tables for Albert Bernis, the impresario of El Liceu, who sent him a note suggesting they meet at six o'clock this afternoon. Not accustomed to be the first to arrive, Granados pulls the note out of his vest pocket. Yes, he's come on the designated date and time, so he finds an empty table. Bernis arrives within minutes, followed by the same young soprano from València, Amparo Alabau, who'd been with him the day Granados and Albéniz discovered Morera's treachery–along with Lucrecia Bori, another young soprano from València, on her way to Milano to study with Melcior Vidal. She's being touted as another María Barrientos.

Bernis is effusive, though the two men hadn't ever been friends. Granados hadn't seen the impresario since that day with Albéniz, when Niubó came to confirm their worst fears. Today Bernis is in the role of the grand seigneur, entering the café with two attractive and promising young singers. Seems frothy as he introduces them. "Maestro Granados, you're surely looking well! Young and handsome as ever." He sits down across the table and motions to the two young women to let him have a few minutes "for private discussions."

Bernis leans over the table and whispers. "That one, she calls herself Lucrècia Bori, in fact she's from the Borja family in Gandia. You know the Borjas? I mean, know of them? Pope Alexander–those Borjas. Lucrezia Borja–infamous for her palace intrigues, decadence, cruelty, and poisonings. Seems this one doesn't want to have to carry that burden around, so she changed her name to Bori. Don't blame her, right? Those Borjas! But a splendid voice! Milano's her next step. Melcior will bring her to a higher level. She'll be an exceptional Carmen. A very pretty one." Bernis takes huge satisfaction in being mentor to young operatic aspirants–and the prettier the better, as he confesses to Granados. "Ah, you know, if they're good to look at and have some feeling for acting, their voices are bound to sound better. Isn't that so?"

Granados nods. He hopes Bernis' mood is a sign he likes the score of *Follet*. Looking over at the two young sopranos seated two tables farther back, he discovers that Bori, the one who changed her name, is gazing raptly at him. When their eyes meet, she runs the tip of her tongue across her upper lip, tosses her head back, and smiles. He looks away.

Bernis changes the subject. "I read your score and the libretto, and was deeply moved," he says. "Oh, a few things to be altered. And the third act isn't quite ready. I loved the prelude! Just brimming with fine music."

Granados holds his elation in check. "So you've decided to present *Follet* at El Liceu? And in Catalan?"

"Yes. And no." The regular season has been set for some time, but there's a break in early April. Bernis offers him a private performance. "That's assuming you'll be able to finish it–by the end of January."

"It's pretty well finished, Albert. In Catalan. As you say, some work is needed on Act Three. I'm doing that. So there's no question of my being finished–you can schedule rehearsals. And I trust you agree I should conduct. Nobody else knows it. But what about finding the right people for the singing roles, and getting the right players?"

"It's always difficult finding the right ones," Bernis admits. "Had the same questions when we did Albéniz, six or seven years ago. Those were fairly successful, considering they were different from what our audience was accustomed to." He pauses. "Too bad we couldn't present his *Merlin* last year."

With good news about his own work in hand, Granados decides to question the impresario. "Didn't you ask him to have it reviewed by a 'committee of experts'?"

"Ah, you know how Isaac exaggerates," Bernis replies. "I wanted the others to see his score, and the next thing I heard he was leaving town in a fit of anger. Who knows, if only he had a little patience."

"Have you thought that sending it to a committee was probably the coup de grace?" Granados asks. "After what happened with Morera?"

"Yes, yes. I'm not naïve. Been at El Liceu a long time, Enrique, you know that. And I've learned to listen to people who can help me or hurt me. That's why I listened to Rafael Moragas before I made a decision on your *Follet*. 'Course for just one performance, we needed some financial help."

"You mean help from–shall we say, mutual friends?"

"You know who they are," Bernis replies. "Very good friends of yours, and always very generous."

"I see." Granados imagines Salvador Andreu and Eduardo Condé.

"Of course, I wanted to do it anyway. But I have to keep the books balanced, know what I mean? Moragas seems especially keen on having your work presented, and I value his opinions. Especially since he'll be reviewing our season for *La Publicidad*, so it's best not to offend him. You have a very influential coterie of admirers."

Granados thanks Bernis, tips his hat to the young sopranos, and leaves the café, heading up La Rambla.

*How sweet! My opera–at El Liceu. Must let Mestres know! Fortunes rising. So Bernis liked it. Thrilling–*Follet *will be seen and heard. No matter just a private showing. If all goes well–if the audience is moved if the reviews are good then* Follet *will be on its way!*

Carmen asks him to play it again, and this time she listens more carefully. "Ah, this is the prelude for Act Three."

"Yes," Granados replies. The Cussó is losing its tune, but since Carmen and Salvador have offered him their place in Sant Gervasi while they're on vacation in Puigcerdà, he's reluctant to ask them to bring the tuner back.

She puts her hand on his shoulder. "It's the storm scene, continuing from the love scene in Act Two."

He nods. With Carmen, there's another pair of ears to help him measure his progress; he trusts her judgment.

"It's the same piece you played for me before. But not really the same."

"I've changed it over and over again. Don't want it to sound like the storm in *Rigoletto*, and don't want people to think I've just reworked a scene from *Die Walkure*. So I've changed it over and over. Have to get this right–it sets the stage for Act Three."

"And the overtone is one of tragedy," Carmen affirms. "Not just a physical storm. And not followed by a gentle calm."

"Exactly. You do remember."

"Mmhmm. It's followed by sadness in the soul of the poet, and at the end, Follet throws himself off the cliff in despair."

He nods, pleased that she recalls the story.

"He's an idealist, that's obvious," she says.

Granados plays the piano line from the love scene.

"Yes. You've carried his idealism right into my heart. That's wonderful!"

He plays the piano part of the prelude to Act Three again, stopping to make small changes on the composition pad, and near the ending he stops. "I'm getting the flashing lights."

"Lights? What lights?" Carmen asks.

He places a hand on his temple and forehead. "It's the headache coming."

"Can I help?"

He walks over to the couch. "Yes. I need to lie down for a while. It's better if the drapes are closed."

"I'll do that. Can I get you anything?"

"Do you have any chamomile tea?" he asks.

"Yes, and I have some rosemary oil, from what the girls and I gathered in Puigcerdà. Would that help?"

"Oh, yes. Splendid. Carmen?"

"Yes?"

"I'm sorry to be a burden. With these headaches I just can't do anything but lie down in the dark until the pain goes away."

"You're not a burden. Make yourself comfortable, and I'll be back with the tea."

When she returns from the kitchen, his face is contorted in pain. She sits down on the couch next to him, removes his tie, unbuttons the collar of his shirt, and unfastens the gold cufflinks on the starched cuffs. She holds the cup of tea while he takes a sip and keeps it close to his lips until he signals he's ready for more. After the tea, she combs his hair back with her fingers, and opens the bottle of rosemary oil.

Granados lays in the dark, at the outset trying to repel the pain as it strikes like flights of sharpened arrows. After a while he's able to sleep, waking and dropping off for several hours. When he can lift his head and look around the room, he's disoriented at first, then remembers he's at the Andreus' villa in Sant Gervasi. Quiet except for the horse and carriage traffic on the Carrer Mayor de la Bonanova. The pain has subsided a bit. He hears the traffic, smells the oil of rosemary that Carmen rubbed on his forehead and temple, and sees that the light–which in its afternoon brightness was piercing the drapes when he lay down–has dimmed. He's about to swing his legs over onto the floor when he hears footsteps coming up the steps.

The light from the hallway sets Carmen's dark brown hair aglow and her hips sway as she walks across the piano salon. "You were sleeping like a baby," Carmen says, smiling and holding up the bottle. "Did the oil help?"

"Yes. It made me forget the pain."

"Rosemary is supposed to be blessed with special powers. Bringing us love, fidelity, remembrance. The magic of rosemary is in the fragrance. You can sniff it while visualizing a long and healthy life. Sniff it to clear your mind."

Spring, 1903

In late March, Granados writes to Albéniz, now living in Nice.

> My dear friend 'Saco:
>
> Next week is the premiere of *Follet* at the Liceu, and you can only imagine what kind of frenzy I'm experiencing. Not only must I put the finishing touches on the score, I've been rehearsing the orchestra and singers, for I wouldn't have wanted anyone else to conduct on that occasion. Collaborating with Mestres has once again been very satisfying.
>
> At last *Follet* will be performed, though I must note this is only for a private audience, yet it's the only way Bernis would accept it. However, if it's received well, doors will open at other venues.

I believe *Follet* is one of my best works so far, and since you've been my constant friend and colleague in trying to establish Catalan lyric theatre in our city, I plan to dedicate this work to you, my dear 'Saco.

All is progressing well at the academy, and when I've survived the premiere of *Follet* I'll resume work on a long piano suite, as well as a piano and violin piece to be performed next summer. Not to mention the next collaboration with Mestres, based on his poem 'Gaziel.' As you can imagine, all of this will keep me quite busy.

Please be assured of my deepest friendship, and don't forget to give my blessings and abraçadas to Doña Rosina and the children.

Your faithful and devoted friend,
Enrique

Tonight *Follet* is to be premiered at El Liceu. Granados wonders how an event that he'd despaired of ever occurring has arrived in such haste. For better or worse, too late for more revisions. The players have their music and the singers have memorized their roles. Whatever he's created will be performed in the orchestra pit and on the stage of El Liceu tonight.

His horse-drawn carriage takes him down La Rambla, slowing for the late afternoon shoppers leaving La Boquería market. The carriage turns right at Carrer de Sant Pau and bounces on the cobblestones for a short distance before stopping. He steps down and enters through the stage entrance. The doorman, whom he's seen every day during rehearsals, greets him and in an excited voice says, "Mestre Granados, it makes me very happy and very proud to have a Catalan opera presented tonight. Catalan–sung for the very first time! I'm very, very happy. Bon sort, mestre!"

Granados thanks him and enters the place he's always regarded as an impregnable fortress. Not simply because of El Liceu's longstanding disdain for works of local composers; nor the exclusivity of the Cercle del Liceu, a club reserved for the richest and most powerful of the alta burguesia–so emblematic of the ruling class that just ten years ago the anarchist Santiago Salvador lobbed two bombs into the orchestra pit, killing twenty people; nor El Liceu's extraordinary opulence, which rivals Milano's La Scala, the Palais Garnier in Paris, and the Statsoper of Vienna, as well as most of the gilded cathedrals of Europe; nor the echoes of music by Rossini, Donizetti, Bellini, Verdi, and more recently,

Wagner; nor having the audience sit on five gilded levels of a cylindrical space surrounding and looking down at the conductor's podium. Sitting in that audience tonight will be music critics for the daily papers and weekly magazines who are poised to render their judgment.

Countless times, Granados has passed by El Liceu. For years he's looked across La Rambla at the theatre from a table at Café l'Opera, always with an outsider's view of it. The distance between him and El Liceu has been palpable and foreboding. He's come tonight as composer and conductor of the orchestra–the center of attention. Despite this, Granados still doesn't feel he belongs at this place. Over the years, he's come here for the Italian operas, and for Wagner's *Tannhauser*, *Lohengrin*, and *Tristan and Isolde*. If Verdi and Wagner were still alive, they'd belong at El Liceu. He's also seen Richard Strauss conduct his works here; watching him, he knew that Strauss belonged here too.

Granados tries to relax in his dressing room.

Thank God the headaches haven't come today! Dreadful to be struck down this night of triumph! Thank God!

Until tonight, Granados has come to El Liceu as part of the audience, on some occasions sitting as a guest in the private boxes of Eduardo Condé and Salvador Andreu. He was once invited to the Smoking Room of the club, where he admired the twelve paintings done by Ramón Casas for the Cercle del Liceu depicting elegant, sophisticated women of the alta burguesia listening to music.

Casas can't sing on key yet he belongs here. Not always–when he came back from Paris his paintings were thought in bad taste–now he's admired. Attitudes can be changed. Not impossible for me to change them.

It's time to leave his dressing room and go to the orchestra. He adjusts his white tie and collar and straightens his coattails. On the way he's is greeted by Bernis.

"Maestro–my most sincere wishes for success tonight!" It's Bernis' effusive tone of voice.

Granados bows and thanks him. In their last conversation, after Granados complained about rehearsal time for the orchestra, Bernis said–in his impresario's voice–that he'd make arrangements for more time. Nothing was done.

Bernis adds, "And I believe the tenor will be suitable after all. He's been sounding better. Don't you agree?"

The title role is always a major factor in an opera's success, and this is especially true for the tenor singing *Follet*. Granados has been unhappy with the one contracted by El Liceu, and after early rehearsals he urged Bernis to find someone more suitable. Nothing was done, so Granados has coped with this by raising the volume of the orchestral accompaniment in those passages where the tenor's weakness is most noticeable. And he hopes the tenor will be inspired tonight.

As Granados leaves the backstage area, Bernis tells him the house will not be full; tonight's audience consists of private boxholders and season ticket holders. "They're educated, and willing to experience new works," Bernis says, "and tonight should be no exception. Again, best of luck."

Granados hears applause for the concertmaster, and the orchestra players' last minute adjustments. From where he's standing behind the curtain on the edge of the stage, he looks out at the ornate interior of El Liceu. He hears the buzzing of the audience mixed with the fine tuning of instruments, and blinks with the array of lights reflected from the four carved, gilded tiers of balconies hanging over the main floor and the fresco-inlaid ceiling–like a royal jewel box turned inside out. He waits for his moment to walk down the steps and to the podium.

It's my time now.

The performance is over and most of the audience retreats to El Liceu's "sala de descans"–a reception room that is the gathering place for the "bones families" of Catalan society as well as for Barcelona's political leaders. The walls of the sala are decorated in burnt rose, with faux columns rising ten meters high, painted in crème with gilded sconces mounted two-thirds of the way to the ceiling. An immense chandelier hangs over the center of the wall-to-wall carpeting–carpeting so thick that women who are frequent guests of the male club members have learned to lift their feet as they move across the room, and neophytes are marked by their embarrassing stumbles in the deep pile. In contrast with the ornate theatre of El Liceu, however, the décor of this sala is characteristically muted. As if to underscore that most of the adult males of the alta burguesía will, come morning, be back at work in their textile mills, steel, cement, and paper factories, banks, and distribution facilities. No lounging about for them. Tonight, however, they've gathered for an opera by one of the better known local composers.

Granados stands inside the main entrance to the sala de descans, alongside Salvador and Carmen. Eduardo Condé, his first patron, greets him with enthusiasm; his wife and children, all former students of Granados, are excited to see their maestro. The audience, in slow procession, comes past and as Granados is introduced to them he receives a predictable phrase or two–gracious, in the manner of a wedding reception. To each one, he bows slightly at the waist and tilts his head, never losing eye contact.

Granados knows this audience was not enthusiastic about *Follet*. He detected that early in Act One, and in the muted applause after the love duet in Act Two, and in the buzzing of conversation during the prelude to Act Three. It was these people, now offering their patinated words of praise, who chatted amiably throughout the performance. Whose applause at the conclusion was brief and polite. For the works of Verdi and Wagner, there would have been more respect and surely more enthusiasm.

Granados, though emotionally and physically drained from the performance, replays the problems that were all too clear at the podium. Having to drown out the tenor, the soprano stumbling twice in the love duet, the chorus composed mainly of voice students, the orchestra needing more violins and cellos and rehearsal time.

There were times when it was just right. To satisfy this crowd requires far far more. If one could ever manage that!

Salvador introduces him to Josep Monegal Nogués, the man who succeeded Bartolomeu Robert as mayor of Barcelona. "All of Barcelona is proud of you tonight!" Nogués exclaims. "At last an opera by a Catalan!" Either the mayor doesn't recall Felip Pedrell's work last year or Albéniz' two operas here, or he's being overly polite.

"Oh, I'm certainly not the first, Mayor," Granados replies, "but I'm flattered you took the time to come. I hope you enjoyed it."

When the mayor has moved on, Salvador whispers in Granados' ear, "That fellow's worth cultivating, Enrique. He's not only mayor, he's also president of the business association. Very well connected! Some day soon we'll have lunch–you can ask him to be on your board of trustees."

Apel.les Mestres joins them to receive accolades. He and Granados congratulate each other, overlooking the problems they experienced bringing the work to El Liceu.

Granados is introduced to Ramón Godó, publisher of the Barcelona daily *La Vanguardia*, and his cousin, Juan Godó, a textile maker and mayor of Igualada. Granados recognizes the name–would they be related to his student, Clotilde Godó? They shake hands and move on for a conversation with Salvador.

Ferran Fabra, Marquès de Alella, stops to offer a warm tribute. Fabra's father, who died last year, built an industrial and banking empire and served briefly as mayor ten years ago. The year before his death he financed the construction of the observatory on the top of Mount Tibidabo. Close associate of Salvador Andreu.

Carmen steps in front of Granados and scrutinizes his tie. "Is there something the matter?" he asks.

She laughs. "Just making sure your tie is straight–here comes more of the nobility."

Granados is amused as he watches a small parade of Catalans whose loyalty to the government in Madrid was cemented forever when the Queen Regent and her son, Alfonso XIII, granted them royal titles. The Baron of Quadras arrives first. He's a successful textile manufacturer with woolen mills in Barcelona and Sabadell. Next are the Baron of Bonet, professor of plant physiology at the University of Barcelona, and the Baron of Viver, a cement-plant owner who's president of the council of Barcelona province. The three barons are somewhat courtly and circumspect; they're followed closely by their wives and children, who after nodding and mumbling a few words of praise move quickly on.

"Do you know these people?" he asks Carmen when the last of them has filed past.

"Heavens, yes!" she whispers. "And except for Bonet–who knows more about plants than anyone in the entire world–they're insufferably boring."

A pair of familiar faces appear: Ramón Casas and Santiago Rusiñol. They're more voluble than the nobility, more generous in their praise. "It's your best work, Enric," exclaims Casas.

"Yes, indeed–it's your best," echoes Rusiñol. "Now that you've got this behind you, you must join us one evening. Like we used to at Quatre Gats."

Granados compliments Casas on his paintings that hang on panels in the Smoking Room of the Cercle. "One of my favorites is *Ball de tarda*–it was in the show for *Pèl & Ploma*."

"Yes," says Casas, "at Sala Parés. Three years ago. I'd have thought you were too busy with your music to remember that."

"No, Ramón," Granados says, "have you forgotten my true love is drawing? Not trying to make music for places like this. And your *Ball de Tarda*–with light pouring onto the couples on the dance floor and the swaying of skirts and the serious look of the men dancing with their fedoras–how could I forget it?"

Casas laughs. "Well, our conservatives are more comfortable with that kind of painting. Women in their place. Not like the women I painted in Paris. Not like real women."

"Nor the one driving an automobile," Granados replies. "That's pretty bold."

"Yes, but she could be sitting in the driver's seat and thinking about driving–someday. The pensive look, you know?"

"You didn't fool me," says Carmen.

When Casas and Rusiñol move on, Carmen tells Granados she plans to offer El Liceu four paintings by her brother Francisco, which will hang with the works by Casas in the Smoking Room. "I think he'd want them to be there," she says.

Granados knows them. They're portraits of a young woman dressed in pink, sitting on the beach at Lloret de Mar; of two women and a girl gathered on the edge of a pond; of a young woman caught in mid-stride with a bouquet of flowers at her feet; and of a young woman, dressed in a ball gown, looking over her shoulder as her male companion writes a note in his dance card.

"Yes, he painted the first three in Paris! The pond must be in Puigcerdà."

"Of course–good eye!" says Carmen. "You noticed the little island in the pond."

"What clinched it was recognizing you. Though when I asked if you'd been his model, he'd never say 'yes' or 'no.'"

She smiles.

"It was you," he insists.

"It doesn't matter. The secret is gone with poor dear Francisco."

"D'accord. But the woman in the low-cut pink ball gown–that one must have been you."

Carmen rolls her eyes. "I never wore a gown cut that low. Nor am I that well endowed!"

"Dear Carmen, you could wear a painter's drape over your head and still be the most stunning beauty in the world."

"Obviously, dear Enrique, all this excitement has disturbed your brain."

"Yes, dear Carmen, but not my heart."

In the next few days, critics write their reviews. And with them, the euphoria of *Follet*'s long awaited premiere at the Liceu begins to fade. Not that they're critical of the music. They simply confirm Granados' sense that his music doesn't quite belong at El Liceu.

Rafael Moragas, who's written his review for an upcoming issue of *Pel & Ploma*, arrives at Granados' office the next day. He's a short young man of twenty, still finishing his degree at the university but already well regarded in literary and music circles. Sitting at the small table in Granados' practice room, he arches up and leans over the table, his small eyes flashing.

"How can you tolerate that crowd of monarchists?" he says. "Their biases would test the patience of a saint!"

Granados nods, grateful to have the young critic articulate what he's been troubled by since last night's performance. "Rafael, you didn't come over here to tell me that–did you?"

"No, I came to show you the review, which I'm taking to my editor. Here it is: I recognize the difficulties you've encountered getting this work to El Liceu. And getting it across to the audience. Then I write: 'We are certain that if the artists'–mainly the tenor, but the soprano wasn't first-rate either–'had been better endowed vocally, if the orchestra had been allowed more rehearsals, and if the organizers had denied entry to all the members of the Liceu (or to anyone who presented himself only with these meager qualifications) that the resulting *Follet* would have been completely different.' And, maestro, that's exactly how I feel about last night!"

"You noticed the noise," Granados says.

"Yes, constant chattering. Clacking like ducks! The height of rudeness!"

Granados smiles. "Well, I can't dispute what you've written. In fact, it sounds like words from my own mouth."

Moragas holds up a hand. "Yes, and I wanted to say something about your artistic development. Here it is. 'The Catalan master has been able to demonstrate how far his artistry has evolved since his earlier works.'"

"That's very generous, Rafael. Thank you."

Two days later, the critic Suárez Bravo writes in *El Diario de Barcelona* that *Follet* is not an opera; it is a poem that has been dramatized, but in which the predominance of the lyric element is so accentuated that the movement of the characters around the stage is hardly necessary to produce all of its effect in the soul of the hearer...in *Follet* the musician is a poet who interprets another poet."

In other reviews, the love duet was compared with the Act Two duet of *Tristan and Isolde*, and the quality of the music was praised. There's support among the critics that El Liceu should offer a public presentation of the opera. Enough favorable comment to encourage Granados to seek more venues for *Follet*.

At the end of the week, Granados climbs the staircase to his residence. Amparo extends her short arms to welcome him and they sit on the large divan in the front room.

"I hoped to see the children before bed," he says.

"They're all down, except for Eduardo. I said he could read in bed. But you'll see them in the morning. They're very excited about going to the park with you."

He takes her hand. "Thank you, Titín."

"Good Lord, for what?"

"For everything. Taking such good care of our children. All the things you do to make this a good home. For all of us. And for not complaining about all the time I've spent on *Follet*."

Tears rise in both their eyes. "Oh, bother. It's just that I so rarely hear you say those things."

"Yes. I'm balancing so many things out there, and I don't remember to take the time."

"About *Follet*, my dear, I think it's your best work, and I don't care what the snobs at El Liceu think. It's your best work! And you will get it presented again. Hear me?"

Summer, 1903

Granados interrupts her after a few measures of the Andante from Schubert's third sonata. "Now please start over," he says. With Carmen and her family on summer vacation in Puigcerdà, Granados is using their villa in Sant Gervasi, and on this day the only lesson on the schedule is with María Oliveró. So she was invited to come here.

"You want this played differently?" she asks, without taking her eyes off the sheet music.

His reply seems laconic. "Yes. Do it the way I showed you."

"With more expression?"

"Of course. It's Schubert–not Bach. And this is a pianoforte."

She turns to him, rolling her eyes, and smiles. "Of course."

"It's a Cussó. Good enough and recently tuned."

"Yes, Maestro Granados, but you're used to it," she says. "You come here all the time. I've never been here. The action on this piano is different."

Oliveró finishes the andante. "Is that satisfactory?" she turns her head toward him but avoids eye contact. Her fingers are suspended just above the keyboard as she maintains the posture that her maestro requires of his students.

"That's better." He looks up from his chair, down the keys and up her arms to the straight line of her shoulders.

Oliveró stands up. "That's all for today, maestro?" Her voice is low, flat, and unassuming. She looks around the piano salon; being in this unfamiliar place feeds her infatuation. She imagines he's lord of the manor, and impossibly out of reach. Despite their flirtation. Despite furtive touching and rapt endearments, still impossibly out of reach. As if she never kissed him. She imagines him lord of the manor, and despairs of ever becoming his lady. She scolds herself for being so weak, and vows to ask God for forgiveness.

"I'd like to see more preparation for the next lesson," Granados says. "You can play this better."

She looks at him, extracting and embracing the implied compliment. "Yes I can, maestro," she says, smiling. "And I will."

If Granados was disappointed in the tepid response to *Follet* at El Liceu and lacking any prospects for additional performances, he takes some measure of grim satisfaction that Morera–who broke up the Teatre Líric Català, was unable to get his *Emporium* performed in Madrid. Morera is now back in town hoping to persuade Albert Bernis to premiere the work at El Liceu.

More satisfying, Granados' *Impromptu* for piano solo and *Melodía* for violin and piano were premiered two nights ago at the Teatre Eldorado by one of his piano students, Ferran Via, and the violinist Lluis Pitxot. Suarez Bravo, in his review for *El Diario* praised *Melodía*, saying "the melodic interest unfolded alongside the artfulness of the work's overall development." Granados is pleased with the review, as well as with his student's performance and the enthusiasm of the audience. Moreover, the young Barcelona soprano, María Barrientos–once a student of Granados, has debuted at El Liceu and La Scala and is preparing for her first bel canto role at London's Covent Garden. Joaquim Malats, his friend since they studied together with Pujol, has just won first prize for piano at the Conservatoire de Paris and the renowned Diémer prize, positioning him for a successful concert career. And the virtuosity of three-year-old Paquita Madriguera, "La Nena" to Granados, is dazzling instructors and students at the academy.

Josep Altet, the young assistant hired to help Granados keep abreast of his complicated life, steps into the practice room and interrupts Granados' lingering pleasure. "You have a student waiting," he says.

"Yes? Which student?"

"It's Senyoreta Godó." Altet's face suggests a knowledge of her reason for waiting. "She's been out there for some time."

"Then send her in."

Clotilde Godó enters and stops just inside the door.

Expecting her customary vivacity, Granados is jarred by the frown across her forehead and along her downturned mouth. "Yes, come in, Clotilde. Please sit down."

"I don't want to take much of your time, maestro."

"Don't be foolish. What is it? The Beethoven?"

She shakes her head. "No, it's much worse than the Beethoven."

He laughs. "Sometimes I want my students to reach for the stars, and I end up pushing them over the edge."

"No, it's not that. I have to leave the academy."

He's unprepared. Clotilde has been making excellent progress in her first full year, and soon will move up to the intermediate level. Though her innate talent may never bring her to the concert stage as a soloist–it's challenging for her small hands to reach a tenth–she prepares well for her lessons and plays with confidence and obvious delight. At the academy she brings smiles and laughter to everyone; her humor is quick, self-deprecating, and tasteful. Empathy with others has made her one of the most popular students. Surely Clotilde can't be discouraged with her progress. "You're doing well here," he says, hoping her decision isn't final, still oblivious to the reason.

"You're right," she replies. "And I give you credit for showing me how to play. But it's not about music. It's about the rest of my life." She raises her hands and covers her eyes, then breaks the few moments of silence with a doleful sigh. "I'm sure you've guessed what this is about."

Now it's obvious. "You're going to get married."

"Yes," she says, turning her head and glaring out the window.

"Well, that's very sad news–for us. All of us. Your friends, and of course for me. But for you, Clotilde, it's the beginning of a new adventure."

She shakes her head. "No, it's not an adventure. This isn't *my* idea. It's my mother's. I've just reached eighteen and it's time–she says–for me to leave my girlish life behind. Vida de niña."

"Surely it's not a child's life to study the piano," Granados says.

"No, but my future husband does not approve. As long as I can play for a few minutes–to amuse him–that's sufficient."

"Your mother picked this man?"

"Yes. My father's too busy with other things–just wants my husband to be from a good family."

"And he is?"

"Oh yes. Juan Marsans–son of a prominent banker. You've heard of the Marsans?"

Granados shakes his head.

"Well, it doesn't matter. Juanito's not my choice! He's spoiled, he's a 'principito'! And there's something hidden about him, something deep inside. In the shadows. And shouldn't I be able to choose? We like to say here that we're so advanced, so progressive. We say Catalunya is the source of such artistry and wonder, that we're more advanced than the Madrileños. If you ask me, we're stuck in mediaeval times, we're just as backward as anyone. Should I be thankful my feet aren't bound as they are in China? I'm not!" She turns to Granados with a small curl of a smile. "Well, enough of this, now you have the news and I needn't worry any more about how I'm going to tell you."

"I'm very sorry," Granados says.

"Yes, I know. You're very kind. I'll miss you–our lessons. I must go." She steps forward, slides through a stiff, respectful abraçada, and is gone.

The deep, sonorous cello notes of nostalgia permeate the practice room as he watches Clotilde leave. A recurring longing for what might have been.

Another goodbye. Will miss this one, her zest and joy. Making the most of her talent. Generous. Always a smile. Difficult to say goodbye!

The following week, Tomás Bretón, director of the Conservatorio de Madrid, announces a contest with a cash prize for the composer of the best Allegro de Concierto. The winning work will also be the exam piece for students graduating in piano. Granados recognizes this as more than a contest; it's an opportunity to gain recognition beyond the restrictive attitudes of his hometown. He knows there will be many entries, but he resolves to compose the winner.

Puigcerdà, August 1903

In the afternoon and early evening, women in casual blouses and skirts and men in summer suits and straw hats sit at tables along the promenade that surrounds the pond in Puigcerdà, enjoying the sun and breeze while watching a parade of walkers and bicyclists. Long strings of colored lights hang from the chestnut and willow trees that form the outer perimeter of the promenade; after dark they'll be switched on for the *Festa de l'Estany*, an annual festival celebrated in the community surrounding the pond. The event is sponsored by

Salvador Andreu, who built his enormous xalet–evocative of vacation villas in the Swiss Alps–overlooking the pond fifteen years ago. And by buying up most of the adjacent land, Andreu ensures that his neighbors are friends and family members.

During the summer months the town overflows with vacationers, and when the xalets are filled to capacity hotels such as the Tixaire and Fonda de Europa accomodate the overflow. The Andreu xalet, which in royal circles would be classified as a palace, stands at the southeastern edge of the pond, and though nearby homes seem designed to rival it in size and elegance, they fall short of its magnificent proportions, fine detail work outside and within, and its towering cupola, which rises as if to challenge the distant Pyrenees. Not to mention its accomodations for up to forty-five guests. During the *Festa de l'Estany*, when many of the cultural elite of Barcelona come to stay with their friends in Puigcerdà, all are invited to attend house parties in the xalets, to graze along long tables of food and wine, and in the largest of the gatherings to enjoy the music of soloists and small, impromptu groups. Over the years, they might find Mathieu Crickboom on the violin or Isaac Albéniz at the piano, while among the guests of Andreu and his neighbors are writers such as Narcís Oller and Francesc Mathieu along with the poet laureates of Catalunya, Victor Balaguer and Joan Maragall, and painters Antoni Fabrés, Lluis Graner, and Santiago Rusiñol.

Across the pond is an art school founded by Pere Borrell, who was born in Puigcerdà and whose students included Adrià Gual–librettist for Granados' *Blancaflor*–and Josep-Victor Solà i Andreu, nephew of Salvador. Before his death, Carmen's brother Francisco Miralles was associated with Borrell and his school. Illustrating the multiple connections–familial, collegial and financial–among festival celebrants.

There's no more regular summer visitor than Granados, who's called upon to organize the music at Xalet Andreu. This afternoon, he and Andreu have rounded up an impromptu chamber music group that will play tonight. "Our family orchestra," Andreu calls it. The ensemble varies from year to year, so consequently does the selection of music. Granados often performs as a soloist, but he prefers to conduct the chamber group and showcase the talent of Paquita Andreu, the oldest daughter and most devoted student among the children. Andreu plays the harmonium. Crickboom leads the string section. A family friend and father of Granados' student Mercè Moner is on cello, as is Frasquita Vidal, Lluisa's sister, whose family is here for the festival. There's a young student who lives nearby, Jordi Garcia, who can barely reach the top of his bass viola, and a bassoon player from the nearby village of Bellver known only as Eusebi, who simply materializes in time for the recital and contributes an energetic woodwind sound. This year the ensemble also includes Carmen, who brought her harp to Puigcerdà for the summer, and the guitarist Miquel Llobet, a prize student of Francesc Tàrrega, whose performances in many of the great salons of Europe brought him fame in the 1880s. Llobet has arranged his friend Albéniz' piano solos *Granada* and *Asturias* for the guitar; they've been received with enthusiasm.

Granados turns to the Andreu's daughter, Madronita. "And will you take a turn on piano?"

She holds up a camera. "This year, maestro, if you don't mind, I'd like to be the official photographer. I have this new camera from Amèrica. It's a 'Kodak.' You can take one hundred fotos with this little black box. Compared to pianos, a better use of my talent."

"Very well. All right, senyores, perhaps we should start with pieces we all know," says Granados, delighted with the size and diversity of the group, yet recognizing the additional challenges. "Do we all know *Eine Kleine Nachtmusik*?"

There's a murmur of assent. "Everyone? Carmen?"

"Maestro, I knew you'd suggest it," she replies, "so I've been practicing."

"Outstanding!"

"And hope not to embarrass the rest of you," she adds.

"Others?"

Among the suggestions are Schubert's *Trout* Quintet, Fauré's *Festival* Quartet, Brahms' Opus 40 Trio, and Beethoven's Trio in D major.

"Maestro," asks Paquita, "could you play the Schubert and the Fauré? You've never assigned those to me–I'd like not to embarrass the group."

Granados nods. "Yes, of course, Paquirra," he replies, using a nickname. "I'd forgotten. On those pieces, I'll conduct from the piano."

"Enric," asks Llobet, "how about your *Trio*?"

Granados looks over at Crickboom and with a toss of his head asks for his opinion.

"I'd love to do it," says Crickboom. "Do you have the music?"

Granados laughs. "Yes. But I haven't played it for some time. And *I'd* like not to embarrass the group!"

With that, the whole group is convulsed in laughter and whatever intent there may have been to have a long, serious rehearsal wanes. After playing through the suggested pieces, the Fauré is dropped and Granados' *Melodía* for piano and violin, played by the composer and Crickboom, is added. Llobet will play two of the Albéniz transcriptions for guitar, then Granados will conclude with the Allegretto from *Valses Poéticos* and his favorite encore piece, one of his Spanish dances.

After dark the decorative lights shower the promenade with confetti of yellow, green, violet, and red light–described by Joan Maragall as being "fruits of fire"– while the festive crowd moves from xalet to xalet. The traditional *Hymn to Cerdanya* erupts from time to time, and with it small circles of celebrants clasp hands and dance forward and back. In the large salon that extends toward the pond from Xalet Andreu, the impromptu chamber group is surrounded by a rapt audience that is willing to stand, packed together like sardines, to hear the music up close. The festive mood allows the ensemble to slip and recover, forget and recall, even to stop and start over. Granados opens with the Schubert, then waves Paquita over and together they play the piano part, side by side. The mood is contagious with all of the players smiling and cheering for each other–except for Eusebi the bassoon player, who plays intently as if this recital is his only event of the year. It may be just that. After the concluding chamber piece by Brahms, the audience applauds with gusto and Granados, after taking his bow, moves from player to player to ensure that the crowd gives each one an ovation. Llobet sets up a chair and footrest for his guitar solos.

Granados is giddy with the whirling sweep of emotion in the room. He looks at Carmen, still seated by her harp. Wisps of dark brown hair have fallen over her forehead and her expression is pensive, as if she's just stepped out of the portraits by her brother, the ones she donated to El Liceu, the ones for which Granados is convinced that she was her brother's model. A sudden torrent of adoration grips him, bringing tears to his eyes. Carmen–is there no limit to what she does well? So many dimensions: elegant hostess for this festive gathering, partner of the famous Doctor Andreu, mother of six lively children, patroness of the arts, tonight the harpist in the family orchestra, a generous and nurturing friend with unquenchable spirit, a messenger who cares more about truth than the taste of the message. As if she's Granados' Athena, whose heart was torn for the wise Odysseus and who saved him from destruction–not from softness and weakness but from wisdom.

Llobet finishes and is applauded. Time for Granados to return to the piano. He plays his two pieces, oblivious to his surroundings. The ovation for Granados' Allegretto from *Valses* is exhuberant and sustained and as he bows, he thinks how different this evening is than the one at El Liceu! This isn't an audience looking for something not to like. This audience knows who he is, what he's trying to express. He belongs here, not at El Liceu. In this place with these players, this audience and the Andreus. Granados plays *Valenciana* from the Spanish dances, his first composing success. As if he's come full circle: returning to Puigcerdà where he composed *Valses*, where Andreu agreed to be patron of the academy, where time and again Carmen has jarred him with her intuition and wisdom. Without her, he's aware, his journey would be unbearable. Once more, a whirlwind of applause. Crickboom, whom he left to start a rival music school, still his constant friend and admirer, comes over after Granados has taken his final bow.

"It doesn't matter how many times I've heard you play those," says Crickboom, extending his arms in an abraçada. "I'm just astonished. And wasn't this fine tonight?"

"Yes, Mathieu, truly it was. And weren't you absolutely brilliant in the *Trout* and the *Melodía!*"

They stand together in passionate admiration until they're interrupted by Andreu, who leads Granados toward the area where a buffet supper is being served. "Before I forget, Enric, I want you to know how terribly pleased I am with the academy." His eyes twinkle and he strokes his long gray goatee. "I'm so very proud to be your patrón. Please know I consider it one of my best decisions ever." He claps Granados on the shoulder. Granados is stunned; it's the first time he's heard this kind of compliment.

Andreu leads Granados around the buffet table, where they both take a glass of cava, and introduces him to General Josep Joffre of the Army of France, standing side by side with Santiago Rusiñol. Joffre is a solid man of fifty with graying hair and moustache, dressed in mufti tonight. When greeted in Catalan, Granados recalls what Albéniz said about this unusually cultural military man who was born in the French Catalan region of Roussillon, who shares Albéniz' devotion to the table. That means, de rigueur, a large lunch and another substantial meal in the evening.

"General," says Granados, "my friend Isaac Albéniz says you're the only one man who appreciates escudella more than he."

Joffre laughs. "You know, maestro, that may be, but there's nobody who can touch Albéniz in sheer quantity consumed. Brindis to him," he adds, raising a glass of cava. "And here's to you–that was a magnificent performance. Frankly, much more enjoyable than going to the Palais Garnier."

"That's very generous, General."

"Ni parlar-ne. Not generous." He turns to Andreu. "Tell me, Salvador, why don't we see more of Granados in Paris? Are you keeping him to yourselves?"

"Not at all, Josep," Andreu replies. "I'm sure he'd come–are you suggesting a 'command performance'?"

After a bumpy daylong ride from Puigcerdà, over the high pass at Toses and down the rocky mountain valleys of the Serra de Mogrony, the six horses pulling the large overland carriage are reined to a stop in front of the Hotel Monestir facing the Plaça Gran in Ripoll. From this market town, renowned for its monastery and mythic title, "cradle of Catalunya," there's a morning train to Barcelona. Granados dozed intermittently during the day, with occasional brief conversations with a young couple from France who spent the day kissing and fondling each other, and a quiet young man from Martinet headed for Morocco with the Spanish infantry. As the carriage stops in front of the hotel, casting a beam of yellow light from the lantern mounted above the drivers' buckboard, the lathered dusty horses snort with impatience for the water and feedbags waiting in the stable, and Granados alights, followed by the porter carrying his baggage.

At the desk he's handed an envelope addressed to "Maestro Granados." For a moment he fears it's a note from Amparo about an emergency at home. Who else knows he's en route from Puigcerdà? But as he opens the envelope, he realizes it's not from his wife.

> Querido Maestro:
>
> Welcome to Ripoll where the rivers Ter and Freser come together! I arrived here with my sister and cousin after a splendid week in the area of Olot. I have a small gift for you, and would be delighted to bring it to your room. Please return this envelope to me in room number 27, so I'll know you've arrived. How anxious I am to see you again!
>
> With devotion,
> María O

Granados reads it again, and there's no ambiguity. María Ojeda is here at the Hotel Monestir. Waiting for him. He puts the note and envelope into his coat pocket and follows the porter to his room.

María here—how? How would she know? Why? Wasn't it clear we said goodbye? No—she's here!

He's lying on his bed when he hears a knock on the door. Backlit by the sconces in the hallway, María Ojeda is a tall, wavering shadow. She takes one step forward and kisses him gently on the cheek. "Are you going to invite me in?"

"Of course." She's wearing a dark brown traveling coat with a hood that frames the swirl of dark hair pinned to the top of her head. And black ballet slippers. He sees that she's carrying an overnight bag. "This is certainly a surprise," he says. "How did you know I'd be here?"

"Well, I've been missing you. Really missing you! So I asked your new man, José, when you'd be back in town. He told me when you were due back at the academy, so I worked backward. So."

"So this isn't just a coincidence."

"Not precisely. But is anything in life truly unplanned? I was going to Olot anyway–to stay with my mother's family, and my sister and cousin were agreeable to returning today. And since this is where one catches the train back to Barcelona–it just so happens."

Olot–Calixto was there with the Army.

"And the others–they're here with you?"

"Yes. But I have my own room. And I said I'd be retiring early."

He shrugs, numbed by how adroitly she's organized this rendezvous. "So here we are in Ripoll," he says lamely.

"Yes indeed, and that's very significant. Why? you ask. This is the place where the rivers Ter and Freser come together, just as you and I have."

Granados is amused, and decides not to remind her that he'd ended their affair. "I see. And which are you, the Ter or the Freser?"

"Oh, it's just a romantic notion, but that is the right question: which are we? The Freser becomes part of the Ter in this very place, and only the Ter flows all the way down to the sea. So if you're taking me into you and I'm becoming part of you, then you are the Ter. But when I take you into me and you become a part of me, then I become the Ter. Have I lost you?"

He shakes his head, yet savors her notion. "After a long day in the carriage, I'm willing to be either."

Carmen would ask a different question. She'd ask are you taking from her or her from you?

"If you wish," says María, "tonight I'll be the Ter. But there's another bit of intrigue. Both of the rivers originate way up in the Pireneus near the border with France. The Freser runs down through Ribes and the Ter runs down through Camprodon and Sant Joan. And they meet here. But this is the intriguing part: they both *originate* within one kilometer of each other."

"Yes?"

"It means they're just like us."

As he ponders this, María carries the overnight bag to the coffee table, then turns to face him. "Are you hungry?"

"Yes. Why?"

She smiles. "I'm glad you're hungry because I'm starving! I've brought us a little supper." She reaches into the bag, extracts a linen cloth and spreads it over the coffee table. Then she removes a small loaf of bread, a block of cheese, two pears, a bottle of red wine and corkscrew, two ceramic plates and matching cups, linen napkins, and a pair of small knives. She hands him the corkscrew. "Would you open the wine?"

Granados sits down on the couch, removes the cork and pours the wine. María arranges the food on the coffee table, cuts slices of cheese and pear, and sets them on two pieces of bread. She hands one to him. "Bon profit, maestro," she says lifting her glass, then sits down–leaving a discreet space between them.

"Yes, bon profit," Granados replies. "I'm curious–are you planning to remove your coat?"

She laughs. "Oh, I hope so."

"Can I hang it up for you?"

"Yes, that would be very gallant. But I'm afraid it's all I'm wearing."

After they've eaten and drunk the wine, María pulls a small, narrow bottle from the bag. "This is your gift."

He takes it, dizzy from the wine and the anticipation of watching her remove her coat. Feeling her long, smooth body next to his once again. Seeing no label on the bottle, he looks up.

"It's ratafía," María explains. "From a friend of my cousin who lives in Olot. His name is Josep Gou, and he calls this 'Ratafía Russet.'"

"Oh, a kind of cognac?"

"No–not made from grapes. They've been making ratafía since the Middle Ages. Mixing green nuts and many kinds of herbs and some type of pure alcohol in a large glass bottle, then setting it outside on the night of Sant Joan. It sits for forty days of sun and forty nights and then, according to Josep Gou, it's ready."

"Forty days and forty nights. Does that mean it's touched by the spirits?"

She puts her index finger on the tip of his nose. "It will do you no good to distract me with your play on words. Some things, like this, you must take on faith."

"So it's more than a beverage to put you asleep after a meal?"

"Oh yes, they say it's an elixir, to cure aches and pains of all kinds. They claim it can cure anything."

"Even migraines? Stomach problems?"

"So they claim. Even heartaches." She pours a small amount.

"It's very sweet," he says.

"Yes. And very soothing." As she moves closer to him on the couch, the top of her coat falls open. "Close your eyes and relax, Maestro."

The sorcery of the wine and ratafía and now her fragrance take hold. She asks him to open his mouth. Not too wide. He feels the sticky wet tips of her fingers sliding across his lips and the aroma rising and the sweet taste of the ratafía dripping on his tongue. Still with eyes closed, he feels her head settle onto his shoulder.

Tiana, Autumn 1904

"This is without doubt the best shoulder of goat I've ever tasted!" says Albéniz as he gnaws remaining bits of meat from the bone that he holds in both hands. "Except in that little place in La Seu."

Granados shrugs, not invested in the rating system for shoulders of goat, and dips a slice of bread into his fish soup. He's just arrived to stay with Albéniz at his family vacation place in the village of Tiana. They're dining at the Café Giral, a block downhill from the main street that runs through the village.

Tiana hangs on the maritime slopes of the Littoral range of mountains north and east of Barcelona, in the region known as Maresme. A riera or large drainage ditch runs through Tiana, sparing its residents from the rampaging spring torrents that rush toward the sea. Perched higher on the mountain is the French Carthusian monastery of Montalegre, dating back to the early 15th century.

Located less than an hour from the center of Barcelona, Tiana's tradition as a detached rural center for vineyards and wine-making is now challenged by an increasing number of summer places built by the alta burguesia of the Catalan capital. To get here, Granados took the main coastal train this morning from the Plaça Catalunya to Montgat, and a carriage up the mountain to Tiana. Though he's familiar with the Maresme, the remarkable ease of access is evident for the first time today. One could live in Barcelona and find a quiet place to work here in Tiana, or work in the city and enjoy the relaxed pace of life in this village.

Albéniz is recounting his frustration in getting *Merlin* presented in Madrid. "Chapí told me it would be premiered sometime between October and December, so I got to work on having it translated to Castilian. And I thought I'd also get *Pepita Jiménez* performed. I did a private run-through for the critics and opera buffs, took them through the score on the piano and even sang some of the vocals. Imagine, with my voice! And out of that came some flattering comments, so–I thought–at last I'd found a venue. But there were no offers. Then this fellow Marabini of the Teatro del Retiro came forward–that scoundrel wanted to stage it without paying me a single peseta! Well, that was the end of my hopes of doing anything in Madrid, so I went back to France."

Albéniz asks the waiter to bring another carafe of wine, and continues: "Rosina was in Paris with the children and I was in Territet in the Swiss Alps with Money-Coutts. And his impossible wife Nellie. Not saying I was without certain diversions–you understand, I'm no saint." He tells Granados his wife Rosina was unhappy and he wasn't very productive living like a gypsy, living off his patron Money-Coutts, so finally he found a place in Nice. Money-Coutts was very accommodating, albeit they fought over whether Albéniz should live in furnished apartments or move his own furniture about from place to place. "He's more than a patrón," Albéniz concedes, "he's a very fine friend. A bit strange about some matters, and his wife is a shrew! Ah, just another woman. Can't expect much more." Albéniz is grateful for Money-Coutts' patronage, which allows him to live without the stress of avoiding the bill collectors. Still, the gypsy life is not very glamorous: wherever he goes, he's a foreigner and regarded as a threat to the local music establishment. Albéniz lights up a puro.

"And your health?" Granados asks.

Albéniz sighs. "Not so good. The doctors say I have an inflammation in my kidneys. That explains the sharp pains. At times it's so excruciating I can hardly stand it. The pains seem to stay longer and longer. But enough about my life, how are things going for you?"

"The academy's going well. Wonderful students, including a four-year-old prodigy. Our children are all fine, all six of them. And no more!" Granados describes the private performance of *Follet* and his frustration in finding a public venue for it. They commiserate about the attitude in Barcelona toward local composers. He tells Albéniz of his intent to enter Bretón's Allegro de Concierto competition, his hopes of winning it, and his concern there will be intense competition. If his is selected, Granados says, it will present a real challenge for Bretón's students.

"I saw young Falla in Madrid," says Albéniz. He played some of his *La Vida Breve*–very impressive–and told me he too plans to enter Bretón's contest. There'll be no shortage of entries."

"I've also been working on a piano piece that I've named *Escenas Románticas*. From intense feelings of passion. And love."

"Love? Source of all evil! Sanctified by poetry and music!" Albéniz exclaims. "Isn't it enough we perpetuate the species? Beyond that, hunh–love's just the seed of bitter fruit!"

Granados is surprised by Albéniz' misogynous and acrimonious remarks. Usually his friend's sunny, optimistic moods offset his own melancholy. "Well, 'Saco, can't feelings of love be the source of great inspiration?"

Albéniz squints across the table. "Ah, so there's a woman involved with this new piece?"

Two of them. Too complicated to explain. Even to 'Saco.

"As you say, none of us is a saint," Granados replies.

"Oh, God, I can only hope that this one is just another dalliance. But who am I to give advice? I do caution you, 'Ric, be careful of ladies who pretend to be sincere. All are deceitful, yes, but the witches who ply us with sincerity, rhapsodizing about the elixir of love, they're the worst!"

Granados counters. "And you don't allow for any exceptions?"

"Yes–my long suffering Rosina. Most of the time. And of course your saintly Amparo."

They're interrupted by a man who crosses the room from another table. He looks remotely familiar to Granados, and is more easily recognized by Albéniz. "Buenas tardes, maestros," says Juan Godó. They shake hands. "I couldn't help recognizing you, Maestro Granados. We met at El Liceu after the opening of your opera. I found it exquisite! And my daughter, Clotilde, was one of your students. And of course it's good to see you again, Maestro Albéniz. Are you gentlemen here for the fiesta?"

The maestros aren't aware there's a fiesta in Tiana.

"I'm just getting to know this town," Godó explains. "Spend most of my time in Barcelona and Igualada. But isn't this a lovely place to get away from the mad rush? Could you gentlemen be persuaded to come to my place tomorrow evening? I'm having a few friends and neighbors over, and would be honored if you could stop by." He turns to Albéniz. "You know where it is, don't you, maestro? Carrer Llaurador. Nothing formal. About eight o'clock then?"

Godó has the bearing and swagger of a successful industrialist, and political skills honed as mayor of Igualada and member of the Catalan parliament. His invitations are invariably accepted. Tilting his head to salute the maestros, he rejoins his table.

After Godó's party has left the restaurant, Albéniz says the villa belongs to Godó's relatives. He uses it as a place to retreat from his textile business in Igualada and his political activities. "So he came to your opening at El Liceu?" Albéniz asks.

Granados explains that their meeting was as brief as a handshake, that Godó was in the reception line with his cousin, the publisher of *La Vanguardia*. Andreu knew them. "He knows everyone," he adds.

"And Godó's daughter was one of your deixeblas?"

"Yes–was. Unfortunately, she got married. Which I'm told had the blessing of the Pope."

"A marriage made in heaven."

"Not exactly," says Granados, recalling Clotilde's description of her husband to be.

"Well, learning piano is just a social skill for the princesas."

Granados objects. "No, 'Saco, this one's unusually talented. Not a concert player, but a very hard worker, an excellent learner. I'm sorry she had to stop. She was like sunshine at the academy. Everyone was sad to see her leave."

"Especially her maestro," Albéniz notes. "Is she the one who inspired your romantic piece?"

"Heavens, no!"

The porter takes their hats in the spacious entryway of the villa on Carrer Llaurador. He leads them through a large parlor and down a long hallway to a salon where Juan Godó greets them. Godó introduces them to his brother-in-law Jaime Armat, the owner of the villa, who makes a cryptic remark about "Juan's recent interest in music."

Godó replies, "But Jaime, wasn't it Voltaire who said, 'Work keeps us from three great evils, boredom, vice, and poverty'?"

"I believe that depends on the kind of work it is," says Granados. "Surely Voltaire was not thinking of making music."

"Touché," says Godó. "But Jaime's been so busy he's failed to note that I've always loved music, especially opera, and these gentlemen are composers of operas. If you cared a bit about music, Jaime, you'd have a grand piano sitting right over there." He points to the corner of the room.

"I've no objection to your buying one and putting it there," says Armat. "Since the only one who ever plays is Clotilde."

Godó motions for a waiter. Handing them glasses, he explains that the white wine comes from the nearby vineyards of the Marquès d'Alella–adding as if he were a huckster that this wine won a gold medal at the Agricultural Exposition of 1891. Albéniz and Granados tip their glasses and offer compliments. "Just a bit of sweetness," says Godó. "That's the Pansá Blanca grape. Makes all the difference!"

"Does the marquès make the wine himself?" asks Albéniz, not intending it as a serious question.

Godó is undeterred. "No, but he's certainly keeping an eye on anything that carries his name. They say his father spent a lot of time in the vineyard. Would you like to meet him?" Without waiting for a response, they're led across the room. The marquès, who shook his hand after the performance of *Follet*, treats Granados like a long-lost friend. He rhapsodizes about "the splendid new opera." Soothing words, even if he is just being polite. Granados compliments the marquès on the wine.

"My family has been making vi blanc since the 17th century," says the marquès. "I should hope that by this time we've figured out how to do it right."

Granados and Albéniz are introduced to most of the guests, who–as soon as it's polite to do so–revert to their conversations about business, trade, and politics. Not the conversation of Barcelona's modernistes and bohemians, nor the polemics of rabid Catalan "independentistes." Pragmatically, they curry favor with the monarchy, swearing loyalty to Madrid in return for being left alone. These are men whose fathers and grandfathers were the original "indianos"–who sailed to the West Indies, applied their business acumen, and reaped the rewards. Their ethic: if it was good for business–including slavery, exploitation, colonialism–it was above reproach. The old indianos resented the crown and the military for blundering into the disastrous war six years ago; these men are learning to live with disaster.

The Spanish Army–my grandfather, my father, my brother–protected their colonial empires. Don't hear much about that any more.

Following the war, the enterprises of the indianos were scorned by the intellectuals at home and attacked by indigenous survivors of colonialism across the ocean. Now their descendents–including some of Juan Godó's guests in this villa tonight, drinking wines of Alella and smoking Cuban puros–confront new fears: that Madrid will betray them by weakening the tariffs that protect their industries, that their workers will join labor unions, ratcheting up the demands for higher wages and better working conditions.

Most of their conversation is alien to Granados' realm of pianos and singers and impresarios and students and composition pads filled with lines and dots, but his incessant curiosity, his devotion to a wide range of reading, and his association with Eduardo Condé and Salvador Andreu have equipped him with a better understanding of the joys and sorrows of the alta burguesia than has the life of Albéniz. In this gathering, Albéniz is truly an alien. But though Granados can follow what these men are talking about, he doesn't find their viewpoint persuasive.

Juan Godó grips Granados' elbow lightly from behind and leads him away. "There needs to be a piano in this corner," he says. "Some day. My daughter Clotilde wants one 'like the one my maestro plays.' Do you know what she means?"

"Yes. It means she wants a Pleyel."

"French?"

"Yes. Made in Paris."

"And is it the very best?" asks Godó.

Granados considers the question. "It's one of the best, and I'd have to say, without being disloyal, it's better than the pianos made here. Though the Cussós are very good. I don't believe your daughter would be unhappy with a Cussó."

Godó shakes his head. "My daughter is very strong-willed, as you may have noticed. And very insistent that her piano be a Pleyel. She was bitterly disappointed to leave your academy. Very bitter. Well, it was a family matter. She says a Pleyel would be a consolation prize."

Granados laughs, understanding more than he wants to disclose. Quite a consolation prize!

"Well, to put it to you directly, I'd like you to find her one of these Pleyels."

"Senyor Godó, I'd love to help, but I don't expect to go to Paris until sometime next year."

Godo raises his palms. "Oh, no. It's not an urgent matter. If I could tell Clotilde you'll find her a Pleyel when next you're in Paris, she'll be ecstatic. Ec-static! Perhaps you have no idea how much she idolizes you."

Granados shakes his head. "Sometimes students–"

Godó clasps Granados by the shoulder. "No, I haven't been clear. Not just your being a great pianist. She says it's the way you treat your students. Very demanding, yes, but you care about them. You want them to find their own way. Do you know how rare that is? Do you know, maestro, those are the very things which differentiate the merely competent businessmen and the great ones? Did that ever occur to you?"

Granados looks into the eyes of Juan Godó and sees the boundless energy and passion of his daughter.

José Altet, his young assistant, brings Granados the telegram from the Conservatorio de Madrid, signed by Tomás Bretón. "Congratulations on winning the competition for Allegro de Concierto. Your piece will now be the required examination for all graduating piano students. The jury had a difficult task deciding which of the twenty-four entries would be declared as finalists. You and José Guervós and Vicente Zurrón were the finalists. But the jury had no difficulty selecting your entry as the winner, by a nearly unanimous vote. Incidentally your friend, the young

Falla, received honorable mention. Once more, please accept my most devoted congratulations on your selection."

Granados' work on the piano piece–inspired by raw passion with María Ojeda and sporadic interludes of coquettish mischief with María Oliveró–is nearing completion. He's settled on the name *Escenas Románticas*. From Ojeda comes the unrestrained passion of the third movement: *Lento con Éxtasis*–slow with ecstasy. An emotion so intense it cannot be expressed in words. So he gives it a title that Robert Schumann once used to symbolize such intensity.

And from Oliveró–who in her two weekly lessons has heard bits of it–comes an elegance teased from him, a delicacy that soothes him, an adoration that has been unwavering. Oliveró, who keeps her blouse buttoned up to the top, who's as demure as the other one is provocative.

"Romantic scenes–escenas románticas." The name he's given to the new piano suite. There have indeed been several romantic scenes, but not with Oliveró. Not with this sweet and devoted sixteen-year-old. One day he asks her to stay after her lesson.

"Yes," she says. "If that's your desire." She holds her breath.

"I'd like to play this new piece for you. All the way through."

She smiles. "Oh, I'd be honored."

"You're sure you can stay?"

She turns her head slightly, probing him with her wide upturned eyes, unsettled by his hesitation. "Yes, if you desire."

"I'd like you to tell me how it sounds. If it moves you."

"It *will* move me," she replies. "And I'm honored to be asked."

"You've honored yourself. You've been my student for six years, and you've worked so very hard to become a good pianist. And I've become very fond of you. Very fond. You've helped to inspire me to write this piece, this *Escenas Románticas*, and I'd like you to be the first to hear it."

The next day, Granados opens a letter from Oliveró.

> Beloved Maestro,
> Being with you yesterday was the closest I've ever come to romantic love, and to fearing the death of that love. Would that time could stand still when we are together! I offer you

a portion of this poem by Joan Rois de Cornella, a Catalan troubadour of the 15th century. Surely he was not writing of courtly love from afar!

> If the siren sings best in time of storms
> then I must sing, now misery torments me
> so fiercely, that my thoughts are taken up
> with instant death; they cling to nothing else.
> But if you let me die beneath your mantle,
> close to you, my pains are at an end;
> like a bird dying in a perfumed bed,
> happy to know its life has come to that.

Know my dearest maestro, that my life has come to that.

María O

He reads the letter twice and sits at his desk, listening to the sound of students practicing down the hall before hiding Oliveró's letter under a stack of sheet music on the shelf above the keyboard of his piano.

After her next lesson, he sits next to her at the piano and they talk in whispers about their love. Their cautious, fragile, illicit love. She kisses him twice as she runs her fingers through his thick hair, then stands and gathers her sheet music and hurries out the door.

The next day, another letter arrives. This one includes a poem from William Butler Yeats "The Lover Tells of the Rose in His Heart."

> All things uncomely and broken, all things worn out and old,
> the cry of a child by the roadway, the creak of a lumbering cart,
> the heavy steps of the ploughman, splashing the wintry mould,
> are wronging your image that blossoms a rose
> in the deeps of my heart.
> The wrong of unshapely things is a wrong too great to be told;
> I hunger to build them anew and sit on a green knoll apart,
> with the earth and the sky and the water,
> re-made like a casket of gold.
> For my dreams of your image that blossoms
> a rose in the deeps of my heart.

At her next lesson, Oliveró demonstrates how well she's prepared for her lesson, playing the Schubert Sonata in D with unswerving intensity. He compliments her.

"Thank you," she replies in the voice of any student whose good work is being acknowledged. Then she raises the pitch. "This is a wonderful piece of music. Do you know Schubert wrote it in the mountains of Austria, just as you wrote *Valses Poéticos* in the Pyrenees?"

"I didn't know that. Very interesting."

"What a tragedy Schubert died so young. Imagine, just thirty-one!"

Granados nods, not wanting to engage her in a personal dialogue–not here in his office, not today. "I'd like you to continue working on the sonata. Next time we'll talk about a new piece."

"I'd like to play one of yours," she says.

He shakes his head and says in his maestro's voice, "You know I assign those only to the most advanced."

"And I'm advancing. Your words."

"Yes, and I hope someday you'll be playing my pieces. All in good time, María."

As she leaves his practice room, she hands him an envelope. In the note, she thanks him for "being so gracious and sweet." And she encloses an excerpt from "Eternal Love," by Gustavo Becquer.

> The sun could cast an eternal shadow,
> And the sea could run dry in but a chime;
> The earth's axis could break
> Like crystal fine.
> Anything could happen! Death enswathing
> Could cover me with its mournful attire;
> But in me your love's flame
> Could never expire.

At the end of the poem, Oliveró writes:

> It's occurred to me, dearest maestro, that in all this time we've been together I've poured out my heart and soul to you, offering my most cherished poetry and asking for nothing in return. I wonder, sometimes in the middle of the night I wonder since I'm not with you, if you truly know what our love means to me. I can only hope you treasure it and respect the depth of what I feel. I can only ask that you'll always allow me to inspire you.
>
> María O

He places this letter atop the growing stack under the sheet music on the corner of his piano.

Escenas Románticas is to be premiered on November 20 in a concert sponsored by l'Unión Musical. The program includes Granados playing his Allegro de Concierto and, with violinist Sánchez Deyà, Beethoven's *Spring* Sonata. Three days before the performance, Oliveró arrives for her lesson. She plans to attend the premiere of *Escenas* with her parents. "My father's a great admirer of yours," she says.

"Your father?"

"Yes. He was at El Liceu for *Follet* and came home fuming because of all the rudeness. My father has many faults–no question–but he loves your music. And that makes up for a lot, far as I'm concerned."

"I'm glad you'll be there. *Escenas* is a special piece."

"It surely is for me."

"More than you know." Granados hesitates, then finishes. "I'm going to dedicate it to you, María. Without you, I couldn't have composed it."

His words catch her as she reaches to place her sheet music above the keyboard. She loses her balance and grabs the corner of the piano. "No, no. Don't play with me, don't play with me!" She turns her face, suddenly streaked with tears, and breaks into high-pitched laughter. "Oh maestro, you're not playing, are you? You're serious. My God! I never imagined! No, no. You dedicate works to people like Joaquim Malats and Isaac Albéniz. To people like Eduardo Condé. And to your son. I'm nobody compared to them. I'm just a student–not even an acclaimed student. Just someone who wants more than I can have, who dreams of more. But who am I to have such a glorious work of art dedicated to me?"

Granados takes her hand. "You? Your spirit is in this work, just as the valleys of the Pyrenees guide the rivers. The music comes from my heart and soul, yes of course, but bringing it to the surface is just the first step. Our times together have been 'escenas románticas.' Who are you, María? You're my inspiration for this. I'm proud to dedicate it to you!"

On the printed program distributed at the concert, the name of María Oliveró is printed under *Escenas Románticas*. The critic for *Revista Musical Catalana* notes that both of the evening's artists, Granados and Sánchez Deyà, are applauded with great enthusiasm by the audience. Beyond mentioning that *Escenas Románticas* is on the program, he makes no comment on the quality of the work.

Tonight Enrico Caruso sings the Duke of Mantua role in Verdi's *Rigoletto* at El Liceu. After triumphant debuts at La Scala, Covent Garden and the Metropolitan, he's in Barcelona for the first time after yet another success earlier this month, in Paris. Caruso's reputation is soaring. El Liceu's audience, fascinated with anything Italian, is expected to embrace the celebrated young tenor from Napoli in his most popular role, in the most renowned Italian composer's celebrated work, set in Italy and conducted by another Italian. Granados, who receives complimentary tickets, is eager to hear Caruso in the role.

At midday, the migraine returns, and Granados leaves the academy to spend the afternoon writhing in bed. Amparo cares for him devotedly, bringing cups of tea, rubbing his forehead and temple with oil, and keeping the sounds of their energetic children, including the newborn Paquito, under control. So Granados is unable to attend today's reception for Caruso, and the first of two performances.

The following afternoon, with the pain diminishing, Amparo sends José Altet over to El Liceu to arrange for Granados to attend Caruso's second performance. When it's time to dress, she helps him with the studs and cufflinks of his dress shirt, ties his bow, and dispatches José to find a carriage to take him to the opera house.

As Granados enters the stage entrance, the doorman sings out, "Bona nit, Mestre" and Granados tips his hat. Inside, an usher takes him to see the impresario.

"We missed you last night," says Bernis. "You weren't feeling well?"

"Just a bit indisposed," says Granados. "I'm better today. How did it go last night?"

Bernis hesitates. "Oh, I think he captured them, at least with *Questa o quella*. Which he encored. But the coloratura–the Cuban, she missed her notes in the duet *E il sol del'anima* and that started it."

"Started it?"

"Well, there was some hissing and Caruso was offended. In spite of this he recovered and encored *La donna è mobile* three times. But at the end there was almost no applause and he was absolutely furious. Afterwards he and I had some unpleasant words and things back stage have been very, very tense. Like a bomb about to go off. You know singers. More demanding than kings and emperors, and this one–well, what can I say? Very temperamental, very Napolitano. Would you like to meet him? He speaks quite passable French."

Caruso emerges from his dressing room. A barrel of a man in the red and gold costume of the Duke of Mantova. Bernis introduces Granados with a bouquet of compliments. They shake hands. "So your own opera was presented here?" says Caruso.

"Yes, last year. A private performance."

"Congratulations, maestro! I wish you success, and I hope we'll meet again. Somewhere–Paris, London, New York."

"Yes, I hope so," Granados replies. "I'm looking forward to hearing you tonight. And to many 'bravos.'"

Caruso snickers. "Ah, yes, the 'bravos.' With this crowd, there's no guarantee."

Once again tonight, Caruso's authoritative bel canto voice fills El Liceu and after an enthusiastic applause for his aria *Questa o quella* he encores it. Granados thinks he's captured them entirely. Once again, however, there's a problem with the duet, *E il sol dell'anima*. Tonight it's Caruso, not Esperanza Clasenti, who misses the high notes, singing flat, and from the audience come hisses and a few catcalls. Then, with an opportunity to recover after a resounding cheer for *La donna è mobile*, the tenor does not encore the aria and moves on. This engenders more hissing and catcalls, so that even when Caruso leads the stirring quartet in Act Four, there is only sporadic clapping. At the end of the opera, the audience expresses its disapproval with the most perfunctory applause.

Afterwards, in the crowded Cafè de l'Opera, Granados sees Bernis entering with his assistants. The impresario is red-faced as he arrives at the bar and calls for a glass of anís. "You saw what he did? You saw that?"

Granados shrugs. He heard Caruso miss the notes in the duet, but was surprised by the rudeness of the audience, and thought the tenor was justified in taking offense.

Bernis is fuming. "But the audience deserves better, don't you think, when they come to hear the best? And when he refused to encore the *La donna*, he knew he was provoking them, and he simply didn't care! With an encore, they would have forgiven him. I told him he only deserved to be paid half his fee and he cursed me in three languages. Said I was a criminal. No, senyor, that's what he is! I'd like not to pay him at all!"

"I hope the audience will forget it before he comes back," says Granados.

"Come back? Hah! He said he'd never sing again in Barcelona."

Now Caruso. Another leaving Barcelona, never coming back. And some of us can't leave.

Granados sees Carmen standing in front of a millinery shop on the Passeig de Gràcia. "I like the one you're wearing," he says, stepping up behind her.

"Oh! You startled me." She turns and pulls him into a long abraçada. "I've been so busy, haven't even stopped at the academy. I've missed seeing you, just this way–without Salvador and the children. Everything's all right?"

"I've been so busy–haven't had any time to shop for hats."

She pushes him away. "Oh you! I'm not really looking for another hat. Don't even wear the ones I have. No, I'm waiting for Madronita to finish her ballet class. But you've not answered–how are you? Your headaches?"

"I still have them. It's my fate. Otherwise, things are going well. You were at the Principal for the prelude from *Follet*. The review was stupendous!"

"Yes, the one in *Diario*. How could I forget? I know how you struggled to get *Follet* presented. How could I forget the critic's very words? 'Deeply felt melodies' and 'lustrous orchestration.'"

"Yours is like the voice of an angel from heaven. Thank you for caring so much about my work!"

"I never asked, but I trust you found Sant Gervasi a good place for concentrating on your work."

A slight shiver goes through him–images of long, erotic scenes last summer with María Ojeda, while the Andreus were in Puigcerdà. Is Carmen probing for something? "I found it ideal," he says, back under control. "Thank you."

"Well, it's yours, whenever we're out of town. How are Amparo and the children?"

"All fine, thank you. You know we've had little Paquito."

"Yes, I stopped to see him. And Amparo was very cordial, considering I'm supposedly the villainess. He has your giant eyes. I'm so envious!"

Paris, Spring 1905

José Altet unloads the baggage onto a cart at the street entrance to the Estació França. Granados follows the porter bearing his luggage cart to Track 5. He'll be overnight and most of the next day on the train, passing through Perpignan, Marseilles, Dijon and Lyon before arriving in Paris.

As he boards the train Granados enjoys the novelty of being among the passengers stepping up from the platform of the Estació França and climbing on board–after so many times being the one seeing passengers depart. So many times saying farewell and "bon viatge" to Casals and Albéniz and Malats, then walking back from the terminal and out onto Marquès de l'Argentera, disconnecting from his departing friends even as he wishes them well, pushing through the lingering remnants of envy that serve no purpose other than to deter him from his work and inspiration. After so many times seeing his friends off to Paris, he's on his way there too.

He invited Amparo to go with him, seeing a way to recognize her daily burden of managing the household, bearing and raising the children, seeing that food is on the table, ensuring that home's always a comfortable place for him. He wanted to thank her.

"We can't afford it," she said, as guardian of the budget.

"Yes, we can," he replied, prepared for her skepticism. "This has been an extraordinary year. The cash prize for Bretón's contest. And I've been paid quite well for concerts. Especially the ones with Ysaye and Crickboom. And they're paying me to come to Paris. Also, Salvador just donated some extra money for travel–said it's 'beneficial' for me to get away, said I'd be 'inspired' in Paris."

"You're sure that was Salvador–not Carmen?"

He repressed his annoyance. "It was Salvador. So, Titín, I invite you to come with me. We'll both be inspired."

"Very well. But you're just counting all the money you've brought in this year and not what's gone out. You always forget about that."

"You're saying we've been spending too much?"

"That's no secret, is it? This place is very expensive."

"Titín, you insisted on having a larger flat–room for all of us."

"Yes. But the cost went up again this year. And your need for clothing and all those little things you fancy so, that hasn't changed. I'm not blaming it all on you. One more mouth to feed. Medical bills. Yes, you've done better this year, bringing in more money, but we've spent it all."

Sensing that her resistance was stiffening, he held his response.

"And what about little Paquito?" she asked. "He's so young, so frail. You'd want me to leave him with the nurse?"

Granados shrugged. "Well, she has been caring for him. I can't make that decision for you."

Next morning, she thanked him for inviting her and told him she would not go to Paris.

So he is traveling alone, with much to anticipate. Seeing Joaquim Malats again, rehearsing with Jacques Thibaud and Eugène Ysaye, giving a concert at the Salle Pleyel with Crickboom. Casals is still touring the Americas, so he won't see him until September. How splendid, however, just to be in Paris again! Going back to all the old places: the Rue de Trévise where he lived with Ricard Viñes; La Salle Erard, where they played Chopin's Rondo for two pianos; and the tiny flat he took to be closer to Francesc Miralles and his coterie of "bohemios" who drank absinthe and smoked hashish all night long, whose intense conversations were both stimulating and frightening to the twenty-year-old Granados.

Joaquim Malats is still aglow from winning the Diémer Prize last year, and enjoying the surge of bookings that followed. It's his first week back in Paris since February. "I have to tell you 'Ric, getting booked is the only bright side," he says, nodding his angular head up and down. "Yes, I'm doing well now–that is, better than before. But there's no glamour at all in going from city to city like a gypsy." He stops, eyes searching. "You've heard all this."

"Yes. From 'Saco."

"Of course. So I won't bore you with details."

Granados shakes his head. "We always think the sun shines brighter on the other side. After a year of it I'd probably be tired of the gypsy life too, but I'd just like to find that out for myself! You understand?"

"Of course. And from the other side of the hill, I envy you being able to stay at home most of the time. You can watch your students grow and not have them waiting endlessly for you to return for the next lesson."

"Though teaching can be a curse," Granados says.

"That pays the bills."

"Yes."

"And I miss being home, 'Ric. This place!" Malats waves his hands in an arc above his head. "This is not home. It's wonderful, it's marvelous, it's the glittering city of lights. But home? I think not!"

"It's the cultural center of Europe, 'Quinito."

"To be sure. A grand place for the French–if they come from families with money and can afford to pretend to be starving artists! But for me? I've been hissed and booed for playing too much of that 'awful Spanish music.' So, if they want Chopin and Liszt, that's what they get. As for the Diemer, thank God for that, but I had to be so much better than the others for the judges to get over their attitude that anything coming from the south side of the Pyrenees isn't ever quite good enough."

Granados is treated like royalty at Salle Pleyel. There's nothing the staff won't do to make him feel more at home. Andreu's words spring into his head, one of his oft-repeated homilies: "The path to success is making your customers–your audience, in your case–feel like they're at home. It allows them to hear what you're telling them. I don't care if it's here in Catalunya or Paris or even in Buenos Aires. Pharmaceuticals or piano music. Worth remembering." So Granados wonders, has the staff at Salle Pleyel heard the renowned Doctor Andreu's prescription for success?

The concert with Crickboom at the Salle Pleyel is received with enthusiasm. After each of the Beethoven sonatas, there's sustained applause. To the extent that his ears can measure, the Scarlatti transcriptions bring an even more ardent response. Followed by three encores. The audience rises and a large contingent gathers in front of the stage. There are many fervent handshakes and much Gallic adulation. When the last of the crowd heads for the door he asks Monsieur Savard, the director, for a moment of private conversation.

Savard's exhuberance is brimming and Granados waits for it to abate before telling him he wants to buy a grand piano.

Savard seems offended. "Maestro Granados, is yours not satisfactory? We would give you another one. That is no problem."

"No," Granados explains, "it's for a student of mine. Her family wants her to have the very best and surely I could only think of Pleyel."

Savard frowns. "One of your students? A prodigy, n'est-ce pas?"

No prodigy. Not her. Plays with heart and soul. Brought sunshine. Not even my student any more.

Granados smiles. "I have some very fine students and I have some who are not. This one, she's close to the top level but will never be a concert soloist. Still she plays with all her heart and soul. That's why I want this student to have your very finest. Not just any Pleyel–your very finest. You understand?"

Savard's face reddens. "Maestro, you're suggesting there are pianos with the name 'Pleyel' that are not the very finest? Surely you don't believe the Americans' lies, that Steinway is a better piano. Surely you don't believe them!"

Not having heard what the Americans say–and not caring–Granados ponders how to cool this hornet's nest. Sudden inspiration. "Those whose conduct gives room for talk are always the first to attack their neighbors," he says to the Frenchman.

Savard looks stunned. "Why, that's from Moliere!"

"Yes, indeed. And since I promised my student I'd find a Pleyel for her–and I don't intend to dishonor that–let's make arrangements for you to ship a Pleyel grand to Barcelona."

Granados is walking the beach at Sant Salvador with Casals. It's an overcast day in late September and the surf is docile. Casals' busy schedule of concerts leaves him only a few days to spend in this place that has been his refuge since childhood. All year he's been touring the United States, this time on his own, and returning to Brasil, Argentina, and Uruguay with Harold Bauer. Then back to Paris for a few days, and concluding the year with a tour of Europe. "Next year, I'm going to settle down. A bit," he tells Granados. "I'll be moving into a new place in Paris and I hope to spend some time there! Promise me you'll visit."

Granados knows about Casals' devotion to daily exercise, but he's amazed at the pace being set on this stroll, especially since Casals went for a long swim in the morning, then played tennis with some Englishmen who were staying next door. "We played doubles," Casals recalls, "and I was on the losing side. You know how much that irritates me! But it's a great sport. You should take it up, 'Ric."

Granados lets it pass. Over the years Casals has urged him to exercise, even giving him one of his tennis rackets last year. The racket is stored in a closet, reappearing only when Granados' son Victor pulls it out and–until it's wrested from him–uses it to hit grapes and figs out the window. Granados, reasonably fit from walking around Barcelona, pulls alongside Casals. "Tell me about this President Roosevelt."

No urging is required: Casals enjoys retelling the stories of his adventures on the road. "All right, the President's wife is the organizer of these musical evenings at the White House. Not the President, though he sat through the concert for nearly two hours–right there in front of the rest of the crowd, and I watched carefully to see if he'd nod off. Amazingly, he didn't. 'Course he did have a kind of far-off look while we played–I could see that because I didn't play until mid-point in the program, and it seemed to me here was a man who'd much rather be outdoors, much rather be on the back of a horse out in the wild western part of Americà."

Granados is fascinated. "You were watching the same man who led the charge against the Spanish army in Cuba."

Casals pauses. "Sure he's famous in Amèrica for that, but I didn't feel any resentment–our government in Madrid should never have gotten us into that stupid war!"

Granados lets it pass. "Did you meet Roosevelt personally?"

"Yes–very briefly after the concert. He told me the cello is his favorite instrument." Casals laughs.

"Well, he is a politician. What do you suppose he tells the pianists?"

Casals isn't in a mood to be needled. "Not so fast. There was an American piano player–the name Ward Stevens comes to mind–who said the President told him the same thing. That the *cello* was his favorite!"

"Mmm. Suppose he was forced to practice the piano as a boy. When he could have been outside climbing trees."

"You know, that might be it," Casals says. "Speaking of pianos, the one in the White House is a gold Steinway. I'm not joking, its case is covered in gold leaf so that the reflection is blinding! Gold eagles lunging out at you from the legs. You'll see when it's your turn at the White House."

"No, Pau, that will never happen. I'm not crossing the ocean! No matter. How did you arrange to play there? Which of your many admirers?"

Casals raises his hands without breaking stride. "I simply don't know how it happened. Furthermore, I was given top billing over the two Americans on the program. Truly a mystery."

"Perhaps a peace offering from the victors."

"More likely the President had nothing to do with the concert and Mrs. Roosevelt did it all. The most interesting thing was that certain informality of the Americans. The people invited that night were the same as the royals and aristocrats in Europe, but significantly different. I don't know, maybe it's the classlessness of America."

One story follows another. While on a South American tour with Harold Bauer, Casals learned that Camille Saint-Saens was on board a ship moored in the Montevideo harbor. He arranged to be taken there, snuck up behind Saint-Saens as he was composing–frightening him nearly to death–and ended up talking all night with this Frenchman who'd been a mentor in Paris for both Casals and Granados. And in Rio de Janeiro, Casals and Bauer "rescued" a young American pianist, Ernest Schelling, who'd been touring with Loie Fuller–notable for using diaphanous scarves and Chinese silk butterfly wings in her interpretive dances. When Fuller's group broke up, Schelling was stranded in Rio. Casals and Bauer organized a concert with Schelling, and all were paid in cash.

"We had a grand dinner afterward, and stayed up all night carousing. Slept until late morning and got up to discover we'd been robbed. All the watches, billfolds, cufflinks, even the studs from our shirts–all gone. But the thieves forgot to look in the suitcase where we stashed the cash."

"And this Schelling," asks Granados, "is he a fine pianist?"

"Yes, he's fine enough. Not a virtuoso–not like you. Incidentally, how did you find Paris?"

"It's been a while, but it's still magical. You know it better. There's a kind of zestful energy–it's missing in Barcelona. Lots of memories, Pau. Nostalgia for the time I was there with Viñes and Francisco Miralles."

"Ah nostalgia! Maybe Shakespeare had it wrong. Maybe that's the green-eyed monster."

"I mean, life was so much less complex then."

Casals' voice rises. "Despite your being so sick you couldn't attend the Conservatoire? No, I'll concede there's a place for remembering the past. Honoring it with our memories. But not blindly, not excessively. Where does that get you? Spaniards are paralyzed with longing for a lost empire. Catalans are paralyzed by memories of lost nationhood. Widowers are paralyzed by loss of their women. No, 'Ric, wishing to bring back the glories of yesteryear can be extremely debilitating. Do I wish I lived in the time of Bach–so I could play the 'unaccompanied suites' for him? Ah, the power to choose when we're born–that would be ideal, wouldn't it, but that's not reality. We don't get to choose when we come into this world. Wanting that only distracts us from living our lives now in the present, and projecting ourselves into the future. If we can't accept our present lives, we're condemned to stay on the edge of life, never quite experiencing it."

The first week in October, Granados climbs the stone staircase to his flat. He stops halfway to the landing to catch his breath. With fading euphoria after the premieres of his newest works, he's back to the long days of teaching and endless hours of introspection. Troubled by questions raised by Casals: where is he going as a composer? He resumes climbing up the stairs and opens the door.

Amparo is sitting on the high-backed chair in the entryway. From his first glance at her face and years of learning the signals her body transmits, he knows that something dreadful has occurred. At first, he's petrified by the thought something has happened to one of the children. On closer scrutiny, he sees that she's holding a stack of letters in her trembling hands. Instantly, he knows they're the ones from María Oliveró that he's kept hidden under the stack of sheet music on his piano.

"You have a lot of explaining to do," Amparo says. It's her harshest tone of voice. "She signs these letters 'María O'–who is this young strumpet? A student of course. I know which one, I've seen her. Tall and beautiful. What a fool I was to trust you with her!"

Tall and beautiful–María Ojeda. She has them mixed up. Could her confusion about the two María O's provide him with a defense? No, there is no defense. He dedicated the piece to María Oliveró, put her name on the music for all the world to see. And her letters have spoken. First to him, now to Amparo. Immobilized, he shakes his head.

"This is how you honor your vows?" Amparo cries. "Having a romance with a student! Then dedicating *Escenas Románticas* to *her*! How dare you dishonor your family! You may as well cut my heart out!"

"I have nothing to say. You've said it."

"But I'm not finished!" she cries. "These letters are now mine." Glowering at him, Amparo lowers her voice to a snarl: "I will keep them to ensure that you abide by my conditions. How else can I trust you?"

"I know it's too late to say I'm sorry. But I *am* truly sorry for the pain I've caused. What conditions?"

"Yes, it's too late, maestro!" She pauses, fighting off grief and panic. "These are the conditions: first, you'll tell this young María Oliveró you will not see her again! She must leave the academy. Second, the piece you dedicated to her will not be played again–never during your lifetime! And finally, you'll become the husband and father you're committed to by the vows you took!"

She has the letters and saw the dedication. Must swallow this. Played with fire. Now's time to pay.

He breathes deeply. "You have every right to be angry, Titín. All right, I won't see her again. And I'll devote myself to you and the children. But it's unfair to keep my work from being played. My work is my life."

"Perhaps you didn't understand me, Enrique. These conditions aren't negotiable! And I'll keep these letters, so if you do not live up to every one of the conditions, they will be shared with our children–and you'll leave this home forever! Do you understand?" She stops on the brink of a tirade. "Why should I ask you? It doesn't matter if you understand. Just live with these conditions, and you can stay here with your children! That's the last word!"

Chapter Six

Barcelona, Autumn 1905

Granados sits at a cluttered desk in the large space that serves as his office and practice room at the academy. He listens to the starts and stops in the rooms down the hall, voices of instructors, and the footsteps of arriving and departing students. Earlier, he marveled as the prodigious Paquita Madriguera, age five, finished her lesson with an early Mozart sonata. It's for students like her that he founded his academy.

This one plays so well—astonishing! Such intensity—large dark eyes. Immaculate oval face. World won't have to wait long for her!

He listens to the chatter of birds in the trees along the sidewalk on Carrer Girona, and to the faint but jarring sound of trains running up and down the new line on Carrer Aragó. It's one o'clock, the last lesson period before mid-day's break. The time when María Ojeda would come for her lesson, before Amparo found the love letters and poetry of María Oliveró. Before both Marías had to leave the academy.

From time to time, José Altet inquires: would the maestro like to fill this open time with another student? And after Granados says he needs the time "for other matters," his assistant backs off. Granados saves fragments from those lustful and romantic interludes, those "escenas románticas," preserving this hour like a souvenir, like an unbroken shell from a walk on the beach. Every week he has this hour, a time for sadness over the abrupt break with his young devotees; a time for needles of shame, incessantly probing and searing—because he couldn't pretend those interludes were harmless when he knew they were bartered for Amparo's trust in him; a time for solitude, because the idea of letting another one into his private life seems abhorrent; and a time for relief, because Ojeda's adventurous way of bringing them together was a mixed blessing, both thrilling and stifling. So sweet, then sweeter, then just a bit too sweet, like crème brulée with one dollop too many of sugar. Occasionally, as a master juggler he'd feel overwhelmed; he'd feign a migraine to take leave of her. But the recurring theme is of sadness. Of a darker hue, like a base paint first applied to a canvas, upon which other colors can be applied. Not simply from the loss of a ravishing source of energy and inspiration, but also from the loss of a piano work that he considers among his best. *Escenas Románticas*—music rising from his heart and soul, not to be played publicly until his death.

Not fair—having to give that up! To make peace. The letters—could have said they were Ojeda's—spared Oliveró. No, not after the dedication. Was fated—both had to go. But not the music!

Several times he's asked Amparo to relent—just on this condition—but the effort seems only to harden her. Last week he tried again.

She spun around, rising to the tips of her toes, and hissed her reply. "No, no, no! How many times do I have to say it? I will not negotiate on this. I don't have to. When will you understand?"

In his most conciliatory voice, Granados said, "I've apologized every way I know how, Titín. I've agreed to live a different life. I'm spending more time at home, more time with the children. But this piece—my art. My reason for being alive. It's not fair it can't be shared with others. Do you really think it's fair?"

She snapped, "And you think it was fair for you—married, father of six children—to carry on with one of your young students? You dare speak to me of fairness?"

"But to bury this work forever—" he implored.

"It's not forever, only as long as you're alive," she said. "It could be played at your funeral—but over my dead body!"

Amparo's answer is immutably "no." It's the answer he's obliged to give Tomás Bretón when he's invited to Madrid to play *Escenas* at the Conservatorio. And his response to Malats, who heard Granados play it last October and wants it for a recital at the Salle Pleyel in Paris. Until Amparo relents, the answer is "no." So Granados clings to fragments like the open lesson time before the midday break. And from some murky place where creativity and revenge are joined, he revives the

Lento con éxtasis movement of the banished work. With minor revisions he renames it *El poeta y el ruiseñor*–after all, he is a poet; and the sound of a nightingale is unrelated to the Marías. He transforms that movement into a new work that he plans to send to his publisher in Madrid.

Granados is not avoiding Carmen, but with her coming to the academy less frequently and evenings at the villa in Sant Gervasi not conducive to private conversation between them, he's been spared having to explain why both María Ojeda and María Oliveró suddenly vanished after years of lessons with him. It's been a taboo subject with the academy's staff except for Domènech Mas, who'd known Oliveró at the choir of Sant Pere and suggested she audition with Granados. Granados asks Mas to help her find another place to continue her studies.

It's uncharacteristic for Carmen, who surmises what's transpired, to forever avoid the subject. One day, she breezes into Granados' office during the open lesson time, closes the door, takes off her wide-brimmed hat with a cluster of purple feathers, hurries the customary abraçada, and sits in the chair next to the Pleyel. Her voice is cordial. "You're working on something new?"

He sets his pencil on the tray below his composition pad and pushes back from the keyboard. "Yes. *Gaziel*. It's the next one with Mestres. For next season. Shorter than *Follet*, less ambitious."

"Less romantic?" Her voice teases.

"Well, there are three characters. The poet, his beloved, and a Mephistopheles type of character."

"Who causes trouble for the lovers."

"Precisely. I'm just beginning. Not a very complicated story."

"You mean not very dramatic."

He plays a few measures from the opening part.

"Nice. I like it," Carmen says.

He looks up, sees her smile fade. "It's not what you came for."

She shakes her head. "You have dark lines under your eyes. Not sleeping?"

"It happens when I begin a new piece."

She smiles. "Or when your life has been turned upside down."

He pushes on. "You didn't come to watch me compose."

"No, I didn't. Salvador hasn't received anything from you for several weeks. Are there no bills to be paid?"

He points to the clutter on his desk. "Oh, I've gotten behind in my paper work. I'll find them right now–and you can take them to Salvador."

"No. I'd like you to gather them, review them, make a summary of what needs to be paid, and send them over to Salvador. And that's what he'd like. My dear, you don't want to annoy him. He's very forgiving–up to a point." There's annoyance in her voice.

"I'll take care of it this afternoon." He pauses. "That's all you came for? Truthfully?"

Carmen frowns. "That's not enough?"

He notices the tiny lines spreading out from the corners of her eyes. The rest of her face is smooth as polished marble. She's wearing a tan suit with pleated skirt, and a lace-trimmed blouse buttoned up to her neck. An elegant senyora of the Passeig de Gràcia. He gestures toward the hat. "Reminds me of *Pel & Ploma*."

"Thank you. It's flattering to be compared to those pretty young models."

"You're far, far prettier."

"And your eyes are aging. Truthfully? I came to get the business straightened out between you and Salvador." She pauses. "And I want to know how you're doing. How much you're suffering."

"Oh, that." He looks away.

"You brought it on yourself–you deserve to suffer. But it's more difficult than you imagined, isn't it? Like a doctor telling you to give up something you crave. Quite difficult. You still haven't recovered, have you? You still crave her."

He shakes his head.

"Well, if you don't want to talk about it–"

"No. I'll talk about it–with you."

"She made you feel desirable again," Carmen says. "More than a dalliance, wasn't it? I could see it coming, and I tried to warn you."

"Yes. I didn't listen. Willing to take the risk. And it was more complicated than I imagined. Much more."

"Did I miss something?" asks Carmen.

Yes. Everyone did. Except me. Why hide it?

"There were two Marías," he says.

Her eyes widen. "Two? Oh, my Lord! Two Marías! Who was the other one?"

"Amparo found her love letters. I dedicated the piece to her, put her name on it–she had to leave."

"You mean María Oliveró?"

He nods.

"You were involved with her too?"

He shakes his head. "Not the same way. Sweet and innocent–compared with the other."

"So they both inspired you?" Carmen asks.

"They were both important. In different ways. The third movement–*Lento con éxtasis*–that was from Ojeda."

"Lento, con éxtasis," Carmen echoes. "My, my. What passion! So intense you couldn't name it. Like Schumann. You were in deep. Way over your head."

"Never again."

Granados looks up from his chair alongside the Pleyel. His student, Ricard Vives, has interrupted Robert Schumann's *Fantasy in C major*, raising his hands from the keyboard to exclaim, "Oh, maestro, I don't know where I am!"

Granados shrugs. "And neither do I," he says. Vives, a promising nineteen-year-old who came to the academy to finish his studies, has just been saved from ignominy, yet gently chastised.

Acadèmia Granados continues to flourish. By elevating his best student, Frank Marshall, to deputy director in charge of piano studies, Granados is relieved of much of the daily administrative burden. Marshall also takes over teaching some of the advanced students, allowing Granados more time for composition. Growing closer to the director, the twenty-two-year-old Marshall thinks of himself as "the spiritual son of Granados." With Carmen's prodding and assistance, Granados is keeping the business affairs in order, and Salvador Andreu remains a contented patron. So, as he steps out of the potpourri of piano music in the building at the corner of Carrer Girona and Aragó, Granados' mood is of satisfaction: one of his dreams is being fulfilled.

This morning he's heading for the Café de l'Opera to meet with Lluís Graner, whose unusual financial success as a painter led to his becoming the impresario of a new theatrical program known as the Espectacles-Audiciones Graner–the third iteration in the struggle to establish a Catalan lyric theatre. Granados hopes that today's meeting with Graner will result in an agreement to present his Catalan lyric dramas, including "*Follet*," at the Teatre Principal.

Carrying a thin sheaf of notes, he walks three blocks down Carrer de Girona to Gran Via, then over to Passeig de Gràcia, and descends through

Plaça Catalunya. The street sounds today seem springlike, though the leaves of the deciduous trees are losing their bright green and the birds are gathering food for the winter. On the edge of the Plaça, he looks down Carrer de Fontanella and sees the edge of the building where his academy was first located. Where he and María Ojeda became lovers.

Push that out of mind. Live for today tomorrow. Graner wants Follet*—good news. Moving forward.*

At Café de l'Opera, Granados finds Lluís Graner sitting at a large table in the back room with five others. He's disappointed to see Morera there, and one of his students. Arriving at the table, he recognizes Antoni Niubó—the mattress-maker of Gràcia and Morera's close associate at the meetings four years ago, and Santiago Rusiñol, who always encouraged Morera's zeal for modernisme. The sixth man is a young writer, Josep Carner, who's collaborating with Morera on a new work.

"We're planning for the winter season," Graner says, leaning forward. "And I'm so excited about the talent we've brought together!" He motions to Morera and Rusiñol. "To open, we have *El comte Arnau* from Maestro Morera and our young friend Carner."

Morera interrupts to launch a windy description of the Catalan legend on which the work is based. Assuming the role of historian and genealogist, elaborating on the symbolic importance of the count, and making the point—several times over—that this work is ideal for the opening of the new season. Patriotically nuanced.

His monologue is cut off by Niubó, who suggests that Graner continue. "Later we'll have works by Pedrell, Lamote, and young Pahissa," says Graner, sounding pleased to be back in control. "And imagine having Adrià Gual, whose many talents know no limits, and magnificent sets designed by Salvador Alarma and Miquel Moragas. Just imagine, I ask you, all of these talents coming together! That's the vision for Espectacles Graner—a synthesis of all of the arts. Combining poetry and music. Drama and stage design. And very soon: cinema. Very soon! I'm certain we'll have no less than overwhelming success!"

Granados is impressed by Graner's enthusiasm, yet wary of impresarios, especially when they predict overwhelming success. He's uncomfortable that all of the men at the table are somehow connected to Morera. And Morera's surely more than Graner's music director; he'll also compose at least half of the works presented during the season. He's the musical core of this venture, with others dancing on the edges. "Well, it's a wonderful vision, Lluís," Granados says to Graner. "Truly grand. You've clearly devoted a great deal of thought to this, and I compliment you."

"Thank you, maestro."

"But surely you're not including me because of the fortune I have to invest in your espectacles."

Graner laughs, gracious as he preserves the levity. "Your observation is quite astute. I'd never think of asking you to be an investor, especially not when Niubó has sold so many mattresses this year and comes to us with sacks of gold. No, not your money, maestro. We want your Catalan lyric works. They'll give what our vision needs to succeed. Isn't that right, senyores?" His eyes circle the table.

The nuance of Graner's voice increases Granados' discomfort, but he plunges ahead and asks, "In other words, you'd be interested in having *Follet* presented next season?"

Graner frowns. "You say, *Follet*? No, we're thinking of your shorter work, *Picarol*."

Granados shakes his head. "*Picarol*? That premiered four years ago. Look, *Picarol* is a good short work, but *Follet* is a much better one, and would be very well received by audiences interested in lyric drama. And it's only been performed once–privately. So you could claim you're offering the world premiere."

"I'm sorry," says Graner. "We did consider it and decided it wasn't exactly what we're looking for."

Morera waves his hands. "Oh, Enric–for a work like *Follet*, you should try to get Bernis to present it at the Liceu. He's just agreed to do my *Emporium* as well as *Bruniselda*."

Granados is stunned. No luck trying to convince Bernis to include *Follet*. And Albéniz left town when Bernis turned down *Merlin*. Yet Morera's getting not one but two of his operas presented. Morera's still everywhere. Granados turns and speaks directly to Graner. "Let me understand this, Lluís. You want to present *Picarol* and you're not willing to present *Follet*. Am I correct?"

Graner tips his narrow head up and down slowly, and replies, "Correct. And we'd like to consider new works in future seasons."

Granados, thinking of *Gaziel*, says, "Well, I've just started a new collaboration with Mestres. You say you'd like to consider new works. I'd like something more than what you're offering."

"What do you have in mind?" Graner asks.

Granados has a subliminal image of his friend Albéniz plunging headlong into Morera's cuadrilla. "I will agree to your including *Picarol* in the upcoming season if you agree to present *Gaziel* in the following."

Graner leans back. "But we have no idea what this *Gaziel* will be. Whether it'll be right for our Espectacles. That's a lot to ask."

Granados looks around the table. Silence. "What? You have no idea what this work will be? Whether it will be right? Are you saying a work of mine would not be right? Are you *trying* to insult me?"

Now Graner's voice brims with contrition. "Of course not, maestro. Your work would be a marvelous addition. But you're asking us to accept a new work–without even seeing the score."

"That's correct. But you're not taking a risk on an unknown composer. What's more, I'm sure *Gaziel* will be very popular."

"You're asking us to make an exception for you."

Granados leans forward. "Not at all. Most of the new works you're planning for next season are even bigger risks than *Gaziel*. Are they not?"

Graner looks to Niubó and Rusiñol. They both nod their heads, however slightly. He turns toward Morera, who shrugs. "All right, then, I'll agreed to what you're asking." He stands and extends his hand. "Welcome to Espectacles Graner," he says.

Autumn, 1906

The train carrying Granados toward his visit with Albéniz in Tiana enters Badalona, once reliant on commercial fishing and agriculture, and now an industrial complex. The fishing fleet is home with its catch on this bright, windy morning in mid-September. The air above Badalona is hazy with particles from factories making petroleum products, fertilizer, perfumes, distilled spirits such as anís, printing inks, and from a number of small tanneries. As it emerges from the polluted zone, the train runs closer to the Mediterranean and the air is clear enough for Granados to see sunlight flitting across the long rolling waves.

The train passes the distillery where Anís del Mono–a more benign, sweeter Catalan version of absinthe–is produced. Granados is reminded of the poster contest sponsored by the company's owner, which was won by his friend Ramón Casas, whose series of colorful posters were judged best in a show at the Sala Parés gallery. Distribution of the posters, depicting sultry women in gaudy flowing gowns enjoying a glass of the liqueur, served to popularize both Anís del Mono and Ramón Casas.

Two nights ago, Granados saw Casas at an exhibit of sculpture by another friend, Ismael Smith, at Sala Parés. Casas, who entered his forties still unmarried, appeared with Júlia Peraire, an eighteen-year-old seller of lottery tickets, less than half his age, with whom he began a love affair earlier this year. Not unattractive, with wide-spaced eyes glowering under bushy dark eyebrows, she seemed to be trying to appear unabashed by Casas' worldly crowd.

Granados was cornered by Smith, the featured artist, who claims that his father, a boat-builder down the coast in Tarragona, was from a Catalan family named Esmíth, which anglicized the name. A claim as bizarre as Smith himself. Pixylike in face and stature, the twenty-year-old dresses fastidiously, looking very much the banker, scorning the uncouth style of most bohemians.

Smith leaned close to Granados to say, "I told you my father was a builder of boats. Yes, I'm sure I did. He dropped dead the night he heard of Spain's defeat by the Americans. When he was younger, he worked with Narcís Monturiol. Surely you know who he was."

"No, I'm sorry," Granados replied.

"You're jesting. Monturiol? Inventor of the submarine? The boat that goes under water. First in the world. You know what *it* was called?"

Granados shook his head. "No. Sorry, Ismael. Don't know much about submarines."

"It was called *El Ictineo*. The fish-boat. Point is, my father worked with Monturiol to build that fish-boat. When they demonstrated it–right here," he says, pointing in the general direction of the harbor, "the Queen Regent was so impressed she commanded the Navy to give Monturiol some money, but the admirals betrayed him and refused to help, so the second *Ictineo* had to be scrapped and his company went bankrupt and later there was an argument about who had invented the submarine, Monturiol or Isaac Peral, but finally Peral himself admitted that Monturiol's came first. And you know what?" asks Smith, not waiting for a response, "If we'd helped Monturiol, I mean our government, Spain would be the strongest naval power in the world and when it was time to fight the Americanos *we* would have won–not them. Think of that! The government in Madrid deserved to lose the war, with the cruel way they treated the Indians." Smith leaned forward and lowered his voice. "He's buried in Figueres, you know."

"Your father is?" Granados wipes the spray from Smith's monologue.

"No. Monturiol. And speaking of cruelty, can you imagine how horrible to imprison Oscar Wilde! For what? For having 'contrary sexual feelings'? That's a crime? Should be a private matter, not for the government to come to your home and tell you how to live. You agree?"

As the train leaves the pollution of Badalona behind, passing between vegetable farms and vineyards toward the next coastal village of Montgat, Granados agonizes over his failure to find a venue for *Follet*. Last spring, after it was rejected by Graner, the management of Teatre Bosch offered to include it in the spring season, and for several weeks announced rehearsals and the opening date. Granados was thrilled–at last a venue for *Follet*–but though time passed and rehearsals were further delayed and he became frustrated, he was assured that *Follet* was still in the theatre's plans for the season. Then without further notice, the management announced that two other works would be presented on the night set aside for the opening of *Follet*, and the season ended without it being performed.

"We decided it was not right for us this year," he was told by an assistant at the Teatre Bosch; the impresario was "unavailable."

"Not right for you?" cried Granados. "It was right for you when I called you two weeks ago, and now it's not right? You expect me to believe that? What's the real reason?"

The assistant–caught in the middle and obviously powerless–merely shrugged.

Were the fates conspiring? Was there a curse on "*Follet*"? Carmen tells him not to despair. But there must be a curse–people changing their minds and canceling. Could it be Morera? He quickly dismisses this. Morera's too busy with his own works–the lyric drama *Comte Arnau*, which ran for two hundred performances, and his two operas accepted by El Liceu. Morera's still popping up everywhere, but bitterness won't help. Barcelona is a small place, and Granados has to live with him.

Granados, Albéniz, and Malats are in Tiana's Café Giral, having lunch and trading stories. The village is celebrating its annual festival, and a concert has been arranged for this afternoon at the Sala Peralt to benefit the poor families of the community.

"The whole village will be there," says Albéniz, scraping out the last of a large bowl of lamb stew. He reaches across the table with both hands and rips off a large chunk of bread. "And people come over from Alella, where, as you know, they make the most exceptional wine." He raises a glass of it. "It's a great time in Tiana, so Rosina and I always make sure we're here. And this concert–to raise money for the poor–is a really fine idea, but not mine. It came from a young woman who lives here–a former student of yours, 'Ric. Clotilde Godó. Remember her?"

Dazzling smile. Left to marry. Found her a Pleyel in Paris.

"Of course," he replies. "A good student. And a ray of sunshine."

"She'll be at the concert," Albéniz says, "and I'm sure she'll be excited to see her mestre again. Now we'd better decide what we're going to play."

"Would you play a piece or two?" Malats asks Granados.

"How about the new one, 'Ric?" asks Albéniz.

Granados gives him a probing look. "What new one?"

Malats intervenes. "He already knows, 'Ric. I said you'd composed a piano suite that you weren't–well, not quite able to play. I hope I didn't say too much."

Granados shakes his head. "You–you're like a pair of vultures circling a carcass. The piece you're suggesting is the one I agreed *not to play*, the one Dona Titín asked me not to play again. If it's still a mystery, use your imagination."

"The love-struck student?" asks Albéniz, playfully.

Granados tries to shake it off. "Since you know the whole story, can we leave it now? It's been a long time."

Too long. The Marías. Voices fading. Fragrance fading like dew on morning grass. Like a sonata's last chord.

After they agree on the concert's program, Albéniz orders a round of brandy and clips the tip of a puro. "All right, let's have Malats tell us what's happening in Paris. God knows I've not been there much."

Malats laughs. He's a reluctant source of gossip. "You want to know what's going on with Casals? I don't really know. He has a new student, a Portuguese girl named Suggia. She played with Moreira De Sá in Porto, that's where Pau met her. She's much taller than Pau–'Ric, did you meet her?"

"No. Pau wasn't in town when I was there."

Malats continues. "She's obviously quite talented. Came to Casals at the request of her mother. No, let me finish. She's talented, but very temperamental. And headstrong? I'd use the word 'feroç'–ferocious. You know the type."

"So is she Pau's deixebla. Or more?" asks Albéniz.

Malats raises his hands. "She's around all the time and plays with Pau's tertulia. She appears to be living there."

"Good for her," says Granados. "And my news about Pau is that he and Alfred Cortot and Jacques Thibaud have formed a trio. Here's a brindis to them!" He raises his glass. "Well, back to this table–'Saco, what are you working on?"

Albéniz says he's all but given up trying to launch a career in music drama and opera. There's a singular lack of interest in works like *Merlin*, which he considers his best. "I have just so much time, and have to decide where to put it. So why not go back to where I began–the piano? Do something that will remain when I'm gone."

"Can you tell us more?" asks Granados.

Albéniz nods. "I think of it as 'new impressions' for the piano. It's name is *Iberia*. The first book is finished and most of the second. I let Blanche Selva play the first book last May–at Salle Pleyel. A very fine young pianist." He turns to Malats. "But my dream is to have you, 'Quinito, take the whole work on tour, to every important venue in Europe. You've been in my mind as I've worked on it. Remembering how magnificently you played *Triana* for me last week–perfectly, I'd have to say! So with your interpretation, perhaps my efforts to scribble all those notes haven't been in vain." He calls for the waiter to bring dessert.

"Thank you. I'm honored," replies Malats. He turns to Granados. "These 'new impressions,' as 'Saco describes them, are simply brilliant!" He pauses to cough. "But before I go out again on a long tour, I've got to regain my strength. I have this nagging cough that won't go away. I was completely exhausted from going to Amèrica last year. But I'm eager to take *Iberia* on tour."

"Oh, 'Quinito," says Albéniz, "it can wait for you to get rested. You know, some of it's still difficult for me to play. But that's not a problem, you play it so splendidly," Albéniz says.

Malats turns aside and endures an extended spell of coughing with his mouth covered by a handkerchief.

The concert in Tiana is a great success, with every seat filled and throngs standing in the back, spilling out the main entrance. Albéniz and Malats play several two-piano pieces of Saint-Saens and Albéniz' *Rapsodia española*. Granados is introduced to the audience and plays one of his *Danzas Españolas* and Allegro de Concierto. The audience insists that all the players return for encores.

After the concert, Granados sees his former student Clotilde Godó walking down the center aisle with a man whom he recognizes as her father. He hasn't seen her in more than three years, since she left the academy to be married, and it's the first time he's ever seen her outside of his practice room. At first glance, she appears to have lost much of the girlish vivacity that endeared her to the instructors and students of the academy. She seems almost solemn, as if bearing the burden of a great loss. Her dark brown hair is wrapped in a swirl at back of her head, and she's carrying the kind of voguish hat that Carmen might wear along Passeig Gràcia or on the boardwalk in Puigcerdà.

Granados and Juan Godó greet each other with a stiff male abraçada, and Clotilde follows with one of respectful modesty. "We're honored to have you here in Tiana," says Godó. "Maestro Albéniz told us other musicians would be coming, but having *you* here is indeed an unexpected blessing. Can you imagine whose idea it was to have this benefit?" He tilts his head toward his daughter.

"It was Maestro Albéniz's idea," she says to Granados in a hushed voice. "I just helped with details."

"In other words, you did all the hard work," says Granados.

Godó claps his hand on Granados' shoulder. "Why, I've entirely forgotten, maestro. I must thank you for finding the piano in Paris!"

"Well, you did thank me, with a most gracious letter."

"Oh, the letter. That's barely sufficient, considering how important the piano is to Clotilde."

"I was pleased to do it–for one of my favorite students," Granados says. Turning, he sees a hint of her contagious smile.

Godó asks, "Maestro, would you join us this evening at the casino? We have a fine time there, and we'd be honored if you–and Maestros Albéniz and Malats–would be our guests."

Tiana's casino serves as a social gathering place for families of the alta burguesia who've built summer homes here, and some of the established, long-term residents of the village. Because of this week's annual festival and the late afternoon concert, the casino is packed. There's a continuous popping of corks pried from bottles of cava. Albéniz wastes no time in lining up at the buffet table and gathering a mound of food. Juan Godó enjoys introducing his guests, the renowned musicians, to his neighbors. Granados is dizzy with the blur of unfamiliar faces and jumble of unknown names. He's accustomed to being among the familiar audiences of Barcelona, and being here reminds him of his tour around Spain last spring. Utterly fatigued after so many introductions, required to respond graciously to the chatter of praise. This is easier, though. Albéniz is the main attraction, well known in Tiana after years of spending his vacations here.

"Maestro Granados?" He turns: Clotilde. She leans closer. "I'd like to show you the Pleyel–the one you bought for me. It's just two blocks from here. Can you come? Please come," she adds, with a hint of urgency. "We can come right back."

He nods and follows her out the front door of the casino.

Eyes seem older. Darker, sadder—used to sparkle. Her laughter brightened those days! Three years ago? Like yesterday.

Clotilde leads him up the main road, which runs through Tiana and up past the Carthusian monastery of Montalegre, then climbs over the Littoral Range of coastal mountains. A moonless night, away from the glow and smoke of the city, stars seeming to hang just out of reach. The breeze has blown away the clouds, cooled the village after a hot afternoon sun, and is now rocking the upper limbs of the poplars along the road. They walk past homes set back from their protective walls, and when the road bends slightly to their left Clotilde places a hand on Granados' elbow to guide him toward a large iron gate and dark outline of the Godó villa, barely remembered from his brief visit three years ago.

The porter lets them into a spacious entry hall with curving stairs ascending to the second floor. Clotilde leads Granados down a wide hallway to the left, passing through two large darkened spaces to the room that he remembers from Juan Godó's gathering. Straight ahead in the corner is a Pleyel grand piano, gleaming in the light from the gas lamps, the one he selected in Paris after her father said Clotilde wanted a piano "like the one my maestro plays" to assuage her bitterness over having to leave the academy.

Granados sits down on the corner of the piano bench and lifts the keyboard cover. "Your father said—when Albéniz and I came to visit—that there needs to be a piano right here in this corner. He was very serious. And very prophetic."

She laughs. "It was so sweet of him to buy this for me. And so kind of you to go all the way to Paris to select it."

He laughs. "Well, I'd like to take credit for going there just to buy this for you, but truthfully I was at Salle Pleyel for a concert, so it wasn't as gallant as you might think." He laughs again. "I told your father there were other pianos—some made here, like the Cussó. I thought he'd be interested in something made here. 'Oh no,' he said, 'my daughter is very strong-willed and she wants a Pleyel!' "

"Thank you," she says, her face brightening. "No matter how ungallant it may seem."

"The Pleyel was Chopin's favorite. Made his Paris debut at Salle Pleyel and owned one like this, made in 1839. Chopin said when he was in good form and strong enough to find his individual sound only a Pleyel, and nothing else, would suffice. I'm pleased you can have one, Clotilde."

"Maestro, I have a favor to ask." Her voice is anxious. "You found this piano for me and it hardly seems fair I should ask one more thing of you. But I'd like to come back to the academy. To study with you again. I imagine it's more difficult than ever to be admitted, and I wasn't your most talented student. And

I imagine you're even busier and haven't time for older students. Or not for those who aren't perfectly excellent. Just the same, I wonder if there's a chance you'd take me back."

"Oh–I'm confused," he says. "There were reasons for your leaving–they had nothing to do with your talent. Your father said you were unhappy about it. I saw that you were unhappy, but I understood. Have you changed your mind?"

"Not my mind. That's not it. I never changed my mind. I *never* wanted to leave the academy!" Clotilde walks around the Pleyel and sits on the far corner of the piano bench. She lifts strands of her hair up over her ears and raises her face, tilted slightly. Her eyes seem to be searching for a sign that she may proceed.

He nods, and when she still hesitates he nods again–several times, to show he's ready to hear whatever she has to say, prompting her as he would a soprano poised for the first notes of an aria.

"It's a long story," she says, guardedly. "More than you have time for. To begin with, my marriage to Juan Marsans was arranged for me. I finally gave up trying to stop it. I consoled myself with all the tragic love stories, with all the men and women who couldn't be with the ones they loved. Why should I deserve any better? I thought of Tristan and Isolde. Francesca and Paolo. And from your own work, Follet and Nadala."

Granados is surprised. He never discussed that work with her. "You know the story of *Follet?*"

"Yes. I was at El Liceu that night. My point is, so many love stories ending tragically, and here I was with my marriage arranged, mostly by my mother, for reasons that had nothing to do with love. That was the first chapter–it goes on and on. Are you sure you want to hear more?"

"Yes, as I'm sure you'd like someone to hear it."

"Someone I can trust?" Her voice wavers.

"If you will," he says.

Clotilde breathes deeply. "All right. It started with an extravagant wedding and a reception quite suitable for a princess." She laughs. "I guess that's what I was: una princesa. You called me that once."

The wedding Clotilde tried to avoid was celebrated by all of the good families of the alta burguesia and by the royal family of Spain, including King Alfonso XIII. And blessed by the Pope. So with all of those royal and religious auguries, the marriage should have been off to a good start. Blessed by everyone except the bride, Clotilde says. And it didn't take long for her husband to confirm her worst fears about him. Not merely a man who believed he was entitled to nights with other women–why should she be surprised? She began to see that as a peculiar kind of blessing. So peaceful not having him around. And then he'd come home, most of the time bleary-eyed, and somehow their marriage would be reconsummated.

"I was pregnant just a few months after our marriage," she tells Granados. "Hoping that with a baby he might change, hoping for the best in him. But several days later, the baby died. A little boy. And my life with Juan went back to its old pattern. If anything, he was even harsher and ruder and stayed out more. The next year, I got pregnant again and once more the baby died soon after birth. A little girl.

"Of course," she says, "I blamed myself. Was nature trying to tell me something? I needed someone to comfort me, to convince me it wasn't my fault. I wished for too much! He made me feel worse, acting as if the deaths of our babies were completely my fault!"

Clotilde says her husband treated her as if she had leprosy. "He never hit me, but may as well have–he threatened to hurt me. His words were like knives. He spent even less time at home, and finally, after he'd been gone for three nights in a row, I told him I didn't want to see him again. And I moved back to my family's home. Now, maestro, thanks to the Holy Father, the marriage has been annulled. Thanks to God!"

"You've had a dreadful experience," Granados says, shaking his head.

Hearing his gentle voice, she's unable to hold back the tears. "It was dreadful! Thank you. I have no right to ask you to listen."

"No, you have every right. I chose to listen."

"If you knew, I hoped you'd understand why I want to come back to the academy. That's all I want, not sympathy. Can you see that music is my passion, my only passion, that it comes from deep within me? That I'm not a dilettante!"

Granados shakes his head. "Dilettante? I know you're not! You were a good student. You worked very hard. There's no need for you to be tested again."

"Oh, maestro, I would work even harder! I don't know how not to."

He raises his hand. "From what you've said, you're ready to come back. How could I turn you away? All right. The answer is yes. We'd have to find time in my schedule."

Excitement is returning to her voice. "Oh, you'll take me back? Maestro, that would be so wonderful!"

At this moment, he remembers there's an open time on his weekly calendar. The time he's been preserving ever since the departure of María Ojeda. "Could you come in at one o'clock on Wednesday?"

Clotilde slides down the piano bench and puts her hand on Granados' shoulder. "Thank you!"

The garden stretches downhill, lit only by a row of lamps along the terrace. The view extends from a ridge off to the left, on which most of the village is built, to a ridge on the right that descends to Montgat. The space in between provides a clear view of the sea reflecting the light of the moon.

"I've left out a few things," says Clotilde, who's leading Granados around the villa before their return to the casino. "When I moved back to my family's home, one thing was obvious: I was no longer their little girl. Being treated that way was more than I could bear. My father–he's been very kind, asked how I'd like to live in Tiana." This villa that has become her home belonged to an uncle who rarely used it, so her father bought it as a place for Clotilde and her Pleyel. At a safe distance from the social whirl in the city. "A place for healing," she says. "A private place. For a new life of my own."

"Your spirit is remarkable," Granados says. "Truly, it's a rare gift. I'm not the only one at the academy who'll be happy to see you return."

Clotilde stops and turns to face him. "Before we go back, would you permit me one more very small privilege? It's not often that an illustrious composer comes here. And next week I'll be your student once more and you'll be my maestro. So just this once, would you please indulge me? I've been reading the most inspiring poem, and I'd like to recite it. Would you permit me?"

"The poet?"

"I think you'll know him."

He nods, and watches her turn toward the sea as she begins to recite.

> I know there are those who ask:
> why do you not still sing
> those same wild songs of yesteryear?
> They do not see the work of just an hour,
> the work of a minute, and the wonders of a year.
> I, now an aging tree, used to moan so sweetly
> from the breezes when I began to grow.
> But the time has passed for youthful smiles:
> so let the hurricane move my heart to song!

"It's Rubén Darío," he says.

Paris, May 1909

Good news in the Barcelona daily papers. Music critics announce that the Paris Conservatoire has selected Granados for the jury of the prestigious Diémer piano competition. Winning the Diémer helped Joaquim Malats launch his successful European tour three years ago. Granados and several others, including the esteemed Gabriel Fauré, will award a first prize to the pianist whose performances over the past three years have been most distinguished. Granados is the first person from south of the Pyrenees to be asked to sit on this jury. He's flattered by the invitation, though amused by this burst of adulation from hometown critics who usually trivialize him with the sobriquet: "our Granados." He leaves Barcelona in eager anticipation of two concerts booked with Jacques Thibaud and a chance to see Casals again.

Paris. For Granados, the mesmerizing and raucous city of his young adulthood. The first place where he lived away from his family. A bewitching swirl around Francisco Miralles and his circle of absinthiate bohemians. Bistro glasses filled with cloudy white liquid, as bland to the eye as cow's milk. Once swallowed–not so bland. Hallucinations, as experienced by the Bulgarian countess who leapt through the glass window of Montmartre's Auberge de Clou, intent on flying back to her home in Sofia. Pungent vapors from hashish; Granados tried it just once and coughed for hours. And the lingering spectre of Carmen Miralles in the sketches and canvases of young women in her brother's studio.

Paris, where a bout of typhoid kept Granados from taking exams for the Conservatoire. Instead, he took private lessons from Charles Wilfred de Bériot, in a piano class with the twelve-year-old Maurice Ravel. From Bériot, who made students from Spain feel welcome, Granados learned the importance of refinement in tone production and pedal technique, and Beriot encouraged his innate talent for improvisation. Paris, where Granados composed nearly forty miniatures and sketches for the piano, and developed many of the themes that later emerged in *Danzas Españolas*. Where his efforts to interest music publishers in his work were unsuccessful.

The most gratifying aspect of going back to Paris is seeing Casals again and staying with him at his small home on Rue Villa Molitor, in the Auteuil district on the southwestern edge of the city. "I love it here!" says Casals at the front door. "After living out of a suitcase for years, what a joy to have a home in Paris!" He leads Granados out to the small garden of rhododendron and rose bushes, surrounded by a bamboo fence and a row of poplar trees. Not far from the center of Paris, it's quiet in the garden except for a faint rippling of poplar leaves and the rich sonority of Saint-Saens' Sonata in D being practiced in the music room by Casals' young student and lover, Guilhermina Suggia.

Casals has known Suggia for ten years, since he met the eleven-year-old prodigy on tour in Portugal. When she arrived in Paris seven years later, Casals agreed to give her lessons and was asked by her mother if he'd provide her a room in his house–under the watchful eye of Madame Coderq, Casal's starchy housekeeper. So enchanted was Casals by Suggia's angular beauty, talent, exuberance, and sudden bursts of laughter–though dismayed by her fascination with the bohemian life and her flirtatiousness–that he soon proposed marriage. Wary as a leopard on the edge of the hunter's camp, Suggia withheld her response, wisely seeing marriage as a threat to her own career.

Granados has only met Suggia once, when Casals brought her to Barcelona two months ago for a Lenten concert that included their joint performance of a concerto for two cellos, written for them by Emmanuel Moór, Casals' Hungarian composer friend and frequent guest at Villa Molitor. The Barcelona newspaper *La Actualidad* ran a front-page photo of Casals and Suggia with a headline that said the two cellists were husband and wife. Casals, who in public treats his most talented but exuberant and temperamental student with gallantry, was upset.

"She plays quite well," Casals concedes, "but she's wild–like those horses–the mustangs, the ones American cowboys have to break."

Granados is amused by the image of Casals astride the tall, fine-boned young woman who speaks Catalan, French, and Castilian with the gliding, sensuous diphthongs of her native Portugal. He's not the protector Suggia's mother had in mind.

"What ever happened to Ruiz?" asks Granados.

"You know he's now Picasso," Casals replies, not trying to conceal his disdain. "He came back to Paris with Sebastià Junyer–who paid his rent. He's living in Bateau Lavoir–a very disreputable place, crawling with bizarre artists. I hear he's with a gypsy guitarist named Fabián, also a painter. Whose interest in Picasso is–shall we say?–not normal. Last time I ran across him, he'd just discovered a new way to understand the meaning of love."

"Did he share it with you?" Granados asks.

"He would have," says Casals, "but I don't smoke opium."

Granados asks if there's news of the Nins.

Casals frowns. "I don't think it's going well. Just a chance encounter with Joaquín, in front of one of those seedy bars in Montmartre. He was very upset when I asked about Rosa. Jumped up and down and shouted some very nasty things about her." He changes the subject. "You haven't asked about Albéniz."

"I missed seeing him last summer in Tiana," Granados says. "I spent most of the summer in Puigcerdà."

"Of course, with Doctor Andreu. Well, I visited Albéniz in Cambo-les-Bains. Not long ago. And he's not well. Not at all well."

Granados shrugs. "Ah, you know our 'Saco, he's always had intestinal problems. Won't ever listen to the doctors. You know how stubborn he is."

Casals shakes his head. "No. This time, I'm afraid he's pushed it too far. And–" Casals stops, attentive to the music coming from inside. "You'll excuse me. She's playing the Saint-Saens all wrong. Too much vibrato. Plenty of talent, but she's so willful!" He stands up. "You'll excuse me, I've got to correct her before it becomes a bad habit."

Lunch is at Casals' favorite restaurant, Boeuf a la Mode, where Joaquim Malats joins them.

"How's the gypsy life?" asks Granados as the waiter brings menus.

Malats smiles, shakes his head. "Bookings are down. Can't win a Diémer Prize every year."

Casals interprets. "Means he's not doing a concert every night."

"Don't believe him!" Malats tells Granados. "The only pianist playing every night is Jan Paderewski."

"What about Paderewski, Pau?" asks Granados. "Does he still think you're 'predestiné'?"

Casals laughs. "Of course! But he hasn't heard me play for years. Am I not too old to be 'predestiné'?"

"I saw him once, on tour," says Malats. "He's living near Lausanne, and quite lavishly! I'm told he spends money faster than he makes it, so he has a grueling concert schedule. He looked about to drop dead any minute."

Tonight there's a gathering and informal recital at Villa Molitor. The first of the guests arrives shortly after eight: Jacques Thibaud, a tall French violinist, dressed in a three-piece suit with floppy silk tie. Granados performed Beethoven's Sonata for piano and violin with Thibaud at El Liceu last November, and they're booked to play again next week in Paris. "Jacques is the one who supposedly fell like a star from Heaven," says Casals. "Like all of us, he was playing in a café until he was suddenly 'discovered!' Now if he'd only practice more, he'd be the equal of Ysaye."

Thibaud throws up his hands. "Ah, but you wouldn't want me to embarrass Eugène. He likes being the best."

Afred Cortot, the pianist and conductor, is next to arrive. Granados met him five years ago at Salle Pleyel. Cortot is a full head taller than Casals, like Thibaud is similarly endowed with dark waves of hair, and dressed with the same elegant Parisian style. The conversation is in French, and Granados strives to regain the facility he acquired when living here. He's able to follow the discussion, since it centers on the music to be played tonight. Something by Schumann; they settle on *Adagio and Allegro* in A flat for piano and cello. And Mendelssohn's *Trio* in D minor.

Casals turns to greet a new arrival. Mieczyslaw Horszowski, not yet sixteen, a child prodigy whose remarkable maturity in his debut in Vienna six years ago propelled him into a tour of Europe, soon followed by a debut in the United States. Such a large name for such a tiny person.

Another guest arrives: violinist Fritz Kreisler, the Viennese who dazzled the Warsaw Conservatoire when he won first prize and graduated at age twelve, followed by a tour of the United States at fourteen. Kreisler all but disappeared for nearly a decade before reviving his career in New York, London, and Berlin while still in his early twenties. Granados was introduced to him three years ago by Casals, who shared a booking agent with Kreisler. The same agent who'd tried to persuade Casals to wear a hairpiece–to appear more the virtuoso–and having failed in this, decided to spread a rumor that Casals was going bald because he'd given so many locks of his hair to rabid female admirers.

Merciless in criticizing those who are unwilling to devote time to practice, Casals once confided to Granados, "Fritz Kreisler is a genius, and the most charming man in the world, but when it comes to practice, he's worse than Sarasate! Worse than you!"

Granados watches Casals standing in the center of his guests. Dressed tastefully, but not with the flamboyance of Thibaud, Cortot, and Kreisler. Far shorter than the others, except for Horszowski, and the only one without a full shock of dark hair. Yet Casals stands out–powerful, authoritative, compelling. His intensity seems like the engine of a new motor car.

Casals drinks from the odd-shaped glass Catalan carafe, and passes it around. The regulars in Casals' tertulia have learned how to raise it above their heads, tilting it just enough to direct a stream of wine into their mouths, without spilling on their starched white shirts. "The wine's from Priorat," says Casals with obvious pleasure, "near where I was born."

"Why, it's almost black!" says Thibaud, holding the carafe up to the light. "But so rich–bursting with fruit!"

"The grape is Garnacha. It's a secret of the monks at Scala Dei." Casals begins an explanation of how he's able to bring this wine to Paris, then stops himself. "Well, you didn't come for wine chatter. To the music!"

They begin the first part of the Schumann, the adagio, with Casals' cello carrying the slow melodic line and Cortot, on the upright piano, completing the phrase with a high delicate counterpoint. In the year of its composition, 1849, Schumann completed nearly forty separate works, despite considerable disruption for him and his family from the fierce war being waged around their home in Dresden. There's no explanation for Schumann's being able to keep that pace with a war going on around him.

Poor Schumann–tragic end. What happened to his mind? Syphilis came back to finish him. Poor Schumann! Ended in asylum. Died alone.

As they finish, Horszowski, leans over and whispers, "I'd like to play that someday–with Maitre Casals."

Granados nods. If this young man is a good as Pau claims, he'll surely be playing with him someday.

Next they play the andante from Mendelssohn's *Trio*, beginning with the piano and soon joined by the cello and violin. Peaceful and sweet and slightly lilting, coming to a partial resolution, then the piano moving forward, still "tranquilo"–gently, then all three coming together with slightly more intensity, followed by a series of passages where first one then another instrument takes the melodic line, and finishing with three exquisite bars of piano solo. Granados is always moved by this piece.

The andante–so sad, so sweet! Mendelssohn also died young–same age as Mozart. What a loss!

The next afternoon, Casals and Granados walk along the edge of the Bois de Boulogne, a short distance from Rue Villa Molitor. They stroll in the Parc de Bagatelle, circling the petite chateau and its Anglo-Chinese garden regarded by Parisians as yet another folly of Marie Antoinette. "But look over there," says Casals. "Not so foolish. They've just put in an enormous rose garden. I'm told there'll be nearly ten thousand roses, more than one thousand varieties!"

"More trivia for your brain," says Granados. "But you're right, they are stupendous."

"Isn't this gorgeous? And just wait 'til June when they're all in blossom."

They exchange smiles and continue their walk down a winding footpath cut into the greenery, emerging onto a meadow surrounded by ancient oaks.

Casals stops. "Tell me, what are you working on?"

"Well, I have another short lyric work with Mestres. Perhaps another after that." He tells Casals about the symphonic poem based on Dante's *La Divina Comedia*.

Casals nods. "What's happened to the idea of a piano suite based on Goya?"

"I haven't given that up, Pau, but it's so loose and fragmented in my mind. Can't seem to find the time and place to work on it. So many interruptions. Someday I'll get back to it."

"And your long piano piece? I still haven't heard it."

"You mean, Allegro de Concierto."

"No. I mean the other one. That Crickboom asked you to play at Salle Pleyel."

Granados knows that Casals will be relentless in pursuing the answer. "You mean *Escenas Románticas*."

"Yes. That's one."

"Titín and I had a terrible fight, Pau, and I agreed not to play it. Ever." He pauses. "It was dedicated to one of my students."

"And you had a little dalliance?"

"No. More serious." Too confusing to explain there were two Marías.

"And Amparo found out."

"Yes."

Casals is silent. After a while, he says, "Can I give you another piece of advice?"

Granados nods.

"If you're going to have romance, have it in Madrid or here. Look up that Frenchwoman. Silvia. But not at home."

Casals has touched a hidden nerve. Granados once dedicated a piano solo–*A la Cubana* to Silvia de Sa Valle, a vivacious Parisian friend of Francisco Miralles, who'd been among the few to encourage Granados to work on his compositions. Years later she came to visit Francisco in Barcelona just as Granados was finishing *A la Cubana*, so it seemed a perfect time to thank her. He hadn't thought about Silvia for a decade. "No! No more romances for me, Pau. Not anywhere."

"Hear me, brother. You're a romantic and you *will* succumb again. I render no judgment. I've never led a saintly life, but even without a wife I resist temptations back in Barcelona. That's my home, my family's there, and everyone knows everyone. The attitude is more–shall we say?–provincial. Here it's different."

"Thank you for the advice," Granados replies.

"If you wish, I'll find you a nice woman for your visits to Paris. No complications."

"No thanks."

This evening there's another gathering at Casals' place. The English pianist Harold Bauer arrives with Isadora Duncan, an American dancer. Granados watches her float through the entryway like a modern Cleopatra on the tips of her toes. She's wrapped in layers of transparent gowns, and barefoot. Casals says he isn't impressed with the "originality" of her dancing, but seems intrigued by her ability to mesmerize Bauer, Auguste Rodin, and the English stage designer, Gordon Craig–who follow her like a pack of dogs, along with others of lesser celebrity.

"And who are you?" she asks Granados.

He doesn't find her beautiful except for the marvelous cheekbones. But her utter confidence and assumption of allure gives her radiance. Her eyes dance in, make contact, and dart away. Granados says he's a pianist from Barcelona.

"Ah, Barcelona. What a lovely place! So nice of you to visit this little village on the Seine. Do you speak English?"

He shakes his head. "A little–not much."

"Parles-toi francais?"

"Oui."

"Then you and I will get to know each other in French. What could be better? It's the language of love, is it not?"

"The French would like us to believe that, yes."

"Touché, Monsieur Granados. You remind me of my friend Blériot–he's the airman who plans to fly his little aeroplane over the channel all the way to Dover. I hope he makes it. I love the airmen. Not just up in the air, you understand. Do you know the airmen?"

"I'm afraid not."

"Do you know the Steins?"

"I'm afraid not." He hopes this parlor game will end.

"They were my neighbors in California. People with money. Gertrude and Leo. They've come here to look for art. Matisse and Braque and the Spaniard–Picasso. You must know the Spaniard."

Granados smiles, recalling the street kid with fierce eyes who used to come to Quatre Gats. He'd seen Picasso's *La Celestina*, the walleyed procuress of Barri Xines, and some of the others with the blue caste, and he much preferred the earlier sketches of characters in the bars and cabarets of Barcelona. "I used to know him, slightly."

"Oh–what a faux pas! Here I assumed everyone in Spain knows everyone else. How uncouth! My apologies. Well, Picasso's a fascinating man," says Duncan. "Smoldering eyes. Though I haven't had the pleasure." She laughs. "So different from Pau, who doesn't approve of my dancing. Why should *he* care if I wear nothing underneath?"

"They're very different," Granados says, ignoring the tease. "Pau is devoted to his cello and Picasso is devoted to Picasso."

"Picasso wouldn't care if I walked down the street nude. As for Pau, you have to admire anyone who finds such joy in the Bach unaccompanied cello suites. I sleep through them. I'm more like Picasso–living on the edge of disaster. I need more than Bach. Now, Monsieur le Pianiste, have *you* seen me dance?"

"I haven't had the pleasure. Where do you dance?"

"Why, everywhere! The Folies Bergere, the best grand salons of Paris, the Bayreuth Festival, my own school of dance. Anywhere with a flat surface."

"At the top of the Tour Eiffel?" he asks.

Her laugh is like breaking glass. "Why no, I've never been booked there. Have you been to the top?"

"I watched them build it."

"Oooh, you must be simply ancient!"

"It was twenty years ago."

She closes her eyes and rolls her head. "I was just ten years old–couldn't possibly remember. Before I forget, you must come to my next performance. Oh dear, it's not 'til July. Don't suppose you'll stay that long. You must see me dance." She wraps an arm around him, her breast pressed against his elbow. "If you come to my flat, I'll dance for you. Would you like that?"

He nods, amused by her aggressiveness.

"Call me. You simply can't go back to Spain without seeing me dance. Promise?"

"Of course."

"I must get back to Harold. He likes me to touch him," she adds, looking down, "when nobody's watching. He's married, you know." She places a hand behind Granados' neck and rises on her toes to kiss the corner of his mouth. "Au revoir, and I trust it will be soon."

At lunch the next day, Casals discusses the menu with the waiter. "He says the foie gras is exceptional," Casals reports. "And the salmon–provençale, with shavings of fennel. And, of course, the French cava."

The waiter asks. "Shall I bring the champagne? The Dom?"

"Yes," says Casals, winking over at Granados. "You may bring the cava at once." When the waiter has gone, Casals is delighted to have annoyed the waiter. "They can't stand my saying that champagne and cava are the same. It's like a declaration of war. And it's so amusing, because it's made in France and Catalunya exactly the same way. Well, I don't have to tell you about the French."

Casals asks about Granados' visit to the home of the Nins this morning. Granados leans forward. "Joaquín was out of town, but I saw Rosa and the children. The girl is a toddler, and there's a baby boy. Rosa seemed very strong–at first."

Casals asks, "At first?"

"She was proper, cordial. Obviously glad to see someone from Barcelona. As if Barcelona has become her home. Her daughter, Anais, seems very frail. She had typhoid and looks as if she almost died of it. So thin. Patches of hair have fallen out. The little boy, he couldn't be healthier. Fat cheeks, big blue eyes, blonde. Perfectly Dutch. But there's something wrong with between Rosa and Joaquín."

Casals shakes his head. "Wrong? How would you know?"

"I'm not sure–I think he's treating her badly. I saw bruises on Rosa's neck and arms. She was trying to hide it."

"What a swine!" exclaims Casals. "Quin canalla!"

Granados and Casals are walking again on the edge of the Bois de Boulogne. "I haven't heard any complaints about Morera," says Casals.

"I have none."

"What? You're saying Morera has mellowed?"

"Not at all. He's gone. Went bankrupt, and decided to go back to Argentina where he grew up. Said he'd make his fortune there and return."

"That's a surprise!" says Casals. "You said he was doing well. He was 'everywhere.'"

"He was. *Comte Arnau* was extremely popular. Why not? It's the myth of ancient Catalunya–performed more than two hundred times. He also had most of the works in the next two seasons with Graner. And was being paid as music director. I can't explain his going bankrupt. Rusiñol says it was some farm he tried to establish, near Sitges. 'Tiago says that's what finished him."

"A farm? Que curiós!"

"Can you imagine Morera milking cows?" Granados asks.

They enjoy the image. "No," Casals replies, "because with Morera, the milk would certainly be sour."

"Exactly. It's his attitude. I don't think he'll do any better in Argentina."

"Now tell me about your work," Casals says. "You were about to premiere *La Divina Commedia*."

"Yes–*Dante*. I did finish the first two parts, and had a private performance at the new Palau. I'm not trying to follow the *Commedia* detail by detail, just giving my impression of the myth. Love as the means of spiritual perfection. The ill-starred love of Francesca and Paolo. For the next part, the death of Beatrice–what a tragedy for Dante!–I'm taking the colors from Dante Gabriel Rosetti's painting: violet and carmine and green, trying to paint them with the orchestra."

Granados isn't surprised to learn there's another gathering tonight. "Not just musicians," says Casals as they wait in the garden for the first arrival. "Zuloaga's bringing a dancer, who claims to be Spanish–Tórtola València. Seems to have a herd of men in pursuit. Not just Zuloaga–also Rodin, and last year it was Eugeni d'Ors."

"Our d'Ors? From Quatre Gats?"

"The very same–he was here for a couple of years. Then this past winter she seduced the young Duke of Leicester. I've heard that Rubén Darío also succumbed. And so many rumors–a prince who committed suicide after she rejected him."

"She's been quite busy!"

"I saw her at the *Folies* last year. She's simply–simply stunning! But she must be busier avoiding the suitors than bedding them down."

"I don't blame her. If she marries, the husband will kill her career."

Casals seems irritated. "That's not always true."

"Pau, I'm just trying to be realistic. Most talented women don't quit because they're tired of pursuing their art. They quit because their men won't let them continue. Take María Barrientos. Sang at El Liceu and La Scala and Covent Garden–on her way 'til she met the Argentine, and then? Zip–off she went! Retired! You see my point?"

"I suppose that bothers you," Casals says. "Would you have it different?"

"Yes. Wouldn't you?"

"I told Suggia she wouldn't have to give up her career if she married me. She didn't trust me."

"Would you?" Granados asks.

Casals is obviously suppressing a smile.

At the gathering, Granados sits with three comely sisters named Chaigneau: Therese–a pianist, Marie–a mezzo, and the third, whose name he's forgotten–a violinist. They're attractive and vivacious and raptly devoted to Casals. With them is Colonel Georges Picquart, whose angular and inexpressive face, flat voice, and formal conversational style belie his fame as a hero of the notorious "Dreyfus Affair." As Casals and Thibaud tune their instruments, Cortot flips through the music for Schubert's *Trio* in B flat.

Granados watches Tórtola València, the young dancer who arrived with Zuloaga, as she slips a long cigarette holder into her crimson lips, draws on it, and blows a stream of smoke rings. She's barefoot, dressed in a diaphanous garment that rises from her bare calves and clings to the uncorseted curves of her body. He gets up and crosses the room, gives Zuloaga an abrazo, and kisses the perfumed hand of the dancer. She offers a quick greeting, then turns and leaves them as the iconic sculptor Aguste Rodin arrives.

Zuloaga, a painter resembling a shorter version of Granados with a black beret, motions for Granados to step out into the garden. "What have you heard about Albéniz?" he asks, his dark Basque eyes probing.

Granados hesitates. "Only that he's not feeling well. But he hasn't been feeling well for several years. Have you seen him recently?"

"Two months ago. He was here to see doctors. Then he took the family down to Cambó-les-Bains. Seemed much weaker, I'm afraid." Zuloaga's concern is evident.

"Still smoking puros?"

Zuloaga shrugs. "No. He was giving away his best ones."

Giving away his best puros—a bad sign. 'Saco seemed much weaker? Need to see for myself that he's all right.

"Then I'm going to stop there on my way home," Granados says.

"If you do go," Zuloaga replies, "give him a big abrazo for me."

"I was born in Sevilla," explains Tórtola València. "My parents took me to England when I was three, and I went to British and French schools. So I speak many languages—all with a foreign accent."

Up close, Granados notices the thick blackened eyebrows, theatrical accents around her eyes, and the short dark curls of hair parted down the middle. Tórtola is never quite still: a twinkling spray of reflected light from her pearl-and-diamond earrings; below her strong chin, a triple string of pearls undulating across a band of flesh that extends from shoulder to shoulder above the filmy folds of her gown. "Your parents are from Catalunya?" he asks.

She smiles. "You heard that from Pau. My parents abandoned me and went to Mexico and died. Which version of my origins do you want to hear? Pau wants me to be Catalan. Others to believe I'm descended from Spanish royalty or that I'm a gypsy, from Romania. Or Algerian—una mora. I encourage them all to believe whatever they want."

"It makes no difference to me. You're a dancer. I'm a pianist."

"And a composer. I've heard your music. It's fine, fine music. Would you compose a dance for me?" She laughs at his frown. "No, not tonight—some other time. Some time before my bones begin to stiffen." She extends one leg forward, between his, and raises her hands to form the shape of a butterfly.

"Why not? I could improvise and you could dance," Granados says playfully. "But I would need a piano."

Her laugh is loud and salacious. "Would a Bechstein be satisfactory?"

"A Bechstein?"

"A concert grand. A gift from the most adorable man, at the Wintergarten last year. He was a baron or a count—one of those, doesn't matter. He became quite attached, and sent me the Bechstein as a token of his devotion. And, maestro, you've just lost your excuse not to come."

She stands behind him as he plays arpeggios on the Bechstein. "Do you like my pearls?" she asks, handing him a glass of champagne.

He looks back over his shoulder and sees them glistening in the candlelight. She bends at the waist and now the pearls are clicking under his nose. "Yes, they're very nice. Another token of someone's devotion?"

She laughs softly. "No. I bought these for myself. They were supposed to be genuine, but the price was so low I took them for costume jewelry. They looked dead–no life, no radiance. To my utter surprise, after a few days I noticed the pearls were regaining their luster! But how? I talked to jewelers, I went to the library, I asked everyone wearing pearls for their opinions. And I was astonished to learn that some people have the kind of skin that deadens the luster of pearls, and others have skin that brings dead pearls back to life. The magic is in the secretions."

"And you have the magic."

"Oh, you're too smart! And later, when the Parisian doyennes heard about this, they asked me to wear their pearls for a few days. They even pay me to revive them."

Still leaning over, she separates the top folds of her shawl. "Look," she says, grazing the exposed flesh with the middle fingers of each hand. She waves the finger tips under his nose. "My magic secretions. Smell the fragrance. Magic so strong you can smell it and taste it."

"Then are those your pearls?"

She places her bare arm along his back. "Mmm. Good question. Enjoy the mystery?"

"You're a woman of mysteries. Who you are, and where you came from. And which man can claim your love?"

She shakes her head. "Who I am? No mystery–I'm a dancer, from everywhere. Who claims my love? No man. It belongs to my dance. Now, would you like to watch me?"

He takes off his jacket and adjusts the piano stool. At the outset, he plays a series of his compositions...*Danza Gallega*, which he dedicated to Casals, *Danza de la Rosa*, and *Jácara*...he doesn't finish any of them and shifts into pure improvisation, lost in his music.

Tórtola drifts into his consciousness as she glides barefoot into view at the far end of the Beckstein. She's flung the shawl and wears a sleeveless, low-cut blouse studded with tiny red silk roses, which descends from her broad shoulders over her breasts, then narrows sharply at her waist before flaring out over the top of a pleated flamenco skirt. She stretches, moving slowly, waiting for the right moment to join with the music rising from the Bechstein. Even in slow motion an earthy intensity surges from her thighs. The filmy skirt swirls around her bare knees. Her dark oval eyes are fastened onto his even as her face moves in every direction, following the quick patterns of her arms and hands. Twisting backward and from side to side as her feet remain planted, her contortions are dramatic, as if she's testing the limits of her litheness. Tórtola is dark and savage, with ferocity barely under control, not light and airy. Guided by impulses, not limited by classical training, she is agile and predatory like a large panther, then menacing like a coiled serpent. Her arms rise and twist, suddenly floating like palm fronds in a sea breeze. Candlelight reflects from the silver tiara holding the swirl of hair atop her head, from the rings on every finger and the bracelets clicking together on her forearms.

From memory, he plays the opening measures of *Triana* from Albéniz' masterpiece, *Iberia*. Triana–the gypsy quarter of Sevilla, which Tórtola claims as her birthplace. But it's not for Tórtola that Granados chooses *Triana*. It doesn't matter to him how she responds, or if she does. This *Triana* is for Albéniz.

Tórtola pulls the pins, removes the tiara, and shakes her hair free. She poses with one arm raised high and the other folded under her breasts. She is motionless as the music–unfamiliar to her–rolls out of the soundboard.

As he plays through the first theme, Granados is transported back to Barcelona, when Malats premiered this piece and moved him to freely flowing tears, and later when Malats played it for Albéniz and his family at the Teatre Principal. Now he prays for his friend's health, while his left hand continues the syncopation and his right hand introduces the second principal theme of the "sevillanas." The sinuous dancer, with sweat dripping off her arms and shoulders from the late spring Parisian heat and humidity, twists her fingers overhead and pumps her knees, and her throaty cries evoke gypsy gatherings around fire pits on the banks of Sevilla's languorous Rio Guadalquivir.

Tórtola València–the voluptuous, untamed fantasy of so many princes, poets, and painters–who momentarily provoked Granados to a precipice where he longed to reach out to touch her, smell her, and taste her, now suddenly has lost him. His mind is already en route to Cambó to see Albéniz.

On Granados' last day in Paris, after a farewell luncheon for the Diemer jury and his final concert with Thibaud, Gabriel Fauré hands him a large envelope to take to Albéniz. "This should cheer him," explains Fauré. "It's a letter from Claude Debussy, informing him that with our recommendation–Claude, Paul Dukas, Vincent d'Indy, and I–the French government has awarded him the Croix de la Légion d'Honneur."

"That's splendid news!"

"We thought we should do something. He's been so generous, helped so many others."

"He's the most generous man I know," replies Granados. "And one of the dearest. I'm sure this will bring him a speedy recovery."

Cambó-les-Bains

Granados gets off the afternoon train from Paris and spends a mostly restless night at a noisy hotel in the resort town of Bayonne. The next morning, after sending telegrams to the Barcelona dailies about the letter from Debussy about Albéniz' decoration by the French government, he catches a local train that runs parallel to the river Nive descending to the Atlantic coast.

Cambó-les-Bains is a market town in the foothills of the westernmost stretch of the Pyrenees. As the French name indicates, it's noted for the recuperative powers of the waters from hot springs. Despite being well inside the French border, the Cambó area is unmistakably Basque. Audibly so by conversation in the streets, and by the names of the nearby peaks of Artzamendi and Atchuléguy, and the villages of Jatxou, Urcuray, and Itxassou. An old Basque adage–"Kambo leku ederra da," extolling the beauty of the area–gave the town its name.

Three kilometers upriver from Cambó is the Pas de Roland, where the legendary Breton warrior is said to have crossed over the mountains with the imperial army of Charlemagne late in the 8th century. On their way, the invaders looted and plundered the countryside belonging to the Basques–the only people on the Iberian peninsula who'd been able to remain free from Muslim domination. As the Franks returned from Zaragoza, which had been promised to Charlemagne by the Moorish governor, the Basques attacked them, seeking revenge. Roland was among those killed. With passage of time, his role in the Franks' invasion of Iberia became ennobled in the legendary *Song of Roland*, and the campaign of plunder was idealized as a holy war against the Saracens, with no mention of the looting and plunder. That version proved more satisfying to French patriots than to the Basques, who still remember such painful details.

Albéniz' original reason for coming to Cambó was to take its waters. For years, the doctors have recommended this for his digestive problems, along with curbing his voracious appetite. The therapeutic benefits of these waters are believed, at least locally, to have been enjoyed by the Roman legions of Julius Caesar, but its current popularity comes from the 18th century visit of Marie-Ann de Neubourg, Dowager Queen of Spain, who came to Cambó upon her doctor's advice and reportedly felt better after the visit. The word spread.

Albéniz' father Ángel was born in the Basque city of Vitoria in Alava province, less than two hundred kilometers' drive westward from Cambó, and though Ángel lived most of his adult life far from his birthplace, he still identified with his Basque origins. Albéniz, other than while giving concerts in the Basque Country, and in writing the "zortzico" for piano that he dedicated to his Basque friend Zuloaga, considers himself a son of Catalunya. His choice of Cambó to recover from his illness is based more on the reputation of its waters than proximity to his father's homeland.

The walkway up to the Chateau Saint-Martin, where the Albéniz family has taken a large suite, winds through a garden of hydrangea shrubs that will blossom in mid-summer with large balls of pink and blue. Rosina Albéniz greets Granados at the door. After a warm abrazo, she takes his fedora and waves him toward a cluster of chairs in the living room. "I wanted to make sure you'd come before letting him know," she says softly, motioning toward a closed door across the room. "Just to be sure."

"But Rosina, I sent a telegram. I said I'd come."

She walks over to where Granados is sitting, and replies in a hushed voice. "Yes, but one of his oldest friends–they were students together–said he'd come and Isaac was very excited, and then this old friend did not come. Isaac was depressed for days. So I was just making sure."

Granados notices the deep lines under her eyes and the downturned corners of her wide mouth. After a quarter century of living bravely with her delightful and exasperating husband, Rosina seems finally to be deflated.

Which old friend? Fernández Arbós?

"How are you and the girls?" he asks.

"We're managing."

"And Alfonso?" he asks, referring to their son.

She looks away. "We haven't seen much of him. He's in London." The closed door swings open and Albéniz' nineteen-year-old daughter Laura comes into the living room. She closes the door softly and gives Granados a lingering abrazo.

Rosina asks her, "Does he know he has a visitor?"

Laura shakes her head.

"Would you let your father know?"

Granados is perplexed. He expected to see Albéniz come barreling through the door with his face beaming.

Laura explains, "He's in bed, maestro."

"In bed? I had no idea."

"We moved the piano into the large bedroom," explains Rosina. "He loves it when visitors play for him. And there are rose bushes on the patio outside his room–with this late spring they're still not in bloom. And of course this upsets him quite a bit."

Laura, a painter who's been serving as her father's secretary in recent years, walks over to the desk and picks up an envelope. "This just came from Money-Coutts. Says he can't come. Says his wife Nellie has business in London and *she* can't travel alone. So *he* can't come!"

Rosina shakes her head, takes the envelope, and removes the letter. "Damn him! He's in Paris–at the Ritz! So close and he can't come? When it would mean so much." She catches herself and lowers her voice. "Victor said no bad news, Laura, so you must tell your father that Money-Coutts has been delayed, that he'll be coming soon. No bad news."

Granados wonders why they're trying so hard to protect him. He's the toro–doesn't need any protection. And won't he find out they've been lying? And be furious? "Who is Victor?" he asks.

Laura explains it's her cousin, Victor Ruiz Albéniz, son of Albéniz' sister Clementina. "He's a physician in Madrid, and he's been our medical director. Though there's a local doctor who comes up every day from Bayonne." She rolls her head toward the closed door. "And Victor's also our music director, since he's quite a good violinist. The other day he played a piece from the *Siegfried Idyll* that my father enjoyed enormously. He'll be here today."

A short, balding man with a stethoscope hanging from his neck comes out from the bedroom and Laura goes in. Looking over the rimless spectacles perched on the tip of his nose, he starts to give Rosina a report on Albéniz' condition. Seeing Granados, he stops.

"It's fine, Doctor Rostéguy. This is Maestro Granados. He's part of our family," says Rosina.

Doctor Rostéguy tells Rosina that Albéniz' condition has stabilized. His urine looks better. Has he complained of nausea? No? How about vomiting? The doctor turns to Granados. "He's suffering from uremia. It's a toxic condition that results from his kidneys not being able to process the waste in his blood." Now he turns back to Rosina. "I'd prefer not to increase the morphine. The side effects can be constipation and urine retention, which is precisely what we're trying to avoid."

"I don't like the morphine either," says Rosina. "But he's been asking for more."

"Well, his respiration seems stable. Has he had problems breathing?"

Rosina shakes her head. "If so, he's not going to tell me."

"All right. You say Doctor Ruiz is coming this afternoon. I'll leave a note for him, and he can make the decision about the morphine." The doctor picks up his hat and black bag and leaves.

His urine looks better. Morphine? Problem breathing?

Laura appears at the door to the bedroom and motions for Granados to follow. He enters and sees his friend of nearly three decades, his entire adult life. Albéniz–always larger than life itself, always the energy source, whose generosity toward friends in need and confidence in their success is always inspirational–now lies flat on his back in bedclothes. Even with a thick mass of hair and beard still untinged by gray, he appears to Granados to have aged since the last time they met. His face is pale. Dark shadows ring his eyes. As if a lifetime of profligacy has finally caught up with him.

"Hola, little brother," says Albéniz. "I heard your voice out there with the women. Come, don't be afraid. What I've got isn't contagious." They exchange an awkward abrazo. Albéniz raises his arms, then lets them fall. His voice is still spicy, the raspy growl is there, but some of his words are slurred. "You are my little brother, you know that. I never had a brother, so I claim you. Maybe that's Alfonso's problem, we never made a brother for him. You look very dashing–ah, Paris will do that, n'est-ce pas? Les mademoiselles de Paris–ooh, la, la! How are you? You can't possibly be doing as well as you look." He cackles.

"Paris is still full of trouble," says Granados. "But I managed to dodge it. Never mind me, 'Saco, I came to see how *you* are."

Albéniz smiles. "There's no shortage of doctors popping in and out of here and women wringing their hands about the color of my urine. The worst thing, I've had to give up puros–my smoky inspiration–and it's been ages since I had an escudella."

"You'd even settle for one without the peus de porc?"

Albéniz' eyes widen. "I would not! And compromise my standards, after all these years? I'd die first! Please spare me, God, I've done this to myself with gluttony. Spare me!"

"I just want you to get better, and bless us with another *Iberia*."

Albéniz closes his eyes. "I've had millions of ideas as I lie here. Good ones, too. Too weak even to scribble notes on a page. Tell me how *Iberia* is doing. I don't get much news."

Granados hesitates. There was no discussion of Albéniz' masterpiece in Paris, nor has *Iberia* been performed in Madrid or Barcelona since Malats introduced it two years ago. "I hear only the most extravagant compliments," he says.

"From every place it's played, from little coteries of people who never agree on anything. On this they all agree, your work is immortal." He's joined Rosina and Laura in protecting Albéniz.

"And in Barcelona–the world's biggest small town?"

"Ah, you remember the reviews in *La Vanguardia* and *El Noticiero*. They showered you with praise."

"Yes, and about time. How about the Parisians? Debussy hasn't always showered me."

Granados reaches into his coat pocket for the letter from Debussy. "Well, let me read this–from Claude himself." He unfolds the paper: "Mon cher ami: I am delighted to inform you that upon recommendation of Fauré, Dukas, d'Indy and myself, the Republic of France is awarding you the Croix de la Légion d'Honneur. Congratulations! Wishing you a speedy recovery. Claude"

When Granados looks up, he sees tears forming in the corners of Albéniz' eyes. He leans forward. "So you see, dear 'Saco, everyone congratulates you on your splendid achievements. And now you must get well. You must give the world more."

"I would settle for being able to get out of this stinking bed," Albéniz says. "What illness can do to ruin the creative spirit."

"You'll get up. You're strong and with all this excellent care you *will get better. I'm sure of it!*"

"Excellent care? This doctor, a Basque you know–with the most Francophile manners. Though he must be Basque, claiming that hydrangeas are excellent for healing kidney problems. I suppose I'll be cured when they start to blossom. I'd settle for roses." He turns his head toward the patio. "Of course I'll get better–but what's better? All of my joys in life have been taken away–puros, my favorite dishes, red wine and cava, being able to travel, playing my favorite music. Not to mention composing. Not to mention, shall we say, the entire realm of lust. The cruelty is endless, 'Ric. Now Victor is holding back on my morphine–does he want me to suffer?"

After listening to the hushed voices in the living room and seeing Albéniz' suffering firsthand, Granados' optimism is draining away. As if a strong tidal undertow is drawing him down, pulling him out to sea. As if it's the very terror that keeps him a safe distance from the surf. He resists the feeling of helplessness. "Would you like me to play?" he asks with as much brightness as he can mobilize. He steps over to the piano.

"Yes, that would be splendid. Can you play *Triana*?"

Granados hesitates. "No, 'Saquito. That belongs to Malats," he says. "After hearing him play *Triana*, it's unimaginable for me to try."

Albéniz cocks his head, a gesture from his better days. "Very well. Play something else.'"

Granados has already chosen *El Polo*, from the third book of *Iberia*. After one of the oldest and most sorrowful of flamenco songs. The sonatalike piece evokes a melancholy without consolation. As the principal theme begins, Granados sees Albéniz' instructions on the sheet music: "dolce en sanglotant"–sweetly sobbing. The air of melancholy, persisting throughout the piece, ends with a lush, rising virtuosity.

Albéniz nods his approval. "Is that the first time?"

"Oh, I've had the music and thought about it–quite a bit. It's such an emotional piece, but I haven't really learned it."

"Just the same, you play it brilliantly." His voice is more animated.

Rosina, Laura, and her older sister Enriqueta have entered the bedroom. Granados now plays his Allegro de Concierto, which elicits a feeble clapping of hands from the bed, and after a brief pause he begins the third part of *Escenas Románticas*. No longer titled *Lento con éxtasis*, it's now *El poeta y el ruiseñor*, and played only in private. Played often at Andreu's villa late in the evening, before Salvador pulls out his watch and escorts him out the door.

"Meravellós!" exclaims Albéniz, now propped up with his elbows. "That's the one?"

"The one?"

"You know," he says, lowering his voice so the women won't hear. "With the student."

"Oh yes. Yes. The price I'm paying for domestic tranquility."

Albéniz laughs so hard he begins to cough.

"I'll play one of yours. You choose."

"Remember *Mallorca*? Color and sunlight and the flavor of almonds and olives," says Albéniz.

Granados nods. It's a piece that Albéniz composed nearly twenty years ago, about the time of Granados' *Danzas*. Before they both turned their attention to composing operas, before the many ups and downs with the Catalan lyric theatre, with Morera, with El Liceu. So to begin this exquisite piece, tender and sweet, this sensuous barcarole evocative of Chopin, Granados goes back to that long ago time of rollicking youth and restless energy and boundless hope, composed in the year Laura Albéniz was born, the year he first performed his *Danzas* at the Teatre Líric and was sought after by Ramón Casas and his crowd of bohemians, two years before he met Amparo. As he plays for his bedridden friend, all these echoes rush through his mind and he's grateful to be playing, absorbed in his most inspired interpretation of Albéniz' work. If he were simply listening, his whole body might shake apart. When he finishes, the overtone of sadness in *Mallorca* lingers and tiny bursts of sobbing pervade the bedroom.

When Victor Ruiz arrives, it's time for Granados to leave. He leans over and kisses both of the bushy cheeks. "Now hear me, 'Saco, you're going to get on your feet again, and come down to see me and I'll take you to Can Culleretes and you can have the shoulder of goat–"

"No, Culleretes has the good escudella. Shoulder of goat in that little place in Tiana. Remember?"

They exchange smiles.

"How *would* you remember?" asks Albéniz. "You always have fish stew."

"You get well and we'll get a bottle of the very best cava, and I'll smoke a puro."

"*You'll* smoke a puro?" asks Albéniz.

"When you get well, yes."

"Surely that'll inspire me. Do you think we should write an opera together? A sequel to *La Boheme*. Opening scene: two aging composers arrange to meet for lunch."

Granados laughs. "I'm sure the crowd at El Liceu would be delighted."

"El Liceu? Piss on El Liceu! We'll open at La Scala!"

They shake hands. When he releases his grip, Granados feels Albéniz hold on. "I've been working on something new, 'Ric. A series of pieces for piano. I have a name: *Azulejos*."

Bright colored tiles in the Andaluz sun. "Azulejos–a beautiful word," says Granados, "and I'm sure it will be splendid."

As he prepares to leave, Granados is embraced by Rosina and Laura. While they wait in the lobby of the Chateau Saint-Martin for a carriage to take Granados to the train station, Victor Ruiz thanks him for coming. "It means so much to him, maestro. He talks about you incessantly. I play for him–not with your kind of virtuosity, and I sing for him. Two weeks ago, he got so excited over a little bit of Chopin that he got out of bed to improvise on the theme. So sad, he couldn't even move his hands over the keys. So sad to think it would come to this."

Granados is still resistant to the significance of Ruiz' anecdote. Still in denial about the gravity of Albéniz' condition. He listens as Ruiz describes the medical problems.

"You know about the uremia," says the young physician. "And my uncle is suffering from kidney failure. It's not reversible."

Uremia? Kidney failure? Not reversible?

Granados' anxiety rises. What more is there to know? "What do you mean, 'not reversible'?"

Ruiz pauses. "Maestro Granados, what I mean is, he's going to die."

No! Not 'Saco–not my older brother. Makes no sense!

The fragile crust that Granados has spread over the truth is finally pierced. There's pounding behind his eyes. His legs are folding. Denial is no longer there for him to clutch and hold onto. Laura steps close to him and puts her arm around his waist. She is sobbing too, but her tears have flowed for so many days that this time they're for her father's friend.

Granados cries out. "No! His work's hardly begun! He's just arrived! He cannot die–there's so much more! What can be done?"

Laura takes his hand. "His music will not die, and there is something you can do for him. He's been working on this piece he calls *Azulejos*. He said yesterday that if he isn't able, he'd like you to finish it. Would you be willing?"

Barcelona

The funeral for Isaac Albéniz takes place four weeks after Granados' visit to Cambó. In the early morning of June 5, his casket is unloaded from the train that carried it down through the Basque country and Navarre and rural Catalunya to the Estació França. The point of departure for so many Catalan artists and musicians heading to Paris, Rome, Milano and Vienna is now the funeral parlor. During a nightlong vigil by his friends and colleagues, the public files past his corpse. The following morning, a swelling crowd hears the municipal band play Siegfried's funeral music from Wagner's *Die Gotterdammerung* as the casket is loaded into the hearse. The Orfeó Català sings Fauré's *Requiem*. Down the Passeig de Colom, then up through the winding streets of the old city, past the Iglesia de Mercé—where Isaac Albéniz and Rosina Jordana were married twenty-six years ago. The procession cuts through the Plaza Real to La Rambla, with the cadence of Chopin's *Funeral March* filling the cloudy, hot, and humid summer morning, stopping in front of El Liceu, then moving on to the grave site in the cemetery of Montjuic. As the ceremonies are concluded, Granados sees the anguished face of Albéniz' prodigal son, Alfonso, who'd been in London when his father died.

Two days after Albéniz' burial, Granados experiences a wrenching pain in his upper abdomen. His physician rules out a heart attack and hypothesizes that it's a digestive problem. "You say the pain is here?" he asks, placing his fingertip over Granados' sternum.

"That's where it's the worst."

"And you have pain below here?"

"Some, yes."

"A sharp pain or an aching pain?"

"Aching, I'd say. But it is painful."

"Have you been watching your diet?" the doctor asks.

Granados smiles, thinking of how Albéniz' would taunt him for always ordering fish soup. "I'm not eating large quantities of anything."

"You've lost ten kilos. That's quite a lot, Maestro. I'd suggest you try to eat a bit more, mostly rice and bread. You're not smoking?"

"I never have."

"Very well." The physician looks down at the chart.

"Then what is my problem?" Granados asks.

"From what I can see, I'd say it's your ulcer. Or it could be an irritated esophagus. We'll treat you for the ulcer."

Thank God—not my kidneys! Too soon to follow 'Saco. Work's not finished. Please God—more time!

Albéniz has been six weeks in his grave. When Malats, on tour in Germany, heard about the illness—but not its final outcome, he wrote to Granados and vented his outrage: "Albéniz will not die!" He could not have known that three days earlier, after bringing her father a red rose that had finally bloomed on the patio, Laura Albéniz saw him sink into a coma and watched him pass away.

So many have died or gone away. Granados' father and brother, both Spanish Army officers, both Calixto; seeing them to slow and painful deaths. His librettist Josep Feliu, dead before *María del Carmen* opened. His first mentor, Joan Baptista Pujol, dead ten years now. Pere Romeu dead despite his devotion to good health. Francisco Miralles, more vulnerable than anyone knew. And now Albéniz, leaving the world his masterpiece, *Iberia*. Granados wonders what would be left if his own time were up.

Those who haven't been taken by death are also gone, scattered all over the world. Casals and Malats and Ricard Viñes and Miquel Llobet–all living in Paris and touring the continent. Falla, though not a close friend like the others, also in Paris. Another mentor, Felip Pedrell, living in Madrid. Crickboom back in Belgium. His rival Morera gone to Argentina, bankrupt. Graner, also bankrupt, now in New York. Rusiñol mostly gone to Mallorca or somewhere on the move. Casas–traveling with Charles Deering, his American patron; when he's in town, the young model with the eyebrows is always with him. And the best singers have left too. María Pichot and Andres de Segurola established in New York. Barrientos retired in Argentina to raise a child. Lucrècia Bori off to Italy. And Conchita Supervia, just fourteen years old, touring South America.

Granados is alone in his room at the academy. Since lessons won't resume until September, both days and nights are quiet here. Quiet, except for the sound of steel rolling on steel as trains pass through l'Eixample on nearby Carrer Aragó. Quiet, except for the sound of his improvisations on the piano.

It's mid-July. He spent the early evening preparing a report that he'll take to Salvador in Puigcerdà. He'd be there now, but the trip to Paris and Albéniz' death changed his vacation plans. He plans to leave town after celebrating his birthday with Amparo and their children.

During the school year, Granados spends most weekday evenings at Salvador and Carmen's villa in Sant Gervasi, and most of his summer break at their xalet in Puigcerdà. In effect, he's become a "satellite" of the Andreu family–despite Amparo's obvious dislike for how he's divided his life into distinct compartments, despite her complaints that he spends more time with the Andreus than with his own family.

During his evenings at Sant Gervasi, his pianistic improvisations are often interrupted by the Andreu children–especially Paquita, now a handsome young woman of twenty, raptly devoted to the piano and to her maestro. So devoted that her younger sister, Madronita, teases her about being "love-sick" over him. When the children aren't with Granados at the piano or hovering nearby, Andreu often brings his guests to the music salon to listen to Granados, or assembles a group to play with him. As a result, opportunities for creative interludes at Sant Gervasi are rare.

Granados' work is not progressing well. Nearly three years have passed since the lyric opera *Gaziel* was presented by Graner, and more than a year since the one and only private performance of the first two books of *Dante.* Since then, with dozens of ideas whirling through his head and a few measures from each scattered on the pages of his composition books, no cohesive piece of work has emerged. So he spends his time at the piano improvising; he can do that effortlessly.

Granados stops and goes over to his cluttered desk. In a stack on the farthest corner, he finds the folder with his notes on Goya's *Caprichos* sketches. Several of them, which seem based on Goya's knowledge of the Spanish royal court and his relationship with La Duquesa de Alba, are especially intriguing. *Nadie se conoce*–a carnival scene expressing the view that everything is pretense; *Que sacrificio!*–a young woman being sacrificed to a grotesque but rich older man; *Bien tirada está*–the elegant silhouette of a young prostitute; *Volaverunt*–of a young woman flying through the air with butterfly wings; two sketches of the same woman, both simply entitled *La maja*, and *Quién más rendido?*–depicting an indifferent lady being courted by a man on his knees. To Granados, the lady is La Duquesa de Alba and the man is Goya.

He looks through his notes from a decade ago, some of which he used for *Ovillejos*. The notes represent the failure he told Casals had broken his heart. But he saved them, convinced there's value in some of the scattered fragments, hoping that with the passage of time and the maturing of his artistry they can be reshaped into a piano suite. As the music leaps into his head, he realizes how much work is required to bring this to fruition. More than getting butterflies to move in concert, more than getting nightingales to sing in unison.

Work and time and peace of mind. No distractions. No dancing from project to project. Work time peace of mind. When? Where?

On the fourth Saturday in July, Granados walks down Carrer Girona to the pharmacy to pick up a refill for his ulcer medicine. Outside, two men argue about the general strike that the federation of unions has called for Monday. One of the men complains that the loss of just one day's production will mean delays in shipping his customers' orders; the other views the strike as a benign opportunity to let the workers blow off steam. He contends that in the sticky heat this time of year productivity has already collapsed. Neither of them, dressed in linen suits and straw hats, are in sympathy with the strike, but the difference in how it affects them is sufficient for an argument. At least on this Saturday, when there's nothing else to argue about.

Inside the pharmacy, two smartly dressed women of l'Eixample chat about the events of the past week while they wait for their medicine. The older woman says, "Last week we went to the port to watch our soldiers off to Morocco. The Marqués de Comillas let the army use his ships–quite generous, don't you think? But it was his wife's idea–a splendid one, to give rosary beads and scapulars and medals of San Cristóforo to the soldiers. So God would bless them. And we all handed out cigarettes. Pity these poor men! Some no older than my own sons, off to fight the Moros in the mountains. What a shame!"

Granados would like to remind her that few of the sons of the alta burguesia are sent off to fight the Moros–their families pay for less privileged men to take their places in the army–but it's not worth mentioning. Not even if he knew this woman, not even to honor the service of his grandfather, father, and brother.

"That was good of them to be so generous," said the younger woman, "because within days hundreds of our men were killed in the Rif Valley."

"Yes, and my gracious, who'd have expected the Moros to know how to fight? It must have been a sneak attack."

"How distressing–now there are meetings and protests, and Monday–they say, there'll be a general strike. We'd best do our shopping today."

The older woman frowns. "Yes, but didn't the government ask them not to strike? My brother says they'll be thrown in jail if there's trouble."

"That may be, but there can't be enough jails for all of them if there is a general strike. I'm going to be safe and do my shopping today."

"Well, I suppose. But isn't this strike just for one day? Surely we can do our shopping on Tuesday."

Granados has been hearing such conversations all week. He grasps what's behind the unrest in Barcelona, but hasn't kept track of the events leading to a general strike. Ordinarily, he'd be better informed simply by listening to evening conversations in Sant Gervasi, but the Andreus have been in Puigcerdà for more than a month. Andreu is always well informed: his enterprises are affected by local decisions about street construction and tramvia routes, and by trade policies with foreign countries. If his workers are unhappy, their work suffers; if they're on strike, no pharmaceuticals can leave his plant on Carrer de Folguerolas. But this flare-up of Catalan *Sturm und Drang* can't possibly affect Acadèmia Granados, already closed for the summer.

The next afternoon, Granados takes his six children–now ranging in age from seven to fifteen, on a jaunt to the top of Mount Tibidabo. They hold hands as they ride the main north-south tramvia up to a little plaza on Passeig de Sant Gervasi, just two blocks from the Andreus' villa. The next leg of their outing is on Tramvia Blau, painted the color of the sky, which runs up Avinguda Tibidabo to the base of the funicular railway. As they wait on the lower platform he shows the two youngest, Natalia and Paquito, how high the cable car will take them.

"The little blue tram and this railway were built by my friend, Doctor Andreu," Granados explains.

"Is he a real doctor?" asks Eduardo.

"He's a doctor of pharmacy–very famous for his little pills. Also very wealthy."

"Not a doctor who puts a stick on your tongue and asks you to say, 'ahhhh.' Not that kind of doctor."

"Well, Eduardo, there are various kinds of doctors. Doctor Andreu makes medicines that help people feel better. That's important too."

"But Papa," says Enrique, "how can someone who makes pills build these things we're riding on?"

"He doesn't build them–personally. He's the one who arranges for streets and houses and tramvias and funiculars to be built. He's like the impresario at El Liceu–who doesn't sing or play in the orchestra, but *arranges* everything."

"I'd like to meet him," Eduardo says.

"Why, you have! He's an older gentleman with a white beard. His wife is named Carmen. They live in the big villa on Sant Gervasi. I took you there once–I'm sure you have met him."

Eduardo cocks his head. "Yes, once. Mamà says that's where you go after work. She says you go there every evening. I think Mamà doesn't like that place, but I'd like to go there again."

Granados frowns. "Eduardo, I go there to give lessons to the children. And they're much older than you. There'd be nothing for you to do."

Riding up in the cable car, Granados points out the observatory built by Camil Fabra, the Marquès d'Alella.

"If he's a marquès," says Eduardo, "he must be a friend of the famous Doctor Andreu."

"Matter of fact, he *was*," says Granados. "He died, but his son–who's also a marquès–is continuing his father's work."

"So if the father is a marquès, the son becomes one too?"

"Yes. It's a title given by the King."

"How about composers?"

Granados shakes his head. "No, kings don't make composers."

"No, Papa," says Eduardo, determined to make his point. "If a composer dies, shouldn't his son continue his work? Like the son of a marquès?"

"Of course. But you'd be foolish to wait for me to die. Be a composer if that's what your heart tells you to be. Pay attention to your heart." He looks around and counts only five children. After a frenzied search, Victor is found under a bench in the back of the cable car.

On top, with a panoramic view of the the city, Granados points out familiar landmarks: the Cathedral, La Rambla, Plaça Catalunya, Ciutadella Park–where they go to the zoo–and the port area filled with freighters, fishing fleets–and pleasure craft.

"This is where the Temple of the Sacred Heart will stand," says Granados as they walk past a massive construction site.

"A temple?" asks Solita. "I thought that's where Jews go to pray."

"You're correct. But it's also a special kind of large church for Christians–for atonement."

"What is atonement?" asks Enrique.

Granados hesitates. "It's the reconciliation of man with God."

Victor points out the main tramvia lines on the streets below, the horse-drawn carriages, and the new motor cars. From Tibidabo, they're small dark specks. "Motor cars–much faster than horses! Papa, can we get a motor car?"

"Someday–perhaps."

"I'm going to have one when I grow up!" says Victor. "I'm going to have the Hispano Suissa. The fastest in the whole world!"

Granados is amused. With each day, there seem to be more of the motor cars on the streets, competing for space with trams, horse-drawn vehicles, bicycles, and pedestrians. Barcelona's industrialists and artists are setting the trend, and there are now several hundred motor cars in the city. The Andreus have a Rochet-Schneider sedan, made in Lyons, and a smaller, racier Hispano Suissa, built in a factory near the Sant Antoni market. "Mark my words," Andreu said recently, "these contraptions will become more and more a part of our daily lives. And they'll begin to create problems we can't even imagine." His remark seemed prescient the following week when a motor car ran over a pedestrian, and a group of incensed bystanders destroyed the vehicle. Granados enjoys riding in the motor cars and he'd like to have one too, but it's a luxury–not required to get where he needs to go. Besides, there isn't enough money, not now, but that will come.

Granados leads his children along the ridge near the top of Mount Tibidabo, to the site of an amusement park being built by one of Andreu's companies. He points out La Mentora, an experimental physics museum built by Ferran Alsina, who left a partnership with the tycoon Eusebi Guell to start his own factory.

"Is he also a marquès?" asks Eduardo.

"Eusebi Guell? No, he's a count."

"I mean the other one."

"Alsina. Neither a marquès, nor a count. But–anticipating your next question, he also is dead."

"Papa," asks Enrique, "what is experi-metal physics?"

Granados laughs.

"And please tell me," says Solita, "what is physics?"

Eduardo has been pondering the meaning of today's excursion to Mount Tibidabo. "My heart is speaking to me, Papa," he says.

"Yes?" Granados replies.

"It's telling me not to build anything up here. All the ones who did are dead."

The next day, Granados has two lessons scheduled in the l'Eixample homes of his students. After the first lesson, he catches a tram on Passeig de Gràcia, heading north. The conductor tells him there's been trouble ahead; the tram won't be able to take him beyond the corner of Travessera de Gràcia, a crosstown route.

"What kind of trouble?" Granados asks.

"It's the strikers. They overturned a tram on Ronda de Sant Antoni, and as I was leaving Plaça Catalunya some of them threw rocks. You'll see the broken windows in back," he says, motioning with his head to the seating area behind him.

"Travessera is fine," says Granados. From there, it's a short distance to the home of his last student today. He rides the nearly empty tram for a dozen blocks, noticing how few people are on the sidewalks, how the normal pace of life in his industrious city has slackened. As he steps down from the tram, he's approached by three men who form a half-circle in his path.

"Don't you know there's a general strike?" says the one who's carrying a stack of leaflets.

"Yes, I heard. But the tram was running, so I took it." His response is cautious and respectful.

The striker hands a leaflet to Granados, and a quick glance reveals that the federation of trade unions is condemning this tramvia company for disregarding the work stoppage. "The trams are owned by the Marqués de Foronda," explains the striker. "Did you know that? He's a Gallego, and he brings his workers all the way from Galicia–to keep the union out! We're shutting him down, so you'd better not plan to be riding any more trams. Do you understand, senyor?"

Granados nods.

"All right, then. You can pass."

The three men step back and Granados continues up Mayor de Gràcia. Other than a bakery and two butcher shops, all its stores are closed. There are a few horse-drawn carriages moving on the street, and one motor car is parked in front of a restaurant. A patrol of four mounted cavalry passes him, and the echo of hooves striking the paving stones drowns out the mumbled conversations of neighbors who stand in tight clusters to share fragments of news and rumors about the strike. In the next block, Granados is alarmed to see that a tram has been overturned and positioned as a barrier to block the street. On top is a group of strikers, whose overalls and visored caps set them apart from the suited and straw-hatted middle class residents of the neighborhood. And from him, in his dark suit and straw hat.

The strikers wave signs proclaiming "Worker Solidarity!" and "End the Bankers' War!" and "Long Live Anarchy!" Granados circumvents the toppled tram, avoiding eye contact with the strikers. It's not their fault, really. Once again Spain has sent its young men into battle. Shipped them off to foreign deserts and swamps to protect the interests of the rich and powerful. Granados wouldn't do that, but it's not his job to step in and try to stop it. Surely he can get around without the trams for a day.

Tuesday morning. What was supposed to be a one-day general strike has escalated into a major confrontation between the anarchists and trade unionists in the streets, and various units of guàrdies–civilian police–who've been deployed to contain them. Many people, including Granados, are unaware that the strike has expanded to most of the urbanized area between Sitges and

Mataró, a distance of seventy kilometers, and that the anger directed against tramvias yesterday is now aimed at churches, convents, and religious schools. The first building to be burned, shortly after midnight, is the Convent of the Marists in the parish of Sant Andreu de Palomar, but that's in a remote part of the city and Granados has no way of knowing about that.

Today is his forty-second birthday. He plans walk down to the tailor shop to be fitted for a new suit, have lunch with Joan Llongueras at Set Portes near the harbor, and later have his birthday dinner with Amparo and the children. Tomorrow he plans to leave for five weeks in Puigcerdà. A splendid vacation. Perhaps some time to work on the Goya-esque music.

Granados weaves through the narrow streets of the old city, detouring around a few crude barricades constructed of paving stones, doors, signboards, couches, and metal bed frames. The men and boys who are standing by the barricades ignore him as he passes, intent on his destination: the Hungarian tailor's shop on Carrer d'Avinyó, near the church of La Mercé. He has to wait for two other customers at the tailor shop. Then the fitting is not correct; the pants are too large at the waist, the jacket too generous from his ribcage down.

"You've lost weight, maestro," says the tailor.

"Yes. Being more careful about what I eat. Doctor's orders."

"Well, your waist is three inches smaller than last year. And the jacket doesn't fit at all. Are you planning to stay in this size?"

Granados smiles, envisioning the inconvenience of recurring trips to the tailor. He admits to being a bit thinner than he'd like to be, and asks for more room around the waist.

The tailor says the suit will be ready in a week; Granados thanks him.

"Unless this strike gets worse," adds the tailor. "Like yesterday on La Rambla! You heard about that?"

Granados shakes his head.

"They came over from El Raval," the tailor says. "A rough bunch! Call themselves 'The Young Barbarians.' You know, followers of Alejandro Lerroux. They're the ones behind it."

"I've heard of Lerroux," Granados says, "the so-called 'Emperor of the Paral.lel.'" Lerroux, a former journalist with a talent for whipping crowds of workers and anarchists to a frenzy, is relentlessly anticlerical, loathing the conservative Catalanists of the alta burguesia and church. His core constituency lies with migrant workers of El Raval, who also resent how they're treated by the Catalanists.

"I didn't think you'd know of him," says the tailor. "You being a famous pianist and composer. Different world, right?"

"I have heard a lot," says Granados, thinking of Andreu's long tirades against Lerroux and the anarchists. That he listens to respectfully and chooses not to challenge. It is not his world.

"Well, enough of that," the tailor says. "You'll stop by next week?"

Granados remembers he'll be with the Andreus in Puigcerdà. "No, I'll be out of town. Could you deliver the suit?"

"I'd prefer seeing you in it again, maestro. "But if you trust me–"

Granados grins and nods. "These days, if not you–who can I trust?"

When Granados emerges on Carrer d'Avinyó, he hears the sound of gunfire as it bounces against the stone buildings of the old city. He's sure it's gunfire, recognizing it from his stay in Olot where his brother Calixto was stationed with the Spanish Army. Crack, crack, crack–exactly like the sound on the army's firing range. Only now the sound is close by.

As he starts up the street, a man steps in front of him and warns that a crowd of protesters is marching toward the Capitania General, headquarters of the local garrison. "They're coming this way because the guàrdies are waiting for them on La Rambla. And today they're armed!"

Granados hesitates. "I'm trying to get back home. To Girona and Aragó."

"I suggest you cross over to the Mercat Born, then go north to l'Eixample. And senyor–stay away from the churches and convents."

"Oh?"

"See that smoke in the sky?" cries the man, pointing overhead. "Smell the smoke? They're burning churches and convents. Even parish schools. You'd better get out of here!"

"Thank you!" shouts Granados as he hurries into the first of a zigzag series of passageways by which he can traverse the old city and arrive at the Mercat del Born. He stops at the edge of the open space of Plaça Santa María. As he dries his forehead with a handkerchief and loosens his tie and vest, he realizes that his route is taking him past the church of Santa María del Mar. The sound of gunfire pierces his ears. He's startled, and after pondering his choices, decides that taking a sharp right turn onto Carrer Espaseria will allow him to circle around the church and find his way to Mercat del Born. He looks over his shoulder, stunned by the sight of armed young men assaulting the church and the guàrdies and civilians defending it. Several of the combatants have already fallen in the plaça.

Not a strike! It's war! They're shooting! Trying to burn Santa María!

He hears more shooting and as he breaks into a run, his tie and jacket flapping behind him, he's grabbed by two uniformed guàrdies who stop him with stinging grips on his arms. "Not so fast, senyor. Where are you going?"

He tries to break free. "I'm trying to get away–trying to get home! I'm not involved in this!"

"We'll see. Come with us." They take him to their office on Marquès de l'Argentera, next to l'Estació de França. "Come back here," says the guàrdia who seems to be in charge, and they wind through a labyrinth of offices to a room with a square table, four chairs, and a hanging lamp that blinks on and off in no discernible cadence. From the rooms around them are cries and shouts followed by silence, then more cries. A short man with a goatee that glistens in the blinking light enters the room. The interrogator of this unit. "Let's find out who you really are, senyor," he says. It's the voice of one who's used to having control of the streets, and fears he may be losing it. "To begin, you say you are Senyor Granados, but you have no identification. None at all. You were near the church of Santa María while it was being attacked, and we arrested you running away. So we need to know who you are and what you were doing there. Do you understand?"

"I understand," says Granados, "but apparently you don't! I was coming from a fitting at my tailor's shop on Avinyó and I heard the crowd coming that way and decided to avoid the trouble, so I ended up at the plaça in front of Santa María and when I heard the shooting I tried to get away as fast as possible. Your men stopped me and brought me here."

"So that's your story?"

Granados cannot hide his resentment. "That is the truth!"

"If so, why can't you produce a single piece of evidence that proves you're Señor Granados? Have you no identification? Have you no papers or bank statements or letters that would help us know who you are?"

Granados shrugs. He's never been asked to prove his identity. Oh, there are critics and impresarios in this city who don't care who he is or what he's just composed, but at least they know him. To them, he's just "Nostre Granados"–talented, but not good enough to compete with the Italians and Germans and French. This is a different challenge. He must prove to these guàrdies that he is "Nostre Granados," that he isn't an anarchist provocateur sent to Barcelona to oversee the burning of churches and convents. "What can I say? I'm Enrique Granados, a music teacher, and I live with my family on Carrer Girona number eighty-nine, at the corner of Aragó. Don't take my word for it. Ask anyone who's involved in music here, ask them who I am."

"But you have no identification–on a day when there's fighting in the streets. Why is that?" asks the man with the goatee.

"I understood it was just a one-day general strike–yesterday. Didn't realize there was a war going on today. And I didn't expect to have to prove my identity. I simply came down here for a fitting at my tailor's. Why would I carry papers to prove who I am? My tailor knows me."

"That's not the point. Not today, with the mob attacking churches and convents. You took a big risk coming down here. This is a battleground, and those people shooting at the church are anarchists, violent people who are hostile to everything that we treasure in España. They're the ones who bombed El Liceu, you should know about that if you *are*–as you claim–a musician. They're bomb-throwers! They've declared a war on our government for sending troops to Morocco. If they disagree with that, there are peaceful ways. Even a general strike can be forgiven. You'll notice, senyor, that we didn't fire on them when they came down La Rambla yesterday and surrounded the Capitania. Not a shot. We're not the ruthless killers they are–they're burning our churches and convents and schools!"

Granados looks back without blinking. "I am not involved, capitan," he says. "I am a music teacher with a wife and six young children and I simply want to go home."

Their eyes remain engaged. The interrogator must decide whether to send him over to the prison at Montjuic or release him.

"I'm going to release you," he says, "so you can go home. But if you're arrested again, we won't be so generous."

Shaken, still breathless, and resentful of being treated like a criminal, Granados leaves the office of the guàrdies and crosses over l'Argentera in front of the Estació França. He turns up on Carrer de Comerç that skirts his home parish of Sant Pere de les Puel.les, just a few blocks from home.

There are barricades blocking all of the side streets that converge on Carrer de Comerç. Today the men standing by the barricades are armed, and there are fewer pedestrians walking the streets simply to satisfy their curiosity. Granados sees three dark, billowing plumes of smoke rising ahead of him, another two off to his left, and several more off to his right. His eyes burn from the particles of ash dropping from the plumes as they rise high above the city. His nose stings, his throat is parched. He wonders how the firemen will be able to respond to so many blazes at the same time, then it strikes him that the proliferation of barriers throughout the city has rendered the fire department useless. Proceeding up the street, he maintains the pace of a pair of armed men ahead of him.

Not too fast. Nor slow. Eyes forward. Don't look back. Blend in. Be inconspicuous.

Granados realizes, as he enters the open space of Plaça Sant Pere, that he'll pass close to another church. His church, the Romanesque Sant Pere, where he and Amparo were married nearly seventeen years ago. That bright day in early winter, with his mother and sister and brother, wishing his father had lived to see that day, and eager to move ahead into the unknown.

Titín and I—lovebirds! She glowed like a paloma in the bright sun. Appeared suddenly as if dropped by angels. Eyes dancing like candles.

Granados met Amparo twenty years ago at a palatial country estate outside València. Her family was invited to hear the young pianist from Barcelona, and after the recital he was invited to return. He rejoiced when, after several months of long train rides and hurried parlor chats and passionate letters, Amparo's father sold his business in València and moved the family to Barcelona. They were married within a year, and two summers later their first child, Eduardo, arrived on the day after Granados' own twenty-seventh birthday. Followed by five more children.

Women do the hardest work! Carrying them, giving birth, caring for them while fathers go on with their lives. Not surprising Titín would resent young women flirting. Not easy for women like Titín.

Granados heads up the sidewalk on the west side of the plaça, intent on passing through the area without incident. A large, noisy crowd has gathered in front of the church. Waving signs, raising clenched fists, shouting political slogans: "Visca l'anarquia! Visca l'anarquia! Anarchy forever!"

In the middle of the plaça is a wrought-iron modernist street lamp rising from a water fountain. Granados sees a young priest in a small cluster of people holding buckets, presumably filled with water. An exercise in futility if the agitated crowd decides to burn the church. And he sees three men appear in the main doorway of the church, carrying torches. The priest seems oblivious to their intent. Granados crosses the plaça.

"Can I help you?" asks the priest, who looks too young to shave.

"Father, you're in great danger—you should leave at once!"

"And you are Senyor—?"

"Granados. This is my parish. I was married here. My children were baptized here."

"It's been a terrible day! I'm Father Trias. All day, we've had this mob threatening to burn the church."

"Where are the other priests?"

"They left with the sisters. I decided to stay. I had no choice."

At this moment, there's a bellow from the crowd. Granados and the priest turn to see flames rising from the Gothic main doorway and the two matching windows on either side, from the windows on the floor above, and from the row of broken stained glass windows in the Romanesque nave. They hear the cry: "Visca l'anarquia! Let's burn them all down!"

Granados leans toward the priest. "Father Trias, this is going to get more dangerous. Come home with me."

"You are very kind, but I can't leave my church."

As Granados watches the priest return to the water fountain, he calls out one more time, hoping to convince him to leave. Turning toward home, he sees a group of four men traversing the plaça, cutting him off. Within moments, he's surrounded.

"Where are *you* going?" asks the apparent leader of the group.

"I'm trying to go home," Granados replies.

"Home? From where?"

"From my tailor's shop. On Carrer Avinyó."

"And what's your tailor's name? Doesn't he know there's a complete work stoppage?"

"I don't know, and I won't tell you his name. Why do you need to know?"

"We'll decide that. What is your name?"

"Granados. Enric Granados."

"And why were you talking to the priest?"

Granados glowers at him. "I was telling him to get out of here. That's all. Do you plan to harm him?"

"Of course not. We don't harm priests or nuns. Not the live ones. Just the mummies." The group joins in his amusement.

The shortest member of them, carrying a rifle, asks, "What kind of a name is Granados? Certainly not Catalan."

"I was born in Lleida. I'm a music teacher. I live on Carrer Girona, at the corner of Aragó."

"Can you prove that? Papers? Identification?"

Granados hesitates. "No. I'm not carrying them. Didn't know I'd be in a war zone."

The leader of the group laughs.

"Perhaps you don't understand," Granados tells them, "I'm not involved in this!"

"Look Senyor Granada," says the leader, "or whoever you are, you *are* involved because we're not going to release you until you prove who you are and explain why you were talking to the priest for so long, and why you won't tell us the name of the tailor who could help explain why you're out today in the middle of this war. For all we know you could be an agent sent by Madrid."

"I've said all there is to say!"

"All right, come with us."

Granados pulls away. "I want to go home. I'm not involved in this!"

The leader takes a pistol out of a pocket in his overalls. "Perhaps this will help you understand."

"But I'm not involved in this!"

"How not? If you are Catalan, as you claim, this is a struggle for the people of Catalunya. Against the crown and the aristocracy, against the military, and most of all against the bishops. Together they have deprived us of our birthright. Once we tossed bombs–thinking that would get their attention, that would make them change. It didn't. Now we have other ways to get their attention."

Granados is led around the Arc de Trionf, then up Carrer de Ribes which runs on a diagonal line to the north and east. At the Plaça de les Glòries Catalanes–as large an open space as the Plaça Catalunya itself, they take the Avinguda Meridiana through the industrial zone of El Clot. Ahead on the broad boulevard, the church of Sant Martí de Provençals is belching flames and smoke. As they approach, Granados sees what appear to be crude stone sculptures resting against the outer wall of the burning church.

"Those are mummified cadavers," says the leader with the pistol. "Priests and nuns."

"You removed them from their crypts?"

"That's right."

They cross Meridiana and descend through an alleyway that leads them to the back of a two-story building. Two men on guard with rifles challenge them, but yield after a brief explanation. Inside, Granados is taken to what appears to be a kitchen, with a large round table in the center and chairs all around it. "You may sit," says the leader with the pistol.

In a few moments there are footsteps and the door opens. A wiry man in his forties enters and sits at the table across from Granados. "What is the problem with this one?" he asks the others. The leader with the pistol tells him Granados was talking with a priest while they were burning the church of Sant Pere, that he claims to be on his way from his tailor's shop yet is unwilling to reveal the name of the tailor. That he has no identification.

The interrogator turns to Granados. "What do you have to say?"

"My name is Enric Granados. I'm a music teacher and I live on Carrer Girona number eighty-nine. This morning I thought the general strike was over, so I went down for a fitting with my tailor on Carrer Avinyó. This is the second time I've been stopped trying to go home. And I'm not involved in this! What you are doing has nothing to do with me!"

"You are wrong about that," says the interrogator, rising from his chair. His eyes probe over the tops of his rimless glasses. "Incidentally, my name is Josep Miquel. I belong to the PRNC, which in case you don't recognize it is the party of Catalan Republicans. This morning we assaulted the headquarters of the Guàrdia Civil in my neighborhood and burned the church of Sant Andreu and a convent. And some other church buildings. You say you are not involved, Senyor Granados? I'm sure you haven't been too busy to notice the bombs set off in several of our industrial plants. Of course, it's all to easy to blame the anarchists–the truth is, these bombs are being planted by the guàrdies in order to discredit those of us who stand up for our rights! Very clever: they get even with the anarchists, and they keep the industries of Catalunya from becoming too powerful. That's the cleverness we've learned to expect from the guàrdies who take their orders from Madrid!"

Granados shakes his head, unable to follow the man's argument. Struggling to control his exasperation.

Miquel continues. "You say you're not involved? When the Comte de Romanones can bring the national army in to protect his iron mines in the Rif, when his friend the Marquès de Comillas–his partner in the mines, provides his own ships to carry the young soldiers of Catalunya to their deaths, when his banker friends like Girona bankroll the filthy scheme, when the fine women of l'Eixample go down to the port and give the departing soldiers religious medals? Medals! Is that fair exchange for their sacrifice? Why don't the good families of Barcelona send their own sons to fight in their wars, instead of paying fifteen hundred pesetas to excuse them from serving? Now, aren't these enough reasons for you to be involved? No, I suppose not. You know who Lerroux is?"

"Yes. He's a deputy from El Raval." The less said the better.

"Lerroux says we should wreck this unhappy country, destroy its temples, tear the veil from its novices and raise them to be mothers who can civilize our species. And finish off the gods. Well, that's the work we've begun. And before it's over, everyone will be involved, even if–like you–they're naïve enough to believe they can avoid it. And if some of us have to die, isn't it better to die on the doorsteps of our homes than be stabbed to death by the Moros in the Rif?"

Granados shakes his head.

"Now, about your identity. Where were you born, Senyor Granados?"

"In Lleida."

Miquel jerks his head back. "No! You're Lleidatà? So am I!"

Granados is relieved. "I hope that means I'll get home tonight."

Miquel presses him. "You say you're Lleidatà? All right, let's find out! What's the name of the river that runs through it?"

"El Segre."

"And who is the annual festival named for?"

"Sant Miquel."

"And what do we call the olives that come from there?"

"Arbequinas. They're very small."

"And what would you find if you went to the top of the hill?"

"You'd find the old castle and the cathedral. If they haven't been burned!"

"That's not amusing," Miquel replies. "Well, those are easy questions. You could answer them with a trip to the library. Here's a final question: who is the piano virtuoso from Lleida who now lives in Paris?"

Granados smiles. "It's Ricard Viñes," he tells Miquel. "He was my roommate when I studied in Paris."

Miquel settles back onto his chair. Turning to the men who brought Granados from Sant Pere, he says, "Papers or not, I'm sure of this one's identity. He's Lleidatà–not an enemy. Naïve, yes–thinking he can avoid being involved in this fight. But not dangerous. We will release him." Turning to the man with the pistol, he adds sternly, "And you will escort him to his home. Safely, you hear?"

On the way, they pass the burning Convent de les Caputxins. In front is a row of mummified cadavers. Granados is too numb from the gyrations of this day to react, but the images are etched in his memory.

Part III

Chapter Seven

Barcelona, July 1909

Doctor Salvador Andreu hurries back to Barcelona when he hears about the week already described as "Setmana Tràgica." Tragic Week–there's no other name for it. Out of devotion to his city and concern about his extensive financial interests, Andreu intends to find out what happened, how it happened, and what can be done to prevent its recurrence. He finds a consensus among his peers that someone has to pay for the chaos and violence. But who? Could the series of events preceding it have been anticipated? If so, why weren't steps taken to prevent it?

Andreu's employees return to their jobs the following week, as do most other workers. Owners of businesses and factories are willing to pay them for time off, hoping to restore normalcy, hoping for a quick return from sanguinary to sanguine. Since the owners are paternalistic, they continue to disregard the seeds of rebellion long since sown.

In the aftermath of Setmana Tràgica, Andreu finds medical and funeral services overwhelmed, especially in Barcelona, where street battles were fought by guàrdies and armed insurgents in the workers' districts of Clot, Sant Marti, and San Andreu. Five guàrdies, three soldiers and eighty-two civilians were killed; thirty-nine guàrdies, twenty-seven soldiers, and one-hundred-twenty-six civilians were wounded. No priests or nuns were among the killed and wounded. Mummified cadavers–disinterred and propped up against the exterior walls–have been replanted. Their identities are contested: church officials claiming they were priests and nuns, church-burners saying they were victims of torture by priests and nuns. Though there are several unconfirmed reports of exhumed nuns being danced with in the streets, only one of the perpetrators–thought to be mentally ill–is identified and arrested on this charge.

From his political contacts, Andreu learns that at least two hundred alleged agitators, all Spanish citizens, are to be deported to undisclosed foreign shores; many hundreds–more than can be counted as they're incarcerated–are under arrest for a variety of offenses; and an estimated two thousand more have fled across the border to France to avoid arrest.

Sixty-seven religious buildings are still smoldering when Andreu returns to Barcelona, most of them burned by the anarchists. Fourteen churches have been partially or completely destroyed, along with twenty-seven schools of various religious orders, three parish schools, six cloistered convents, nine convents of religious orders dedicated to charitable causes, six residences of religious orders, and two centers offering services to workers and their families. From his villa in Sant Gervasi, Andreu can see thin ribbons of smoke still rising from the ashes. A dreadful sight. Heart wrenching, and to a disciplined man like Andreu, shamefully unnecessary.

There's also an onerous political price to be paid. The national government of Antoni Maura, a Catalan whose conservative party has been in power just two years, is under pressure to resign. This could split the party in two. Maura's response is to veer more sharply to the right, leading a faction that appeals to the most violent, youthful extremists.

Taking the analytical approach in which he excels, Andreu concludes that the alta burguesia–clinging to its conservative version of Catalanisme–cannot fathom how an ordinary general strike could lead to such chaos and violence. Consequently, it sides with those who want to eliminate anyone labeled "revolutionary." This threatens the Catalan alliance of left and right, which has been pressuring the central government in Madrid to grant more autonomy to Catalunya. Francesc Cambó, a leader in the moderate group favoring Catalan autonomy within Spain, now faces a tough race for reelection to the parliament. He is caught in the middle, between extremes.

Anguished by the sound of citizens pitted against each other and the sight of burning churches and convents, Andreu's friend Joan Maragall writes some of his most inspired poetry. He reflects on the events and their implications for Catalunya, laying the responsibility for Setmana Tràgica on the alta burguesia. Maragall's most provocative lines–written after attending mass in a burned out church–are excised by the conservative publisher, Prat de la Riba, who allows only the poet's hopeful lines to survive:

> All of us who were present at the Sacrifice
> celebrated on that simple table before the damaged crucifix,

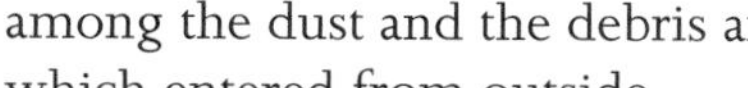

among the dust and the debris and the sun and the wind
which entered from outside,
were feeling still around us the trail
of destruction and blasphemy
which had so recently passed through that same air...
It filled us with a new, active virtue,
as only the first Christians could have experienced it, persecuted
and hiding in a corner of the catacombs,
delighting above all in the beginnings
of the mystery of redemption.

And Maragall seizes Gaudí's gigantic temple, Sagrada Familia, as a symbol of rebirth–recalling that while smoke from nearby convents and churches swirled past its spires, and ash rained on Antoni Gaudí as he prayed in the open that which would someday be the main nave of his most ambitious work, Sagrada Familia was spared by the anarchists.

But in the cultural life of Barcelona, the mood is changing. Faith in the Catalan "belle époque" has been undermined. After two decades of blossoming, the cultural garden of Catalunya seems to be withering. Setmana Tràgica has provoked a wave of soul-searching and criticism of "bohemianism," and the post-Romantic illusion that Catalunya could somehow remain a solitary oasis of industrial and artistic progress in a troubled Spain still staggering from the losses of 1898. A common refrain among the alta burguesia is that Setmana Tràgica was God's punishment for the excesses of modernism and secularism–twin catalysts in the resurgent cultural life in a city that looks to Paris rather than Madrid for inspiration. Andreu hears the refrain, and sullenly disagrees, unwilling to bear the brunt of the industrialists' ire.

Finally, there's widespread pressure to make someone pay for the bloodshed and widespread disruption. The man chosen to be scapegoat is a fifty-five-year-old anarcho-unionist, educator, and publisher named Francesc Ferrer i Guàrdia. Though Ferrer openly has espoused a revolutionary overthrow of the monarchy, led by radical republicans, he was not even in town until the eve of Setmana Tràgica, and there's no evidence that he was its prime instigator. In fact, the spontaneous and chaotic nature of the week's events suggests there was no prime instigator. But the guàrdies have waited three years to avenge Ferrer's alleged involvement in an attempt by Mateu Morral–who once worked for Ferrer's small publishing firm–to assassinate King Alfonso XIII on his wedding day in Madrid. (Morral, whose bomb missed its target but killed twenty-four bystanders, was arrested, then managed to escape and commited suicide in order to avoid capture. Ferrer, after several months of detention, was released for lack of evidence.)

But Ferrer's most telling liability is his success in establishing lay public schools in centers created by Lerroux's republicans. This is viewed by the church and the alta burguesia as heresy, as is his association with Lerroux and other anarchist and unionist leaders. He's arrested a month after Setmana Tràgica as he leaves his home in Alella, reportedly bound for the French border. After a perfunctory trial, in which no evidence is presented against him, Ferrer is executed by a firing squad in the courtyard of the prison on Montjuic, while troops of white-capped cavalry are deployed on the roads outside to keep any protesters at bay. To Andreu, this is an act of vengeance unsupported by evidence.

Ferrer is the scapegoat, but not the only one to pay. Four others are shot, while thirteen of those condemned to death are spared and sentenced to long terms in prison. In fact, the first to go to the wall is Josep Miquel i Baró, leader in the area of Sant Andreu del Palomar—who identified and freed Granados after his detention by the anarchists at the burning church of Sant Pere. Ferrer and three others follow Miquel to the courtyard of the Montjuic prison: Ramón Clemente i Garcia, who danced with a mummified nun—executed not for his choreography, but for erecting barriers in the streets, though what differentiates Clemente from hundreds of other men and boys who committed the same offense are the first-hand accounts of his danse macabre; the other two are Antoni Malet i Pujol, accused of setting fire to the church of Sant Adrià de Besòs, and Eugenio del Hoyo, a member of the security guard who fired on the Spanish Army troops sent by Maura's government to quell the uprising.

Followers of the anarchist Alejandro Lerroux—"the Young Barbarians"—are regarded as most responsible for turning an ordinary general strike into areawide and armed chaos, yet Lerroux has not been arrested. It's rumored that the authorities in Madrid believe his extremist views are thought more harmful to the cause of Catalan autonomy if he's left on the streets than if martyred by a firing squad.

Spring, 1910

Granados passes through the Plaça de Sant Pere, glancing over at the burned church. Every window is fire-scorched and the main doorway boarded up. Soon after the torching of the church, Granados received a note from Father Trias, thanking him for "standing with me on that tragic day, and caring for my safety." The young priest was spared by the mob, though he had to suffer their taunts until they dispersed at nightfall.

Memories of Setmana Tràgica still haunt Granados. Though he could have taken a different route today, he chooses to pass by Sant Pere. Curiosity draws him back, and a certain bewitchment with the events of that day: the fateful choices, the ironies, the improbability of falling into the hands of an anarchist leader who came from Lleida, his home town. Granados survived and his captor, Josep Miquel–to whom he had to prove his identity–was executed. On that day, he was a stranger to the guàrdies and a stranger to the anarchists, in a city that takes his music for granted. Surely Mozart didn't have this problem in Salzburg.

Setmana Tràgica represents more than a shock to Granados' sensibilities. Along with the loss of Albéniz two months earlier, it has rekindled a sense of mortality and an anxiety to leave a more lasting legacy, as his friend did with *Iberia*. But how can he realize this aspiration to create a masterpiece based on the art of Goya? How and where and when?

Granados stands at the intersection of Carrrer Girona and Carrer Ausiàs Marc, looking up at an imposing, five-story building in the early modernist style. Girona, number 20. Designed by Enric Sagnier i Villavecchia, and built between 1888 and 1890 for the family of Roger Vidal. Sagnier, though not as well known as Gaudí, Domènech, and Puig, has become the architect preferred by the wealthiest of the alta burguesia. Next month, Granados' will move his family and the academy to this new home.

Girona, 20. Granados first heard about it from Dr. August Pi i Sunyer, after last month's directors meeting at the academy. Pi, who moved with his family to a flat on the fourth floor of the building three years ago, learned that the owner was planning to move out and rent the "principal," or owner's residence. "The academy needs more space," Pi said, "and this is large enough for your family and the academy–even as it grows."

Before touring Girona, 20, Granados talked to Andreu, interrupting him while he was playing his organlike harmonium in the music salon at the Sant Gervasi villa. "It's eight hundred square meters," he told his patrón, "there's additional space on the street level, and in between the ground floor and the principal. We could expand the academy for some time to come."

Andreu nodded; a sympathetic gesture. "Well, it seems reasonable. But more expensive. Indeed you do have a growing number of students–if you're collecting from them."

"Salvador, I *am* collecting from them. Believe me, there's no more charity!"

"All right," said Andreu, returning to the harmonium, "you have my backing. Now show me how to play this Saint-Saens!"

Granados is familiar with this neighborhood, has walked every street of it. Up and down Carrer Casp and Ausiàs Marc. Most of the buildings are of early modernist style, most designed by Gaudí and Domènech. Multicolored stone construction, with flowers and vines carved in stone, across balconies that undulate beneath curved, asymmetrical windows. Iron grille balconies on the higher floors, curving faux columns, and cylindrical galleries projected out over the sidewalk. Rolling rooflines topped with statuary, baubles, and abstract gargoyles. And just as there seems to be a pattern, the next block offers yet more surprises: faux columns in the shape of trees, appearing to support a five-story edifice. And across the street from Girona, 20, the Laboratorio Nordbeck, with a façade of carved mahogany, stained glass, and a wrought-iron sign: "Farmàcia." How convenient for someone who frequents pharmacies. What a splendid neighborhood for his family and his academy.

Granados admires the carved stone balconies and iron grille-covered windows of the façade, which is set diagonally to face the intersection. And he's enthralled by the space behind the façade. In the majestic atrium with three-story columns of modernist Corinthian, light streams down from skylights five stories above. A cantilevered marble staircase, with iron balustrade of flower and tendril designs, provides exclusive use by the family living in the principal residence. At the top of the stairs is a pair of tall gleaming mahogany doors with carvings of flowers. To the left of the doors, and in contrast with the curves, is a tall stained-glass window–emerald green, amber, and clear–composed entirely of straight lines that form triangles, quadrangles, and trapezoids. Above the window is a brass lamp, also with modernist curves.

The residence area is stunning. A reception hall, inside the imposing doors and stained-glass window. A ceiling six meters high, composed of panels in which crème maple leafs are affixed to a salmon background. All around the room, a pale green frieze with sculpted arrows and leaves and blossoms. A reception hall in which one could receive royalty.

Granados marvels at the large music salon, with windows looking out over Carrer Girona. An enormous room, combining the pastels of peach and light green, with a frescoed ceiling and gilded trim along the upper corners of the imperial space. Enough space for recitals, with players at one end facing an audience of perhaps as many as fifty or sixty. And from wall to wall, an elaborate decorative tile floor, composed of tiny pieces of hand-placed squares, set in patterns of red and mauve and gold, with a dark brown border along the edge of the floor. Behind the salon, a large space that could handily accommodate two pianos or formal dining for up to two dozen guests, embellished by a fireplace at the far end, a ceiling of carved mahogany, and frescoes of palms and pear trees in blossom against a pale blue background.

At the end of the east-facing side of the residence, a corner study, with windows on two sides and a balcony offering a view of the intersection through the leaves of silver maple trees. The study is enriched by a burnished gold tone on the walls and ceiling, with voluptuous circles and sweeping half-circles, and gilded trim along the upper cornice. A study that could please an emperor, or at least his kapellmeister.

Girona, 20, is a place that is affordable only with patronage from Andreu. Despite this, and chronic frustration over the lack of fulfillment and recognition as a composer, it's a place that allows Granados to feel he's finally arrived.

May, 1910

Domènech Mas and Frank Marshall are waiting just inside the main entrance of the academy. With the school year ending, final exams must be scheduled and decisions made on which of the students will receive awards, prizes, and promotions to the next level. "And also," Granados says, "we need to send notes home with the students who haven't paid tuition." Mas and Marshall nod in unison, both surprised that the director is showing concern about a matter that is rarely discussed.

Granados asks how certain students are progressing. "La Nena" Madriguera? Mercè Moner, Juli Pons, and Clotilde Godó?

"La Nena is wonderful," says Marshall. "She's learning Schumann's *Tema con Variaciones*. She insists she's ready–today–to play at the Palau. 'Go slow,' I told her, 'you'll get there.' And she gave me a look that was like a bolt of lightning. 'Yes, can we make it tomorrow?' she asked. Tomorrow!"

All three men laugh. "Well, before long," replies Granados, "she will indeed be ready."

"She has a childlike belief that anything is possible," says Mas.

Granados stares at him. "Well, isn't it?"

"Of course, mestre."

"And the others?" asks Granados.

Moner and Pons are doing exceptionally well. And Godó is making good progress.

"Just good?" Granados asks.

Marshall answers. "As you know, Senyoreta Godó works very hard, as hard as any of our students. But she's not at the top level. Which reminds me, she has a lesson with you today. And Llongueras is back–wants to see you. I said he could see you at noon." He points to his watch.

Joan Llongueras is a thirty-year-old pianist, composer, poet, and music critic. He's intrigued by a method pioneered by the Swiss music educator, Emile Jaques-Dalcroze, based on coordinating music with body movements–and intended to give students a more immediate experience of music than traditional methods. Llongueras has just returned from studying with Dalcroze in Geneva.

"Please sit down," Granados says to the thin, excited Llongueras, whose arms are whirling as he paces in front of the piano. "Or my neck will stiffen just trying to follow you around!"

Llongueras stops. His angular face with high forehead and acquiline nose are frozen in a grin. "You see how excited I am? You understand? Why, just watching what they're doing with Dalcroze, the dancing and chanting, the improvised music, it's amazing to watch students become so involved that they forget they don't know anything about music! It's not possible to describe it in words, but I swear, maestro, I swear it's the most exciting discovery I've ever made!" He loses his balance when he stops pacing.

"Yes. Sounds very intriguing. What will you do with this discovery?"

Llongueras raises his hand. "Ah, I thought of that all the way back from Geneva. You see, I want to introduce it here–at the academy! And also to my friends at l'Orfeó. I believe it will sweep the country! But if I started here, with you, that would make it seem less revolutionary."

Granados laughs. "Or make people think we're both crazy."

Undeterred, Llongueras asks the obvious question. "If you're willing to help me introduce it, whom would you choose for the first students?"

Granados shrugs. "That's easy. We'll start with my own children. Eduardo first, then the others. Why not? When do you want to start?"

"You mean, try it out with your children? To see if it works?"

"I don't mean that at all, Joanito. We'll start with my children next week. And when classes start again here in September, we'll offer it to everyone. Isn't that what you want to do?"

Llongueras face reflects his amazement. He expected a barrage of questions, a siege of skepticism, a host of conditions.

Clotilde Godó is early for her lesson, entering his office with a resplendent smile. "I have a surprise for you, maestro," she says.

"You've memorized the Beethoven?"

"Yes. But that's not it." She adjusts her pile of wavy dark hair, held up with a pair of pearl-inlaid combs. She teases him with a glance from the corners of her eyes.

He feigns contemplation. "Mmmm. You're getting married again?"

Her laugh is playfully scornful. "I'd expect that from other men, but not from you!"

He shrugs. "I give up. I'm just too stupid."

She shakes her head. "There may be some who'd believe that–not I. All right, you tried your best. Come outside–I'll show you my surprise."

She leads him to a shiny black-and-tan motor car parked on Carrer Girona.

"This is your father's?" Granados asks.

She laughs again without modesty. "No. It's mine. It's the Hispano Suissa."

"And you know how to drive it?" he asks.

Clotilde reaches into her black beaded handbag and retrieves a folded document. "My license, maestro. It's the first ever issued to a woman in Barcelona. Would you like to see how well I drive?"

He hesitates. "How did you learn?"

"I have brothers and they are my slaves."

"Like Circe."

"Yes."

"Does your magic protect your passengers?" he asks.

"So far I haven't had to use any magic. We'll see, won't we?"

"You'll be missing your lesson." It's his last diversion.

"That's right. And I'll work extra hard to make it up. Now, that's settled. There's just one thing I need help with. See that little handle–in front?"

He crouches down, having watched the Andreus start their motor cars.

"Yes–down below," she says. "When I give the signal, just crank it a few times and the motor will start. Are you willing?"

They start the car, and Granados climbs into the seat next to Clotilde. "This certainly is a surprise," he says as the motor car leaps forward.

She drives them up Carrer Girona to Diagonal, where she turns left toward the town of Sarrià. After weaving through a mélange of tramvias, horse-drawn carts and carriages, motor cars, and bicycles at the intersection of Passeig de Gràcia, they pass the construction that will extend Carrer Balmes north of Diagonal–a project conceived and promoted by Andreu to develop his land in Sant Gervasi and Tibidabo. Beyond Balmes, Diagonal becomes a country highway, surrounded by long rows of trees that separate the large agricultural estates of Sarrià.

"Are you frightened?" cries Clotilde.

"What?" The sound of the motor and rush of wind are deafening.

"Are…you…frightened?"

"Of…course…not!"

She makes a sharp turn in the form of a letter "U" and heads back on Diagonal. Then–instead of retracing their route–she swings the motor car down to the right toward the Plaça d'Espanya, where Gran Via and Avinguda Parallel meet in a six-pointed star radiating out from a circle. Tramvias arrive, are turned around here, and head back in the opposite direction. There's also a generous amount of foot traffic, which–in combination with the ingress and egress of vehicles and beasts of varying sizes, rates of speed and means of locomotion–makes threading through the plaça a formidable task. Clotilde navigates her motor car, with Granados holding on firmly, briskly through the melee without hesitation.

"Wasn't…that…fun?"

"Yes! Yes! Can't you…go faster?"

Back at the academy, he invites Clotilde to stay past her lesson hour. "I have a surprise for *you!*" he says, placing a composition pad on the piano.

"You've learned the Beethoven?"

His laughter fills the large room. "You're making fun of me."

"Yes." She points to the composition pad. "Is that *Azulejos?*"

He is off balance. "I told you about it?"

She smiles. "Yes, maestro, you said that Señora de Albéniz gave it to you after her husband died. Said you were guarding it with your life. Hoping to finish it soon."

"That's right. And I'm nearly finished. The difficulty is preserving the style of the first sixty measures–where he stopped." He feels tears forming in his eyes at the memory of their last visit. One year ago today.

"A wonderful friend, wasn't he?" Clotilde asks.

He looks at her soft empathetic eyes and nods. And nods again. After a few moments he explains: "He finished sixty measures, and I have to add at least that many. I want most of all for this to remain his work. Would you like to hear what I have?"

As she listens to it for the first time, remembering Granados and Albéniz together in Tiana and sensing the great love between these men–like brothers but more intimate with each other than her own brothers–Clotilde begins to tremble. The piece is evocative of Albéniz' *Iberia*, which she heard Malats play at Teatre Principal. It begins so gently, the treble notes falling like water in a mountain brook. Now, reprising the theme, it's like sunlight reflected by the colored tiles, the azulejos. Like walking the streets of Andalucía looking into sunlit entryways and seeing tiles from floor to ceiling, as far back as the eye can follow. Now the theme is repeated in the middle of the keyboard, with the shadow of melancholy and an ominous hint of beauty that can never be heard. And finally, seeking resolution, a more hopeful and ascending sonority.

Granados stops. "That's as far as I've gone. Last night I sat for hours, just improvising. I went to a distant place and when I finally stopped I was no longer playing his music."

"You haven't decided how to end it?" asks Clotilde.

He ponders this. "How to end it? Oh, I know how it ends. But getting there–much more difficult!"

"It's extravagantly beautiful," she says. "But surely you know that."

"Yes. You could play this, Clotilde."

"No, not after hearing you."

"Nonsense. When I've finished, I'd like Malats to premiere it, but I'd also like you to learn it. I insist, you could play this."

She shakes her head and changes the subject. "What else have you been working on, maestro?"

He chuckles, admiring her poise. "Well, there are quite a few new ones. I thought–after Setmana Tràgica–I'd be paralyzed, I'd just want to hide in a dark room. Instead, that horrible experience reminded me to make the best use of my time. While it lasts. So I've completed one called *Valse de concert* for solo piano. I'm finishing *Cant de les estrelles* for piano, organ, and chorus–it's a Catalan translation of a poem by Heine. Another one, *Elisenda*–is based on a poem by Mestres–for piano, voice, harp, string quintet, flute, oboe and clarinet. There's a lot of scoring for all the parts. And the last–I hope–of the lyric dramas, *Liliana*, from another poem by Mestres. Let's see, then there's *L'ocell profeta*–a *lied* for voice and piano, from a text written by the Contessa del Castellà. Also *Seis estudios expresivos*–one part based on a Mestres poem. And Sonata for violin and piano, which I'm dedicating to Thibaud. I think that's all."

Still leaping from one to another. Like crossing mountain streams on paths of slippery rocks.

"What about *Dante?*" Clotilde asks.

Granados sighs. "Ah, there's always *Dante*! Always a hope and a promise and never quite finished. Just one private performance–the first two parts, but too little time to rehearse. I set it aside for a bit, then revised it last winter for a premiere at the Palau–that went much better. I've done some work on the third part and there's a fourth to follow. It's time to finish it–I'm not being fair to Francesca and Paolo, am I?"

Clotilde shakes her head. "It's not a matter of being fair to Paolo and Francesca–what a sad story! How she loved him yet she was married to his brother. After being deceived. She only consented to marry believing that Paolo would be her husband. Such a sad, sad story!"

He's surprised. "You know it?"

Clotilde holds up both hands and recites from the mezzo soprano part, Francesca's lament in Canto V of *La Divina Commedia*:

> Time and again our eyes were brought together
> by the book we read; our faces flushed and paled.
> To the moment of one line alone we yielded:
> it was when we read about those longed-for lips
> now being kissed by such a famous lover,
> that this one (who shall never leave my side)
> then kissed my mouth, and trembled as he did.
> Our Galahad was that book and he who wrote it.
> That day we read no further.

Clotilde adds: "The Pilgrim is so overcome with pity for the lovers he 'swoons as though to die.'"

Granados claps his hands. "You've heard the music?"

"Both performances."

"Then you understand what I'm trying to do."

"Yes, you're taking colors from Rossetti's painting," Clotilde says.

"Exactly! Trying to paint with the orchestra. It's so difficult to describe."

"That may be, but I'm sure what's really difficult–what I can't begin to imagine, is transforming painting into music."

"Yes! And that's what I'm trying to do with the work of Goya–I won't even try to describe that." Granados points to his chest. "It's been here inside me for twelve years, ever since I went see his work at the Prado. Always inside me–whether I wanted it there or not, whether I liked it or not. I'm sure it will give me no peace until I release it."

"Perhaps you need to get out of its way and let it come out," she says.

Out of the way? Sounds easy. She means–what?

"When? And where?" he asks. "And how do you think I'd be able to do that? Get out of its way?" His voice drips with frustration.

She responds calmly: "When? This summer–why wait? Where? A suggestion–if you'll pardon my boldness: my home in Tiana, and you have been there. I have a Pleyel, as you know. How? I'll leave that to you. You're the composer."

Granados shakes his head. "Thank you, but it's not possible. There are several problems. You're my deixebla. I'm a married man. And much older."

She laughs and shakes her head. "Ah, Maestro Granados!"

"You find me amusing?"

"Yes. Absolutely! Perhaps you have me confused with some other deixebla. Younger than I." She laughs again. "Furthermore, I'm not inviting you to my bedroom. I'm just trying to be helpful, and if you're looking for a place to work on your Goya, Tiana might be ideal."

"Well, I have plenty of places. The academy will be closed 'til September. I'll spend most of the summer with the Andreus in Puigcerdà. There's no shortage of places."

She cocks her head and pushes forward. "I'm sure that's true, maestro. But didn't you just tell me you've had Goya inside you for twelve years? Twelve years, and Goya's still inside you–trying to get out."

"You're suggesting I come to Tiana so Goya can get out?"

She laughs again, softly. "Yes. I live alone except for the staff. There are no children. No interruptions. There's a Pleyel that was built for concerts, simply aching to be played by a virtuoso. You could use me to help you–only as you wish. I'd do anything helpful. And you can get to Tiana in about half an hour."

"But it would compromise you," Granados argues. "Tiana's a small village."

Cotilde shakes her head. "Compromise *me*? I'm already the eccentric woman who lives alone in the big villa and invites her bohemian musician friends to come up and play for her. After all, I don't fancy you and I dancing naked in the garden!"

His mood lightens. "Half an hour by train to Montgat?"

"Yes. And I can pick you up there."

He smiles at last. "In your Hispano?"

"Yes."

"Poor old Goya."

"Say again?" Clotilde asks.

"Poor old Goya. If we come up that winding round in your little motor car, he'll take flight of me."

"Well, he's been down there quite a while," Clotilde says. "I thought you wanted to get him out."

Francisco de Goya y Lucientes, rivaled only by Diego Velásquez among the greatest Spanish painters, has been crouching in Granados' mind ever since that first visit to El Prado museum in 1898. Granados remains most intrigued by the *Caprichos* sketches, which depict the glamour, indolence, arrogance, and daring of the majas and their men, the majos, in the streets of Madrid. He's fascinated by the supposed romance between Goya and La Duquesa de Alba, and by speculation that she was the model for his Maja portraits. And he's titillated by the notion that this wealthy and powerful aristocrat disrobed and posed for Goya, letting him drape her in a shawl—even more provocative than baring her flesh.

In the summer of 1796, Goya traveled by coach across mountains, plains, and rivers from his home in Madrid to Sanlúcar de Barrameda. He was invited to Sanlúcar by La Duquesa, whose large country house—one of seventeen residences—was in the middle of a nature preserve at the mouth of the river Guadalquivir, not far from where Crìstofol Colom left the safety of the Iberian peninsula and headed across the Atlantic to find India. Sanlúcar, in southwestern Spain, is noted for its sherry wine, redolent of the salty air, and its proximity to the large estancias where most of Spain's fighting bulls are raised. It's as distant from Madrid as any place in the country, so Goya's was not a casual journey.

María del Pilar Teresa Cayetana de Silva y Álvarez de Toledo, 13th Duquesa de Alba, had recently buried her husband. Thirty-three and childless, she invited Goya to stay with her during the obligatory period of mourning. María Teresa, as she preferred to be known by friends and lovers, was a stunning woman, wealthier than the Bourbon kings, graceful and intimidating, with curly raven hair tumbling to the small of her back, dark extravagant eyes, a waist that might be encircled by a man's hands, the exquisite oval face of a porcelain doll, intelligence, wit, passion, and spontaneity. La Duquesa often dressed in the costume of the majas–a peasant dress with a tight waist, trim open jacket, and towering black mantilla. A Gypsy style, which appealed to those aristocratic women who dared to assail social conventions. Surrounded by a retinue of younger men, who swarmed like bees in search of nectar, La Duquesa would flaunt her maja wardrobe at the opera and chamber music concerts.

As official painter of the Spanish royalty, Goya had done a portrait of both La Duquesa and her late husband the previous year. And upon entering her free-spirited life, even before the demise of her husband, Goya became one of her favorites. After La Duquesa's first sitting for the portrait, Goya confided to a friend that she asked him to paint her face, so he accommodated her and she left his studio with it painted. "Better than a painting on canvas," said Goya. This anecdote, and Goya's sketch of La Duquesa's dying husband–attended by a pair of donkeys in doctor's gowns, with a tiny figure of La Duquesa sitting on the edge of his bed–suggest to Granados a relationship more personal than between artist and his subject.

Goya was fifty years old, and deaf following a near-fatal illness five years earlier, when La Duquesa invited him to Sanlúcar. There he joined the collection of outcasts upon whom she would shower love and devotion. For Goya, it was a welcome respite from the political crossfire at the court in Madrid, the languor of his marriage to Josefa Bayeu, and the daily stress of coping with a raucous urban scene which for Goya was now soundless. He stayed for several months with La Duquesa. After his return to Madrid, she began an affair with the torero Pedro Romero, followed by a series of liaisons with a wide variety of men, including Manuel de Godoy, Prime Minister of Spain.

During his stay in Sanlúcar, Goya filled a notebook, *l'Álbum de Sanlúcar*, with pen and ink drawings that depicted the daily life of La Duquesa and her household: her royalty leaning out of a window, breasts falling from a loose undergarment; pulling up a stocking on one of her parted legs; lying unclothed under a single bed sheet with her knees raised; lifting her skirts to display a bare bottom; sitting naked on the edge of her bathtub; swinging her legs out of bed; and having her long hair combed by the servant girl, Catalina. These drawings suggest to Granados that she and Goya were lovers, or at least that she allowed him to be with her and see her in the most unguarded of poses.

After Sanlúcar, when Goya had been replaced by the torero and other men, his depictions of La Duquesa were less idyllic, often filled with bitterness and rage. In the next two years, Goya created the *Caprichos* series–some from the drawings he'd made in Sanlúcar, sharpened by his growing disenchantment with the cruelties and idiosyncrasies of the Spanish nobility. Cynical and biting, they also represent Goya's critiques of the falseness and pretense of the entire human family. Rich men who sacrificed young women, as well as church leaders, politicians, and La Duquesa. In one of them, Goya is groveling in front of her, with the caption: "Which of them is more overcome?" In another, being carried off on the backs of three men, one of them resembling Pedro Romero. In a third sketch, as a double-headed creature with one face toward Goya and the other staring up at the sky.

Upon her return from Sanlúcar, La Duquesa dictated her last will and testament, leaving everything to people who were unrelated to her by blood or class–her beloved outcasts and servants. And she included the only surviving child of Goya, his son, Javier. She and Goya remained friends, and he was reportedly present at the dinner party in her Palacio de Buenavista the evening of July 23, 1802, after which she became seriously ill. She died the following day, before reaching her fortieth birthday. Other attendees that evening were Prime Minister Godoy and his estranged wife, as well as aristocrats who were close to both Queen María Luisa and her son, Prínce Fernando–who at the time was busily plotting to seize the throne and collaborate with Napoleon to deliver Spain to the French empire.

With the presence that evening of so many people who might benefit from the death of La Duquesa, it was rumored she'd been poisoned by one of them. Within days, Queen María Luisa was wearing La Duquesa's pearls and diamonds, and Godoy was given the use of her palace. He confiscated her collection of paintings, including the formal portrait Goya had painted.

Granados mourns her as if she'd been his own friend and lover. He's outraged by what he considers blasphemy by Prince Fernando, Queen María Luisa, and Godoy. He's impressed that Goya portrayed women with much complexity, and in many different situations–not just as ornaments. He concludes that Goya reveled in the company of women, respecting them more than most men of that time, that Goya enjoyed women of substance in his life–who were friends and confidants, not only his lovers. Granados sees parallels with his own life, and his friendships with Carmen Miralles, Lluisa Vidal, and the feminist leader Carme Karr.

Granados keeps circling back to the *Caprichos*, and Goya's satirical targets: marriage among the privileged class, contrived marriage in which the bride and groom were pawns in a game of chess; victimized young women married off to unattractive older rich men; betrayal by lovers; lives full of pretense; failure to judge the real value of people; and using charm to deceive. In one of the sketches, Goya satirized the Queen and her lover, Godoy. In another he showed La Duquesa, with butterfly wings atop her head, being transported by three men–a metaphor for Goya's discovery that she was addicted to "a powder from the Andes," which put butterflies in her head but warded off demons.

Granados appreciates Goya's cutting blade of satire, and sees an obvious comparison with life among Barcelona's alta burguesia. But how to infuse his music with a Goya-esque satirical edge?

In a letter to Malats, Granados is effervescent. "I fell in love with Goya's psychology, and with his palette. With him and with La Duquesa de Alba; with his lady Maja, with his models, with his quarrels, his loves, and his flirtations. The white rose of their cheeks, the flaxen lace against the black velvet, the bending bodies of dancing creatures, hands of mother-of-pearl and of jasmine resting on jet-black trinkets–oh, how they've overpowered me!"

Granados also admires Goya for remaining an observer of the sanguinary struggle for power over Spain, and for unceasing adherence to his art. Goya hunted with the aristocrats, sat in their tertulias, dined at their tables, drank their wines and spirits, slept with some of their women, and watched them plot against each other. As a keen observer in these lofty circles, he took what he'd seen and converted it to the art of oils and ink. Never belonging to the circles. Yet Goya, who resisted taking sides, was caught in the midst of violence–as Granados was in Setmana Tràgica. Close to the vortex but not involved, not overcome. Though Goya is eulogized as a Spanish patriot for his paintings of the horrors of the war, Granados sees that the painter never lost his perspective. Violence by both sides is portrayed as disaster.

As Granados returns to the challenge of converting Goya's oils on canvas and ink on paper to piano music, the spirit of the painter roams again in his homeland. A wave of rediscovery sweeps across the Iberian peninsula, just as the idea of Goya-esque music stirs again within Granados. Not only is Goya's body repatriated from Bordeaux to Madrid, his outrage during the war against Napoleon is now molded into an oddly prideful patriotism in the wake of the disastrous war of 1898. There's renewed admiration for Goya's portraits of women; he's even described as a forerunner of the French Impressionists, who aren't especially thrilled to be indebted to a Spaniard. Miquel Utrillo calls him "the father of the new painting." Blasco Ibáñez writes a novel titled *La Maja Desnuda*, about an artist influenced by Goya's painting and his attitude toward the world around him; the painter is described as savoring "the delights of her naked body, fragilely beautiful, luminous, as if the flame of life were burning inside it, and shining through the pearly flesh." Francisco Villaespesa's drama in verse *La Maja de Goya* is published and performed in Madrid. Blanca de los Ríos eulogizes Goya in her novel, *Madrid Goyesco*, crediting him with "anticipating the snapshot and impressionism" and declaring that Goya painted "what no one had painted before: movement." And Rubén Darío includes the poem "To Goya," in his new volume of poetry–a quasireligious, fervent song of praise. Goya is ubiquitous as painter of his people, lover of women, and chronicler of the disasters of war.

As he's pulled into this mélange of memories and rediscoveries, Granados identifies more and more with Goya: the artist sitting on the edge of the inner circle, just as Granados sits on the edge of Barcelona's alta burguesia. Goya as a satellite of La Duquesa and the royal family; Granados of the Andreu family. Some of Goya's finest work was inspired or provoked by La Duquesa–the sketches he made at Sanlúcar, many later emerging in the *Caprichos*, and in the voluptuous lines of the Majas. She was a muse of Goya, light and dark. While in Granados' life, there's been no muse to inspire and provoke him.

June, 1910

It's late spring, awaiting the official arrival of summer. There are constant reminders: climbing vines beginning to flower up and down the streets of l'Eixample, newborn birds embarking on longer treks away from their nests, the breeze coming straight across the Mediterranean from North Africa, and the pace of life slowing as families who can afford to depart for vacations along the coast and up in the mountains.

Acadèmia Granados is closed for the summer, though some students continue weekly lessons in their homes. Only six of Granados' students are scheduled during the summer, one of them Clotilde Godó. He's told them he'll be going to Puigcerdà for six weeks, that their lessons will resume in late August. The students are grateful for a summer break–except for Clotilde, who's asked him to give her six weeks of assignments in advance before he leaves.

Ah, Puigcerdà! In two days he'll be there, sitting in the garden with Andreu, looking across the pond at the last sunlight of afternoon on the jagged peaks of the Pyrenees, watching couples and families strolling on the boardwalk, waiting for the sky to fill with stars. Puigcerdà, with Carmen and her children–who've touched him and made him their unofficial uncle, not to replace Francisco Miralles but to remind them of him, an uncle to witness their lives as they move on through this new century. From the same flesh and blood, but so different: Paquita Andreu, one of his protégées, who treats him with a mixture of reverence and coquetry; Madronita, forging ahead on her own path, with passion for photography and filmmaking; Carmen, seemingly headed along the more traditional path of her mother and namesake; Salvador the son and Pepe–who at nineteen asks to be called by his adult name, José–both following their father's path in the profession of pharmacy; and Juanito, still called "el niño," whose ambition at fifteen seems to be driving a sporty motor car and offering rides at breakneck speeds to the young ladies who flock to him at social gatherings.

Puigcerdà! Another wonderful summer, organizing the Andreu family orchestra with the usual combination of volunteers who materialize to play their chosen instruments. The annual squabble in which they beg to play his own chamber music at the Festival of the Pond. "Please, Maestro Granados! Please, Enric!" they will implore once again, and the answer will be the same: "No."

Today is the last lesson for Clotilde Godó before Granados leaves town. Tomorrow he'll catch the train for Ripoll, and after a night there he'll climb into the Andreu's Rochet-Schneider and be driven up the winding, bumpy mountain roads to the valley of Puigcerdà.

"I guess this is 'good-bye' for a while," Clotilde says. She tosses a dark curl from her forehead and fixes her eyes on his, at an oblique angle.

He looks at her, seeing sunlight set half her face aglow in the mid-afternoon. "Yes, I guess it is," he says. "Until I return, I wish you a very delightful summer."

She laughs. "Hmm. Summer. It's all the same. Summer, autumn, winter, and spring. Song of autumn–in springtime. That's by Darío."

"Is that so?"

"Remember it?

> Youth, treasure only gods may keep,
> Fleeting from me forever now!
> I cannot, when I wish to, weep,
> And often cry I know not how…

"And here's the ending, maestro…"

> I sought for the prince in vain,
> He that awaited sorrowing.
> But life is hard. Bitter with pain.
> There is no prince now to sing!
>
> And yet despite the season drear,
> My thirst of love no slaking knows;
> Gray-haired am I, yet still draw near
> The roses of the garden close…

"You changed 'princess' to 'prince,'" Granados notes.

"Of course I did. Wouldn't you?"

"I wouldn't need to." He laughs softly at his quip. "Well, Clotilde, I'll see you again in August," he says, rising from his chair.

"Yes. I suppose your work can wait."

"My work? What work? Would you care to explain?"

She shrugs. "Nothing to explain. I said, 'your work can wait.' When you decide to do the work from Goya, my offer remains."

Her offer! How foolish not to remember! How thoughtless!

The following morning, Granados sends a telegram to Salvador and Carmen, saying he won't be able to come to Puigcerdà until later in the summer.

Tiana

Granados has decided to go to Tiana without a ready explanation for Amparo. On the eve of his first day there, he tells Amparo that Andreu invited him to use the music salon at the Sant Gervasi villa, a "quiet place" to work on the Goya-esque composition. He says the invitation came from Salvador, with no mention of Carmen.

Amparo asks, "Why not work right here in the salon?"

He says there's too much noise with their houseful of children.

She insists she can keep them from interrupting. "I know this Goya work's very important to you."

He says he needs to be away from the place of his daily routine. After all, he's trying to go back one hundred years, all the way back to the time of Goya. Madrid in the early 1800s, not today's bustling l'Eixample. Says he needs a place far removed from the rest of his life.

"But Sant Gervasi is not far removed from your daily routine, it's where you go every evening," she replies.

Amparo wants to say more, to tell him once again how painful it is to wait for him every evening, and–after putting the children to bed–to wait alone until finally she hears the sound of the Andreu's chauffeur bringing him home from Sant Gervasi and the slow cadence of his steps as he climbs the stairway. She knows he's become like a satellite of the Andreus: he fits nicely into their enviable style of life, he's useful to them, he enriches their tertulia, whereas she does not. She's from the ordinary, industrious Catalan middle class, in which men are expected to take the initiative and women to hope for the best. And she wants to tell him the children don't even ask any more if he'll be home before their bedtime. Instead, she holds back.

"You see," Granados explains, when fewer words might be more persuasive, "the Andreus will be up at Puigcerdà for the summer. All summer. So I'll have their place to myself. All to myself."

Amparo recognizes the mannerism of deceit–the repetition, but she can't find words to rebut him. She knows this man, oh yes, she's known him since he came to València to play a recital, when she fell in love with him instantly. She's always known that this artist, this impractical bohemian would fill her life with romance and daring, known that he'd love her and frustrate her and perhaps often break her heart. That he'd spend more money than they had coming in. Ah, but he was so much more interesting than Ramón, the young man who'd been courting her for three years. Ordinary industrious Ramón, whose father owned a large store in the center of València and could have provided her a comfortable life. But her desire for comfort faded when the young pianist from Barcelona with the large eyes and refined manner came to town. Once he teased her heart and made it pound deep in her breast, the tenuous courtship with Ramón was over. Were it not for Granados, she'd have accepted earnest Ramón, lived with him and their children in València. A very predictable life. Now, eighteen years and six children later, she's weary, she's lost her shape and her hair is turning gray. She knows the time of lustful passion is over, and periodically wonders if Granados is involved again with another breathless, devoted deixebla, another whose narrow waist and high breasts and enraptured eyes have lured him into yet another escapade. Perhaps another María is out there now, waiting for him.

"I'll just be spending the days, just days," he says, "and coming home in the evenings. That's to say, most evenings, evenings I don't fall asleep at the piano."

Amparo has been hearing Granados talk about the music based on Goya for a dozen years, ever since his excited return from the visit to the Prado Museum. She's pleased to hear he's returning to it. She's become wary and skeptical from his expensive failures with the subscription series for orchestral and chamber music, and then the Catalan lyric theatre, then his difficulties getting *Follet* presented. She's watched him gain the outer edge of prominence and recognition–with the promise of financial rewards–and then lose his place on that edge, spiraling away. So she's eager to help him, not wanting to hold him back.

Amparo feels justified in punishing him for her heartbreaking discovery of his affair with María Oliveró, and won't ever consider reprieving him for that. She wishes there'd been a less onerous penalty than banishing the piece, the lovers' song, altogether. Astonished and strengthened by her own ferocity in confronting him, she's now able to control her fears and recognize that setting him free to work on the Goya music, letting him choose a place that he believes to be "far removed," offers her the best chance to help him. If he's being drawn into another immature dalliance, he'll end up paying the price for that too, but how can she prevent it? It's like telling her children not to play with fire and hearing them cry when their fingers are burned. She can't spare them the consequences. Especially Victor, very much his father's son.

Trying to release him, Amparo is amused by her own intensity. "It sounds like you've considered this carefully," she says. "Either that or you're becoming more skillful in deceiving me. If so, what can I do but hope you'll have more sense than your son Victor? If you must go to Sant Gervasi, Dios te guarde–God protect you." She pauses and smiles. "And who am I to know better?"

Granados is prepared for a longer discussion, if not an outright quarrel. "Yes. Well, I'm glad you agree."

"I know how important this is."

"Titín, I truly believe I'm on the brink of something magnificent."

She smiles again. "Then who am I to stand in your way?"

"It's very decent of you. Very understanding."

She takes his hand and squeezes. "I wish you well, mi amor. Go find your Goya."

Granados' train arrives in Montgat. The last time he stepped off at this seaside town, four years ago, he was going to Tiana to spend the weekend with Albéniz. To play in the benefit concert, during Tiana's late summer festival. That same weekend, Juan Godó invited him to the Casino and Clotilde took him to her home, to show Granados the Pleyel that he found for her in Paris. She seemed darker then, and less effervescent. She asked if he'd accept her back as his deixebla and he agreed. Standing by the Pleyel, she said her new home in Tiana afforded a safe distance from Barcelona and the inconsolable memories of life there. A place for healing, she said, a private place. A place of her own. And later, walking through the garden redolent of lavender and roses, she recited a poem by Darío.

"Maestro Granados!"

Clotilde's voice is bright and lyrical. He turns and sees her standing by her motor car with an air of indolence. Charmed by this, he walks across the driveway of the Montgat train station.

The sea breeze flattens a cotton dress against her thighs and waves loose wisps of her hair above her hatless head. Her face is tilted up as if to scrutinize him as he approaches. "Are you willing to take another chance with me?" she asks.

She's pointing to the passenger seat of her motor car. "Of course I'm willing," he says. "In fact, just imagining this ride with you made the hair stand up on my arms. Why else would I accept your invitation?"

She laughs as they converge with a stiff abraçada. "Well, you *aren't* too old and sanctimonious, are you? Come, and hold onto your hat!"

From the rail station, Clotilde wheels her motor car through Montgat, past bakeries, dry goods stores, meat and fish shops, small cafés, fruit and vegetable stands, and purveyors of wines and spirits. It clatters up narrow streets of paving stones, passing pedestrians who've had ample warning from the rising whine of the Hispano Suissa engine and have prudently flattened themselves against walls and windows. On the other edge of town the road becomes a steep, rocky path–designed for horses and bicycles, barely wide enough to allow two vehicles to pass. Each time they swoop around a wagon loaded with hay or farm animals, Clotilde is brimming with glee as she waves to the farmer.

Granados clutches his hat with one hand and the edge of his seat with the other as the motor car climbs toward Tiana, kicking up billowing clouds of dust in its wake. On both sides of the road are Catalan masias–farmhouses made of stone, surrounded by vegetable gardens and plots of grain, with grazing sheep and goats, all clinging to the steep slopes that run between the sea and mountains from here to the French border.

Men and boys working their land stop to watch them pass. Motor cars are no longer a novelty, but the sight of this sleek and sporty one–driven by a young woman–is worth a break in the day's tilling and weeding. By the roadside, chickens scatter, dogs leap and bark, and children jump up and cry out, all of their sounds lost in the roar of the passing vehicle.

The drive up to Tiana is otherwise uneventful until they round a sharp corner and find themselves converging on a pair of goats who've chosen the center of the road for a midday coupling. Granados shuts his eyes and braces himself with his legs, waiting for the impact. Instants that seem like minutes come and go as he feels the car swerving–first to the left, then to the right–in a fluid motion, never jerking as when a panicky driver jams the brakes. He opens his eyes and sees they're still climbing toward Tiana with a clear road ahead.

"That was close," she says. Her inflection is nonchalant.

"I thought for sure we'd hit them!" he says with amazement.

"And I thought they'd pull apart and we'd go between them," she says, turning with a smile toward Granados. "But they didn't, so I had to go around."

"You didn't use the brakes."

"No. Too late for that. I must say, those goats didn't seem to care at all that they were about to be destroyed. Simply too busy."

His composure is returning. "Well, they *are* goats."

"Yes. But so different from humans? Pleasure comes first."

He laughs. "Oh, there are plenty of differences."

"Oh?"

He releases his grip on the back of the seat. "Not worth mentioning, especially when you're busy driving."

"Of course, maestro," she says, feigning servility.

Near the edge of town, the road appears to be merging into a wider concourse, below ground level and several meters deep, twice as wide as the crude pathway they've been climbing. "What is this?" he asks.

"They call it the Riera de Tiana."

"An arroyo? Drainage ditch?"

"Up here, they use the Catalan. Yes, a drainage ditch."

The riera runs through the middle of the village. It was built to guide the springtime flood waters through Tiana without carrying away its residents and their homes. From early summer until late winter, the riera is a causeway for wagons, bicycles, pedestrians, dogs, and recently the occasional motor car.

"I've never seen a single drop in this riera," says Clotilde as she cruises through the light traffic. "Some of the old people talk about a great flood many years ago, but I've never seen a drop."

"So if we were driving up and a great flood was coming down, we'd be in trouble. I'd rather not die that way!"

The riera levels off at a wide clearing on the Tiana slope, where Clotilde stops the car by the side of the road and turns to Granados.

"I've heard of your phobia, maestro. About water and drowning. If you don't mind, could I ask where that comes from?"

He hesitates, preferring to change the subject, but her candor is disarming. "I was just a boy," he explains, with no reason to distrust her, "we were living in the Canarias. One day I was with my friend Pepe, we were at the beach, splashing each other. There was another boy, Luis–you see, I haven't forgotten his name. This Luis began to say bad things to me. 'You're not from here,' he said, 'you're a cubano.' He must have heard my father was born in Cuba. 'And I said, 'I'm not cubano. I'm Spanish.' Then he said, 'Sí, tu eres! You are cubano, Kee-kay.' I said, 'Don't call me that! My name's not Kee-kay, it's Enrique!' I splashed him, and suddenly he pushed me down under the water, and I swallowed a lot of it and began to choke–I thought I was going to die! I could hardly breathe but I could run, so I ran home. Crying all the way."

Clotilde, seeing his hands shaking, reaches across and puts her hand on his shoulder. "That must have been horrible. You weren't from there, and he was taunting you. Making fun of your name. So it made you feel like an outsider, not belonging."

He shook his head. "Is that something you learned at colegio? Or from Doctor Freud?"

"Neither. Just watching and listening and thinking about things. I could be wrong."

"No, you're not wrong." He looks up the riera, as if seeking a new subject. "Someday I'll come up this riera on my motorcycle!" he says, propelled into a fantasy jaunt.

"Your motorcycle?"

"Yes. Someday I will have one. Not the kind with only two wheels. I'll have a sidecar, so I can take a passenger. So it won't tip over."

"Would you take me for a ride?"

"Only if you're able to learn Allegro de Concierto," he says.

She laughs at the non sequitur. "But you won't assign that to me!"

"You're not ready."

"And you're not ready for a motorcycle," she says, engaging the gear and steering the Hispano Suissa back into the riera. After a short distance, they leave it behind, turn to the right, and climb a steep hill. Off to their left, he recognizes the wall that surrounds her villa and the row of cypress trees rising above it.

She parks the motor car in the courtyard and leads him inside. Before going to the music salon, she shows him the lavatory and a small study off the main entrance hall where he can rest. "The divan is very comfortable," she says. "If you simply want a siesta, it's dark and quiet there. Come, let's give you a chance to do some work."

The Pleyel stands where it was four years ago, in the corner with light from two sides. Across the salon is a second piano, a Bechstein. Granados sits down at it, raises the keyboard cover and plays a few arpeggios. "Not a bad sound," he says.

"It was a gift from my uncle. He said he won it at the Casino, but he has a vivid imagination. I'm happy to have it, in case people want to play twin pianos."

Granados stands up and goes over to the Pleyel. More arpeggios. "I shouldn't complain, but they're both somewhat out of tune."

"Yes. I've engaged the tuner to come up tomorrow."

"I didn't give you much notice," he says.

"That's right. But we'll manage. I'm going to leave you now. If you need anything, I'll be close by."

Granados has been improvising for more than two hours. Taking a measure or two from his old notes on the Goya-esque music, he meanders in a formless reverie. Majas and majos dart from the shadows, dancers whirl, lovers embrace, men philander, women flirt, men argue and fight, trust is broken, nightingales sing, men and women suffer and die.

Suffer? Die? Where is this going? Being here–does it make any difference? She's generous–trying to help–but make any difference?

He stops and looks out the window and over the gardens. Clotilde stands motionless, surrounded by her roses–pink, red, and yellow–and framed by a row of cypresses behind her. He opens the door and steps onto the terrace. "The flowers are beautiful," he says.

Her own reverie has been interrupted. "I'm glad you're here. Aren't the gardens splendid? Come, smell the roses and the lavender. Listen to the birds. And to me. I've reworked that poem by Darío, the one I recited the last time you were here."

"He has a flat across the street from Paquita Madriguera," says Granados.

Clotilde is undeterred. "Darío? Oh, I'd like to meet him. Someday. But today, just listen. It's a brighter version."

> I sing now
> with that harmonious madness of yesteryear
> I sing now
> with the labor of the minute, the wonder of the year
> Merely a tree
> I generate love from the breezes
> and I grow
> with a vagrant and sweet sound
> and I grow
> while a hurricane moves my heart

He's moved by the fervent affirmation in her voice. Looking across the garden, and through gaps between the cypresses, he sees clouds covering the sky all the way to the horizon, above a calm and gray sea. He feels her hand take his arm as he falls in step, down the middle path of the garden.

There's a persistent, solo fruit fly in the music salon of Clotilde's villa in Tiana. It returns again and again to alight on the waves of Granados' hair, breaking his concentration on the Goya-esque composition. He shakes his head to catapult the insect and when that fails, he puts down his pencil and reaches up to slap at it. And to miss. At last the pest departs, leaving Granados to contend with a swarm of ethereal creatures buzzing inside his head, in patterns as random as the peregrinations of the fly.

He's chosen an opening theme from a tonadilla–an early 18th century song for voice and piano, this one composed by Blas de Laserna, a contemporary of Goya. The easy part is borrowing these eleven notes; not as easy to render them in a series of variations. For Granados, that means endless variations. His inherent genius for improvisation–refined from countless evenings sitting at pianos in Rusiñol's seaside retreat in Sitges, in the Sant Gervasi villa of Salvador and Carmen, and at their xalet in Puigcerdà–brings this demanding feat within his grasp, while it would be unreachable for most of his contemporaries. Along with many of his previous works for piano, this music is only playable by an authentic virtuoso. "I will try to play your new piece," Malats once told Granados, "and I'm honored you'd ask me, but truly, Enric, only you should play it!"

Goya. La Duquesa. Majo and maja. Black eyes. Madrid. Coquetry in the streets. Flattery and deceit in the palace. This Capricho that Capricho. Endless flirtation. Two aristocrats–no sincerity–taking advantage of each other. No there's much more–a love story. Where's this taking me? Must be more than fascination with myths–more than collage of Caprichos. Otherwise another failure. It's time for Goya. Now or never. Here it comes. Eleven notes teasing me. Need to take hold of them!

When, after two hours of improvisation, Granados stops to wipe the perspiration off his face and loosen his tie and collar, he hears Clotilde calling to the gardener from the terrace outside of the music salon. He looks at the composition pad with the same eleven notes scrawled in haste on the top line. He'd borrowed the notes, he'd taken hold of them as he desired, and after he'd brought them to light it was as if a myriad of cocoons were opened, from which countless multicolored butterflies could embark on their summer flight, the zenith of their short and vivid existence. Great brilliant flights of color soaring from the keyboard, breaking the sunlight into millions of slivers and sparkles. Music from sunlight, as if from the luxuriant palette of his friend Joaquim Sorolla, colors from all over Spain, hues of seaside and mountains, dancing with pure joy. Granados imagines the room filling with them, then bursting out to fill the Tiana sky. Which of them must he catch and hold onto–at least long enough for them to enter his right hand and reach to the tip of his pencil, long enough to form a series of lead dots and streaks on his composition pad? Which of them? Which of them? Having to choose could bring madness!

He stands up and walks to the window. Clotilde sees him and motions him to join her on the terrace.

"I heard you stop playing," she says, tilting the wide-brimmed straw hat to the back of her head. Her oval face is radiant, her wide mouth gleaming. "I heard ornamentation. Extraordinary. Building on a simple theme. Am I correct?"

He nods. "Yes, building–but I have just eleven notes on paper. That's all. The rest? Just exercise for my fingers."

She resists. "Oh, no, it was much more. What you have is very rich and very deep!"

"But it's like a giant flock of butterflies," he laments. "Millions of colored wings beating in unison."

She ponders this. "Well, then, you have to catch some of them."

"Precisely. That's why I stopped–to avoid madness!"

She lifts her hands. "You'll not go mad here, maestro. You may become weary of too many roses, too much quiet, too many cypresses swaying in the breeze, and soon the dusk, the end of the day, but there *will be no* madness! Come, sit here with me. I have three surprises for you."

He smiles. "You are a wondrous fount of surprises, mi hija."

"I'm not your daughter," she says quickly. "Your chauffeur perhaps, and your student. Here's the first surprise–from Tennyson."

> Now sleeps the crimson petal, now the white;
> nor waves the cypress in the palace walk;
> nor winks the gold fin in the porphyry font:
> the firefly wakens: waken thou with me.

"That's splendid!" Granados exclaims.

Clotilde continues. "And the second is from–oh, it's a secret, I want you to guess."

> When I am dead, my dearest,
> sing no sad songs for me;

plant thou no roses at my head,
nor shady cypress tree.
Be the grass green above me
with showers and dewdrops wet;
and if thou wilt, remember
and if thou wilt, forget.

I shall not see the shadows,
I shall not feel the rain;
I shall not hear the nightingale
sing on as if in pain.
And dreaming through the twilight
that doth not rise nor set,
haply I may remember,
and haply may forget.

He shakes his head, eyes misting with tears. "That's so sad! Like something I'd write. Still, I don't recognize it."

She laughs softly. "You'll be upset if I have to tell you."

"Sounds British. Or Irish. Lyrical–'sing no sad songs for me'–has to be an Irishman."

"Give up?" she asks, obviously pleased.

He nods.

"The poetess is…Christina Georgina Rossetti."

"Rossetti?"

"The sister of Dante Gabriel–"

"–who painted Dante and Petrarch!"

"As you would say, 'precisely.' Did you catch the twist in the second stanza?"

He frowns. "Twist? Oh, my Lord, yes! In the first stanza she's unwilling to have her lover troubled by her death, then in the second she doesn't seem terribly eager for her lover to join her in Heaven."

"In fact," Clotilde adds, "she may hardly remember him."

"I know people who'd be shocked by that."

"Yes, and I'm delighted you're not among them. I ran across it the other day and thought of you. Rossetti–it reminded me of your *Dante*."

"My *Dante*?" Granados lowers his voice. "Another dream burst."

She waves her hand. "No, not burst. Simply not yet fulfilled. Someday your *Dante will* be celebrated. And this one as well–your Goya-esque music, your lonely eleven notes. Now, if you're willing–here's the third surprise, from Darío–his 'To Goya.' "

Your mad hand limns
the outline of the witch
huddled in the shadows.
And learns an abracadabra
from the goat-footed devil
with a twisted grimace.
A muse proud and confused,
angel, spectre, medusa:
such is your muse…
The dead yellow light
of the terrifying nightmare
gleams in your chiaroscuro,
or makes your brush light up
red lips of honey
or carnation blood.
Your feminine angels
have murderous eyes
in their heavenly faces.
With capricious delight
you mingled the light of day
with dark, cold night.

Eyes closed, Granados nods. "That's our Darío. And that's our Goya. It's about the Caprichos."

"Yes, but your Goya-esque music is so much more!" she argues. "Not just the brilliance in colors and light, not just Goya's darkness and Sorolla's sunshine, your music has both light and dark–joy and sadness." Clotilde catches her breath and thrusts her face closer. "Listen–I have an idea–will you listen?"

"I am listening."

"About capturing some of the colors splashing in your head, I have an idea. If you'll trust me, if you'll give it a chance. Now listen: there are two pianos, and two pianists. Though maybe it's one and a half. Never mind. I think the way for you to capture the colors–the butterflies, if you will–is to hear the music played back, to be able to step back and hear it. So you hear what you want to change and what you want to keep and what you want to throw out."

"Hmmn. Interesting idea," he replies. "Let me think about it."

At the end of the first week his work is progressing at a snail's pace. He plays the first two pages for Clotilde, who stands behind him and looks over his shoulder at the composition pad.

The sound of it thrills her. "Will you let me play it?"

He shakes his head and plays it over again.

"Please, I'd like to try."

"It's not ready," he says.

She notes the nuance: the *music* is not ready, not: she's not ready. "Please, let me try."

He pushes the chair back and steps over to the end of the keyboard. "You may try."

Clotilde studies the notes. "Pedal here?" she asks, pointing to the last measure of the first bar.

"Yes, but staccato. And down here."

She nods, and begins. Her playing is tentative, slower than the way he jotted the notes on the pad. Despite many years of practice in sight reading, she struggles with the density of this piece and its constantly lush ornamentation. With a torrent of notes to play with both hands. After the last full measure, she returns to the opening and plays it again, this time less tentatively. She plays it three more times without asking for guidance. "I'm still not sure of the pedal," she admits.

"You're a little light," he says. "And here," he adds, pointing to the fourth bar on the first page, "you need to pick up the tempo. Ah, but you're doing quite well."

She smiles and plays it two more times. "How does it sound to you?"

"You're doing quite well."

"No, I asked: how does *it* sound? Not me."

He smiles. "Oh, I'm so used to being maestro, and you're asking about the music. It sounds fine, except I'd change this." He leans over, picks up the pencil and inserts three grace notes. "Play that bar over."

She plays it.

"That's better," he says, reaching over again and penciling in three more sets of grace notes. "You see what I'm doing?"

She nods. "Do you see what *we're* doing?"

He stares at her, as if startled by the concept that they're engaged in some form of mutual endeavor. In a collaboration. He recognizes it's her idea, which she tried to explain to him earlier in the week. At the end of the day when he wasn't paying attention. "Of course," he replies, having regained his aplomb.

"Are you ready to hear my idea? Again?"

He laughs. "As ready as I was to take that first ride in your little motor car."

She reaches out and touches his shoulder as if to assure him this will not be like dodging traffic on the Diagonal. "Good. Here it is, again. After you've finished for the day, I'll make a copy from the composition pad. I'll do it every day, piece by piece, so I can learn it overnight. The next day, you'll listen to me play it and make notes on what you want to change. Then while you're moving on to a new piece, I'll put your changes in my copy. At the end of the day I'll play the new version for you. We'll work piece by piece, back and forth, with you playing the first version on the Pleyel, then listening to me play it on the Bechstein, followed by the changes, back and forth, from piano to piano." Clotilde pauses. "Now, does it make any sense at all?"

He reminds her that he always composes at the piano, always listens to himself play. He's not going to change that.

Her face lights up, as if she knew what his response would be. "Of course, maestro, I don't want you to change that. But you're a brilliant improviser–your spirit and your fingers move so quickly that you can't catch those millions of butterflies flashing in the sunlight. You send them aloft–it's vivid and it captivates you–but you don't catch very many of them. Isn't that right?"

"You're right," he concedes.

"So your wonderful gift of improvisation just makes it *more* difficult for you to compose a complex work like this one. You simply can't keep pace with yourself, and you lose much of the brilliance."

He frowns. "And your idea is to slow me down so more of the butterflies can be caught?"

She nods.

"But if I do this, and know you'll be playing it, won't that cause me to compose music that is easier–so you can play it?"

She frowns at him. "I don't believe you'd do that. Would you?"

He shrugs. "I don't know. It just crossed my mind."

"Well, you're thoughtful and considerate–indeed you are, but composing is your purpose for being, you know that, and this work can be a masterpiece. I don't believe you'd jeopardize it just to do me a favor."

"With your idea, it will be very slow," he says.

She laughs. "We do have plenty of time, don't we?"

He shakes his head, overcome by her insight and logic. "Yes, we do have plenty of time."

So they work together, as she suggested, for several days. The first piece, derived from the *Capricho* "Tal para qual" and evoking levity and flirtation in the streets of Madrid, begins to take shape. Every night, after driving Granados to the train station in Montgat, Clotilde plays his music, over and over again until the notes begin to blur on the page and she feels her hands cramping.

In the middle of the next week, his migraine returns. With the first tremor of pain he wonders if he should hurry home before it hits with full force. Instead, he asks Clotilde for water to wash down his medicine and goes to the study to lie on the couch, seeking relief in the darkness.

Clotilde stands in the doorway. "Is there anything else?"

He shakes his head, then asks if she has some tea. As she turns to go, he remembers how soothing it had been when Carmen rubbed his forehead and temple with lavender oil at Sant Gervasi. He asks for that too.

Granados drinks the tea and lays back while Clotilde applies the oil. His eyes are closed, her fingers move softly, the fragrance of lavender has a calming effect, the room is entirely dark except for a sliver of light entering under the door, and there is no sound whatsoever. He falls asleep.

When he wakes, the room is still dark, but the sliver of light is gone and he realizes it's nighttime–he can't stay here, he must leave and take the next train home. The pain still throbs in his temples. He puts on his shoes and opens the door to the entry hall. Clotilde is waiting.

"You were sleeping so peacefully," she says, "but I was just about to wake you. I know you can't stay."

On the way to the train station in Montgat, she says she heard him talking in his sleep.

He quips, "You're sure it was me?"

She laughs. "You were the only one sleeping in the study. Yes, I'm quite sure."

"What was I saying? Reciting poetry?"

"Oh, it didn't make much sense, except you repeated the name 'María Teresa, María Teresa,' over and over. 'Don't die, María Teresa, don't die.' Who is *she?*" asks Clotilde.

Granados is relieved he wasn't calling for one of the departed Marías. He assumes that wouldn't matter to Clotilde, but if he repeated their names in his sleep at home, Amparo would not be as understanding. "María Teresa was La Duquesa de Alba," he says. "So I was dreaming of her and Goya. That's good. But I don't remember the dream."

"And you didn't want her to die."

He shakes his head. "No. Goya was shattered by her death, even though they were no longer lovers. She was just forty years old."

"And you were shattered in the dream."

He nods.

"So sad, to die so young!" Clotilde says, taking his hand. "With so much to live for."

"Many believe she was poisoned. By someone working for the queen, who was threatened by La Duquesa. That's part of the myth. But nobody knows. What does it matter? She died too soon." He opens the car door.

"Are you going to be all right?" asks Clotilde.

Coping with daggers of pain in his head and squinting against the bright lights of the train station, he asserts, "I'll be fine. A day or two and I'll be back." He leans toward Clotilde. "That is, of course, unless there was poison in your lavender oil."

She shakes her head. "No poison, maestro, surely not while you're working on the Goya piece. Poison only if you gave up on it."

"If I did that, I'd deserve to die."

In the days following his recovery from the migraine, Granados works on the first piece, "Los requiebros"–based on the coquetry and flattery between the mythical maja and her lover, the majo. He envisions a scene in which the maja plays the role of temptress and seductress, a creature of coquetry and lust, leading the majo with the passion she arouses, leading him to ruin and death. The maja is not unlike La Duquesa de Alba tempting Goya. He composes it as a "jota"–the renowned dance form of Goya's home region, Aragon. He passes the theme back and forth between right and left hand, weaving in the throbbing sound of guitar strings being plucked. He surges into improvisation on the theme, then stops himself in order to pencil in the melodic line before it escapes. In his scribbled notes, he varies the mood: tenderness, grace, fervor, vivacity, caprice, spirituality, elegance, daring, gallantry, tranquility, gaiety, nonchalance, passion, brilliance. All of the mood swings reflective of his own life, sudden and unexpected, which in the aggregate form a distinctive pattern. He infuses the piece with lilting romance and soaring hope, contrasting with and lifting the music above the cynicism and satire of the *Caprichos*, concluding with a sweeping arpeggio.

Granados finds Clotilde in the garden, sitting on a bench in the shade of a cypress, absorbed in a book. "I've finished the first piece," he says, more drained than celebratory.

"Dios mío!" she exclaims, putting the book aside. "O, maestro, how wonderful! Can I hear it?"

He plays it for her, several times. She asks to play it and he rises from the Pleyel.

"I'll play it on the Bechstein," she says.

"No, play it here."

She plays through the early pages with assurance despite her lack of virtuosity, and stops at the final section. "Yes, I see what you've done. I must wake up my left hand." She plays through the final three pages, stopping at the composer's note: Con molta gallardia. "Oh my–I'm not playing it with enough authority."

"Play it again," he suggests.

This time she plays it Con molta gallardia.

"Much better. But I need to make a change." He reaches across Clotilde and sweeps up through the arpeggio with his right hand, then strikes the final chord. "Here," he adds, picking up the pencil. "Here, just these three little grace notes. Right here." In a crouch, with the pencil in his teeth, he plays the final seven measures. "Yes, that's better."

For the second piece, "Coloquio en la reja," Granados envisions a scene in which the lovers are conversing through the iron grille of her window. He's made a pen-and-ink sketch of the scene: a royal crest on top of the window frame, the pale face, sultry eyes, and bare shoulders of the woman inside, and the shadowy silhouette of the man, grasping the grille and wearing a cape with crested hat, which evoke a balcony painting by Goya. The protective grille represents the gap between the aristocratic woman and her impoverished suitor. Or La Duquesa inside, looking out at the Goya. A dialogue of femininity and virility. Unrequited desire woven with melancholy. Her refinement, his coarseness. Shadows heighten the mystery, making the engagement seem furtive, illicit, and ultimately doomed. Both yearn for each other and suspended in time, neither are able to transcend the barrier. The music, slower and sweeter than in the first piece, drifts back and forth between the lovers, its bass notes imitating the flamenco guitar. As with the first piece, he and Clotilde follow their method of collaboration to capture the escaping splashes of color and light.

In the third piece, "El fandango de candil," Granados creates a scene of nocturnal revelry in the light of the street lamps. The music suggests a popular dance of Andalucía, the fandango, but Granados' interpretation is more refined, more complex, poetic, and subtle than the raucous and bawdy music of the archetypical bars and cabarets depicted in Bizet's *Carmen*.

In mid-July, Granados begins work on the fourth piece, "Quejas, o la maja y el ruiseñor," which takes place in a moonlit garden. The maja, surrounded by the perfume of her flowers, sings of her love, and a nightingale emerges from a leafy enclave to answer her with his own trilling, melancholy song. Granados transforms a theme from an old Valencian folk song into a series of dazzling variations, each more colorful and fragrant, culminating in a hypnotic cadenza, a brilliant flourish imitating the mournful song of the nightingale. The nightingale, which symbolizes the joy and sadness of love, the lament and rapture of love, both esctasy and agony.

After several days of work, long days at the Pleyel and long nights for Clotilde applying all of her technical skills to each day's portion, the duet between maja and nightingale emerges. Now there are four pieces, comprising the first book of the work that he's named *Goyescas* or *Los majos enamorados*–majas and majos in love. He plays all four pieces through, over and over, penciling in more corrections. The last time through, he softens his touch on the final few measures of the duet between maja and the nightingale.

"I need to stop here," he says, sitting with Clotilde on a marble bench in the garden. "It's time to go up to Puigcerdà and rest my soul."

"But you're not finished with Goya."

"There are more pieces, of course. At least two, possibly three more *Goyescas*."

"*Goyescas*. I like the name," she says. "When will you go?" she asks, imagining how quiet it will be here without him. "Tomorrow?"

He hesitates. "I'll spend the weekend with my children, and go up next week."

She nods, looking across the garden at the terrace and the windows of the music salon. Late afternoon shadows have crept across the rosebushes and are climbing the cypresses. Soon it will be time to take him to the train station.

"I have something for you," he says, reaching into the pocket inside his coat. He unfolds a sheet of stationery. "I'll read it if you like."

She holds her breath.

"It's a little poem I borrowed from Mestres. He didn't give it a name, but my name for it is 'Sueños del poeta'–the poet's dreams."

> In the garden of cypresses and roses
> resting against the pedestal of white marble,
> waiting for his time,
> the poet sleeps, dreaming…
> At his side, and caressing his forehead
> the Muse watches over him.

"It's not much." He looks up. "Oh, I've made you cry."

Clotilde takes the handkerchief from his pocket and wipes her face. "It was so white. Perfectly white. Now, look at it. Oh, it's such a beautiful little poem, you are the dearest man in the world! I'm going to–" She stops herself.

"I'm going to miss you," he says. "How can I possibly thank you for the *Goyescas?* This little poem–it's a way to dedicate these *Goyescas* to you, the only way I can. You've seen my note: 'play this with the jealousy of a wife and not the sadness of a widow.'"

"Yes, and I know you can't possibly put my name on the first edition. I know. The price you'd pay would be too great. But this means more to me, maestro. This means so much more than a formal dedication!"

He hands her the poem, with his signature at the bottom. "There will be music for this. It's already up here," he says, pointing to his head. "And, incidentally, I *do* have a name."

"Enrique. It's just, I'm so used to your being my maestro."

He laughs. "Well, I'm flattered you stayed with me all these years. I'm terribly hard to please."

She smiles. "I was so terrified of you. So terrified." Her eyes fill again with tears. "I never thought you'd approve of my playing."

"Never approve? Clotilde, mi querida, do you know how beautifully you've played for me this summer? You've played like an angel!"

At the train station, she gets out of her motor car and walks him over to the track. The coastal train is in sight, clattering in from Mataró. Clotilde puts her arms around Granados and holds him. She feels his arms tighten around her.

"You'll miss your train," she says at last. "Go. God be with you. Que te vayas con Dios."

Puigcerdà

Two days later, during his journey from Barcelona to Ripoll, Granados dozes and watches the hilly, rocky gorges of the Catalan countryside whizzing past. Thinking of *Goyescas*. Of going to Tiana nearly every week day. Clotilde and her garden of roses and hydrangeas. The nightingales she says come to sing when night falls, after he's gone back to the city. Wondering what fates may have guided him to her.

My student for eight years. Just a child then. Radiance–bubbles rising in cava–buds opening. Devoted always prepared. Not the most talented. Devoted always. Now a woman–more than youthful sparkle–now she has shadows. We all have them. Romantic–clear from the poetry she recites. Not yearning for what she can't have–or is she? Not like my yearning. To hear the nightingales sing in her garden.

As the train climbs from Vic to Manlleu, and follows the Riu Ter to Sant Quirze and Torelló and its last stop in Ripoll, Granados is awake and his head is buzzing. Book One of *Goyescas* is finished, though a piece of music is never finished. So many ideas for revisions–small but not trivial. Like floating grace notes. Is there too much repetition in the fandango? He needs to play it again. Book Two is next: interpreting the *Capricho* "Love and death," followed by an epilogue. When will he have time to finish it? Summer will end all too soon, the academy will reopen. Will there be time to keep going to Tiana?

Xavier, chauffeur for the Andreus, stands on the platform of the rail station in Ripoll, waiting for Granados to step off the train from Barcelona. He intercepts the luggage cart and leads the porter and Granados to the black Rochet-Schneider town car parked in front of the station. Xavier, who once drove horse-drawn coaches for the Andreus, has moved to the horseless carriage with alacrity. In the city, it's Xavier who drives Granados and other guests from the villa in Sant Gervasi to their homes. During the summer, with nimble hands he maneuvers the large vehicle up the narrow, switchback roads originally built just wide enough to allow two horses to pass without incident, climbing over the pass near Queixans and descending to the wide valley of Puigcerdà. Xavier manages to avoid oncoming vehicles with a penchant for intimidation, relying on the oncoming drivers to use caution. To date, all of the Andreus' guests have arrived safely.

Carmen, having heard the Rochet-Schneider roaring up the drive and bouncing into the courtyard, waits for Granados at the tall, arched main entrance, above which are a pair of stone shields–on one a carved lyre, on the other the carved head of a Wagnerian maiden.

"My dearest Enrique, you're just in time for the Festa," she says, opening her arms wide for an abraçada. "We thought you'd never come," she adds, still holding him. "Perhaps you'd abandoned us."

"No, I've been hard at work. And just finished Book One of *Goyescas*. At last, after so many years. And I tell you without any doubt, it's my best work ever! That's why I didn't come earlier, you know that."

She draws back to challenge him. "Better than *Danzas*? Better than *Valses*? *Follet*? *Dante*? Better than the one you're not permitted to play anymore?"

"Yes, Carmen, better than all of them!"

"Splendid! Then I'm glad you abandoned us."

"Hardly that. I'm sure you found solace with a little jaunt to France."

"That's not the point," Carmen replies. "You know I can't just sit here all summer like a rock. Not the point at all. You and I have things to talk about! But come, Salvador is relaxing in the garden, and Paquita's most especially keen to see you again. Every day she asks, 'When is my maestro coming?' Without fail, every single day. Oh dear, could that child be infatuated with you?"

"Please–I've just come all the way from Ripoll. Risking my life, careening up the mountain with your Xavier."

"Indeed you have," says Carmen. "But it's your fault for coming up so late in the summer. Don't think it's been easy protecting your favorite room. And yes, even *I've* been longing for you."

"Even you?"

They both laugh.

"Come. Salvador asked to see you the minute you arrive."

Andreu sits on his chair in the garden overlooking the pond. "Now, Enric, you say this *Goyescas* is your best work ever. Are you saying that to justify abandoning us?"

"Salvador, there's no doubt–this *is* my best work ever! La millor! I'll play it for you tonight."

"If that's so, I'm delighted. Waiting for you, I've been sitting here thinking about our family orchestra. We haven't played much this summer, not without you. But the Festa begins this week, and we'll need adequate rehearsal time. We should start tomorrow."

Granados is amused by the zeal with which Andreu approaches the upcoming concert by the family orchestra. As if it were the introduction of a new pharmaceutical, or another housing project. Who else in this vacation haven of the alta burguesia would be so concerned about getting adequate rehearsal time?

"Yes, of course," says Granados. "Tomorrow. Whom do we have this year?" He knows those who are not coming to Puigcerdà: Crickboom, moved back to Belgium; Albéniz, dead more than a year; and Tàrrega, who died last December.

Andreu responds with a listing of players. Family members, of course, they've already been practicing their instruments. Paquita on piano, mother Carmen and Madronita on harp, young Salvador and Juanito on cello, daughter Carmen and Pepe on violin, and the doctor himself on harmonium. Granados will conduct, and replace Paquita for the more difficult pieces, such as the Fauré quartet. And, if he's willing, would the maestro play two or three of his own pieces? The Allegretto from *Valses*, perhaps, and one of the *Danzas*, and something from the new work.

"Those are the family players," Granados notes. "Who else?"

"Miquel Llobet will be here tomorrow, so we'll have a guitar. He told me he's done a transcription of your 'Danza Number Five.' And Doctor Moner will be here to strengthen the cello section. Also, Jordi Garcia–the young man who plays contrabass. Why, you'll never recognize him–he's grown up like a poplar tree, and he's finally taller than his instrument!" Andreu snickers. "And of course our friend Eusebi will come over from Bellver with his bassoon. Amazing–every year when it's time for the Festa, he just arrives. Then disappears for the rest of the year. Strange little fellow, but he plays quite well, don't you think?"

Granados nods.

"We'll have plenty of guests for the Festa. Francesc Vidal and his girls, Lluisa and Frasquita."

"Hardly girls, Salvador," Granados points out.

"Yes, point well taken. As for the guests? Joan Llimona arrived yesterday, and Maragall said he'll be coming. He's been very sick, you know."

"I didn't know."

"You've never cared for his politics. Too conservative for you, isn't he? Like Llimona. Too close to Bishop Torras." Andreu assumes that since Granados has been privy to so many political discussions at Sant Gervasi, he's bound to recall at least the essence of them.

Granados shakes his head. "Salvador, you know I don't care for *anyone's* politics!"

"Fair enough. Maragall has zigged and zagged, hasn't he?"

Granados chuckles. Andreu seems intent on eliciting an opinion. "If you insist, I did note that Maragall held the industrialists responsible for Setmana Tràgica. After that, one of his poems was refused publication. So he's not always with the conservatives, is he? As for Llimona, he certainly showed his colors when he threw Rodin's nude into the rubbish pile!"

Andreu is surprised. "Well, that's bold talk from someone who doesn't care for anyone's politics."

Granados backs away. "I didn't say I agree with Maragall. After my own experience that day, I'd say a plague on both houses."

"Well, I'd say a plague on the trade unions. And a plague on their friends, the anarchists."

Granados is uncomfortable when he hears Andreu disparage the trade unions, or espouse the theory that those with wealth are the natural aristocracy–deserving the largesse, but he regards his patrón as the most deserving of those with wealth, since from modest beginnings Andreu built his reputation and fortune through hard work and perseverance, skill and daring. Andreu seems the antithesis of those third- and fourth-generation aristocrats whose idle lives are arranged to aggrandize their power–even if that requires them to marry their cousins and consort only with their own kind. Andreu's not like those who seem dwarfed by their names and titles, wastrels in their ducal palaces. Those who resent his phenomenal success.

It troubles Granados to hear persistent rumors that the renowned Doctor Andreu built his fortune by shady or illicit tactics. "How could he make that much money just selling little pills?" goes the refrain. "There must be more to his story, more than just the pills. Something not quite–shall we say, honorable?" Yet those who disseminate these rumors weren't paying much attention when young Salvador Andreu earned the degree in pharmacy that permitted him to be known as "Doctor Andreu." Nor did they discern that putting this "brand name" on the products coming from his laboratory made them as recognizable as any commercial product in Catalunya. They're not privy to his keen understanding of the tangible advantage of giving superior service to his customers. And they don't know that at midnight, when many of the city's industrialists are still dining or carousing in the Barri Xinès, Andreu is pulling a gold watch from his vest pocket, popping the lid, peering down through his bifocals, and announcing that his guests must depart so he can be at work promptly in the morning. But Granados knows; he's heard the "Doctor Andreu Story" over and over again, watched him up close for nearly two decades. Granados so admires his patrón that he defends him if he hears a disparaging comment. Alas, he realizes, the rumors "of something not quite honorable" will survive, titillating, a justification for those who've squandered their ancestors' fortunes.

Paquita Andreu is waiting for Granados in the music salon, brimming with curiosity and flirtatious energy. "It's been far too long," she pouts. I've nearly forgotten how to play! It was cruel of you–cruel to make me wait so long!" Her voice is teasing.

He sighs, feigning exasperation, and sits down at the Cussó. It's out of tune. "How long since the tuner was here?"

Paquita laughs. "No sooner is he gone, the pianos need tuning again. Why doesn't he just stay for the summer? No, no–Mamá won't hear of it." The piano tuner, a wiry bald Italian named Flavio, comes up several times each summer. Not trusting the railroad porters, he sits with his tool kits on the train from Barcelona to Ripoll, loads them onto one of the carriages leaving for Puigcerdà, and upon arrival carries them up more than two hundred stone steps to the elevated center of the city, then through the narrow streets to the Xalet Andreu. Paquita rolls her eyes. "One day, he'll just drop dead halfway up those stairs. Piano tuners aren't meant to be mountain goats!"

As Granados opens up a copy of Book One of *Goyescas* and places it on the piano, Paquita sits down beside him on the bench. She sees that it's the work inspired by Goya. "You've named it! *Goyescas*–oh, it takes my breath away!"

He plays through the first piece of Book One with a pencil clamped between his teeth. Paquita leans forward, eyes dancing, her hands clasped as if in prayer.

When he stops, she exclaims, "Oh, Dios Mío, there are millions of notes. I could never play it. But it's so gorgeous! Oh, maestro, it's perfectly gorgeous!" She takes the pencil from his teeth. "Don't ever, ever change a note!"

He laughs, and reaches up to make a penciled correction. "I have a few tiny changes, if you don't object. I won't ruin it."

"What ornamentation! Oh, no, I could never play it."

"You must have patience." It is his maestro's voice.

She frowns. "Patience? I'm twice as old as that Madriguera girl. Twice as old! And *she*'ll be able to play it, won't she? Won't she?"

Granados shrugs. "Yes, someday. But La Nena Madriguera–she's not normal. She's a prodigy."

"Like you." Paquita's voice wavers.

He nods.

"Not normal?"

"That's right."

She chooses her words carefully. "People envy the prodigy, but there must be a dark side."

"A dark side?" he asks.

"I mean, it's mostly a blessing, but if you're a prodigy, people have such high expectations. How difficult to live up to that!"

"Perhaps, but what does it matter? Now then, you are *not* too old, nena. Someday you'll be able to play this."

She stands up, pulling her shoulders back. "You call me 'nena'? Do I look like some 'nena innocent'?"

He shakes his head.

"Don't you know I'm twenty-one, maestro? Old enough–if you weren't like an uncle to me!"

He starts to reply, to tell her he's more than twice her age. That's not the point, so he desists. It crosses his mind that Paquita's the same age as María Oliveró.

She checks herself. "I'm sorry, Uncle Maestro Granados. I've embarrassed you. I'm so sorry. I'm just frustrated. I love playing the piano, it's the only thing that arouses me, truly arouses me. But, in truth, I'm not going to be a concert pianist. If I work hard, I can be a good pianist, maybe even very good, but no more. No more than that. And if there were just one place for someone like me to play–not El Palau, not Salle Pleyel, just a simple place to play for small groups, to enjoy my music, to play short unimportant recitals. That's all. Do you think it's too much to hope for?"

"No, it's not," he replies. "And I apologize for calling you 'nena.' You are a beautiful, talented woman and I'm proud to be your maestro–and your uncle."

Paquita smiles. "You'd help me find a place where I could give unimportant recitals?"

"Yes."

Her voice is singing again. "Would you come for a ride in my little car? Oh, say you will! We could drive up into the mountains, we could have lunch in France."

The image of her dark blue Hispano-Suissa, shaped like a bullet, leaps into his head. "Would you be terribly hurt if I declined?"

In the evening, the Andreus and their guests gather in the music salon to hear Book One, and Granados sits down at the Cussó. He's just cut twenty measures from the fandango piece–concluding they're redundant, and made a few other corrections. He asks Paquita to be his page-turner. She waltzes across the room, enjoying the recognition.

Afterward, Andreu is effusive. "You were right, it *is* your best work ever!" he tells Granados, clapping him on the shoulder.

Though awash in adulation, Granados waves off a tremor of giddiness and holds fast to a lucid judgment. "Thank you," he replies, "I believe it is, yes. The masterpiece."

Andreu waves his index finger as if to scold. "Not *the* masterpiece, Enric. No, this is only the first in a series."

Granados is touched. "Thank you. Only because you–"

"Nonsense," says Andreu, placing his index finger above Granados' heart. "Here's the wellspring–in here!" The patrón's face is filled with joy and celebration. "Now then," he adds, ever the pragmatist, "we need to rehearse tomorrow. Shall we say one o'clock?"

Carmen and Granados are walking around the pond. When they reach the opposite shore, she suggests they take one of the rowboats, and though he protests that being on the water makes him uneasy, she persists. The sun is nearly overhead as they push out from the landing dock. Across the way, the mirror-smooth water is broken, and tiny waves slurp against the retaining walls that contain the pond. Small flocks of mallards, widgeon and geese paddle to the far side as the rowboat, with Carmen at the oars, crosses over to a gazebo that was built ten years ago in the middle of the pond. The white swans, following the black one, are cruising away from the promenade as strollers walk past.

"Salvador is thinking about your idea," says Carmen. "Your Sala Granados. The way you've described it, a recital hall for solo and chamber music. He said it's not a business decision–more a matter of civic pride. Something worthwhile for the community."

"He and I haven't discussed it for a while," Granados says. "I wasn't sure he'd make another investment, when he's already done so much."

She stops rowing. "Your best chance is Paquita. You understand?"

He shakes his head. "Paquita? I know she's frustrated because there's no place for her to perform."

"Dear Enrique, you'd do well to watch more closely. Salvador will not throw his money around, but he will respond to his heart. And his heart–his weakness, is his children."

Granados is surprised. Andreu's weakness was always Carmen. "You're not his weakness?"

She tosses her head and looks at him from the corners of her eyes. "Not so much. Not any more. It's the children's turn." Her voice is tinged with melancholy.

He shakes his head, fending off the implication. Not wanting to recognize her vulnerability. "It's always their turn," he says. "Your six children and mine–the nature of life. You and I aren't young any more. Sad but true."

"Of course, you're still surrounded by students–that must keep you young. All of those young women." Carmen turns and stares at him. "Which of them has captured your heart this time?"

He stares back. "There *is* nobody!"

"Who was able to keep you in Barcelona–instead of coming here?"

"That's not it, Carmen. There isn't anyone."

"Am I to believe you created this masterpiece–this *Goyescas*–at home?"

"No, of course not," he replies. "All right, I've been going to Tiana, working with one of my students."

"Ah, isn't that what I just asked?"

"It isn't, not exactly. This isn't a love affair. She's a young woman who's been a student of mine for eight years. She has a home in Tiana and a Pleyel. And a Bechstein. She helped me capture the butterflies–I mean, showed me that I had too much flying around in my head and wasn't able to keep up with it. She made me listen to the work I was doing, piece by piece, day by day. And became a kind of collaborator. I'm not sure I could have composed it without her."

Carmen thrusts her head close to his. "Who is she?"

"Clotilde Godó."

Carmen takes a deep breath. "We know the Godós. From Igualada. She's not an ingénue like the last one, is she?"

"No, she's not an ingénue. She's twenty-five, Carmen."

"But you're involved with her."

"I'm not. Please try to understand! She offered me a place to get away from everything, to go back to the time of Goya without an endless series of interruptions." He leans toward her, and his voice is assertive. "She's not an ingénue. This is not an affair!"

"All right, then," says Carmen. "I don't know her. I just know you have a wife and six children. Oh, Dios Mío, Enrique, you're forty-three years old now–I love you, I'll always love you, I'll always want the best for you, I'll always believe in you. I'm tired of lecturing you–I'm not your mother. I just want to be your friend!"

Barcelona

"Lluisa says your new piece is spectacular," says Carme Karr. "It's the one I've heard about for years? From Goya?"

Granados nods, wondering how many people he told in the twelve years since his visit to the Prado. "Yes, it's the one. At last!"

Granados is meeting this morning with Karr and Lluisa Vidal in the office of the women's magazine *Feminal* on Carrer Mallorca, in the heart of l'Eixample. Karr, the editor, sits in a lacquered wicker chair with her back to a tall, polished mahogany desk, its shelves and compartments stuffed with books, publications, and bulging files. On the writing shelf, folded down, is a bouquet of red and orange roses–the colors of the Catalan flag–framed by a display of pointed palm fronds. Karr is dressed in a dark blue suit and white blouse with ruffles at the collar and cuffs. She is a handsome woman in her mid-forties, with serious, probing green eyes and light brown hair gathered atop her head.

Vidal, sitting next to Granados, leans toward Karr. "It's absolutely ravishing! The ornamentation–simply overpowering! The same enchantment as *Iberia*."

Granados shakes his head. "Oh, Lluisa, it's kind of you, but nothing can be compared with *Iberia*."

"How did you find the time?" Karr asks Granados.

"Well, the academy was closed for the summer, so I had two months with no interruptions. The music had been in my head for years–haunting me, giving me no peace of mind. Like butterflies. It was time to let them out."

"Though it's never that easy," replies Karr. In addition to editing *Feminal*, Karr is music critic for the periodical *Joventut* and composer of a lyric drama that was presented at the last Espectacles Graner two years ago. And five years ago, she published a collection of songs, including one named "Death of the Nightingale."

"No. Never easy to decide what's worth keeping," replies Granados.

"Well, I hope you'll be having a private recital," says Karr, "before the entire world hears it. And you'll not forget me, will you?"

"You have my solemn word," he says, but his eyes forsake him. The word 'solemn' seems to invite duplicity. He's learned that if people say, 'quite sincerely,' then be careful–what they're about to tell you is probably not true. Forget the words, watch the eyes. He looks at Karr, then Vidal.

All three are convulsed in laughter.

Karr is considered the city's leading advocate of better education for women, and equal opportunity in professional careers. Equality is her banner: freedom for a woman to choose the traditional role, and that–Karr argues–is an honorable choice, but if she chooses a career, there should be no artificial obstacles. Though antipathy toward Karr often rises with the billowing cigar smoke in the lounges of the men's clubs, she enjoys more tolerance in Barcelona than she would in most cities of Spain.

Lluisa Vidal has been a friend of Granados since the tertulias at Els Quatre Gats. With her father and sister, she's been a frequent guest of the Andreus in Puigcerdà: seated at the table when Andreu announced his backing for the new Acadèmia Granados nine years ago, and in the music salon when Granados played Book One of *Goyescas* two weeks ago. Lluisa paints luminous landscapes and portraits of women and children, and in a more prosaic use of her talent she's been the illustrator for *Feminal*. She's now an attractive, slender woman in her early thirties, whose appearance and mannerisms are more conservative than of most art students returning from Paris. Vidal says she went there to improve her craft and become a professional painter, not to plunge into la vie bohemienne. "I can drink absinthe right here at home," she reasons, "if I choose that kind of poison!"

Granados listens as Karr and Vidal describe a series of articles planned for *Feminal*, about opportunities for Catalan women in music. The series will feature women who've been successful in various musical careers, describe the time and effort required for success, and identify obstacles faced by women.

"Why me?" he asks.

Karr smiles and explains, "You're the one prominent performer, teacher, and composer who's stayed in Barcelona over the past two decades, so your views are especially valid." She pauses. "And some intangible factors. So are you willing to answer some questions, and be quoted?"

"I'll try," he says. "What are these 'intangible factors'?"

Karr smiles. "Just my way of saying, you're one of very few men who wouldn't try to convince us that women belong in the home."

"But my own wife *is* in the home," he replies.

"Yes, but isn't that by choice?" asks Karr.

He shrugs. "You're saying this serious of articles isn't about my marriage. Fine."

"Let's move on," says Karr. "Here's the first question: in music, does a young girl have the same opportunity as a young boy?"

Granados understands, and offers a nuanced reply. "Well, for children with an unusual talent for music–let's say the prodigies–there's opportunity for both boys and girls. I've had both at the academy. However, I'd have to say that parents of the girls may not make the same effort to find superior maestros as parents of the boys. But assuming they do receive the same instruction, there's no reason girls can't advance just as fast as boys."

"Are you speaking of the piano, or all instruments?" asks Vidal.

"Piano, certainly. Even though having smaller hands is a disadvantage." He holds up his enormous hands. "Women can also play violin. Or cello, like your sister. And reed instruments. It's less true of the brass and woodwinds. I don't know why."

Karr probes. "Is it about size? Physical strength?"

He chuckles. "Well, I've never seen a woman playing contrabass."

"You're saying girls don't start with a big disadvantage," Karr says, "and experts in education say that adolescent girls mature earlier and are better students than boys. Then why aren't there more women in the orchestras and in chamber groups? Why aren't more women launching careers as soloists?"

"Good questions," Granados replies. "First, the impresarios and conductors choosing players for an orchestra are all men. Chamber groups seem to form at the soirées where it's typically men getting together without women. As for soloists, it's far easier for men to get around from city to city. If women aren't escorted, their reputations are at risk–which can hurt bookings. It means the cost of two people traveling, hotels, meals, and all the other expenses. Those are big obstacles!"

He continues. "If we go back to the eighteen-year-old woman who's interested in a musical career, that may be *her* dream–but since she's probably from the alta burguesia, her mother has already picked out a future husband and is busy arranging a marriage. So many promising young women simply disappear," he says. "Their talent is confined to those sweet little home recitals to entertain their guests. Nothing too serious. Chopin is fine, but Beethoven's too heavy, if you know what I mean."

"Aren't you describing an impossible situation for women?" asks Karr.

"Difficult but not impossible," he replies. "There are extraordinary girls who can be successful soloists. Such as Paquita Madriguera, a student of mine. I predict that if she can resist getting married, she'll be one of the world's best. Her mother's more interested in her piano career than getting her married off. That's now–but Paquita's only ten."

"And the singers?" asks Karr.

Granados smiles. "Ah, we need women to sing soprano, don't we? There aren't any more castratos. We've produced marvelous sopranos here–Barrientos, Bori, Supervia, several others. Also, Gaetana Lluró–she studied with us, had her debut two years ago. Supervia debuted in Buenos Aires last year–only fourteen. And Barrientos had an incredible career, all over the world–until she married some gaucho from Argentina and he retired her! Had a son last year, and I don't think we'll ever see her again. What a loss!" He shakes his head.

"So what you're saying," says Karr, "is that women's careers in music reflect the traditions and customs of our culture. Is it that simple?"

"I don't know," he says. "I'm part of our culture. My own life is full of contradictions. I haven't always given women the respect they deserve."

Dalliances. The Marías. Telling Amparo my work this summer was in Sant Gervasi. Many many contradictions.

"Well, you have the decency to admit it," says Vidal. "How many would?"

Tonight, at the suggestion of Rafael Moragas, music critic for *Pèl i Ploma*, Granados will play Book One of *Goyescas* for a small, private audience in the large salon of Girona, 20. Moragas, though still in his late twenties, for years has been an unabashed enthusiast for Granados' music. In a review of the private performance of *Follet*, he assailed "the small-minded businessmen" who dictate taste at El Liceu. Then, after making peace with the Cercle del Liceu, he was hired to assist Albert Bernis in bringing Wagner's complete tetralogy *Der Ring des Nibelungen* to El Liceu. He's now the impresario's favorite for the job of artistic director. Moragas' excitement over arranging tonight's intimate recital is evident. "I'm so honored that you'd do this," he tells Granados with ingenuous sincerity.

According to Moragas, it's a fine group to hear the new work. Some old friends, like Joaquim Pena. But a mixed group, not just the musical crowd. Moragas says that all of them "were thrilled to be included." He's also invited Isolde Wagner, daughter of Richard Wagner and granddaughter of Franz Liszt, who by chance is in town. Moragas suggests that Granados play Liszt's Sonata in B minor, and perhaps the piano adaptation of Wagner's prelude on the death of Isolde, "La Mort d'Isolda." And at the end, his own *Goyescas.*

Granados is riding home in a horse-drawn carriage, up the wide Via Laietana that was carved two years ago through the heart of Ciutat Vella, the oldest sector of Barcelona. It's a hot and dry late summer evening. The rains will come again in late October, but until then the air will be filled with a fine dust from construction all over this booming city, kicked up the north-south streets by the siroccos, steady and oppressive, which drive across the Mediterranean from northern Africa. Fine weather for the pots of geraniums hanging from the balconies, as long as they're not allowed to dry out. The time of year when maple trees give up their seeds, which spin downward in parabolic arabesques, when the hydrangeas begin to wilt even as the bougainvilleas become more dazzling, when the grapevines and wisteria begin to harden for the winter. When at night the snails come out of their dark corners and resume control of the rocks.

Granados wonders if the fates are once again playing with him. He couldn't find a venue for *Follet* anywhere. Can't play *Escenas Románticas* ever again. *María del Carmen* had its short run and is forgotten. Allegro de Concierto is a rigorous test for students at the Madrid Conservatory, but the rest of the world won't hear it. The lyric dramas had their seasons and have been forgotten. The first half of *Dante* is hardly in demand. He's still asked from time to time to play the *Danzas* and *Valses*, but he composed those works twenty years ago. He's had no real success since those. Now, with *Goyescas*, people are talking. This one depends only on his own ten fingers. No impresarios cutting rehearsal time. No missing players. No sopranos fighting with tenors on opening day. No ignorant aristocrats and self-proclaimed experts. Tonight some important critics will hear him play it. On his own Pleyel.

Isolde Wagner! Imagine—Wagner's daughter Liszt's granddaughter coming to hear Goyescas! *Fates, are you with me?*

The guests are gathering in the music salon, standing around the Pleyel. "I hear you've composed a masterpiece," says Joaquim Pena, who since collaborating with Granados and Albéniz to establish the Associació Wagneriana has been an informed and fair-minded music critic. "Nobody will celebrate more than I. Felicitats!"

"To be safe, Joaquim," Granados replies, "you should reserve judgment until you hear it."

The guests are no strangers. Josep Pous, a novelist and journalist and, less successfully, a dramatist; in the aftermath of Setmana Tràgica, Pous was imprisoned for an article he contributed to a political journal. Manuel Rodriguez, art critic and painter who taught at La Llotja school and is chief art critic for *La Vanguardia*. Romà Jori, journalist and painter, who's edited a number of liberal publications in the city; he's a vocal advocate for Catalan solidarity. Jaume Brossa, an influential modernist writer who was exiled by the Spanish government a dozen years ago, and continues from his base in Paris to stir the political pot in Catalunya. Alexandre Soler, a theatrical designer who composed a work based on lyrics by Verdaguer, which premiered at the Tívoli. Gabriel Alomar, essayist, poet and politician, who writes for *El Poble Català* and talks of blending messianic, mystical modernist theories of art and the social mission of the artist. Except for Moragas, all are in their mid-thirties, with careers in ascendancy, and a few years younger than Granados.

They are joined by Salvador Armet, a music critic, folklorist, and Comte de Castellà, and his wife, the Comtessa, who's also a music critic and composer. And by Isolde Wagner, the oldest child of Richard Wagner and his second wife, named after the ill-fated heroine of her father's opera, *Tristan und Isolde*, which premiered in Munich the year of her birth. She is with her husband, conductor Franz Beidler.

A few minutes past nine, Granados walks to the piano and the guests sit in a half circle around him. Standing at the keyboard, he says, "Tonight I'll play the works of two immortals and something new from a local composer who is virtually unknown." Isolde Wagner and her husband are perplexed until he repeats it in French. "Ah," she says, "c'est très amusant."

"Maestro," says the Comtessa, "would you agree that I am the only composer here who is truly unknown?"

Granados bows and sits down. The Pleyel was tuned this morning, and before the guests arrived he played through the three pieces, so he's confident and relaxed as he begins. The Liszt Sonata is an inveterate selection in the piano repertory, and Granados provides a stirring, romantic interpretation. Next he plays the Wagner prelude to the death of Isolde with a soft, almost muffled sonority. The room is filled with bravos after each of these pieces, along with extended clapping by Isolde Wagner. The room is hushed as Granados begins the bass notes leading into "Los Requiebros," the first of the *Goyescas*.

When he finishes, the audience stands up and applauds for several minutes. Over and over: "Bravo, Maestro!"

"You took me back to Madrid!" cries the Comtessa, rising to her toes. "I heard them dancing in the street, reciting poetry in the gardens. I felt the passion of the lovers. And the melancholy–in the end, overcome by optimism. And yes, the trilling of the nightingale! So utterly Spanish, so like Madrid in Goya's time! There are no superlatives to describe how deeply this touches me!"

Isolde Wagner asks, "And you will name this *Goyescas*, after the painter Goya?"

Granados nods. "I haven't made a final decision. I also like *The Majos in Love–Los Majos Enamorados*."

The Comtessa steps forward. "Granados, don't look for another title. The title is *Goyescas*. There's no other for this masterpiece!"

Igualada, September 1910

Granados is on a train heading for Igualada, to meet Clotilde at her father's home. Juan Godó has arranged for him to give a recital at the town's new theatre, sponsored by Igualada's industry and agriculture association–founded by Juan Godó. From his seat in the coach section, Granados looks out, seeing vineyards on both sides of the track and grape pickers lifting full baskets onto wagons that will carry them to the winery to be crushed.

Two weeks ago, during Granados' brief visit to Tiana after returning from Puigcerdà, Clotilde told him her father was showing a keen interest in her maestro. "He's more than just curious," she said. "Of course he thinks the world of you–as my maestro. But he looked at me–you know that fatherly look, and asked if there's anything more between us."

Granados froze. "And I should hope you told him, no–there's nothing more."

She laughed. "Would it matter if I told him we're having a torrid affair?" She seemed unable to contain her glee. "Of course that wouldn't be true. And I never lie to my father."

"If you told him that, I'd soon be hearing a loud knock on my door. Your father and brothers coming for revenge."

She waved an index finger, one of several adorned with rings, in front of her pursed lips. "There, I've gotten you all excited. I just mention it because Papá knows perfectly well you and I've been spending time together. He doesn't need me to tell him that."

Granados was puzzled. "How would he know?"

She laughed. "He hasn't succeeded in business and in politics without very strong intuition. What's more, he sees me happy for the first time in years. So his not saying anything critical means he's accepting–he approves of you."

"But when he asked if there's anything more, what did you tell him?"

"Since we're not having an affair, since I'm merely helping you compose your *Goyescas*, I told him the truth. And my reason for mentioning that he's curious is to prepare you for some tantalizing questions when you come to Igualada."

Igualada is an energetic industrial city about sixty kilometers northwest of Barcelona on the west bank of the Riu Anoia. Since mid-18th century, the availability of inexpensive power from the river and the lesser militancy of its worker syndicates have enabled Igualada to become second only to Barcelona in the textile and garment industries.

Igualada has also been home to the Godó family since the original Ramon Godó and his son–Ramon Godó i Mas, arrived here in the 1760s from the tiny hamlet of Valldellou, located in the rocky sierras on a tributary of the Riu Noguera north of Lleida. The weaving shop that they established in Igualada was the cornerstone of the future Godó empire. A grandson, Antonio Godó i Domingo, expanded the family operations into dyeing of fabrics, mostly cotton. A mill for spinning cotton was added in the 1840s. Antonio's son, Leopoldo Godó i Llucià, entered the realm of politics and served in the Catalan legislature, and his brothers, Juan and Ramon, were both mayors of Igualada. Two of the third-generation Ramon's sons, Carles and Bartolomeu Godó i Pié, moved from the family's tight little industrial colony to Barcelona, where they established a factory to make textiles of jute, and the daily paper, *La Vanguardia*. Carles' son, Ramon de Godó i Lallana, founded a plant to supply the newsprint for the newspaper. The Godós of the fifth and sixth generations remain active in Igualada politics, and have expanded their influence in the government of the capital city.

Juan Godó i Llucià, born in Igualada in 1855, is a cousin of Carles and Bartolomeu. He owns a large textile factory (Igualadina Cotonera), is mayor of Igualada, and a member of both the Catalan legislature and the Spanish national parliament in Madrid. He married Adela Pelegrí from Sant Serni, another hamlet on a tributary of the Riu Noguera, not far from the place where the original Ramon Godó was born. Three sons were born to Juan and Adela–Juanito, Ramon, and Pompeyo Godó–before the arrival in 1885 of their first and only daughter, Clotilde Godó Pelegrí.

In the early 1890s, in order to attend to his business and legislative interests in Barcelona, Juan Godó purchased a large home on Rambla de Catalunya in l'Eixample, and while he continued to divide his time between the capital and Igualada, the new home became the principal residence for his wife and children. Shortly before the family moved from Igualada, Clotilde was sent off to Colegio de las Damas Negras, a secondary school, where she excelled in piano and was considered by the nuns to be a prodigy.

"Oh, I cried for weeks when they sent me there!" she told Granados one day in the garden of her home in Tiana. "I was so homesick! And my mother refused to visit me. She refused! She told the nuns, 'When she's done crying, I'll come to see her.' God rest her soul!"

Juan Godó and his family would often stay at the villa in Tiana, a vacation home of a distant relative, "Tío Jaime" Armat–considered to be an uncle–an architect who seemed too busy to use the villa. After Adela Pelegrí's death in 1906 and the annulment of Clotilde's marriage to Juan Marsans–approved by Pope Pius X–Juan Godó purchased the villa from "Tio Jaime" as a residence for Clotilde.

A carriage is waiting for Granados at the Igualada train station and he's driven to the Godó home on Rambla Nova. "They all live in that part of town," he's told by the driver, who speaks Catalan with a Basque accent. On the steps leading up to a broad front porch of the home, Granados is greeted by Juan Godó as if he were visiting royalty.

"My daughter's thrilled you could come," says Godó after the kind of abraçada ordinarily reserved for close family members. "And so am I. How long has it been? Three, four years? I've been so busy with business–and trying to keep Catalunya on a steady course, and you–so busy giving vent to your creative juices."

Granados nods. Juan Godó reminds him of Salvador Andreu: there's passion and soul under the imposing veneer of success. "I'm flattered you'd invite me, Don Juan," he says.

"This town is so excited! You've no idea. Imagine, *the* Maestro Granados coming here! And everyone knows you're the maestro of three talented Igualadinas, daughters of this humble little city. Can you imagine all three of them from here?"

"Yes. It is remarkable. Your daughter and La Nena Madriguera and Rosita Artés–all from here. What's the secret?" asks Granados, "quality of the water? Fragrance of the gardens?"

Godó laughs and winks conspiratorially. "Perhaps it is those things. But perhaps it's finding the right maestro, don't you think? And buying the best pianos for our daughters! Or perhaps it's a mystery you and I will never solve. Come, there are refreshments inside–and I imagine you'd like to prepare for the concert. Clotilde's anxious to see you, that's no secret."

While Granados stretches his hands with arpeggios and a few minutes of improvisation on the Cussó, Clotilde sits in a wicker chair by the window overlooking the gardens of the home where she spent her childhood. She's dressed in a white chiffon frock with puffy sleeves, cut low enough for comfort in the sweltering late summer afternoon but on the safe side of risqué. Around her long, graceful neck is a collar of tiny pearls and her hair is gathered and wrapped with matching pearls. When Granados looks up from the keyboard, he sees her eyes, the color of roasted almonds, watching him, seemingly mesmerized, like those of a child. He looks at her fine, high cheekbones, her ivory complexion, arched brows, and zestful mouth. For nearly a decade Clotilde Godó has been a composite of the music she plays, the sound of her laughter, her high spirits, her buoyancy, her impassioned reading of poetry. How seldom he's actually looked at her. When he stops playing, the spell is broken.

"Will we hear something from *Goyescas?*" she asks.

He shakes his head. "I wish I could, but there's an agreement with El Palau. The first public performance will be there in March." He pauses. "Too bad, because I'd like to give you credit–here in your home town–for making *Goyescas* possible. But not this week. Later on, yes."

She rises and glides across the tile floor of the salon. "You mustn't feel obliged. I helped, yes, but you're the composer."

"With thanks to Goya."

"If you will."

"And to you," he insists.

"Thank you. Someday I'd like my father to hear it. Privately. Could you play it for him–someday?" she asks, reaching out to touch his shoulder.

The fragrance of lavender is enticing. "Of course."

"Papá's helped me so much. He didn't like Juanito Marsans, but Mamá was charmed by him so that sealed my fate. I knew it wouldn't last. Knew it from the day we arrived in Paris—our so-called honeymoon. And life with Juanito got worse, not better. Mamá was ill for a very long time, then dying, so I couldn't upset her, but after the second baby died, there was no more reason to stay with Juanito and I went to my father. He supported me without hesitation. He was like a rock to cling to. He also said my mother wouldn't last much longer—that was a shock—said he'd help me have the marriage annulled. After she was gone. So I left Juanito—no regret at all—and moved back home. We told Mamá I was home to help care for her. After she died—and with her pain it was a blessing!—Papá asked if I'd like to live in Tiana. He'd talk to Tío Jaime, who never used the place. And after I moved there, Papá talked to his friend at the Vatican—someone close to the Pope. I'm so fortunate to have a father who understands. That's why I'd like you to play *Goyescas* for him."

The concert is held at the spacious new music hall built by a civic group—Circulo Mercantil—also headed by Juan Godó. Every seat is filled to hear Granados play the music of Schumann, Mozart, Albéniz, and Liszt. Men stand side by side in the back of the hall, holding their jackets, and outside a spillover crowd is poised in silence to catch the music as it drifts their way. After the Liszt, sustained applause and echoing of bravos subside only when Granados returns to the Chassaigne. Now he plays his favorite encore piece, "Danza Number Seven," and after more applause, the allegretto from *Valses Poéticos*.

Flowers are brought on stage while the crowd stands at their seats, and Granados steps forward to thank the mayor and "everyone who made this concert possible." He thanks Igualada for making him feel as if he's home. Then he compliments the city for producing three of his finest students. "My hope," he says, "is that all of them—Paquita Madriguera, Rosita Artés, and Clotilde Godó—will all be invited to play here so Igualada can hear the prodigious talent of its very own."

After the concert, Granados returns to the Godó home for a private reception. Though he's used to such events, the accolades today are notably exuberant, and seem to him more heartfelt and genuine, coming from people for whom a concert is a special occasion, not a common occurrence.

As guests begin to disperse, Juan Godó invites Granados to take a stroll in the garden. They walk to the far end of the property, then stop under an arbor wrapped in a climbing wisteria vine that is past its time of flowering, past the redolence of its purple blossoms. Godó turns and places his hand on Granados' shoulder, as if father to son.

"She's a very special child," he says, "you know that. Perhaps you don't know the circumstances. Clotilde was only eight when her mother became seriously ill for the first time. Looking back, that was the beginning of the end. It meant I had to be more of a parent for her than I'd been for her brothers. I wasn't prepared to become father and mother, but that's what happened. So for me Clotilde is a very special child. Strong-willed–they say she gets that from me. Of course I love my boys–they're good boys, but this one is very, very special. You understand?"

Granados nods, wholly absorbed.

Godó makes eye contact and continues. "So we get to what's on my mind, and I must be absolutely candid with you. Being so close to my daughter, knowing her so well, I may have powers of observation that most fathers don't have. I have to tell you–I've never seen Clotilde so happy. I've never seen her glow as she has the last few months–since you began coming to Tiana."

Granados braces himself. "You know I've been working there?"

Godó chuckles. "Do I look like someone who wouldn't know about things that are important to his family?"

"No, you certainly don't."

"So you'll understand why I'm concerned about Clotilde's involvement with you. Her maestro. A married man with several children who cannot offer her any assurances."

Seeking to clarify, Granados pushes back. "Forgive me, Don Juan, but you're talking as if something's going on between us. Perhaps you've made assumptions, incorrectly. Your daughter Clotilde and I are *not* involved–only in the music. If you see me as one of those bohemians who has no principles, no morals, no ethical standards, you are wrong. That is not who I am!"

Godó holds up his hands. "No, maestro, I'm not suggesting you're a bohemian. Not suggesting you've done anything harmful. Just saying, you and Clotilde spend a lot of time together, and it's been an inspiration for her. The two of you together at the villa in Tiana day after day. Let's be candid–you're a most attractive man, an older man. I've heard the women gossip, they say you're 'handsome as the devil.' So please listen to my concern: whatever happens between you and Clotilde–I don't want her to be hurt. Can I count on you–can you assure me she won't be hurt by *whatever* may happen with you?"

"You can count on me," says Granados.

Sant Salvador

Pilar Defilló de Casals is a strikingly handsome, once pretty woman in her late fifties, who tonight presides over a dinner assemblage that includes all three survivors of the eleven children born to her. The oldest of them, Pau, who for years was the marrow of his mother's existence, sits at the far end of the table. Granados, Amparo, and Guilhermina Suggia sit across from Casals' considerably younger brothers, Lluis and Enric, both in their late teens. Enric is becoming an accomplished violinist and Lluis, a student of agriculture, is planting the garden and a small vineyard around Villa Casals under the vigilant eyes of his mother.

Defilló turns to Granados, sitting next to her. "You asked how we found this place. It's the very place where I used to visit with little Pau when he could barely walk. We'd stay in a guest house just down the beach from where we're sitting tonight. I'd watch him play for hours on end while he learned to swim, my how he learned to swim! After my husband died, I decided to build a place far from the cities. A place for all of us."

Casals rises, glass in hand, to toast his mother and thank his brother Lluis for planting a small vineyard on the far side of the area devoted to flower and vegetable gardens. With the toast, he becomes the center of attention. As a raconteur, he's intense and dry, very fond of depicting his life on the road with twists of irony. In recent months he's performed in Vienna, Budapest, Geneva, Warsaw, Nice, Brussels, Amsterdam, Frankfurt, Marseilles, and London. For Granados, romantic names of places that he's never seen.

Casals describes meeting an English composer, Donald Tovey, and their blossoming friendship. "Why you can sing the violin part of an obscure Hayden quartet, and Tovey will know every single last detail of the work! I've never met anyone with such an amazing memory."

"And such an amazingly high opinion of himself," Suggia whispers to Granados. She stretches her tall sinuous body, in summer lace of ochre and burnt orange, toward him, the olive skin of her oval face bathed in candlelight. She giggles, just loud enough to interrupt Casals' monologue.

Casals lowers his head, which is prematurely bald except for a dark half-circle around the back, riding just above his ears. He glares at Suggia before continuing. "And what a fine sense of humor. Tovey can do the most hilarious parodies of Handel–who took himself much too seriously."

Meanwhile, Suggia places her hand–hidden by the table cloth, lightly on Granados' knee. Barely audible, she whispers, "And Handel's not the only one." Audible enough to interrupt Casals again.

Granados inches away from her.

Casals plunges ahead. "Where was I? Oh, yes, Tovey. We played at Aeolian Hall in London, and it went so well they booked us to return next summer."

His mother initiates a short burst of hand clapping. "But we haven't heard about your latest visit to Russia. Was it as exciting as the first?"

Casals frowns. "Indeed not." He turns to Granados to explain. "That year, Lenin called a general strike. The Czar's troops fired on workers at the Winter Palace. Hundreds fell dead. Then more strikes and they shut down the rail system–just when I was en route to a booking in Moscow. So after thirty hours on the train from Berlin, we were stopped at the Russian border and told we could go no farther. It looked as if we'd have to turn around and go back–thirty more hours! But there was a Russian general on the train–he'd been at one of my concerts in Berlin so he recognized me. This splendid general found me a seat on an emergency train taking important people to St. Petersburg. When I got there, Alexander Siloti–who persuaded me to come in the first place–said there was no way for me to get to Moscow, but he'd just learned that Eugène Ysaye was stopped by yet another strike in Warsaw, so Alexander arranged for me to take Ysaye's place. That was my debut in Russia."

Granados shakes his head. Except for the violinist Ysaye, all people and places he can only imagine.

The memory of his journey softens the unbroken brow over Casals' dark eyes, and his excited voice rises to the upper register. "What a debut! The power plants had been knocked out by the strikers. Absolutely no electricity. Hundreds of candles were lit in the Hall of the Nobility–what a name! The place was filled with women dressed in furs that covered them head to toe, and gowns from Paris, and jewels glittering in the candlelight, and men smartly dressed in suits from Savile Row or dress uniforms covered with ribbons and braid–what an audience! And with all of my luggage back in Lithuania–where the train was stopped–I had to perform in my business suit. The audience was anxious to hear the great Eugène Ysaye, not knowing of the substitution, so when Siloti led me onto the stage–I was carrying my Bergonzi–there were peals of laughter. Not cruelty, just surprise. Well, we started playing the Saint-Saens concerto and–do you know?–after the opening, the audience was on its feet, shouting, and doing that typical Russian hand-clapping, in perfect unison. Needless to say, the reviews were fantastic!" Casals looks down the table at Granados.

Granados smiles.

The Saint-Saens–yes you must have astonished those Russians! Brought them to their feet.

Casals looks around the table, eager to convey what he'd experienced. "Russia–what a stupendous place! Huge concert halls, excellent sound, filled with intelligent, appreciative audiences. How they roar and clap their hands. Truly, Russia is just bursting with talent. And how they drink! All the Russians drink vodka day and night. You can't imagine what's it's like to be there."

"So Russia quieted down since your first visit?" asks Casals' mother.

"Yes, it is quieter. On the surface, at any rate. There's so much extravagance among the royalty and artistocrats, but the distress is obvious. You see it everywhere. The rich ones flaunt their luxury–scandalously! My most horrible memory is of leaving a palace one night after playing for a Russian prince and his guests. On the way, there was a double line of the prince's servants, and as we approached they threw themselves down onto the floor. I was appalled! There was no way to get through that corridor without stepping *on* the servants. 'Walk over them,' the prince told me, 'that's what they're here for.'"

The next day, Casals and Granados walk on the beach, past the stone pier at the far end of the inlet where swimmers' heads bob up and down in the gentle surf. As they walk, Granados hears their feet falling on the crusty sand in the cadence of three steps to four, as if in three-fourths time. Casals plodding ahead–one-two-three-four, and Granados loping alongside–one-two-three. They've walked together so many times–in Barcelona and Madrid and Paris–and though much has changed in their lives, they're walking on the beach of Sant Salvador in three-fourths time.

"Your new work is extraordinary," says Casals without breaking stride or turning his head, which is nearly hidden under a straw hat.

"Truly?" Granados asks. After he played Book One last night, everyone was lavish in praise, but he knew Casals would wait until their walk on the beach to discuss it.

"My brother, surely you know it. You know it's a masterpiece. You don't have to be modest with me."

"Would you say it's 'meravellós'?"

"Absolutely!" says Casals. "And I'd add, since you're inclined to be outrageously modest, that your *Goyescas* is also distinguished, memorable, exceptional, astonishing, spectacular, magnífic, breathtaking, formidable, fantastic. Yes, and miraculous! Need I go on?"

Granados shakes his head. "Fine. I won't be outrageously modest, Pau. As I finished it, I immediately thought of you–who believed in me when many others took me for granted."

Casals plods ahead. "Brother, you've always been special, always. When you first told me about this idea of putting the colors of Goya into music, I knew–and I told you, there was nobody else who could do it but you. Only you–didn't I say that? I did–we were waiting for my train to Paris. We walked in the park–I knew it then, I've always known you were the only one." Now he stops and turns to Granados. "And the only mystery is, how *did* you finally create this? What was it–after all these years?"

Granados is not surprised at the question. In fact, he's asked it of himself. What was it? After so many years? After carrying all of those butterflies in his head, all of those radiant sparkles, what was it? "Pau, the idea was there all along," he replies, "but what may have opened my heart was what happened last year."

"What happened?" Casals asks. "What are you saying?"

"Well, I visited 'Saco last summer and discovered he was dying. And he had a new piano piece–'Azulejos'–that he'd never finish. Rosina gave it to me after he died, saying 'Saco wanted me to finish it for him. And I played for him in his room in Cambó while he lay dying, and oh, just seeing him that way! Not our old 'Saco, not the one who'd devour an entire escudella i carn without taking a breath, not the 'Saco who created *Iberia*–the most magnificent work by anyone in our country. I came home knowing he'd composed his masterpiece–*Iberia*–and it would be his finest legacy. I also knew it was time to get on with my own important work. Not let myself be defined by others, not by Morera and the dragons at El Liceu, not by anyone! It was time for me to make a supreme effort to create a masterpiece of my own. And I was haunted by the memory of the song of the nightingale, which I heard for the very first time in Paris, early one morning. 'Saco was there with me, and Malats and Viñes. I couldn't let life pass me by without bringing that mournful sound to life once again."

Casals maintains his pace on the beach. "And that's all?"

"No. After returning from Cambó and seeing our friend buried, then–unexpectedly–I got caught in Setmana Tràgica."

Casals, who heard about that traumatic week when he returned home last fall, expresses concern about the rising level of violence to settle political matters in Catalunya. "But how did that affect your doing this *Goyescas?*" he asks.

Granados is eager to explain. "Oh, it was such a horrible experience, and it taught me that life is indeed fragile–more than we like to accept. Our lives can be ended in an instant. It could have happened to you in Russia. It could have happened to me right in my own neighborhood. And given that, I was compelled to put my heart and soul into creating works of real significance. Not just to satisfy the tastes of dreadful impresarios and fickle audiences. Setmana Tràgica reminded me that life is very short. Only a few chances to do what we're here to do."

Casals nods, and looks up. "And what else?"

"What else? Why should there be 'something else'?"

Casals shrugs and laughs. "Because there usually is."

Granados pushes back. "You mean, it wasn't enough that 'Saco died and I was captured by both sides in the street fighting? Those events weren't enough to push me forward with *Goyescas?*"

"Oh, surely you were pushed forward. I have no doubt. But this idea had been inside you for a dozen years, and if memory serves me you have quite a busy life–children, friends, students, patróns–all making claims on your time. I know what that's like. Yet you've just finished the first book of a genuine masterpiece! One I'd would compare to *Iberia*–and you want me to believe you simply picked up your pencil and wrote it out–in between all the interruptions? I should believe that's what happened?"

Granados looks away. "No. It didn't exactly happen that way. Look, Pau, there were no interruptions while I was working on it. The academy was closed for the summer. And instead of going to Puigcerdà, I stayed home."

"And composed it at home. With your six children?"

Granados shakes his head. "Not exactly. I don't want to mislead you. I composed it in Tiana."

"Tiana?"

"Yes, in the home of a student who lives there. A good student. She has a Pleyel and a Bechstein."

"So there *is* a woman," says Casals without expression.

"No, no–you don't understand. She helped me. She played back parts of it after each day. So I could hear where it needed revisions."

"You stayed there with this woman? Young, I assume."

"Of course not. I went there in the morning and came back in the evening. And not so young. Older than your Suggia!"

"I would hope so!" Casals retorts, parrying the thrust. "Now, does Amparo know about your going there?"

"She does not. You know how jealous she gets. I told her I was using the Andreus' place in Sant Gervasi, told her I needed to be away from the routines of life in order to recapture the time of Goya. And that part was absolutely true."

"But not the part about Sant Gervasi."

"No."

Casals stops and turns to Granados. "Well, fine. That's the 'something else' I was probing for. And this woman, what is she? Your muse?"

Granados hesitates. "If you mean, could I have done it without her? I'd say, no, probably not. Going there nearly every day, having her help in deciding which of the millions of butterflies to keep–that was very important. No, it was essential! But if you're suggesting she's 'una musa romántica'–as from Homer? She's not that kind of muse. She–Clotilde is her name, she was my helper, just that."

Casals frowns and a smile curls the ends of his mouth. "Well then, if it's based on Goya, would this Clotilde be your Duquesa de Alba?"

"Surely not! I'll dedicate the first three pieces to three of our finest pianists–Sauer and Risler and Viñes. And the fourth, the 'Maja and Nightingale,' to Amparo."

Casals nods and turns to resume his walk up the beach. "That's very wise of you, brother. 'Course I don't believe some young student could make a difference. Nor help you very much. Since this one truly *is* a masterpiece, and I was stunned when you played it last night. Others will be stunned, some just curious. And if Amparo finds out about your going to Tiana, I forbid you to agree you won't ever play this one!"

"I'd never agree to that," Granados says.

Tiana

As he prepares to leave this morning, Amparo chides him: "All the time you're not out of town, you're working. All the time." But her voice is gently probing and lacking a critical bite.

"You always say that," he replies, more concerned about getting to the train station. Not hearing the softer tonality in her voice.

"You've always been working. But more so the past year. Every single waking moment goes into your work. I know. I know."

He nods. "It's true. I've started a lot of new ones, and they're all in my head at the same time. Titín, you know I had to finish the first book last summer. Now it's *Liliana* and Book Two of *Goyescas*. Suddenly–so much to do and all at once."

She laughs. "Suddenly? I've been your wife for nearly twenty years, and this isn't 'suddenly.' Well, 'to give the devil his due'–that's Cervantes, dearest–I'm not as illiterate as you may think, just because I don't join the Señora de Puig and her kind, the refined women of l'Eixample, in their boulevard life on Passeig de

Gràcia, shopping for new hats, shopping for new dresses and gowns. Yes, I've read Cervantes! In fact I seem to know Don Quixote all too well. Ah, but that's another matter. Mi amor, *Goyescas* is surely worth every minute you spent on it. Every minute! If Pau says so, it's surely a masterpiece. Sometimes it's hard for me to say nice things or fawn over you, but not for a lack of understanding. Or that I'm not very, very proud of you. *Goyescas* is truly extraordinary. And thank you for putting my name on it."

En route to Tiana, which he's visiting for only the third time since completing Book One, Granados is so engrossed in his notes for the orchestral score of *Liliana* that he's oblivious to the train's arrival at Montgat. Only a tap on his shoulder by the conductor, who recognizes him from his daily itinerary last summer, spares Granados a trip up the coast, leaving Montgat and bound for France. With Clotilde sitting in her motor car at the station.

Clotilde starts toward Granados as he alights on the platform at Montgat. She's suddenly aware that her excitement to see him again is on public display; she's not unknown in Montgat. She hesitates, tilting against him as they stumble into an awkward abraçada.

"I've missed you!" she says.

"It's just a few weeks."

Clotilde rolls her eyes. "Oooh, only a man would say that! A few weeks–after seeing you nearly every day. Only a man!"

"Ah yes, men are horrible! But this man missed you too."

She looks up. "You did?"

"You know that."

"Yes? Let's go home."

On the ride up to Tiana, which Clotilde drives with customary aplomb, she thanks him for sending her Matilde.

"Matilde, who worked for my family? You saw her?" Granados asks.

"Yes. She said you were most generous after your wife dismissed her. You told her I might be looking for someone." She shakes her head. "Truth is, I found her on the street, sitting on a bench and sobbing. She said she'd just been fired by your wife. Didn't give a reason."

"Amparo had this bizarre notion that the girl was flirting with Eduardo. Said she'd known for years that Matilde's a little tramp, but I kept protecting her, and now that Eduardo's eighteen Matilde had to go."

"Well, I showed her around," says Clotilde, "and decided to hire her. I was showing her around and we came to the music salon. She walked over to the piano and stared at it for the longest time. Then she turned and said, 'El Mestre'—in a curious voice as if she'd solved some sort of puzzle."

"I'm 'El Mestre'?"

"Yes indeed. Later she told me that when she'd launder your clothes she'd find the stubs of your train tickets to Montgat. Nearly every day, she said. Then she'd destroy them so your wife wouldn't find out."

"Find out? Matilde couldn't have known I was coming here."

Clotilde smiles. "It's not about knowing, it's purely woman's intuition. After several years working for your family, suddenly she found these train stubs—all of them 'Barcelona-Montgat'—and she never overheard any conversation about Montgat, so with an active mind and lots of time to explore the world of fantasy, she imagined some shadowy sensual mystery—it would intrigue her and feed her longing for the kind of life she hoped to find when she left her tiny village."

Granados shakes his head, wishing that Matilde also found the love letters from María Oliveró. That would have saved a lot of grief. And saved *Escenas románticas*. He turns to Clotilde, who's just slid the car around a truck on a sharp curve in the road to Tiana. "You got all of this just chatting with Matilde?"

"Of course! And she kept your secret—ever loyal to 'El Mestre.'"

When they arrive at Clotilde's villa, Matilde is waiting at the front door. Bowing her head, she says in a barely audible voice. "Thank you very much, Mestre Granados. Moltes gràcies."

In the music salon—while Granados arranges his composition pads, takes off his jacket, and exercises his hands at the Pleyel—Clotilde arranges a tall vase of fresh flowers from her garden. From across the Pleyel she asks, "Did you play it for Maestro Casals?"

"Oh, indeed I did. He said he was astonished." He laughs. "As if I'd never composed anything! And," he adds, savoring the memory, "he believes it's my masterpiece."

"Marvelous! That seems to be everyone's response."

"Yes. Of course, everyone who's heard it is predisposed to be generous. All of them, so far, are aficionados."

She shakes her head and raises the palms of her hands. "Aren't you being a bit gloomy? Is there any doubt in your own mind?"

He smiles. "That was a bit gloomy. And no, I have no doubt."

Why not enjoy the praise? When there's sunshine don't look for clouds. Thank you Clotilde!

He continues. "At any rate, Pau said he was astonished. Amazed I'd been able to capture the images from Goya, especially after my first attempt failed. Pau knows me like a brother, so he kept probing, kept probing. Not satisfied that it resulted from Albéniz' death and Setmana Tràgica. He asked, 'What else? What else?' Probing as only he can. Very skeptical. Wouldn't accept that I just picked up my pencil and wrote the notes down–not with all the interruptions in my life."

"And so you told him about coming here." Clotilde seems anxious.

"Yes. He said: 'So there is a woman.' As if that were the heart of the matter. Suggesting a young woman, like Suggia–a student and lover. He was especially worried that I'd dedicate *Goyescas* to you. Of course, he meant publicly–putting it on the music."

"No. You honored me in a private way. I'll always cherish that."

He nods. "I told Pau I plan to dedicate the first three parts of Book One to Sauer, Risler, and Viñes, all great pianists. And the fourth part to Amparo."

Clotilde nods. It's no surprise to her.

"Pau asked why the nightingale would burst into song with the jealousy of a wife–not with the sorrow of a widow. He suggested a certain irony in my dedicating the fourth part to Amparo. But the maja's not a widow, she's just melancholy and missing her majo, wanting to be with him, wondering where he is. Nor is she a wife, though she could still be jealous."

Clotilde asks, "Wasn't Casal's question about the nightingale–and what his song represents?"

Granados shakes his head. "No. It was about my notation, for someone playing the piece. I wanted the tension that comes with jealousy, not the sorrow from a loved one's death. That will come later."

"Well, if it's in the notation, I agree. It's not a widow's lament."

"Exactly. But Pau had several questions. He wanted to know if I stayed here with you. I told him no, of course not! I also told him you weren't so young."

Clotilde laughs. "Oh? Aren't I?"

"You know what I mean."

"What else did you tell him?"

"He wanted to know if you were my muse. I told Pau I couldn't have done this without you. Without your being with me, without your help."

"That's very flattering," she says.

"It's not meant to be. I said I couldn't have done it without your help, but you aren't una musa romántica, not in the Homeric sense."

Her face brightens. "You mean,

Among all men on the earth the poets
Have a share of honor and reverence
Because the muse has taught them songs
And loves the race of poets…

Is that what you mean by Homeric?"

"You're amazing!" he exclaims.

"I'll accept that. But please don't make me your muse. Your muse must be la maja. La Duquesa. La maja with the nightingale. La maja that is España. La maja eterna, whose song is the sea breeze sighing in the maple trees and moaning in the pine boughs. Please don't make me your muse!"

They look at each other across the Pleyel.

Muse? All this talk of muses. What are you then? Your voice–the sea breeze. You are singer and maja. You helped this come to life.

Clotilde breaks the silence. It's time for her to meet with Jaime, the young gardener hired the same week Matilde arrived at her door. "He claims to know how to care for animals," she tells Granados as she opens the door to the terrace. "If so, that's a blessing. We certainly have a fine little zoo down there, don't we?" She laughs. "It's just possible we have too many animals. Though I love them all. I can't ever say no!"

Granados stops his arpeggio and turns. With her hair pinned high, her long neck reminds him of the swans on the pond in Puigcerdà. Her dress is silvered by the pale autumn light and fluttered by the breeze.

"And," he says, "I also seem to have too many delightful creatures–only mine are flying around in my head. It's comforting to know someone else who can't say no."

Clotilde steps back toward the piano and places her right hand on his left shoulder. "Thank you! You've touched me–one more time. Understanding about my animals. Here's a little verse that says it best."

Give all to love;
Obey thy heart;
Friends, kindred, days,
Estate, good fame,
Plans, credit and the Muse,
Nothing refuse."

"Coleridge?" Granados asks.

"From Emerson's 'Give All to Love.' Now enough of this chatter. You tend to your creatures and I'll tend to mine."

Granados and Clotilde are sitting in the garden. As the sun descends toward the ridge, the air is cooling as the cypresses cast long shadows on the stone wall separating her property from the narrow cobblestone street leading up from the riera.

"You were working on *Liliana*?" she asks.

He nods.

"When will you begin Book Two?"

"As soon as possible! And I'd like your help, if it's not too much–"

"Of course. You're welcome here–any time."

"It won't be as easy as last summer." The logistics of getting up to Tiana have been on his mind for several weeks, ever since his walk with Carmen in Puigcerdà. He's rescheduled a few of his students, allowing him to break away from the academy in the early afternoon. By arriving in Montgat around two o'clock, he'll have several hours each weekday to work on Book Two. He's told Amparo that he'll be busy preparing for the opening of *Liliana* and finding venues for revivals of *Follet* and *Dante*. Adding that Rusiñol invited him to come down to Sitges any time he needs a quiet place to work, and that, as usual, he'll be going to Sant Gervasi to spend evenings with the Andreus. In turn, with the same pretext, he told Salvador and Carmen that he'll be arriving an hour or two later than in the past, and perhaps not every evening. In effect, following his instinct, he's recreated another compartment in his life, so that he can go to Tiana.

"Then you'll leave here in the early evening?" asks Clotilde.

"If the Andreus are expecting me, yes. If not, I'll stay later."

"Later, but before the nightingales sing."

"Yes."

After a long pause, Clotilde turns to him. "Incidentally, I'd like to return to the academy for my lessons."

He ponders the suggestion. "You could have a lesson when I'm here. Any time."

She shakes her head. "No. I'd like to separate your being here to work on *Goyescas* with my need to keep improving. When I come to the academy, you're the maestro and I'm the student. It's very clear and uncomplicated. But it's different here, very different since last summer."

"Yes it is different," he replies, recalling a conversation with Paquita Andreu. She preferred the impromptu lessons with him in Sant Gervasi, their brevity and flirtatious informality. He told Paquita she'd progress faster if she came to the academy. "I agree," he tells Clotilde, "it would be better if you came in. Not here."

"Perhaps it's a matter of discipline," she says. "Keeping everything in its proper compartment. That's it?"

He's amused to hear that word from her. "Before the nightingales sing. Some day I'll stay over, just to hear them," he says.

She laughs, shaking her head. "No you won't. It's a pretty idea but you will *not* stay here for the night."

Granados is intrigued with the idea. "Some night, then, I'll come up to visit you, just to hear the nightingales. I'll come on my motorcycle–straight up the riera!"

"Oh, my. You don't even have a motorcycle."

"I will have one," he says with widening eyes. Suddenly what's been a casual fantasy has become an ambition. "A red one with a sidecar, and I'll take you for rides in the hills. We'll go to Alella, we'll go to Mollet, we'll go to Vallvidrera, even to Olot."

She laughs. "I'd give anything to hear you roar out of the riera and slide to a stop in my driveway. Will you wear goggles? Will you look like one of those dashing aviators?"

"Definitely not. But come I will, you can count on it. You have my solemn word!"

"Oh, dear me," she says, convulsed in laughter. "There's nothing solemn about this, nothing at all!"

It's nearly time for her to take him down to the train.

"And everything's going well at the academy?" she asks.

"Yes, amazingly well."

"I ask because you haven't said anything." She tosses loose strands of hair off her forehead.

In response, Granados compares his work as a maestro to gardening. First, preparing the earth. Then planting the flowers and nurturing them. Watering them, propping them up with stakes, tying them if they're climbing vines, removing the weeds, then waiting for the blossoms. "I've watched you out here," he says. "It reminded me of starting the academy. Now it seems to have a life of its own. What's the difference? The students!" he exclaims. "They're just like flowers in your garden! Where to begin? Of course–Paquita. A treasure! You may not know Ricard Vives, who studied with Nicolau. He's coming for some advanced work. Federic Longàs–a marvelous pianist, and he comes while Malats is on tour. Not to forget Juli Pons."

"Oh, Juli. He's a dear soul!" says Clotilde. "He says you read him poems during his lessons."

"Of course! I want him to understand that music is not just the black and white keys, not just about pedal technique. It's more. It's romantic visions, of lakes with cruising swans, enchanted mountains and forests, epic tales of love and death. I want him to learn how each fragment adds to the artistry. Of course I read poems to my students. And excerpts from literature."

"You've only read once or twice to me," she says.

Granados realizes he's talked himself into a corner. With Clotilde, the emphasis is on helping to improve her technique; with students who are more advanced, he infuses their studies with poems and prose. He avoids a reply that would make her feel slighted.

"Well, you haven't. Have you?" she insists.

He turns and points to the book of poems by Darío, which she's been holding on her lap. "No, but you and I've been reciting poetry to each other for some time, several years in fact, so it's hardly necessary during your lessons."

She laughs. "Ooooh, bravo for you, maestro! Most especially when I need to work on my technique. True?"

"I don't recite Darío with anyone but you," he says, struggling to retain his composure, but failing to effect the maestro's voice. The proper voice in conversation with a student.

"We talk of nightingales," she replies, "and courtly love from afar. Reciting poetry. And your catching the last train from Montgat." She looks away, riffling the pages of the book with her thumb. "Do you like his 'Poem of Autumn'?"

"Another one about autumn? Seems to be Darío's favorite season."

"Perhaps not his favorite, but a season for inspiration. It must put him in a melancholy mood," she says, scanning the first long title poem in the book. "Especially here, toward the end. Shall we take turns reading the verses? I'll begin":

> Delight in the flesh, the reward
> which today bewitches us,
> and later is transformed
> to dust and ashes.

"It's your turn," she says, holding the book in front of him.

Granados reads:

> Delight in the sun, in the pagan
> light of its fires;
> delight, because tomorrow
> you'll be sightless.

Clotilde reads:

> Delight in the sweet harmony
> invoked by Apollo;
> delight in the song, for one day
> you'll have no voice.

Granados:

> Delight in the earth, which is
> surely a burial ground;
> delight, because as yet you're not
> under the earth.

"And here's the ending," she says, still holding the book in front of him, and leaning onto his shoulder.

> The salt of the sea in our veins
> is welling up within us;
> we have the blood of sirens
> and of tritons.
>
> In us the evergreens and laurels,
> and the density of foliage;
> we have the flesh of centaurs
> and of satyrs.
>
> In us Life exhibits
> strength and warmth.
> Onward! to the kingdom of Death
> along the pathway of Love!

Clotilde closes the book and sits upright. "You see, he returns to hope at the very end."

"It's pretty gloomy. Though it could be one of his best."

"A masterpiece?" She takes the thought from the edge of his mind. "Could be," he says.

"So you and Darío both finished a masterpiece at about the same age."

"Same age?"

"Yes, both born the same year."

He shakes his head. "I didn't know that. Perhaps that explains why."

"Why his words are so resonant?"

"Yes. Just speculation."

"But not foolish," she argues. "He's a romantic, just like you. You're both poets. Dare I say you're both adventurers, both dissatisfied with the ordinary?"

"On the other hand, he works for the government. And as a journalist–which I wouldn't care for. Travels all over–which I might do if I didn't have to cross the oceans. And time and again he's been in trouble over women." Granados grins. "Can we change the subject?"

It's not easy to recapture the spirit of collaboration and surge of creativity that graced the composition of Book One last summer. The first part of Book Two is derived from the tenth of the *Caprichos*, titled "El amor y la muerte." Goya's etching depicts a grief-stricken woman comforting a man whose agonized expression suggests the imminent approach of death. His sword lies at his feet. He fought a duel and suffered mortal wounds. The eyes of both are closed; their mouths are opened in cries of love and anguish. Their love led to conflict, drawing of swords, violence, death, anguish. An inexorable sequence–how dreadful! Goya captures the deepest of sentiments: intense sadness, nostalgic love, the final tragedy of death.

Granados is also intrigued by the ninth *Capricho*, titled "Tántalo," which depicts a man wringing his hands in grief over a pretty young woman, who is either dead or dying. His face and his compact body could be Goya's. Her face is that of La Duquesa de Alba in the portraits by Goya. The man is tormented, pathetic and helpless. Is he too caught up in his grief to revive her? How ominous! When he sketched the *Caprichos*, Goya was bitter over the end of his romance with La Duquesa. But soon after he was crushed by her death, haunted by what he could have done to save her.

El amor y la muerte. The theme of love and death. Music to be played with animation and drama. With much expression and sadness. Opening with heavy bass notes, the foreboding sounds of impending tragedy. Savagery and lyrical dignity. Violent mood swings. As in Book One, lustrous ornamentation. Jeweled harmonies. Stunning rubato–notes drawn out that deviate from the tempo. Some butterflies recaptured from Book One, flying in new patterns, reflecting new colors. Once again the theme of the maja in the garden with the nightingale. A change in the maja's voice, as if grief can engender happiness, or somehow they can be entwined. And now it's an aching not merely from absence, but for the complete loss that follows death. Ending with a slow tolling of the bells.

"It's very rough. Needs a lot more work. A lot more." Granados says to Clotilde after several days. "I didn't expect it to take this long." He shakes his head. "Well, no sense rushing it. I want brilliance to the very last note! If it takes longer, I'll need perseverance."

"And patience, my lord, which is the very essence of genius."

He smiles. "Where's that from?"

She shrugs. "Oh, I just made it up."

He's delighted. "Now that's brilliance!"

"Is it time for a stroll in the garden?"

They walk around the beds of roses to a row of hydrangeas that are in their most extravagant bloom. They stop at the bench surrounded by eucalyptus trees that separate the flower garden from Clotilde's rows of vegetables, sloping down toward the pens and coops where she keeps her collection of animals.

"I have to confess," she says. "And I don't know how to say it–I hope you won't be offended. But if you are I have to say it anyway. We talk of patience, of making sure your brilliance is sustained to the very last note. I understand your being anxious to finish, you have so many others to tend to, so many other works rising up, so many more masterpieces to be composed. I want to confess that this work that brought you and me together, this *Goyescas* is the one that means so very much to me. The one that gave me a vision of becoming more than just another deixebla who's infatuated with her maestro–yes, let me finish–who's limited by the rules of our culture, who's forgotten when the next student comes along. So it's not about you or about me or about us, it's about this work."

She continues. "But I know we're going to finish this some day, in the not so distant future, and then–I'll be your student and you'll be my maestro. When that day comes and *Goyescas* is sent off to the publisher, that day will be like the piece you've been working on, where grief engenders happiness, that day will be the beginning and the end of–God knows what!–and I dread that day because I don't know what kind of day it will be for *me*. As if I matter that much. So I confess that if it takes longer for you to finish *Goyescas*, that would be fine with me, and I know that sounds selfish. It's just that I'll miss you when this is over. That's all, very simple. I'll miss you."

He understands. "You're afraid that when I've finished *Goyescas*, I'll move on, not be interested in you any more. I'll have gotten what I needed from you and then I'll move on. That's what you think?"

She rises to her feet and looks out over Tiana, across the coastal plain to the shimmering last flecks of light on the Mediterranean breakers. She sees a large steamship leaving the harbor, heading down the coast.

"Oh, how do I say it? Of course I want more. Of course I do! But not the part of you that Amparo already has. It would be so difficult to fall in love with you, knowing that nothing could come of it except heartache, like the lives of Tristan and Isolde, like Goya and La Duquesa. But if I had to choose that kind of fate or living without you, living without love, I'd rather be Isolde, rather that than never being truly alive. Wouldn't you? But if I were to fall in love with someone like you–with you, it would have nothing to do with what you and my father discussed in Igualada, it would have nothing to do with your feeling obliged to him. That's not my concern! Please, if I were to ever fall in love with someone like you–with you, I hope you'd please respect my choice!"

Granados rises and takes her hand. "When I first heard the song of the nightingale, it made my heart sing, drowning me in the trilling of that mournful song. What a time! I was so young, and life offered me such unlimited possibilities! And I carried the sound of that nightingale in my heart for years and years. I let it out in the 'Siesta' portion of *La Aldea* and again in the third part of *Escenas Románticas*, and now again in *Goyescas*. And I still wonder, why is the nightingale so important? When the other birds sing all day long, why does he sing at night?"

Clotilde turns and takes his other hand. "Then, who *is* the nightingale? Is it you? Or our favorite poet, Darío? If it's you, and you'd sing only at night, only when others are quiet–I don't want that for you. I want your song heard day and night! I want you to be a nightingale who sings by day and night."

"I've been longing to hear the song of the nightingale again. This time to hear it with you."

Clotilde pulls her hands away. "Some day. Perhaps. Not tonight. The last train leaves in twenty minutes. It's time to go."

"My dear, if it's not too much trouble, I'd like to stay until your nightingales begin to sing."

She laughs. "Oh, my dear, it's not a question of being too much trouble. But you have a family expecting you to return. You can't put them through that."

"I won't, not tonight. Tonight they'll be content–believing that I'm with Rusiñol in Sitges, and returning to them in the morning."

"Oh, my!"

Barcelona, March 1911

Tonight *Goyescas* will be premiered by Granados at El Palau de la Música, the newest and finest concert hall in Barcelona, and the apotheosis of Catalan modernist architecture. The city's other great hall, El Liceu, had been the top venue for opera for six decades, so since El Palau opened three years ago it's been embraced by lovers of orchestral, chamber, and choral music.

El Palau was built near the upper end of Via Laietana, a modern thoroughfare that slashes through the old city, connecting the port with l'Eixample. Six blocks west of the church of Sant Pere, where Granados was arrested for the second time during Setmana Trágica, and four blocks from his home. El Palau occupies a smallish site surrounded by narrow streets and apartment buildings. The architect, Lluís Domènech, argued for more space, but the opening of Via Laietana had driven up prices of real estate in that sector, so he settled for a site that didn't permit easy viewing of the façades, domes, and mosaics that distinguish El Palau's exterior: busts of Palestrina, Bach, Beethoven, and Wagner above the main entrance; on the façade above the carriage portico, a sculpture depicting archetypal Catalans gathered around a nymph representing folk music; and, watching over the sculpture, Sant Jordi–patron saint of Catalunya, holding the Catalan banner.

Inside, Domènech was required to build an auditorium with at least two thousand seats, rehearsal rooms, and the sizeable backstage space required for a concert hall, and to provide office and archive space for El Palau's main tenant, Orfeó Català–the choral group that spearheaded the raising of funds. His solution was to "float" the concert hall on the second level, with a double staircase for the audience to climb from the ground floor foyer. In the foyer and up the staircases, the audience experiences a display of Catalan craft and decoration intended to suggest the heroic proportions of a Wagnerian extravaganza. On the way up, the audience passes a dizzying collection of pink stained glass, twists of metal, tiles of pale ocher and aquamarine, balustrades of golden glass, and continuous streams of light passing through or reflected by an eclectic array of shapes.

The most dramatic sculpture waits in the oval shaped, glass-walled auditorium itself: a proscenium that frames the organ above the stage. Designed by Domènech and sculpted from ghostly white pumice by Didac Masana, it provides a startling contrast with waves of colored light flooding the auditorium from the sides of Domènech's "glass box" and descending from an enormous stained-glass skylight that plunges like an inverted fountain. The sculpted proscenium depicts the entire range of music envisioned for El Palau, from Catalan folk frolics and dirges to classical music for voice and instruments. On the left side, facing the stage, is a bust of composer Josep Anselm Clavé, along with the subjects of his lyric drama, *Els Flors de Maig*. On the right is another bust of Beethoven, flanked by Doric columns. Between the columns a cloudlike swirl rises and is transformed into Wagner's Valkyries on their winged horses, riding hard toward Clavé. On the back wall of the stage is a colorful arrangement of sculpted muses on a background of broken ceramic tiles, holding a variety of musical instruments. El Palau is a visual extravaganza.

Tonight will not mark Granados' first appearance at El Palau, though it will be the most significant. Soon after its opening, he performed with violinist Marià Perelló in a short program that was not well attended. Two months later, he staged the first two movements of *Dante* for a private audience, with critics concluding that with only two rehearsals the work was not ready. During last year's Lenten season, when a revised version of the same two movements was presented to a public audience, the reviews were more positive. And last November, Granados and Jacques Thibaud offered a concert at El Palau for a capacity audience, followed by good reviews.

Performing six of his own works tonight requires Granados to be on stage for nearly three hours. The audience, filling every seat, has high expectations. Those who expect an evening to glorify the folk music traditions of Catalunya will be disappointed. In contrast to the inaugural program of Catalan music, plus Bach and Handel, Granados's works are derived from other parts of Spain and Europe: *Valses Poéticas*–premiered in Madrid and not heard in Barcelona until four years later; *Azulejos*–according to Albéniz inspired by the ceramic tiles of Andalucía; Granados' transcriptions of sonatas by the Italian, Scarlatti; *Allegro de Concierto*–which won Bretón's contest at the Madrid Conservatorio; and *Goyescas*–inspired by the etchings of an Aragonese artist who lived most of his life in Madrid. Even the concluding work, *Cant de les Estrelles*, sung in Catalan by the Orfeó, is based on poetry by the German Heinrich Heine.

Despite the demand for seats tonight, the concert was scheduled only after Granados submitted a formal proposal to a review committee. To avoid a repeat of Albéniz's failure to gain approval at El Liceu for *Merlin*, Granados wrote his friend Malats, disclosing that he'd "written a collection of *Goyescas*, works of great sweep and difficulty," and asking him to join El Palau's review committee to help bring about a favorable decision. Since Malats is a Diémer Prize winner and spends most of his time touring Europe, he's no longer looked upon as merely "local talent"–nobody refers to him as "nostre Malats." This politically astute move was not Granados' invention, being first suggested by his confidant and neighbor, Dr. August Pi i Sunyer. It apparently tipped the scales: despite Malats' touring schedule and persistent illness that prevented his attending sessions of the review committee, he was able to champion the new work by mail.

The inflammation of Granados' digestive system recurs shortly after a light lunch: rice and chicken soup, two slices of bread smeared with ripe tomato, three slices from a pear, and a glass of white wine. Eating alone, perusing the choral score of *Cant de les Estrelles*. As he returns to the music salon, he feels the first fluttering of nausea. He stops, waiting for it to pass, and when he feels his lunch storming up from his stomach, he rushes to the nearest bathroom—between the kitchen and the salon, and heaves into the toilet bowl. Kneeling on the tile floor, he feels his head pounding and a wave of fever rising up the back of his neck, bound for his temples and forehead. From repeated bouts, he knows that diarrhea is lurking and will soon arrive.

Thank God it's not the migraine! Can't let it destroy this day. Audiences don't forgive pianists with bad stomachs. It must go away!

After the first attack, Granados makes two more hurried trips to the bathroom. Dry heaves and diarrhea. He's comforted by the likelihood that with his digestive system thoroughly emptied, he won't have to dash off the stage of El Palau tonight in the middle of *Goyescas* for another round of abdominal discharge.

While he dresses, Amparo brings a pot of tea, laced with honey, which he sips cautiously. Onced dressed, with help from Eduardo in getting his white tie to stay perfectly horizontal, he walks to the entry hall where Amparo and the children are gathered. The soft light of late afternoon, descending through the skylight at the top of Girona, 20, is converted to amber and green beams by the stained-glass window and dances on the children as they twitch and jostle.

Eduardo and Solita, young adults in formal attire, step forward to give their father solemn abraçadas; Solita whisks a few flakes of dandruff from his shoulders. "You're very handsome tonight, Papá," she says. Enrique, frowning and serious in a dark gray suit, says nothing as he embraces his father. Victor lurches forward to say, "Good luck, Papá," and lurches back. Natalia curtsies and gives him a radiant smile. Paquito, who at age nine has to be nudged forward by Solita, cries, "Hurry home!" as if Granados were leaving for an extended trip.

Amparo stands by the mahogany doors–twice her height–which are open to the landing at the head of the curving staircase where José Altet waits to descend to the street with Granados. Earlier today, Amparo fought off recognition that great success this evening could widen the crevasse between her and Granados, exacerbating their differences, propelling him to those glittering faraway cities where he'd be praised and fawned over and tempted by women who'd want a whiff of fame up close. She resisted fears that he'd leave her–the dogged practical wife, talented only in the domestic arts–farther and farther behind. She halted her slide toward despondency, chiding herself for such indulgence, assuring herself that she was indeed irreplaceable. Now, as Granados steps toward her, she rises on her toes to pull him close to her and kiss him lightly on the side of his neck. "I've given José a pot of tea–you can sip it in your dressing room."

He thanks her. "That's sweet. I'm much better."

She squeezes him again. "I'm very proud of you. This will be a magnificent night. The skeptics will forever be silenced–and it's about time!"

He laughs. "Dear Titín, you know they'll never be silenced. They're like vampires–need fresh blood every day."

She bristles at the suggestion. "After tonight, I dare them!"

The audience rises and applause fills Domènch's "glass box" as Granados enters the empty stage. He bows to his left–then to center, then to right–and walks back to the Chassaigne concert grand. He arranged for Flavio to tune it this morning so it would hold its brightness through the long night of energetic fingering.

Without hesitation, Granados prepares to play *Valses*, the first major work in his romantic-modernist period. No less than Henri Collet compared it to the music of Schubert, others heard echoes of Chopin. It was very well received and raised expectations for the composer then in his early twenties. Granados dedicated it "to my friend Joaquim Malats" and tonight, before beginning, he closes his eyes for an image of Malats' angular face.

Here's to you 'Quinito–wish you could be here.

Carmen sits with Salvador and their six children in the family box, below and to the right of Beethoven's statue and the fog from which the Valkyries soar above the stage. The first measure takes her back to the summer when it was composed…walking into the music salon of the xalet in Puigcerdà while Granados played it for her brother, remaining motionless until he finished, hairs erect on her arms. It was mid-August and dusk had settled over the pond and there was sunshine on the tops of the mountains across the French border. Soon it would be time to move her household and children back to Barcelona. Living on Carrer Aragó, hoping to move into the new villa in Sant Gervasi by springtime.

Carmen hears the familiar sequence of waltzes. As always, just a bit different than the last time. After the jaunty spirited introduction, the first waltz is sweet and melodic, and is followed by the regal waltz, then the slow and tender one with the delicacy of a rose petal, then the playful one that gives way to the elegant one, then the sentimental waltz which evokes the soft breeze off a lake in the early evening, followed by the short energetic lively one, the sequence of waltzes culminating with the coda and a rephrasing of the first, melodic waltz. Carmen hears all of life's longings and the fading of its occasional joys, astonished how much time has passed since that summer, and is grateful to Granados for carrying her back to that splendid time in her life.

Her reverie takes her to the day Granados burst into her brother's atelier in Paris, drenched by the spring rain–how thin and awkward he seemed! Most resembling a drowned rabbit. And then she heard him play, in a place where her brother would gather with his bohemian friends to drink anís and smoke hashish and rail against authority. The drowned rabbit came in dry clothes, hair cut short and moustache trimmed, bright and intense as he sat down at the upright piano, and he played, oh how he played! One could hear a pin drop. Instantly she recognized his majestic talent. Had no doubt there was genius in that smoky room.

The critics have heard *Valses* before, so it's not of much interest. Their attitude: it's pretty, charming, romantic, somewhat engaging–though it doesn't challenge the listener. Tonight, if history is to be made, if there's to be a compelling story for their readers, it will be the three works heard for the first time. The audience enjoys *Valses* and there is sustained applause.

"Azulejos" is next. Granados waits, taking a few moments to remember Albéniz. While completing the unfinished piece, he wondered if the spirit of Albéniz was guiding him; tonight, mindful of how much he owes to his late friend, he imagines exactly how Albéniz would want it to be played for its world premiere.

Spirit please flow to my hands. Here's a brindis, 'Saco! Celebrate with Heaven's finest cognac! And a puro—if they allow them there.

Albéniz's widow Rosina and his daughter Laura are in the first balcony, under the Andreus' box. As Granados begins and establishes the opening theme, Rosina is reminded of Albéniz's struggle to stay at the piano during their last winter on the French Riviera. She remembers his insistence in the last days at Cambó that she give the manuscript to Granados, hears an echo of his raspy voice: "Only to 'Ric. He'll know how to finish it." And Granados' promise that he'd "guard it with his life."

Laura Albéniz recalls Granados breaking down when told that her father was going to die, and his despairing voice: "No! His work's hardly begun!" She listens carefully, confident of recognizing the last measure written by her father and the first by Granados, but she misses it, so entranced is she by the notes that—just as intended—evoke the arrays of azulejos, the colorful tiles sparkling in the Andaluz sun.

Sitting on the lower level of El Palau with most of the music critics, Frederic Suárez Bravo of *El Diario de Barcelona* jots these notes: "This is clearly a work in the style of Albéniz, which Granados has successfully carried through. This is one more piece of *Iberia*."

There's considerably more fervor in the applause, with a sizeable contingent rising to their feet and the air pierced with numerous exclamations of "Bravo!" Granados takes a deep breath and sets the score for the next piece, the fourth sonata by Scarlatti, which he transcribed for the piano several years ago. It's glorious music, enjoyed by the audience. Since they've heard it, the critics find nothing of special interest. After bowing quickly, Granados prepares for *Allegro de Concierto*, which he also dedicated to Malats.

You should play this 'Quinito. Also Azulejos*—that was intended for you. Here's to you!*

As Granados begins *Allegro*, Paquita Andreu—sitting in her family box, is intimidated by the thought of performing this piece. "Me play this?" she asks herself. "Only my maestro could play this!"

On the other side of the auditorium, María Oliveró–sitting with her father, mother and sister Mercedes–listens intently to *Allegro*. She remembers Granados working on this piece while he was composing *Escenas Románticas*. When she was enraptured. She hasn't seen him since a chance encounter on Passeig de Gràcia last spring–how awkward he seemed to her. Seeing him on the stage tonight, immersed in his art, jostles her memory: her audition with him and her fear of rejection. Ten years working so hard to please him, knowing she could play well, though never well enough to be a concert performer. Never here in El Palau. She became his student at the age of ten and continued until she'd become a woman. Infatuated with him from the outset, in a young girl's way, idolizing him for his genius. In adolescence, fantasizing about him, flirting with him, teasing him, then a series of slips. Or so it now seems. All of those years as his student and nothing more. Until–when did they cross the line? How did it happen? She remembers wishing for more with him, not daring to ask for more, and as she watches him tonight it occurs to her that the affair may have been her petty illusion, something she craved, a dream rather than something that actually happened. Was it an illusion?

María wonders why Granados hasn't included *Escenas Románticas* in the program tonight. Unaware of his agreement to refrain from playing it publicly, she wonders: why not the one he dedicated to her? There must be a reason, perhaps more than one, but tonight she can only wonder.

During the intermission Granados returns to his dressing room, threading his way through members of l'Orfeó's choir waiting backstage for the final number. Perspiration runs down his face and he's relieved to slump into a chair. Is it the fever or excitement? He raises his right wrist to his forehead, at first feeling nothing, then realizing it's the wrist with the small bronze casting of the head of Beethoven mounted on a red leather band.

No fever–right Beethoven? If there's fever does it matter? Two pieces left then back home to collapse.

José Altet brings a cup of tea. "There's more honey in this one," he says in a nurturing tone. "Mestre hasn't had anything to eat for hours. That's not good."

Granados chuckles. "Not good, but better than having to leave in the middle of *Goyescas*." He closes his eyes and breathes deeply.

Now–back to Goya and the streets of Madrid the sound of feet dancing and powerful currents drawing lovers together and the mournful song of the nightingale.

"It's time to go, mestre," Altet says.

Granados is greeted with thunderous applause that reverberates off the glass-filled arches surrounding the concert hall of El Palau. It subsides only when he steps forward to the edge of the curved stage, standing where it might be imagined that the stony eyes of Clavé and Beethoven are staring. He bows in three directions and announces *Goyescas*.

"I had another name for this piece," he explains while the audience holds its breath to catch his words, "it was *Los Majos Enamorados*. But since I've tried to take the art of one of our greatest painters and interpret it with the piano, the name *Goyescas* seems more fitting. I hope you'll enjoy it." He returns to the Chassaigne.

The audience and critics hear the opening motif that recurs over and over, rising and plunging, arriving and fading, gleaming with ornaments, ceaselessly overlapping. Weaving new motifs that echo each other. Tumult and sudden rapture. The ecstasy, thrill, and danger of being carried away. An ubiquitous shadow of melancholy. Love and death intertwined and telescoped into each other. Over and over the colors and fragrance of roses. Heat shimmering and rising from the streets. Evoking a panoply of delights, some impossible to describe and others elusive and forbidden. Men and women glimpsed in passing, embellished for a moment or two until they vanish, specters of the immediate past. Murmured secrets, love declared with passion, whisperings in dark corners. Strangers whom we recognize as ancestors. Patterns of leaves and ripples as if a breeze were stirring the surface of a lake. Clouds soaring high and promising a perfumed journey to the ends of the earth. Tonight *Goyescas* begins in the streets of Madrid, but as the work progresses the audience is transported to the streets of anywhere, and the drama is not just about majos and majas, it's everyone's story.

Clotilde Godó sits in a box with her father, across the concert hall from the Andreus. She leans forward as Granados begins, concerned about how pale he looks. Clotilde knows every note, she's played every note, she's heard the work evolve day by day. She braces for the changes he's made since last summer but early in the piece, as she hears the "poco più animato," she's drawn into the music and along with most others at El Palau tonight she hears it as if for the first time.

The critics have been waiting for this. Their pencils are busy as they jot notes that will form the substance of their reviews. Joan Salvat of *Revista Musical Catalana* is sitting next to Josep Marià Folch, writer for several magazines including *Revista*. Salvat scribbles: "The impression is not startling, since Granados' works are lacking in violence... but buried within the sentiment–a sweet tranquility...it's the work's principal charm...this is the best of his piano work–brilliant, it will remain in the piano repertory."

Rafael Moragas, who organized the private performance of *Goyescas* last fall, leans over his notepad and jots: "The portrayal of street life in Madrid now takes on universal significance in this brilliant performance at El Palau." Carme Karr, sitting with her husband, journalist and playwright Josep de Lasarte, turns to him and whispers, "I love it–so somber, so playful, so dreamlike." Granados' friend and fellow Wagner enthusiast, Joaquim Pena, shakes his head repeatedly and wonders how he'll be able to sound like a critic in his review. His jottings include: "There's a vast richness of ideas and rhythms." Writer and journalist Marc Jesús Beltran of *La Vanguardia* notes that the response to this new work "is the kind that marks an epoch in musical history." The Comtessa de Castellà looks down at her notes: "dancing in the streets...poetry in the garden...always the melancholy overcome by optimism...trilling of the nightingale–so Spanish, so like Madrid in the time of Goya! No superlatives to describe how this touches me!" Scattered throughout the audience, other critics jot down their impressions: "glorious ornamentation...sheer opulence of imagination...richness of melodic invention...modernity in harmonies...captivated by lovers conversing through the window."

As Granados finishes, Carmen tries to hold back her tears, then resigns herself to the emotions taking over. Putting her arm around Paquita, whose tears are also streaming, she tells herself this is no time to hold back! María Oliveró tries to subdue her response, still protecting her parents, but it's no use; she lets the tears fall. And Clotilde, knowing that this masterpiece is part of her and attached to the deepest layer of memory, where it's indelible and forever part of her, rises with the audience for an ardent and exuberant outpouring of affection.

Throughout the concert, Amparo sits with the children in a box reserved for celebrities. Her mind drifts in and out of reverie. Their first meeting: Granados came to play that day for the Carbajosa family at their estate outside València, a former monastery surrounded by gardens and orchards redolent of orange blossoms. The Carbajosas–friends of Granados' father–invited the young pianist to perform at their large gatherings of family and friends. On that day, her family was included–the Valencian merchant Francisco Gal, his wife Francisca Lloberas, and daughters Paulita and Amparo. She recalls how thin and fragile he seemed to her. And, after they were bonded in love for music, how romantic he'd been! Her heart would sink when he left for Barcelona, and leap when he'd return to the Carbajosas. From what seemed a great distance came tender letters, addressing her as "my treasure," asking Amparo "to pardon all his whims," once declaring that she possessed "such beautiful affection that you could declare war on all of the hearts and then show them mine, and cry out 'learn to a love a Titín, you idiots!'" He was so sweet, she reflects, so earnest and yet hilarious, so handsome, so artistic, so passionate. In some ways so helpless! And as she looks at him now on the stage of El Palau–not so sweet, the ripened maestro but more handsome than ever, still earnest and hilarious and yes, passionate. And still so helpless! But this is a night for Amparo to forget all the peccadillos, a night to embrace this man of hers, this father of her six children.

Chapter Eight

Barcelona, Spring 1911

A wave of admiration is swelling for Granados and *Goyescas*, beginning with his private recital and peaking with the premiere at El Palau de la Música. Even music critics who concede his wizardry in playing the music of Beethoven, Chopin and Schumann, but have previously discounted his own works, are joining the chorus of adulation. Granados is surprised, elated, amused and–given the impermanence of cresting waves that must in due course fall–he's wary and a bit unnerved. He cajoles himself.

Carmen would call me idiot. Enjoy she'd say–don't look for the dark side! Clotilde would laugh. They'd both want me to revel! Revel!

Fragments of laudatory reviews of *Goyescas* still echo: "an intensely expressive pianist with delicate refinement... temperament of feminine subtlety expressed in manly fashion... Granados, the poet of the piano... interpreter of prudence and energy and elegance... to give a perfect concert requires more–must fall into the right hands... this most personal of his works reaches beyond to the artistically universal... blending of three arts: painting, poetry, and music... what genius and poetry, is combined to realize this idea... he made us live in a world that no longer exists–the memory is true art... the ovation was the kind that heralds an epoch... creates delight and beauty like the exquisite aroma of a flower... exquisite poetry and tender elegance... tonight's performance was received with an thunderous ovation for his incomparable works of art."

Why not revel with reviews like these? Why not?

The wave isn't confined to music lovers. Barcelona's political and business leaders are keen to honor him, so a committee is formed to plan an homenatge

–a ceremony of homage–in one of the city's most venerated places, El Saló de Cent. It's headed by Domingo Sanllehy and Apel.les Mestres, whose verse was the inspiration of Granados' five lyric dramas. Sanllehy–former mayor of Barcelona, member of Catalunya's parliament, three times president of the Cercle del Liceu, and married to the daughter of the banker and industrialist Manuel Girona, reputedly the wealthiest Catalan. These names at the top of the invitation ensure a room full of Catalunya's political, commercial, and cultural elite to honor Granados.

El Saló de Cent–Salon for the One Hundred–was built to provide a permanent meeting place for members of Barcelona's provincial Council, or parliament. Established in 1274 to represent a broad range of interests and classes, the Council was regarded as one of mediaeval Europe's unique political innovations. It also proved to be one of the more durable, lasting 440 years until it was abolished by the French Bourbon king, Felipe V, victorious in the War of Spanish Succession. Since then, all major decisions have been made by the central government in Madrid, but El Saló de Cent remains the meeting place for the city council and a favored site for ceremonial events.

Granados is greeted at the main entrance by José Maria Orriols, editor of *Revista Mundial*, a monthly magazine devoted to promoting the commerce, industry, trade, and tourism of Catalunya. Orriols–dressed in a grey jacket, black vest, and pin-striped trousers–is a tall, sleek man with receding black hair, combed back and secured with thick hair creme, a long curving nose, sharp protruding chin, and dark thin arching eyebrows. This afternoon he's attentive to Granados to the point of making him nervous.

"I can't exaggerate our delight in having you with us today, maestro," Orriol says as he leads Granados up a long flight of stone stairs.

Granados is amused. "I should be the one delighted for such an honor. I'd have come today if they had to carry me on a stretcher!"

Orriol leads Granados to a podium at the far end of El Saló. It's draped in crimson velvet with a border of harvest yellow, embroidered with the shield of Catalunya.

Granados glances at a copy of the agenda. "You want me to speak?" he asks. "I must confess, oratory isn't my forte."

"Oh, just a few words–after you receive the plaque and a special gift." Orriols rattles off a long list of expected attendees. It includes most members of the Barcelona city council; Mario Sol, mayor of Granados' hometown, Lleida;

several members of the provincial and national parliaments; Enric Prat de la Riba, cofounder of La Lliga Regionalista; Joaquín Sostres Rey, a monarchist who expects to become mayor of Barcelona later this year; the Marqueses of Alella and Marianao and the Comte de Vinatesa; business leaders from the flour milling, textile, and railroad industries; prominent bankers and financiers; and Pere Guerau Maristany Oliver, leading exporter of Catalan wines, recently named Comte de Lavern by King Alfonso XIII.

Intrigued by the auspicious list of guests, Granados wonders what would motivate them to pay homage to a hometown musician. He looks up at the stone arches. Compared to the floral glitter of El Liceu and El Palau, this space is plain and predictable. A secular throne room. A space intended for debating ordinary matters of the day—water and sewers and police, streets and roads, building permits, taxes. Andreu would be perfectly at ease here, artfully convincing council members to widen this street, seal off that one, and to do whatever might ensure success for his pharmacies and real estate ventures. To Granados, these dignitaries are just names. He notes the dimensions of the salon, is thankful they've not asked him to play.

Acoustics would be dreadful! Still it's an honor—must learn to revel!

"And, maestro, we have proclamations from no less than three hundred and sixty-eight cities and towns!" says Orriols, exuding pride. He leans toward Granados in the empty room as if to make sure nobody can overhear. "Quite honestly, there are places on this list that I'd never heard of. Yecla! Have you heard of Yecla? Casalla de la Sierra? Guernica-Lumo? Ciudad Rodrigo?"

Granados laughs. "That's remarkable—do you suppose they've actually *heard* my music in those places?"

Granados is heartened by the arrival of his staff and the advanced-level students from the academy, along with critics Joaquim Pena and Rafael Moragas, stage designers Miquel Moragas and Ricard Alarma, and dozens of writers, scholars, architects, and artists.

Andreu breezes into El Saló, pumping hands with the politicians, as comfortable here as Granados expected he'd be. He gives Granados a long abraçada. "Quite a gathering, mestre. I'd have to die to get this many people together."

Granados laughs. "Salvador, this many would gather just to hear you on the harmonium!"

"Hear *me*? Hunh! Not to hear me, no senyor, to hear the Orquestra Andreu i Granados."

Santiago Rusiñol arrives arm in arm with Eugeni d'Ors; they swap anecdotes with Granados about the nights when the teenagers–d'Ors and Ruiz Picasso–were allowed to sit with the established bohemians at Els Quatre Gats; about the night d'Ors read his gothic story at Rusiñol's villa in Sitges while Granados played his improvisations far into the night with the surf breaking on the rocks below.

D'Ors leans toward Granados and in a low voice says, "How we talked about Goya–how we adored him! Remember? And now, Enric, you've done it! I knew you would–felicitats!"

Granados asks when d'Ors' new novel will be published.

"Ah, *La Ben Plantada?* I promise you'll get your own copy the very first day! And I think you'll recognize her."

"I'll recognize who?"

D'Ors laughs. "My heroine. La ben plantada. Teresa. Oh, you'll recognize her–just as I recognized La Duquesa de Alba in *Goyescas.*"

It's time for the formal ceremonies. Orriols reads a proclamation: "The genius of Enrique Granados is not merely recognized by the people of España but also by music critics and colleagues of Maestro Granados. Yet these were not the only factors. There was also the 'secret' that he is a member of the Permanent Tribunal of the Doctorate of Music in Paris, France! That's right, our own Maestro Granados! He's very modest, you know."

Our Granados–must learn how to revel in this! So revel!

Orriols continues. "Tonight, in addition to all of you distinguished men who've come to honor Maestro Granados, we have proclamations from no less than three hundred sixty-eight cities and towns in España!" He pauses and picks up the list of proclamations.

Ay Dios Mío! Will he read the entire list? Yes, he's going to!

Indeed, nothing will deter Orriols from his task. At the end of his extended time at the podium, he hands a large silver plaque and a small box to Granados–the special gift. Inside is a gleaming gold ring with a square-cut diamond. The plaque commemorates the occasion with a bas-relief bust of Granados and a likeness of Goya's *Capricho,* "Tal para cual."

María Luisa–the Queen–and Godoy. When he was army officer. Not just men who are corrupt. They're two of a kind. Procurer and procuress. Amusing they put that one on this plaque!

The mayor of Lleida steps forward and raises his glass. "Brindis!" he exclaims. "Here's to Maestro Granados–I'm so very proud to be mayor of the birthplace of our distinguished guest of honor!" He turns and gives Granados a warm abraçada.

Granados looks out at the gathering of the rich, powerful, wise, and talented who've come to honor him. Touched and somewhat disoriented. Is this what he's been waiting for? He thanks Orriol before turning to the guests. Still a bit numb, he shakes his head, then grasps the podium with both hands. "Thank you for coming tonight. I'm exceptionally grateful. But I tell you, good senyores, most generous senyores, I'd be eternally grateful if instead you recognized Isaac Albéniz–the greatest of our composers–as you recognize me tonight, and I ask you to spare nothing in bestowing these same honors to the beloved composer of *Iberia*. How much I'd enjoy this kind of recognition for *him!*"

Paris

When Granados arrives at Casals' home in the Villa Molitor, Madam Coderq greets him at the front door. She takes his hat and leads him back to the small garden. In the music room Suggia is practicing a piece by the Hungarian composer Emanuel Moór. The early spring flowers are budding and the songbirds are courting. Casals rises and after a hearty abraçada he hands Granados a copy of the magazine *Le Monde Musical*.

"This is for you," says Casals. The magazine is opened to a long review of Granados' performance of *Goyescas* at La Salle Pleyel three nights ago. "I come home from London and find you've become a beloved celebrity–*you*, my old Catalan brother! Paris isn't a city that squanders praise–you know that, but today they can't say enough fine words about this Granados." He points to the magazine. "The review is simply lluminosa. And rare in this city of lights. So come over–sit down and enjoy it!"

Granados reads every word of the review, relishing some of the phrases again and again. Spiced with flourishes of Gallic hyperbole. According to the critic for *Le Monde Musical*, Granados as a pianist "is the equal of the great maestri of the keyboard today. The sonority he produces is amongst the most beautiful, the most varied and the most expressive that are known today; his performances are always driven by the highest and purest sources of great art." As for his own compositions, the reviewer continues, "in all of these pieces is the hand of a maestro, a hand that has a rare gift for firmness in rhythmical and melodic design, with a color reminiscent of the great Spanish master...with planes, reliefs, shadows, bright lights that make *Goyescas* a singularly attractive work that can be ranked alongside *Iberia* by Albéniz. It was an unusual stroke of good luck to be able to hear this work performed by the composer himself, an experience that will not be equaled for a very long time. Rarely have such artists come to Salle Pleyel, rarely has the auditorium been so vibrant, so enthusiastic, so truly entranced as it was by the exceptional artist from Barcelona."

Granados couldn't have asked for a better audience at La Salle Pleyel: a galaxy that included Camille Saint-Saens, Gabriel Fauré, Jules Massenet, Jacques Thibaud, Edouard Risler, Charles de Beriot, Eugène Ysaye, Vincent d'Indy, Alfred Cortot, Louis Diémer, Ricard Viñes, Maurice Ravel, and Claude Debussy.

My revelry continues! They gave me the piano—Camille Pleyel's favorite. And the French government gave me a medal. Granados now Chevalier de la Legion d'Honneur. But no horse to ride up Champs-Élysée? They wouldn't let me study at Conservatoire—now make me Chevalier. Vive la difference!

Granados' daydream is interrupted by Suggia, whose heels click on the flagstones as she glides across the garden, a large cat on the prowl. As he rises she slides her hand across his cheek and gives him a warm abraçada. "Hope I'm not disturbing you," she says. She smells of Paris.

He holds up *Le Monde Musical.*

"Glorious review, don't you think?"

"I hope it's not a case of mistaken identity. Where's Pau?" he asks.

Suggia's laugh is scornful. "Aghhh! He's been upset all day about the bridge on his cello. Thinks it's coming loose. I looked at it and think it's purely his imagination. But you know Pau, obsessed with his cello—his instrumento." She gives the last vowel a long Portuguese U-sound. "It's always about some part of his beloved cello. The soundboard. Or the strings. Or the finger board. Or the tuning pegs. Today it's the bridge. He'll spare nothing for his cello. And what about me?" she asks, her voice rising. "What about me? I wish he'd be obsessed with my parts!" She raises her hands, drawing the tapering fingers slowly up her body in twin arcs, across the top of her skirt. The sinuous gesture traces ten shadows across the upper part of her blouse, illuminated by the afternoon light that is slicing through gaps between the poplar trees in Casals' garden.

Granados knows there's mischief behind her smile. "Please, 'Mina! Pau's my oldest, dearest friend. If you're trying to get his attention, I don't want to be a pawn in your game."

Suggia steps back. "Forgive me, maestro. I didn't mean to offend you. But he leaves me alone here for days and weeks. He returns from London—for just two days!—and spends the day fretting about his cello. It's as if I'm not even here! Then he's off again—to Budapest!"

Tiana

The village is baking on this breezeless midsummer day. As Clotilde drives into Tiana, rings on her fingers flash and sparkle in the sunlight. Granados watches her with appreciation and endearment. "I've missed you too," he says, shifting his stack of composition pads to his right arm and reaching over to touch the pale, lustrous skin flowing from neck to shoulder. "I've missed you–every single day," Granados says as she maneuvers her car onto Avinguda Onze de Setembre.

Clotilde smiles. "You've said that twice."

"Yes. Am I distracting you?" he asks, withdrawing his hand.

"Not distracting. Making me warm all over."

"Not the sun?"

"No, it's you. Please don't stop. You've been away so much."

He breathes deeply. "Yes, trying hard to revel in all the attention. I'm not very good at it–still a neophyte at this reveling!"

Clotilde is amused. "You'd better get used to it. I know you have a whole new cloud of butterflies waiting to burst forth. So many, if they flew over us now they'd darken the sky."

He laughs. "You're my dearest fanática. I'd be content simply to finish *Goyescas* in a month. I have to finish it before the academy opens."

"Isn't that two months from now?"

He shakes his head. "Yes, but I promised Salvador and Carmen I'd come to Puigcerdà the third week in August. Salvador even had the Festa delayed so I'd be there to lead the family orchestra. You'd think the orchestra was more important than his businesses."

She laughs. "Perhaps it is! What's wrong with that?"

"So I have the entire month for the fifth and sixth parts–then *Goyescas* will be complete."

Clotilde nods, reassured that their collaboration is being extended. "All right, then. You'll have the house and the pianos. And I'll keep them in perfect tune. And you'll have me."

"That's the best of all," he replies. "You're always in perfect tune."

"Ooooh, dear me! If you have just one month, there'll be precious little time for that kind of revelry. That will have to wait. And I command you to stay healthy. Fish soup or chicken soup every day. No migraines."

"I'm bound to have one of them."

"I'll ask La Virgen to spare you." Her voice is unwavering.

"How can I fail–with you and La Virgen?"

"That's enough," she says, wheeling her car into the courtyard.

In the privacy of Clotilde's music salon they turn to each other in a lovers' embrace. At last, Granados relaxes his arms and breaks away. From the stack of composition pads he retrieves a large envelope. "This is for you," he says.

Clotilde's face is aglow as she opens the envelope. "Oh! I wonder what this is. Must I guess?"

"No. It's the Private Edition."

Clotilde reads the cover page. "Private Edition of the first book of *Goyescas* (*Los majos enamorados*), printed in Barcelona, 1911. Copy issued to Clotilde Godó Pelegrí. Copy Number Two."

"Please turn it over," he says.

She reads the handwritten inscription on the back of the page.

> "To Clotilde Godó
> Greetings from your maestro.
> Enrique Granados
> Barcelona in the year 1911
> month of June."

Clotilde looks up. "But this is your Private Edition!" she says in a choked voice. "Given only to the *most* important people. Patrons. Royalty. Dignitaries. Family. The closest of friends."

"Yes. So I've given copies to the Andreus and the Condés. And to friends like August Pi i Sunyer. I've sent them to Pau and Malats and Viñes. And Beriot and Crickboom and Bretón. Who else? Of course, Pedrell. And the mayors of Barcelona and Lleida. Monsieur Lyon at La Salle Pleyel. And–oh yes, to Rosina Albéniz. I also have one for the King. And at Sorolla's suggestion, one for the Hispanic Society of America in New York. Who else? Marshall and Mas and Llongueras." He raises his hands. "I've forgotten the rest."

"And you've included me–with all of *them*?"

"Of course!"

"Why is my copy marked with the number '2'?"

He smiles. "They're all numbered. One through fifty."

"But this is Number Two! My copy. Why?"

"Because you're very, very important to me. Because without you there would be no *Goyescas*."

Clotilde shakes her head. "I don't know what to say." She recovers. "Would you be offended if I asked who received Number One?"

Granados laughs. "Ah, that's an excellent question. Number One is for King Alfonso XIII."

Granados plays the opening figure of the fifth part of *Goyescas*, making corrections with a pencil. The theme is love and death, and it's derived mainly from Goya's tenth *Capricho*, depicting a grief-stricken woman holding her dying lover who–judging by the sword lying at his feet–has been mortally wounded in a duel. This fifth part also echoes the tragedy of the ninth *Capricho*, depicting a distraught man holding a dead or dying woman on his lap.

The ten bass notes of the first measure are dark, intense and ominous. A theme of death. Granados intends to shatter the poetic elegance of the maja's lament in the previous part; he will repeat the opening figure often as a reminder that death is always close by, even during fleeting spells of gaiety, passion and joy. In measures eleven and twelve, the maja's lament from "The Maja and the Nighingale" is heard again, then sharply interrupted by the jarring theme of death. In the second part, her lament was for the absence of her lover. Now it's a lament of helplessness and grief as he dies in her arms. In measure twenty-one, the theme from "Coloquio" returns, echoing the adoring conversation through the window. Three measures later the theme of death returns with an ominous chord, a reminder this is the lovers' last conversation.

Clotilde sits down beside him and scrutinizes the composition pad. "I see you're bringing back the lament from Book One," she says, pointing to measures eleven and twelve. "And weaving them into a different tapestry with this heavy opening figure. A darker tapestry."

He nods. "A despairing one."

"It was absolutely jarring to hear the interruption. It made me hold my breath."

He smiles. "Good! That's what it's supposed to do."

"Will you also reintroduce 'Requiebros' and 'Fandango?"

"Yes. They'll come back too. You'll recognize them but they won't be exactly the same."

She points to measures eleven and twelve again. "You've marked this 'Lento' here, but wasn't it 'Andante melancólico' in the original lament?"

"That's correct. But when it's reintroduced, there's a melancholy of despair and grief, not just a longing for the absent lover. And also a reflection of *Capricho* number nine, with the man in grief over a dying woman. Both sides of the dyad, trapped between love and death. So in this part, the lament, should be a bit slower and more fragile."

She nods. "But I hear love trying to overcome death. The maja trying to affirm that love will prevail."

"What a joy it is to work with you!" he says.

She shakes her head. "No–it's my joy. One more question, if I may."

"You certainly may."

"With all these fragments, the tonality's a bit confusing. You start with B flat minor, then you start to wander. It could be bewitching but also bewildering."

Granados drops his pencil. Her intensity is endearing and he cannot control his delight. "You think I'm wandering?"

She hesitates. "Yes, I think you are. *Aren't* you?"

"Would you be surprised if I closed this part with a G minor chord?"

She smiles. "Oh no, mi maestro. There is nothing about you I'd find surprising!"

Puigcerdà

Flavio the piano tuner is waiting with his tool kit and suitcase in the main courtyard of Xalet Andreu as the driver Xavier slides the big black Rochet-Schneider to a stop with his usual panache. Granados steps onto the cobblestones as Carmen appears in the front doorway of the chalet.

"Here you are–at last!" she exclaims as they greet each other.

"Only slightly worse for wear," Granados replies with a quick motion of his head toward Xavier. He's regaining his balance after the long drive.

"But isn't this a splendid day to drive through the mountains, mi querido?"

He laughs. "Yes, quite splendid, I'll grant you that. I could see all the way down–where we'd die if Xavier drove off the road."

"Oh, that's nonsense. Xavier's an excellent driver–we haven't lost a single guest. Well, not yet. And he's far better than my two young lady race drivers, who miraculously survived crashing into each other!"

"Paquita and Madronita? Of course you're joking."

"I wish I were! Don't think Salvador was pleased, having to pay for repairs. He admitted it was better than repairing the girls." Carmen laughs. "Enough of this. He's pacing in the garden, dreadfully anxious to talk to you. Keeps muttering, 'where's my conductor?' You know how intense he gets. He's had the children practicing every single day."

Andreu is far more amiable than in Carmen's description. Not surprisingly, the first matter is to set a time for rehearsal, but having dispensed with that, he announces that work has begun on the recital hall. Sala Granados.

Granados is delighted. "That's wonderful! Is it on Tibidabo, the site you showed me?"

"Yes, indeed. Número 18, Avinguda Tibidabo. Using the plan you and I reviewed. Recital space, practice rooms. I didn't cut anything out."

"Salvador! It's been a dream for so long! And now it's coming true. How can I thank you?"

Andreu smiles and strokes his white goatee. "Assuming you're ready, I'd like to hear the rest of *Goyescas* this evening. Naturalment, after our rehearsal."

Of course, first things first. "I'm ready," Granados says. "And it's playable! Needs some fine tuning, that's all."

"Speaking of tuning, we had Flavio here this week."

"Yes. I saw him in the driveway."

Andreu nods. "Xavier agreed to drive him down to Ribes."

Granados is appalled. "But he just brought me up from Ripoll. How long can Xavier keep on driving?"

Salvador laughs. "You put Xavier behind the wheel and he'll drive forever. Don't worry–he won't kill the piano tuner."

Paquita Andreu is ecstatic. Her father gave her the good news about the recital hall this morning, so when Granados enters the music salon she rises and runs from the piano to greet him. "Oh, maestro–I'm so happy! I'm just dizzy! It's been a dream for so long! I thought it would never happen! Most dreams don't. How can I thank you? How?"

"Thank me?" Granados cocks his head.

"Yes, thank *you!*" exclaims Paquita. "Father would not build a recital hall for a pianist of ordinary talent, not even his daughter."

Not going to argue with her. She wouldn't understand.

Paquita motions for Granados to follow her to the piano. "You told me to be patient, not to be in a hurry to play *Goyescas*. So I have been patient, oh so patient! Painfully patient! I've been working on the Mendelssohn."

"That's good. I'd love to hear it."

"And also *Azulejos*, she says. "Mamá brought me the sheet music from Paris."

He shakes his head. "I would not have assigned that to you."

"I know. That's what Mamá said, but won't you'll help me with it?"

He is resigned. "Of course. I know when I'm outnumbered."

"And one more thing, maestro." Paquita reaches behind the printed sheet music and pulls out a composition pad. "I've been working on some music of my own. Hunhh–it's nothing, compared to yours. But I'm quite pleased with it. Some day, perhaps, could I play it at Sala Granados?"

"Why not? But first, I'd like to hear it."

"While you're here? Splendid! If Father will leave us alone between rehearsals!"

He laughs. "Let's hope he will."

Paquita steps close to Granados. "And I'd like you to drive over to France with me. Lunch some day. To celebrate Sala Granados."

He shakes his head.

Por dios! Drives just like Clotilde. Must pray to St. Christopher!

"You don't ever give up, do you?" he asks.

"And you, maestro? Do you give up if it's something you really want?"

He seizes upon one last ploy. "But if I went with you, wouldn't the others be jealous?"

Paquita laughs. "The others? Of course not! Carmencita is married now–she's our perfect doña de la casa. Madronita? She has photography–her only true passion. And the boys? Salvador and Pepe are like acolytes for Papà–farmacías, medication, pills, money–and Juanito lives only for tennis and golf–and the girls. That leaves me, the only real aficionada. Mother says it's what she hoped for, we'd all find something enthralling, not march in step like Prussian soldiers."

"Your mother said that?"

Paquita smirks. "No. I made it up. But she *might* have said it."

Granados is walking around the pond with Carmen. A storm swept in from the high Pyrenees last night, leaving a dusting of snow below the tree line on the nearby mountains. It's considerably cooler than yesterday afternoon, and they both have cashmere scarves draped over their shoulders.

"How many times have we walked like this?" she asks. "Hundreds of times? Thousands?"

He ponders the question. For at least twenty years. Several times during each of his visits. "I'd say hundreds, not thousands. Whatever the number, I thank God for them. And for you."

"I pray there will be hundreds more," Carmen replies.

"I can think of nothing better."

"Yet we may not be so fortunate."

What is it? Bad news from a doctor? She's seems robust as ever.

"What do you mean?" he asks.

"Oh, I don't mean to frighten you. No, there's nothing wrong with me. I should live to be an irascible old lady. It's just that we can't know how many more years we'll have. God takes us when he chooses, not when we're ready to go. It's the apparent randomness of who goes when and why. I couldn't imagine Francisco dying so young."

"Or 'Saco. Even younger."

"Precisely. Of course, and I wonder what if they'd taken better care of themselves?'"

Granados nods. Albéniz's gargantuan appetite, his devotion to brandy and puros. Miralles' bohemian life style in Paris. "'Saco didn't take care of himself at all," he says, "as for Francisco? I loved him like my own brother. He was–different, wasn't he?"

"You knew that and I knew that, but we're not supposed to let it pass our lips. All of us are different from each other, aren't we? But he was so very different–"

"In a way that was unacceptable," he replies. "And unmentionable. Not for me, not for you. But for most people, especially in this part of the world. At this time."

She shakes her head. "I remember people wondering, why isn't Francisco married? Why doesn't he have a family? He's so handsome. Talented. Worldly. So kind and thoughtful. Muy caballero."

"And how lonely he must have been, surrounded by people whose lament was that he wasn't more like them." Granados takes her hand. "But I doubt that had anything to do with his dying so young. Any of us could die tomorrow."

"I know," she says. "I didn't mean to suggest he'd still be alive. No, it was related to the randomness of when we die. That's all. God bless our dear Francisco. Thankfully, my God is a god of acceptance, and that's why I know my brother is with my God. He hears my prayers." Carmen stops and turns to Granados. "I've never asked you this–what do you pray for?"

He prays very seldom, but the answer is close to the surface. "I pray this world will some day be a place where differences are celebrated, not stigmatized. Where beauty is revered–more than power and wealth. And those who are divergent or bizarre or eccentric are treated like our brothers and sisters."

Barcelona, February 1912

The site that Andreu selected for Sala Granados is on the east side of Avinguda del Tibidabo, the avenue running up the middle of an affluent neighborhood being developed by him. Tramvia Blau–a sky-blue electric trolley car–runs up and down the avenue, from Passeig de Sant Gervasi to the base of a funicular railway that ascends to a plaza below the peak of Mount Tibidabo.

Years ago, when Andreu bought the land in the Tibidabo area, it seemed too far from the heart of the city to attract new residents. But he foresaw that the shortage of land between the urbanized area of Barcelona and the Collserola mountains was bound to inflate the value of his investment. And to hasten his payback, he convinced the city council to extend Carrer Balmes into Sant Gervasi. That would have a catalytic effect on his developments in Sant Gervasi and Tibidabo.

Sala Granados' neighbors are large villas and small palaces of three and four stories, surrounded by stone walls and iron fences, most of them gated and separated from the street by curving driveways. Distinctive for their size though not for architectural daring. Their owners are members of the alta burguesia who relish being seen as pacesetters, and who enjoy Tibidabo's cleaner air and superior view of the city below. Andreu is fond of saying that without exception they asked to purchase property in Tibidabo. He was in no rush to sell them the real estate.

The parcel of land proposed for Sala Granados was still available because its back portion falls off into what was once a ravine carved by the spring rains coming off the Collserola. So any building must be sited close to the street, making it impractical for construction of a large villa or small palace.

Avinguda Tibidabo, Number 18 stands at street level with an unpretentious front façade abutting the sidewalk, rising only one story to a terrace level enclosed by a balustrade. Three tall entry doors are framed by fluted Ionic columns with scroll-like capitals. Above the middle door are the simple block letters: "ACADEMIA GRANADOS." Inside is the lobby, and behind it is a plain vaulted two-story auditorium with an elevated stage and one level of seating for no more than two hundred. On the level below the auditorium is a cluster of practice rooms for the academy, opening up onto a crude terrace, in need of landscaping, which overlooks the former ravine. So the sloping land of Tibidabo, 18, a challenging site for a villa, is quite suitable for this building that tucks the space for music lessons and rehearsals under the auditorium. And what it lacks in elegance of design and décor, it recovers in functionality.

Granados' original idea was a recital hall for soloists and chamber ensembles, a less commercialized place where new talent could perform and new works could be heard. Before they're beaten to death by the critics. Works that would never be presented by El Liceu or El Palau. The idea was amplified by a growing need for more practice rooms at the academy, which could not be accommodated at Girona, 20. And an even broader vision emerged, which Granados described to Andreu with enthusiasm: a place of union between composers and performers and those who enjoy their music, a place that serves the art of music and becomes a sanctuary for it, a place for people to come and breathe the air of creativity, and a place of sensitivity, where students can face the challenge of performing an entire program for a special but still rigorous audience. There's no comparable place in the city, no place in the entire country. Nor is there any place for poets and composers to come together, or for the new works of Granados and others to be heard without the fanfare and politics of El Liceu and El Palau.

After seeing that Andreu recognized his broader vision, Granados added the coup de grace. "And–not least of all–to give musicians a place to perform that doesn't require they be the very best, only that they be devoted–completely loyal to their art," he told Andreu.

"You mean musicians like our Paquita?"

Granados hesitated, wondering how Carmen would advise him to respond.

"Well, if it helps Paquita," Granados said, "that's an added blessing. She can be part of the vision, because not everyone who loves music can be the very best, and they too deserve a place like this."

The auditorium is filled this evening, with a congregation of students from the academy standing behind the rows of seats. Moderate, elegant, tasteful, and gleaming white, the space reflects Granados' vision. No banners, no flags. For tonight's audience, it's a haven from the chill wind sweeping uphill from the Mediterranean, as well as a nexus brimming with promise, buzzing with opening night excitement.

Tonight's invited audience was chosen by Granados and Andreu one evening in November at the villa in Sant Gervasi. The Andreu family is seated on the right side of the front row, separated by a center aisle from the Granados family. The audience includes Granados' staff at the academy, his musical colleagues, students and former students, friends of Granados and the Andreus, selected music critics, city officials, the marqueses of Alella and Marianao, the Comtessa de Castellà, and a priest from the parish church of Sant Gervasi, who's been invited to give the blessing. A young Mexican journalist, Francisco Gandara, who interviewed Granados earlier this week at Girona, 20, stands in the rear with the academy students, scribbling notes. At the last minute, a seat is added on the left side of the front row for a representative of King Alfonso XIII.

When Granados walks to the Pleyel–the piano he received in Paris last April, Camille Pleyel's favorite–the audience rises and greets him with deafening applause. He bows, dignified and serious, and in a voice wavering with emotion thanks everyone for attending. He turns and motions for the Andreus to rise. He struggles to maintain composure and clears his voice. "Without my dear friends, Salvador Andreu and Carmen Miralles, I would not be here tonight. You would not be here. This perfect gem of a recital hall would not be here. So join me, please, in recognizing them!"

After the applause, Granados plays three of the pieces that he's preparing for next month's concert with violinist Jacques Thibaud at El Palau: Chopin's "Nocturne and Ballad," followed by Brahms' Third Piano Sonata and Beethoven's *Patetique* Sonata in C minor. The applause is progressively more exuberant. After the Beethoven, someone in the middle of the auditorium cries out, "Maestro–play something of your own!"

Granados raises his hands, and turns his head from side to side. "Maestro–play one of yours!" cries another voice. Now there's a chorus of voices, now a cascade. "Yes–one of yours! Yes, Maestro Granados, please! One of yours!" He looks over at Salvador and Carmen and sees they're both nodding their heads.

No escape tonight. Have to play one—but which? Everyone's heard Goyescas. *What have they not heard? Yes—*Dante!

Granados shrugs, announces that he'll play "a sketch," and sits down to play an excerpt from "Paolo e Francesca," the second movement from his unfinished symphonic poem. The applause is deafening. He bobs his head, not quite comfortable with the adulation, and licks his lips nervously.

The audience surges forward and surrounds him, grasping his hand, clasping him in abraçadas, and pouring torrents of congratulations over him.

Paris, Spring 1912

Granados has been invited once again by Gabriel Fauré to be a member of the Diémer Prize jury. He departs from Estació França and makes the familiar journey through Marseilles, Lyon, and Dijon, arriving at the Gare de Lyon in the southeast sector of Paris. He's looking forward to seeing some old colleagues on the jury, playing Book One of *Goyescas* for Fauré at the Conservatoire, and giving a private recital of *Goyescas* at the apartment of Joaquín Nin and Rosa Culmell. Joaquín, Rosa and their three children still live mainly in Brussels, but they're in Paris this month while Joaquín gives classes at the Schola Cantorum. For Rosa, it's a chance to have their nine-year-old daughter, Anais Nin, examined by a specialist in children's diseases.

On the evening of the recital, Rosa opens the door for Granados. He barely recognizes her. Anais' susceptibility to illness, her own stressful marriage to Joaquín, and frequent moves with three children have aged Rosa well beyond her forty years. Joaquín, in contrast, looks younger than his thirty-three years. He could be Rosa's son.

Tonight—dressed in the manner of aristocracy, lean and handsome with dark blue eyes and auburn hair—Joaquín moves about the apartment with an intense nervous energy, infallibly courteous to his guests, who include Granados and Manuel de Falla. Words glide from Nin's mouth as he greets his guests. "I'm so enormously pleased you could come. This place? Just rented for the month. Of course we're normally at our villa—near Brussels. Would you care for some champagne?" He apologizes to Granados for "the indelicate condition of the piano," indicating he was too busy to have it tuned.

Granados walks over to Falla, a thin man in his mid-thirties with a hawk's nose and a balding, wedge-shaped head. He's dressed in a black suit, looking dour as a priest. Both studied composition with Pedrell, so their conversation begins with Granados telling Falla that when he was last in Madrid he wasn't able to see their old maestro.

"I miss him," says Falla, "but I don't miss Madrid. I could die of frustration there, looking for a venue for *La Vida Breve*. Not that it's been much better here. In fact I've gone to Milano and Brussels and London to find a venue. No success, not yet. But I've met more interesting people here in Paris. Debussy. And Paul Dukas, who's tried to help me. And Stravinsky and Ravel. So I'm happy to be here. You know I wouldn't be here at all if it weren't for Casals. He got me a fellowship."

"And your new work?" Granados asks.

"Yes, our friend Viñes introduced *Cuatro piezas españolas* and I'm working on some 'canciones populares'–Spanish themes. And there's a chance to get *La Vida* performed in Nice."

Rosa comes into the salon to introduce her children to the guests. Anais is a dark, thin girl with large eyes, whose gaunt visage makes her seem older than her nine years; she reaches out for Granados' hand with long, graceful fingers. Thorvald is seven, a solemn husky blond and blue-eyed boy, reflecting his mother's Danish heritage. Three-year-old Joaquín, with mischievous eyes, reminds Granados of his own son Victor. "He's already learned to climb up onto the piano bench and play chords," Rosa says with evident pride.

"His parents are both fine musicians," replies Granados, "so he has an advantage."

Rosa winces at his comment. Shaking her head, she discloses in a lowered voice that her husband has forbidden her to perform. "I can't talk about it now," she says, and herds her children off to meet the other guests.

As requested, Granados plays Book One of *Goyescas* to an intimate group that is eager to be enraptured. He follows with the excerpt from *Dante*, which he'd played at the opening of the Sala, then *Allegro de Concierto*. For an encore he plays the seventh *Danza*. He stands up and motions for Falla to take over the piano. Falla leans close and says, "It's a wonderful work, Enrique. I've never heard any finer. What I especially love is the elegant way you take us from melancholy to spontaneous joy. I know it comes from deep within you."

Later in the evening, Rosa takes him aside and asks if he'll meet her in the morning. "I can't tell you why," she whispers, watching Joaquín over Granados' shoulder. "There's a place on Avenue Montaigne, Café Marcel. Can you meet me at ten o'clock?"

Rosa is late. As Granados sips his coffee at Marcel's sidewalk table he wonders if she's been detained. Not likely. Solid and practical, Rosa wouldn't forget. Joaquín's a friend, so is his meeting with her disloyal? But she sounded desperate. What's it about? Money? Malats told him Joaquín goes on tour without knowing if he'll be paid. Said Joaquín tours like a prince. Luxury hotels. Finest restaurants. Expensive women. Rosa could be looking for money. If so, Granados wouldn't be her best prospect.

At around ten-thirty, he sees Rosa scurrying up Avenue Montaigne and stands to greet her. Her mouth is taut as she apologizes for being late. "I expected him to leave for Berlin early this morning," she explains. "He had a tantrum–one of his silk shirts wasn't back from the laundry. Back in Brussels, I would have had it ready. He screamed a lot until finally his cab arrived–but he didn't hit me. Not this morning."

Granados winces. "Rosa, I have to tell you, I'm appalled to hear about this!"

"Yes, but Carme Karr told me you'd listen."

"Carme?" He wonders what links the editor of *Feminal* and this handsome Danish woman who grew up in Cuba and lived only briefly in Barcelona.

"She's a friend of mine. She knows everything I'm about to tell you."

Rosa leans forward and tells her story. Joaquín is clever enough, she explains, to be a perfect gentleman when anyone else is present. "He goes from being a noble prince to a monster when we're at his mercy," she says.

The inevitable clash of cultures and strong wills in the marriage is exacerbated by Joaquín's failure to achieve the recognition that he believes is deserved.

For Joaquín, as Rosa explains it, relying on her family to maintain their lifestyle is a source of shame and bitterness. Joaquín has spent much of his time performing in solo concerts throughout Europe and in his native Cuba, while Rosa has delivered three children in five years in three different countries, and is raising them. Joaquín often says he didn't want the children, and at home he ridicules them, especially Anais. As his treatment of the children has become more harsh, Rosa has become more protective. If they misbehave, he grows rageful and beats them savagely. He attacks Rosa for neglecting the children and for trying to revive her singing career. If a fight breaks out, Joaquín locks the children in their bedrooms so they can't see him beating their mother. Or he locks her up and beats the children. Once, in a rage, she tells Granados, he beat a neighborhood cat to death.

"Worst of all," says Rosa, "he's a shameless predator–he made sexual overtures to my sister Juana when she lived with us, and he boasts of women chasing him when he's on tour. He has no more interest in me as a woman, but he's begun to fondle our daughter–and she is only nine!" For the first time Rosa bursts into tears.

Granados closes his eyes. What he's heard far exceeds his darkest suspicion. He's embarrassed for thinking Rosa was coming to him for money. That Joaquín would be neglectful and abusive is not as surprising as Rosa's descriptions of his rage, cruelty, and perversity.

"We should not have married," she says. "We are predestined to bring out the absolute worst in the other. Sometimes I wonder what would have happened if I simply didn't fight back."

Granados raises his hand. "No, Rosa! Absolutely not! He's become a monster–you've done nothing to deserve this!"

"That's just what Carme said. 'No, Rosa, you've done nothing.' All right. I'll put that out of my mind."

"You must leave him and get the children away from him! What can I do to help?" Granados asks.

She shakes her head. "Right now? Nothing. Yes, I have to get away from him. I'd like to bring the children to Barcelona. Would you help me get established? I don't know anyone there, and you know everyone."

"Of course I'll help you," he says.

"I'm so concerned about the children," she says, her voice breaking. "I don't know how to protect them."

"Can I make a suggestion?" Granados asks. "Leave him without delay, and save the children!"

The turbulence of ideas and feelings fills Granados with a whirlpool that threatens his balance. How could Nin–the precocious young man from Cuba whom he knew, or thought he knew, at Quatre Gats–have become such a monster, abusing his wife and children?

Tiana

Clotilde is in her flower garden, admiring the full bloom of the peonies–pink and light blue–when she hears an unfamiliar rackety sound coming up the hill. The sound, from an unknown source, grows louder as it reaches the side street and turns into the courtyard of her villa. She's annoyed that the serenity of a brilliant summer afternoon has been interrupted, and turns from her garden with reluctance.

Matilde is in the courtyard staring wide-mouthed at a strange black motorcycle equipped with a sidecar. The rider is dismounting as Clotilde approaches. She stares at him–dressed in a tan suit with matching shoes, a visorless leather rider's cap, and goggles.

"Good afternoon," says the rider.

Instantly she recognizes the voice. "Whoever you are," she says, "you do a perfect imitation of Maestro Granados. Tell me, for what purpose are you creating this disturbance in my courtyard?"

Granados pulls off the goggles and cap. "I've come to take you for a ride," he says, beaming.

Clotilde shakes her head. "You look entirely too pleased with yourself. Would you mind turning off that engine?"

He turns to the motorcycle–where is that switch? He turns back to Clotilde and shrugs. "I learned how to start it and how to drive it and how to stop it," he explains. "But he never showed me how to turn it off–or I've forgotten."

She's delighted with his discomfort. "But that's the reason for the sidecar, is it not?"

He looks perplexed as the engine whines on. "For the sidecar?"

"Your mechanic can ride along. Then if there's a problem–"

He feigns annoyance.

"Will you allow me a suggestion?" she asks, having decided to help him solve his problem.

He nods. "Of course! Do you think me too proud?"

"You? Oh, heavens no! There's an ignition switch–right there," says Clotilde, pointing to a spot just behind the handlebars. "You might try that. Is this machine yours?"

He laughs. "You remember, I told you some day I'd ride up the riera on a motocicleta and carry you off to the mountains."

"Dios mío–you came up the riera?"

"Of course. After watching you dodge horses and wagons and goats and dogs and people on the road from Montgat, I thought the riera would be much safer. And it was!"

"And you're quite certain I'll ride with you?" Clotilde asks.

"Yes–considering how many times I've risked my neck in your car."

"You're terribly pleased with yourself, aren't you?" She enjoys seeing him off balance. "And what does Amparo think of it?" she asks.

He hesitates. "She hasn't seen it yet."

"Oh, you are so dreadful! You know that? And unpredictable. And impractical–"

"Not impractical–to the contrary," he replies. "This is ideal for running about town, going quickly and easily back and forth from home to the Sala. And for coming to Tiana. Not being dependent on others."

"But I love coming down to Montgat, waiting for you. It's a special moment in my day. Waiting for you to get off the train. I love that first moment, the moment of first seeing you."

Granados retreats. "I won't always ride this. Only in good weather. When I'm not exhausted. Never when you want to come and meet my train. I love that first moment too."

"I love the moment and I love you," says Clotilde.

Late in the afternoon, they go for their first ride together on the motorcycle. Up the winding mountain road from Tiana to Martorelles, then northeast–parallelling the coast to Vilanova del Valles, continuing past the road that leads down to Alella until they arrive at La Roca del Valles just as darkness falls upon them and light rain begins to fall. Then down a narrow, wet stretch of road to Argentona. From there, skirting the edge of Mataró, they turn south on the coastal highway with raindrops pelting their heads and shoulders, and pass through Vilassar de Mar, Premià de Mar, and Masnou before reaching Montgat. As the rain intensifies they begin the final leg up to Tiana. At the outskirts of town Granados heads the motorcycle toward the riera.

Clotilde shouts a warning that is lost in the roar of the engine. "No, not the riera! No! It's raining! Not the riera!"

Before leaving, Granados and Clotilde joked about the riera being safe enough unless there's a deluge of water coming down from the Collserola. As he drives the motorcycle into the riera, there's a brief, frightening image of a wall of water coming down and sweeping them away, but he discards this and turns his mind to the more immediate task of dodging any rocks or debris that remain from the spring rains. He's relieved to see only a few shallow rivulets coming down the incline.

Now he can hear only one sound above the roar of the engine. A sound muffled by the wind whistling over his leather cap and goggles and the scarf that she insisted he wear. Not until he slows down at the top of the riera, and enters the side street below Clotilde's villa, does he recognize the sound. It's not the roar of raging waters coming to sweep them away. It's the ecstatic and uncontrolled torrent of Clotilde's laughter.

Midsummer, 1912

Granados and Clotilde manage to see each other nearly every day–except on weekends, which he reserves for his children. She comes to the Sala for her lessons on Tuesdays and Fridays; hers is the last lesson of the day. Two or three evenings each week he goes to Sant Gervasi and spends the evening with the Andreus. The other evenings he rides his motorcycle out to Tiana, returning to his home around midnight. For Amparo, he attributes his daytime absences to the doctor's advice: "Get away from your work and take long walks in the afternoon." If he returns home later than midnight, Andreu's hour to chase his guests away, he tells Amparo he's been dining with friends. To mask his deception, he draws from a wide range of those who might invite him to dine.

Granados and Clotilde have become more careless about being seen together, which inflates the number of people who observe the renowned musician of elegant dress and jaunty air as he strolls with the comely young lady, so evidently of the alta burguesia, ripened, effervescent, and adoring. Only Amparo is oblivious to their rapturous strolling, for which the only lucid explanation is that they are lovers.

During the long mid-afternoon break, the Barcelona version of the "siesta," they often rendezvous at a dairy store–una lleteria–on Passeig de Gràcia at the corner of Aragó. This began with another of the doctor's recommendations: yogurt for Granados' digestive problems. "You won't drink milk? Ach! Yogurt is better than milk," the doctor said. "I guarantee it'll settle your stomach!" Granados tells this to Clotilde, lampooning the doctor with a German accent, and obviously pleased there's something he can enjoy taking for his running battle with gastrointestinal pain. It gives him a sound medical reason to meet Clotilde at the lleteria, and thereafter to stroll with her on the sidewalks of l'Eixample.

"If it's yogurt every day for you," says Clotilde, playfully, "I'll have to drive in from Tiana to make sure you follow your doctor's advice."

In mid-July, Granados is on his way to the lleteria when he's hailed by his friend Carles Pellicer, a painter who's also frequent guest of the Andreus. "Hola, Enric. Do you have a moment?"

"Hola, Carles. What's up?"

Pellicer looks up and down the street and lowers his voice. "I'm sorry to say, I may have caused a problem for you with the good Doña Amparo."

Granados' mind races to recent conversations with his wife.

Titín hasn't been upset–except about the motorcycle. And the usual complaints.

"What problem, Carles?"

Pellicer voice is apologetic. "I had no idea, my good friend. No idea. When I saw Amparo on the street the other day I asked her, 'Where in the devil is that rogue of a husband Enric? Haven't seen him in a thousand years!' And I knew instantly I'd said the wrong thing. Instantly. Because she said, 'How strange, he said he dined with you last night at your home.' And my mind was racing–what could I say? I tried to pretend I'd been jesting–about not seeing you in a thousand years–but I could tell from her face that my pretense was a failure. She broke off the conversation and headed up Gràcia. I wish I'd said nothing–I'm sorry!"

"Carles, I don't blame you. It's not your fault–you had no idea. If there's a problem, it's of my own making."

As he continues up the street, Granados ponders his predicament.

She must suspect there's a woman. Yet says nothing. So unlike her. Got angry about my buying new suit! Now says nothing. Why not?

When he arrives at the lleteria, Clotilde–always punctual, is not there. As he orders his yoghurt, the proprietor recognizes him and motions for him to come around the counter. "Mestre Granados," he says, "I have a note from la dona–the one who meets you here."

Granados opens it. "Mi querido, I forgot to tell you I'll be with two of my aunts from Igualada this afternoon. Hasta mañana, alma mía! C__ " Granados thanks the proprietor and turns to leave.

"Mestre Granados, do you have a moment?" asks the proprietor. "I'm sorry to trouble you," he says in the same apologetic tone as Pellicer's, "but a woman came in the other day–I did not know her. She was short. Older than you and me. Said she'd come to meet you. So I told her–I told her that you'd already been here that day. That you usually come with your wife early in the afternoon. And I immediately knew that she–not the other lady–must be your wife. How stupid of me! I'm terribly sorry if I've caused a problem, mestre!"

Granados thanks him and leaves.

First Pellicer. Now this. She must know there's another woman. Should have been violent explosion. Why not?

They find other places to rendezvous. Later, Granados would wonder why they chose Gaudí's enormous Temple Expiatori de la Sagrada Familia. Later, he'd see the profound irony of this choice.

Sagrada Familia was launched by an arch-conservative cult–the Spiritual Association for the Devotion to St. Joseph, known as "the Josephines." Under their leader, a bookseller and amateur flautist named Josep Maria Bocabella y Verdaguer, the Josephines started to raise money to build a temple for people to pray in and "do penance for the sins of secularism and modernism." They selected a site in the northeast portion of l'Eixample, where the surrounding land was still mainly devoted to the grazing of large flocks of sheep. They chose, intentionally, the most unfashionable part of l'Eixample, removed from Passeig de Gràcia in distance as well as in state of mind. The original architect, Vilar, quit two years after the cornerstone was laid for Sagrada Familia, and the Josephines looked for a replacement.

Gaudí, a conservative Catholic extremist, impressed them with his proclamations of piety, but a more likely reason for his selection was that Bocabella had a vision of their "temple of penance" being built by a true Aryan. More precisely, someone with blue eyes. When Gaudí came to be interviewed, staring at the committee with his piercing blue eyes, Bocabella was said to have suddenly decided he was their builder. And they gave Gaudí a free hand to modify Vilar's ordinary neo-Gothic design.

Gaudí has done so with relish, designing enormous paraboloid arches and curved columns that transmit Sagrada Familia's weight straight into the ground without conventional Gothic buttresses, choosing the complex geometry of nature in free-flowing and sinuous forms, and introducing non-Gothic color with millions of pieces of tiny ceramic tiles. Somehow it has escaped the Josephines' notice that Gaudí's grand design is prototypically modernist, so with construction expected to continue for decades to come, the truly penitent will never lack cause for seeking forgiveness.

A quarter century later, the Josephines have tapped their best sources of funds, and Sagrada Familia is no longer a bustling project with more than three hundred laborers. Only the crypt, apse, and Nativity façade are nearing completion, and the project faces a long struggle to realize Gaudí's ambition. The Catholic archdiocese of Barcelona, which already has a cathedral, and the city of Barcelona refuse to finance the project. Now, with "noucentisme" taking hold among the cultural elite of the alta burguesia, Sagrada Familia has become the object of scorn, derision, and ridicule.

Gaudí, knowing that Sagrada Familia will not be finished in his lifetime, treats the slowdown as a sign from God that he should reflect on his design and create a legacy for future architects and builders so they won't deviate from his vision. He's become more reclusive, spending most nights sleeping in his office in the crypt below the temple. For years a vegetarian, he's reduced his intake of food and beverages until his clothes hang on him like rags. His ruddy complexion has turned chalky from the plaster dust around him, and the long hours hunched over his drafting table. He's also let his hair and beard grow and, except for allowing the nuns of St. Joseph to trim them, he appears more and more as a white-haired derelict, as a hermit.

To raise enough money to retain a few assistants, Gaudí knocks on doors in the neighborhood, imploring with his probing blue eyes, begging for funds. He's quick to approach anyone who appears to have any wealth with such intensity that when members of the alta burguesia are in the vicinity of Sagrada Familia they cross the street to avoid the emaciated old solicitor.

But for Granados and Clotilde, Sagrada Familia is ideal. They're unlikely to be recognized here, since their friends and colleagues live, work, and play far from this part of town. With construction all but halted this year, the unfinished temple is a haunting but distinctive trysting place. The site is enormous, suitable for meandering through its arches, climbing its stairs and ladders, sitting among sculpted rock and tiles, and trying to imagine how it will finally appear years from now, perhaps beyond their own lifetimes. It reminds them of classical antiquity, ruins of Moorish fortresses, and mediaeval castles on the plains of Castile. It becomes their own alfresco theatre in which to recite and read poetry of Darío and Schiller and Valle-Inclan, to sit thigh by thigh holding hands, dreaming of a romantic idyll. Here they may become Tristan and Isolde or Dante's Francesca and Paolo.

One day, as they stand sunlit near the intricate towering Nativity façade, an old man creeps up behind them, so soundlessly that he's close by when his raspy voice startles them and they spin around. "Senyores," he repeats, "if you please, I'd be grateful to accept a donation to help us continue our work here."

"Aren't you Senyor Gaudí?" Granados asks.

"I am," says the old man. "Do I know you?"

"We met once, through Francesc Vidal. Years ago."

"Ah, Vidal," says Gaudí. "One of our finest decorators. We worked together on furniture for Guell. Vidal's daughter, God forgive her, is one of those feministes! But he's a good man. Don't see him much any more. Don't see much of anyone. So you're a friend of Francesc? Your name?"

Granados introduces himself.

"Yes. Mestre Granados. You're one of my favorite músics. Your work is very romantic. I admire your not going along with all the modernists. You're not one of them! And who is this? Your senyora?"

Granados hesitates, then answers, "No, she's also una música and a friend of mine." He presses five pesetas into Gaudí's hand.

Gaudí knows the woman is not Granados' wife. "Molt de gust, senyora," he says, extending his bony hand.

"Molt de gust," she replies, reaching into her handbag and pulling out a leather purse. "Senyor Gaudí, I'd also like to make a small donation." She hands him one hundred pesetas.

Gaudí takes the money, eyes glowing. "Ah, senyora, you are far too generous! I will pray for you, senyora."

Clotilde has taken care to cover the book of poety by Darío. She tells Gaudí how they enjoy coming in the afternoon to Sagrada Familia. "Of course, Senyor Gaudí, if I were to give you a donation every day, I would soon have no money. But I'll send you small amounts from time to time."

Her grace and candor bring tears to his eyes. "You are generous, senyora. You will always be in my prayers. I will light ten candles for you this very evening. What else can I do to thank you?"

Clotilde doesn't hesitate. She learned quid pro quo from her father. "When we come, as we do often, and you see us here enjoying your magnificent temple, please don't feel obliged to ask us for donations." Her gaze is unwavering.

Now there's a rare twinkle in Gaudí's eyes. "I respect your sentiments, senyora. But I can make no such promise."

The following week, as the midsummer sun scorches the city below, Granados arrives at the Sala, half an hour late for a lesson. The front door is opened by the housekeeper, who tells him that Senyoreta Godó is waiting for him downstairs. Strange, it's not time for Clotilde's lesson. Hearing her play a Chopin prelude, his pulse quickens. He follows the sound to the largest classroom, closes the door behind him, and walks over to the large divan as she finishes the piece.

Clotilde rises from the piano stool and crosses the room. "I thought I'd surprise you," she says, standing close to the couch and reaching down to run her fingers through his thick, swept-back hair. "I wish I had hair like this," she says. "Are you happy to see me?"

"When my eyes meet yours, my heart knows, and leaps with joy."

"You're much too sweet," Clotilde says, lifting her skirt and lowering herself onto his lap. She kisses him. "I've waited forever for that."

He laughs. "You've waited since yesterday."

"That's forever!"

"This *is* a surprise," he says, wondering if he's forgotten today's schedule. There's a piece missing. "I'm sure you don't have a lesson."

"No. Mine was yesterday. And the day after tomorrow. Why?"

"I thought I had a lesson at eleven. Ah well."

"You're a curious man," she says, softly kissing his eyes.

"How am I curious?"

"You ride up the riera, on your motocicleta. With the rain pouring down. You're so fearful of getting on a boat, so terrified of drowning. Yet you'd race up the riera, not knowing what was coming down."

He shrugs. "We weren't swept away. It was just a bit wet."

"Not swept away there–I'm swept away by you," she says, kissing him again. "But that's not what's curious. It's that you didn't know how much water was coming down, and still you kept on climbing."

Granados ponders. It's obvious to him. "You should know, mi alma, that when I face something that truly frightens me, I don't run away from it. I run into it and force my way through."

The door to the classroom suddenly opens and Paquita Madriguera take two steps into the room. She stops. Her face is fixed in disbelief, as if unsure what she's seen.

Clotilde jumps up, straightens her skirt, and walks back to the piano with her face turned away; Granados commands Paquita to wait outside. Soon after, Clotilde leaves and Granados calls out for Paquita to come back in for her lesson. After playing a few scales and arpeggios, she begins *Ronda* from Beethoven's Second Sonata–which he critiqued after her recital at El Palau. Suddenly he cancels the lesson. "Is your mother at home, Nana?" he asks in an agitated voice. "I want to see her right away! Go at once and tell her I'm coming!"

Paquita flees the Sala and hurries home, fearing that she's made some horrible mistake–perhaps she didn't work hard enough on the Beethoven.

Granados races his motorcycle down Avinguda Tibidabo, crosses the intersection of Sant Gervasi with a prayer that nobody's coming from his right or left, then makes a rapid descent on Carrer Balmes to the home of Enrique Madriguera and Francisca Rodón. He parks the motorcycle and strides to the front entrance.

Dios mío! Now this! Nana's lesson time–how foolish to forget! There we were–she saw too much! Must talk to Francisca–must convince her it's only Nana's imagination.

"Come in," says Francisca Rodón at the door, "and follow me." She leads them into a parlor in the front of the house and they sit down face to face over a coffee table.

"What did Nana tell you?" asks Granados.

She motions for him to relax. "We have plenty of time, Enrique. And plenty to discuss."

"What did she say?"

"She told me she arrived late for her lesson and the moza let her in. The moza told her you'd just arrived in that little bit of an automobile–"

"It's a motocicleta. With a sidecar."

"Yes. My, my. A grown man like you. The moza told her you'd just arrived and were downstairs. Paquita said there was a woman with you."

"Did she say who?"

Francisca sighs. "Of course she did. She recognized Clotilde Godó. A student of yours, she said." Francisca pauses. "I've known her and her family for many years."

"Yes, I imagine so. Did Nana say what she saw?"

"*What* she saw? Oh, Enrique, por Dios! She's just twelve and her entire life is piano. She isn't interested in anything else. You know that!"

"She has two eyes," he insists, "and all I'm asking is, what did she *say* she'd seen?"

Frasquita sits upright in her chair. "She told me nothing. She's terrified that you're angry at her. Says you were rude and cut the lesson short and sent her home. She's afraid she's done something horrible. Like not practicing enough. Is there any reason for her to be afraid?"

"Of course not, Francisca. She's absolutely my favorite student and I'm deliriously proud of her. That's not why I came here."

Francisca gives him a thin smile. "You came here to explain what happened. That's fine. Why don't you tell me what my daughter *might* have seen?"

He shakes his head. "If she thinks she saw something, it's probably her imagination."

"Oh? That's why you sent her flying home and came roaring down here on your moto-ci-cle-ta? Her imagination? Please, Enrique, we've known each other so many years, you don't have to hide from me. I'm a friend of Amparo–a good and loyal friend. And I'm also a friend of Clotilde's family. So you can see how I'd feel caught in middle of a nasty situation. But it's not my business, so I won't say a word to anyone."

"Then you *do* know something?"

Francisca smiles. "Don't be clever, Enrique. You keep dodging around, trying to get me to tell you what I know–without telling me a thing! I'm tired of this game of cat and mouse. What I know is that you're having an affair with Clotilde. You see her nearly every day. Your passion speaks loudly. Strolling on Gràcia. Spooning yogurt into each other's mouths. Holding hands at Sagrada Familia."

"You've seen us?"

She shakes her head. "I don't need to. The entire town knows about this romance. Seems that poor Amparo's the only one who doesn't. Do you seriously believe your affair is a secret? Of course you don't."

"What do you suggest, Francisca?" His voice wavers.

Her eyes widen. "You'll not get any advice from me! Figure it out for yourself!"

Sant Salvador, Autumn 1912

Pablo Casals' seaside village is celebrating its annual fiesta, and the town's folk ensemble is playing in the plaça as Granados and Amparo arrive for a five-day visit. A time for dancing on the beach in front of Casas' vacation home, and for revelry late into the evening. The cellist's Catalan patriotism outweighs his ordinary disdain for any music that is too folksy or conspicuously popular.

"The sardana is different," he tells Granados as they watch the circles of dancers on the beach. "It's been our dance for ages–do you know they've found etchings of sardana dancers in the caves of Cogul? It's not about musical taste, it's about patrimony!"

Granados laughs. "You've been down in the caves again, Pau?"

Whether the dancers in the caves of Cogul were indeed dancing the sardana is not certain. One theory is that ancient people in northern Iberia paid homage to the heavens with dances by the light of the full moon. From the 14th century there's a description of pilgrims dancing "the round dance" at the monastery of Montserrat. And in the late 16th century the name "sardana" appears in writing, though often written "cerdana" and confused with the Pyrenees region of Cerdanya. There's no doubt, however, that this music and dance form have become identified with Catalanism, along with the region's ubiquitous red-and-yellow banner, and resurrection of its language. In the mid 1800s, the traditional sardana with its rigid rules was lengthened and rendered far more complex by composer Pep Ventura and choreographer Miquel Pardàs.

By 1900 the sardana, embraced by intellectuals and politicians, spread from the northeastern Empordà region to most of Catalunya. Men and women, rich and poor, conservatives and liberals now joined hands raised high at village festivals, at the hallowed monastery of Montserrat, and at the Festa de Mercé in Barcelona. These days, they dance tiptoed to music composed not solely by Ventura but composers of some stature, including Morera, Juli Garreta–a favorite of Casals–and Joan Manèn. Sardana dancers must memorize the number of short and long steps contained in each piece, and the formulae are complex–indeed bewildering to the neophyte. The folk ensemble that plays the music, the cobla, was in mediaeval times a small group of minstrels, but as the sardana evolved it's grown to a contingent of eleven musicians in which wind instruments prevail.

Casals, with his wide-brimmed straw planter's hat perched on his eyebrows and ears, sits on a beach chair watching the patterns of the dancers, refilling his pipe, awash in the sounds of the cobla. While he can sit for hours, his guests are not as enamored of the sardana, though Donald Tovey, the English composer who's become a great favorite of Casals, has ingratiated himself with his host by composing a sonata for cellos that incorporates a variation of sardana music.

After an hour, Granados slips into the music salon with the young pianist from Poland, Mieczyslav Horszowski, whom he met at Casals' home at Villa Molitor. There are three pianos, the Cussó and Dietrich uprights and a Pleyel grand that just arrived from Paris–and they're all out of tune.

"It's a game Pau's been playing with me for years," says Granados.

"Just imagine him with a cello that's out of tune!" replies Horszowski.

"It would never happen."

Tovey has taken charge of activities for Casals and his guests, and with auspicious gusto. Granados and Horszowski try their best to avoid him. Tovey's schedule entails breakfast at nine, swimming at ten, a stroll on the beach at eleven, tennis from noon to two, lunch and siesta, another stroll on the beach at four, a game of catch with beach balls at five, tennis again at six, music recital at eight, and dinner at ten-thirty, followed by another short stroll on the beach. He's made no allowance for this September's unusually hot weather.

It's now ten o'clock–nearly time for dinner, and since the second round of tennis Casals has been watching the dancers. Tovey takes a restless, solitary walk on the beach, pondering what went wrong with his schedule of activities. Amparo sits on the veranda with Suggia in idle conversation, waiting for dinner, while Granados plays excerpts from *Goyescas* for Horszowski, who was away on tour when it was performed at Salle Pleyel.

Around the dinner table there's a kaleidoscope of moods. Casals is ebullient, energized by watching the sardana and the prospect of a late-evening recital that he's added to Tovey's schedule. Suggia, at the far end of the table from Casals between Granados and Tovey, is restless. Tonight her long hair has been released from the bun in which it's usually gathered, and it covers her shoulders, reflecting the candles' glow. She's deeply resentful that Casals hasn't paid any attention to her since they came down from Paris two weeks ago. Annoyed with his spending so much time with correspondence from around the world, holding court with what seems a random mélange of drop-in visitors, and playing cello the rest of his waking hours. Now there's a houseful of guests, for nearly a week.

Tovey, whose great height is compromised by bad posture and clumsiness, whose attire–though he's dressed by the tailors of Savile Row–manages to look unkempt, sits between Suggia and Amparo. He's chafing because his first-day schedule was disrupted. Insistent on the last word in every discussion, Tovey is finding tonight's conversation much less stimulating than chats he enjoys with Casals in London. Horszowski is delighted merely to be here, to sit between Casals and Granados, but he's wary of Covey's ambitious schedule. Amparo, between Tovey and Casals, is content to be relieved from a few days of the chores of managing the household and six busy children, and from wondering, always wondering, how badly Granados will disturb what should have become–for a woman approaching her fifties–a settled and nontraumatic life. A life without new contraptions like motorcyles, a life without another young paramour.

Granados, between Suggia and Horszowski, is pleased to be with Casals again and eager to play the piano part of *Elisenda* for his friend tomorrow. He's annoyed–not simply by Tovey's schedule but by his aggressive need to dominate the discussion of every subject, without exception–and irritated by Tovey's assumption he's an expert on everything. And Granados is anxious and bewildered by Amparo's silence, when by now she surely knows about Clotilde.

The conversation is in French, their only common language, with occasional bits of Italian, English, and Portuguese. Casals and Granados converse with each other in Catalan. Amparo is isolated, waiting for Granados to translate summaries of what's said in French into Castilian.

With Casals and Tovey engaged in an old dispute over the design of a poster in London that featured the name CASALS and omitted the other players, Granados feels Suggia's toes sliding up his left leg. It's no surprise, considering her past flirtations. With as much caution as he can muster, he waits to catch her eye. He will signal her to stop it with a quick shake of his head. But there is no eye contact; he soon realizes that her body is twisted toward Tovey. With a rustle of silk, her hips swivel away from Granados and her left hand slips under the tablecloth. What he felt was her right leg grazing him as she stretched toward the Englishman. He watches as Tovey slips his right hand under the tablecloth, never varying the cadence of his repartee–once again seizing the last word from Casals.

The next day, Suggia raises the stakes during the morning swim. Granados and Horszowski refrain, sitting on beach chairs and observing the others. Casals and Amparo, who enjoy swimming, stroke back and forth in the water just beyond where the waves are breaking, while Suggia follows Tovey as he floats with the current toward the fishing pier down the shore from Casals' property. Granados watches as their bobbing heads converge and remain close until they return to shore several minutes later. He sees Casals standing on shore, glowering at Suggia but saying nothing.

During the tennis match, Suggia claps whenever the tall, clumsy Tovey hits a ball past Casals. And when the group turns to a game of catch, Suggia aims the ball at Tovey's crotch and smirks playfully with her sensual, upturned mouth as he blocks it with both hands. Throughout the day, she laughs at any comment by Tovey that could be considered amusing, and sits next to him on the veranda, across from Casals.

Before dinner, Granados plays the piano excerpt from *Elisenda* for Casals. "It's meravellós, 'Ric! What is it?"

"The first movement of *Elisenda*–from a poem by Mestres. We premiered it at the Sala–your brother played with us. I'm glad you like it."

Casals is emphatic. "I love it! You should have this piano piece published separately."

"Yes–a fine idea! And when I do, I'll dedicate it to you."

As they leave the music salon to prepare for dinner, Granados sees two silhouettes on the veranda, one slouched, sitting close together. He turns and sees Casals' eyes burning with rage.

At dinner, Casals puts Suggia between him and Amparo, as far away from Tovey as the table is long. He's no longer the attentive, engaging, stimulating host. Suggia sits silent and stiff in her chair. Her hair is back in the customary bun, as if it were a peace offering. Tovey, seeming oblivious to the rising storm at the other end of the table, is engaged in a lively debate with Horszowski over the piano style of Artur Rubinstein. Granados has lost his appetite after feeling abdominal pains while dressing for dinner. Without waiting for everyone to finish dessert, Casals summons the moza to clear the table and stands up. "You'll forgive me, senyores," he says with tightened lips, "it's been a long day and it's time for us to retire." He takes Suggia by the hand and leaves the dining room.

Casals' guest bedrooms are on the second floor of the main structure at Sant Salvador. Granados opens a pair of French doors and steps onto a terrace above the veranda that overlooks the narrow beach and the sea. Casals' bedroom and bath are on the first floor, tucked behind his study so that ordinarily a conversation there would not be audible in the guest bedrooms. But this is not an ordinary moment, and as Granados walks out from the bedroom where Amparo has already retired, the angry voices of Casals and Suggia echo down the hallway below. Voices that become high-pitched and reedy as anger overflows. Granados is grateful to be above the fray.

The fight seems to be escalating. Granados hears Casals berating her for flirting with Tovey. "Do you know how offensive that is? Do you?"

"Ah! You're offended?" her voice is teasing.

"I am! And it's not just your puta behavior today. You've been flirting with him since he arrived!"

"You call me a puta?" Now she's irate.

"I said puta behavior."

"Puta! Then you're a puto!"

"I will not tolerate any more of this!" he cries.

"And I will not be neglected any longer–I'm leaving!"

"You can go–I don't care! You'll have no career without me!"

"I have no career *with* you!" shouts Suggia.

Casals forges ahead. "And what music will you play? Rontgen, Moór–they're friends of mine! You're not good enough to play Bach!"

"Those friends of yours? Their music is horrible! You're the only one who can't see that!"

Casals embarks on a new line of attack. "You wouldn't have gone to Russia without me! If you leave, you'll sit and rot in Portugal!"

"Portugal? I'm going to London! As for Russia–I never wanted to go there. It's a dreadful place!" After a brief pause, Suggia launches her own thrust. "You go to Russia for the women with breasts the size of your head!"

"Which yours are not!"

"Oh! How would you know? How would you *know*?"

"I'd know if I could find them!"

Suggia's scream, followed by the sound of breaking glass. "That's it–I'm leaving!"

"You're nothing but a puta!"

Another scream and more glass breaking.

"Puto! Puto! Puto!"

Granados hears a door slamming, and Suggia running down the hallway, screaming and crying. More glass breaking. Then sobbing.

At breakfast, Casals tells his guests that Suggia left early this morning. Nobody asks for an explanation. Casals turns to Tovey, who's been abnormally silent. "Are we swimming at ten?" he asks in a terse voice.

Granados is as astonished by Casals' self-control as he was overhearing the raging battle last night.

Amazing! Pau's expert at pushing things out of his mind. So self-sufficient. Great friend but doesn't need anything anyone. Only his cello.

On the last day at Villa Salvador, Granados and Amparo walk up to the fishing pier. She's dressed in an off-white summer dress and sandals. Exposure to the sun and swimming every day have restored the rose and ochre tones to her face. Her dark auburn hair, gray strands carefully tinted, waves in the breeze and gleams in the sun. Her vigorous strides through the sand remind Granados of the young woman in València who'd captured his heart. Years ago. How many? More than he cares to count.

"Have you wondered why I've haven't said anything?" she asks.

Their stroll has been silent, and his mind wandering. Just now, to one of the tonadillas, an aria for voice with piano in the popular satirical style, on which he and Fernando Periquet–the notable Goya-phile–are collaborating.

La maja de Goya–not just another woman to pose. Not just any maja–LA MAJA. THE maja. La maja de Goya. La-da-da-da-da-da-da-da-da-da-da-da. La-da-da-da-da-da-LA-MA-JA-DE-GO-YA.

Amparo repeats the question: "Haven't you wondered?"

"Sorry–I was daydreaming," he replies. "Have I wondered why you haven't said anything? Said *anything?*"

She stops walking, and waits for him to turn and face her. "I think it's time for us to come to terms with your romance."

Granados is stunned, but the lack of anger in her voice is in sharp contrast with how she confronted him about María. He nods, hoping she'll continue.

Admit nothing unless necessary. The safest course.

Amparo glares at him. "Look, I know about you and Clotilde Godó. I'm no fool. In fact, I've suspected it for over a year and just refused to admit it. That's my weakness. Yours is that you always need some woman to drench you with love. Perhaps you can't help it. Or you don't want to."

"Titín–"

"No, let me finish! No screaming, no tears this time. I'm drained. I've used up all the tears. Let me finish. I know this is a serious romance–not another dalliance with an adoring deixable. She's not as young as the others, is she? And she has known heartache, so I guess she has enough sense to know what she's getting into. God help her if she doesn't. As for me, I've known you too long and there's nothing that would surprise me any more–except in your music."

She pauses and takes a full breath. "This has nothing to do with that, but your *Goyescas* is truly remarkable. It is a masterpiece. There will be more. And I know she had something to do with it. Women just know these things. And I'm jealous, oh, you can be sure of that! But not enough to kill you. Not enough to leave you–we have six children who need both of us. Strange to think this, but I'm jealous enough to wish *I'd* inspired *Goyescas*. I do wish that. But to the point–I'm asking you for only one very important thing. As long as this lasts–and for all I know it'll be over in a month or a year. As long as this lasts, I ask just one thing. If you agree, we can live in peace. Or in armistice. I don't want to go through what Pau and Suggia went through. Yes, I heard it."

Amparo turns her eyes on him, like barrels of a shotgun. "I demand only this: you will not dishonor me! You have been very indiscreet–the whole town knows your little secret. But I won't be dishonored! I demand that you not continue to flaunt your love affair in public. That you not cause people to say, 'oh, poor Doña Amparo, we're so sorry for her, she's a martyr, she's a saint to put up with that scoundrel!' That does nothing for me, and surely nothing for you! And if you will honor me by discretion, if you don't cross the line, we can all live in peace."

"And how will I know the line's been crossed?" he asks.

Amparo gives him the merest trace of a smile. "My husband. Mi amor. You can count on me. I will be the first to let you know!"

Barcelona, October 1912

One month after returning from Sant Salvador, Granados receives a telegram from Ricard Viñes, announcing the death of Joaquim Malats in a private hospital for tuberculosis patients near Paris. Despite knowing of the illness for more than three years, despite Casals' pessimism when they discussed it briefly during that turbulent week at Sant Salvador, Granados has been resistant to the gravity of the situation. Just as he was with Albéniz.

How foolish to pretend!

In the telegram, Viñes relates that he visited Malats the previous week, and was shocked to see how the disease had "drained the vitality from our genial and talented friend." With Albéniz and Malats gone, only Granados and Carles Vidiella remain from Joan Baptista Pujol's most esteemed protégés.

Too young! Poor 'Quinito! Did he work himself to death?

November

Granados has arranged to meet Ernest Schelling for the first time, following the American pianist's initial concert at the Teatre Principal. Over the years,

Granados has heard Casals speak of Schelling, and two months ago at Sant Salvador he learned that Schelling would be coming to Barcelona, and anxious to hear *Goyescas*.

As José Altet opens the cab door in front of Girona, 20, he hands Granados a pass for the theatre. "You'll be in a box on the first balcony," he says. "Bona nit, mestre." Granados thanks him and settles into the cab as Altet closes the door. Arriving as the lights dim, Granados settles into his seat just as the audience rises to applaud. Schelling walks across the stage. Granados instantly sees the striking resemblance.

Dios mío! Am I dreaming? No–I'm here on the balcony. Schelling's down there.

Schelling is tall, slender, dignified, simmering with energy. Black hair flowing back from a wedge-shaped face, and luxuriant moustache. Glowing eyes and an aquiline nose.

We're not identical–but could be my brother.

After the concert–music of Chopin, Liszt, and Schubert–Granados goes to Schelling's dressing room backstage. Schelling stands more than six feet high, half a head taller than Granados, but otherwise the physical resemblance is striking.

"Pau says you're like a brother," says Schelling in French.

"Then you and I must also be brothers," replies Granados.

"Absolutely–nous sommes freres! Well, I'm ready to leave this place. And I'm famished!"

"There's an excellent place nearby. Albéniz and I used to go there when he was in town."

"Albéniz? Well, if he liked it, that's good enough for me!" says Schelling.

They are in the back room of Can Culleretes, at the corner table.

"You knew Albéniz?" asks Granados.

"Knew him?" asks Schelling. "Not really, though I met him when he came to Paris in the spring of Eighty-nine. I was studying with Moszkowski."

"Ah, Moritz. We've been on the Diémer jury together."

"I was very young then," Schelling adds. "Only thirteen. Albéniz was a giant! He came to the Salle Erard and played his own works–I'd never heard them. Well, I was captivated! Especially by 'Torre Bermeja'–the sound of a Spanish guitar. That was astonishing!"

Granados nods. "I was at that same concert," he says. "Also very young–twenty-two, living in Paris with my friend Ricard Viñes."

During dinner Granados and Schelling discover several similarities. Both showed prodigious talent at an early age. Lived in Paris at the same time. Both had careers interrupted by illness; for Schelling, a serious bout of neuritis when he was sixteen. And both were born on virtually the same day, July 26 and 27.

"Our stars must be aligned," says Schelling. "If you believe in astrology. Do you?"

"I don't know what it is. Some kind of sorcery? Merlin's magic?"

"Not exactly. It's–well, an arcane sort of quasi-science, going back to mediaeval times. Though I have a friend in London–he plays first violin for Sir Henry Woods, and he swears by astrology. He's a decent fellow, and otherwise quite sane. Claims he bets on the horses based on astrology. And claims to win."

"Really?"

Schelling shakes his head. "Quite amazing. He's forever trying to get me into it, but my life is so hectic, when would I have time? Except when I'm at Céligny–our place in Switzerland, though it's rather doubtful there are astrologers hanging about there."

"It's a way to predict the future?" Another mysterious door opened.

"Ah, wouldn't that be splendid!" exclaims Schelling. "I'm not at all sure, but I did visit an astrologer once, just to get a reading. She was very eccentric, but I didn't let that get in the way. She told me I'm a Leo, that's my sign. A lion. The king of beasts. Strong-willed, you know?" He chuckles. "And she said, 'Your Leo is rising,' so that meant I'm a double Leo. She guessed I was an actor. I told her she was wrong–I was a pianist. She persisted. 'No,' she told me, 'if you play the piano it's because you've created that role for yourself.' 'What role?' I asked. So we went round and round."

Actor? Created the role? Yes of course!

"Forgive me," says Granados, "I think I know what she meant. And I know absolutely nothing about this astrology. I think she meant you decided at some point what you were going to be, and then you created that role for yourself just as an actor would create 'King Lear' or 'Hamlet.' Except you've shaped your whole life to be a pianist, so the role *is* you."

However deep the instantaneous rapport, their lives have also been quite disparate. Schelling's family could afford to send him to Paris when he was not quite five. He's performed all across Europe, from England to Russia, and throughout North and South America. He's studied with Georges Mathias–a student of Chopin, with Moszkowski, Theodor Leschetizky, and Jan Paderewski. He'd like to have more time to devote to composition, but unlike Granados he's not obliged to teach in order to make a living. As a result of his tours, he's met and befriended hundreds of musicians and members of the cultural elite, especially in New York, London, Berlin, and Paris. He's become a personal friend of the German royal family, and he's befriended and played bridge with Spain's King Alfonso XIII. Schelling is married to Lucie Draper, from a prosperous Boston family; they have no children. Two years ago, the young couple purchased the chalet "Garengo" in the Swiss village of Céligny, near the Lake Geneva chalet of Paderewski.

"I tracked Paderewski down in Philadelphia," Schelling tells Granados, "hoping he'd accept me. Instead he nearly broke my heart! 'You may have little technique,' he told me, 'no repertory, and a poor touch. But you have something. I see there's a spark in you. Come to Switzerland, and let me find out what it is. I will take you under my wing as my only student. I shall be glad to do something for an American boy.'" Schelling laughs. "Well, I could hardly pass up that offer, so I went there and studied with him for four years. Never worked harder! There were many times when I thought my fingers would fall off!

"Thinking of that time, if I chose a role in life, I'd be a mountain climber. For one thing, you meet the most interesting people. Once I ran across two German lads and we decided to make a climb together. We were forced to take refuge in a mountain inn, and what do you know? There was an old piano, so while a snowstorm roared around us I played for these Germans. One of them asked who in the devil I was. I told him, and he said his name was Wilhelm. Not just any old Wilhelm–he was the Crown Prince of Germany–the Kaiser's son! He introduced me to his family, and when I returned to Europe for my honeymoon, we stayed with the Kaiser's family."

The next day, Granados plays the entire *Goyescas* piano suite for Schelling on the Pleyel in his music salon at Girona, 20. Then they discuss the work for nearly three hours in the study. Schelling wants to know everything. How did Granados discover Goya? Why the *Caprichos*? Why these *Caprichos*? How did he conceive of putting Goya's art into music? How did he decide on the street dance, the lovers' colloquy through the window, the maja and nightingale, love and death, the appearance of the ghost? When and how did he compose the work? Did he go about it in the same way as with previous works? Will there be more *Goyescas?*

Schelling sits on the edge of a chair in Granados' study, his eyes gleaming with excitement, listening intensely. Several times during their conversation, he breaks in to finish Granados' sentence; often their heads nod in unison. And Granados' initial caution about revealing how *Goyescas* was created is dispelled by the American's obvious, palpable enthusiasm for this work, especially his obra mestra.

"It's perfectly marvelous," says Schelling. "You've played it here and in Madrid. And in Paris. This needs to be heard everywhere! I could arrange concerts for you in London and in New York. Would you be interested?"

Yes want it heard everywhere. But going to those places means getting on a boat.

Granados shakes his head. "I'm afraid not, Henri." he replies using the French equivalent for Schelling's pet name. "I have too much going on here."

Undaunted, Schelling gives a quick toss of his head. "Another time, then. But would you allow me to learn it and play it when I'm in New York and London?

"Yes–I do want *Goyescas* to be heard."

"I realize it's a difficult piece–don't think I'd embarrass you."

"Of course you wouldn't, Henri. I'd be honored."

Schelling gets up from the chair and walks to the window. He stretches his hands over his head, just as Granados would, and with the midday sunlight flowing around him, he becomes the silhouette of Granados. When he turns around, he asks, "Have you thought of making an operatic version of *Goyescas?*"

Granados' face radiates a sudden exhilaration. "Yes! Of course! I mean, I haven't thought of it, not until this instant. But of course I *should* think about it. Of course! You've just given me a gift. A treasure!"

Schelling smiles. "It's just an idea. Easy for me to suggest. Much more difficult for you–finding a librettist, expanding it to full orchestra and all the voices. Well, you know that better than I. You've done it before. So you could do it again, especially with this music."

El Liceu won't take it. Just another disappointment.

"I don't think there's an audience for it here," Granados says.

"Oh? Why not? You're a native son!"

"That's part of the problem. The audience here is mesmerized by the Italians. If it's not Donizetti or Verdi, there's no interest. Albéniz went to his grave without a venue for *Merlin*. This is not the place for an opera about the majas of Goya. Very frankly, I was concerned when I heard you were coming here for a *series* of concerts. In Barcelona, if you give three concerts, the first is to warn the public, the second to invite them, and the third, a danger!"

Schelling waves his hands. "All right, forget Barcelona. But I tell you, there is an audience for it in Paris!"

"In Paris?" Opening night for an opera based on *Goyescas*. Riding down Boulevard des Capuchins, turning up l'Avenue de l'Opéra. Entering Charles Garnier's mammoth neo-Baroque palace, which crouches at the end of the street, its seven arches like elongated mouths yawning to swallow the aristocracy of the Second Empire of Napoleon III, its opulent foyer and marble and onyx Grand Staircase built for strolling, chatting, flirting, sipping and ogling–more intriguing than what's on stage. "Le Palais Garnier?" Granados asks.

"Absolutely! I know the artistic director, Jacques Rouché. In fact, I know him quite well. When you're ready, I'll arrange an audition. You can count on it!"

Schelling's suggestion sets Granados' imagination ablaze. Over and over he envisions climbing the Grand Stair Case of Garnier's monumental palace with Schelling, accompanied by a deafening applause. He imagines the street scene from Book One on stage, and the maja's garden. Seeing a *Goyescas* opera in Paris–won't El Liceu be envious? Casals was right–this American is invaluable. Knows everybody, and all doors open for him.

Prior to the appearance of Schelling, there was no shortage of projects to nurture, especially a promising collaboration with the Goya-phile Fernando Periquet on a series of "tonadillas" for piano and voice. Thus far, Granados has sent Periquet six pieces of music based on "imagined situations," but he's expanded his own role by sending verses to accompany the music to the librettist. That doesn't prevent Periquet from penning his own verses and sending them back to Granados. A time will come to reconcile the two libretti. And there are new "tonadillas" hovering in Granados' head, just out of reach. There's also a piano piece that Granados envisions being played with the two books of *Goyescas*. It's based on another Goya sketch entitled "El pelele," depicting a group of women tossing a dummy stuffed with straw into the air with a blanket.

Granados' life is further complicated by the arrival in Barcelona of Rosa Culmell and her three children. When she comes to his office, Rosa ruefully admits to making another effort to salvage the marriage with Joaquín Nin, instead of taking Granados' advice to leave him. For this, Joaquín repaid her with a cloying campaign to seduce the fifteen-year-old daughter of his wealthy Cuban patrons, who'd come to live with the Nin family in a rented beach house. To Joaquín's surprise and dismay, the girl told her parents she'd fallen in love with her host, whereupon they shipped her back to Cuba for a hasty marriage with a more eligible suitor. Then Joaquín left the beach house and returned to their home near Brussels, and after a few weeks informed Rosa he was leaving her, noting that he'd sold most of their possessions. He suggested she go to Barcelona to live with his parents. For a short time, Rosa Culmell's sisters helped her as she sold off the remaining possessions and arranged for travel to Barcelona. So here she is in Barcelona, staying with her in-laws, with no money to live in a place of her own.

"I need to work," she says to Granados in a flat tone, "and Carme said you'd be able to help."

"Yes," he replies, "of course I'll help." Indeed the solution to Culmell's acute problem presents a salutary arrangement: Granados adds a mature vocalist to the academy's staff, with the temperament to coach young sopranos, most notably the promising Conxita Badia; Badia and Culmell are available to sing his "tonadillas" in their formative stage; and Culmell's youngest, Joaquinito, is enrolled at the academy to learn music theory instruction from Badia.

Tiana, Winter 1913

After working for two hours, Granados pushes his chair back from the Pleyel in Clotilde's music salon. He invites her to come over. She sits down, puts her arm around his waist, and scrutinizes the composition pad. "This is delightful. 'El pelele'–I can just see them tossing the dummy filled with straw–then you take me beyond that with these cascades and torrents. Difficult–not for you, just for us mortals."

"You'll be able to play this," he replies.

"We'll see." Another glance at his notes. She nods. "Perhaps. Then explain how–in addition to this and everything else–you're going to create an opera based on *Goyescas?*"

"I'll find a way."

A frown covers her face. "Oh, you'll find a way? Mi amor, you raced up here on your moto and burst into my quiet little world, after not being here since before the holidays, and then talked without stopping about this Schelling and taking your opera–which you haven't composed–to l'Opéra de Paris, and then you buried yourself in this new piece. Since you learned how to turn off your noisy little moto, I wonder, could you please turn off the moto in your head? And tell me, please, how is this Schelling–this americano magnífico–different from the other americanos, who are only interested in money?"

"You think that? Why?" he asks.

"I haven't met many of them–but my father has, and you know Juan Godó–he's not disinterested in money, not at all, but he doesn't believe money is the only important thing."

Granados shakes his head. "Schelling is different. Money is not important to him. Music is his passion. He seems quite genuinely excited by *Goyescas*, and wants it heard everywhere. As I do. He wants me to play it in London and New York, but I told him I'm too busy to go to those places."

Clotilde smiles. "Which is not the full story."

"That's right. But Schelling is learning *Goyescas* and he's going to play it in New York in March–in the Carnegie's Hall. Just imagine! And he'll soon have a booking for London–in the Queen's Hall. That's enough to convince me that Schelling is different from the Americanos your father knows from his textile business."

Clotilde smiles. "You're saying I've prejudged him?"

"Well?"

"Perhaps I have. Mi amor, I'm thrilled that *Goyescas* will be heard in London and New York. Fine, let's talk about the opera. Who'll write the libretto?"

"That's the very question I've been trying to answer. Of course, there's Fernando Periquet. He introduced me to Goya. And we're working on the 'tonadillas.' So I know what he can do. And yet–"

"You're wondering if he can write a libretto for l'Opéra de Paris?"

"Exactly."

She takes his hand. "I don't have an opinion, and I should not. And I know you'll proceed carefully and make a thoughtful decision. The music is maravillosa, there's no denying that. If I were you, I'd ask this Schelling what you need for an audition with l'Opéra de Paris. That will help you decide how to use your time." She pauses. "I suppose your other choice is to write the story yourself. Let Periquet–or someone else–create the verse to support it. After all, Wagner wrote all of his own librettos."

Granados shakes his head. "Wagner was a poet and a composer."

"As are you, mi querido."

He shakes his head again. "It would be one more enormous project. On top of everything else."

"Yes, but summer will come–not too long to wait. You can put the other pieces aside and devote yourself to the opera. If you come here, I'll see your time is well spent. And keep you healthy."

"Yes, healthy! Thank you. Especially now–no time to be sick!"

For several months, Granados has avoided telling Clotilde about his conversation with Amparo at Sant Salvador. He prefers to think of it as a private matter, in its own compartment. There was no ultimatum, as with María Oliveró. Amparo only asked for respect, discretion. Then why tell Clotilde?

Her garden is bedded down for the winter. The maple and poplar trees at the far end of the property have dropped their leaves, and the evergreen cypresses are tinged with brown. With less foliage, the sounds of the animals and birds rise from the pens and cages. Crowing of roosters, snorting of pigs, and the staccato bleating of goats. Sounds of life, which contrast with the dormancy of the garden. "Have you lost your passion for yogurt?" she asks. "We haven't been there since last summer."

Granados dissembles. "I've been so busy since then," he replies. "José brings me yogurt at the academy."

"And it's been a while since we've gone to Sagrada Familia."

He chooses to deflect this with humor. "Ah well, it's just that I can't afford to give five pesetas to Gaudí every time we go there."

Her laughter sounds forced. "Those are good enough reasons," she says. "But they're not the real ones, are they?"

"No, they're not." At length, he recounts the conversation with Amparo.

When he's finished, Clotilde rises from the garden bench and walks down the center aisle between the ghostly shapes of hydrangea bushes covered for the winter. Granados watches her, relieved of the burden of withholding this, but concerned about her reaction.

There's no sparkle in Clotilde's voice, just resignation and a tinge of sadness. "It's no business of mine," she says, "I'm simply sorry you didn't tell me sooner."

In the months following Schelling's visit to Barcelona, he and Granados stay in touch by mail and telegrams. A common practice for the peripatetic American, but for Granados–whose life and work has been concentrated in the area of Barcelona–a novelty requiring him to discern where to send his replies so they're received in timely fashion.

London, Paris, Berlin, Rome, New York, Chicago, San Francisco, Philadelphia. Schelling moves from place to place. Malats called it "the gypsy life." Poor Malats! Schelling can do it. Not me.

After Schelling's first American performance of *Goyescas*, he sends Granados a copy of the review in the *New York Times*, which Schelling says is the country's most prestigious newspaper, and with it a letter in which he translates the article: "Mr. Albéniz saw Spain through the veil of the modern Frenchman. Mr. Granados is submitted to no such foreign influence. That Spain that is embodied in his music is authentic, yet what he has written is a personal, individual expression." A critic for the *New York World* also praises the work, which he claims "is supposed to illustrate a little slumming expedition to Madrid by the Duchess of Alba and her lover the painter Gorja." Schelling writes, "I pointed out the connection to the works of Goya, but the critic didn't quite understand. It's my fault for not taking more time to explain, and his fault for being in a big hurry to finish his review. Typical of we Americans!"

Schelling writes that while in Chicago, he met with the general director of the Chicago Grand Opera Company, hoping to convince him to present the opera. As yet there's no firm commitment. "Hope you're making good progress," he writes.

Progress? Not much so far. Haven't decided on the libretto. Chicago? Dios mío—half way around the world!

Granados replies with a long description of his work with Periquet, explaining that the Spanish "tonadilla" is similar to the German *lied*. "I'll describe one of them. In 'Maja dolorosa' there are three kinds of pain or grief: the immediate pain after the death of the majo, the pain of teardrops, and the pain of remembering it." And to show Schelling a relationship with the operatic *Goyescas*, he writes, "This collection is written in the classic style. They are however original pieces and not reiterations of familiar ones. I've wanted to create a collection that will serve as a document for the opera. And please note that with the exception of 'Requiebros' and 'La maja y ruiseñor,' none of the *Goyescas* include popular themes. I've made them in a popular style, yes, but they are true originals. I imagine them setting the atmosphere for the narrative of the opera."

In a subsequent letter, Schelling describes a conversation with Rudolph Schirmer, the eminent New York music publisher. He states that a contract with Schirmer will be far more beneficial than Granados' current ones with publishers in Madrid and Paris, and promises to arrange a meeting with Schirmer. Granados can count on several thousand francs a year, paid in advance against royalties.

Paid in advance! No time to waste. Must finish Tonadillas*—decide on the libretto. Schelling will have me booked before there's an opera!*

Tiana, Spring 1913

"How long will you be in Madrid?" asks Clotilde.

Granados looks up from the Pleyel. "About a week. Long enough!"

"Oh yes." She turns and points to the composition pad. "What name will you give these pieces?"

"I've been calling them *Tonadillas in the Ancient Style*."

"Will you get more verses from Periquet in Madrid?"

Granados rolls his eyes. "Por Dios, I surely hope so! Most of them are mine, with my music. Then Periquet changes them. And we send them back and forth until there's some kind of agreement–or we're exhausted. Like this one–still unfinished. I'll play it again. Here's the verse." He hands her a notebook, and Clotilde reads it aloud:

La maja dolorosa

I ardently treasure those memories
of my gallant love who was my glory.
He adored me fervently and faithfully
and I gave my whole life to him.
A thousand more I would give if he wished,
for in deep love anguish is only a blossom.

When I think of my gallant love
I'm engulfed by dreams of a time gone by.

Neither in El Mentidero nor in La Florida
did a more handsome man ever stride.
Under his broad-brimmed hat I saw his eyes
fixed on me with all of his vitality.
Whomever they looked upon inspired love,
for no deeper gaze can be found in the world.

When I think of my gallant love
I'm engulfed by dreams of a time gone by.

Clotilde shakes her head in amazement. "It puts me right into the streets of Madrid. Goya's just around the corner."

"I've intended that there be no separation," he says. "Goya lives in all of them."

Clotilde points to the second stanza. "Tell me, do his eyes *inspire* love in whomever they gaze upon? Or is *he inspired by* whomever he gazes upon?"

"Pheewh! You have a sharp eye. Read it again."

"'Whomever they looked upon inspired love'–now, if you change it to 'que a quien miraba enamoraban,' it's not ambiguous. Those who *receive* his gaze are enamored–*he* isn't."

"You're absolutely right!"

"But I know virtually nothing about your Goya," Clotilde says.

"Doesn't matter–you caught the nuance of this line!"

Later, they drift out from the music salon onto the terrace overlooking the garden. Wordlessly, when deliberation is superfluous. The harbingers of spring abound in the budding of deciduous trees, the rising of yellow daffodils, and the sounds of migratory birds. Most exciting, the nightingales are returning from North Africa. Are those who sing male or female? Is their androgyny inherent in the beauty of their song? Then why do they sing in the gloom of night? Do the nightingales hide such sorrow that only by singing in the night can they find relief?

"I have a little poem from Valle-Inclán," she says as they reach the garden bench.

"One of his erotic tales?" asks Granados.

"I'd have thought better of you!" she teases. "No, he may be a rogue, but this isn't roguish. It's called 'Miracle of the Morning,' and I discovered it waiting for the sound of your moto. It was quiet and I thought of you–the sound of you coming up the riera." She laughs. "Would you like to hear it? All right, here it is..."

> A bell rang out
> in the crystal blue
> of the sacred morning.
> A country prayer
> which quivered in the blue
> sanctity of the morning.
> On the old pathway
> the nightingale was singing
> with a luxurious trill.
> The village bell
> with its voice told
> the bird to sing out.
> The village bell
> in the glory of the sun

was the Christian spirit.
As it tolled it scattered
the fragrance of roses
from La Virgen María.
This sacred fairy tale
reminds us of a song
in an old fable.
Bell, little bell with sacred beak–sing
while the miraculous rose blossoms.

Madrid

When Granados arrives to work with Periquet, he has music for ten pieces, a full set of *Tonadillas.* There will be revisions–that's an inescapable part of the process, but with Granados it becomes an extended continuum. Partly due to his skill in improvisation, and partly from his reluctance to reach closure while ideas for improving a piece are still swirling in his head. He's been known to release a piece to one of his publishers if there's a financial crisis, but ordinarily every one remains a work-in-process. Even after printing, when the sheet music can be purchased and played by strangers in most large cities of Europe, Granados feels no obligation to desist from further revisions. His assistant at the academy, Frank Marshall, says he's never heard Granados play one of his pieces twice in the same way.

Tomás Bretón, director of the Conservatorio in Madrid, is providing a practice room in which Granados can work with Periquet. If they complete *Tonadillas* this week, Granados can move on to the opera version of *Goyescas*, and make a decision about the libretto.

Periquet draws upon the vast store of knowledge he's accumulated about the iconic Goya. He's fond of pointing out that "Goya would say this" or "Goya would do that," using a detail he's discovered in his research to prod Granados toward his viewpoint. Both men are intensely devoted to this project, but while Granados can slip off into a reverie or toss off a harmless jest, Periquet guards his devotion like a novice praying the Rosary on Holy Friday. In a disagreement, Periquet resembles a lively fox terrier, Granados a lean pointer of upland game.

"Could you play that again?" asks Periquet. Granados plays the music for "La maja dolorosa," as Periquet scrutinizes the lyrics. After the first refrain, Periquet holds up his hand. "Here's the part," he says, then reads the verse aloud: "... 'under his broad-brimmed hat I saw his eyes fixed on me with all of his vitality. Whomever he looked upon was enamored, for no deeper gaze can be found in the world.'"

"That's correct," says Granados. "As you wrote it, the *majo* is inspired to love all those his eyes gaze upon. And I don't think that's what you intended, Fernando, so I changed it."

Periquet flares. "Not what I intended? So you changed it? You're trying to tell me what I intended?"

Granados shrugs. "If that's not what you intended, it's easily changed. If you did intend it that way, we have a problem of content. Which is it?"

Periquet stands up and walks away from the piano. Beads of sweat course down from the top of his bald head, are diverted by his bulbous nose, and run under thin wisps of dark hair swept forward above the oversized ears, that are red from tension. Turning, he asks how Granados could understand what was intended. Or is he challenging Periquet's intentions? "It's not inconceivable," he argues, "that Goya could fall in love too. He was forever on the prowl."

Looking across the room at his fitful partner, Granados is tempted to retaliate, but realizes that two dogs barking leads only to stalemate. "Yes, but the maja in this piece is describing a majo who was 'her glory, to whom she gave her entire life.' She says his gaze was so powerful that those he looked upon were enamored of him." Granados softens his voice. "Let me pose the question in a different way. If the majo's gaze upon a woman inspired love *in her for him*, then the lyrics should read, 'que a quien miraba enamoraban.' Ten beats. Que'a-quien-mi-ra-ba-e-na-mo-ra-ban. Am I correct, Fernando?"

Periquet blinks and answers in a sullen voice. "Yes, maestro. You are correct." He pauses. The next words are in a suddenly imperious voice. "I will make that change," he concedes.

The next issue is the length of Periquet's long ballad in verse that opens "La maja de Goya." It's a tale of Goya, in which his passionate idyll with a married woman is interrupted by the arrival of her irate husband. The woman covers her head with a drape, leaving the rest of her nude body uncovered. Goya steps between them and challenges the husband: "This woman you want to take away from me, you say she is yours. If so, by looking at her you'd know if she is indeed. And you'll see that this woman has never been your wife." The husband walks around the woman twice, scrutinizing her nude body, and finding nothing that is familiar, apologizes to Goya for making a mistake. The narrator, a woman who admires Goya, then breaks into song:

> Never in my life will I forget
> that precious, dashing image of Goya!
> There is no woman nor maja nor lady

who does not miss Goya now!
If I found someone
who would love me
like he loved me,
I would not envy–no,
nor yearn for
more happiness
nor good fortune.

"Except for these eleven lines at the end, you didn't write music for the singer," says Periquet. "Why not?"

"There is music to go with the verses," replies Granados, "but I envision the singer telling the story, not singing it, then singing the conclusion. That separates the tale of Goya from the storyteller's feelings about him. I think it will be more dramatic."

At the end of the fourth day at the Conservatorio, when they've resolved all but one or two of their disagreements, Periquet announces that he's arranged for a presentation of *Tonadillas* at El Ateneo de Madrid in late May. He and Granados would appear with the playwright Manuel Linares Rivas, who'd give a short lecture on the historical and current forms of the tonadilla, followed by selected pieces played by Granados and sung by the actress Lola Membrives.

Granados is reluctant to introduce *Tonadillas* publicly in this setting. "I don't agree, Fernando. El Ateneo isn't the right venue to premiere this."

"What's not right? You know, maestro, I live here and I should know which venue is right. We can't just drop these pieces on the musical audiences without the proper context."

"I beg to differ," says Granados. "You don't have to be a music historian to appreciate this work. If we're trying to revive a genre that has been neglected, we must do it in the modern context. Wagner didn't present a lecture before the premiere of *Lohengrin*, did he?"

Periquet starts to object, but on this issue decides to compromise. "All right, then we'll just present one or two of our pieces. Not an official premiere. Is that acceptable?"

Granados shrugs. "If you're asking, will I come for this event? Yes, I'll come. But I want *Tonadillas* to be premiered in Barcelona. And I want Conxita Badia to sing them."

The following day, Periquet suggests they go to the Real Academia de Bellas Artes for an exhibition of Goya's paintings, including the formal portrait of La Duquesa de Alba that was in her home, when she died.

"Look at her!" says Granados in an excited voice. The portrait, towering over them in the poorly-lit gallery, shows La Duquesa in a white gown with a modest scoop at the neck, a bright red sash around her narrow waist, a matching bow above her left breast, and a necklace of red gemstones. Wavy, raven hair falls in cascades onto her shoulders. Her face is cocked slightly to her right so that the dark brown irises look back at the viewer from the corners of her eyes. Her lips are drawn together in a flat line. She stands with a small white Pekinese at her feet, her right arm extended at an oblique angle to her body, and index finger pointing enigmatically to the earth outside the frame of the portrait.

"She looks hesitant, cautious," says Periquet, stepping back and cocking his head. "Almost self-conscious–how unusual!"

Granados shakes his head. "I don't see caution. It's as if she's trying to suppress an eruption of laughter at a playful remark by Goya. She's trying to maintain her dignity."

"I don't know. When this was done, she and Goya hardly knew each other. It was before their romance, while her husband was still alive. I don't mean she'd be hesitant about who she was, but I imagine her being wary of the life and times of that period."

Granados nods. "And surrounded by scoundrels?"

"Oh, indeed. Yet energized by scoundrels."

"Including Goya?"

Periquet turns. "He had many women, yes. But he truly loved La Duquesa. She broke his heart."

Granados sighs. "She loved looking like a maja and living that kind of life. She couldn't be true to any man, even Goya. That's the meaning of the *Capricho* 'Volaverunt'–La Duquesa borne on high by two-faced creatures, floating upward with arms stretched like the wings of a butterfly. Or the goddess of infidelity."

As they leave the exhibition, Periquet asserts: "The story of Goya and La Duquesa is one of the great love stories of all time. We must capture it in the opera!"

"The opera?"

"Yes, the one you and I discussed–the operatic version of *Goyescas*." Periquet glares at Granados.

"I don't remembering discussing any operas with you, Fernando."

Periquet looks puzzled. "When you came here last winter and we talked about *Tonadillas*, I asked if you'd be interested in an opera based on *Goyescas*, and you said yes, that was a very interesting idea. Don't you remember?"

Granados does not remember. He's irritated by Periquet's presumption. "Fernando, I think all these pieces are 'goyescas'–the ones I wrote for piano and the tonadillas–because they're all inspired by Goya. Goya–goyescas. But truly, I don't recall discussing any opera with you."

Periquet is undeterred. "Let me ask you a different question. Are you interested in creating an opera with your 'goyescas'?"

Granados reflects and answers. "Yes, it's an intriguing idea, Fernando. In fact, my American friend Schelling suggested that when he was in Barcelona. I told him the same thing–it's an intriguing idea. An opera inspired by Goya. About majos in love. The piano suite is a good starting point. Of course, there's no libretto. Not even a story."

Periquet seizes the moment. "I can do the libretto! Who else has my passion for Goya?"

"No question, you have the passion. But do you know how to write a libretto for an opera? For an opera premiered at Palais Garnier?"

"Garnier? You mean l'Opéra de Paris?"

"Yes. Schelling said he could arrange an audition with the artistic director, Jacques Rouché. As soon as I'm ready."

"Then shall we work together on the opera?" asks Periquet.

Granados remembers Goya's La Duquesa suppressing a smile, and laughs. "Do I have a better choice, Fernando? Ah well, here's to the majos in love!"

Barcelona

Pigeons gather at the edge of puddles left by last night's rain as Granados walks across Plaça Catalunya, returning home from the mechanic's shop where he's taken his motorcycle to be serviced. Ordinarily, tasks like this are assigned to José Altet, but on this first day of summer recess for the academy, Granados seizes a chance to stretch his legs and enjoy a solitary stroll along Carrer de Sant Pau–to the corner where El Liceu faces La Rambla, then across to Café de l'Opera, where only the waiter who brings coffee recognizes him–then out into the morning sunshine again, heading up La Rambla, where the flower markets are at their most resplendent in early June.

After those rollicking months of reveling in the adulation poured upon him for *Goyescas*, this year seems to be tempered by a sense of measured progress toward the ultimate goal: to have his work recognized by a universal audience. Adulation can only go so far if one hasn't truly achieved success. More than simply shimmering like dawn on some remote, undefined horizon; arising like the outlines of landfall after a long sea voyage.

Schelling's premiere of the piano suite of *Goyescas* in New York was a step in this direction; he's booked to repeat it in London next December. In a letter, Granados tells him how grateful he is for the effort to get the opera *Goyesca* performed. He also thanks Schelling for arranging a contract with Gustave Schirmer to publish several of his works. The extra money is indeed welcome. In the same letter, Granados asks what will be needed for an audition with Jacques Rouché at l'Opera de Paris.

Schelling replies, that Granados will be asked to play the piano version of *Goyescas*, and should bring an outline of the libretto, with two scenes fully orchestrated and lyrics for the singers. Granados expects to be prepared for the audition in August. If Rouché accepts, Granados hopes the opera, which he still calls *Los Majos Enamorados*, can be presented during next winter's season.

The summer is full of promise. This month, while Granados works on orchestration for the opera in Tiana, Periquet is completing the outline of the libretto. Next month, Periquet will come down from Madrid and work on the scenes to be presented in Paris. The collaborators will work at the country house that Granados has been renting for family vacations up the coast in Vilassar de Mar. To ensure even more isolation, Granados has hired a neighboring farmer in Vilassar to build him a small shack–"una tartanita"–beyond the vegetable garden. He visits the site with Eduardo and tells him, intending to jest, that he built this tartanita with his own hands. Surprised when his son believes him, Granados decides to incorporate the fable into the story of composing the opera. It amuses him to imagine people pointing to the little shack, exclaiming, "Can you imagine? Granados built it with his own hands!"

Schelling has invited him to stay in Céligny in August, and Granados hopes by then to have what he needs for the audition with Rouché. He imagines going to Paris, meeting Schelling there. Then, while waiting for a decision, he'll go to Puigcerdà, where he'll continue work on the opera. In September, the academy will open again, and he'll spend a week with Casals in Sant Salvador. A long, fine, productive summer.

In the last week of June, Granados feels a sharp, cramping pain in his lower abdomen. For two days it comes and goes, but with each episode the pain is more intense, and takes longer to subside. He waits for it to recede. Though the doctor has warned him that an absence of pain is no guarantee it won't return some day, he's been free of digestive problems for more than a year and has erased the warning from his mind.

On the third day, Granados recognizes the familiar sequence. First the sharp, cramping pain in his lower abdomen. Then diarrhea and rectal bleeding. A loss of appetite. Pain in his legs and arms and shoulders. Fever and chills. And after a few days of rest in bed, clear liquids and bland food, the symptoms will begin to diminish. That's the familiar sequence. This time, however, the symptoms persist for a second week. The doctor visits him every other day, assuring Amparo that Granados' affliction is not contagious, and leaves prescriptions for diarrhea medicine, an ointment for the sores in his anal area, and herbal supplements to replace the nutrition he's unable to retain. Amparo cares for him day and night, brings his meals and medicine, keeps air circulating in the bedroom, reads him *La Vanguardia* every morning, and goes through the mail with him every afternoon. She's also the doorkeeper, bringing the children in for brief visits and shuttling them out when she sees her husband's strength begin to ebb.

On a good day, Granados can get up, walk to the music salon, and practice for half an hour before the dizziness takes over. On a fair day, he can sit up and read for a while. On most days he lies flat, his mind meandering from one fragment of music to the next, without the strength to write the notes. Some evenings the fever rushes to his head like a forest fire and he wonders if his brain will be consumed; other days, in spite of the prevailing summer heat, he curls up to repress a shaking chill. He agonizes over the work that's not being accomplished, and despairs over the loss of these weeks that promised to be so fine, so productive.

Could still go with Schelling to Paris. If this goes away!

But with each passing week, going to Paris becomes more unlikely. What could still be is becoming what might have been. "Why don't you just shoot me?" he asks Amparo one day when she brings him the ointment for his anal sores.

She laughs. "Shoot you? I've got to fatten you up first."

"Don't make me laugh. It hurts to laugh."

"All right then, no more talk of shooting."

Granados reaches up and takes her small hand. "Titín, you are so incredibly patient with me. I'm not a very good patient, am I?"

Amparo gives him a thin smile. "You're a very sick man, and you're my husband. You think I'm going to let you suffer?"

In the third week, Granados begins to pass blood with his urine; he learns from the doctor that he also has an infection in his bladder. "It's painful but not serious," says the doctor, "but in a weakened condition you're liable to these kinds of infections. You must avoid contact with anyone who might expose you to other diseases."

Granados finds the strength to chuckle. "Doctor, I have no contact with anyone except my family–and you!"

Every week, Granados asks José Altet to call his students and cancel their lessons, and gives him notes to be delivered to Clotilde in Tiana. "This is between you and me," he says in a low voice.

"Of course, mestre."

The summer that he hoped would be so productive is unraveling. There's been no progress on the opera since the onset of the abdominal pain. He writes a note to Periquet informing him of the illness, promising to make up the time when he's back on his feet. "I'm sure this will pass in another week," he writes, "so please work hard on the libretto and please be patient." With each week this becomes more illusory.

With no abatement in the illness after three full weeks, Granados writes Schelling in Céligny, explaining that "work on the opera has been delayed because I've been immobilized by a bad inflammation of the bladder and an infection in my digestive system. I remain hopeful that Periquet will finish the outline of the libretto this summer and that I'll soon recover. I look forward to visiting you at your chalet in Switzerland, no later than late August."

In the last week of August, he writes Schelling again. "I apologize for not informing you earlier, mon cher Henri, but I've been in bed with this illness for more than six weeks, and I've lost ten kilos. My pajamas used to fit me quite well, and they're like a tent. I'm very thin and I'm just now beginning to feel better. Consequently, I'll not be able to visit you in Céligny. This is a list of the pieces that I'll send to Schirmer as soon as I have the strength: '*Impromptu*,' '*Sérenade goyesca*,' '*Prelude in D*,' '*Marche Militaire*,' '*Dansa à la Cubaine*,' two of the '*Spanish Dances*,' and '*Valse de Concert*.' I also hope to prepare two more works for Schirmer: '*Valses Poéticos*' and '*Cant de les Estrelles*' for piano, organ, and choirs–and a very important work. Cher Henri, please know that I'm terribly disappointed to have missed seeing you and your good wife in Céligny."

Granados is heartened by a reply from Schelling, announcing that Schirmer will send a contract and Spanish translation to Granados along with a check for three thousand francs as an advance payment on royalties for the first six months. He reports that Schirmer is also interested in Granados' Catalan lyric operas and will do "whatever is required to have them receive a fitting performance, either in Paris or some other capital of Europe."

Three weeks later, Amparo writes Lucie Schelling that "my husband has been very ill for the longest time, so we couldn't come to visit you in Céligny. Of course we're both terribly disappointed, but I'm especially sad not to have been able to meet you. Thankfully, he's beginning to spend more time on his feet and, of course, at the piano. He has an important concert to prepare for in Madrid next month. I hope you'll renew your invitation next summer, and if so we'll be delighted to come to Céligny."

Four days later, Granados writes Schelling, "I'm still convalescing from this long illness but I've agreed to go to Madrid to play at the state visit of the new President Poincaré of France. In sickness or in health, it's the lot of the artist! Nobody notices. But by then, I expect to be feeling much better. Unfortunately, since I've lost so much weight, I'll have to be fitted with a new suit, so M. le President de France doesn't think they've brought in a scarecrow to play for him. Since that is my only performance in the remaining months of this year, I'll be able to devote the rest of my time to the opera so that we can go to Paris for an audition next spring."

Clotilde is waiting for Granados at the Montgat station. She hasn't seen him since the day before the onset of abdominal cramps. Three unbearable months ago. When he steps down from the coastal train, she's jarred by his gaunt appearance. The loss of more than ten kilos accentuates his oversized head. His starched collar is too large and his suit coat too baggy in front. There are deep umber circles under his large round eyes. She hurries across the platform as he shuffles toward her. She is crying as they hold each other in a long abraçada.

"I had nightmares about you dying," she sobs. "You were dying and I couldn't be with you. They wouldn't let me come. I was desperate to see you. They kept grabbing me and pulling me back and I knew you were in there dying. It was so horrible!"

Winter, 1914

The first letter from Schelling in the new year comes inside a large envelope along with copies of reviews from the London papers. Schelling writes: "I hope this letter finds you fully recovered from your long illness and in good spirits once again. Your work was very well received by the audience at Queen's Hall, in spite of your not being here to play it! My friend Sir Henry Wood was enormously impressed with *Goyescas* and is eager to meet you to discuss other works which could be performed here. You and I didn't have much time to discuss *Dante*, but I mentioned it to Sir Henry and he seems interested. Do you have a completed score for it? I'd could take it to him on my next visit to London. As you know, I've sent a copy of *Dante* to Leipzig, hoping Schirmer will review it when he gets there and let me know if he wants to proceed with a contract. Meanwhile, I've enclosed copies of the reviews. You'll notice that the *London Times* critic loved your music but thought I could have played it better. I hope your work on the opera goes well. I'm looking forward to seeing you in the springtime."

Granados writes back. "I read the English newspapers and I'm delighted to think that my work has made its way–thanks to my great friend and artist–among the world's more important audiences! It's too much for me! Thank you, a thousand times, merci!"

Memories of last year's illness are receding, except for a residual bitterness over time lost and a continuing fear of its return. "You're a lucky man," the doctor told Granados during an exam just before the holidays. "Many people die of this, because there is no medical cure for the problem and in a weakened condition, they're vulnerable to other diseases."

"In other words, it can come back any time?"

The doctor nods. "Yes. That's what I've been telling you for some time, maestro. Any time."

"So I have to live with this, knowing it can come back any time?"

"I'm afraid so."

Paris, Spring 1914

In April, Granados performs at Salle Pleyel. In addition to playing both books of *Goyescas* and two of his *Danzas*, he introduces *Serenata* for piano and two violins, and finishes the long recital with *Tonadillas*, sung by the French soprano Matilde Polack. The audience seems captivated by the melodic grace, directness of expression, and simplicity of the tonadillas. Granados' piano, often imitating the rhythmicality of the guitar, supports but never overwhelms the exquisite delicacy of the vocal lines. After the recital, he's greeted by the music critic Georges Jean-Aubry, to whom Granados recently sent a long, thirteen-page letter with a synopsis of the plot and numerous excerpts from the score of his lyric drama *Liliana*. Jean-Aubry, considered one of the severest of Parisian music critics, is effusive in his praise.

Granados is even more excited when Jacques Rouché of the Paris Opéra comes up, introduces himself, and expresses his enthusiasm.

"Our friend Schelling told me I must come tonight and hear you play these Goyas," he says. "He played one of them for me–'Coloquio,' but said he could not do it justice. He insisted I hear *you* play it."

Granados thanks him.

"Schelling says you have an opera derived from these piano Goyas," says Rouché.

"Oh, yes. I've been working on it for more than a year."

"I'd like to arrange an audition. Could you be ready in June?"

June? For the Paris Opéra–how about tomorrow?

"Of course, Monsieur Rouché. You set the date and I'll be honored to submit the work."

"Excellent! I think the Academie de la Musique Francaise would be a splendid sponsor for the premiere. I look forward to seeing you in June."

Next, a man and woman approach Granados to introduce themselves as Robert and Mildred Bliss. Friends of Schelling. Mildred is a strikingly handsome, tall regally dressed extrovert of thirty-one with lustrous chestnut tresses; Robert is more reserved than his wife, clean-shaven with heavy-lidded pale blue eyes, a lean and dapper man of thirty-six, a career diplomat who for the past two years has been Secretary of the American Embassy in Paris. They've been "fanatiques" about *Goyescas* since Schelling played Book One for them last year.

"Henry said we simply must hear you play it," says Mildred, still holding Granados' hand. "And we weren't disappointed. Far from it. Forgive my boldness, maestro, but we'd like to invite you to our home–of course at your convenience. Henry said you'll be back in Paris in June. We'd be honored if you could play some of your work for our guests. I trust that wouldn't be too much to ask." She holds eye contact with the allure of a modern-day Carmen. Robert steps forward and hands him an engraved card:

Embassy of the United States of America
Robert Woods Bliss
The Secretary of the Embassy to France

"I'd be honored to come to your home," Granados replies.

Schelling said expect me back in June? That's when Rouché will arrange an audition. Everyone seems to know about June.

Two days later Granados is notified that the government of France has awarded him the Medaille de la Legion d'Honneur for his performance at Salle Pleyel. The next day, he's invited by Jacques Pillois, a composer and musicologist, to attend concert versions of Stravinsky's *Sacre du Printemps* and *Petrouchka*, conducted by Pierre Monteux of Diaghilev's Ballets Russes–who's also conductor of l'Opéra de Paris. On the day of Granados' departure for Barcelona, Jean-Aubry's review appears.

"Granados interprets his music in a manner which is beyond the ability of even the best pianists. For that reason, one truly has not heard his work except by him. Of the first book of *Goyescas* I'm convinced that it is among the finest works ever produced in Spain, along with those of Albéniz, Falla, and Turina."

Barcelona

The train from Marseilles brings Granados back to l'Estació França. Back from triumph in Paris to Amparo and their children, back to the academy, back to Clotilde, and back to the practical need to prepare his opera for a June audition with Jacques Rouché.

He sends a letter to Schelling, accepting the invitation to stay at Céligny to work on *Los Majos Enamorados*–after the l'Opéra de Paris makes its decision. "I am so glad to have a great friend like you, and you will find in me what is not very easy to find: the deep gratitude of a heart that will never deceive you."

Friendship like this not easy to find–very rare. Found it with Pau. And 'Saco. And 'Quinito. So many blessings!

Granados is energized by the success in Paris, but sobered by the enormity of the work ahead. Taking the art of Goya and converting it to music was a splendid idea. Preserving it in his imagination was a source of great satisfaction for many years. Composing the piano suite required him to make the most concerted, sustained effort in his life. But now an even larger challenge looms: completing work on the plot and outline of the libretto, and scoring two entire scenes for the orchestra along with the singing parts. Not for presentation in the amiable confines of Sala Granados, where he can control every aspect of the performance. What's at stake this time is a decision by Jacque Rouché and his colleagues at the Academie de la Musique Francaise to present *Goyescas* next season at Palais Garnier. Or not to present it.

Collaboration between a virtuoso who's widely revered as a musical genius and a journalist who aspires to write for the stage was bound to be difficult. Even more so with them living at opposite ends of the long train ride separating Barcelona and Madrid, and with Granados' continuing reservations about Periquet. Further complicated by Periquet's belief that Granados should adapt his music to the words of the libretto, as is traditional in opera, and Granados' conviction that the libretto should follow his music. Periquet claims he wrote the libretto based on an agreed-upon plot so that Granados could let his fancy roam over the scenes that are built from Periquet's verse. "It's nearly impossible to create a libretto from the notes of your music," he argues. Eventually, however, Periquet yields.

Granados still wants the main characters to be Goya and La Duquesa de Alba, not fictional ones, but he's restrained by the knowledge that most operas about historical characters have not been successful. Even describing them as "a famous artist, lover of a duchess" and "La Duquesa" is unlikely to disguise whom they're intended to be. Periquet is constantly trying to simplify the story and Granados keeps changing it, seeking more complexity.

"I want this to be the simplest thing I've ever written," Periquet says with ill-concealed exasperation.

"And I'm trying to give it more depth," replies Granados, "to make it more dramatic, as it will need to be to sustain the audience's interest."

"But if you keep changing everything, we'll never finish!"

"Fernando, if I don't keep making it better, it shouldn't be finished!"

In the first outline sent by Granados to Periquet, the opening scene takes place in front of a ducal palace that resembles Palacio de Buenavista of the Alba family. The duchess and her lover the artist enter the palace, both dressed in majo style, while the "Requiebros" music from *Goyescas* is played. The next scene shows the lovers in the "Coloquio" duet at the window of the palace, followed by the "Fandango" dance scene in front of the palace. Some kind of incident provides a conflict between the lovers. The next scene is at the royal palace of Aranjuez, with more aristocrats in majo dress. A captain of the guards flirts with the duchess, and when her lover appears the two men have a sword fight, the lover is mortally wounded and expires to the music "Amor y Muerte."

In the second outline, there are revisions of essentially the same scenes. The first one is set in the meadow of San Isidro, near Madrid, and begins with the music of "El Pelele," followed by a scene in front of the duchess' palace. The garden scene at Aranjuez involves only the maja and nightingale.

The third outline involves a much larger cast. The rivalry for the duchess' affections now occurs when an art student and a military officer both flirt with her. In the second scene, the student and the duchess sing a love duet through the grille of a window. Music from the last piece in the piano suite, "Serenata del Espectro," foreshadows the death of the lover. It is followed by the dance scene, the duel and the lover's death.

In the fourth outline, Granados opens with "El Pelele" and the arrival of the heroine, who is named Constanza, and in a second carriage one D. G. Lucientes–borrowing the family name of Goya's mother–who arrives for a duet with Constanza.

After several more iterations, the collaborators settle on a principal male character–Fernando, a captain of the Royal Guards, and a principal female, Rosario, an aristocrat. Conflict arises when they are brought together with the torero, Paquiro, and his woman, Pepa, who represent the authentic majo and maja of the streets in Goya's Madrid. Granados and Periquet also select two scenes for the audition with Rouché: "Coloquio"–the lovers' conversation through the window, and "La Maja y el Ruiseñor"–the maja in the garden with the nightingale. Periquet has written verse to fit Granados music…

Por qué entre sombras el ruiseñor entona su armoniosa cantar?	Why does the nightingale pour out his harmonious song in the dead of night?

The oversized envelope from New York arrives later in April. Inside is a formal, engraved announcement from Madame Pilar de Casals and Madame Frank J. Metcalfe–mothers of the newly married Pablo Casals and Susan Metcalfe. The marriage took place in New Rochelle, New York on April 4. Granados, not having seen Casals since the stormy visit to Sant Salvador a year and a half ago, is stunned by the announcement.

Pau married! Susan Metcalfe? Sounds American. He's never mentioned her! That's so like Pau–secretive about personal matters.

Granados and Amparo send Casals send a telegram of congratulations and two weeks later they receive a letter from him, posted in London. "I cannot tell you how joyously my life moves," he writes, "all is changed for me and already I can see it in my face. I know and count on your affection and friendship–this word is to tell you that your friend is happy."

Carmen is waiting for Granados at the sidewalk café on Passeig de Gràcia. Earlier in the week she took him aside after dinner at Sant Gervasi, while Andreu was escorting two of his physician friends into the music salon for brandy and cigars. "I never have a minute to see you–except at this circus," she said. "I'm dying to hear what's going on in your life."

She watches him walk up the boulevard. "How are you, my dearest?" she asks after an affectionate abraçada. "Still look a bit thin, aren't you? I've tried to fatten you up, but all you ever eat is soup and bread."

He shrugs. "Doctor's orders."

She laughs. "You? Taking someone else's advice? How amusing!"

"Seriously, I can't afford to lose any more time. Besides, I've taken your advice quite a bit, no?"

"Ah, that's debatable. Now, tell me your news."

Granados describes his visit to Paris and the upcoming audition with l'Opéra de Paris; the medal of La Legion d'Honneur; his progress with Periquet on the opera version of *Goyescas*; an invitation from the American diplomat Robert Bliss to play at his Parisian home; Schelling's insistence that Granados come to Céligny in June and work on the opera; Schelling's performances of *Goyescas* in New York and London, and the excellent reviews; the letter from Schelling advising him that Sir Henry Wood wants to perform *Dante* in August or September; the Barcelona premiere of *Tonadillas* with Conxita Badia at the Sala in June, and Badia's booking to sing it at El Palau later the same month; the agreement with a New York publisher, Schirmer; and completion of *Elegia Eterna*, dedicated to María Barrientos, who's back from Argentina and is booked to sing it in London.

"My, my! Paris, Switzerland, London, New York. Are you telling me our favorite composer from this backward little country is making a splash in the great cities of the world?" Carmen's voice brims over with delight.

He laughs. "You asked for the news. Though I never know when I'm at risk of receiving your honey-tipped barbs."

"And I'll never let you know," says Carmen. "Well, it's perfectly marvelous. Truly–no jest. I was so worried about you last summer. Sitting up there in the mountains, thinking about you, not hearing from you, knowing you were very ill."

"Why, I sent notes to you and Salvador!"

"Yes, very cryptic little notes. You're a brilliant musician and a fine artist, but as a writer your pen is out of ink! So I asked Salvador to talk to your doctor and find out how seriously ill you might be. He told us not to worry–you were not going to die."

"I wish he'd told *me* that!"

Carmen shifts gears. "Now tell me about your romance in Tiana."

"Clotilde? She's been wonderful!"

"Are you attentive to her?"

He shakes his head. "Attentive? Of course! Why do you ask?"

"It's none of my business, of course, but when you told me Amparo found out about the two of you and was very–'understanding' was the word you used–I just wondered if that wasn't a very clever way of letting the romance run its course. Very shrewd, to let it come to an end on its own. Since all romances have a way of doing that."

"You wanted to know about Clotilde. The answer is, she's fine. A strong beautiful gracious loving woman. Ben plantada."

"Ben plantada? Like the woman in Eugène d'Ors' novel?"

"Yes. And I cannot tell you how joyously my life moves."

"Mi amor, that's all I wanted to know," says Carmen, taking his hand. "The rest of it? Just leaves, blowing in the wind."

Paris, June 1914

Granados takes an overnight train to Paris and arrives in the late morning of the twelfth of June. His room–at l'Hotel Bristol on the Place de Vendome–has been reserved by Schelling, who arrives in the late afternoon from London. After a brief, affectionate reunion in the lobby, Schelling asks Granados if he sent the vocal part for *Tonadillas* to the American baritone Emilio de Gogorza. And have the rest of the pieces been sent to Schirmer?

Granados affirms he sent everything to Schirmer; the vocal part was sent to Gogorza last month.

Gogorza attended the presentation by Granados and Periquet at the Madrid Ateneo last month, and told both Granados and Schelling of his interest in singing the tonadillas. Schelling suggested he sing them at the home of Robert and Mildred Bliss when Granados will be there. Schelling arranged for the Blisses to invite Gogorza, then asked Gogorza and Granados to correspond about appropriate gender changes. In a telegram to Granados, Schelling noted that "Señor de Gogorza is a singer of international reputation who can help you get *Tonadillas*

performed in Europe and the United States." Granados welcomed Schelling's advocacy, and conceded that switching genders was indeed feasible; in a letter to Gogorza that accompanied the score, he indicated it'll be the majo–not the maja, singing of his love, he doesn't want to live without *her*, and so forth. In the second piece there'll be some verses that don't precisely rhyme, but someday–after he's completed the opera–he can rewrite the tonadillas for a male vocalist.

"So Gogorza got the scores. Excellent," says Schelling as he and Granados walk up Rue Tronchet to the restaurant. "Now then, here's what I've arranged for this week. Tonight we're dining with Gogorza and his wife Emma Eames–she's a soprano who retired a couple of years ago. There's a marvelous little place just three blocks away–you won't be disappointed with the soupe de poissons. Oh yes, been meaning to ask: did you send the string parts for *Dante* to Sir Henry?"

After receiving the score from Schelling, Sir Henry Wood promptly decided to include it in the next Promenade concert series at Queen's Hall in September. "I worked on it," Granados replies, "but simply ran out of time. I'll finish before August–that's when he needs the string parts."

"Superb!" says Schelling, tossing his head. "Now where was I? Yes–the next day–it's the fifteenth, we have the audition with Jacques Rouché at l' Opéra. And the recital you've prepared for Robert and Mildred is on the twenty-first. I'm hoping to leave the next day for Céligny. Would you come home with me?"

Granados struggles to digest Schelling's breezy preview of events, and wonders if all Americans are this well organized. He thanks Schelling for the invitation to Céligny, but says it's important for him to return to Barcelona to finish the work on *Dante* and send it to Sir Henry. If they receive good news from Rouché, he'll then come to Céligny.

"If we receive good news?" asks Schelling. "You mean, when!"

Yes. Must be optimistic. Suppose that's very American.

"Yes, mon ami–when we get the good news," Granados replies.

"Well, then, by all means finish *Dante*. I hope you'll stay in Céligny for a good while."

"Yes, Henri. It sounds idyllic."

"It is that," says Schelling, "but Céligny's also a fine place for you to work on the opera. So why not stay the summer?"

The Paris home of Robert and Mildred Bliss is large enough to accommodate dozens of guests for dinner and a recital in the adjacent salon. As secretary of the embassy in an important post like Paris, Bliss is entitled to an entertainment allowance, generous enough but still not sufficient for this baronial residence overlooking the Seine. For the Blisses, that's no hindrance.

Born into a wealthy family in St. Louis, Robert Woods Bliss was educated at exclusive boys' schools in Boston, and at Harvard. After graduation he joined the U.S. Foreign Service, which recruits most of its diplomats from East Coast universities such as Princeton, Yale, and Harvard. He served in Puerto Rico, Venice, St. Petersburg, Brussels, and Buenos Aires before assignment to Paris two years ago. Mildred Barnes Bliss was born into a prominent family in New York City, also educated in private schools. They were married four years ago when Robert was still in Brussels. Fluent in Spanish and French–and childless–they have the time and money, along with passionate interest in the cultural life of wherever they're sent by the U.S. Department of State. With considerable aplomb, Mildred mixes continental artists and musicians with the international diplomatic crowd and their well-traveled American friends. Tonight she serves a six-course dinner culminating in a soufflé Richelieu to eighteen guests, including Schelling and the de rigueur coterie of European counts and countesses, barons and baronesses. Three dozen more guests from the Bliss' social and diplomatic circles are invited for a postprandial gathering in the music salon, where this afternoon Granados and Gorgoza rehearsed the three tonadillas of "La Maja Dolorosa" at a concert grand that Salle Pleyel sent to the Bliss' home at Granados' request. Granados is grateful it's been properly tuned.

Granados arrives while the guests are finishing dinner with coffee, cognac and a compote de fruit. The butler escorts him to a parlor adjacent to the entry hall, where after a few moments he's greeted by Mildred. She's dressed in a revealing gown by Premet of pearl tulle, sleeveless, trimmed with a sash of hyacinth violet mousseline de soie, and suspended by strings of pearl; it's this year's "Tango" look that has captivated the couturiers of Paris and their most daring clients. Mildred's chestnut hair is piled high and secured with a pearl clasp. She extends a long bare arm toward Granados and curls her long fingers around his hand, pulling him toward her.

"Oooh, bon soir, Maestro Granados! I'm perfectly delighted you've come!" She gives him a French buss on both cheeks while her long string of pearls clicks the studs of his jacket. "I do hope you're not inconvenienced. I think you'll find this evening very, very informal."

Granados recognizes the mannerisms of a seasoned and polished hostess. Mildred has lingered in his memory as a cosmopolitan, handsome American woman with an alluring passion for music. Tonight he finds her stunning:

probing green eyes, thin Athenian nose, New World élan, wide mouth turned up in a playful smile, and wrapped in an audacious dinner gown. Yet though outwardly seductive, she exudes assurance and invulnerability. The frontiers are clearly marked. She's scarcely older than Clotilde.

"Señor de Gogorza just arrived," says Mildred, leading Granados down a gallery of expensive art to the music salon. "He promised me an English translation of 'La maja dolorosa.' Or is it 'el majo'?"

Granados laughs. "Gogorza's 'el majo'–not exactly what I had in mind originally. To me, el majo was Goya and La Duquesa de Alba was la maja. But the tonadillas aren't just about those two–they're about all men and women in the time of Goya."

Mildred stops, standing between a Degas and a landscape by the obscure Argentine painter Fernandez, a souvenir from the Bliss' three years in Buenos Aires. "Is it too simplistic for me to say you're describing men and women of any time, not just Goya's? For instance, if a lover cries out, 'Oh cruel death! Why hast thou betrayed me? You stole my beloved one at the height of our passion. I cannot live without him. It is death thus to live.' That's not just about Goya's time. It could be me, in grief over a dead lover, n'est-ce pas?"

He's surprised to hear his first "La Maja Dolorosa" translated into French. "That's very close. Is that your translation?"

Mildred demurs, turning her eyes away. "Yes, in a way. Señor de Gorgoza gave me that piece in English, and I translated it to French. Forgive me if it sounds amateurish."

"No, I'm impressed. It's very close. You've captured the feeling."

"You haven't answered my question, maestro. It's not just about Goya, is it? I could be about me, n'est-ce pas?"

He's delighted with the question. "Yes, it could be you. Or about me. Love and death comes to all of us, all men and women. For all I know, there's someone *you* can't live without."

"Of course, I'm not saying it's about me or that I've had a dead lover. I'm not saying that. Why, it could be merely fear of a lover's death." Her voice suggests the first crack in her composure.

"Yes it could be, Madame Bliss."

"I'd much prefer you called me Mildred. Especially since you implied that you and I are–what did you call it in your letter? 'almas amigas'?"

Doesn't miss a thing! Yes that was in my letter.

"What I meant," he says, "was that only someone who's a soulful friend could understand the delicacy of my artistic spirit. You seem that kind of person."

She bows, exposing the curve of her breasts. "Thank you, maestro. I'm honored."

"Enrique, s'il vous plait."

She takes his hand. "Yes, Enrique. Very well, that's settled. Here's Señor de Gogorza," she says, guiding Granados into the music salon.

En route to the audition at Palais Garnier, Schelling describes the dynamics of the trio who will render judgment on the opera: Jacques Rouché, whose job is to look at the artistic merits of new works such as *Goyescas*, and to recommend those he wants to include in the upcoming season; André Messager, a composer and conductor; and Frederick Broussan. "When he was at Covent Garden," explains Schelling, "Messager conducted the British premieres for Saint-Saens and Fauré and Massenet. So he's predisposed to like new works like *Goyescas*. As for Broussan, I hardly know him. Jacques says he favors romantic operas. He'd love *Boheme*."

The three Frenchmen are smoking at a round table next to the Pleyel grand in a recital hall under the stage of the auditorium of l'Opéra de Paris. They hold their Gauloises with palms inverted, cupping hirsute chins as they inhale, drawing the pencil-thin cigarettes away as they release plumes of blue smoke into the room. A mannerism, perhaps intentional, which suggests languor and disinterest. And heightens stress for those who are being auditioned.

Granados plays both books of *Goyescas* and *El Pelele* for the first time without a predisposed, passionate audience. He knows this is an audition, not a tour de force for family, friends, and fanáticos at Sala Granados or Salle Pleyel. For the first time, nobody rushes forward with a bouquet; there are no encores. And though Granados understands the difference, the absence of any fervor at all is disconcerting.

At least Bernis would applaud—even if he then took me over to Café de l'Opera to say it isn't right for El Liceu.

After an awkward pause, Granados comes to the table to give a quick summary of the libretto. He hands the outline and scoring for the two scenes, "Coloquio" and "Maja y Ruiseñor," to Rouché. He also passes around the pen-and-ink sketches he's made: one is called "La Maja en el Balcón," an impressionistic glimpse of a maja, with one pale hand resting on the wrought-iron railing of a balcony, looking at the viewer with eyelids lowered in sadness or longing; another shows the caped back and black hat of a military officer who's standing outside a grilled window, conversing with the ghostly white face of his maja; the third is of a maja dressed all in black with hair cascading down to her waist—as La Duquesa de Alba was fond of appearing—with a white fan and the white curve of her breasts drawing the viewer's eyes up to her face. At once beguiling and carnal and demure.

"These are superb!" exclaims Rouché. "Are they by Goya?"

Now Granados is amused. "By Goya?"

"Well, they're very good," says Rouché, bolstering his comment. "They really convey the spirit you're describing–the time of the majas, their mysterious allure, the romance of the streets of Madrid. Parfum in the air, the clicking of castanets and strumming of guitars. The dancing of feet on cobblestones. Mais oui, these sketches completely capture it!"

Granados nods. "I hope so, Monsieur Rouché."

Rouché leans forward. "And are they by Goya?"

Schelling intervenes. "No, Jacques, they are by the maestro."

The three Frenchmen pull out their packs of Gauloise. "Extraordinaire"–repeated over and over.

"Maestro Granados," says Messager, "these too should be hanging in the Prado!" There's a twinkle in his eye.

"Monsieur Messager, you flatter me. Not the Prado. But perhaps the Louvre would be interested."

Dead silence, followed by an explosion of laughter.

Granados takes advantage of their disarray. "Alors, messieurs, I have many passions, of which sketching is only one. Many years ago–as a student of de Beriot–my friend Francisco Miralles used to show me how to render acceptable sketches. He was a wonderful mentor, an extraordinary friend. But after sober reflection, though sketching was a passion, it wasn't the most important one. So I remained with music. But I'm glad you like my sketches."

Broussan asks the first question. "Maestro Granados, could you explain the difference between a majo and a maja?"

"Yes. Rosario, the heroine, is dressed as a maja and her lover, Fernando, is a military officer."

"Ah, then he's a majo. Trés amusant! So it's a question of gender, n'est-ce pas?"

"Yes, men are majos. Women are majas." Granados searches Broussan's face to discern if he understands.

Trés amusant! Spaniards always "amusants" to the French. Gracias a Dios they didn't conquer us and make us French!

Granados looks from Broussan to Messager to Rouché. "In the time of Goya, the aristocracy would dress in the manner of the flashy people of the street," he explains, hoping they won't identify that period with the Spanish urging from the French army under Napoleon, and reminding himself that this is 1914, with the fate of his opera being decided. He dismisses a sudden urging to compare the maja to Marie Antoinette in the bucolic dress of a country maid.

She lost her head ten years before Goya painted the disasters of the war. No more sly remarks. Just answer their questions.

"Not only the aristocracy, messieurs–a military officer such as Fernando or an artist such as Goya might appear in the street dressed as majos, just as the La Duchesse d'Alba would dress as a maja."

At last, Broussan is nodding. "Most interesting. Merci, maestro."

"And the scene in the garden–what does the nightingale represent?" asks Messager.

"The maja, Rosario, is missing her lover, Fernando, and the nightingale appears in the dark garden to sing. And she–in a dreamlike state–asks why the nightingale pours out his mournful song in the gloom of night. Is it a grudge he bears against the king and he's trying to right a wrong? Or does his breast hide such sorrow that he finds relief in the darkness by sadly singing songs of love? In either case, his song is mysterious, surrounded by dark shadows. But we sense from this scene that the song of the nightingale is a hymn of love." Granados stops, feeling tears rise in his eyes. "Does that answer your question?"

After nearly three hours, Rouché stands up to conclude the meeting and guides Granados and Schelling through the corridors and stairways of the Palais Garnier to the Place de l'Opéra. "Maestro Granados," he says, "I'm enchanted with your opera *Goyescas* and will recommend it to my colleagues. I wanted them to hear the piano suite–as I did at Salle Pleyel–and I believe they're very impressed with the work. In other words, there's excellent chance of presenting it in our next season."

"Jacques, that's wonderful!" exclaims Schelling, grasping his hand. "When will we know of your decision?"

Rouché holds up his hands. "Ah, Henri, you know this business. There are so many things I cannot control. I think the impresarios will accept my recommendation, then we'll hope for no malicious acts of God."

Schelling steps forward. "But Jacques, how soon will you be able to let us know–barring acts of God?"

"I'll let you know within a week," says Rouché.

As they wait for a cab on Place Vendome, Schelling turns to Granados. "You were magnifique, mon frere! And the way you knocked them off balance–not the Prado, perhaps the Louvre. That was delightful!"

"There were moments when I wondered."

"That's precisely what I'm saying–those were the moments when you were magnifique!"

"To be honest, Henri," says Granados, "I wanted to tell them how I resent their air of superiority. But I'm older and wiser. I know better."

"As do I. Don't forget, the French have no more regard for Americains than they do for Spaniards. To them, we're simply barbarians."

"And we're just second-class Frenchmen, n'est-ce pas?"

"Alors, barbarians–francaises inferieures. No difference."

"I only hope their decision will be positive," says Granados.

"Yes, that's the American spirit! Or is it Catalan? At any rate it's time for you and me to celebrate a job well done! D'accord?"

Barcelona

Two days after returning from Paris, Granados comes home around midnight to find Amparo waiting for him, waving a slender yellow envelope.

"It's a telegram. I think from Paris," she says.

Heart pounding, he lays a stack of composition pads on the table in the entry hall, and reaches for the envelope.

Can't open it–what if it's bad news? Better wait 'til morning. No–that's ridiculous! Another sleepless night? All right–ready now.

He raises the envelope and squints at it, holds his breath, then inserts his index finger under the flap at the corner and pulls gently.

"I know it's good news," says Amparo, with her arm around his waist. "It simply must be!"

Granados takes the telegram out of the envelope and unfolds it.

> [MON CHER MAESTRO GRANADOS]
> [I HAVE THE HONOR TO [INFORM YOU THAT THE OPERA <GOYESCAS> HAS BEEN ACCEPTED FOR NEXT SEASON OF THE OPERA DE PARIS] [WE ARE PRIVILEGED THAT THE WORLD PREMIERE OF YOUR WORK WILL TAKE PLACE AT

THE PALAIS GARNIER]
[WITH GREAT RESPECT AND AFFECTION] [JACQUES ROUCHE]

"You're shaking," says Amparo. "It's all right. It's all right. Tu sueño–your dream has come true!"

"I must let Henri know I'm coming to Switzerland."

Granados decides to leave for Céligny on June 29. When Amparo hears of his intention to spend most of the remaining summer there, working on the opera, she suggests he invite Solita to come along–realizing their oldest daughter will soon be leaving home to start a family of her own.

"It may be your last chance," says Amparo.

"My little Solita? Oh, you mean her flirtation?" he asks. Though he has no objection to the young medical student, Rossend Carrasco, it seems inconceivable that one of his children is on the brink of leaving home. He wonders if that means he might soon be a grandfather, then dismisses that.

"Our little Solita is eighteen. And not so little. I don't know how much she cares for Rossend, but she's certainly prepared. Núbil. Any fool can see that." Amparo laughs. "Even you."

The next morning, Granados autographs a photo for Robert and Mildred Bliss and dispatches José Altet to post it. The formal portrait shows Granados in a vested white linen suit with a cravat tied scarf-style. Light reflected from his face and suit offer contrast with the dark background, and dramatize the meticulous trim of his moustache and the lidded geniality of his eyes. The inscription is unadorned: "With all good wishes to M. and Mme. Bliss Enrique Granados Barcelona 28 juin 1914"

That's brief. Much more to say. Instantaneous rapport with Mildred. She appreciates my artistic spirit! Robert doesn't seem to mind her flirting. It's safe and she's safe and we're safe. Mildred and Robert–lives seem blessed—such generous spirits!

Tiana

Clotilde hears the whine of his motorcycle and walks to the courtyard. Since his return from Paris, they've been together only once, the afternoon before he received the telegram from Rouché. He was edgy then, meandering in anxiety, not knowing there was good news waiting for him at home. She hasn't seen him since, though he called her and read the telegram. Read it twice. And tomorrow he'll be leaving again, this time for Switzerland, this time for most of the remaining summer. They talked of her joining him there for a few days, but now with his daughter going along that's no longer possible. Clotilde wonders if that's the reason for Amparo suggesting that he take Solita, then scolds herself for letting a setback so trivial turn to pettiness. She reminds herself she'll not ask for anything that isn't his to give, she'll concentrate on whatever she can to enrich their time together, and avoid making him feel she's become another one of his many obligations. No, she vows, she'll never let that happen, she'll never leave their remarkable garden untended.

The motorcycle skids to a stop and Granados, without removing his rider's cap or turning off the engine, walks toward Clotilde. By the time he reaches her she hears his excited voice.

"Come away with me, fair maiden! The sun is shining, the birds are singing, the sprites are dancing. O, come away, fair maiden!"

She laughs. "If you think me the fair Dulcinea, alas sire, you're sadly mistaken. And how might you be called, knight so bold?"

"If you are Dulcinea, I hardly know thee. Nor could I be the Knight of the Sorrowful Countenance." He strikes a señorial pose with his arms crossed.

"No my lord? I'm dismayed, for if you were indeed that great knight of La Mancha you'd remember this: 'Journey over all the universe on a map, without the expense and fatigue of traveling, without suffering the inconveniences of heat, cold, hunger, and thirst.'"

"I'm impressed, Fair One, but you forgot the part about longing for the absent lover."

"No, it's Cervantes who forgot to include that."

He steps forward and embraces her. "You're still disappointed about not coming to Céligny."

She nods. "It was a pretty little dream."

"We both dream. And that's why–if the opera's accepted–you will come with me to Paris."

"Paris? For the premiere? Oh, yes, that would give me such joy!" She catches herself and gives him a searching look. "Are you quite serious?"

"Serious? To show you how serious, listen Fair One, I'll sing you my reply." He begins Alfredo's part in the duet from the final act of Verdi's *La Traviata*, his voice breaking as he reaches for the notes high in the tenor range.

Null'uomo o demone, angelo mio	Neither man nor demon, my angel
mai più staccarti potrà da me.	can separate you from me.
A Parigi, o cara o noi lasceremo,	We'll leave for Paris, oh my darling,
la vita uniti trascorreremo:	and we'll always be together:
De' corsi affanni compenso avrai,	the pain of the past will be healed
la tua salute rifiorirá.	and your health will blossom.
Sospiro e luce tu mi serai,	You'll be the light of my life
tutto el futuro ne arriderá.	and the future will smile upon us.

"Bravo! Bravo!" cries Clotilde, jumping up and down. "No man ever sang for me!"

Granados clears his throat. With voice recovered, he asks if she noticed the slight change in the verse.

"Of course I did–you've taught me how to pay close attention! Verdi has the lovers leaving Paris to start a new life, and you have us going *to* Paris. Oh, you're far too clever!"

"We'll see how clever I am when it's time for the premiere. But on this splendid day, will you come away with me? I'll take you up to Cànoves."

Clotilde shakes her head. "Where's that?"

"Well, it's in the direction of Paris," he says, laughing. "No, seriously, it's a very picturesque ride. A beautiful little village. Very old, in the midst of a forest on the side of Serra Montseny. I'll show you the Great Chestnut Tree, which is hundreds of years old, and the hermitage of Sant Salvador in Samulús. Please come, fair maiden!"

Clotilde takes his arm and leads him toward the house. "Thank you, kind sir. There's only one thing I ask for–before we ride up to see the Great Chestnut Tree. Before we plunge into the forest. Or see a hermitage. One thing only, mi querido, this last day before you leave. But first, please turn off the engine–on your moto-cicleta. And come with me."

Celigny, Switzerland

Amparo and the children come to l'Estació França to see them off. Solita and her mother cry in each other's arms when it's time for boarding. "I can't help it," says Amparo, "it's the first time I've watched my little girl go away. No–you're not my little girl any more, I know. I still can't help it. You write now, don't forget!" she exhorts her daughter. "Tell me all about Switzerland. Practice your French. And don't forget to write!"

Granados sleeps all the way to the French border. He's exhausted by the hectic pace of the last few days. Finishing the string parts for *Dante*, reviewing the libretto with Periquet, writing a letter with the good news to Salvador and Carmen, two jaunts up to Tiana and one with Clotilde to Cànoves, and packing for an extended stay in Céligny. Too preoccupied with boarding the train this morning to see the story at the bottom of the front page of *La Vanguardia* about an archduke being shot somewhere in the Balkans, too exhausted to overhear the excited voices in the next compartment. Soon after dozing off again, he feels the brakes slowing the train. "We're in France!" exclaims Solita.

Granados sits up and looks out the window at the town and harbor of Collioure, and the Cote Vermaille stretching north toward Marseilles. "Solita, this area's called Roselló. They speak Catalan here."

"But we're in France, aren't we?"

"Oh yes, we are. But just as Barcelona is a long way from the capital in Madrid, this is a long way from Paris."

"I don't see any flags of Catalunya. Look over there–le tricolor de France. Do they think of themselves as Catalans, as we do?"

He smiles at Solita, sees a bright, curious, attractive young woman of eighteen. His eyes, mouth, and acquiline nose are set on Amparo's round face; she's dressed in a tan suit for travel, with a maroon scarf tied at the collar of a pearl-white silk shirt. While her older brother Eduardo has a taut smile and seems ever purposeful, Solita–without the burden of having to follow in a father's steps–has an impish genial smile and the capacity to savor what for her has been a comfortable life. She enjoys being courted by the young Dr. Rossend Carrasco and regards him as quite suitable, but has not been swept off her feet. Sensing that a marriage proposal is forthcoming–unless she outright refuses to see him–she's been trying to deflect her mother's impatience. "Mamá, I'm in no hurry. I have plenty of time–the rest of my life–to be married," she says, "so there's no need to lose my mind and rush into it." Nothing she might say could make Amparo more anxious.

"Well, Father, do they–think they're Catalans?" she asks again.

"That's a good question, Solita. Some say this region's just another part of Catalunya. Same language, same food, same history."

"Papá, can we speak French on this trip?" she asks. "Seulement francais? I must improve before we reach Céligny."

In Marseilles, Granados and Solita take a stroll through the station–a chance to stretch before the ride north to Lyon, where they'll catch their train to Switzerland. All around them are travelers diving into newspapers, while others hold impromptu forums about the likelihood of war. "La guerre–c'est inevitable! Non, ce n'est pas inevitable! La guerre–c'est impossible! Let the Austrians fight. Let the Germans fight. Nous n'avons pas besoin de guerre! Who needs war?"

Granados, his curiosity piqued, stops at a kiosque and buys a newspaper. The front-page story–with banner headline–is about yesterday's killing of Archduke Franz Ferdinand, nephew of the Austro-Hungarian Emperor Franz Josef, in the Bosnian capital of Sarajevo. The assassin, Gavrilo Princip, was arrested at the scene of the murder and incarcerated. The Austrian government is investigating. Though Princip and the other terrorists are Austrian subjects, it's reported that they were armed in Serbia and smuggled back into Austria by a Serbian nationalist organization. This has fueled speculation that the Austro-Hungarian Empire will soon declare war on Serbia. It's also reported that the Empire has asked for support from Germany, another member of the Triple Alliance, to deal with Serbia. Granados looks up from the paper and watches the flow of passengers to the newsstand.

Thank God España's not involved! We had our disastrous wars. All wars disastrous. Thank God France isn't involved!

"I don't understand this talk of war," says Solita. "Will España be in this war? Does this mean Rossend will have to go?"

Granados shakes his head. "You know I don't get involved in politics, and this is a good example why not. But you shouldn't worry about your fiancé. España will be neutral just like Switzerland. It's a shame all countries aren't neutral–we could eliminate war. But don't worry, this war won't touch us. We can be grateful for that."

Solita smiles, relieved. "Gracias a Dios."

Céligny is a tiny enclave nineteen kilometers north of Geneva, closer still to the French border. Like Puigcerdà, its remote location and view of distant mountains have made it a favorite of the wealthy and renowned. In a mild, temperate climate, many of its large estates have lawns that roll down to a thin strip of beach along the shores of Lac Léman, and on the hillsides there are small orchards and vineyards. On a clear day there's a view across the long lake to Montreux and the snow-capped mountains that surround the Alpine resort of Gstaad. And on a very clear day the highest mountain in Europe, Mont

Blanc, is visible. Céligny, not a busy tourist destination like Gstaad and other Swiss resorts, has preserved its tranquility. From the tiny rail station there's a short drive around the village square, past the l'Hotel du Soleil and up a narrow winding road to "Garengo"–the chalet that Schellings bought four years ago.

Henry and Lucie Schelling are at the station platform when Granados and Solita arrive, both in matching English riding attire: jodhpurs, boots, white blouses, twill jackets. Lucie is a slender, tall, regal, and lovely woman of intellect and wit, ripening in her early thirties, ruddy-cheeked and green-eyed, with short curly chestnut hair. Her instinct for making people laugh–and for making outrageous comments–once set her apart from the other debutantes in Boston and Bar Harbor. Her daring and canny sense of just when to spice a conversation with unvarnished language both stuns and delights. Her affluent family blessed her marriage to Schelling seven years ago–despite his peripatetic career as a musician–because his father was European-born, respectable, and scandal-free, and because both Lucie and her mother found Schelling irresistible. And because Lucie–like her husband–is intent on getting her way.

While the chauffeur takes the baggage to their town car, Schelling pulls Granados aside. "I'm just ecstatic about l'Opéra de Paris. I wasn't surprised–Jacque was so impressed after hearing you play *Goyescas* in April. No–not surprised, but it's such good news!"

"And there's so much work to be done," says Granados.

"That's precisely why I wanted you to come here." Schelling lifts his arms overhead. "Can you imagine a more perfect place to work?"

"I can't tell you how grateful I am. And Solita was just thrilled to be invited."

"She'll have the time of her life!" says Schelling. "Riding, swimming, tennis, boating–I have a fast boat you know–biking, picnics, tea-dances, band concerts, and a swell group of young people, just her age, and are they excited to meet a Spanish girl! I'll say! She's in for the time of her life!"

As they climb into the town car, Granados is buoyed by their arrival.

Like coming home. Like arriving in Puigcerdà. Warmth and affection. Henri's remarkable. Such zest for music–brought us together. And unquenchable enthusiasm. Amazing charm.

The first thing Granados notices about Henry and Lucie Schelling's chalet "Garengo" is the courtyard of rectangular stones, cut with precision and laid down like bricks, and an imposing fountain that rises from an elongated octagon of flowers and shrubs. Across the courtyard is a twelve-room three-story villa built in the 18th century, constructed of granite cut to rectangles, with a grand entrance and reception hall providing access from the courtyard, a pair of verandas in the rear that overlook another fountain surrounded by formal gardens, and a rushing stream that plunges through a series of hanging gardens toward the lake. Ornamental trees and shrubs everywhere, and a carriage house large enough to accommodate the Schellings' three horses. The second thing Granados notices is the large white dog that bounds across the courtyard.

"Ah, here's Nicki–some new people to sniff," says Schelling, stepping down from the town car. The dog rushes to him, its white tail a wagging blur, and receives the desired scratching of ears and neck. "Down boy, down Nicki." Schelling turns to Granados, who hesitates to step down. "Oh, he looks mean but he's just a big puppy with lots of energy, wanting to play, wanting to be our companion. Come over, I'll introduce you."

Before dinner, Schelling invites Granados to stroll in the garden. "It will be busy while you're here," he says. "This is a gathering place–not an accident, it's what I hoped it would be. Pretty obvious, Lucie and I aren't going to devote our lives to raising a bunch of children. So you'll see a parade of people coming through, and I don't apologize for it, though I did invite you to come here to work on the opera. It's still a fantastic place for that, but just the same you'll be exposed to the parade. Tonight Josef Hofmann will arrive from Paris. You haven't met him, though I'm sure you know of him–you'll enjoy him enormously. Next week you'll meet my old maestro Paderewski. Jan and Helena live up on the north side of the lake near Lausanne, about forty kilometers from here, and they'll come down for a couple of days. Also Fritz Kreisler's coming on Sunday. Won't stay long–he's going back to Vienna. You've met Kreisler?

"Once or twice, at Casals' place in Paris. A few years ago."

"Speaking of Casals, weren't you surprised to hear he's married Susan?"

Granados shakes his head. "Completely surprised–I've never even heard of her. Have you?"

"Oh yes, Susan Metcalfe's a fair–not a good–soprano. Not going to have a career, though she gives a few concerts in America every year. And she's sung a few times over here. She's known Casals for years. Probably ten, since before Suggia, but I've never heard her mention him other than respecting his virtuosity. And he–well you know him better than I–he's never mentioned her at all. So it's a splendid mystery."

"I hope to see him on my next trip to Paris."

"I'm not sure you'll find him there–I've heard they'll move his things to London. Ah yes, I forgot to mention that the Blisses will also be here this week. Two of my absolute favorites! They'll be arriving Monday afternoon. Forgive me, but isn't Mildred stunning? Stunning! Well, I don't have to tell you that. But I confess to finding her one of the most alluring women I've ever met. You know, of course, she's entirely devoted to Robert. That's a blessing because Paris is full of scoundrels. And some really fine gentlemen who also are attracted to her, like you and I. Hopelessly married, aren't we?"

Granados gives him an enigmatic smile. Except for the Blisses, it'll be a parade of musicians from Poland, Germany, Austria, España, America. "A very impressive group, Henri."

"Well, they were impressed to hear *you'd* be here," says Schelling. "No, seriously! I do hope you'll play *Goyescas*. Hofmann said he'd play some Chopin tonight. He plays with extraordinary delicacy! You're bound to enjoy him. And the others have all promised to play next week."

Schelling has a collection of seven Steinway pianos at Garengo. Three are located in the music salon; the others in the living room, Schelling's study, and in two guest cottages close to the chalet. Hofmann is at work in one of the guest cottages, preparing for his annual American tour. The day after he leaves, Paderewski and his wife will occupy the same guest cottage.

"I compliment you on your pianos," says Granados after Schelling shows him the music salon.

"The people at Steinway have been very generous," Schelling says with charming nonchalance. "What's more, they provide me with a piano every time I have to cross the ocean."

Granados has been able to spend the first two days at work on the opera, thanks to the abundance of Steinways, and Lucie's willingness to take Solita shopping in Geneva, making sure she's kept busy with the young people of Céligny.

"A precious young woman," Lucie tells Granados, "she's sweet, she's bright, she's funny! My compliments to you and your wife. And I wouldn't be surprised to see a lovesick suitor or two follow her back to Barcelona. Tongues out, hearts pounding. Ah, to be young and succulent!" She strikes a bewitching pose.

On the third day after Granados' arrival, Schelling takes him for a hike in the nearby hills where they enjoy panoramic views of Lac Léman and–since it's an unusually clear day–the towering Swiss Alps in the distance. Granados brings a sketching pad and returns with four quickly rendered landscapes. He'll give one to Lucie and take the others back for Amparo, Carmen, and Clotilde. He promises to do a sketch of Schelling and Nicki, having noted with amusement that the wavy outline of the dog's ears is identical to the curve of his master's moustache–except upside down, like a reflection in a mirror.

With each passing day, there's more talk in the capitals of Europe that the assassination in Sarajevo will trigger a general war on the continent. Two days after Granados and Solita arrive in Céligny, three of the terrorists who assassinated Archduke Franz Ferdinand confess they were armed and aided by Serbian nationalists in their deadly mission, and high officials of the Austro-Hungarian Empire resolve to make Serbia pay for it. A swift military strike would not be difficult, and would convey to all nations–friend and foe alike–that the empire is willing to punish any group that challenges its suzerainty. And Serbia is considered more a backward pariah than David to the empire's Goliath, especially because nine years ago some of its army officers killed their own king and queen, threw them from a palace window and hacked them to pieces. Serbia's demise would stir little sympathy in the rest of Europe.

But the Austro-Hungarian leaders are reluctant to mobilize against Serbia, leaving their border with Russia unprotected, so instead of a decisive strike they seek to persuade the German government to join in the war of retribution. This complicates decision making and serves to alert the Russians, whose sympathy with Serbia as a kindred Slavic state has thus far been tempered by its own internal problems. However, the specter of German involvement heightens Russian concern, and because Russia is allied by treaty with France, it raises the alarming possibility that England, aligned by another treaty with France, could also become involved. Italy, by virtue of its alliance with Germany and Austria-Hungary, would also be obliged to join the conflict. So what might have been a quick, brutal attack on Serbia by the Austro-Hungarians now contains the embers of a conflagration that could engulf all of Europe.

Yet while ministers plot and scurry from office to office and military commanders ready their forces for the possibility of combat, news and rumors are far slower arriving in Céligny, and conversations are far less intense away from the capitals of Europe. And though the threat of war is a favored topic in the cafés of Geneva and Lausanne and around dinner tables in the chalets, it's hard to imagine a general war–however devastating to the combatants–disturbing the tranquility of this lovely valley in neutral Switzerland.

"What about this talk of war?" asks Granados when Schelling and Nicki appear on the veranda to be sketched. "Could it keep me and Solita from returning home?"

"Certainly not!" exclaims Schelling. "You can put that out of your mind. After the assassination fades in the memory, we'll get back to our lives. Won't we? Now, would you like to hear about the letter I just opened from Campanini?"

"Campanini?"

"Ah, Cleofonte Campanini. His older brother is the tenor, Italo Campanini, who sang in *Faust* its opening night at the Metropolitan. Italo became an impresario and brought Cleo over to conduct the American premiere of *Otello*. After that, Cleo conducted at La Scala and Covent Garden until Oscar Hammerstein hired him to help establish the Manhattan Opera House. To rival the Met. He soon had a falling out with Hammerstein, and went to the new opera company in Chicago, first to conduct, then as general director. That's where he is now."

"You knew him in New York?" asks Granados.

"Yes. And was impressed by his interest in new operas and the great number he introduced to America. Three by Massenet, Debussy's *Peleas*, one by Wolf-Ferrari, several others. At any rate," says Schelling, "I talked to Campanini about *Goyescas* and got a note back saying that he'd be happy to receive a score of the new opera by Granados. To be presented next season, after its premiere in Paris. Also, Rudi Schirmer says he'll talk to Gatti-Casazza at the Metropolitan about having it performed there. He thinks that's the best place for an American premiere–not Chicago–says he prefers it from every point of view. That's Schirmer–I haven't even talked with Gatti about your opera."

"I'm confused, Granados says. "So many possibilities, but the opera's been accepted by Paris. Why talk to Chicago and New York?"

"A very good question. It's something I learned from Sir Henry."

Sir Henry Wood. My score for Dante *should have reached him.*

"He's also interested in 'Los Majos'?" Granados asks.

"No, we were grouse hunting together, in Scotland, and I learned a valuable lesson: in the field you don't put all your hopes on just one bird. You see one up ahead and you think: 'That's my bird,' and the bird flies off–well, it hasn't agreed to be your bird, and meanwhile you've missed all the other birds sitting in the trees watching while you pursue 'your bird.' The dogs are trying to tell you about the others in the trees; the dogs are watching you like you're daft."

On July 7—the day the Austro-Hungarian Imperial Council of Ministers meets in Vienna to discuss military action against Serbia—Henry and Lucie Schelling host a dinner at Garengo for their eight house guests. In addition to Granados and Solita, they include Jan and Helena Paderewski, Fritz and Harriet Kreisler, and Robert and Mildred Bliss. Before dinner, Paderewski plays one of his signature pieces, Beethoven's sonata "La Appassionata," and his own composition, "Fantasie Polonaise." Kreisler and Schelling play the host's Sonata for violin and piano. And Granados plays Book One of *Goyescas*.

Schelling leads the guests to dinner, down a long candlelit gallery through a gauntlet of medieval suits of armor and a collection of halberds—axes designed to split a helmet, collected by his father. "That one's from Spain—sixteenth century," he says, turning back to Granados.

Granados retorts, "Mais non, Henri. That's from Spain—in 1898. Why do you think we lost the war against America?"

The guests are still rhapsodizing over *Goyescas*, the last piece played before dinner. Granados, walking with Paderewski and Mildred Bliss, recognizes this was the host's intention, and he's grateful. Paderewski confesses to Granados, "This place is so inspiring—one of the few that Helena and I visit willingly. Otherwise we insist that people come to Morges." He then turns with a dancer's grace and kisses the hand of Mildred Bliss, continuing without a moment's pause, "This place is blessed with the company of the most dazzling women!"

"Jan, you say the most beautiful things," she replies. In her sleeveless turquoise tulle gown by Paquin, barebacked, bare shouldered, and hanging by a pair of rhinestone straps, with a hemline several inches above her ankles that twirls as she moves, she's been receiving a disproportionate share of admiring glances from the men. She knows the elegant Paderewski is a charming, inveterate hand-kisser. "Your words are sheer poetry!"

Ignacy Jan Paderewski was born in a small Polish town, son of a land agent with ties to the nobility and a professor's daughter who died soon after his birth. His family recognized his pianistic talent and arranged for lessons with the best teachers they could afford. He entered the conservatory of Warsaw at age twelve and after completing his studies lived modestly on income from teaching and composing. Married at age twenty, he lost his wife shortly after the birth of their son, who was born disabled. A trip to Berlin, where he met Richard Strauss and Anton Rubinstein, provided the break Paderewski had been waiting for. He went on to advanced studies in Vienna with the legendary Leschetizky, who later taught Schelling. After teaching in Strasbourg, Paderewski went to Paris when he was twenty-eight, and was a resounding success.

Within two years, Paderewski toured most of Europe, becoming a favorite in London, and made his American debut at Carnegie Hall. That led to frequent tours in the U.S.A. and Canada, as well as in South America, Australia, New Zealand, and South Africa. His striking appearance–a blond, leonine mane, sensual mouth, and offstage sartorial elegance–and his Old World charm, hypnotic stage presence, and imaginative performances endeared him to audiences around the world, though not always the critics. He would shrug them off with, "It is not a question of how the music is written, it's a question of musical effect." And musical effect was Paderewski's forte. He married again, to the actress Helena Gorska, who'd befriended and supported him during his lean years in Warsaw, and they settled in his recently acquired villa at Morges with his son, who soon died just short of his twentieth birthday.

Despite a late start, Paderewski is now the highest-paid keyboard artist in the world. He owns a large estate in Poland and lives an extravagant life at his Swiss villa, where he entertains in royal style and is usually surrounded by a gaggle of servants and admirers. This lifestyle, combined with his generosity toward those suffering in his occupied homeland, require Paderewski to follow a grueling schedule of concerts. He confesses to his closest friends that life on tour has become "a kind of torture" that leaves him without desire to play.

So he's lightened his punishing itinerary, though always willing to perform in London, where his popularity has never waned, and where he and Muriel Draper–the American wife of singer Paul Draper, and half Paderewski's age–are having an affair. This was the primary reason for his being in London nine days ago, when Archduke Franz Ferdinand was being shot dead in Sarajevo. Paderewski was playing a Liszt sonata on the Bechstein concert grand in Mrs. Draper's music salon, converted from a stable and decorated in Florentine splendor, while she lounged in his silk robe on one of the gigantic cushions scattered about the tile floor, swilling champagne from Moet & Chandon–said to be the preferred beverage of King Louis XV's mistress, Marquise de Pompadour, who considered champagne to be "the only wine that leaves a woman beautiful after drinking"–and munching hors d'oeuvres from the catering service of the Hotel Savoy.

"Granados, your piano suite is magnificent!" It's the voice of Fritz Kreisler, walking behind him. "You played one night at Villa Molitor–one of your other pieces, and it was quite good–but this new one is magnificent."

At thirty-nine Kreisler is as handsome as any leading man of the stage, with charismatic charm and genuine warmth that endears him to friends, colleagues, and people on the street who have no idea who he is. He's as well liked as his American wife Harriet is loathed–she publicly mocks and embarrasses him, telling even new acquaintances that "Fritzi might have amounted to something if he hadn't been so lazy, if he'd been willing to practice more."

Kreisler was born in Vienna and began to learn violin at age four, playing with his father, an amateur violinist. He entered the Musikverein Konservatorium at age seven, the youngest student ever accepted. After completing his studies and winning several prizes, he moved on to the Conservatoire de Paris at age twelve. At fourteen he toured the U.S.A., assisting Moritz Rosenthal, and after mixed success returned to Vienna to pursue studies in medicine. While back in Vienna he also satisfied his military obligation to the empire, serving for two years as a junior officer in the Kaiserjaeger Regiment. His commanding officer was Archduke Eugene of Habsburg, grand-nephew of the Emperor and an amateur singer with whom Kreisler presented sporadic recitals. Eschewing careers in medicine and the military, he returned to his first love at age twenty-one, building a repertory for the concert circuit and composing a number of works for violin. Kreisler returned to music virtually unknown, long forgotten for whatever scant reputation he'd earned as a prodigy, and was able to reestablish himself only with the most intense devotion.

Kreisler's virtuosity is unique. He practices very little yet achieves an amazing expressiveness and sweetness of tone, seemingly without effort. His use of an intensified vibrato, regardless of the tempo, gives his music a certain magic that others find difficult to emulate. He plays with overt emotionalism and sentimentality that are popular with today's audiences, especially when he plays the Viennese pieces. Though some critics have labeled his style "exaggerated," Kreisler remains unafraid of playing from his heart, and many critics are swept along with the audience as he renders a stirring, affective poeticism. In this summer of 1914, Kreisler is in the top ranks of world violinists, with packed houses and raves virtually assured, especially in the U.S.A.

Since Kreisler's former unit in the Austrian army would be mobilized if the empire's dispute with Serbia escalates, he and Harriet are keeping a watchful eye on events, and he is in daily contact with friends and family in Vienna. In the music world where he's lived most of his life, nationality is rarely a barrier between artists, so he's unmoved by the passions that engender conflict between nations. He agrees with most of his countrymen that the Serbs are uncivilized, and difficult neighbors in the Balkans, but that's as close as he'll come to being adversarial. If his regiment is called up, Kreisler will honor his homeland and report for duty, but he prays that will not be necessary.

To celebrate the four nations represented around the oval table tonight, Lucie Schelling and her ambitious chef have prepared an array of courses. After a round of sparkling cava from Catalunya, the meal begins with a Catalan favorite, Pa' amb Tomaquet–toasted bread smeared with tomatoes and drizzled with oil, served with Arbequina olives from Granados' hometown of Lleida; followed by a Polish dish for special occasions, Szpinak–a spicy soup of spinach, beef, and potato; then Austrian Rehbraten–roast of venison with noodles and red cabbage, served with a red Sandbechler wine from Innsbruck; and several desserts, Austrian Apfelkuchen (apple cake), Polish buckwheat and raisin pudding, American-style apple pie, and Crema Catalana. Thick black coffee arrives with Swiss dark chocolates and French Armagnac.

The dinner conversation is light and amiable, spiced with anecdotes about travel. Nothing controversial. Very simpático. Very gemutlich. A purring sense of well-being. When a silver box of cigars is offered to the men, Lucie rises and nods to Helena, Mildred, Harriet, and Solita; all five excuse themselves. The five men gather at the far end of the table.

Schelling wastes no time in asking the question: "Well, gentlemen, are we headed for war?" He looks around, and sees four heads shaking. "Fritz, what are you hearing from Vienna?"

Granados has been in a reverie, thinking of his opera, the vocal exchange between lovers in the garden.

Headed for war? Over a ridiculous dispute in Serbia? Henri's trying to liven up the conversation.

Kreisler says his friends and relatives are hopeful that his government will pressure Serbia to respond to its demands arising from the assassination. It can be settled without declarations of war. There's no need to involve other countries.

"What did you learn in London, Jan?" Schelling asks.

Paderewski was not in London for that purpose, but in his travels he's been constantly in touch with Polish independence groups. "I talked to someone who just returned from Warsaw. He thought the Russians would not jump in to help the Serbs, since they also regard them as Asian barbarians. I hope that's true, because if the Russians do come to the rescue of Serbia, they'll have to push through the Austrian sector of Poland as well as fight the Germans up north. Nothing could be worse for my people! But I don't think it will happen."

Schelling turns to Bliss. "Robert? What's your view of this from Paris?"

Bliss has been monitoring the build-up of tension, because if the Russians were to jump in with Serbia, France would be obliged to come to the defense of Russia.

And President Poincaré leaves this week for a state visit to Russia. For Bliss, personally, a post in the middle of this turbulence can only enhance his diplomatic career; far better than being in Puerto Rico. Bliss measures his words as he explains that America is only an observer, that she's unlikely to become involved even if a general war breaks out on the continent. "President Wilson is implacably opposed to our involvement in Europe's disputes," he says with a clipped voice, "and the American people would be very unhappy if he changed his mind."

Schelling makes an effort to sum up. "All right then, messieurs, can we stop worrying about a war? Haven't our governments learned there's nothing to be gained by war–everyone suffers–and there's everything to be gained by peace? Ah, let's hope so! If there's peace, we can continue to travel whenever there's an audience waiting to hear us. But if there's war, we'll not be passing through the battle lines to play our pianos and violins."

"If there's war," Kreisler says, "I'll have no choice. I'll be in it with my regiment."

"Fritz, you have no business in a war!" says Granados. "You're a violinist–one of the best in the world. Not a warrior! You hate violence as much as I do!"

Kreisler's voice softens. "You may be right, my dear Enrique. But also I am an Austrian. And I cannot change that."

"And that's the dilemma, isn't it?" asks Schelling, tossing his head. "We are men of many roles. Some of them in conflict."

"If there is a war," says Bliss, "let's face it, we'll all be affected, all of us, even if we belong to a neutral country. Let's hope it blows over as it has before."

"I will certainly drink to that," says Granados.

"Robert's correct," says Paderewski, "if there's a general war, nobody will escape it. We'll all be in harm's way. Wasn't it John Donne who wrote: 'No man is an island'?"

"That's a good argument for nobody starting a war," says Granados.

Schelling raises his glass of Armagnac. "Hear, hear!"

The next few days at Céligny evoke Granados' summers in Puigcerdà. Outside on the terrace, bright sunshine and fresh mountain breezes; inside the stone walls, a delicious coolness and serenity. And quiet–only the sounds of birds. Anyone who can't compose here should give it up! Today he's revising Periquet's verse in the lovers' scene in Rosario's garden.

Rosario: Yes, life is all thorns, but my caresses will ease your pain. And you will enjoy life seeing yourself in my eyes.

Fernando: Ah, Rosario, you calm my heart, and you flood my soul with passion!

Rosario: Ah, blessed are the bonds of love.

Fernando: I feel the power of those that bind us.

Rosario: I shall fall into your arms crazed with love. Yes, I adore you! When you aren't here, I weep sadly, thinking of your passion.

Granados' music is dramatic, taking themes from the piano suite and building them for a full orchestra, yet he wonders: is there enough tension in the plot? Is the situation between the lovers equal to the music? There is no answer, just a nagging question that has persisted since he began his collaboration with Periquet.

Granados drifts away from the opera, playing music as it enters his head. Not *Goyescas*–it's the third movement of *Escenas Románticas*. Which he hasn't played for a while, though it's always with him. Never far below the surface. Especially this movement: "Lento con Éxtasis."

He doesn't hear Mildred until she's crossed the room and is standing beside the piano. It isn't the sound of her that breaks into his consciousness, it's the slight stirring of air in the music salon and a trace of her Parisian cologne. She's a tall wraith, backlit by the sun, coming into clear focus: dressed in a pale green taffeta afternoon dress, trimmed in ruffles–at the elbows, the modest neckline, and the hemline just above her slender ankles. A perfect complement for her sunlit chestnut hair. Her dress is cool and airy with simple lines. Elegant and practical for summers in Céligny. Suggesting rather than defining the shape of her body, unlike the gown she wore the other evening, when Granados noticed Paderewski rising to his tiptoes for a better view.

"You always look–perfect," he says.

"Aren't you dear? Perfect is what I'm supposed to be, as wife of the Embassy Secretary."

Granados smiles. "And what does *he* have to be–as husband of Mildred Bliss?

She laughs. "What an unusual question! Nothing of course. I mean, he is the Secretary. Oh dear, you're playing with me!"

"Yes."

"I won't let you. What was that music?"

He turns from her bright green eyes and points to the composition pad. "It's a scene between the lovers. In her garden. I'm trying to balance the orchestra and the singers. And if the music isn't simply in the background, if it's blended with the voices, each part must carry the same message. Of sadness, or affection, hope, longing, desire, foreboding. In this scene I've tried to infuse a hint of the tragedy to come." He notices Mildred's widening smile.

"Not this music, mon cher. I can read these notes. I was asking about the music you were playing when I came in."

"That music? Oh, just something from long ago. Very long ago."

"So long ago it still moves you when you play it?" Mildred asks.

He shrugs. "Of course it still moves me. All my work moves me."

"Do you *remember* what you were playing?" she asks, stepping closer.

"Yes. The third movement of *Escenas Románticas*."

"Romantic episodes! Would you play it for me?"

He hesitates. "Yes, of course I'll play it for you." He closes his eyes and takes a deep breath. From time to time he's played it for himself, but never at home and never at the academy. Never for anyone else, except Clotilde. He plays the third movement. After the lyrical opening and the trilling arpeggios, he arrives at the twenty-eighth measure, marked "apasionadamente" on the score–and marked indelibly in his mind because this is where the ecstasy bursts. As he plays the melodic octaves, he feels a wave of longing rise through his fragile core. There's no pain, just a tremolo–as if a set of strings inside him were being bowed with vibrato. Not a wave that slaps and stings, rather one that caresses–as if flesh were being brushed with the softest velvet.

As he finishes, Mildred's cheeks are streaked with tears. "It's a love story," she says in an unsteady voice. "Slow–so marvelously slow, like the onset of lasting love. And when you play the octaves, the ecstasy. That's what I felt. Ecstasy! At the end, the trilling of the nightingale. You've just filled me with sadness and longing." She shakes her head. "Mon Dieu, what am I saying? I'm sorry. Your music took me back to a place I thought I'd left behind." She looks down across the piano, probing with her emerald eyes. "Who was she?"

How to explain? No time for evasion.

"Her name was María," he replies. "She was a student. A good pianist. There's no way to explain."

"It's not necessary." Her voice is like the soothing waters of a spa.

"It was very complicated. There were two Marías. And there were times they got blended in my mind. It sounds insane. Not really. I was trying hard to keep everyone separate–in their own compartments. I thought I could. Foolish of me."

Mildred shakes her head. "Not foolish. I do that too. But why haven't I heard this piece?"

"I dedicated this to the student, and then my wife found out. I agreed not to play it."

She clasps both hands over her mouth. "No! But it's like losing one of your own. I mean, it feels just like that!"

"I agreed to it. And now I've told you far too much." He shakes his head. "I couldn't hold back with you."

"I know that. And I'm flattered. No matter what, please know you never need to hold back with me."

A month has passed since the assassination in Sarajevo. The Austro-Hungarian government did not take quick and decisive action, choosing instead to consult its Triple Alliance partner, Germany. When a list of demands are finally received in Belgrade, the Serbian government is inclined to accept them, believing the matter can be resolved by Serbia and Austro-Hungary without assistance from others. Before Serbia responds, however, information comes from the Czar's country palace that the Russian mood is ardently pro-Serbian. Emboldened by this, the Serbs send the demands back to the Austro-Hungarians, attaching conditions. Clearly an affront. Both Serbia and Russia begin to mobilize their military forces. As Britain and France try to persuade Russia to cease its mobilization, the German ambassador in St. Petersburg warns the Czarist government that mobilization will force Germany to follow suit, which would make war all but inevitable. The Austro-Hungarians, seeking to finesse proposals for outside mediation of their demands, decide finally to declare war on Serbia, hoping the Russians will stay clear. But until the Czarist government stops mobilizing, Austria-Hungary cannot move on Serbia and leave its frontier with Russia vulnerable to attack.

So although none of the major powers are militarily prepared to go to war, in fact would rather not, mobilizing for that possibility engenders mobilization on the other side. Without any agreed-upon mechanism to stall this process and negotiate an end to the crisis, as was done last year and five years ago, Europe lurches toward a general war that could involve all but a few neutral countries.

Day by day in the last week of July, as prospects for peace worsen, Schelling's protects Granados from whatever news or rumors he receives. He sees no value in interrupting his friend's work on the opera. At last, he must inform him, for two reasons. First, tonight there'll be a special dinner to celebrate

Schelling's thirty-eighth birthday, July 26, Granados' forty-seventh on the 27, and Paderewski's "name day"–birth date of his patron saint, on the 31. With Jan and Helena Paderewski coming for dinner, Schelling won't be able to suppress discussion of the impending war. Second, because as mobilization fever breaks out in Paris, Berlin, Vienna, St. Petersburg, and London, the logistics of transporting hundreds of thousands of men and horses to the frontiers is certain to require all of Europe's rail capacity. From conversations in Geneva this morning, Schelling fears that Granados and Solita will not be able to secure rail passage through France if they don't leave in the next two or three days. He decides to tell Granados this afternoon, before the celebratory dinner.

"It's precautionary," he explains to the stunned Granados as they sit on the veranda, "but the French are bound by treaty to go to war if Russia does, and the Czar seems to be relishing a fight with the Germans and Austrians. If that happens, every train in France will be diverted to move troops. At the very least, you'd be unable to get back home for several weeks. That's if the war doesn't come to Lyon, which would mean a much longer delay."

"War? What madness! What madness! You're saying all of Europe is about to go to war over what happened in Sarajevo?"

"Yes, except for the neutrals–Switzerland and España. Belgium's also neutral, but if the Germans attack France, they're right in the path of it."

"That's ridiculous! It's all ridiculous! And–it's wrong!"

"I agree," says Schelling. "It's ridiculous and it's wrong. But we're not powerless. We can get you back home safely. So I've arranged for your travel on the first day of August. That's in three days. You'll need to get ready. And let Solita know. And let your family know you're coming home." Schelling hesitates. "And you should not pack anything of value–including manuscripts. Carry them, and don't let them out of your sight. There's no telling what might happen if your train is stopped."

Tonight's birthday celebration is muted because of impending war. Rumors and anecdotes are retold again and again, as if it would be disrespectful to chat about matters of lesser consequence.

Paderewski breaks into tearful rage, lamenting the horrors of having his homeland overrun again by warring armies. "All over Europe there are patriotic celebrations in the streets and young men putting their affairs in order as they wait to be called to military service," says Paderewski. "Except in Poland. Our young men are fearful of being marched into battle against their own countrymen. Against their own families. Can you imagine how horrible that would be?"

"I heard from Kreisler yesterday," says Schelling. "He's leaving for Vienna by week's end. Harriet's going with him to work for the Red Cross."

"Fritz is in an infantry unit," adds Paderewski. "He won't be needing his violin until this is all over. He'll be needing a rifle–to shoot at Russians!"

"That is insanity!" says Granados.

Schelling stands up and raises his glass of wine. "My friends and dearest Lucie, may I propose a toast? We're not at war–at least not yet, so let's drink to peace! Let's have a moment of silence to pray for peace…and let's also drink to good health and long life and our passion for music! May these be years of great creativity for us–so that on that day when we are called, we'll leave this world a better place, blessed with the music we've composed and played. Here's to all of us who are celebrating birthdays, and to all of the many times we'll come together again in friendship and love."

Granados and Solita leave Céligny on a cloudy Sunday morning, the first day of August, and cross the border without incident. The next leg takes them to Lyon, where they transfer to a train bound for Marseilles. It's here, in the Lyon terminal, that the newspaper headlines seem larger, darker, and more urgent:

> AUSTRIA, RUSSIA MOBILIZE FOR WAR FRANCE URGES THAT CZAR DESIST MOBILIZATION MAY BRING WAR DOES TREATY BIND FRANCE TO WAR? IS WAR INEVITABLE? WILL GERMANS ATTACK FRANCE? POINCARÉ URGED TO MOBILIZE GERMANS DECLARE WAR ON RUSSIA WILL BRITAIN SIDE WITH FRANCE? GERMANS DEMAND INVASION ROUTE IN BELGIUM LARGE CROWDS IN MUNICH

Also in the Lyon station, young men in uniform are leaving their families to return to their units. "Au revoir! A bientot!" Their wives and parents wave hats and handkerchiefs, crying out as the soldiers board the train. "Farewell! See you soon!" The spirit of these departures is buoyant, as if the travelers are headed for holidays at the beach. The sound of "La Marseillaise" played by a civic band echoes in the station, mixed with train announcements and occasional shouts: "Vive la France! Vive l'armée!" Only the most pessimistic observers predict that in less than three days General Otto von Emmich's task force of the German Second Army will cross the border and exchange fire with Belgian cavalrymen.

Barcelona

Granados arrives home with most of Europe on the brink of war. But with Spanish neutrality assured, the news here is slow arriving and sketchy. After spending most of June and July away from home, he feels a curious detachment, letting Solita rave about her vacation in Switzerland, hoping there will be an end to the excited questions. It's impossible for him to suppress his anxiety about the war and what devastation it could bring. And anxiety about the innocent people caught in its path. Kreisler, most immediately. And everyone else who tours the Continent–Schelling, Paderewski, Casals, and Viñes. Paris might be captured by the Germans. What would that mean for Robert and Mildred Bliss?

Gracias a Dios–España is neutral! Gracias a Dios–my sons won't be drafted!! Gracias a Dios–we will survive this catastrophe!

On the third day after returning, all of the declarations of war are reported, even in the Barcelona newspapers, along with news of German advances through Belgium toward Paris. Granados is eager to see Clotilde again after the long absence. As he waits for José Altet to bring his motorcycle from the garage, Eduardo enters his study and hands him a telegram.

From Paris! Must be Robert or Mildred. No it's from l'Opéra de Paris. From Rouché. Let me see.

> [MON CHER MAESTRO GRANADOS] [ON BEHALF OF L'OPERA DE PARIS I REGRET TO INFORM YOU THAT SINCE OUR REPUBLIC IS IN GRAVE DANGER OF WAR WE ARE OBLIGED TO POSTPONE THE OPERA SEASON THIS YEAR] [WE HOPE THE WAR WILL BE VICTORIOUS AND SHORT-LIVED] [WE HOPE TO PRESENT 'GOYESCAS' SOMETIME IN 1915] [WITH RESPECT AND AFFECTION] [JACQUES ROUCHE]

"What is it, Papa?" asks Eduardo.

Overcome by grief and unable to speak, Granados hands his son the telegram.

Chapter Nine

Barcelona, Autumn 1914

"Sauf évènement imprévu"–that was the vital phrase in the letter from Jacques Rouché, the letter that confirmed that *Goyescas* would be presented by l'Opéra de Paris in the early part of 1915, or at the latest during the course of the year.

"Sauf évènement imprévu"–"barring an unforeseen event." It was the only condition placed on Rouché's commitment. When he received Rouché's letter of acceptance in late June, Granados paid no attention to those three words buried in the long first sentence. In the excitement of having *Goyescas* accepted, all he could think of was fulfillment of a dream: his work would be heard around the world, with the premiere in Paris as the first step. Now in sober reflection he realizes that those three words could justify reneging on the commitment for any event that was "unforeseen." A general war in Europe fits that description, but so might Jacques Rouché's having a toothache. In retrospect, Granados realizes that his opera's future is tenuous indeed, that no dream will be realized until the house lights dim, the performance begins, and the critics heap praise on it. He chastises himself for thinking otherwise.

A letter arrives from Schelling, explaining that the postponement wasn't entirely due to the war. Financial difficulties, he writes, caused the impresarios–Messager and Broussan–to withdraw from l'Opéra de Paris. But Rouché is staying on, committed to its survival. Even had the war not broken out, Schelling says the premiere of *Goyescas* would have been delayed. For that reason, he argues, "we should go to work convincing the Metropolitan to schedule it for a premiere in New York next season." He reminds Granados of Sir Henry

Wood's hunting advice: don't concentrate on only one bird. "That means we should talk to people in New York and Chicago and Buenos Aires–anywhere there isn't a war!"

Anywhere there isn't war? Should be everywhere! Peace everywhere not soldiers killed and wounded, families and friends suffering.

It's easy for Schelling to say, go to the Americas and England and Argentina, but those places require getting on a boat. Granados' life at the mercy of icebergs and weather, the helmsman's skill and the captain's judgment. And the whims of the god Poseidon. An infinite number of unforeseen events lurking out there. Easy for Schelling, who crosses the ocean with grand pianos supplied by Steinway, who crosses without fear. It's not enough to merely create an opera, not enough to work with Periquet and his many idiosyncrasies. Granados now faces the necessity–no longer the choice–of crossing the ocean, to avoid this unforeseen event, this shameful war.

In Céligny, before the war broke out, life seemed so orderly. He'd devote his time to finishing the opera; after returning, he'd visit Salvador and Carmen in Puigcerdà, meet Casals' wife Susan in Sant Salvador; and spend blissful afternoons and evenings with Clotilde in Tiana. In September, he'd reopen the academy. Then back to Paris for rehearsals of *Goyescas*. Then opening night–the lights of Paris in Clotilde's eyes. Life revolving around devotion to the music inside him, over which he's powerless. Music that gives him no peace until he finds a way to let it out. Everything and everyone else relegated to the proper compartment–family, patrons, friends, colleagues, students, his lover. Life with a nice rhythm, a gentle momentum.

But now, with the war and postponement of the premiere, the number of variables has increased, answers to everyday questions are more elusive, more effort is needed to maintain the fine lines he's drawn.

Tiana

On the eve of Granados' departure for Puigcerdà, Clotilde is empathetic and nurturing. "Remember how strong you've been," she says. "Don't forget how many obstacles you've overcome. It hasn't been easy, but you have persevered. This is a temporary setback." And she's come to believe that his American friend, Schelling, will help him find a venue for the opera. "They're good at this kind of thing, the Americanos," she says, an admission she'd judged Schelling prematurely. "You know, mi querido, they're very persuasive–this one loves your music and seems to know everyone in the world. You have a woman who totally adores you. And you have your magnificent talent. So let me see you smile again –oh, that's much better!"

Puigcerdà

Andreu encourages him to forget about Paris and seek a premiere for *Goyescas* somewhere in the Americas. "The French have chosen war," he says with disdain, "instead of an opera season. In fairness, it wasn't their first choice. Thank God we're not involved! In fact, if the rest of Europe is bent on war, it'll be good for Catalan industry. I dread saying that–it's no consolation, but it's a fact of life. And," he seeks to reassure Granados, "this ill-considered war will not last long. You can take comfort in that. You can bet on it!"

Carmen, in their walk around the pond, is uncommonly gentle with him. "I know it's a terrible disappointment," she says, "but you'll soon look back and laugh at how wretched it made you feel." She laughs softly. "You'll celebrate how wonderful it is to no longer feel wretched."

He laughs. "And you call *me* romantic?"

"Besides," Carmen adds, "you have people who care deeply about you, who love you, who believe in you. People who know you're our finest composer. And I–who've loved you forever–know there are swarms of what you call butterflies just bursting for freedom, and we'll all be blessed as they reach the sunlight."

Sant Salvador

A month later, walking the beach with Casals, Granados learns that his old friend will be moving to New York until the war is over. "Susan and I thought of shipping everything to London," says Casals, "but London's only useful if you can tour in Europe and Russia, and all my favorite venues are shut down by the war. So I may as well concentrate on the Americas." He laughs. "Besides, my bride would much prefer New York. That's obvious. Oh, she's charmed by my family, I'm sure of that, but she thrives on the pace of New York. Finds this place too small, too slow. All of which I adore. Susan's a New Yorker–when you come over, you'll see what I mean. And you will come over, won't you?"

"I can't wait forever for Paris," says Granados. "And Schelling says the Metropolitan is the best place for the premiere–if they accept it. They haven't yet."

"Then you'd get on a boat and come over?" Casals looks up, probing.

"If I have to, yes. I'll get on a boat. Unless I can get Louis Bleriot to fly me over."

Casals is amused. "Bleriot! You know his nickname: 'the one who always crashes.' He was lucky just to get across the channel in that contraption. Damned lucky. If you're waiting for Bleriot, you'll have a long wait! Airplanes are just a daredevil's plaything."

"If I have to, Pau, I will get on a boat!"

Meanwhile, Granados' correspondence continues with Jacques Rouché. He asks for a commitment to relinquish any rights if the opera cannot be presented in 1915, so he can pursue other venues. He receives a prompt but enigmatic reply: "We will brilliantly celebrate our victory with all the artists of Latin countries; we will exalt the light of their genius against the darkness of the barbarians." Meanwhile, suggests Rouché, the libretto should be translated into French. Granados writes back that he's willing to give Rouché exclusive rights through the end of 1915, but no longer.

The next letter from Paris begins in a conciliatory vein, and asks Granados to appreciate Rouché's predicament: "I understand your impatience and the inconvenience of waiting. I cannot promise that *Goyescas* will be the first opera presented to the public. For many reasons. Especially because I believe the first opera will necessarily be patriotic. However, I can promise that within six months of reopening l'Opéra de Paris, your work will be presented. Would that be satisfactory to you? After all, there are three major tasks to be done—rehearsals, building the sets, and making the costumes."

Two weeks later, without receiving a reply, Rouché writes again, suggesting two possible solutions: The first provides for the opera to be presented within six months after the end of the war, with Rouché sending him an advance payment. The second provides for Granados to contract with other opera companies, and commits l'Opéra de Paris to present *Goyescas* within two years after its reopening. "You seem to believe," writes Rouché, "that after the war *Goyescas* will not be well received here. I am sure that you are in error. There will be a great swell of enthusiasm and an ardent desire to revive it. In any case, I leave you completely free to decide given the fact, as you point out, that the war, beyond our power, prevents us from honoring the contract. You would be free to have *Goyescas* presented in America, but I ask that you reserve for us a priority for Europe. I wish you great success for your beautiful work in the United States while we look forward to a première at l'Opéra de Paris, after the victory of our country, and you can be assured of the most fraternal homage that we can bestow upon you."

Schelling hasn't waited for Granados and Rouché to find a venue. Even before the audition with l'Opéra de Paris, he elicited a promise from Rudi Schirmer to talk to the impresario Giulio Gatti-Casazza about an American premiere at the Metropolitan. At every opportunity Schelling has promoted *Goyescas* with Otto Kahn, chairman of the board of the Met, and other board members. One of these, Clarence Mackay, the multimillionaire founder of a large telegraph company, has been a close friend of Schelling's since Clarence's mother recruited the seven-year-old Schelling, a student at the Paris Conservatoire, to play for Clarence in Mackay's Paris home. So with Rudi Schirmer working the "inside" strategy–persuading Gatti-Casazza–and Schelling his own "outside" strategy with board members, he's never doubted that *Goyescas* will be accepted by the Metropolitan.

Schelling's considerable powers of persuasion are also aimed at Granados, who clings to hopes for the war to end soon and the opera to premier at Palais Garnier. Granados' optimism was initially fueled by Casals, who reported that last fall's annual tennis tournament at St.-Cloud, just outside Paris, hadn't lost any of its prewar luster. Casals was confident that by spring 1915 the war would be over and he'd resume his touring in Europe. But other than Casals' limited view, the news from Europe's battlefields was anything but cheerful. The initial exuberance of the crowds, the strains of national anthems, the jaunty cries of "au revoir–a bientot!" and "auf wiedersehen–bis bald!" soon died in the winds of war. When General Emmich's troops–slicing through Belgium–ran into unexpected resistance in the first days of combat, they retaliated with a harshness that earned them international opprobrium. The German thrust, aimed at surrounding and capturing Paris, was stopped at the River Marne by the armies of France and Britain under the unified command of Marshall Josep Joffre–lover of Catalan food and culture.

"You remember him, don't you?" asks Andreu after reading accounts of the battle at the Marne in *La Vanguardia*. They are sitting in the music salon at Sant Gervasi, waiting for Paquita to play the Mozart she's been practicing for her first recital at the Sala Granados.

"Joffre? Joffre? No, Sal, I don't remember him."

"You met him, ten years ago in Puigcerdà. You played 'Allegro de concierto'–I'm pretty sure of that, and he enjoyed it quite a lot. Remember the French military officer? The Catalan from Roselló? The man with–." Andreu curves his hand over an imaginary pot belly.

"That was Joffre?" exclaims Granados. "Yes, he's the one 'Saco met in a restaurant somewhere. That's Joffre? Even 'Saco was impressed by his prodigious appetite."

"Well, I hear that Joffre's a brilliant general, but with his own unique priorities. That he's very devoted to the table, and allows nothing whatsoever to interfere with lunch, even during a crisis." Andreu chuckles. "A true Catalan, devoted to the table. Though I believe Napoleon lost the battle of Waterloo because he tarried too long over lunch, giving Wellington the superior position for the afternoon's battle."

Granados is amused. "How naïve of me to believe you're merely an expert in pharmacology and miracle cures and real estate," he says, enjoying a rare chance to take a playful poke at his patron.

"Have you forgotten my expertise in organizing the family orchestra?"

Joffre's adroit blocking of the German advance on Paris stirs a wave of optimism, albeit short lived, among those who aren't close enough to the front to observe that the adversaries are now engaged in a death lock that kills more than 300,000 Frenchmen and the same number of Germans in the first four months.

Given this carnage, perhaps the least of the continent's concerns is the fate of artists and musicians as they flee belligerent countries in droves, seeking refuge in neutral Switzerland and rekindling their careers in the Americas–in blessed isolation from the war. Not all are able to escape. Granados learns, in a letter from Casals, that Eugène Ysaye slipped past the German advance in Belgium and is now in London, but Mathieu Crickboom has vanished; Jacques Thibaud and Maurice Ravel are driving ambulances in Paris; and Alfred Cortot is employed by the French Ministry of Culture.

In a letter from Schelling, Granados learns that Fritz Kreisler and his wife Harriet were taking the waters at a Swiss spa when the Austro-Hungarian Empire went to war. He resigned his officer's commission two years ago, but upon arrival in Vienna Kreisler was welcomed back by his Kaiserjaeger Regiment and promptly sent to the Russian front. In a fierce engagement, Kreisler was wounded when an attacking Cossack sliced open his leg before taking a fatal shot from the violinist's revolver. He was found by his orderly several hours later, in a heap of dead and wounded men in front of the Austrian line, and shipped to a field hospital. Back in Vienna he was declared permanently disabled and unfit for further military duty, then discharged. Within three months after the outbreak of war Kreisler arrived in New York on the SS *Rotterdam*, and embarked on a series of performances. At Carnegie Hall the audience responded with fascination and rapture as the wounded war hero limped onto the stage with a crutch, carrying his violin. "It's a tribute to America's firm detachment from the war that it matters not which side Kreisler was fighting for," wrote Schelling.

Granados is incensed.

Doesn't matter which side–Kreisler should be carrying violins not guns! Which side? No good side in war. Goya saw cruelties on both sides. Both sides in Setmana Trágica–a plague on both houses!

The other war news–with personal significance–arrives in a telegram from Periquet, informing him that the Parisian writer Jean Marliave, who'd been engaged to translate the libretto for *Goyescas* into French, was killed in action at Charlerois, on the River Sambre, during the third week of war.

Early in the New Year, the last bit of encouraging news emerges from the Western Front: on Christmas Eve, troops on both sides called a truce and came out of their trenches to celebrate the holiday together. They exchanged food and wine, faced off against each other in games of football, and sang Christmas songs. "Joyeux Noel" and "Stille Nacht" and "Good King Wenceslas"–sung by cold, frightened, and weary men and boys who until that night were trained and directed to destroy each other, sung in rough voices by ordinary soldiers who expected by now to be back home with their friends and families, sung with voices that doubtless strayed off key–except at two points in the line, where German tenor Walter Kirchoff and French tenor Victor Granier enriched the sound of holiday carols. This amazing truce, reflecting a consensus of trench-bound infantrymen with front row seats for the horrors of war, might have held, but the generals on both sides realized that the order and discipline of their ranks was threatened by this spontaneous flight toward peace. The truce was swiftly quashed and the errant Yuletide celebrants were replaced with fresh troops untainted by the delirium. So the Christmas Eve pause in the carnage was broken, merely a suggestion of what might have been.

Granados is distraught and saddened by news of the broken truce. He remembers the faces of the men and boys in the train station of Lyon: standing straight in their clean uniforms, their jaunty voices assuring loved ones they'd be back home by Christmas.

How many have fallen? How long before generals and politicians see there's no sense in this outrageous war?

"I lost everything! Everything! All because of this war!" Ismael Smith stands in the middle of his exhibition at Sala Parés, his reedy voice bouncing off the walls where his sketches hang. However grave his misfortune, Smith is dressed as fastidiously as ever, looking more the financier than the eccentric artist. Granados, the intended receiver of his complaints, waits until he's finished.

"You say you left your sculptures in a warehouse, and they disappeared?"

Smith shakes his head wildly. "No, no, no! That's only part of it. Now, listen," he chides Granados, "I had a friend in Paris, a woman friend, and when her illness became more serious I moved in with her so she'd have someone. She couldn't afford a nurse. I let my own flat go and put my sculptures in storage in a warehouse on the edge of the city. I thought it was a safe place. But then the war began and my friend was dying, so I stayed with her night and day. I was holding her hand when she died. Have you ever been with someone dying?"

"I haven't," Granados replies. His father died in the next room while Granados was consoling his sister; his brother died in the middle of the night, with only a nurse in attendance.

"It was horrible!" says Smith. "I could feel the life escaping her and I waited for *the* moment and then I realized–Dios mío!–it had passed. She was a dear, dear friend and I've had very few of them in my life, except for my brothers. Zuloaga and I used to be friends, years ago we'd meet every day at the Lion d'Or. And Laura Albéniz–always a friend. And Eugène d'Ors. And you've been a friend too, 'Ric, but this woman was *very* close–intimate–that close." Smith pauses as his eyes fill with tears. "That close."

"What happened to your sculptures, Ismael?"

"Paris was a crazy place!" Smith recalls. "The Germans invaded Belgium heading straight for Paris and the French soldiers were marching around in circles. People crowded around for announcements being posted on the walls around Les Invalides. I ran down to the warehouse where I'd taken my sculptures and found the military in control of it. I tried to explain that my art work was inside, years and years of work, and I wanted to get it out, but the corporal in charge would not let me through. I asked him if my sculptures were still inside–he just laughed. 'You think you have sculptures in there, Spaniard?'

I said yes, I'd rented space for them and paid a year in advance. He laughed again. 'You better go home Spaniard,' he said, 'everything in this building was taken out when we moved in.' I asked if he knew where 'everything' was taken, and he just laughed again. I sat down on the sidewalk and cried."

Granados shakes his head. "I can't imagine losing so much work. It's very sad."

"The French don't give a damn about any of us. We're just Spaniards! They look down on our painting and sculpture. Even our music, isn't that a fact? But I wasn't the only one who got caught in the war. You know what happened to Rodin? Even the great Rodin was ordered by the government to move all his work to a basement in the Hotel Biron. Art's not important any more. Only war! There was an American woman with him, one of his students. Perhaps one of his lovers–he bedded down with every last one. Her name was Malvina Hoffman. Interesting woman. Tall and voluptuous. I wanted her to pose for me, but when she had Rodin–why *would* she? She went back to New York."

"Where do you plan to live?" asks Granados.

"I'm going to London. They selected some of my work for an exhibition of modern Spanish art. My brothers are going there with me. I think it's a safe distance from the war. And it's the only place left in Europe, so it should be a good place for refugee artists."

"I wish you well, Ismael. I hope your bad luck is behind you."

"If you ever come to London, promise to let me know."

"I promise," Granados says, "but I have no intention of going there. I prefer to stay on terra firma."

March, 1915

The envelope is printed with an unrecognized address: Santiago-Echea, Zumaya, Guipúzcoa. Apparently somewhere on the Basque Coast. Granados opens the envelope and reads the short letter:

> Mi distinguido amigo: I've been in Madrid for several days, where I had the pleasure to meet Señor Periquet; a very simpático person, and terribly absorbed in the time of Goya. We talked at great length; and we were in agreement. He understood very well that veracity, or authenticity in the theatre can at times result in disaster. I also saw Antonia Mercé, who calls herself 'La Argentina'–an extraordinary dancer and ideal for your masterpiece. Let's hope now that this horrible

slaughter will soon end; and that we'll able to get back to work. You may count always on your friend,

Ignacio Zuloaga

Granados forgets about Zuloaga's letter until ten days later when a note arrives from Antonia Mercé. "Distinguido Maestro Granados," says the note, "I'm in Barcelona to do a show at l'Imperial. Since our performance is not until next Tuesday, I hope you and I will have time to discuss dance music for my repertoire, as well as your opera *Goyescas*. I'd be thrilled if we could meet after tomorrow's rehearsal. With the greatest admiration, Antonia Mercé"

Mercé's second note, to set a time and place, is delivered by José Altet–who relates he was summoned to the Hotel Oriente to pick it up. Altet boasts of dodging the scrutiny of Doña Amparo.

"Oh? Why would she care, José?" asks Granados. "I barely know this ballarina."

Altet steps back, admonished. "Molt ben, mestre. But you've said I can't be too discreet, right?"

Granados laughs. "Yes indeed. My very words."

"And this one, this Argentina is a very great beauty. Best that Doña Amparo doesn't see her. Forgive me, mestre, but those green eyes–she could melt a man with those!"

Mercé was born in Buenos Aires–hence her stage name after the country of her birth–she moved to Madrid as a child with her parents, both Spanish dancers; began lessons with her father at four, and debuted with the Royal Opera Theatre in Madrid at nine. At eleven, she was prima ballerina. About that time she first met Granados, became infatuated with him, and began pestering him to write some music for her. After her father died–when she was fourteen–Mercé gave up classical ballet to train with her mother in Spanish folk dancing. Without apology, she took her passion from the Royal Opera to the music halls and cafés of Spain.

Blessed with prodigious talent, she's helping to popularize flamenco, whose heart and soul belongs to gypsies dancing barefoot around campfires late at night. As her art evolves, Mercé's reputation grows as "the Queen of the Castanets." She's also creating dances for the music of modern Spanish composers, including Albéniz, de Falla, and Granados. At twenty-four, Mercé is a veteran of the circuit in Spain, and last year was warmly received in London. On that occasion she danced to new music by Manuel de Falla, which he'll introduce this year as "El amor brujo."

"I would like to be considered for the choreography," Mercé says to Granados, sitting across a table at Café de l'Opera. She's dressed in a simple tan peasant skirt and high-necked white blouse with an emerald green jacket. Her voice is calm and professional, her manner sincere and determined. Ambitious, but without stridency. She rations her most conspicuous asset: parrot-green eyes of striking width, enormous when the eyelids are raised. Eyes that complement a wide mouth invariably turned up at the corners. Mercé was told by Periquet that Schelling and Schirmer are trying to arrange a premiere for *Goyescas* in New York.

"Which scenes?" asks Granados. He knows the answer but wants to know how well the dancer has prepared.

She lifts her eyelids. "Señor Periquet made me a copy. To begin with, the opening scene of 'El Pelele'–"

"If that is indeed the opening," says Granados.

"Of course. That's not my decision," she says. "Then in the first cuadro, 'La Calesa'–with Pepa getting out of the carriage. I love this scene! So many possibilities! And then, 'El Requiebro.' In the second cuadro, 'El Baile de Candil.' Followed by 'El Fandango.' Am I correct? These scenes require choreography."

Granados smiles at her, satisfied that she has indeed prepared. "You're correct."

"I've thought a lot about your work," says Mercé, leaning across the table. "It's so beautiful. A bit overwhelming. I'm reluctant to suggest you'd let me work with you, but still I have to ask: could I show you how I'd interpret your music?"

"Show me?" he asks.

"Yes," she replies in a quiet voice. "Don't you have a recital hall?" Mercé's tempered and unassuming ambition is disarming.

In the auditorium of the Sala, Granados rubs his hands to dispel the chill of early March and waits for Mercé to change into her dancing attire. He warms up with a series of arpeggios. Mercé enters the stage from the dressing room, wearing a sleeveless, white V-necked blouse over a dancer's leotard and a flamenco skirt of alternating red white and green circles that, buoyed by a petticoat of crinoline, sweeps out from her narrow waist and falls in pleats to ankle height, exposing her high-heeled black dancing shoes. At the edge of the stage she strikes a classic flamenco pose: one leg thrust forward and her upper body arching back. Slender arms raised, the left one over her head and bent only slightly at the wrist; the right one extended parallel to the floor, bent slightly downward. "Are you ready, maestro?" she asks.

He smiles. "Where would you like to start?"

Mercé saunters down to the piano. "Your music is splendid–with inspired choreography it will be divine! Dance allows our bodies to break free from constraints. From awkwardness, they can return to animal suppleness, the native eloquence of creatures made for movement and the harmony between feelings and gestures." She lowers her throaty voice. "There's a duality between what one feels and what one does–both coming from the inner vision. One way to restore balance is with dance. Are you following me?"

Granados hasn't missed a word. He's enchanted with her voice and the vivacity in her green eyes. "I am your shadow," he says.

"You translate life into music, maestro, and I do it through dance. Seeking harmony in which the soul expresses itself through the movement of the body. It's the meeting place for music, poetry, drawing, sculpture and architecture. Right here," she adds, letting her outstretched hands drift down from her shoulders to her thighs.

Mercé steps away from the piano and reclaims the flamenco pose. "Now let's imagine the curtain has just opened. The orchestra's playing the overture. In the background we see the hermitage of San Antonio." She sweeps her arm in a wide arc behind her as Granados plays the piano part of the opening scene. Now her eyes begin to dance. "There's brilliant sunshine," she says in a lilting voice, "and all the costumes are shimmering with color. Majos brazenly flattering the majas–tirando flores." Her laugh is slightly brazen. "The majas are being coy and flirtatious but nobody's fooled by that. In the center are five women tossing a straw doll with a blanket–el pelele, right? And now the majas break into song. 'Because of love, whoever is trusting and doesn't watch out will become like a pelele. Come my love, so brave and gallant–not like a fool. For a maja is better off alone than accompanied by a fool. Now look how high the pelele is flying–always let the one who loves you fly!' And the majos sing: 'I'd gladly be a pelele if I'm lucky in love! But the most beautiful women are the most dangerous.' And then the torero, Paquiro, steps forward and sings to the majas: 'It's your delicate fragrance, oh flowers of the garden, that enrapture us wherever you go.' And while the singing continues, the majos and majas continue dancing, whirling and flirting with each other continuously until the carriage arrives and Pepa steps out."

As she describes the scene, Mercé moves back and forth with stunning grace, punctuating her words with fragments of dance–now stepping lightly, now exploding in a clacking of heels. "You see, maestro, I believe it's important to open with the excitement of this dance in the street, with all the pride and passion of that time. And yes, its artificiality. We all know what will come of it: love and death. But this first scene is one of limitless possibilities–like the sweetness of new love, just beginning to ripen. Of course that's only my interpretation."

"No, it's more than that," he says. "You do understand–perfectly."

Mercé picks up her castanets. "Would you play the fandango? I'd like to dance it for you."

It begins softly and rhythmically with an insistent beat that prevails throughout. The theme is introduced and repeated. Sweeping arpeggios, punctuated by short passages of melancholy and others of high energy. Mercé's dance seems to reflect every nuance that moved Granados as he composed it. She is tall for a flamenco dancer, but not the slightest bit awkward. Her footwork is confident. Her lithe body moves with the agility of ballet. Her hands are twin troubadours: the eloquence of the dance is the essence of pleasure, the essence of life.

Granados is bewitched. Mercé lacks the raw serpentine allure of Tórtola València, but the differences are not in a lack of grace or fire. Mercé's art is aligned, in a visceral way, with the devotion of the gypsies to the flamenco dance as a release from the joys and pains of life.

Her dancing my music brings tears. Her body hears my music.

She finishes the dance. He watches her approach the piano, hears the heels of her flamenco shoes clattering on the oak floor of the auditorium, and feels her hip press against his as she sits down beside him.

"What do you think, maestro? Have I understood the music–which you pour out in the gloom of night?"

Her words–a paraphrase from "Maja y el Ruiseñor"–reach the inner space that Granados protects against incursions by strangers. He turns his head toward her and smiles.

She looks up. "You'd allow me to work with you?"

He looks at her face. Seems guileless. In her eyes, an intense desire to be included in his opera. "Of course. I'm honored by your interest."

She throws her arms around him, exclaiming, "Oh, maestro, there's no way to thank you–I won't even try!"

"But so far there's no certainty of a venue."

"Oh, I know you'll find a venue for *Goyescas*! If you allow me to work with you, I'll be entirely devoted. I'll place my entire heart and soul on your stage. And never, ever let you down!"

He looks away from her bright green eyes. "You're very kind."

"Won't the premiere be in America? In New York?"

"That's what Schelling's hoping for. I wish it could be in Paris."

"No, it can't be there," Mercé replies. "Not with the war. Aren't you excited about a premiere in New York?"

He reengages her eyes. "I'm excited about a premiere. Not about getting there."

Mercé claps her hands over her mouth. "Oh! Dios mio! Of course–it's crossing the ocean. Isn't it?"

"I'd rather not discuss it," he says, standing up.

She turns to him, wrapping her arms around his shoulders. "Then we won't. But if the premiere is in New York, I will be there. A friend offered to pay my passage over and back–so I'll be there to work with you. If you go, I'll go too."

Granados laughs. "Have you no fear of the crossing?"

"Of course–you think you're the only one? Of course I have fear. Oooh, you're so tight!" she says, digging her fingers into his shoulder blades. "Right here–I can feel the tension. Your shoulders–like cables of steel. As if you're carrying the burdens of the whole world."

He tries to dismiss it. "Not exactly."

"If you want to carry them, I can't stop you. But I could loosen your shoulders–if you gave permission. Would you?"

He shrugs.

"You'll have to be more positive," says Mercé, "or I can't help you much. I'll ask again, maestro: will you?"

"Not unless you call me Enrique."

"All right, Enrique. Is there a place where you can lie down and I can massage your shoulders?"

Only one place to lie down. "Yes, downstairs," he says.

After removing his jacket, vest, tie, and shoes–as instructed, Granados lies face down on the couch in the large practice room. The noise of street traffic and the Tramvia Blau going up and down Avinguda Tibidabo is inaudible here, on the lower level of the Sala. The only sound is a faint rustling at the other end of the room. It reminds him of the afternoon long ago in Sant Gervasi when the migraine struck and he lay on the couch waiting for Carmen to bring lavender oil to rub on his forehead and temples.

Mercé removes her billowing skirt and crinoline petticoat, then her dancing shoes. Once the massage was proffered and accepted, it would have been awkward–no impossible–to proceed in full costume. Massage is common enough among members of a dance company, but now she hesitates. Dressed only in her white blouse and leotard, she's about to climb onto the back of Maestro Granados–the man she's idolized since girlhood–to loosen his shoulders. She could stop now, before wrapping her legs around his hips. No, she cannot. Mercé leaves her regalia in a heap and crosses to the couch on the balls of her bare feet.

Granados feels her hands on his shoulder bones as she swings one leg over him. He feels her muscular thighs tighten on his hips and her pelvis press onto his tailbone. She rubs the upper part of his back and shoulders. At first, as her fingers probe the muscles, he winces.

"Did that hurt?" she asks, stopping.

"Hmmm. Just a little."

"You're very tight in this area," she says with a clinical voice. "I'll try to loosen you up, if it's not too painful. Let me know–"

"I'll let you know," he says.

Mercé resumes the massage, digging her thumbs into the muscles on the insides of his shoulder bones. After a few minutes she asks if he'd mind taking off his shirt. "It would be easier," she says.

"I don't mind," he replies, and when he feels her climb off his back he sits up, unbuttons his shirt and removes it. He reclines again, face down.

Mercé works on Granados' back for nearly an hour. She finishes by running her finger tips over his back, barely grazing his skin. "Well, I've loosened up those cables of steel. My, they were tight! Has anyone ever massaged your back?"

"No. Just my head. I have migraines."

"Well, if I were you, I'd find someone."

Granados turns over onto his back. Mercé is silhouetted by light from the hallway outside the practice room. With her legs still straddling his waist, she raises her slender arms, clasping her hands together, and lowering them slowly to a point just below her chin. Her face is in shadow, but there's enough diffused light for him to see the arches of her cheekbones.

"Do you feel more relaxed?" she asks.

He nods. "Yes. Very relaxed. Half awake, half asleep. You have magic in your fingers. Thank you."

"Would you like me to move?" she asks.

"No. Are you uncomfortable?"

"No."

He reaches up and clasps his hands around hers. He lowers them and kisses the tips of her fingers. "Thank you, magic fingers." He caresses each of them with the tip of his tongue, then releases her hands.

Mercé reaches behind and unfastens the hooks on her blouse. She pulls it over her shoulders, and places it on the top of the couch. Then she bends forward, placing her hands on his chest, just below his collar bones.

Granados feels her hips sliding down and the frontal arch of her pelvis brushing him. He reaches up, runs his index fingers along the outer rim of her ears, down to the lobes where she wears a pair of large gold hoops, across her high cheekbones, and slowly across the narrow gap between her lips, along the tops of her lower teeth. He hears a short gasp and feels her lips and teeth take hold of his fingers.

April, 1915

Antonia Mercé is on tour, performing in Portugal and France. If *Goyescas* is premiered in New York, she'll ask a friend–the young Russian Prince Trubetskoy–to purchase her passage to America. For Mercé, the affair with Granados was tempestuous and satisfying, but mercifully brief. Three days. She was bursting with passion for him, but took care not to lose her head to a man whose life was already overflowing. She gave him all she dared to give, and received as much as she knew he could spare. For three nights, he was an ardent, inspired, and attentive lover; he invited her to choreograph the opera; and promised to compose a piece for her to dance–in New York, if that's where he was bound. He gave it a title: "Tango of the Green Eyes."

Granados receives a letter from Schelling describing conversations with Otto Kahn, board chairman of the Metropolitan, and Schelling's boyhood friend and board member, Clarence Mackay. Based on their promise of support, Schelling is "virtually certain" that the Met board will approve a premiere for *Goyescas* early next year. The general manager, Giulio Gatti-Casazza, "is still hesitant to give it his blessing, but he'll hear from Otto and Clarence, and I trust that will be the end of his hesitation." Schelling adds that the Met will pay for Granados' passage to New York and back, as well as expenses while he's in New York preparing for the premiere. He concludes: "You will hear from me or Rudi Schirmer."

Granados is delighted by the news, but instantly sees the trap: if the Met makes an offer, he will have to take a boat to America. He has come too far to pass up this opportunity. He cannot shake off the feeling of being trapped by unforeseen events.

Good Friday, 1915

After a sleepless night, Granados slips out the front door of his home and walks over to the garage where he keeps his motorcycle. The mechanic tries to engage him in conversation, without success. No aimless chatter this clear and sunny April morning. Granados rides out of Barcelona, headed for the hermitage in the hamlet of Samalús, on the eastern foothills of the Serra de Montseny, about an hour's ride from home. The same hermitage that he and Clotilde visited last October, when the deciduous trees were dropping their yellow and burnt orange leaves. In contrast, today's ride is solitary and joyless, a desperate attempt to find pastoral and spiritual solace.

A disaster! Zuloaga's letter—no hint of what to come. Then Antonia's note. Like most disasters unseen and stealthy. Antonia wanted to choreograph. Took my guard down. Massage set the stage. Can't blame her—my fault. Betrayed Clotilde! Can't forgive myself! Haunts me day and night! Need to be alone! Always quiet at the hermitage. Will there be forgiveness there?

Father Garriga—poet, romantic, and by choice assigned to this isolated parish—has just finished celebrating mass of the Passion for Good Friday in the small chapel of the hermitage where he lives—l'Ermita de Sant Salvador de Terrades. He watches nine villagers climb up the wagon path, heading back to their stone farmhouses. As he stands in the midday sun, listening to the sound of chickens behind the hermitage, the priest sees a tall man standing uphill from the chapel at the edge of a thicket of poplar and chestnut trees. In a few moments, the priest remembers this man coming here last autumn with a young woman—she rode in the little sidecar attached to his motocicleta. He's the musician from Barcelona.

Granados faces the thicket of trees, his face buried in his hands, sobbing grievously. He hears Father Garriga's shoes on the gravel path.

"Can I help you, my son?" asks the priest.

Granados turns and bares his cheeks streaked with tears. "Oh, capellà! My tears will remain in this place to implore God to pardon all of my errors and offenses. So many of them!"

"My son, you know what day this is?"

"Yes, capellà," replies Granados, "today is Holy Friday."

The priest speaks with a gentle voice. "That's correct. The day Jesucristo was martyred on the cross. The day he was cut and wounded for our wickedness, and stripped for our sins. No pain did Jesus refuse to suffer in his own body so he might deliver us from pain everlasting. On this day we receive the gift of the only Son of our God. God did not rescue his only son from pain so that we might be delivered from evil. This sacrifice was to atone for all the sins of the world. And this is the day when Jesucristo cried out to his Father: 'Do not stay far from me, for trouble is near, and there is no one to help. Many bulls surround me; fierce bulls of Bashan encircle me. They open their mouths against me, as would lions that rend and roar. Like water, my life drains away; all my bones grow soft. Father, my heart has become like wax, it melts away within me. As dry as a potsherd is my throat; my tongue sticks to my palate; you lay me in the dust of death. Many dogs surround me; a pack of evildoers closes in on me. So wasted are my hands and feet that I can count all my bones. But be not far from me, Oh Lord! Oh my strength, hasten to help me!' And God did not turn away from him, but heard him when he cried out."

"Oh, capellà! How can God forgive *me*?"

The priest offers a thin smile. "Bow your head, my son. Pray with me..."

> The Lord is my shepherd; I shall not want.
> He maketh me to lie down in green pastures.
> He restoreth my soul:
> he leadeth me in the paths of righteousness for his name's sake.
> Yea, though I walk through the valley of the shadow of death,
> I will fear no evil; for thou art with me;
> Thy rod and thy staff they comfort me.
> Thou preparest a table before me
> in the presence of mine enemies:
> Thou anointest my head with oil; my cup runneth over.
> Surely goodness and mercy shall follow me
> all the days of my life:
> and I will dwell in the house of the Lord for ever.

With eyes closed, Granados recites, "Oh, Lord, I have sinned against heaven and against Thee. I ask for your forgiveness in the name of Jesucristo."

Father Garriga recites a prayer of absolution, prescribes a penance, and gently traces a cross on Granados' forehead. "Ego te absolve. Now, my son, go in peace. May God be with you."

"I'm not sure I understand," says Clotilde. "You went up to Samalús–the little hermitage we visited? Last Friday?"

"I felt as if I was breaking into a thousand pieces," says Granados, closing his eyes. He tells her everything–except what happened with Mercé. "I was desperate. Looking for a quiet place–a place to get all the pieces back together. Suddenly too many pieces to keep track of. I was overwhelmed. Felt like I was drowning."

She squeezes his hands. "Well, it's no wonder. The war. L'Opéra de Paris postponing your premiere. All the uncertainties. And your passionate belief you can do everything–all at once."

"And on top of everything else," Granados adds, "the likelihood of a premiere in New York. On the other side of the ocean."

Clotilde kicks off her shoes and pulls him down beside her on the couch in the music salon. "Mm-hmm. I know–your worst fear."

"And my only choice," he replies. "Pau said London would be the best place–and just a short crossing, but now he's leaving, taking his career to New York. Says London's too close to the war. Says the German submarines are attacking ships in the Channel. So for *Goyescas*, it has to be New York."

"Yes. If your friend Schelling succeeds, you'll have your premiere. Surely there are worse things."

"Yes, like being on the *Titanic*!"

"Mi querido, the *Titanic* struck an iceberg. There aren't any of those between here and New York."

"How can you be so sure?"

She laughs. "This isn't the first time you've mentioned the *Titanic*, so I went to the Compañia Transatlántica the other day. The agent said there've never been any icebergs along the southern route. Now, isn't that reassuring?"

He gives her a thin smile. "Yes, thank you. Of course, my fears are entirely irrational."

"Precisely. That doesn't mean trivial. Having a reason to be afraid isn't the point, is it? Can I suggest you take a big breath and count the blessings in your life?"

The envelope with the letterhead "G. Schirmer, Inc., 3 East 43rd Street, New York, New York" has been sitting on the desk in Granados' study since yesterday afternoon. He's felt no urgency to open it because he's not expecting an advance payment on royalties until September, but today his curiosity prevails and he opens the envelope with his gold letter knife.

> Muy estimado Maestro Granados:
> It is my great pleasure to inform you that we have just agreed upon a contract with the Opera Company of New York, The Metropolitan, for the production of your opera *Goyescas* in the coming season. The opening performance will most likely take place in January 1916.
>
> With your consent, I've begun a search for translators so that the libretto will be available in Italian and French. We will then be prepared for performances of *Goyescas* in Milano and Paris, at the conclusion of hostilities.
> Very respectfully yours,
> Rudolph Edward Schirmer, President

The letter from Rudi Schirmer is a catalyst. Months of uncertainty are replaced with the sweet nectar of relief, and a song of exultation. Instead of waiting for a decision by strangers in a mythic city across the vast Atlantic, the letter marks a decision made well beyond the reach of Granados.

It's decided then. Americà. January. Only eight months. Schelling true to his word. Again! Now no other choice. Time to embrace it.

He walks–nearly running–down the hall and finds Amparo in the kitchen with the cook. He waves the letter from Schirmer. "It's Americà, Titín! New York! El Metropolitano! In January!"

She seems stunned. "Really? That's from Schelling?"

"It's from Schirmer. We have a contract for a premiere in January!"

Amparo smiles. "That's wonderful! Oh, I'm so glad you've found a venue!" She pauses. "That means you'll go to New York?"

"Yes–I have no other choice. Can't sit all my life worrying about crossing the ocean. Have to be there. And Schelling said if they accept the opera they'll pay my travel costs and expenses while I'm in New York."

"You'll have to go over in December."

He hesitates. "Yes, that's right. December."

"Before the holidays."

"Yes."

"Well, you have no other choice." Amparo puts her arms around him. "Congratulations–it's wonderful news."

He grasps her by the shoulders. "Titín, you could come with me!"

She shakes her head. "And where would we get the money?"

"We'll find it! There will be more money. We'll find it somewhere."

She laughs. "You always believe the money will appear as if by magic. And it never has." She shakes her head again. "No, and even if we found it, I couldn't leave the children. Certainly not during the holidays. They'd feel like orphans. No, you must go, but I must not."

Clotilde hears the sound of his motocicleta and places her book on the bench in her garden. By the time she reaches the courtyard, Grandos has dismounted and turned off the engine. He runs toward her, waving the letter from Schirmer. "We're going to América, mi amor! América!"

She squeezes him. "They've accepted it?"

"Yes! El Metropolitano! January! Only eight months! I'll go in December and you'll come over in January for the premiere!"

She raises her hands. "Let me catch my breath."

"I invited you to come to Paris, and they decided to have a war instead of an opera season. But América isn't in the war, so everyone's going there. That's what Schelling says, that's what Pau says. So I'm going there too. I have no choice–I have to be there. It's time to stop sitting and worrying and letting my life pass me by. I'm going and you're coming over too–to celebrate *Goyescas* with me! Say you'll come. Please say you'll come!"

She laughs. "Do I have a choice?"

At dinner in Sant Gervasi, they are eager to hear about the offer from the Metropolitan, and Granados has been eager since the letter arrived from Schelling to tell them. Andreu is emphatic that crossing the ocean to New York will not present problems despite the war in Europe. "My agents say there's been no change whatsoever. Of course, they're taking the southern route to Buenos Aires and Rio but they go on La Compañía Transatlántica–Antonio López' ships–the same ones that go to La Habana and New York. No icebergs. And, thank God, no German submarines! You'll have a fine time as long as they have pianos on board."

"Of course, dear Salvador's an authority on this–not ever having made the crossing," says Carmen in a teasing voice.

Andreu ignores her comment. "Look–as long as there's a war, the opportunity for you is in Americà. New York, Chicago, Buenos Aires. Even London isn't the same as before the war, and you can forget about the rest of Europe. So here's to Americà!" He raises his glass of cava.

In the following week, Granados receives a letter from the Metropolitan's Gatti-Casazza, in which the impresario describes his needs.

> With respect to producing your opera *Goyescas*, send me immediately the sketches for the costumes and sets. I've received from your editor, the firm of Schirmer of New York, the rights of representation for the 1915–16 season. I expect material for the designing of sets. Indicate the division of the choruses. We have 45 men and 55 women. I request that you make final revisions to the score, and send them to me. Tell me if the role of 'Paquiro' is for a bass or a baritone. I'll make every effort for your opera to be presented in the most perfect manner.

Gatti-Casazza adds that the Metropolitan is also willing to pay for travel and living expenses for Periquet through the opening night of the opera.

Just when Granados has pushed through most of his fear of crossing the ocean, news reaches Barcelona that on the afternoon of May 7 a German submarine attacked and sunk the gigantic, unescorted Cunard passenger liner RMS *Lusitania* off the southern coast of Ireland. *Lusitania* listed to starboard and plunged into the sea in less than twenty minutes. Two-thirds of her passengers and crew died, a total of 1,201 lives lost. Details of the attack trickle in every day, along with interviews of survivors taken ashore in the Irish seaport of Queenstown and in Liverpool, the port that was the liner's destination after crossing the Atlantic from New York. There are horrifying photos of orphans, women who lost their children, and dead babies. Survivors tell of the liner's last moments, followed by desperate hours clinging to wreckage in the sea, surrounded by corpses. There are unconfirmed accounts of submarines circling, taunting the shivering and dying survivors, and machine-gunning some of them. A series of sketches by one of the survivors, depicting the death throes of the great vessel, are circulated widely–except in German and Austrian newspapers.

The German press applauds the attack, arguing that it was justified by the fact that the ship was armed, and was carrying munitions and Canadian troops headed for the front. German editorials accuse Cunard Lines of carrying innocent civilians on a warship. Not surprisingly, British press reaction is bitter and rageful, calling the sinking "The Hun's Most Ghastly Crime." British and French papers express hope that U.S. President Wilson will be motivated to do something more than issue harmless protests. Posters that show a sinking ship with victims struggling in the water proclaim: "Avenge the *Lusitania!*" For several days, there are anti-German riots in British cities and demands for deportation of all people of German and Austrian origin. In France there are widespread protests against "German barbarity," and predictions that neutral countries–Italy, Spain, Norway, Netherlands, and the U.S.A.–will now be obliged to join the war on the side of the Allies. The German ambassador in Washington, Count Johann von Bernstorff, expresses "deepest sympathy at loss of lives," but places responsibility on the British government. According to Bernstorff, the British blockade has forced the Germans to launch these submarine attacks.

The immediate reaction in the U.S.A. is shock. Suddenly there are banner headlines about a war that no longer is half a world away. Germany, which has enjoyed a reprieve due in part to the large number of German-Americans in the middle region of the country, is now labeled "the outlaw of nations." When Ambassador Bernstorff comes to New York to attend a charity concert for the German Red Cross at the Metropolitan Opera, he elects to hide out in his suite at the Ritz-Carlton rather than face a pack of reporters, and sends the German naval attaché Captain Karl Boy-Ed to the opera house. Fearing trouble, the Met stations plainclothes police in every corner of the building, removes all of the German flags and banners, and forbids the singing of "Deutschland uber Alles." Captain Boy-Ed and Germany's military attaché Franz von Papen are booed and hissed as they take their seats. The next day, when Bernstorff tries to slip out of town, the pack of reporters intercepts him. They follow him to Pennsylvania Station, board his train, and escort him back to Washington, relentlessly seeking an interview.

With opinion shifting against Germany, President Wilson sends a strong note to Berlin, the essence of which is: "This can't happen again." The *Washington Herald* argues that the Germans, who were guilty of massacres in Belgium early in the war, have now sunk the *Lusitania* and murdered Americans simply because England is interfering with Germany's commerce. But Americans are also indignant that the British Government permitted the ship to enter the danger zone without adequate protection, especially after the German government ran ads in the New York papers warning passengers not to take British ships into the war zones. American confidence in British naval supremacy is shaken, and its politicians and press want to know: Why wasn't the ship convoyed? Why was it approaching the coast of Ireland without escort? Is it because of indifference or incompetence? Or is there some skulduggery behind it?

The sinking of the *Lusitania* and the staggering casualties–so many of them women and children–sharply increase the awareness of the civilian population in both combatant and neutral countries of the drastic consequences of modern warfare. The *Lusitania* was not the only disastrous news of the war in this spring of 1915. Last month's mass slaughter of British and Australian troops as they came ashore on the Turkish penninsula of Gallipoli, and the introduction of poisonous gas by the Germans in the battle for Ypres have sent shock waves through a world accustomed to stability within a framework of international law–today's fragile descendant of noblesse oblige and Pax Britannica. These events mark the end of innocence for citizens of neutral countries who've clung to the belief that the ravages of war will spare them.

Spanish neutrality is never in question, but the demise of the *Lusitania* sends waves of concern through Madrid and Barcelona, and a new wave of panic through Granados. His anxiety is inflamed when the normally dauntless Casals arrives in Barcelona with Susan, en route to the beach home in Sant Salvador. "We were booked three weeks after *Lusitania*," says Casals, "and you know I've never had any fears of crossing the ocean. This time–and so soon after it–I began to lose my nerve! But we'd moved all of my things from Paris to London, so we had to stop there. Except for that, I wouldn't have gone through the war zone."

"You mean England's in the war zone?" asks Granados. "I thought the war was in Belgium and France."

"That's where the trench war is. But German submarines are everywhere–around the British Isles, right in the channel itself."

Soon after, Granados receives a letter from Schelling describing how their friend Fritz Kreisler, welcomed in New York only a year ago as a wounded war hero, is now treated as a pariah because he fought on the same side as the Germans, who are now seen as the killers of innocent Americans on the high seas. "Poor Fritz!" writes Schelling. "He was only being loyal to his homeland. How did he know the Germans would behave like barbarians?"

Quin horror! Great liner sinks less than twenty minutes! Hundreds dead. If it happens to Lusitania *what ship is safe? There is no safety.*

"Truthfully, I can't bear the thought of crossing," he tells Andreu and Carmen after the children have left the dinner table at Sant Gervasi. "But how can I abandon my opera, after putting nearly my whole life into it? Nearly my whole life!"

"Look, Enric," replies Andreu, "if you take the ship of a country that's at war, yes, there may be risk. But the Germans aren't going to attack a ship of a neutral country–Spanish, Dutch, American. What I'm hearing, the war's confined to a line running through Belgium and France, and another where the Austrians and the Russians are having at it. The neutral countries aren't going to get into this. And if the British and French push the Germans back to their own border, the war will be over. I hope that happens, because war is indeed horrible! Even though it may be good for some of our businesses here, in the long run it's going to be devastating for the economy of Europe. And after all, aren't we Catalans more European than Spanish?"

Granados resists the invitation to discuss political philosophy. "You're telling me it's safe to go from here to New York?"

"Yes. If you book passage with La Compañía Transatlántica. You'll get on the ship right here, stop in Cádiz, then cross over on the southern route. You won't be anywhere near the war."

Granados makes reservations in first class for himself and Periquet on the SS *Montevideo*, departing from Barcelona November 30 and arriving in New York twelve days later. That means spending the holidays away from Amparo and the children for the first time, but the next departure on the sailing schedule is in late December, which wouldn't permit enough time for Granados to rehearse the orchestra and vocalists for the premiere on January 28.

Granados will not be alone in New York. Pau Casals and Susan will be at home in their new flat on the prestigious upper East Side; Henry and Lucie Schelling will be in their Park Avenue apartment; Robert and Mildred Bliss will come over from Paris for the premiere; Lucrècia Bori, now an international favorite, will sing the role of Rosario in *Goyescas*; and Antonia Mercé will choreograph and dance the street scenes. María Barrientos–her career renewed after leaving the Argentine husband–will also be in New York, preparing for her Metropolitan debut in *Lucia di Lammermoor*, three days after the *Goyescas* premiere; Emilio de Gorgoza is booked to sing *Tonadillas* at Aeolian Hall; former student Conxita Supervia will be in town to promote her career in Latin America; Paquita Madriguera and her mother will come over to line up American bookings, staying with Rosa Culmell Nin on West 75th Street; Miquel Llobet will embark on a tour in several U.S. cities; and some of Granados' musical colleagues who've fled the war in Europe–Kreisler, Paderewski, Josep Hoffman, and Eugène Ysaye–will also be in New York.

And Clotilde will be there, sailing on the next voyage of the *Montevideo* and arriving two weeks before the premiere.

Americà together! As Goya and La Duquesa were in Sanlúcar. Clotilde beside me as curtain rises. So many currents of my life converging. Current's now swifter–days coming weeks passing as if days.

The idea of staging the photos is born in Clotilde's garden on a sunny afternoon in July, soon after Granados and Periquet finish their work in Vilassar and send the score of *Goyescas* to Gatti-Casazza. "What I imagine," says Clotilde, "is my being in black–like the majas in your sketches. White silk under the black lace. Cut down to here," she adds, pointing to the tops of her breasts, "and a peaked hat with a veil falling below my shoulders."

"Which of my sketches?" asks Granados. "The one with the fan? With light falling on the maja's breasts? Yes, you will be La Duquesa de Alba!"

"And you will be Goya."

"Mmm. In costume?" The image of Goya's self-portrait comes to mind: portly body, receding hairline, clean-shaven round face, ruffled white shirt, and painter's smock. "No, I'll wear a dark suit. We'll do it with a piano. With one of the *Caprichos* on the music stand. Number 27–'Quien más rendido'–don't you think?"

"The one Goya said was of him and La Duquesa," Clotilde replies. "The artist and the duchess. Oh, I'd enjoy that!"

"Something to savor when we're in what Cicero called 'the crown of life, our play's last act.'"

"Or as Shakespeare put it, 'when thou art old and rich and hast neither heat, affection, limb, nor beauty, to make the riches pleasant.'"

"Bravo! Of course if I were old and rich, I'd dedicate part of my wealth to providing education for needy musicians. Since I probably won't be, I'll just keep giving lessons."

Clotilde smiles. "My love, you will be old and *beautiful*–and adored by me! And rich enough so you can provide for those needy musicians *and* devote yourself to composing more magical new music."

Puigcerdà

Granados' three weeks at the Xalet Andreu in Puigcerdà have come and gone with the ephemerality of a summer storm, and this is his last day before returning home. Twenty days of rest and twenty evenings of music and conversation have restored his strength and balance, allowing him to improvise and scribble notes on a composition pad–to remind him of the butterflies that he plans to release after *Goyescas* has enjoyed its season of celebrity.

During Granados' stay, Andreu asks about the direction of the academy while its founder is in New York. "I'm sure you've made proper arrangements," he says. "Just the same I'm curious. Can't blame me for that–three months is a long time."

"It is, and I can't. Certainly not, Salvador. Frank Marshall is my deputy director and indispensable assistant. He's absolutely capable of taking my place while I'm gone," says Granados. "He's taken over many of the administrative tasks, and done very well. The staff has great respect for Frank. As for the others–Mas, Llongueras, Perelló–they're excellent teachers. And my own students–especially Gerhard–will work with Marshall. I tell you, Salvador, they'll hardly miss me!"

Carmen stops on the promenade across the pond from Xalet Andreu. "Well, this is the last day, isn't it? 'Til next summer. Dios mío, how fast the time has gone! And the next thing, you'll be in New York."

Granados nods. "The fates seem intent on getting me on a boat. I won't complain any more. All the others have to do it, and they'll be there for the premiere. Pau and Schelling and Barrientos and Paderewski and Kreisler and Bori and Llobet and Gorgoza and La Nena Madriguera and La Argentina–"

"The dancer?"

"Yes. I want her to do the choreography."

"What a shame Amparo can't be there!" says Carmen.

"The Metropolitan is paying for me to come over, but not for her. Besides, Titín says she won't leave the children. Especially not for the holidays."

Carmen squints up at him. "You recited a list of all the people who will be in New York. Is it possible you forgot someone?"

He shakes his head. "I don't think so."

"You know who I mean."

He folds his arms and takes a deep breath. "Yes, Clotilde is coming over–for the premiere."

Carmen shakes her head. "As I said, what a shame Amparo can't be there." She turns and resumes the stroll around the pond.

Granados quickly falls in stride with her.

Hoped this wouldn't come up. Easy for Carmen to render judgment. Life's easy for her. Right and wrong–everything clearly defined.

"I'll miss you," says Carmen, taking his arm. Not wanting their last stroll of the year to end on a discordant note.

Granados looks up, over the swans on the pond and over the rows of poplar trees ringing it, past the foothills across the French border. Above the mountain tree line, the stony Pyrenees rise as if they're spires of nature's cathedral.

Walking around this pond with Carmen. How sweet–serene! This same air breathed for years and years. How fragrant the pines! Years and years walking around this pond. Will we walk here again?

Adéu Puigcerdà!

On August 19, while Granados was relaxing in Puigcerdà, the German submarine U-24 sank an unarmed British White Star Line passenger ship HMS *Arabic* as it approached the coast of England. Forty-four were killed, including two Americans. British news stories charged that the U-boat commander had contravened orders of the German naval high command not to attack unarmed passenger ships without warning. However, the commander claimed he'd confused the vessel for a freighter; the German government quickly blamed the British for the confusion. In fact, the Admiralty had introduced "decoy" ships to the war zone, disguised to resemble ordinary tramp steamers, with guns concealed behind screens on their decks. The purpose was to entice U-boats to the surface, then to sink them. Because of this, the Germans claimed, it was too risky for their submarines to surface and verify that the ships were unarmed; they had to use their best judgment. And on the very day that *Arabic* went to the bottom, the HMS *Baralong*–a "decoy" ship flying the American flag–attacked and sank the German U-27, hunted down and shot some of the submariners floating on the surface, and after killing others seeking refuge on the freighter, threw their bodies overboard. So, with the rules of sea warfare now broken by both sides, the notion of a "safe passage" has become a grim and bloody travesty.

Hearing the news about *Arabic* and *Baralong* shortly after Granados' return to Barcelona, Andreu concludes that the situation is getting out of control. And he's troubled by the sanguine assurances he's been giving Granados. "I'm glad I don't have to go across," he tells Carmen.

"But isn't he taking a Spanish ship? On a southern route?" she asks. "That's what you've been telling me."

Andreu sighs. "Yes. And I've given him the strongest advice to avoid the war zone. There've been no attacks on the Spanish ships. Not yet. What worries me is that this war is different. As horrible as war has always been, there were always certain rules and everyone observed them. Except, of course, the barbarians."

"Well, what's the difference between Germans and barbarians?"

He shrugs. "I don't know. But, it's not just the Germans. Both sides are breaking the rules. Thank God our country's still neutral!"

Tiana

"I've been wondering about New York," says Clotilde. "It seemed such a fine idea. So romantic, such a splendid dream to be there with you."

"And you're wondering if it's the right thing?" asks Granados.

"Yes. But more than that. I'm wondering if Amparo isn't the one who deserves to go."

He shakes his head. "It would be nice if she could be there. But I don't see how. She said she wouldn't leave the children."

"You've asked her?"

"Oh! Not exactly. But she says she wouldn't leave the children. Besides, we can't afford it."

"I understand," says Clotilde. "Still, it's a shame she can't be there. And there is a way. There is. I'm sure you've thought of it."

He shakes his head. "I don't know what you mean."

"Well, I've purchased my passage to go to New York. And I could ask La Compañía Transatlántica to transfer it to her. Surely we can't *both* be there."

"You would do that?" he asks.

"Mi amor, if it's the right thing to do? Yes indeed! And trust me, it might be better for you if she's the one basking in the glow of your triumph. Besides, you'll have more premieres for *Goyescas*. When the war's over, I'll go to Paris and Milano with you. And surely there will be many more operas. I'll go to New York with you for the next one."

You're right. Carmen's right. Amparo deserves to go. But Paris and Milano—your consolation for missing New York—easy for you to imagine future premieres. Not so easy for me.

Sant Salvador, September 1915

Pau Casals leads Granados toward the municipal pier as a gale blows off the Mediterranean, kicking up whitecaps and driving the surf onto the beach. "So Titín will be going with you?" asks Casals. "Maravellós! Susan and I will have a reception for you. It's exciting to think we'll all be there at the same time. And plainly *Goyescas* will be the great success of the season."

"Thank you, Pau. Your words are my greatest solace."

This familiar walk—with you my most constant friend. Can count on you no matter what. You'll always be here to walk this beach.

Adéu Sant Salvador!

Barcelona

In the next few weeks, Granados attends to the myriad of loose strands in his life. He and Periquet sign a contract with the Metropolitan for four performances of *Goyescas*. He agrees to take a set of antique enamels to New York for Doña Francisca Llovera, Amparo's mother, and to look for a buyer. He goes to Madrid for a performance with the Orquestra Filarmónica, and on the same program plays the complete cycle of Beethoven sonatas for piano and violin with Joan Manén. Back in Barcelona, he conducts the inaugural concert of the Association of Chamber Music, of which he's been named the artistic director, and plays the Grieg A minor Concerto that helped him launch his career twenty-three years ago at the Teatre Líric. While he was studying in Paris, he heard Grieg himself play this concerto; soon after, Granados sent his *Danzas Españolas* to Grieg and received an effusive note of admiration. He dedicates this last performance before leaving for New York to the Norwegian composer.

My last performance here—until our return. The Grieg concerto. Like bookends for my career.

Granados never ceases his work on *Goyescas*, making pencil corrections to the score nearly every day. If the libretto requires substantive alteration, he sends a note to Periquet; otherwise, he pencils in his own corrections to the verse. After the academy reopens, he spends several hours with Frank Marshall going over the instructional plans for his own students. He congratulates himself for having mentored Marshall in the past few years; now he can be absent for three months with confidence that the academy will continue to prosper, and that advanced students such as Robert Gerhard will progress under Marshall's guidance.

For some time, Granados has been dreaming about a house of his own. After Andreu's return from Puigcerdà, he asks him to help find a building site in Sant Gervasi or Tibidabo.

"You want to build a torre up here?"

"Yes, Salvador. I'm confident more money will be coming in. You know, I've been paying rent all of my life. That's putting money into others' pockets. I think it's time to put that money into paying off a mortgage. So my children will have a home after Amparo and I are gone."

Andreu beams. "I couldn't agree more! You know, I've made that suggestion several times, but 'til now you've never shown any interest."

"Yes, you have suggested it. And I haven't been interested. But now there will be much more money coming in. I'm sure of it."

"I know just the site for your torre. A short walk from here. Close to the Sala, with a nice view of the city. I'll show it to you tomorrow."

In early November, Granados is stunned by the sudden death of his friend of more than three decades, Carles Vidiella, another "predilecto" student of Joan Baptista Pujol. Vidiella had just returned to his study from an afternoon of giving lessons at the Escola Municipal. He reportedly walked to the window, took a puff of his puro, and suffered a massive heart attack. Dead before he reached the floor. So of the four renowned Catalan pianists trained by Pujol in the late 1870s and early 1880s, Granados at age forty-eight is now the only survivor. The other three–Albéniz, Malats, and Vidiella–have all passed on.

Carles dead! Can't believe it–saw him the other day. Carles' phrasing nearly perfect. Sense of humor–made me blush saying if he were a woman he'd be enamored of me. Carles dead! Slouching with top button of his jacket hooked in the middle buttonhole. And his battered bowler.

Tiana, December 1915

Clotilde holds Granados' hand as they sit on the bench in her garden. It's late in November, the day before he and Amparo are to board SS *Montevideo* for their first ocean crossing to New York.

"Would you read me this little poem?" Clotilde asks, handing him a folded note. "You said you borrowed it from Mestres."

"Ah, 'Sueños del poeta.' Don't have to read it. It's here," he says, pointing to his head. He recites:

> In the garden of cypresses and roses
> resting against the pedestal of white marble,
> waiting for his time,
> the poet sleeps, dreaming…
> At his side, and caressing his forehead
> the Muse watches over him.

Granados looks up. "Oh, I've made you cry. Again."

Clotilde takes the handkerchief from his pocket. "It's the poem–always makes me cry!"

He puts his arm around her and pulls her closer. "You missed one. Here." He wipes a tear from her cheekbone. "I have something for you," he adds, handing her a notebook bound in red leather.

Clotilde is puzzled.

"It's my diary," he says. "I'm not very good at putting things into words, but I've been jotting notes in this little book for some time. Some of it just looking back over my life. And some recent entries from the last few years. About you. About you and me."

She shakes her head. "But why are you giving this to me? It's your personal diary."

"Yes. But I want you to keep it. Just in case."

Her eyes widen. "Oh, nonsense–just in case–you'll be back! You'll be back before the nightingales return–you'll be here to hear them! You'll be back to sit right here–with me–and watch the early flowers, watch the daffodils burst into bloom. You'll be back with me, and the next time you go, I'll be with you. Wherever that is–Paris or Milano or London. Truly, there's no need for you to leave this diary with me."

"Mi alma, nobody would be more grateful–assuming you're correct. But I just don't want this diary discovered by my children or falling into the hands of strangers. There's too much of a very personal nature. I want you to have it, so if somehow I don't return you'll keep it forever–or share some of it with my children, after they grow up."

She reaches up and places her hands around the back of his neck. "You're trusting me with the most personal reflections of your life."

"Yes."

Tears come to her eyes. "I could never have dreamed you would place that kind of trust in me. Perhaps you're not aware of it, but sometimes it's as if I'm still the frightened student coming to audition with the great maestro."

"No–that was long ago. You've become the romance of my life. The sound of your voice is my song of love. I heard it in your voice the very first time I came here. Do you remember?"

She laughs. "Remember? Could I forget the way my throat dried up just before I asked: 'Maestro, would you like to see the Pleyel you bought for my father?' And asked you to take me back as a student. I wanted to run from the Casino, but my legs were too weak."

"I never would have guessed. You were so poised, so confident."

"I was scared to death!" she says.

"Your voice was like the sweetest lyre in the garden of love."

"My heart was racing. As it is now." She takes his hand and places it between her breasts. "Your hands are so large!"

His throat is dry and he too is aroused. "Of all the poetry I've heard, only the words coming from your throat and the tip of your tongue, only your words ever reached me so deeply and touched me where there's joy and then delirium. Only the sound of your voice makes me shake all over. Would you read that poem from Darío? The one you recited the first time I came here?"

"I don't have to read it," she says. "It's here," she adds, pressing his hand more firmly onto her chest. "And always here, mi amor…"

> I know there are those who ask:
> why do you not still sing
> those same wild songs of yesteryear?
> They do not see the work of just an hour,
> the work of a minute, and the wonders of a year.
> I, now an aging tree, used to moan so sweetly
> from the breezes when I began to grow.
> But the time has passed for youthful smiles:
> so let the hurricane move my heart to song!

Granados is trembling, overcome, mute. He wraps his arms around her and places his head on her shoulder.

Adiós, Tiana! Adiós mi amor!

Granados' embarkation the following day is a festival of wine, song, and revelry. The restaurant of the Customs House is alive with the popping of corks and joyful chatting. Victor Granados and Solita's fiancé Rossend Carrasco stroll through the crowd, keeping the stem glasses bubbling with cava. The crowd swells, overflowing to the boardwalk between the Customs House and the octagonal Royal Maritime Club of Barcelona with its flags popping in the breeze. At the entrance to the restaurant, Eduardo Granados stands next to his father, amazed at the burgeoning crowd. Amparo is nearby with their two daughters and youngest son, Paquito. Their son Enrique is with a group of friends from school, listening to two guitar students of Miquel Llobet as they play their maestro's transcriptions of music by Albéniz and Granados. Only those standing close to the guitarists can hear their music above the din.

The makeup and mood of the crowd suggests a wedding reception, not the everyday boarding of a steamship–but it's clearly not an everyday occurrence for a local celebrity to leave Barcelona for distant shores. And to see Granados boarding a steamship bound for America, given his longstanding vow never to do so, lends a special fascination to the event.

Well-wishers and admirers arrive on this Tuesday morning from nearly every corner of Granados' life: close personal friends such as August Pi i Sunyer and Gabriel Miró and their families; Andreu and Carmen and all of their children; three sons of Eduardo Condé; Santiago Rusiñol and Carles Pellicer and their families; Eugeni d'Ors–accompanied by the young painter Josep Mompou and his younger brother, Frederic, an aspiring composer–who gives Granados an autographed copy of his antiwar manifesto written for the Friends of the Moral Unity of Europe; Carme Karr and her husband, Josep de Lasarte; Lluisa Vidal and her sister Frasquita Vidal de Capdevila; faculty members from the academy, closed for the day–Frank Marshall, Joan Llongueras, Domènech Mas, and Adrià Esquerrà; nearly all of the academy's students, including Frederic Longàs, Conxita Badia, Robert Gerhard, Josep Caminals, María Llucià, Alexandre Vilalta, and Mercé Moner; former students, including Ferran Via, Emilia Ycart, Baltasar Samper; the entire Barcelona Trio of Ricard Vives, Marià Perelló, and Pere Marès; one of Granados' most talented prodigies, Paquita Madriguera, with her parents, her brother Enric and four sisters, including Mercedes, an infant peering wide-eyed from under layers of blankets; several of Granados' musical colleagues, including Joan Manén, Apel.les Mestres, Amadeo Vives, and Lluís Millet of the Orfeó Català, and Pau Casals' brother Enric; Frederic Lliurat, a former student of Granados and now editor of *Revista Musical Catalana*; music critics Joaquim Pena, Joan Salvat, and Rafael Moragas, who helped organize the private recital of Book One of *Goyescas* five years ago; Gabriel Alomar, who attended the private recital and complimented Granados for creating an artistic blend which represents "España–the everlasting maja"; stage designers Miquel Moragas and Salvador Alarma; news reporters from *La Vanguardia* and *Diari de Barcelona*; political leader Prat de la Riba, who never misses a sizeable crowd of voters; José Maria Orriols, editor of *Revista Mundial* and host of the homenatge for Granados at Saló de Cent, along with city council member Francisco Carreras, who presided over that event; and, somewhat lost in the multitudes, the family and friends of Fernando Periquet and Miquel Llobet–who are also boarding the vessel for New York.

Also in the gathering outside the Customs House are the young priest from Sant Pere de les Puelles, Father Trias, come to bless Granados' voyage; a flower-seller who walked his cart down from its usual location on La Rambla; Granados' tailor; an old man with six chickens tied together by their feet, for sale at a special price; the photojournalist Frederic Ballell; the mechanic who keeps Granados' motorcycle running; a group of young women practicing figures on roller skates, their long skirts billowing up to risqué levels in the breeze; three pickpockets and four prostitutes from the Barri Xinès, lured by commercial possibilities; two young photographers from the publicity office of La Companyía Transatlàntica Española, which owns and operates SS *Montevideo*; a class of landscape painters from the nearby La Llotja school of art; passersby drawn by the prospect of glimpsing celebrities; and Antoni Gaudí, who passes through the crowd unnoticed.

José Altet weaves through the crowd to Granados' side. "Mestre, it's time for you and Doña Amparo to board the ship. I'll show you the way."

"The luggage is on board?"

"Yes, mestre. And your suite is waiting."

Even with a marked thinning of the crowd, the first-class cabin is tightly packed with those who wish to spend the last few minutes with the travelers. Paquita Andreu clings to Granados, weeping inconsolably. Amparo is flanked by her children, inadvertently arranged in order of birth.

Marshall, Pi i Sunyer, and Miró shake Granados' hand and give him a collegial abraçada. "We'll look in on the children every day," says Pi i Sunyer. "There's no need for you to worry."

Granados laughs. "I won't worry, but make sure you tell that to Titín."

Andreu is next, offering, "You'll have a marvelous trip, 'Ric–find a piano on board–I guarantee you'll have yourself a fine orchestra in no time at all."

"But never as fine as the orchestra of Puigcerdà."

"I should hope not!"

It's Carmen's turn. She holds him in a tender abraçada. "You'll be fine as soon as we get out of here and give you some peace."

"I wish all of you could come with me," he says. "Especially you!"

"Oh, we will–in spirit!" she exclaims with forced gaiety. "Don't worry. The spirits will guide you safely. And your masterpiece will be the miracle of the New York season."

As Granados watches Carmen leave the cabin, a purser in dress whites appears at the doorway and announces it's time for all guests to return to shore. Eduardo gives his parents a sober farewell abraçada, and is followed by his siblings, with Carrasco leading Solita out, Enrique reminding his father of a promise to collect autographs from opera celebrities, and Victor promising to do better in school. Paquito is last. He gives his sobbing mother a final hug, then he's led out by Natalia.

While Amparo unpacks their clothes, Granados reads the publication for passengers of the Compañía Transatlántica. Trivial reading, intended to distract anyone harboring fears of an ocean voyage, with many ads–for "Anis de Mono" of the Vicente Bosch distillery, and the Gran Hotel en La Rambla–and a news item relating that Violet Asquith, daughter of Britain's embattled Prime Minister Herbert Asquith, was married at Westminster Abbey.

As the ship is tugged away from the pier, Granados goes out onto the promenade deck and stands at the rail, Amparo at his side. His eyes sweep across the panorama of Barcelona. On his left is the sugarloaf mound of Montjuic, where the Romans built a shrine to Jupiter and gave it a name: Mons Iovis–which survives in today's Catalan version; where a castle was built in the 17th century to protect the city from seafaring invaders, the castle later converted to a prison and torture center for political prisoners. Montjuic, the site of the Poble Espanyol, a replica of Spanish life and customs; and the city's southwest area cemetery, where Jews were buried from the 11th to 14th centuries, and Albéniz was laid to rest six years ago.

Straight ahead, Granados sees the bronze statue of Cristófer Colom atop a cast iron column fifty meters high, where the base of La Rambla converges with the historic maritime entrance to the city. Colom is said to be pointing west, toward the Americas where Spanish conquistadores did their best to destroy the indigenous civilizations. In fact, the Genoese explorer is pointed across the Mediterranean, in the direction of Libya.

Beyond the monument to Colom, Granados raises his eyes, following the slightly diagonal winding course of La Rambla, past El Liceu and Café de l'Opera and Carrer dels Tallers–where he lived with his family after arriving in Barcelona–past Carrer de Fontanella–the first location of the academy–and the alleyway he'd take down to Els Quatre Gats, over to Plaça de Catalunya and up Passeig de Gràcia through the heart of l'Eixample, farther up to Sant Gervasi and Avinguda Tibidabo, where Andreu built the Sala, then up the mountain to Vallvidrera, where he went to the bittersweet farewell party for Albéniz, then to the point where the rocky peak of Mount Tibidabo meets the china-blue sky.

Granados' eyes drift to the right, where the unfinished spires of Sagrada Familia rise above the neighborhood where his children will sleep tonight, through the Born district where he was arrested for the second time during Setmana Tràgica, across Parc de la Ciutadella–where he spends so many Saturday afternoons with his children–and l'Estació de França–where he's seen so many friends off, wishing them success in their careers, where he departed for Paris at several critical points in his own life over the past three decades, where he left for Schelling's chalet in Céligny with the letter of acceptance of *Goyescas* by l'Opéra de Paris.

Now he squints as haze from the industrial area of Badalona on the eastern rim of the city obscures his view of the rocky hills in which the village of Tiana is snuggled, and he imagines Clotilde standing in her garden, peering through the same haze–as if the intensity of their vision will somehow connect them, looking toward the harbor where SS *Montevideo* is being tugged into the main channel leading to the open sea, its boilers stoked and propellers biting into the waters of the Mediterranean. A fleet of gaff-rigged sailboats, beating against the wind in a weekend regatta, scatters to release the vessel from the port as the coal-fired engines pick up speed.

Coming back–watching this with heart beating wildly. Coming closer and closer to home. Closer and closer to Tiana. Feeling her embrace hearing her voice again.

Adéu, Barcelona!

Gabriel Miró is standing with Pi i Sunyer, their families, and Carrasco. He looks up, past the flock of Granados children who are scattered in a crowd of young friends and academy students, all perched on the edge of the pier for a closer look as the ship pulls away. He looks up and sees Granados, his pale face in shadow, with a somber expression of defeat and anguish, his hands gripping the rail of the promenade deck. As the distance between them widens, the features of Granados' face begin to blur and only his eyes–those enormous eyes–are unwavering, frozen in a longing gaze toward the city of his triumphs and disappointments. And Miró sees a motionless Amparo frozen against Granados, her head on his shoulder, her face smiling, and her cheeks glistening with tears.

After a routine run–down the Costa Daurada and Costa de Azahar, splitting the gap between Cap de la Nau and the Balearic Islands, traversing the Costa Blanca, around Cabo de Palos to the westward run along the Costa del Sol–SS *Montevideo* enters the Strait of Gibraltar, flanked by the Rock on the starboard side and the Ceuta point of Morocco off to port. Midway through the Strait, *Montevideo* is stopped and boarded by French military police. They are looking for the Algerian leader of a small band of saboteurs employed by the Germans to track French shipping in the Mediterranean. The Algerian escaped from confinement in Marseilles and was reported to be heading down the coast to Barcelona.

There's a shipwide search and a knock on the door of Granados' cabin. He wakes up to the voice of a young French naval officer asking Amparo for their papers. As the bright afternoon light floods the cabin, he's disoriented and annoyed as he hears a voice explaining to Amparo in broken Spanish the purpose of the intrusion.

"Señora, if you please would display us your passports," says the apparent leader of the police. "We are at your service to leave you without further molestation." He looks across the cabin at Granados. "And you are Señor Who?"

"I am Enrique Granados," he replies in French. "Of course, we will show you our passports. Titín, por favor."

Amparo is already searching in the large purse where she put their papers and tickets after boarding. "Ay, no!" she says to herself as she finds only one passport: hers. She turns to Granados, "I don't find yours. Did you give it to me?"

Granados shrugs. "No, I thought you had all the papers."

"But you must have shown it when we boarded. I had to show mine."

He shakes his head. "Nobody asked me. I supposed they knew me."

At this point, the policeman steps forward and studies Granados' face. "You say you are Señor Granados, but you have no passport. How is it you have no passport? Where are you going to?"

Granados explains that he and his wife are going to New York for the premiere of his opera. Amparo opens her passport and hands it to the policeman. "You see, I am his wife. We are going together to New York. Apparently my husband left his passport at home."

The policeman studies her passport and shakes his head. "But how is it you could be his wife? It says you are Amparo Gal i Llovera. It does not say you are the wife of any Granados."

In an agitated voice, she tries to explain that women in Catalunya retain their names when they marry. The French policeman responds with a harsh, skeptical laugh. "Ah, so you claim this man is your husband, even with a different name?" He turns to Granados. "And you are a Spanish composer? Are you able to show that is true? That you are not the man we are searching for?"

Amparo steps between the policeman and her husband. "Excuse me, officer, I will bring two other gentlemen who are traveling with us to verify that this man is indeed Enrique Granados. If you will permit me."

An hour later, after Llobet and Periquet are brought to the cabin to confirm Granados' identity, and after a thorough grilling, the French police leave without apology and continue their search of *Montevideo*.

Awakened from his siesta and shaken by the incident, Granados follows his colleagues to an elegant, two-story music salon, where they lead him to an Ortiz & Cussó grand piano in the corner, bolted to the floor. Granados sits down, plays a few arpeggios, and–finding the piano in acceptable tune–plays through Book One of *Goyescas* as a small audience gathers.

Late that evening, *Montevideo* arrives at the port of Cádiz, its last stop before the unbroken run across the Atlantic to New York. Cádiz is located up the Costa de la Luz from the Strait of Gibraltar, on a peninsula that protects a superb natural harbor. The city was founded around 1100 B.C. by the Phoenicians, later became a Roman naval base, was one of the first major cities reconquered from the Moors, and served as the starting point for Colom's second and fourth voyages across the Atlantic. By the 18th century, three-fourths of all Spanish commerce with the Americas was passing through Cádiz. And while the rest of Spain was under Napoleonic rule in the early 19th century, it was in Cádiz that a new Spanish constitution was written and the revolt against French rule was launched. Cádiz is also the birthplace of Manuel de Falla.

When *Montevideo* leaves Cádiz the following morning, Granados walks aft on the starboard side of the promenade deck, hoping to see the area of Sanlúcar de Barrameda at the mouth of the river Guadalquivir, which carried Colom's vessels down from Sevilla on their first voyage across the ocean. Sanlúcar, where Goya and La Duquesa de Alba spent several weeks together in the late spring and summer of 1797. Granados finds Periquet standing at the farthest aft section of the rail, peering intently at the coastline.

"See, where the river empties into the sea," says Periquet. "The water is lighter, cloudier, muddier. Just look beyond that point–it's called Chipiona, you'll see the great marshes of Las Marismas. And look farther–see where the land rises and seems darkened with trees? That's where the Palacio del Rocío was in the time of Goya. It was a sumptuous sprawling country palace with a tall watchtower and more than thirty private apartments. Mostly used by the Dukes of Medina Sidonia for hunting excursions. Goya arrived there in the month of May at the invitation of La Duquesa. They remained together and he sketched her in the most private moments–leaving no doubt, not in my mind, of the intimacy between them."

Goya's sketches were apparently made at all hours of the day and night, with La Duquesa unposed and seemingly unaware of the artist–or at least uninhibited by his presence. The sketch of La Duquesa sleeping, with her hair flowing over the pillow; in a nightgown, arranging her long, dark tresses; bathing at a fountain, nude, with her head turned away; and after bathing, with a maid combing her hair.

Periquet's voice is full of tremolo. "His visit to Sanlúcar was the high point! Imagine how he must have longed for her! Imagine his enormous delight in her invitation. Imagine his ecstasy in becoming her lover." Periquet pauses. "And, then imagine his bitterness and despair when she moved on to other men. But rejection was like a pearl in his oyster, inspiring *Los Caprichos*. How does anyone know when tragedy will be the prelude to magnificence?"

Granados can barely see the place where the land rises, but he imagines an elegant summer palace where Goya sketched La Duquesa lounging déshabillé in the simmering heat of the Andaluz summer.

"Don't you agree?" asks Periquet.

"Mmmn." Granados has lost track of his librettist's monologue.

"I thought so. And isn't this an incredible coincidence–you and I, looking over at Sanlúcar–on our way to putting Goya's art on the stage of the Metropolitan? The gods must be smiling!"

No. If gods were smiling not being hauled off to the high seas where who knows what Poseidon has in store for us!

"Don't you agree?" asks Periquet.

"Mmmn?"

"That it's an incredible coincidence."

Granados nods. "Ah, yes. Very much so." He lingers at the starboard rail long past the time when the dim outlines of Sanlúcar and Las Marismas and the wooded area and the summer palace of La Duquesa de Alba, real outlines or imaginary, have been left behind in the morning haze. He remembers once wanting to go in search of her palace, to be as close to it while he composed *Goyescas* as he'd been to the orchards of Murcia when he created *María del Carmen*, but it never became important enough to make an effort to break away from all the other venues of his life. And now the opportunity has passed, along with the dim outlines, real or imaginary.

Adiós, Sanlúcar!

Shortly after *Montevideo* enters international waters off La Costa de la Luz, it's intercepted again, this time stopped and boarded by a coastal patrol boat of the British Navy, in search of a weapons dealer reportedly heading for New York to procure guns and ammunition for the Turkish army. The Turks have succeeded in stopping the British and Australian invasion of the Gallipoli peninsula, with each side suffering 300,000 casualties in barely two months of carnage, and even though the British now plan to evacuate the peninsula, this boarding of the neutral *Montevideo* is doubtless motivated by fear that the resupplied Turks will mount a new attack as the allies try to withdraw from their ill-advised Dardanelles campaign.

When they arrive to check papers, Amparo sends a ship's purser to retrieve Periquet and Llobet, and after a round of solemn declarations and an exasperated offer by Granados to prove his identity at the ship's piano, the squad leader takes his men away without apology.

That evening, the captain of *Montevideo* invites Granados and Amparo to sit at his table for dinner, and apologizes. "I've never been searched twice in the same voyage," says Captain Massó. "Never. This wretched war! Gracias a Dios we are not combatants! Forgive me, Maestro Granados, I've neglected to say how honored I am that you and your good wife are guests of ours on this run. Honored, absolutely. I've been a fanático of yours since I first heard you play your *Danzas Españolas*. Are you surprised? Yes, I was there–at the Teatre Líric. How many years ago, maestro? Oh, I'd say about a quarter of a century. But I've never forgotten that stupendous recital. Are you surprised? Surprised that some of us who've spent our lives at sea are devoted to the music of Catalunya? And in my case, devoted to yours?"

"Thank you, Captain."

"I have a favor to ask. I've been asked to authorize a benefit for the French Red Cross. Some time during our run to Americà. Would you and your colleague, Señor Llobet, be willing to provide the music?"

"I'd be honored, Capità Massó. I'll talk to Llobet."

New York City

Because of the boardings and unusually rough weather on the Atlantic this early December, *Montevideo* arrives outside the Port of New York late on December 14, nearly three days late. She anchors overnight off the port, and in the morning is guided by tugboats into Pier 8 on the Hudson River side of Manhattan Island.

Emerging onto the promenade deck, Granados' first impression of New York City is the height of the buildings. None of the large cities he's lived in or visited–Barcelona, Madrid, Paris, Marseilles, and Geneva–can compare with this city's vertical thrust of steel and concrete. To be sure, he's seen monuments like the Tour Eiffel, tall spires of cathedrals, and towers of castles and fortresses that rise several stories above the ground, but in New York there are many rows of buildings rising at least ten stories, surpassing those in the European cities, and there are a few "grataceles"–buildings that seem to scrape the sky, which are breathtaking.

Amparo joins him on deck as they wait to disembark. "I told you we'd make it across safely. No icebergs. No submarines. It wasn't worth worrying, was it?"

He laughs. "Of course not, Titín, but don't think I choose to worry. I'd like to jump on a boat without a thought, as some can, but I just can't. You know that."

Amparo takes his arm. "At any rate, here we are in New York."

"Yes, and I'm glad to be here alive!"

At the bottom of the gangplank they're greeted by Francisco Gandara, the Mexican journalist who visited Barcelona at the time of the opening of Sala Granados nearly four years ago.

"Hola–Maestro Granados! Remember me? Francisco Gandara. Bienvenidos a Nueva York!"

The face is familiar. Gandara reminds him of where they'd met.

"Ah yes–Gandara. You came to our home."

"Yes, and since I knew you, Signore Gatti of the Met asked me to help you and Señora de Granados get settled in your hotel. Well, truthfully, I offered–since none of them speak Castilian."

"Thank you, Francisco. That's very kind."

"Ah, it's my pleasure. Maestro, I can't tell you how exciting it is to see you here. Everyone in town is so anxious for your arrival."

"Are you sure they've heard of *me*?"

"Of course they have! Maestro Schelling played *Goyescas* at Carnegie Hall–the most famous sala in America, and the Australian, Percy Grainger, also played your work here. Last month, the Chicago Symphony and Opera performed *Dante*. Emilio de Gogorza has sung some of your *Tonadillas*. Also Rosa Culmell. Of course there's been much advance publicity about your opera and your coming here for the rehearsals. I will do an interview with you for the *New York Times*. Without a doubt, you're already known here–and before you leave, the name 'Granados' will be on everyone's lips. I promise you that, maestro!"

Granados is grateful for Gandara's assistance. For the first time since he went to Paris three decades ago, he's surrounded by hordes of people whose language he cannot understand. Originally, Schelling planned to be at the pier to greet him, and they could have conversed in French, but the three extra days in crossing and Schelling's concert in Boston last night made that impossible.

Along with the incomprehensible babble of voices, Granados is impressed by the quick pace of life in the city he's entering. In comparison, Paris is vibrant and leisurely, Barcelona resolute and industrious, and Madrid formal and austere.

As they emerge from the terminal, a gust of cold wind sweeps down the Hudson River. "What's the best way to our hotel?" asks Granados.

"I've arranged for your luggage to be taken to the Hotel Claridge," says Gandara, "and we could take a taxi cab up Seventh Avenue. That's the best way if it weren't so cold. The cabs are open–no heat, and there's a nasty wind."

"What's the alternative?" asks Granados.

"The warmest way is taking the subway. If you're willing."

Granados laughs. "Why not?"

"Have you ever taken a subway, maestro?"

"No, but it can't be any worse than crossing the ocean."

Part IV

Chapter Ten

New York City, December 1915

Giulio Gatti-Casazza is all business this morning as he faces Granados and Periquet across the large mahogany desk in his office. It's not that Gatti can't exude charm when it serves his purpose. Without it, he could never have hired, coped with, and managed so many operatic tenors and sopranos–artists who would prefer to answer only to God. That he's thrived for so long–ten years at Milano's La Scala and seven at the Metropolitan–is a tribute to Gatti's wide range of skills. Among the sopranos he's directed is Frances Alda, a feisty red-haired diva from New Zealand who followed him from La Scala to the Met, married him five years ago, but refused to take his last name.

Gatti's self-confidence and wry wit are legendary: last year he interviewed a mediocre tenor and suggested that his voice was not ready for the Met. The tenor was offended. "Not ready? Why, when I was with La Scala they thought so much of my voice they insured it for fifty thousand pounds!" "Oh?" replied the impresario, "and what did La Scala do with the money?"

This morning, with two neophytes from Spain, Gatti is a caricature of the impresario with a heart of granite. His office intimidates most who enter it for the first time: a massive desk with corners capped by brass castings of a lion's legs and paws, Persian carpeting, a collection of gold-embossed first editions in the glass bookcase behind him, and sculpted bas reliefs on the doorframes, suggesting the grandeur of Rome. Gatti may have sobbed uncontrollably at the sight of the revered Verdi lying in state, may have consoled a distraught Puccini after the initial failure of *Madame Butterfly*, but this morning it's all business. There are a number of thorny issues to confront with these Spaniards, and the sooner, the better. He could as easily be negotiating the purchase of uniforms for the Met's ushers as welcoming the men who created an opera that will premiere just six weeks from tonight.

"You should know this wasn't my idea," Gatti says, looking directly at Granados without a trace of emotion. He's a year younger than Granados and five years older than Periquet. His features are strong but not handsome: long, square chin, high forehead, carefully trimmed moustache, and a short goatee that is turning gray. His physique and voice could belong to a baritone. "It has nothing to do with your being Spanish. In fact, I'm interested in world premieres from a variety of composers, and I want a variety of nationalities represented–not just Italian–and I'd like to find an 'American Verdi,' if there is one. But I'm not sure about this opera of yours, maestro. I suppose because the libretto is weak," he adds, looking now at Periquet, who begins to react and thinks better of it. "And it's not that I'm adverse to risk, messieurs. I took an enormous risk on Puccini's *Fanciulla del West* in my second season here. No, it's not the risk. It's whether your work measures up. Frankly, you wouldn't be here at all without the 'angel' who was willing to subsidize it."

Granados looks across the desk at the self-confident impresario, impeccably dressed in a dark business suit with vest, white shirt, and dark green tie. "An 'angel'–what do you mean?" he asks. "And what do you mean by 'measuring up'?"

Gatti straightens up in his chair. "It's not for me to discuss your angel. If you don't know who he is, I suggest you ask your friends, Mr. Schelling and Mr. Schirmer–God knows they've promoted your opera! Or ask Mr. Kahn, or one of the board members with such a keen interest in it. Mind you, Granados, I'm not saying it's wrong to have an angel. But this is a short opera and very costly for the time it's on stage. We have to present it with another short opera or the audience will demand a refund. Or run me out of town! There's a large cast, mostly for the street scenes. Three expensive sets. I've sent Antonio Rovescalli to Madrid to study Goya's paintings, and we'll spare nothing in making the sets remarkable. But three sets and four scene changes–including one between the two operas! That's why we needed an angel."

"What other operas will be presented?" asks Granados.

Gatti says there will be four performances, starting January 28. For the premiere, *Goyescas* will be presented with *Pagliacci*, with Caruso singing Canio. "That will ensure a full house," he says. "For the other three performances, it will be paired with *Cavalleria Rusticana* and *Hansel and Gretel*. Gatti explains that this is necessary because the same singers are not available every time. "For your work, I wanted Lucrezia Bori," Gatti says. "After all, she's a Spaniard.

They say she's descended from the Borgias–one of them was a pope–he was the one who reversed Joan of Arc's death sentence. The Borgias would make splendid opera."

"There is an opera, but I don't know how splendid it is," says Granados.

"Yes, that one. But *Lucrezia Borgia* wasn't one of Donizetti's best. Is it true Bori's one of the Borgias?"

Granados shrugs.

"At any rate, Bori has a very serious problem with her throat. I saw her the other day with her entire neck wrapped in bandages–what a tragedy! So I've signed Anna Fitziu."

Granados shakes his head. "I'm disappointed," he says, "but Fitziu's not bad. I heard her sing in Barcelona, and her voice is fine for Rosario. Bori would have been better."

"I'm glad we agree," Gatti says, moving on. "Fernando will be sung by Giovanni Martinelli. He's been all over Europe and had his debut here two years ago in *Boheme*. For Pepa we signed the mezzo Flora Perini. She also was at La Scala and just had her debut here last month in *Manon Lescaut*. Finally, for Paquiro we have Giuseppe de Luca, who also just had his American debut here in *Barbiere di Siviglia*. Big success–he's already a favorite. Of course the conductor will be Gaetano Bavagnoli. Chorus master, Giulio Setti. So you see, messieurs, I'm dedicating only first-rate artists to your work. And I'll do everything in my power to make it a success. Thank the stars you haven't included an elephant!"

"Elephant?" asks Periquet. "Why would we include an elephant?"

Gatti smiles for the first time this morning, cocks his head, amused that he's lured the librettist like a tortoise from its shell, and recounts the saga. In Gatti's fourth season at La Scala, he presented Donizetti's *Linda di Chamounix* along with a choreographic poem that attempted to portray some of the great events since the creation of the world. One of these–Julius Caesar's triumphant arrival in Roma–called for a small herd of horses, an ox, and an elephant to be marched across the stage. Gatti acquired the largest of these beasts–a male named Papus–from Germany, and hired a trainer to prepare him for his operatic career.

"Of course," Gatti recalls, "the trainer assured me he could keep the animal under control–he exaggerated how well he knew his trade." One day Papus became frightened and left La Scala, heading down the street. A crowd gathered, the police arrived and were about to shoot him until the trainer stepped in, explained that Papus was "an artist of La Scala Opera," and managed to get the beast back to his quarters.

"Did this elephant ever perform?" asks Periquet.

"Oh, my yes! With the help of a monkey named Pirri who rode on his back, Papus played his role scrupulously. Was a great favorite. I've known many tenors and sopranos who weren't nearly as well behaved."

Gatti enjoys the vignette. Having relaxed, he asks about their arrival in New York, and if their hotel is satisfactory.

"Thank you for sending the car," replies Granados. He laughs. "It was so cold, we decided to take the underground–the sub-way–and it was quite an adventure! Down in the sub-way, there are infernal caverns. Like a scene from Dante!"

Gatti nods. "I'm sure the weather was a shock, coming from Spain. Actually, it's been milder this year, and so far, very little snow." His voice takes on a faraway tone, recalling his own arrival seven years ago. "I'd never been in America. Didn't speak any English–never had to. And knew nothing about the way of life and customs. My first days here were brutal. I could not have had a colder or more indifferent welcome! Ah well, I thought, I'll stay for five years and save some money, then go back home. But after five, I decided on another five. Learned enough English to get along. Not easy, but what a wonderful opportunity! The Metropolitan. We can be even greater than La Scala. So here I am!" Gatti leans toward Granados. "You should know, maestro, your music is very difficult. When I gave the score to the conductor and concertmaster, they said we'll need a string section full of Paganinis to play it, but somehow we'll manage. I don't tolerate failures, and we'll find a way to play your music. Your friend Casals–the cellist–has asked for the score. He's willing to help with rehearsals. I welcome him, since Bavagnoli has so many other works to prepare for. And you'll just have to work with Bavagnoli–in all fairness, I brought him over to replace Toscanini. To do Italian operas, so–"

"Not Spanish," says Granados.

"That's right. But as I've said, we're going to find ways to make this successful."

"And how do you define success?" asks Granados.

Gatti smiles, like a cat swallowing goldfish. "I'm glad you ask, maestro. Personally, I agree with Verdi, who judged all operas by their measure of success with the public. A few years before he died, Verdi gave me this advice: 'read most attentively the reports of the box office. These, whether you like it or not, are the only documents that measure success or failure, and they admit of no argument, and represent not mere opinions, but facts. If the public comes, the objective is attained. If not–the theatre is intended to be full, not empty. That's something you should always remember.' Verdi's own words. That's how I define success, and I hope you don't disagree."

Periquet's anxiety is evident as he squirms in his chair.

"Another thing, maestro," Gatti continues, as if Periquet were not in the room, "I'd suggest you don't make any more statements to the press about yours being 'the only true Spanish opera.' Personally, I don't believe in talking to the press. I have an annual press conference to announce the schedule for the next season. I hand it to the reporters, and that's about it. You know why? The music should speak for itself–if composed and performed well–instead of people promoting their work or their performances. The very best don't have to do that. Besides, over here people are fond of Bizet's *Carmen* and you'll simply antagonize them if you say yours is 'the only true Spanish opera.'"

"I understand your point about being careful with the press," replies Granados, "and I regret what I said to the reporters. I'd hardly recovered from the trip when they descended on me. But the essence of what I said is true. Rossini wrote *Il Barbiere di Siviglia*–in Italian–without ever having been in Sevilla or even in España, and Bizet wrote *Carmen* without any real understanding of the country. His libretto was in French, not Spanish. The *Habanera* was not his own, it was lifted from a melody by Sebastian Yradier, who was Basque and lived in Cuba. The story was based on a tale by Mérimée, so there wasn't anything authentically Spanish about it! If you'll forgive me, Monsieur Gatti, my experience is that most Frenchmen consider Spaniards to be somehow inferior, no matter what the topic–art, music, food, wine, intelligence, culture–and of course it's evident to anyone with minimal powers of observation. So my statement *was* valid, wouldn't you agree?"

"Your points are well taken," says Gatti, backing up, "but I'd never discuss them with reporters. Now, we haven't discussed dancing and choreography. As you know, we have our own ballerinas here."

"You have Spanish dancers in your company?" asks Granados.

"No. Our lead dancer is from Italia. Rosina Galli. Young, but an excellent ballerina. Danced with the Chicago Opera, and joined the Met when Chicago curtailed their season. It was the war."

"I believe the dancing and choreography should be authentically Spanish," says Granados. "For an opera about life in Madrid at the time of Goya. It's not about some place in Italia. There are excellent Spanish ballerinas."

Gatti raises his hands, choosing to suppress any direct confrontation. "Of course I'm willing to consider Spanish dancers. Do you have any in mind?"

"Yes," replies Granados. "I have someone in mind, who is very familiar with the opera and the dance scenes. Her name is Antonia Mercé. She's also young and attractive–perhaps not as young as your dancer. Antonia's very well known in Europe and is now touring South America. I know she's interested. What would you offer?"

Gatti shakes his head. "I'm willing to consider Spanish dancers, maestro, but certainly not ready to make an offer. I'm already paying Signorina Galli, whether she dances in your opera or not."

"Would you do me the courtesy of explaining what the terms of the contract would be if you accepted my recommendation?"

Gatti ponders. "Well, since I already have a fine ballerina, I wouldn't pay any travel to New York. But I would pay, let's say, three thousand British pounds per month for the duration of the run. For three months, including rehearsal time. That's the most I'd consider."

Granados nods. "All right. Now I've got to find her."

"As long as you understand there is no final commitment," says Gatti. "I've agreed only to consider it."

Granados smiles. "Signor Gatti, you convinced me that you'll do everything in your power to make *Goyescas* a success, so I'm sure you'll 'find a way' to include the very best dancer and choreographer."

Gatti laughs, recognizing that he's been undone by his own words, and reminds himself not to take this Spaniard too lightly.

From the Western Union office on 42nd Street, Granados sends a telegram to Antonia Mercé in Buenos Aires. He invites her to join him as choreographer and principal dancer in the production of *Goyescas*. She sends back a prompt acceptance. She'll come to New York soon after the holidays. Her husband, Carlos Marcelo Paz, will come with her. She apologizes for not having sent him an announcement when she and Paz were married in the Argentine capital last June. She assures Granados that her husband is a good man, and will not hinder her efforts to make the choreography a great success.

Good news! She's married. Will bring husband. Much less complicated. Married an Argentino–how fitting! Unless he locks her up–like Barrientos' ex-husband.

Delmonico's

Henry Schelling laughs with the aplomb of a man who can afford sharing the blessings of his and Lucie's birthright with others. "That's a wonderful question! I'm certain a New Yorker would never think to ask. Right, Luce? Of course not–no one in this city would dream of walking if there's a cab close by."

Granados smiles. "I ask, Henri, because I've seen people jump into a cab on the Broad-way simply to go around the corner! I'd never think to do that."

"Because you're European, and used to walking," says Lucie.

Granados shakes his head. "I'd just never think to do that. Who'd spend the money to go around the corner in a cab?"

"Money? Another wonderful question!" says Schelling. "You see, the people who won't walk a block without hailing a cab–they don't worry about how much it costs. They're more interested in getting there quickly. Time is money."

"And that's a wonderful explanation," says Granados. "People here do move more quickly. Everything moves more quickly."

Schelling turns to Amparo. "Now, do you and the maestro walk everywhere in Barcelona?"

Amparo, not trusting her French, smiles.

Schelling repeats the question, this time "walking" his fingers across the table.

Amparo's eyes brighten. "Mais oui, I do walk. Je suis une–I'm a frugal Catalana. Is that correct–frugale?"

Lucie leans close to Amparo, "Yes, that's correct. Or you can say, 'économe.' And the maestro? Does he walk?"

Amparo shakes her head. "Not so much. He used to walk always, but now he takes great pleasure in his moto. Moto-cicleta?"

Schelling laughs. "And well he should!" he exclaims, extending and twisting his fists as if to rev a cycle's engine. He raises his glass of champagne and offers a toast to his guests.

"Thank you–for everything," says Granados. "To answer the obvious question, Titín and I walked here tonight from our hotel."

They are sitting at a table in the front room of Delmonico's Restaurant on the northeast corner of Fifth Avenue and 44th Street, three blocks from the Hotel Claridge. Founded ninety-two years ago on William Street, near the southern or "downtown" tip of Manhattan Island, by a Swiss sea captain, John Delmonico–who wanted to replicate the Parisian model of haute cuisine–Delmonico's has been a pioneer of "dining out" in a city where a slab of beef or a bowl of stew, accompanied by beer or rancid wine–and served at home–was the custom. Delmonico's has followed New York's most discriminating diners in their migration up Fifth Avenue, to 14th Street, then to 26th Street, and finally to this splendid five-story gourmand's palace in midtown on the edge of the theatre district.

There are other restaurants that aspire to be the choice of today's elite New Yorkers and visiting cognoscenti. The foremost of these are Sherry's, across the street from Delmonico's, and Rector's, located next to the Hotel Claridge. But the many upper-crusters who favor Delmonico's deride these contenders as "lobster palaces"–appealing to a racier clientele, places where a man can bring his chorus girl and dally with her in a private dining room. The police were once summoned to Sherry's to find an exotic dancer known as "Little Egypt" dancing from table to table in nothing more than a pair of mesh stockings. In contrast, Delmonico's–with its mirrored walls, mahogany furniture, frescoed ceilings, softer lighting, and discreet acoustics–feels more like a posh gentlemen's club.

"The first time my parents brought me here," recalls Lucie, "I saw Diamond Jim Brady sitting across the room. Oh dear, it was this very table where we're sitting tonight! He was with his honey, Lillian Russell. Easily the most famous actress in America."

"And I imagine them gorging themselves," says Schelling. He explains to Granados and Amparo that Brady, a railroad tycoon and philanthropist, was a prodigious bon vivant who'd devour a few dozen oysters on the half shell while deciding what to order. A typical lunch might include a pair of lobsters, some deviled crabs, two dozen clams, and slices of roast beef, topped off with one or two pies, washed down not by one of the celebrated sherries or clarets but with the beverages he drank exclusively: orange juice and lemon soda. In the evening–after the oysters–his meal might include a few crabs–soft-shelled if they were in season–several bowls of turtle soup, two whole ducks, six or seven lobsters, a large sirloin steak, a generous serving of turtle steak, and an assortment of vegetables, followed by a selection of pastries and a box of chocolates. Miss Russell, also prodigious at the table, had ballooned her once buxom but alluring shape after retiring from the stage three years ago.

Could 'Saco have kept pace with this Diamond Jim?

"And why this name?" asks Granados. "Did he give many diamonds to the famous actress?"

Schelling laughs. "He surely did–since Lillian was an insatiable collector of jewelry, but he got his nickname by wearing them around his own rather gargantuan belly!"

Schelling planned this evening at Delmonico's, extended and leisurely, to make the visitors from Barcelona feel more comfortable, give them practical suggestions to enhance their stay in New York, and inform them of upcoming events. The grace and lack of apparent intent with which he guides the conversation, and his efforts to include Amparo–pausing so Granados can translate from French to Castilian–aren't even recognized at the time. That is one of Schelling's gifts.

"I'm dying to hear about your crossing," says Schelling, "because I know it wasn't something you were eager to do." He nods across the table.

Granados shakes his head, wanting–now that he's safely on terra firma–to dismiss how much he dreaded the voyage. "Ah, it was a fine trip," he says, shrugging. "We had a decent piano–an Ortiz & Cussó, from Barcelona–and Llobet and I did a benefit concert for the French Red Cross."

"Splendid!" says Schelling.

"Well, a friend of mine arrived from London the same day–Wednesday," says Lucie. "She said the weather out there was terrible!"

Amparo leans forward, nodding. "Yes, it was–very terrible. Un orage, un tempete–for several days. We thought we'd never survive it!"

Schelling congratulates Granados for overcoming his fears.

Granados shakes his head. "No. I haven't overcome them, but I can't spend the rest of my life sitting in Barcelona with the rest of the world waiting for my music. I still have my fears, but I refuse to let my life be controlled by them!"

Lucie turns to Amparo. "Your hotel is close to the best stores, so I plan to be your shopping guide." She elaborates. "Your husband will be busy preparing his opera for its premiere, and all the other events scheduled for him, so I plan to be your personal guide while you're in our fair city."

"I don't want to pose any problème," says Amparo, her face reddening.

"No, it's no trouble, my dear Amparo. Regarde-toi, for me it will be the purest of pleasure. Who else has an opportunity to become the friend and the guide of Madame de Granados? We'll go to Altman's new store. Imagine twelve stories of shopping in an Italian Renaissance palazzo! And they deliver everything to your hotel. You and I, Amparo! We'll have more fun than the boys!"

Schelling turns to Granados. "And I've found you a splendid place to practice. We have a friend, Malvina Hoffman, a sculptor who studied with Rodin–she's quite good. Her late father was Richard Hoffman. Soloed with von Bulow at the Philharmonic. It's his piano, a Chickering, which he left her when he passed away. I've found it quite acceptable. And her home isn't far from the Met."

"Not far?" Granados asks.

Schelling smiles playfully. "Oh, it's an easy walk for any good Catalan. Now, I told Malvina I'd let her know when I can bring you 'round. How anxious are you to practice?"

"Quite anxious. Haven't played much for two weeks."

"Then I'll try for tomorrow or the next day. Meanwhile, Rudi wants you to come for a small reception. Schirmers is on 43rd Street, just around the corner. A short cab ride–no, I'm joking. And Rudi's anxious for you to meet the cultural attaché from Argentina. Seems they want you to bring *Goyescas* to Buenos Aires."

"El Teatro Colón?"

"Yes, indeed. Rudi believes they'll make you a handsome offer. Of course, you'd have to take another boat ride."

"Henri, please put that out of your mind. I will go anywhere to present *Goyescas*."

Can't always be storming on the ocean!

"Bravo! Then I'll make arrangements with Rudi so you can meet the Argentines. Now, let's see–what else?" He reaches into the inside pocket of his jacket, and pulls out an envelope. "Here. I've made you a copy of the events. At least the ones I know about."

Events? So like Henri to have list of events!

Granados opens the envelope and scans the list.

Christmas Dinner at the Schellings
Visit with Archer M. Huntington at the Hispanic Society of America–an award will be presented
Party honoring Granados at Otto Kahn's
Recital with Casals at the Ritz-Carlton Hotel
Robert and Mildred Bliss arrive week before premier
Dress rehearsal of *Goyescas* two days before premiere
Celebration at Sherry's after the premiere hosted by Schirmer's
Recording sessions for the Aeolian Company and recital with Anna Fitziu at Aeolian Hall
Three more performances of *Goyescas* at the Met
Other events to be added

Granados is amazed, delighted, and overwhelmed. He shakes his head. "I can see you've been busy. How can I ever thank you?"

Schelling is nonchalent. "I had no difficulty. Except with Signor Gatti-Casazza."

Granados laughs. "Yes. Presenting *Goyescas* was not his idea."

"It wasn't. And waiting for Gatti to come around would have taken too long. He's an excellent impresario. And likes to be the source of new ideas. But once he sees the light–and now he has, he'll go to the ends of the earth."

"Did having an 'angel' make him see the light?"

Schelling seems unnerved. "Gatti said there was an angel?"

Granados nods.

Schelling takes a deep breath. "I've been meaning to tell you, there is a very generous person who's agreed to underwrite the introduction of your opera. Made all the difference in the Met's decision. And in Gatti's seeing the light."

"Who is the angel, Henri?"

Schelling clears his throat. "Well, there's no reason you shouldn't know. It's Archer Huntington. Of the Hispanic Society." He leans over the table, and says in a whisper, "He wants it to be an anonymous gift, so everyone in town doesn't come knocking on his door."

Huntington, of course. Pieces of the puzzle falling into place.

Schelling, composed again, adds, "Once Gatti put it on the Met's schedule, I went to the others. All I had to do was mention you were coming. You see, New Yorkers love a celebrity, and for the next two months, New York will be yours! You'll be the toast of the town!"

Malvina's Place

Granados is disoriented when he wakes up on a large divan in the studio of Malvina Hoffman's home on East 35th Street.

Where? Tiana? Puigcerda? No. Americà. Nova York. Sculptor friend of Schelling. Malvina. Her father's Chickering. Taking short rest. Sound of klaxons honking outside.

He sits up and puts on his shoes, stands up and looks around the large studio. The piano is across the room, behind a screen arranged so he won't be distracted. Next to the divan is a large fireplace, behind it are bookcases built into the wall, and around it are two lamp tables and a coffee table. At the far end of the studio, bathed in natural light, is a long work table covered with carved stone and castings of plaster and bronze, next to a pair of easels. He remembers the sculptor apologizing for the chill, bringing a large fur robe, and covering him with it as he lay down for his siesta.

After arriving this morning with Schelling, Granados spent three hours practicing on the grand piano made in Boston by Chickering & Sons that Malvina inherited from her father upon his death six years ago. After a lunch of soup, bread, and tea, Granados sauntered over to the enormous, velvet-covered divan–long enough for two people to lie down head to toe and wide enough for three lying side by side. He admired its size for a moment, calling it a "monument du repos,"–which amused Malvina–then flung himself onto it, asking her to rouse him in two hours so he'd be on time for his first rehearsal at the Met.

As he puts on his jacket, he sees Malvina, a tall young woman in her late twenties, walking toward him from her work area. She's dressed in a long beige skirt, white blouse with an upturned collar, loosened blue tie matching the color of her eyes, and an artist's coat that hangs to her ankles. Her chestnut hair is piled onto the top of her head to keep it out of the way, her wide handsome face glows without makeup, and she moves more with purpose than grace.

"You're awake. Are you rested?" she asks. Her voice is deep and a bit guttural.

"Mmnn. Oui, merci bien."

"I was afraid the klaxons would wake you. This used to be such a quiet neighborhood! Oh, I forgot to ask: is the piano satisfactory?"

"Oui, merci."

"I had the tuner come last week. And nobody's played it since. Schelling's the only one who ever plays it. He'll come by at tea-time, lift up the top, and play for an hour or two. Such a dear man! But he's been out of town, and I don't play. My father said pianos should be tuned every single day. He could hear the difference, and I'd venture you can too. Not me. But I'll take your word that it's satisfactory. And I'll keep it tuned. Please come again. You're welcome any time."

"I'd like to come every day–if it's convenient for you. In the mornings."

"Fine, I'll count on you. I can leave a key when I'm out for errands. And we'll have lunch about one-thirty. You can rest, and I'll see you're on your way to rehearsal by four o'clock."

Granados shakes his head. "That would be simply splendid! How might I repay your generosity?"

Her laugh is a guffaw. "Repay me? When I can have one of the great composers playing for me while I work? Why, I'll be the most envied artist in New York!"

Malvina Hoffman is the youngest of five children of the pianist Richard Hoffman and one of his students, Fidelia Lamson. When Fidelia's parents frowned on her romance with a "common musician," the pair eloped. "I know it's common for students to have romances with their maestros," Hoffman says to Granados. "In my parent's case, it wasn't courtly love from afar. Not a bit. It was the real thing."

The real thing. As mine is with Clotilde. Missing her so!

"Before you go," Malvina says, "I've been eager to ask you about the article in the *New York Times* yesterday."

He shrugs. "I haven't seen it. En anglais–I wouldn't understand it. Was it by Francisco Gandara?"

"Yes. With some fascinating details of your life. I suppose you know that, since you did the interview."

"I was told that the article would appear soon, only that."

"Would you like to know what Gandara said about you?"

"Of course."

She goes to the dining table and returns with the article. "The first thing is about Gatti-Casazza being in Paris when the war broke out and seeing an opportunity to get your opera *Goyescas* for the Met. It makes him sound like some sort of scavenger."

Granados' eyes widen. "Gatti? That's a joke! He may have been in Paris, but he's anything but enthusiastic about my opera! What else did Gandara write?"

"Here. An account of you as a ten-year-old student in Paris playing for Dom Pedro, the Emperor of Brasil. The emperor was so pleased he said you were the only majestic one in the room and he kissed your forehead."

He laughs. "I never played for any Brasilian emperor! A few years ago I played for the grandson of the last emperor–the one who was deposed. The grandson's name was also Pedro. He was enjoying life in Paris. How did Gandara get that so twisted up? What else?"

"He says you are an ardent sportsman, an enthusiastic automobilist, and a motor-cyclist. That some of your pupils gave you the motor-cycle on your saint's day. That you were about to start for London and were plunged into gloom because you had to depart for America without taking your first ride on the machine."

Granados sighs. "I'm not any kind of 'sportsman.' Where would I find time for that? Yes, I know how to drive an automobile and a motorcycle. With a side car, so it doesn't tip over. Which some of my students did help me pay for. More or less. But I've never gone to London! What else?"

Malvina hesitates. "Well, here he says you are usually alert and gay, but you have moments of deep sadness, in which you become meditative and melancholy. The slightest gesture can plunge you into what Leopardi–whoever that is–calls passing madness."

"Leopardi? The Italian poet of despair. Wrote about the futility of life and unrequited love. That there's no consolation in this world. I'm not that pessimistic!"

"Ooof! I hope he's wrong! Your reporter friend writes that at such times you complain like a querulous child. Then you smile, once more your lively self. Dear maestro, I'm afraid it's not very flattering."

Not very flattering? Makes me sound like a lunatic!

Granados shakes his head. "The reporter didn't hear these things from me!"

Malvina puts the newspaper down on the coffee table. "It's not for me to judge, but I think you could be more careful with the journalists."

Central Park

Pau Casals leads the way down a path at the upper end of New York's Central Park, skirting the large reservoir a few blocks from their starting point at his home on East 96th Street. As they walk southward, with a row of elm trees ringing the slate-gray water on their right and apartment buildings across Fifth Avenue on their left, he points to the large complex of buildings whose outline is directly ahead of them. "That's the Metropolitan Museum–it's New York's El Prado," says Casals over his shoulder as Granados quickens his pace. As if they were walking in the Parc de la Ciutadella in Barcelona, or the Bois de Boulogne near where Casals lived in Paris, or the beach in front of Villa Casals at Sant Salvador. Casals forging ahead, pointing things out and talking over his shoulder, with Granados trying to keep up. In three-quarters time. Long walks and long talks, this afternoon for the first time in a city of the New World, on the far side of the Atlantic, far from their homeland. It's colder in this new venue, and the wind chills their bones as it whips off the surface of the reservoir.

"How was the crossing?" asks Casals. "Uneventful, I hope."

No reason to deny it. Don't have to pretend with Pau.

"Hardly," Granados replies. "The crossing was very rough! Our ship was stopped twice by military police. And I'd forgotten my passport, so I could have ended up in a French dungeon or the Tower of London! And the weather was terrible. We had just a few hours of calm in the entire two weeks. The rest of the time–we had a storm that never let up. Thought we'd never survive! One afternoon Titín and I lay down in our cabin, embraced each other, and asked God to save us."

"It sounds dreadful. Your worst fears."

"Exactly. But you know, Pau, after surviving such a crossing, I realize I've got to push through these fears. Can't let them rule my life."

Just before reaching the museum, they turn onto the path that leads them toward the West Side. "You must take the time to see the museum," says Casals.

"I've been there already," says Granados. He and Amparo went there on Sunday afternoon with Periquet, who wasted no time finding the three works by

Goya: a large portrait of Don Sebastian Martínez y Perez, clad smartly in a blue and black striped jacket; a smaller portrait, entitled *Jewess of Tangiers*; and one of the *Caprichos*–Number 60, depicting an experiment in which a nude witch is trying to teach a nude man to fly. With an enormous mountain goat looking down on them, two cats, and a skull laying on the ground. The painter's notes are sparse, suggesting that if the man pays careful attention, he can follow the witch into the sky. Granados was much less interested in explaining it than Periquet.

They also saw several paintings by Joaquín Sorolla, two of them on loan from the Hispanic Society of America: *Beaching the Boat, València* and *After the Bath*–depicting a young woman just out of the surf, her wet yellow bathing suit clinging to her, and a young man with a large yellow straw hat holding a white robe that he's prepared to wrap around her. "It's the perfectly gorgeous light of València," says Granados, "and the deepest blue sea. You can hear the surf! And I was captivated by a portrait of Sorolla's wife."

His wife's named Clotilde–throat's parched at the sound of her name!

Granados explains that he saw the Sorolla last month at Rusiñol's place in Sitges. The artist was spending the autumn months at work on a scene to represent Catalunya for the series of large murals he's creating under contract with Archer Huntington, designed to fill an entire gallery at the Hispanic Institute on West 155th Street. Sorolla seemed fatigued, and complained of frequent headaches.

"Huntington," Casals asks. "Senyor àngel?"

Granados shakes his head. "I don't know if he's my angel, Pau. Gatti said there's an angel, otherwise he wouldn't have accepted *Goyescas*, and Schelling–who knows everyone and everything–suggested it is Huntington. I'm just glad to have a venue."

"You've certainly gotten a fast start in this town," says Casals. "You've been to the museum. You've had dinner at Delmonico's. And you've been interviewed for the leading newspaper. I'd say you're getting right into the New York way of life!"

Granados laughs. "No, I'll never get right into this way of life." He admits he's dazzled by the lights of New York, far brighter than in any other city he's seen. The buildings–topped by the world's tallest, the Woolworth–are glittering pinnacles rising to the sky. The pace of life is so much faster than in Barcelona or even Paris. There's breathless haste and constant tension, feverish energy, and impatience at the loss of even one minute. The shiny new hansom cabs are now equipped with meters that keep track of the time and how much money is to be charged. How better to let passengers know that time equals money? Granados is impressed by the importance of money in every small detail of life, and by attitudes that seem based solely on their pecuniary value. "It seems," he says, "that rich people here are desperate to let everyone know how wealthy they are. Wealthy people back home don't do that, except for a few with royal pretensions."

"My wife's a typical New Yorker," says Casals. "She takes the jewels and furs for granted. Loves the fast pace. She'll take a cab ride of two hundred meters and think nothing of it. Put her in Sant Salvador and it's much too slow. She feels like an alien there. Of course, there's the language."

"Ah, the language!" says Granados. "It's just the reverse here for me." He's not able to speak and understand the language for the first time in his life–except briefly in Paris while he was learning French. For various reasons, he never went to Milano or Roma, never to Vienna or Berlin, nor to London. So until he arrived in New York, language was not an issue. He can converse in Catalan with Casals, Castilian with other Spaniards, and French with the Schellings, Hoffman, Blisses, Gatti, Paderewski and Kreisler. But the conversations around him, newspapers and reviews, and the chatter and joking in bars and restaurants are all in a language that is entirely foreign. The disparity in language engenders his feeling of alienation, the familiar old feeling of not belonging. He broods about Goya having to live deaf among people whose voices and laughter, whose plotting and treachery he could no longer hear, whose words of praise and love were simply the movement of lips without sound.

How Goya must have suffered! Yet he persevered.

Casals turns his head toward Granados. "So you played for the Emperor of Brasil when you were ten years old?"

"You read the article?"

"Of course. The *New York Times* is the leading paper in town. Nearly everyone reads it. And how was it you were a student in Paris at the tender age of ten?"

Granados raises his arms and looks to the sky. "You don't really want to know. You want to torture me!"

"Yes," says Casals without expression. "And the motorcycle?" he asks. "Your students bought it for you? I'd like to have such students!"

"It's much more complicated. When Gandara interviewed me back home, he asked about the moto and I told him–because Titín was all ears–that a group of my students had raised the money. She'd have been furious if I'd paid for it myself, and more upset if she knew where the money really came from."

"Your romantic friend in Tiana?" asks Casals.

Granados scowls. "Heavens no! Salvador bought it for his youngest son, Juanito, and when Carmen found out, she put a stop to that. She didn't think

Juanito at fifteen had the good sense to come in out of the rain, much less drive a moto. So it happens I was thinking of getting one, so I could go up and down from home to the Sala–and of course to ride out into the countryside."

"Of course. The countryside around Tiana."

"Yes. And that's truthfully how I got my moto, believe it or not."

Casals grins. "It's far more believable than the rest of the article!"

As they make the turn by the Metropolitan Museum of Art, Granados asks Casals if he'll help with rehearsals at the Met. "From what Gatti said the other day, the conductor's unhappy with the score."

"Ah, Bavagnoli–he's more of a prima donna than the sopranos! But I think the problem is that your score is way above his head. He doesn't understand it, that's plain. You're right, he does need help getting the players ready."

"Will you help?" asks Granados. "I don't see how I can do it alone."

"I do have time to help with the score," says Casals, "but the libretto is another matter."

"I know–I'll find another librettist for the next one!"

"Anything else?" asks Casals.

"Well, the choreography. Gatti isn't very excited about bringing in Antonia Mercé."

"La Argentina? Why not? She'll do a great job. Am I missing something?"

Granados shakes his head. "No, there's nothing. She's simply the best one for the job. No matter what. So I invited her to come up from Argentina."

"No matter that you had a fling with her?"

"I told you?"

"You didn't need to–it was the slight pause before you said her name. But I think the problem is that Gatti also has someone in mind. His bailarina, Rosina Galli."

"Obviously, you know more."

"His bailarina is very young and pretty, and an excellent dancer. And I think she's danced her way into his heart. That could be a problem, especially as you've invited another dancer to come to New York."

As they cross Madison Avenue to the East Side, Granados breaks into Casals' rambling, repetitive monologue about his difficulties with Susan Metcalfe. "Of course there's a lot on my mind, Pau. This is my first time in Amèrica and my first world premiere of a major work. I never got the right presentation for '*María del Carman* or *Follet*, so this premiere takes on even more importance. But it's not the culmination of my work. It's just the beginning! My dream is not about just one opera, it's to become–a nostra pàtria–the same as Chopin was to Poland, and Schumann was to Germany, and Saint-Saens to Francia, and Grieg to Norway. I'm convinced that I can occupy that place! The music is here, and here." He points to his heart and the side of his head. "It's inside me and what I have to do is make a way for it to escape, just as I did with *Goyescas*. Anyway, I had to tell you that. Thank you for listening!" he concludes, wiping away tears before they become tiny globules of ice.

The Oyster Bar

Granados' protegée Paquita Madriguera is in New York to arrange her first American tour. She and her mother, Francisca Rodón, are staying with Rosa Culmell, who's settled here with her children in an apartment on West 80th Street. Paquita and her mother are having lunch today with Granados and Amparo in the Oyster Bar at Grand Central Station, an enormous place under tiled and vaulted ceilings, which clatters with pottery set onto marble counters, and is redolent of its celebrated oyster stew. "A place for anyone craving fresh seafood," according to Periquet, who discovered the Oyster Bar his second day in town, "and an easy walk from the hotel."

After lunch, Granados intends to return to the Claridge for a nap while the women attend a reception hosted by Susan Metcalfe. As they put on their coats and caps to brave the chilling winds of late December, Rodón says she's not feeling well and sends her daughter and Amparo off with an abraçada. She lingers, and when they're alone she turns to Granados.

"Can you spare a moment, maestro?" she asks with palpable irritation.

Granados nods and steps back from the entryway of the Oyster Bar.

"You've been behaving like a child who's being punished for some sort of mischief. Or someone suffering a great deal of pain. What's the matter?"

He dissembles. "Oh, I'm just not feeling well. It's nothing."

"Nothing? You invited us for lunch, and you've acted like a sick puppy the whole time! Do you realize you didn't once look over at Amparo?"

"I haven't been feeling well, Francisca," he replies, with only glancing eye contact. "I had a migraine for two days and a night of fever. I'm worried the stomach problem could come back–I can't let that happen at such a critical time. You know that, Francisca."

"But that's not why you're acting like a sick puppy. Is it?"

Though she's been critical since learning of Granados' romance with Clotilde nearly four years ago, Rodón–a friend of both Amparo and Clotilde–is perhaps the only person with a view of the entire situation, and one of very few to whom he could reveal his torment. There's no point dodging her, so he describes his profound longing for Clotilde. Being away from her for so long.

"Come now!" Rodón says with impatience, "it must give you shame to behave with such indignity. Don't you see how much poor Amparo is suffering? Your attitude is loathsome!"

"I can't disagree with you," he replies, "and it's very bad for me to make her suffer. But sometimes I just can't help it! It's beyond my will and my reason. Francisca, do you know what the poor woman told me the other night? With her eyes filled with tears? She'd taken my temperature and said I had no fever. She told me, 'Enrique, heal yourself! It makes no difference to me that you love her, but I ask you–I beg you, try to heal yourself. If you don't get well, you'll never see her again.' That's pretty impressive, isn't it?"

Rodón glares at him, then bursts with anger. "Enrique–I hate you!"

The Great Caruso

As he's leaving the Met to walk to his hotel, Granados recognizes Enrico Caruso standing on the corner of Broadway and West 40th Street, surrounded by an entourage of admirers. He hasn't seen him since the tenor's first and only appearance at El Liceu nearly twelve years ago, but there's no doubt it's Caruso: the powerful upper body, attired in a light gray, double-breasted topcoat over a dark gray suit, black fedora on his oversized head, light gray spats buttoned over his black shoes–and as Granados comes closer–a brilliant white shirt and bright red bow tie visible at the opening of the topcoat. Caruso is lighting a cigarette, one of the forty or fifty pungent Egyptians he smokes every day, as always through a black-and-gold cigarette holder.

Seeing that Caruso is occupied, Granados starts to walk around him. There is eye contact. Caruso, having been told by Gatti that Granados is in town, hails him. "Maestro! It's Maestro Granados, n'est-ce pas?" He breaks away from his entourage. "Excuse me," he says to them, "I have a very important meeting with Maestro Granados." The two men shake hands and quickly discover they're both heading back to their hotels, located on consecutive corners along Broadway.

"Buon giorno, Signor Caruso!" A top-hatted doorman in a maroon uniform festooned with gold braid pulls open one of the brass doors and they enter the Knickerbocker Hotel where Caruso occupies a fourteen-room apartment on the ninth floor. After seven years in residence, he's known to every concierge, desk clerk, bellman, bartender, waiter, and housekeeping maid in the hotel. He and Granados sweep through the lobby. "Good afternoon, Coxworth...bon jour, Marcel...buon giorno, Raffaello." They enter the softly lit, dark-paneled bar and Caruso asks the maitre d' for a table in the far corner, out of the traffic.

Once seated, Caruso points to a large painting hung behind the bartenders. Divided into three panels, the work stretches nearly the length of the mahogany counter and brass rail of the bar. It depicts "Old King Cole," who in the mythic verse "was a merry old soul, who called for his pipe and called for his bowl and called for his fiddlers three." The artist is Maxfield Parrish, considered a craftsman–not a fine artist–but whose work is better known and admired in New York than any of the Impressionists. In his art, Parrish conveys a romantic vision of life. This endears him especially to women, who display his calendars in their kitchens and at year's end cut off the lower portions, framing and hanging Parrish's illustrations in their parlors and boudoirs.

Caruso recalls their only, brief meeting in Barcelona, while he was at war with the impresario Bernis and much of the Liceu audience. "I'd like to forget that chapter in my life," he admits, thrusting his head forward, "but how can I? The audience was so rude, hissing when the soprano sang 'e il sol del'anima' out of tune. I was offended–for her! They didn't deserve an encore of 'la donna mobile.' Then Bernis said my pay should be cut in half! In half! Santa Maria! Ah well, that was long ago." Caruso reaches across the table and claps Granados' shoulder. He says he's thrilled to be singing *Pagliacci* the same night as the world premiere of *Goyescas*.

"The honor is mine," says Granados, tipping his head forward.

"What a combination are we!" says Caruso. "Enrique and Enrico. Two men with the same name. We should charge them double, n'est-ce pas? Martinelli showed me your score. The duet in the garden, in the third tableau–after the wonderful aria by the soprano. And which soprano? You must be disappointed Bori can't sing it. But this young Fitziu will do well."

"Yes. I heard her sing in *La Traviata* in Barcelona. She'll be fine."

Caruso rambles. He's also scheduled to sing *Rigoletto* when María Barrientos makes her Metropolitan debut next month. And when Geraldine Farrar returns from making a film in Hollywood, Caruso and Farrar will sing five performances of Bizet's *Carmen* at the Met.

"You were right, of course, about *Carmen*," says Caruso about Granados' statement to the press. "Gatti didn't like it, but you were absolutely right. *Carmen* is French, undeniably French, nothing but French. Using Spain as a backdrop. Some of it's quite beautiful, and I've enjoyed singing Don José." He laughs. "But never more than in Spain itself–the only time I've been there since that disaster in Barcelona. You see, we were coming here from Naples and had to stop in Gibraltar, so I thought, what a wonderful chance to have some paella!"

"Paella?" Granados is surprised that anyone outside Catalunya has ever heard of it.

"Ah, but I mean good paella! Not just throwing some clams into a pan of rice. Of course, there was no place in Gibraltar, so we–Bori and Farrar and Giulio Setti and I–crossed the Spanish border and found a tavern that looked just like a set from *Carmen*–even a poster of the upcoming corrida. The tavern keeper said the torero in the poster was Guerrita, who made two thousand dollars for every appearance. When I told him I made even more than that, he was very, very doubtful. He said I looked more like a picador–the one who sticks a lance in the bull?–and he said picadors don't make that kind of money. So I had to admit I was a tenor, and as the words left my mouth, the tavern keeper said 'Madre de Dios, you are Caruso!' and so of course Farrar and I had to sing the duet from the second act for him. We got to the part when Carmen tells Don José, 'Je vais danser en votre honneur,' and we were paralyzed with laughter–neither of us could continue, because Farrar and I, well, we'd been entertaining each other privately in Paris that summer while poor Toscanini was not on the scene to be jealous, so in that little Spanish tavern I took a rose out of the vase–remember the little flower that Carmen throws at him earlier? and the scent of this little flower sustained his love for her during his suffering in prison?–anyway, I got to my knees holding the rose and Farrar threw her arms around me. And for just a moment I forgot we'd gone there for the paella." He shakes his head. "Seriously, we've never sung it so well," he says, his voice softening and dropping well into the baritone range.

Caruso lights another cigarette and orders another bottle of champagne. The flame of his lighter highlights the fleshy expanse of his square clean-shaven face, as well as the dark hedges of his eyebrows and shadows under his generous eyes, the creased corners of his mouth, and the large cleft in the middle of his chin. Through the makeup and headgear that are designed to transform him on stage into the clown Canio in *I Pagliacci*, the nobleman Des Grieux in *Manon*, the doomed lover Rhadames in *Aida*, the cynical Duke of Mantua in *Rigoletto*, the soldier Don José in *Carmen*, and the Parisian painter Rodolfo in *La Boheme*, the audience is willing to forget that this strong paisano face could belong only to

Caruso. Perhaps only in the title role of *Samson* is his identity disguised. But in that role, as in the others, there's always the singular voice.

"And how are you getting on with Giulio Gatti?" he asks.

Granados snickers. "Oh pretty well. I think. At our first meeting, he told me and my librettist that presenting our opera was not his idea. Not his at all! And it wouldn't be presented without a generous angel. He made it clear–quoting from Verdi no less, that unless an opera fills the house, it's not successful–regardless of its artistic merits."

Caruso throws his large head back, howling. "Yes, indeed, that's Gatti. He's like that with everyone. I'd be shocked if he deferred to you because you're new in town."

"He surely did not!"

"We've all felt Giulio's lash. One day I told him about an offer I'd received from Oscar Hammerstein of the Manhattan, the Met's rival. If Gatti ever worried about any thing in this world, it was about losing one of his singers to Hammerstein! So I told Giulio that I'd been offered twice as much as he's paying me. You can imagine that got his attention! The next day, he said he'd match the offer and pay me twice as much. But there was a catch–he'd hire second-rate singers and second-rate players to make up the difference. I acted as if he'd insulted me, and told him I never intended to ask more than two thousand five hundred for each performance. Where did he get that idea?" Caruso takes a cigarette from his holder, inserts a fresh one, and lights up. He blows a stream of smoke toward the ceiling. "You know, that's a lot of money! I never dreamed of making that much. I used to sing the canzoni in a place called Caffè dei Mannesi in Napoli–without that my family would have starved!"

"Yes, yes! I played in a wretched place called Café de las Delicias. Long hours, cheap music, poor pay. But after my father died, we needed the income to survive."

Caruso pulls a gold pillbox out of a vest pocket and swallows two of the pills with a swig of champagne. "Damn headaches!" he exclaims, rubbing the base of his skull. "If they're really bad, I want to kill myself. But I have to sing. Do you get them?"

"I have it up here," replies Granados, placing his hands on his temples. "Mine are the migraines. I must go into a dark room and stay there until the pain goes away. I can't possibly perform."

"Mine are back here," says Caruso. "Feels like a stiffening–a cramping of the muscles in the back of my neck. They're coming more frequently and they're more painful. Like two steel cables pulling the back of my head down. Otherwise I'm healthy–except for the digestive problems that come and go."

Granados chuckles. "I have those too."

Caruso frowns. "We're just like brothers. Two poor boys named Henri, singing and playing in cafés. With headaches and digestive problems. Ah, but you're married with six children. My life has been less–shall we say–complicated."

Granados raises his glass. "I wouldn't bet on that, Henri." As he drinks, he notices a tall young woman with cinnamon red hair swirled to the top of her head, dressed in a long dark blue cape, entering the bar with two older women. The maitre d' shows them to a table in the middle of the room, and as the tall young woman removes her cape she looks over at Caruso and Granados.

Caruso leans over. "Quelle rousse magnifique! Even in this land of beautiful signorinas, this one is remarkable. I can't take my eyes from her!"

With her cape removed, the young woman's slender arms and rounded shoulders and the tops of her breasts are exposed to the flickering light from a candle on her table. Her moss green tulle theatre gown by a Parisian couturier is topped by a tight bodice, beaded and embroidered with rhinestones, and covered by a sheer black tunic. It's brash and provocative, either suggesting that Paris' high fashion cabal still believes the war will soon be over, or that the proximity of battlefields is no reason for couture to be sacrificed. Most especially, it's daring to hang a gown so precariously on such a pretty young American, in a city that would still prefer to keep its back turned to the ancient corruptions of Europe.

"Looking back at a woman can be dangerous," says Caruso, shifting his chair and fixing his gaze on Granados. "I should know. I saw a woman once–quite a beautiful woman, no, a goddess–at the Garden Theatre, here in New York. We let our eyes make love. When we were introduced after the performance, I asked if she'd be at the matinée the next day. I was singing *Tosca*. We met after the performance and there was no turning back." Caruso shakes his head. "Such a splendid woman! Well educated, an excellent pianist, she traveled the world, spoke several languages. And bellissima! Like so many Americanas. Like that one."

Soon after, the young woman comes to their table, her fragrance close behind. Caruso rises and steps lightly around the table. The candlelight dances on the bareness of her extended arm, and as Granados rises Caruso takes her hand and kisses it.

"Buon giorno, signorina," says Caruso with a practiced, syrupy tone.

"'Giorno, Signor Caruso," says the young woman sweetly. "When I saw you, I wasn't sure, but yes indeed, you are il tenore di l'opera Metropolitano. E vero?"

Caruso notes the American accent. "Ah, si. Io sono Caruso."

"Mi chiamo Penelope Havermeyer."

"Ah, Penelope–wife of Odysseus," says Caruso teasingly.

"Yes, I suppose it's a name with great mythological value. You may call me Penny." She turns and introduces herself to Granados. Caruso says he's a "famous maestro" from Spain. "Yes, Señor Granados," she says in flawless Castilian, "I'm so terribly excited about your premiere. I've simply given my heart to Goya. Spent endless days at El Prado. Persuaded my mother to buy one for our home. Bravo to you! Felicitaciones!"

The young woman turns to Caruso. "My family has a box at the opera, and I never miss a performance, and I must confess–if you'll forgive my boldness, I've become quite devoted to you. Your voice, your magnificent stage presence. I'm not embarrassed to say you've become my favorite tenor, ever since your American debut. I heard you sing in Milano the year before, and when you came on stage as the Duke of Mantua, I was swept away. Of course, I was a young girl then. Très ingénue."

"Of course," says Caruso, releasing her hand, and seizing the moment. "Of course you'd not still be swept away."

Her laugh is like the chiming of a treble carillon. "Oh, but I am! Mais, oui! Absolutely. But that's not why I came over."

Caruso's smile stretches from earlobe to earlobe. "Of course not, signorina."

Penelope Havermeyer's pale green eyes cut through the frivolity, and her nostrils flare at the base of a thin, elegant nose. He may be the most famous tenor in the world, but her family was one of the original subscribers when the new Metropolitan Opera was founded in 1880, and since then the Havermeyers have owned their own box. "In fact," she says, somehow blending the dulcet tones of a lyre with the ping of a hammer, "I came over to ask a small favor."

Granados, though her fragrance is pervasive and her allure is bewitching, enjoys the role of spectator.

Penelope wife of Odysseus–young and gorgeous–he'd best not take her lightly. Didn't come over for seduction. Softened him up so he'd let down his guard. Controls his eyes. Now she'll ask for something.

"Ah, signorina. How could I possibly refuse a small favor?" asks Caruso in a voice which might precede his breaking into "La Donna e mobile."

Penelope Havermeyer shuns the *Rigoletto* role of the lovesick barmaid, Maddalena, and stays her course. "A very small favor, Signor Caruso. We're planning a benefit to raise money for the French Red Cross. I've been asked to recruit the artistic talent. Of course I thought immediately of you, Signor Caruso. Who else could ensure a grand success? And I'll use every power of persuasion to convince you to say 'yes.' Will you agree to perform?" she asks.

Caruso shakes his head. "Do you have a date? And a venue?"

"We're planning on the middle of March" she says. At Carnegie Hall, of course. That's being arranged. My task is to convince you."

Caruso laughs. "Well, if we were to meet quite frequently and get to know each other, I'm sure you'd succeed." He hesitates, watching her stiffen. "No, signorina, it's a joke–une petite plaisanterie. No, no. I'd be happy to do it, provided I'm not scheduled to sing that night."

After she leaves their table, Caruso admits to being disarmed by the young woman. "Saying 'yes' to people has caused me a lot of trouble," he sighs. "Ah well! Life can't be so orderly it puts us to sleep. In my complicated life, I need someone to keep everything in its proper compartment. Compartiment–that's what you call it?"

"Yes, it's compartiment–they help me avoid a complete breakdown. I have my students–they're here," Granados says, forming a pair of cylinders with his hands. "And my compositions–here. And my family–over there. And my patrons, Doctor Andreu and Carmen–over here. And so many friends–here and here and here. And–"

"And your lover, n'est-ce pas?" Caruso's eyes are twinkling.

Granados shrugs. "Ah, but I'm too busy for that." He laughs, realizing it's useless to pretend.

Caruso finds this hilarious. "You? Who tries to put the colors of Goya into music? You? From the land of Don Quijote? Pardonnes-moi, Granados, I am only a poor paisano napolitano, but–but, look at you! Look at your eyes–they tell me what your words cannot. Of course, it's none of my business."

"Un moment," says Granados, forming a larger cylinder with both hands and placing it over his heart. "Yes, there is one more compartiment. In here."

"I thought so!" Caruso exclaims. He lights up a cigarette and motions to the waiter for another bottle of champagne. "Too bad Toscanini decided not to return this season. I understand why, but it's still too bad. He would have taken your score and created magic."

"And why didn't he return?" asks Granados.

Caruso nods over and over. "I miss him! You know, for years and years we worked together. How many? Mmnn–I'd say about fifteen, since the new century. Toscanini's wonderful! Difficult. Demanding. He's memorized every single score. And if a singer gets lost, he'll sing it and make you feel like a worm! Oh, yes, I miss him! But you ask why he didn't return. There's no easy answer, but it's about the war. Toscanini–c'est très patriotique. When Italia entered the war, he was loyal to his homeland. I don't understand, you wouldn't understand. Art and politics–bad to combine them. This guerre horrible has alienated him from Puccini, who won't even go to benefits for the victims."

"I agree, it's a guerre horrible," Granados replies. "My country is neutral, so this war has nothing to do with me. But for victims of war–of course I'd help them."

"And we may all be victims," says Caruso. He pulls a pencil out of his jacket, and opens the menu to a blank page. "Do you mind if I make a sketch of you? It's very nice to use my hands and let my voice rest. I enjoy it very much–but only if you're agreeable."

"Je suis d'accord."

"Where were we? Yes, Toscanini. Last summer, after Italia entered the war, he went to the front with a military band–imagine, Maestro Toscanini with a military band! Toscanini's own son was wounded and lying in the hospital at Udine as his father moved with l'armée Italiana to battle against the Austrians. Near Monte Santo. The fighting was terrible, many soldiers falling on both sides. It seems Toscanini was able to ignore the carnage and somehow lead his little band so far into the battle that they were caught in the middle of it. Some were hit by the bullets and shrapnel flying through the air, and the bass drum was destroyed, but there was Toscanini, refusing to duck down, standing tall and directing his players, and after each piece crying, 'Viva Italia! Viva Italia!'"

Granados is astonished at the image of the thin, ascetic conductor standing in the midst of battle.

Caruso continues. "You won't catch me over there, not even singing the battle song from *Aida*–not me. After the war broke out, Gatti collected all of the Met people to take a boat from Napoli. What a crowd! Gatti and Toscanini and Giorgio Polacco and Farrar and Elisabeth Schumann and Frieda Hempel, and also Lucrezia Bori–your compatriote, she and I had just sung the second act of *Butterfly* in Roma, she has a wonderful voice and it's a tragedy she's having such problems with her throat. It was October and most of us were very nervous. We knew there were German submarines, we knew that they were sinking ships everywhere, that they controlled every coastline, and I woke up the first night with a nightmare that we were torpedoed like *Lusitania* and the whole Met company was lost. But the fates were with us, and we arrived safely. I'd just like this war to be over, wouldn't you?"

"This war and all of them," says Granados.

"It wasn't just the war that kept Toscanini in Italia. He and Farrar had been in liaison romantique for several years, and finally Farrar said he'd have to leave his wife or she'd break it off. Divorce was out of the question. He was still in love with Farrar and couldn't stand the idea of working with her after it was over. Soon after, Martinelli sang badly in *Carmen* after I got sick, and that gave Arturo an opening. He told Gatti he was canceling the last six performances and returning home. And *that* saved his life!"

"How?" asks Granados.

"Well, by leaving early and changing his reservations, he missed being on the *Lusitania*–on its very last voyage! Life's strange! Toscanini's frustrated passion for Farrar saved his life!"

January, 1916

The holidays are past, and Granados' life has settled into a New York version of a familiar pattern. After morning coffee he goes to Malvina Hoffman's place, practices for two or three hours, eats lunch with his hostess, takes a nap, then goes to the opera house for rehearsals and discussions in preparation for the premiere on the twenty-eighth of this month. Then back to the hotel and an evening with Amparo, whose days are planned by Susan Metcalfe or Lucie Schelling. Then dinner, usually as guests of the Casals or the Schellings. Weekends spent resting, sightseeing in the city, or with Rosa Culmell and the collection of Spanish and Catalan artists and musicians who come to her apartment, including Francisca Rodón and La Nena Madriguera. Everything nicely in its own compartment. Except for a two-day bout with digestive pains–which Dr. Emile Sarlabous on West 75th Street treated as an ulcer, and a moderate attack of migraine during the last two days of December, for which he was treated by Dr. Fellowes Davis on West 47th Street–Granados' first month in New York has gone as well as could be expected.

When Granados arrives at the Met this morning, there's a note from Gatti-Casazza asking to see him. Sitting in one of the leather chairs while the impresario finishes a phone conversation. Granados only hears portions of Gatti's end of it, but the dulcet tone of voice suggests that it's an unhappy Italian soprano on the other end. "Oh, signorina bella! Please don't ask of me something you know is completely impossible. For you know that if there were anyone in the world I would do that for, it would be you, only you. But I cannot…sì, sì, I will tell her I have an agreement with you. Sì, sì. But the other–what you're asking is not possible. Ah! per pietà! Non posso–it's impossible, even for so great an artist as you, signorina…please, I beg you, please trust me. I have only your interest in my heart."

After concluding the conversation with a dollop of gelato, sweet and cool, Gatti swivels in his chair and faces Granados. "Maestro, we need to bring your opera together without further delay. And bring the singers together with the strings and the rest of the orchestra. I don't need to tell you. But there are only so many days left."

Granados is annoyed at the patronizing tone. "I'm well aware of that, and I think you should pass that same message on to your conductor. I've hardly seen Monsieur Bavagnoli."

"He's no problem. Besides, you and Casals are here every day, so perhaps Bavagnoli doesn't feel the need to step in quite yet. As I told you the first time we met, Gaetano came here to conduct Italian operas."

Granados says, "I'm grateful that Casals is willing, because he can speak English to your players. But we need a decision on choreography."

"That's decided. We're going to use our ballerina–Rosina Galli."

Granados is stunned. "You've decided? But you haven't even seen Señorita Mercé dance!"

"I don't need to," says Gatti in a flat tone of voice. "She isn't going to dance, at least not here. I hope you didn't promise her anything."

Anger rushes to Granados' head. "Monsieur Gatti, we discussed it, and you even told me how much she'd earn for the four performances, so I invited her to come here from Buenos Aires. She's arriving tomorrow. I didn't make a firm promise, mostly because I wanted to extend to you the courtesy of seeing her dance before a final decision."

"I appreciate your thoughtfulness," says Gatti, looking away.

"The choreography is very important, especially in two of the scenes, and Señorita Mercé is ideally suited for it. This is a Spanish opera. Not composed by a foreigner, as were others. It's about Spain. And we can get an ideal dancer who's devoted to Spanish music. Now you're telling me you've chosen an Italian dancer?"

Gatti glares back. "It has nothing to do with her being Italian. She's an excellent ballerina and a member of our company. I've known her since she came to La Scala at the age of six, and I've seen her make excellent progress since then. Do you blame me for using someone I know, and have great confidence in?"

Granados sees no reason to back off. "I offered you the best dancer in Spain and persuaded her to come here–believing that you'd have some confidence in my judgment about Spanish dance! It's obvious you do not!"

"You're missing the point, maestro. If nationality were the criterion, nobody but Austrians could play Mozart. Only the French could play Saint-Saens. Only Italians could sing Verdi. Only Germans could sing Wagner. Don't you see how impractical that would be?"

"I'm asking you to delay your decision until you've seen Señorita Mercé dance. That's all."

Gatti stands up. "I'm sorry. I won't do that. Now, if you please, I'd like to conclude this matter. There's someone else waiting. Bon jour."

Por Dios! Things going well–now this! Like fighting to get into El Liceu. Gatti never listened–why expect more from an impresario? The God of the Met with deaf ears. Antonia arrives tomorrow expecting to work. Serious problem! Need to find venue for her.

Antonia Mercé, still exhausted by a long sea voyage from Buenos Aires, sits with sagging shoulders at a table in the café across 39th Street from the Met. Having just learned from Granados that the offer to choreograph *Goyescas* has evaporated, she's disconsolate and speechless. Her lids, heavy with mascara, hang over the enormous green eyes, and she gnaws on her lower lip. Her husband, Carlos Paz, who's unused to facing problems without the nearby power and prestige of his renowned Argentine family, sits by her side as Granados dispels any remaining hope that Gatti will change his mind.

"You asked my wife to come here without a firm promise from the Metropolitano!" says Paz in an abrasive tone. "Do you know how far it is from Buenos Aires–where we were having summer–to this frozen place? I know. It's twice as far as you came from Barcelona! We would not have come here on idle speculation, maestro! Would you?"

"Señor Paz, it wasn't idle speculation," says Granados, noting that Paz speaks Castilian with a pronounced Italian accent. "I also was shocked the impresario chose someone else."

"And you want us to believe you can do nothing–nada en absoluto–to spare my wife this dishonor? Does her reputation mean nothing to you?"

Granados breathes deeply before responding. "Señor Paz, this is not a matter of my lacking concern about your wife's honor. This is not my fault! If I were impresario, she'd have the job. I'm not. I've said I'm sorry for asking her to come–I wish I'd never sent the telegram! But your wife was very interested in dancing *Goyescas*, and I thought it would be good for her career–it wasn't for any selfish reason! Look, she's accepted my apology."

"Yes, I have," says Mercé in a sad voice. She turns to her husband. "It's not his fault. He was trying to help. Please try to see that, or you'll only make it worse!"

The Hispanic Society of America

Granados and Casals ride up Broadway in a town car sent by the Hispanic Society of America, where this afternoon Granados will receive an honorary membership and a silver medal "for distinguished contributions to Hispanic arts." Casals turns to Granados. "This will be a big day, brother. Archer Huntington's very excited about your opera. Not a big crowd today, and you won't have to play. But real luminaries! You'll meet Otto Kahn, el cap of the board of the Met, and Schelling will be there. And Bori–she did a recital for Huntington just before her throat problems. Also the Spanish ambassador to America–Juan Riaño–they say he's a great fanàtic of your music. It's a big day."

Granados rolls his eyes and looks out the window at the brownstone apartment buildings flying past. "I'm surprised the ambassador is coming. Aren't you?"

"Not at all," replies Casals. "Riaño was assigned to Amèrica with one purpose: to normalize relations after the war, to close the gap. He grew up in England, married an American, and he's an experienced diplomat–the ideal person for healing wounds. No, no. Riaño will seize any chance to show Americans that España isn't a barbaric country, that it's a modern country–" Casals chuckles. "You and I know those are exaggerations! Anyhow, Riaño sees opportunity in promoting the arts and music of España. When I came here for the first time, there was strong anti-Spanish feeling. Anger at the Spanish government in Madrid for oppressing people in Cuba and the other colonies. Riaño figures, what's better than introducing Spanish opera to the Metropolitan? He and Huntington are very much in common purpose."

The Hispanic Society of America is the centerpiece in a cluster of Beaux-Arts buildings that stand on the east end of what was for many years the bucolic Manhattan estate of John James Audubon, a naturalist who combined voluminous research and a talent for drawing in *The Birds of America*, a book that established him as the hemisphere's leading ornithologist. Audubon, who began life as the illegitimate son of a French sea captain and a Haitian Creole, was educated in France and spent decades exploring North America before purchasing thirty acres of undeveloped land in northern Manhattan. Since the 1840s–when Audubon and his sons built their homes near a mansion that served as George Washington's New York headquarters in the Revolutionary War–the growth of New York City has absorbed the surrounding countryside at a steady pace.

Ten years ago, Huntington purchased that portion of the Audubon estate that extends from Broadway to Riverside Drive on the east and west, and is bounded on south and north by 155th and 156th Streets. Three years later, the Hispanic Society opened its doors to the public, envisioned by Huntington as a center for linguistic studies, art, literature, and music of the Iberian peninsula and Latin America. His timing was excellent: with the Independent subway extending its Broadway line to 157th Street, the pastoral idyll of the Audubon estate was a thing of the past.

Archer Milton Huntington was the "love child" and only progeny of Collis Huntington and his mistress, Arabella Duval, a woman endowed with a probing interest in the arts that she's passed on to her son. Huntington is heir to one of the great railroad fortunes in America, built by his father with such California partners as Leland Stanford, Mark Hopkins, and Charles Crocker. Vast amounts of money flowing from the Central Pacific Railroad and the Newport News Shipbuilding & Drydock Company provided young Archer with private tutors and extensive European travel with his mother, who made sure he didn't waste his time in Spain. Not worth visiting, she would admonish. But Archer's interest in Iberia had been kindled at age twelve when he read George Barrow's *The Zincali*, an acount of the gypsy life in Spain, and when, during teenage visits to a ranch owned by his father–which covered roughly one-third of the state of Texas–Huntington rode horses, listened to the stable boys and ranch hands, and learned to speak Castilian.

In his early twenties, he broke away from Arabella on a tour of France and headed for Burgos, home town of the epic Castilian warrior El Cid, giving full vent to his Hispanophilia. Despite a lack of formal education, he became a respected scholar, publishing an English translation of *Poema del Cid*, believed to be the 12th Century work of a monk living in the Moorish kingdom of Zaragoza. Not a trivial task, since the poem rambled on for more than one hundred pages in a language caught in transition from Latin to Castilian. Huntington also began to collect the art and craftwork of Iberia, but only those works that had already been removed from the country of origin. In his early thirties, he founded the Hispanic Society, building for it a modern facility whose amenities include a system of air conditioning with air forced over blocks of ice. His dream: the neighborhood around the former Audubon estate would become an uptown mecca for theatres, galleries, and restaurants rivaling the area around Times Square.

The town car drops them off in front of a massive iron gate bisecting a fence that runs the width of the property. After passing through the gate,

Casals leads Granados up a long flight of stairs to a plaza with formal gardens covered for the winter, then angles to the right and up two more flights of stairs, emerging on a wide redbrick terrace. They walk toward the main entrance to the Hispanic Society, framed by two-story Ionic columns, a pair of sculpted lions guarding the doors, and a Roman classic cornice and parapet with the engraved names of Columbus, Cervantes, San Ignacio de Loyola, and the Portuguese poet Camoens.

Huntington, a handsome man in his mid-forties, is waiting. In his dark suit, high-collared white shirt and plain dark blue tie, beard trimmed short, and wearing a pair of wire-framed glasses, he could be a government official or a diplomat. He is soft-spoken and self-assured, gracious but as dry as a professor of classics. His language is precise and carefully chosen.

"Bienvenidos," he says as he gives each of them a firm handshake. "I'm honored by your visit, pleased you'd take time from your rehearsals to come." He leads them through a room filled with archives, paintings, sculpture, ceramics, manuscripts, and leather-bound books. "It looks chaotic," he says as they arrive at this mahogany-paneled office, "but I know where everything is. You'll pardon my Castilian," he says affably. "When I'm in New York, I begin to lose it. Now if it weren't for the war, I'd be preparing to go back. Very strange, we can't take the steamer across when the spring comes. Little chance of that, with the war going on and on. Something we used to take for granted, right? Gracias a Dios, España's not involved. Nothing to do but wait for the end of it."

Huntington thanks Granados for sending him a copy of the private edition of Book One of *Goyescas*. "It's marvelous music," he adds, "and though I can't play it, I can read the score. I'm so fond of the music of España! People have no idea what they're missing. Granados, Albéniz, Falla—such treasures! I can hardly wait for *Goyescas* to open."

Granados listens carefully for a hint that Huntington is his angel.

Great passion for España—that's obvious. Schelling says he's quiet about his contributions. Doesn't want everyone knocking on his door. Wait for him to bring it up.

Huntington suggests a tour of the collection, and their first stop is an octagonal gallery now being used as a reading room, where Joaquín Sorolla's *The Regions of Spain* will be installed. "My policy," he explains, "is not to acquire a work in the country of origin. The works you'll see were outside España before I acquired them. Otherwise it's plundering, and God knows there's been enough of that in the art world! The only exception is when I commission a work, like the ones being done by Sorolla." He notes that among his acquisitions are three El Grecos; one each by Bartolomé Murillo, Diego Velásquez, and Francisco de Zurburán; four portraits by Goya, and a sketch for his scene of

May 3, 1808 in which Spanish peasants are being executed by French troops; and a painting of Goya's studio in Madrid by Francisco Domingo y Marqués.

"Which Goyas?" asks Granados.

Huntington smiles. "I thought you'd be interested. There's one in particular. We'll see it presently."

As they cross the vestibule, Huntington points to a painting of Christ's crucifixion by Luis Jiménez Aranda, a Spanish Impressionist who trained and worked in Paris. They pass through a filigreed arch into the replica of a Renaissance Spanish courtyard, a two-story atrium with a balcony for viewing the paintings on display on the upper level, with each of the arches around the lower level bearing a coat of arms of the provinces of España.

"There she is," says Huntington in a laconic voice.

Granados is face-to-face with María Teresa, La Duquesa de Alba.

As he freezes, remaining motionless, Huntington recites the title that came with the portrait: *Doña María de Pilar Teresa Cayetana de Silva Álvarez de Toledo, Décimotercia Duquesa de Alba*. As a student of Iberian culture, Huntington knows that Goya's subject was given many more names at her christening, but three given names and three family names seem sufficient.

Granados knows Goya's private name for her. And it matters to him what words Goya spoke to her in a darkened bedroom, the sound of those words surely does matter. But seeing her here is a numbing surprise. There had only been one portrait of her, the one he saw with Periquet in Madrid. Now this one.

María Teresa! Ma-rí-a Te-re-sa! Dios mío! How can you be here? How can you be in New York? And why? Waiting for me? Came half way around the world–to bring Goya to Americà–now you're here waiting for me. Must be losing my mind!

"You seem surprised," says Huntington. "I hope pleasantly."

"Oh yes. Yes. I'm sorry," says Granados, "it's just–I had no idea there was another portrait of her. Nobody told me there was another one, only rumors."

Dutifully and dryly, Huntington recounts the portrait's history. Goya worked on it in late 1796 and early 1797; at the bottom left corner is the artist's inscription: "Goya 1797." He was probably sketching for it when he was in Sanlúcar de Barrameda in the summer of 1796. It remained in Goya's studio for the rest of his life, and when he died in 1828 his son Javier inherited it. Ten years later, Javier sold it to the Louvre in Paris for inclusion in a new Spanish Collection. The French Revolution of 1848 and the Louvre's fleeting interest in Spanish art led to closing the collection, and the paintings were sold. In 1853 it was auctioned in London and purchased by a private party, M. P. Sohège, who kept it in his Parisian home–unseen by the art world, essentially unknown and forgotten–for forty-nine years. In 1902–the centenary of La Duquesa's mysterious death, Huntington stumbled upon it and with a generous offer acquired and brought it to New York, where it remained in his home until the opening of the Hispanic Society eight years ago. Huntington looks earnestly at Granados and Casals. "A magnificent piece, don't you think?"

María Teresa–did you ever see this one? After you took up with other men after you broke his heart did you go to his studio? Did he allow you to see yourself as he had in Sanlúcar?

Anyone entering this main gallery must come face to face with La Duquesa. She's dressed in black, standing on a sandy break in the piney, swampy, foggy wasteland surrounding her palace north of Sanlúcar. Her attire, from the top her head to the pointed high-heeled shoes, is funereal black. The skirt is trimmed with ruffled lace, a mantilla is draped to reveal a gold blouse and the lacy edges of a white bodice, and a crimson and gold sash is tied above her curving hips. The artist's palette and her posture suggest more vibrancy than mourning. Her lips are pursed; she could be on a brink of a smile, or launching an insult. She's less the grieving widow than an aristocrat dressed as maja, bound for a street dance. Granados imagines the romantic and sensual. He notes the heels of her gold-braided shoes don't penetrate the sand. Perhaps Goya wanted her poised as if to rise off the earth, as depicted in the *Capricho* being borne aloft with butterfly wings–a common symbol for fickleness.

"The Duke of Alba died so recently," says Huntington. "I'm sure that's why Goya dressed her in mourning clothes."

"Or he dressed her as a maja," replies Granados, turning from Huntington back to the portrait.

Mourning? Hardly. Inviting Goya to share your intimate moments–bathing having your hair brushed rubbing your body with oils lying on your bed with your hip forming an arc backlit in candlelight waving him to come to you. More likely Goya's mourning for the loss of you! Feet barely touching–prepared to fly away? Odd he placed your feet such a wide angle. So your knees would be parted your thighs spread beneath the gown.

Granados shakes his head at the contrast between this portrait and the other one painted in 1795, the one he saw in Madrid. In that one, La Duquesa was two years younger, her eyes widened in an expression of innocence, with an undercurrent of frivolity and playful sensuality. Wavy hair in a cascade from the pale forehead above her dark eyebrows down to her girlish waist. A white dress bordered in gold thread, red sash around her slender waist, red necklace around her swan's neck, and a red bow above her bodice. A little white Pekinese dog at her feet; her right hand pointed enigmatically off the canvas to her right.

In this portrait, however, Goya betrays his ambivalence: adorning her from worship and craving, blemishing her from rage. La Duquesa's raven hair is covered by a black mantilla, emblematic of Spanish femininity, which provides a frame for her oval face. Heavy dark eyebrows arch above her chestnut eyes as if in surprise. Sunlight falls on her right cheek, with the left in shadow. Her left arm, in a long-sleeved blouse girdled by a row of silver bracelets, is cocked at a right angle with her hand placed on her hip, a gesture of bravado that seems to propel her toward the viewer. Her right arm hangs over her right thigh, with the ivory flesh of her hand drawing the eye down and away from her face; on the middle finger is an oversized cameo-style ring inscribed with her ducal name: Alba. The long ethereal index finger, wearing a gold band, points to the sand in front of her.

Granados moves closer, squinting to read eight large letters etched in the sand: "S ó l o G o y a."

"Yes, there's no question," observes Huntington, after leaving Granados to his reverie. "It says 'Sólo Goya.' Goya's the only one. Remember, those are Goya's words, not hers. All in all, there's quite a bit of emotion in this work. In fact, emotion is its very essence. As it is in your opera, maestro."

Granados nods. His head is swirling with a torrent of words to describe her–stupefying, resplendent, impudent, vivacious, restless, angelic, wanton, languorous, devilish, playful, imperious.

"Sólo Goya"! His desire or fantasy? Wondering–of all those men it's only me? Nearly twenty years older and deaf? Goya claimed her in the sand–what pretense! Arrogant–romantic! Love twists us.

The award ceremony is brief and convivial. Henry Schelling arrives with Otto Kahn, the German-born investment banker who as chairman of the board of the Metropolitan recruited Gatti-Casazza from La Scala. Kahn, who at the urging of Schelling gave his blessing to the premiere of *Goyescas*, and snuffed out Gatti's resistance.

While his staff sets up a small table at the opposite end of the main gallery from Goya's portrait of La Duquesa, Huntington goes to the main entrance of the Hispanic Society to greet the Spanish ambassador. His Excellency Señor Don Juan Riaño de Gayangos, Ambassador Extraordinary and Plenipotentiary of the King of Spain, Alfonso XIII, is a disarmingly affable career diplomat whose well-bred Washingtonian wife, Etonian English, and enthusiastic promotion of Spanish culture have opened many doors in this country that just eighteen years ago defeated Spain and seized its colonial empire.

In appearance and voice, Juan Riaño seems more the English barrister or public accountant than a descendant of Spanish nobility. His receding hair and a trim moustache are turning gray on a square head that sits on a pudgy fifty-year-old frame. He's dressed in a brown herringbone tweed suit, conservative shirt and tie, and cordovan shoes. He and Huntington have become close friends; in the past year he's also befriended Schelling and Kahn. And because of a mutual connection with the late Count Morphy, Riaño and Casals have become friends. Except for Granados, everyone in the circle gathered around the table in the main gallery is well acquainted with the others.

With great dignity, Huntington presents Granados with the Hispanic Society's Silver Medal of Arts and Letters. "We've also honored five others who made outstanding contributions to Hispanic arts and letters," Huntington says, reading from notes in his hand. "The extraordinary painter from València, Don Joaquín Sorolla y Bastida, whose exhibition eight years ago was our very first and which was an enormous success. Don Joaquín is working on a series of large tableaux titled *The Regions of Spain*–which will be installed in what is now our reading room. Also, Vicente Blasco Ibáñez, another Valenciano, whose novels and essays–some a bit controversial–have added immensely to Hispanic literature. And Don José Echegaray Eizaguirre–dramatist, mathematician, economist, and cabinet member–truly a Renaissance man from the Basque Country and, as we all know, Nobel Laureate in literature. And another Basque, the eminent painter Ignacio Zuloaga y Zanora, whose exhibition here was one of the first after we opened, and whose striking scenes hang in our gallery. Last, though certainly not least, Rubén García Sarmiento of Nicaragua. We all know him as Rubén Darío, whose poems of life and hope have stirred the Hispanic world. We were proud to have him here just this past year, when he read a new poem entitled 'Pax!'–commissioned by the Society. But I'm distressed to report that Don Rubén is now back home in Nicaragua, in somewhat precarious health. We all pray for a speedy recovery."

Granados is delighted and flattered to be included in such company, but while listening to Huntington's closing comments, he returns to the afternoons of Darío's poetry in Clotilde's garden.

What was that poem? The one she recited by heart on our last day?

Instead, the lines of Darío's "To Goya" return:

> A muse proud and confused–
> angel, spectre, medusa:
> such is your muse…
> Your feminine angels
> have murderous eyes

in their heavenly faces.
With capricious delight
you mingled the light of day
with dark, cold night.

After the ceremony Huntington asks Granados if he'll write an excerpt from the score of *Goyescas* on one of the pillars in the exhibition hall, preferably near Goya's La Duquesa.

"I'd be honored," says Granados. "If I had time and you were willing, I'd write the entire score on your columns."

It takes Huntington a moment to appreciate the humor. "Oh, that's not necessary, maestro. Just an excerpt." He recovers. "What do you suppose Goya would prefer?"

Granados laughs. "He'd like the maja singing with the nightingale. The maja all alone, missing her lover."

"Of course."

"But what would La Duquesa prefer to see?" asks Granados. "I think she'd like the 'coloquio' with the lovers courting each other through the window."

"It's up to you," says Huntington. "Here's a pencil."

Granados reaches up and begins to write.

La maja y ruiseñor. First four measures. Introducing the theme. Which version? Tiana version? The one Isolde Wagner heard? As played at El Palau? Salle Pleyel? Goyescas *will surely last longer here than at the Met.*

Granados and Casals wait at the main gate of the Hispanic Society for the town car to come around. Darkness is falling and the street lights are on. A biting wind whips up the stone-and-concrete canyon from the Hudson River. As a squall passes, Granados hears a familiar trill. He turns to Casals and whispers, "Listen! I just heard a nightingale!"

Casals laughs. "Oh yes, and I just saw a giraffe running down Broadway."

"No, Pau, listen–I heard one. There's no mistaking that trill!"

Casals shrugs. "And there's no mistaking a giraffe."

The week before the premiere, Granados and Amparo make First Class reservations to return home with Francisca Rodón and Paquita Madriguera on the

Spanish vessel SS *Antonio López*, which departs New York on March 8 and–unless the Atlantic is stormy–arrives in Barcelona on the 19th. Ambassador Riaño procures a new passport for Granados, so if the ship is stopped, there'll be no confusion about his identity. And in a reversal that astonishes Amparo, Schelling, and Casals, Granados signs an agreement with Ricardo Capelli of El Teatro Colón in Buenos Aires for a South American premiere of *Goyescas* in June, which will oblige him to cross the ocean again, less than two months after returning from New York. Capelli offered him fifty thousand pesetas to sign the contract.

Granados is baffled by Capelli's appearance in New York so soon after the arrival of Antonia Mercé and her husband Carlos Paz. Just prior to Capelli's appearance, the Argentine cultural attaché whom he met through Rudi Schirmer had been arrogant and noncommittal. "How did he get here so quickly?" he asks Mercé and Paz, after telling them he's arranged a venue for her performance. "We didn't talk about El Colón until *after* you arrived. Two days later, this man called me. Did he fly?"

Mercé and Paz exchange nervous glances. She breaks the silence. "To tell the truth, maestro, he was on the same boat coming from Buenos Aires. Carlos and I were so grateful to you for getting me the job with the Metropolitan, we wanted to do something in return. Carlos' family is very influential in Argentina, and very interested in the opera."

"So when you saw Capelli on the boat, you told him about *Goyescas?*"

Mercé shakes her head. "No, no. We didn't just run into him on the boat. Carlos talked to the impresario and two of the board members about your opera–in Buenos Aires–and discovered they already knew about *Goyescas* from María Barrientos. They agreed at once to send Capelli to make you an offer."

"Ah, so Capelli was *sent*. Didn't just happen to be on your boat. And I'm the only one who's surprised."

"Yes," says Paz. "El Colón didn't want another city–Havana or Rio–to be the first in South America to present your opera."

January 28, 1916

Tonight *Goyescas* receives its world premiere. It's been five-and-a-half years since Granados finished Book One with Clotilde in Tiana, and nearly five years since the first public performance of the piano suite. Converting the art of Goya to piano music was a formidable challenge; creating an opera has been comparably difficult. Collaborating with an irascible Goya-phile with no operatic experience, who wrote a weak libretto. Contending with a music director who'd come to New York to perform Italian operas, who conducts with the most inappropriate tempos. Staying up all night in his hotel room to compose an orchestral piece to fill the time between scene changes. And chafing under the authority of an impresario who didn't want to present *Goyescas* in the first place, whose disdain for Spanish music and dance is palpable. All of those hazards and barriers have been overcome. Tonight the lights will go on at the Metropolitan. His opera will be heard by a full house.

Across the Atlantic, Europe's war continues–decimating the armies on both sides and bankrupting the combatant nations. Germany's submarine fleet is deployed to interrupt shipping around the British Isles and along the coast of France. General Erich von Falkenhayn reinforces the Crown Prince's Fifth Army and concentrates his artillery for a massive assault on the French line near Verdun. But life in the neutral United States of America is largely undisturbed. The United States Army is limited to guard duty in the former colonies of Spain, intimidating the last dissident American Indians, and helping the Carranza government in Mexico keep Pancho Villa and his revolutionary followers in check.

To be sure, wealthy American travelers complain about missing their annual tours of Europe, refugee musicians from over there search for new venues over here, politicians in Washington debate getting involved in the Old World's nasty war, and German Americans hunker down to avoid the stigma exacerbated by reports of German atrocities. Yet the streets of New York still pulsate with characteristic haste and energy.

There are thirty-five box holders of the Diamond Horseshoe; their families built the Metropolitan Opera House after realizing that no matter how wealthy they might become, the eighteen boxes at the Academy of Music would forever belong to those who made their fortunes earlier. It didn't matter that Mrs. William K. Vanderbilt had a net worth estimated at two hundred million dollars. She was turned down by the Academy as quickly as her chambermaid might have been. For New York's upper crust, a box at the Academy wasn't merely a preferred spot for enjoying the operas; it was the pinnacle of social standing. So in 1880 the new elite–Vanderbilts, Goulds, Roosevelts, and Morgans, along with the Astors and a few other descendents of the early Knickerbockers–decided to built their own opera house and purchased a site on Broadway at 39th Street. It opened with Charles Gounod's *Faust* in late 1883.

Twenty years later, the cream-colored walls–considered unflattering to the jewelry worn by the Diamond Horseshoe's women–were repainted gold and maroon, not coincidentally the colors of the Astor family.

The Met is a splendid new place for boxholder families to be seen by their peer group, which excludes Catholics, Jews, and those who are foreign-born–unless they are titled. So Otto Kahn, a German-born Jew, despite having amassed a fortune on his way to become managing partner of Kuhn, Loeb & Company, and despite, as chairman of the board of the Met, having personally underwritten its losses in the early 1890s, is not permitted to have a box. So the Met is newer, yes, farther uptown, and large enough for ambitious productions, but no more egalitarian than the Academy, which was forced into bankruptcy by its larger, upstart rival in less than seven years.

The Met's ample seating capacity, dedication to solvency, and entrepreneurial attitude allow it to attract New York's burgeoning immigrant population, which brings an inherited devotion to opera from the Old World. This ensures that the main floor and balcony seats will be sold out, revenues will fill the Met's coffers, box holders of the Diamond Horseshoe will hear the best singers the world and–appealing to their residual Yankee frugality–they won't be tapped to cover losses at the end of each season.

Tonight the Diamond Horseshoe is bursting with box holders and their close friends, anticipating one of the high points of this winter's social season. And the rest of the seats are occupied tonight with members of New York's Spanish and South American colony, eager to hear their ancestral language sung for the first time on the stage of the Met. Stacked behind them are five rows of standees, and in the lobby behind them is a crowd of people content simply to be "at the Met" on this auspicious occasion.

Along with opera goers' interest in the first Spanish language opera and its composer, New York's astute merchants have picked up the theme, notably Wanamaker's La Galerie, which advertises "new fashions for women with a Spanish influence." These include creations by three Parisian couturiers, shipped across the Atlantic just in time to be flaunted in the Diamond Horseshoe on opening night: Poiret's "Infante" evening gown, Worth's "Goya" gown of rose satin and tulle, and Lanvin's "Velásquez" evening gown of black silk tulle beaded in crystals. Not to miss the opportunity, an Italian restaurant in the theatre district has added an "authentic Spanish rice dish" to the menu. Nothing fancy, nor authentic: it's a risotto of arborio rice and tomatoes, served with a red rose. And Altman's attracts a throng of au courant shoppers by featuring "Maja" perfumed soap and cologne by Myrurgia.

Granados is oblivious to all of this hoopla. His mind is spinning in several circles, reflecting his concern about making tonight's premiere a paramount success.

Must ignore obstacles—leap over them. Difficult rehearsals. Complaints from players. Bori's throat problems—having to substitute. Gatti's choosing his dancer instead of Antonia. Biggest problem—the libretto. No surprise—misgivings about Periquet from beginning. Next time it won't be Periquet. Find strong libretto first.

In the early afternoon, Granados and Amparo go for a walk in Central Park, close to their new hotel, The Wellington, on 7th Avenue between 55th and 56th Streets. They moved last weekend because of Amparo's complaints about the noise and congestion of Times Square. Because for Granados a hotel is merely a place to sleep, he was willing to accommodate her.

New York City is enjoying a reprieve from the winter with several days of unseasonably mild weather. The temperature reached fifty-five degrees Fahrenheit three days ago, then sixty, a balmy sixty-nine yesterday, and sixty-six today. Warmer than in Barcelona. The sticky snow that fell intermittently two weeks ago is long gone, and the walking path around the Pond is alive with nannies wheeling the well-bundled, privileged infants of the Midtown and East Side neighborhoods, while boys on roller skates, cooped up since late November, fling themselves in restless anticipation of an early spring.

As they walk, Amparo points to the swelling buds on branches of the young oak and elm trees lining the path. "The buds think it's springtime," she says. "I do hope they don't come out too far. Everyone says there's more winter to come."

Granados stops, reaches up, and gently pulls down a branch for closer inspection.

If spring's coming here surely it's coming back home. Buds bursting around the Sala and in Tiana! Home—just an abstraction. Forty more days and we go home. Forty days—longer than eternity!

The day before yesterday, the dress rehearsal—ordinarily performed for a small but appreciative coterie—drew a larger audience than for any Met rehearsal, attended by such notables as the wives of Otto Kahn, Richard Aldrich, and Vincent Astor, son of John Jacob Astor IV, who went down with the SS *Titanic* four years ago. The audience applauded as if it were opening night. Also attending was María Barrientos, who will sing the title role in *Lucia di Lammermoor* in her Met debut three days after the premiere of *Goyescas*. Barrientos, who considers Granados one of her mentors despite never having taking lessons directly from him, sends this note to his hotel: "Dearest maestro and friend–I've just come from your opera with the highest enthusiasm. You will certainly have a real triumph and surely it's what I wish for you with all of my soul. Viva España! María Barrientos."

Dressed in a black trousers and tails, with a white shirt and tie under a biscuit-brown waistcoat from Brooks Brothers, Granados takes a cab from the Wellington down 7th Avenue, through the late Saturday afternoon bustle of Times Square, then three blocks down Broadway to the Metropolitan. The uniformed man at the stage door greets him in Spanish. "Buenas noches, maestro. This is the big night!"

"Sí, sí. A big night, Ramón." For an instant, Granados imagines that he's back home, entering the stage door of El Liceu.

The doorman's name is Ramón Iglesias, from Mayaguez, Puerto Rico–the same town where Casals mother, Doña Pilar, was born. When Casals discovered him busing trays in a diner near the Met, he went to see Gatti and convinced him he must hire some people who speak Spanish. "I told him the Spanish colony is growing fast and they're all opera-lovers," said Casals later, enjoying his achievement. "Gatti may be arrogant, but not dumb. Of course, Iglesias' father originally came from Catalunya, but Gatti wouldn't understand that distinction, would he?"

In his dressing room, Granados takes off the overcoat and leather gloves and slips on a pair of gentlemen's white gloves, flexing his hands to stretch them tightly over his long fingers. Backstage and behind the curtain, two hours before it rises, there's a mélange of orchestral players drifting up from the practice rooms to find their places in the pit; stage crew members being instructed by Jules Speck one last time on the night's major transition: from *Goyescas*–Madrid of the early 1800s, to *Pagliacci*–a Calabrian village of the 1860s. Some of the seventy-six cast members in *Goyescas* are measuring their steps one more time.

Granados stands with a fidgety Periquet on the side of the stage, looking up at the opening set by Antonio Rovescalli, who was dispatched by Gatti to be inspired by Goya's paintings in El Prado. It's a leafy grove on the outskirts of Madrid. In the background is the Hermitage of San Antonio de la Florida, where Goya painted the Miracle of San Antonio de Padua on the ceiling of the cupola in 1798, and where he's now buried; stage right, a restaurant; and a street occupying most of stage center. Granados is pleased with the set, and amused as well as gratified by Gatti's claim that the sets for *Goyescas* are the most expensive of any work ever presented at the Metropolitan.

Some of the audience is already in the house, and Granados senses excitement in their voices. Early to arrive are Hispanics and Hispanophiles wanting to make sure they don't miss a moment of this ethnic festival. They converse excitedly in the aisles. Also among the early arrivals are doyennes of the Diamond Horseshoe such as Alice Gwynne Vanderbilt—an authentic opera buff—who will stay through both operas in Box 4.

Penelope Havermeyer, the young woman who met Caruso and Granados in the bar of the Hotel Knickerbocker, arrives early at her family's box with two of her cousins. She's dressed in Lanvin's "Velásquez" evening gown of black silk tulle—daringly cut and wrapped tightly, with a black lace shawl. Caruso promised to see her tonight in his dressing room—to discuss her benefit concert for the French Red Cross.

Amparo, dressed in the maja style with a gown of green velvet and black lace, will sit in the "composer's box" with Casals and Susan Metcalfe, Henry and Lucie Schelling, Robert and Mildred Bliss, and Jan and Helena Paderewski. Huntington will be in his box with the pianist Teresa Carreño, her husband Arturo Tagliapietra, Andrés de Segurola, María Barrientos, and Malvina Hoffman. Otto and Addie Kahn will be in a box set aside for board members who are not boxholders, with Ambassador Riaño and his wife Alice Ward de Riaño y Gayangos, the Irish-born tenor John McCormack and his wife Lily, Fritz and Harriet Kreisler, and Thelma Cudlipp Whitman, wife of the governor of the state of New York. Scattered throughout the audience are most of the notables who attended a reception at Otto Kahn's in honor of Granados; friends, colleagues, and students of Granados from Catalunya; Antonia Mercé and Carlos Paz; and Gustav White of Schirmer's, who will host a dinner for Granados after the operas at Sherry's Restaurant.

It is finally time. Granados nods and waves good-naturedly across the stage to the chorus master, Giulio Setti. The babble dies down behind the curtain as the slender, hawk-faced Gaetano Bavagnoli paces with his baton on the corner of the stage behind the curtain, waiting for the orchestra to tune up, waiting for a cue from the concertmaster. Now, with the cue, Bavagnoli steps around the orchestra pit and up to the podium.

Granados, eyes closed, hears the overture, half a minute in length.

Dios mío! Too slow—it's not Verdi's Requiem! *Doesn't understand! Cellos too weak—he doesn't care! Calm down. Take deep breath. Ahhhh.*

As the curtain rises, the chorus of majas begins.

Yes—excellent! Thank you!

Four of the majas are tossing "el pelele"—the straw manikin—up and down, and the entire stage is swept with playful energy as the chorus of maja voices sings:

> Whoever is trusting and doesn't watch out–because of love–will become like el pelele…jump up, jump up! A man like this can always be found, for a girl is better off alone than accompanied by a fool!

The majo voices respond:

> I wouldn't change women like these, not even for heaven. The sun would give us little joy, in spite of its power, if there wasn't the love of these women. I'd be a pelele if I could! Young or old, I'll always be a gallant lover. But the most beautiful women are also the most dangerous.

Yes! Bavagnoli's picked up pace. Thank God! Voices are clear–strong. Audience captivated!

Giuseppe de Luca, in the role of the torero Paquiro, is the first of the lead singers to step forward. He flirts with the majas:

> It's your delicate fragrance, flowers of the garden, that enraptures men wherever you go.

The majas disparage his overture:

> This one's love is pretense and deception. It pleases him to be a butterfly and fly from flower to flower. That's why it's best to take him in jest. O! How we love his gallant favours!

The first scene is brought to a close with a duet of choruses. The applause is loud and sustained, with the entire house on its feet.

Yes! De Luca's strong. Audience is with us!

The second scene introduces Flora Perini in the role of Pepa, Paquiro's lover. The majos and majas recognize her as one of their own, as she claims to be. While the people in the street celebrate the love between Paquiro and Pepa, a carriage comes onstage and the aristocratic Rosario steps down from it.

Paquiro sings:

> A dream of a woman! The most beautiful I shall ever see!

Pepa is offended. The majos and majas are skeptical:

> This duchess who's so famous for love–why has she come here? Who is she looking for? What does she want?

With this, the second scene ends. Once more the audience rises to its feet and applauds with enthusiasm.

Fantàstic! Perini's perfect tonight! Audience is thrilled!

In the third scene, Rosario–sung by Anna Fitziu–and the Royal Guards captain, Fernando–sung by Giovanni Martinelli–join Paquiro and Pepa on stage, and the seeds of a violent denouement are planted. In a quartet, Fernando becomes jealous of Paquiro, and Pepa of Rosario. It's followed by a stirring duet by Rosario and Fernando, in which she tries to overcome his jealousy.

The fourth scene builds to an uproarious conclusion, with the majas singing:

> It's the burning sun that kindles our blood–and that's how love is born. El amor–it sets its snares, that's how it's born. And love is the best there is in this life.

The chorus of majos echoes this declaration, and the curtain falls on the first act.

The audience rises again, and with a chorus of bravos! sustains its applause until the four lead singers step in front of the curtain for a bow. The applause continues, and Bavagnoli turns and bows from his podium. Now the chorus of bravos! is punctuated with cries of "maestro!" and "Granados!" When it's apparent that the applause isn't fading, Granados steps out from behind the curtain and bows. The opera house is filled with cheers and exclamation.

Gracias a Dios! Hope my fill-in piece doesn't ruin it!

The orchestra plays "Intermezzo"–the piece he composed overnight, to fill the time between acts. It not only serves its purpose but is warmly applauded as the second act opens.

Excepcional! Gatti said only first-rate artists. Nice balance between strings and woodwinds. Smooth fading out. Fine percussion. Bass player finally learned pace for a jota! Gatti's word was good–though Bori would have been stronger and Antonia should have done the dance. This audience not cold–nice surprise.

The second act opens in a large roadside inn, illuminated only by a lantern that hangs from a heavy beam above the dance floor. The crowd of majos and majas surrounds a couple who are dancing a fandango to the music of a guitar. Pepa and Paquiro belong to this crowd. The mood shifts with the arrival of Rosario and Fernando, whose air of sophistication at this lowbrow party annoys Pepa and leads to a confrontation between Fernando and Paquiro. The majos sing:

> When women are concerned, the only way to settle things is for one to lose his life. Women are always more pleased with a brave man, and they always deny the cowards their love! Women give their passion to the man who's brave, the man who disdains love. If this man brought such a fine lady to this place, he should have known to hold his tongue!

The tension builds. The majas sing:

> Finally it seems that this affair will be resolved in a tragic manner. If two men clash for the love of one woman, the only way out is for one to win her with his life. When two brave men face each other, only the shedding of blood can settle a feud caused by their burning love.

Paquiro and Fernando exchange insults, then threats. Ignoring Rosario–who faints after pleading for them to stop–they arrange a duel. Rosario and Fernando leave and the crowd begins to dance the fandango, a courtship step that was popular in roadside inns during Goya's time.

Granados watches the lead dancers, Rosina Galli and Giuseppe Bonfiglio, trying to see their performance without any of the bitterness he felt when Gatti refused to accept Antonia Mercé.

All right. They dance well. Pace is good. She's not Spanish but still flashes and sparkles.

The dance concludes and the curtain drops. The audience is on its feet again, cheering. The chorus of majos and majas, along with Paquiro and Pepa, take a bow, followed by Galli and Bonfiglio–who are wildly acclaimed–then Bavagnoli, then once again–following cries of "maestro!" and "Granados!"–the composer steps onto the front of the stage and bows deeply, savoring more rounds of echoing cheers. His face is flushed and his heart is racing. In his shaking right hand is the score. He bows again, blows a kiss toward the composer's box, and returns backstage.

An orchestral interlude sets the mood for the third and final act.

At last–splendid scene! Fitziu's best aria biggest challenge. So much depends on her. So young–La Duquesa always young. At last–por fin–la maja y el ruiseñor. She longs for love. Listen well Clotilde–you will hear it! Now! The trilling. Listen well!

The curtain opens on the luxuriant garden of Rosario's palace in Madrid. A gate with a railing is backstage center, behind a stone bench. Rosario, alone in her garden, is listening to the trilling sound of a solitary nightingale in the trees splashed by moonlight. Entranced by its song, Rosario sings:

> Why does the nightingale pour out his harmonious song in the gloom of night? Perhaps he bears a grudge against the king of the day, and wants to revenge a wrong. Perhaps his breast hides such sorrow that he hopes to find relief in the darkness by sadly singing songs of love. And perhaps there is a flower, trembling with the fear of love, that is the enchanted slave of the nightingale!

> Mysterious is the song he sings, surrounded by the gloomy shadows. Ah, love is like a flower at the mercy of the sea! Love! Love! Ah, there are no songs without love. Ah, nightingale, your song is the hymn of love. O, nightingale!

As Rosario enters the palace and Fernando appears, the audience releases a deafening roar of approval. Momentarily, its fervor stops the young soprano Anna Fitziu in her tracks and shakes her. She turns and bows. The roar is sustained. She bows twice more.

Granados watches Fitziu recover with tears flowing down his cheeks, soaking his moustache.

Love—flower at mercy of the sea! Nightingale—your song is mine—hymn of love. Dear Anna—you sang so well! Ay Dios—don't let me explode!

The love duet, sung through the iron grating, begins with Fernando asking if Rosario's been waiting for him. She sings:

> My days and nights are only for you.

He responds:

> A moment ago, one of those doubts that haunt those who are in love crossed my mind.

Rosario:

> What is the cause of your doubt?

Fernando:

> The jealousy I felt when you flirted with him!

Rosario:

> All that you must forget, and now devote your life to love.

Fernando hears a bell tolling ten o'clock, the hour set for his duel:

> Oh, treacherous life!

Rosario:

> Crazed with love, I shall fall into your arms. Yes, I adore you! Te adoro! When you aren't here, I weep sadly, thinking of your passion.

Fernando:

> Oh love! Forever!

Rosario:

> My love! Sí, siempre! No doubts! To cherish forever!

Their duet is broken by Paquiro, who as he passes the palace motions to Fernando that the hour has come for their duel. Fernando tries to break away.

Rosario:

> Won't you stay longer?

Fernando:

> No, no, Rosario! Let me go!

She realizes what's occurring, and tries to hold him back:

> No! I know everything! Do you deny my love this entreaty?
> Por Dios, give me back my peace! Come here, come here!
> Don't give in, por Dios, to blind anger.

Fernando breaks away and Rosario rushes after him as the scene is concluded. The audience brings Martinelli and Fitziu back for three bows.

Can't hope for more! Martinelli magnificent! God bless Fitziu! A triumph!

The final scene opens on the palace garden, deserted, with the icy silver light of the moon shining through the trees. Offstage, the clashing sound of steel blade on blade, then a scream of agony as one of the men is run through with a sword, then a woman's scream of despair. The orchestra depicts a scene of violence and its fateful conclusion. From the left appears Fernando, mortally wounded, leaning on Rosario for support until they reach the stone bench, onto which she lowers him. They pose in a replica of the tenth of Goya's *Caprichos*, representing love and death. The music softens, now full of sweetness and longing. The woodwinds evoke the passion of the lovers, with the basses and cellos suggesting the imminent approach of death. The strings reprise the theme of the lovers' duet.

Rosario caresses Fernando as life drifts from his body.

> It's a dream! Ah, cruel fate! The forces of destiny are blind and treacherous! Fernando, mi alma! Soul of my soul, turn your eyes upon me now! Ah, your suffering tears me apart! Don't you feel my anxiety?

Fernando, pushing away the specter of death:

> I fear it's already pulling on me.

Rosario:

> What do you fear if here there is one who would give a hundred lives for you; one who will never forget; one who feels the thirst of love? Speak and hear me, my darling, for this silence is like a hangman's noose! Look at me, my love! For if you speak you give me life. Habla! Speak to me, my Fernando! Por Dios, have pity on me!

Fernando embraces Rosario and takes his last breath:

> My darling! Adiós!

Rosario continues caressing him, not yet realizing that he's dead:

> My dear Fernando! Why did you say adiós? What are you asking for? These cruel words suddenly kill my hope. Bésame–give me a kiss, and you'll see how my lips will give you strength. Have you ever seen my eyes shed tears because of your indifference? No–I am your love, your support. Come to your Rosario, come!

She sees that he's dead, and sings the finale:

> O, Dios mío! This look that sees nothing. And the lips I kissed, now speechless. And the face rigid. Muerto! Muerto! Dios santo–heavenly God, I've lost all the delight I sought in life! Farewell forever! Por siempre adiós! Life is bondage, but death is more so! O! Mysterio! O!

Rosario falls over his body as the curtain falls. There are several moments of breathless silence, than a deafening applause that makes the pendants of the Met's chandeliers dance.

Granados' face is streaked with salty tears and salty drops of perspiration commingled. He watches the lead singers bow–one by one, then in pairs. Fitziu and Martinelli. Perini and De Luca. The dancers, Galli and Bonfiglio. They turn and bow toward the rest of the cast and the applause surges again. Granados watches Bavagnoli bow to the audience on his left, then center, then right. And still the applause reverberates. Now he hears "maestro!" and "Granados!" along with the bravos and he walks to the center of the stage for a thunderous cheer. He motions for Periquet to join him. Bouquets of flowers arrive and are given to the two principal female singers and to the lead ballerina. The applause continues and everyone on stage bows. Finally, in a departure from one of his strict rules, Gatti sends an assistant out to center stage with wreaths of laurel for Granados and Periquet. More applause.

Otto Kahn walks out with a bronze wreath for Granados. They shake hands as the applause intensifies, and Kahn says with evident delight, "Félicitations, maestro! This is the high point of our season!"

Granados stands, smiling, with a wreath on each arm. His mind slips from one fragmentary image of the past to the next. Numb and thrilled and incoherent, except for the excited voice within.

Ay sí! At last! Per fi! At last! My dream come true! Per fi! Gracias a Dios! At last! At last!

The audience remains standing, sustaining its applause for several minutes more. Throughout the house handkerchiefs are raised to dry the tears. Voices are hoarse from cheering. Held in suspension by the passion of the moment, very few turn to leave the theatre for an intermission that will be followed by the performance of *Pagliacci*. At last the applause begins to diminish and the curtain is lowered.

In the composer's box, an excited Casals turns to Schelling. "I've never witnessed such enthusiasm! It's an explosion! Never before in the theatre! Look at them! Applauding like mad but also crying. Obviously, people from Spain and South America understand the real character of this work. I'm so excited for our 'Ric!"

"I feel sorry for the cast of *Pagliacci*," replies Schelling. "Even Caruso will find this a difficult act to follow!"

Granados roams backstage, thanking the participants. Singers, players, dancers, stage hands. Abraçadas for Fitziu and Perini. He shakes hands with Martinelli, De Luca, and Bavagnoli, puts his arm around Setti and hugs him with special affinity. As Rosina Galli passes by, Granados steps over to give her an abraçada. Turning toward the dressing room, he's suddenly face-to-face with Caruso in Canio's white clown's costume for *Pagliacci*, oversized buttons down the front, carrying the pointed fool's cap. The familiar, oversized head surrounded by a ruffled collar. A broad grin, just as in his self-caricature. "Maestro Henri! A triumph! I've never heard them roar like this! Félicitations! Merveilleux! This city is yours, maestro! And how's a poor paisano like me going to follow such a triumph? Impossible! They will throw fruit at me! Why did Gatti have me follow you?" A loud laugh roars from his massive chest.

"You're very kind, but they won't throw fruit at Caruso."

"I don't care! Let them throw fruit! This is merveilleux! Félicitations! Now I want you to write an opera for me, comprends-tu? Don't forget! Don't forget!" Caruso wraps his arms around Granados and gives him a crushing hug.

Granados reaches his dressing room and stumbles onto a chair. As he closes his eyes, a wave of dizziness passes through him.

They said American audiences are cold–this is overwhelming! Anything but cold. This audience seized every chance!

Granados leaves through stage door and finds a throng of people waiting. As he reaches the 39th Street sidewalk, he's stopped by a couple who live in Brooklyn. The man's family originated in Fuendetodos, birthplace of Goya. "My grandfather was also a painter–of houses!" All three enjoy the joke. "My wife and I are aficionados of opera. Imagine how excited we were to hear you were coming with *Goyescas*! Maestro, would it be too presumptuous for us to ask for your autograph?" The woman hands Granados her program.

"No, not at all presumptuous. Your name is?" he asks the woman, and writes a personalized greeting.

Another couple, younger, intercepts him. They are from Lleida, now live in New Jersey. "Maestro Granados, you and my father were both born in the same town. Perhaps you played together as boys."

"Ah sí, perhaps," says Granados. He recognizes he was born in Lleida almost by accident; that was where his father was stationed by the army, and he only lived there for three years.

Though being from Lleida saved my life!

He signs their program, and sees that the crowd is growing. There are several dozen autograph-seekers, and Granados is high-spirited as he signs their programs. Most of them speak to him in English, and in the context of the interaction, he's able to respond.

An older couple steps up; the man tells him in Catalan that his wife's family is from "near Barcelona."

"How near?" Granados asks.

"A small town," says the woman. "Tiana. Have you heard of Tiana, mestre?"

He nods, and signs her program. "Ah sí–Tiana. A charming place. An enchanting place!"

God give me patience and strength for the next forty days!

When Granados arrives at Sherry's Restaurant, he sees Amparo waiting near the front door. They take several quick steps toward each other and embrace. He recognizes Schelling's voice, leading the other guests in a chorus of bravos.

"Titín," says Granados with a trembling voice, "Titín. I'll never be able to thank you! Without you I wouldn't be here! Tell me how I can thank you!"

With her arms around him, Amparo pulls her head back and looks up. "But you have, my dear. Six times!"

He laughs. "No, no–Titín! *You* raised the children. Por favor, seriously! How can I thank you?"

She smiles and tightens her arms around his waist. "I *am* serious, mi amor. When I look around and see all the women here with their diamonds and pearls, I say to myself: I have the most precious jewels in all the world. Six of them. What could be more precious? And I have you." She pauses, smiling. "You're quite precious too!"

They break apart and Granados goes from guest to guest, abraçadas for all. Casals is the first in line. "My brother, truly I've never witnessed such an explosion of enthusiasm! Mai tan emocionat! Never before! Everyone applauding like mad but also crying! Our people from Spain and South America understand the real character of your work. Visqui Goya! Visqui Granados! Ay, 'Ric, I'm so excited for you!"

The host for tonight's dinner in Granados' honor is Gustav White of G. Schirmer Inc. Sitting around a long table in one of Sherry's most opulent private rooms are Granados and Amparo; the Casals, Schellings, Riaños, Paderewskis, Kreislers, McCormacks, and Kahns; Huntington and Malvina Hoffman; Periquet and María Barrientos. On both sides of Granados and Amparo are Robert and Mildred Bliss, who arrived from Paris on the eve of the dress rehearsal. Mildred is radiant in her copy of Worth's elegant, provocative "Goya" gown of rose satin and tulle with a black lace shawl, for which she was fitted in Paris by a seamstress working under the watchful eye of Gaston Worth, son of the founder. A place has been set for Caruso, who said he planned to come. But the tenor wasn't seen after the performance of *Pagliacci*—except by the doorman, Ramón Iglesias, who saw him come through the stage door of the Met and climb into a La Salle town sedan with a tall, young, and very attractive red-haired woman. Gatti was also invited to Sherry's, but declined.

Louis Sherry, who started his first enterprise—a cart selling candy on Broadway near the Metropolitan—opened this new midtown restaurant at the turn of the century. Along with his nearby competitor, Delmonico's, Sherry seats many of the Met box holders of the Diamond Horseshoe at his tables, and tonight is no exception. But tonight Sherry remains close and attentive to G. Schirmer's table with its collection of international artists, the Spanish ambassador, and philanthropists of the stature of Huntington and Kahn. For the guest of honor, there's a special menu, printed for this table:

Dinner in Honor of Maestro Enrique Granados

Friday, January 28, 1916
Little Neck clams • Blue Points
Cream of celery soup
Broiled Spanish mackerel, Maitre d'Hotel
Hot House asparagus
Roast lamb, mint sauce
English pheasant
Salad
Compote of fruits • Chocolate mousse
Cognac

Sherry returns with a magnum of wine, wrapped in a white napkin, and shows it to Gustav White with obvious relish. White's eyes open wide. "I thought we'd do something a little special for tonight, if you're agreeable." With the host's assent, he directs a sommelier to fill the glasses with the rich tannic garnet-colored Bordeaux wine of Chateau Latour, bottled in 1886. One of four chateaux to be awarded the "1er cru classé" in 1855, a designation that still prevails.

Huntington turns to Kahn. "Will that do, Otto?"

Kahn laughs. "It will do–perfectly drinkable when I had it last week!"

Granados overhears the exchange, and looks around the table. Everyone is sipping the Chateau Latour as if it were vin ordinaire. More bottles arrive. His eyes graze those of the other celebrants. He observes the smiles and satisfaction of the New World's most successful. Casals seems at ease, sitting alongside Susan Metcalfe, who's just had her husband listed in the New York Social Register. Granados wonders: which of these men and women are not at ease? He looks across at Barrientos and Periquet, sitting side by side. Periquet is an actor, so he's unfathomable. Barriento's in a faraway place, in anticipation of her Met debut in three nights. She's "Lucia" now, not the ungainly girl from Barcelona with the stunning voice. She's "Lucia"–the role that will carry her to a second round of prominence. Granados' eyes have made the circuit, and now they return to Amparo. She's delighted to be here. This is a reward for so many years managing the household, raising the six children and waiting for him to come home. His eyes meet Amparo's. He lifts his glass and sips the Chateau Latour. She lifts hers and takes a sip. They clink their glasses.

"This wine will do," says Amparo. "Perfectly drinkable!"

The morning after the premiere, Granados walks down to the Western Union office on 57th Street and sends telegrams back home.

To his children, he wires: DEAREST ONES. A TRIUMPH BEYOND MY DREAMS. WE RETURN EARLY MARCH. I EMBRACE YOU ALL WITH AFFECTION

To Andreu and Carmen: RECEPTION FOR 'GOYESCAS' FAR BEYOND EXPECTATIONS. ONLY REGRET YOU WEREN'T HERE. THREE MORE PERFORMANCES. WE RETURN IN MARCH. UNA ABRAÇADA

To Frank Marshall at the academy: GREAT SUCCESS AT METROPOLITAN. EAGER TO TELL YOU EVERYTHING. PLAN TO RETURN MID-MARCH. ABRAÇADAS TO INSTRUCTORS AND STUDENTS

A similar message to his friends Gabriel Miró and August Pi i Sunyer: OPERA GREAT SUCCESS. MANY THANKS FOR WATCHING CHILDREN. BACK HOME THIRD WEEK MARCH. UNA ABRAÇADA

To Clotilde: OPERA GREAT SUCCESS. LONGING FOR YOU EXCRUCIATING. YOU CANNOT IMAGINE HOW MUCH. 'GOYESCAS' ACCEPTED BY TEATRO COLÓN. YOU MUST COME TO BUENOS AIRES! ARRIVING BARCELONA AROUND 18 MARCH. AN ETERNITY TO WAIT. UNA ETERNIDAD! TE ADORO TANTÍSIMO

When Granados returns to the Wellington, the desk clerk hands him an envelope of white linen paper with dark blue letters in the upper left corner: The White House, Washington, D.C.

It's an invitation from President and Mrs. Woodrow Thomas Wilson to play for family and friends in the East Room of the White House on March 9. Also appearing will be Julia Culp, a Dutch contralto who's well regarded for her interpretations of German lieder.

The President wants me to play! The White House? Ninth of March! Dios mío! We're suppose to leave for home day before. Can't accept–without changing plans. Must call Pau!

He phones Casals for advice. "Too bad about the timing," says Casals. "If it were only two or three days earlier. Of course you haven't much choice. It's a command performance. Like playing for King Alfonso. There's no telling how much it could help your career, especially in Americà–and Americà's the only place left until the war's over in Europe."

"You're advising me to go?"

"Absolutely," Casals says. "I know it's inconvenient. Like most things worth doing. Yes–you should go. And find another boat to take you home."

Granados replies, "We're booked on the *Antonio López*–straight to Cádiz and Barcelona, but it'll be gone by the ninth."

"Then you'll have to find another boat," says Casals. "Or, better yet, wait for another Spanish boat. So you don't have to go through the war zone."

The next morning, Granados accepts the invitation from the White House and walks through yesterday's melting snow to the travel office of Thomas Cook & Sons on 57th Street, where he made reservations for the departure on March 8. The sales clerk, Arthur Bromley, recognizes him and invites him to sit down.

"It's Señor Granados, is it not? Yes, you'd prefer to speak French. D'accord. Now, what can I do to help you today?"

Granados explains that he's been invited to play for President Wilson and needs to change his reservations.

"Félicitations!" Bromley reaches for a directory behind him and flips through the pages. "Ah, here it is. Why, I can get you on the very same ship–*Antonio López*–early in April. Could you stay over?"

And wait another month? Of course not! Already too long. Then another boat to Argentina in May?

"No," he says to the clerk. "We have to leave sooner than that. What other ships are sailing to Europe?"

"Just a minute. Let me consult with one of my colleagues."

Granados is restless. When he told Amparo about the White House invitation last night, she wasn't convinced it would benefit his career, but conceded that Casals was far more experienced in such matters. Granados explained that if he went to Washington, they would not be able to leave on March 8. "Of course," replied Amparo. "If you go, I'll stay here and get us organized. It's a bit confusing. I think you should make the decision–and find us another way to get back home. And the sooner the better!"

Bromley returns, exuding confidence. "I think I've found a solution for you, Monsieur Granados. It so happens the very next vessel available is a very fine liner of the Holland America Line–SS *Rotterdam*–which will leave New York March 11. That's only three days after your original departure on *Antonio López*. Of course, *Rotterdam* doesn't go to Barcelona, but it will get you to England. And from there it's an easy hop across the Channel and you can catch a train on the other side. From Boulogne or Dieppe."

Only three days' delay. Much better than waiting for next Spanish boat. Mildred Bliss said traveling on Holland America was splendid. "So we'd have to go through England?" asks Granados.

"Yes, unless you want to wait for a boat to Barcelona or Marseilles. But that means waiting three, maybe four weeks. The *Rotterdam* doesn't go to Spain."

"I don't want to wait. It means going to London?"

Bromley smiles. "Yes, I'm sorry not to be more specific. You'll want to stay in London, and make arrangements there to cross the Channel."

London–The Royal Opera! Covent Garden! Sir Henry Wood! How to get home from there?

"You're suggesting we go through Paris?"

"Heavens no!" Bromley says, unfolding a map of France. "Look here, you'll go down through Rouen and Tours and LeMans–here, then down through Bordeaux, to Bayonne just north of the Spanish border."

"Ah, I've been to Bayonne." Stopped there en route to Cambó, his farewell to the dying Albéniz. "Hmnn. So we can avoid the war. Fine–I understand. I presume we'd get off the boat in London."

For the first time Bromley hesitates. "Actually, it'll be Falmouth," he tells Granados. The ship will approach England's southern coast, passing Land's End and Lizard Point, and make a stop at Falmouth. A lighter will come out from Falmouth Harbor to take off passengers bound for London. "You'll take a short train ride from Falmouth to London," Bromley says, "where I presume you'll want to stay."

"Yes. Can you make arrangements for us to cross the Channel?"

Bromley leans back in his chair. "Well, I'd like to book your crossing here, but the service isn't as reliable as it was. Before the war. There are steamers crossing the Channel every day, that's not the issue. This far in advance, more than a month–well, by the time you'd be ready to cross, it might be another steamer, don't you see?"

Granados shrugs. "As you say, we can make arrangements for crossing when we get to London."

"Précisément. Now, if you're agreeable, I'll try to get you a cabin in First Class on *Rotterdam* leaving the 11th of March." Bromley estimates the rates for their passage from New York to Falmouth, and rail from the French Coast to Barcelona. It's more expensive than returning on a Spanish boat, but less costly than staying another month in New York. "You should know I'm giving you a good rate, Monsieur Granados."

Granados frowns as he contemplates spending more money.

How much will playing for Americà's President help my career? More expenses to play for him. And delay reaching home. Worth it?

"Do I receive credit for the return trip on *Antonio López?*" he asks.

"Yes, by all means." Bromley reaches for a notepad and pulls a pencil out of his desk drawer. "I can arrange for you to receive a refund from the Compañia Transporte Española. And if you wish, that can be applied to your tickets on *Rotterdam*. But with one caveat, Monsieur Granados. Once you've agreed to this arrangement, I won't be able to get you a refund from Holland America–if for any reason you're unable to take *Rotterdam* on the 11th of March. I want to make sure you understand that."

Granados' nods, but his mind is racing ahead–back across the Atlantic, to the prospect of seeing Schelling's friend Sir Henry Wood about a Royal Opera

Company production of *Goyescas* at Covent Garden. To the possibility of seeing that his art reaches another corner of the world.

Within days of the premiere of *Goyescas*, the major New York newspapers render their judgment. By most of them, the music is praised and the libretto disparaged. Several find faults with the orchestration, its "patchwork construction," and Bavagnoli's conducting. These comments are no surprise to Granados.

The *New York Evening Post* says his *Intermezzo* is the equal of Pietro Mascagni's renowned "intermezzo sinfonico"–composed, as was Granados'–to separate the two acts in his opera *Cavalleria Rusticana*. Granados hopes the comparison won't be prophetic, since after the popular reception for *Cavalleria*, Mascagni's subsequent operas weren't ever deemed its equal.

The *New York Telegraph* praises the opera in a short review:

> There were ecstatic bravos over Signor Granados' music and his biscuit-colored waistcoat as he took the stage repeatedly for bows.

The *New York Herald* review says the premiere marks "a brilliant evening and one of the important social events of the winter," and in assessing the opera, concludes:

> The work takes only an hour in performance, including two entr'actes, yet it calls for four important singers and three complete sets of scenery. This, in itself, is almost sufficient to defeat its chances of performance in most opera houses. One is inclined to ask: was it worth all that?

Writing for *Novedades*, a Spanish language publication in New York, Pedro Henriquez Ureña says:

> The applause was tumultuous, from the close of the first act, and Granados was obliged to take the stage to acknowledge it, along with his librettist Periquet. With 'Intermezzo' there was loud applause, much handclapping, and shouts of 'Olé!' There were tributes for Anna Fitziu after the song of the maja and nightingale. Pride in culture and common homelands resulted in a delirious ovation, but it was contagious for the English-speaking audience, and the entire production was greeted with enthusiasm.

The most heartening review comes from the newspaper with the largest daily circulation. In the *New York Times*, Richard Aldrich compares Granados to Chopin. He writes:

There was ecstatic applause after each of the first two acts and more at the end of the opera. The singers were again and again recalled. Mr. Granados came frequently; Mr. Periquet came; Messrs. Setti, Speck, and Bavagnoli came, and none was left unhonored. Vast wreaths were given the two authors of the opera, a bronze one to Mr. Granados.

The applause on this occasion doubtless had much of the fictitious value of first-night applause, to which was added the element of national pride. But there seemed to be evidence to show that the brilliantly exotic little opera–it lasts hardly an hour–had really made an impression on the general public, and that it may turn out to have more than the transitory attraction of many new additions to the operatic list.

There is no question that the opera is intensely Spanish in its whole texture and feeling; that it is charged with the atmosphere of the country and vibrates through and through with the musical quality of Spain as does no other opera and no other music that has been heard here.

The music is Spanish, coming from the brain and heart of a real Spaniard. Spanish music has occupied a curious place since the exploitation of nationalism in music first began, well along in the nineteenth century. But how many Spanish composers have there been of cosmopolitan standing, known beyond the confines of the Pyrenees, who have done for their native music what Chopin, Liszt, Grieg, Dvorak, the neo-Russians, have done for theirs? Sarasate did something of the sort in the elegant manner of a virtuoso. Isaac Albéniz did something in a more poetical, more suggestive style, though he saw his native land through the veil of the modern Frenchman. Beyond these two it would be hard to name any Spanish musician who has interpreted Spain for the rest of the world till Mr. Granados came with this full-blooded, passionate utterance, sometimes stirring in its characteristic rhythms and frank melody, sometimes languorous, poetical, profoundly pathetic, subtly suggestive.

The Spain that is embodied in his music is authentic. And yet possessing as it does an intensely national color, what he has written is a personal, individual expression. Nor does he fall into the easy commonplaces to which Spanish tunes and rhythms are so often a tempting invitation. There is here something deeper, more profoundly felt. The Spain that is

> pictured in *Goyescas* is something very different from the "hot night disturbed by a guitar" that has been ironically said to be the sum and substance of Spain in music.
>
> Mr. Granados has a rich and unconventional harmonic feeling, though he does not follow those who are most conspicuous in the exploitation of "modern" harmony. His harmonic scheme is elaborate, and gives a peculiar distinction, warmth and brilliancy to his style. This music has a haunting power. It would be too much to say that the opera is a great contribution to modern art, or even that it approaches greatness, but it is genuine and vital."

From Rudi Schirmer, Granados receives a translation of the reviews into Castilian. He reads them over and over, especially the one in the *New York Times*. He savors the tribute, repeating and rewording some of the phrases, and disregards the question of whether *Goyescas* is a great contribution to modern art.

That's for posterity. But at last—at last!—a critic making effort to understand. Brilliantly exotic opera. More than transitory attraction. No question opera is intensely Spanish. Vibrates with musical quality of Spain as no other work ever heard. Except for Sarasate and Albéniz hard to name Spanish composer who's interpreted his country. This reviewer felt it! Music has haunting power. Couldn't ask for more. At last!

Gatti-Casazza, out of hearing range of the critics, offers this cryptic comment to Bavagnoli on the day the reviews appear: "It's not a great thing. It's a sort of symphonic poem with vocal parts—set to a poor libretto. Granados is a man of great presumption. He believes he's written something truly superior—that leaves *Carmen* far behind. I don't agree." Yet *Goyescas* is sold out for its four performances, and when Gatti needs to replace another work scheduled for March 6, he inserts *Goyescas* for a fifth and final performance.

That final staging takes place on March 6. Since Periquet returned to Spain after the second performance, Granados takes tonight's bows alone. The audience responds with enthusiasm but not delirium, perhaps because few of the Spanish and South American colony are present, perhaps because it's the most uneven of the five performances. Bavagnoli seems to have lost his way again with the tempo.

With the conclusion of his opera's run at the Metropolitan, Granados' attention has turned to other venues. Two months after he returns home–sooner than he wanted or expected, he'll come back across the ocean to Buenos Aires, earning far more for taking *Goyescas* to Teatro Colón than he's earned at the Metropolitan. He'll arrive two weeks before the June 2nd opening and stay for five weeks, all expenses paid.

In addition, he receives an unprompted letter from a Señor Florencio Constantino, representing a California group that wants Granados to present the opera five times in the month of May in Los Angeles. In closing his invitation, Constantino wrote: "We have some old Spanish Californians who are enthusiastic to greet the eminent author of *Goyescas* that has been such a triumph in New York!"

Clearly, five performances of *Goyescas* in Los Angeles in May is not possible. At least not this May. Despite this, Granados–unaccustomed to having venues tossed in his direction–inquires about Florencio Constantino, who gave María Barrientos as a reference.

"Florencio? He's in California?" asks Barrientos, shaking her head.

Granados shrugs. "He says there's a group in Los Angeles wanting me to come out and do five performances in May. This May–in two months! Of course I can't–I'll be back home by then. It won't work out this year, but maybe next. I'm just curious."

Barrientos grimaces. "Florencio's a lyric tenor. I sang with him in Italy a dozen years ago. A good mezzo range, but he can't hit the high notes. I didn't see him again until I resumed my career. We did *Lucia* together at the Colón–I'd say five years ago. By that time, he made his Met debut and was quite excited. I think we also did *Rigoletto* at the Colón. But–"

"But?" asks Granados. "What is it?"

"Well, Florencio's a bit strange. Molt estrany, entens? His family's Italian, he was born and grew up in Bilbao, then went to Argentina after some dispute over a betrothal. He tried to explain it to me once, but it made no sense at all. Poor man! So generous! But he took all the money he'd made singing, and he built an opera house in Bragado–a place two hours north of Buenos Aires. Bragado! Right in the middle of the Argentine Pampas! Well, you can imagine, it took him just two years to go broke. To make matters worse, he poked out Giovanni Gravina's eye in a sword fight on stage, somewhere. He was sued for that. So I'm surprised to hear he's in California."

Granados sighs. Another life story resembling a bel canto opera. "Well, I can't possibly take *Goyescas* to California in May. Though it's always nice to be asked."

Despite the lack of time, despite the usual obstacles to mounting a new production, Antonia Mercé's United States debut at the Maxine Elliott Theatre exceeds expectations. The house is nearly sold out, excellent for a Thursday. Mercé is dazzling in a costume designed by Ignacio Zuloaga, dancing Granados' "Danza–Andaluza" for the first time. And the audience applauds wildly after her performance of the elegant, poetic piece Granados wrote for this occasion: "Tango of the Green Eyes." As the ovation continues, she motions to the box where Granados is sitting and he takes a bow. Mercé parlays this success into an afternoon of concert dances booked for three weeks later, before an audience of actors, musicians, and patrons of art. Her career in the United States is launched.

The day after a concert with Anna Fitziu at Aeolian Hall on 42nd Street, Granados returns to the hall, where he's made a number of recordings on Aeolian's Duo-Art "piano roll" system. He's already finished what the contract called for–"El Pelele" and "La Maja y el Ruiseñor" from the opera, four of the *Danzas*, and *Danza Lenta*–so it's assumed he's come back to say farewell. No, he tells them, he wants to do one more recording. And he seems extraordinarily sad. After the staff prepares the equipment, Granados pulls out a scrap of paper with a few notes jotted down, and proceeds to improvise for five minutes.

Granados sits for photographs and reviews copy for a Duo-Art advertisement that will be published the day after his departure. His mood is jovial and his eyes twinkle. "You're asking me to believe *I said* these things?" he asks playfully, holding up the ad copy. "That I really said, 'The tone of the Duo-Art Pianola is exactly the tone of the piano that is played by hand'?" He's assured that is what he said; if he wants to change it, they'd certainly concur. He continues to tease them. "No, those seem the ideal words to sell more of your pianos. And you've paid me well. So those must truly have been my exact words!" For a moment, he watches the Aeolian staff pondering a response, then adds, "Well, I'm not worried. If they aren't my words, gentlemen, I'll be gone before the ad appears."

With reservations made to take *Rotterdam* to England, Granados sends a telegram to Ismael Smith in London, asking if he'd find a comfortable hotel in a convenient location. Smith replies quickly, offering his own residence that he shares with his brothers. Granados sends back an appreciative reply, thanking Smith for his generosity but saying he hasn't been feeling well and would prefer to be in a hotel. He also asks Smith to arrange a meeting with Sir Henry Wood to discuss presenting *Goyescas* at Covent Garden. Smith's reply confirms his willingness to find a hotel; he suggests a meeting with Sir Thomas Beecham, who's just been knighted by King George V and is more involved in operatic productions than Wood. Granados is pleasantly surprised that his somewhat bizarre friend seems able to help make the stay in London worthwhile.

Granados' decision to take *Rotterdam* to London detonates a controversy among his friends in New York. Casals and Schelling agree he had no other choice than to accept the invitation from President Wilson. Knowing his lifelong fear of ocean travel, they're reluctant to advise him about his return passage. Malvina Hoffman says some of her sculptor friends cross back and forth from England without concern. Mildred Bliss, who's remained in New York to see friends and family, asks Robert for advice. He returned to the embassy in Paris in mid-February, and in replying he suggests she reserve a stateroom on *Rotterdam* for March 11th to return through London, where he will meet her and escort her back to Paris. However, Francisca Rodón is alarmed when Amparo tells her of their reservations. She phones Granados at the Wellington.

"I understand you're going right through the middle of the war zone!" she cries. "I know the Spanish boats are smaller and slower and uglier and less comfortable than the luxury liners of Holland. But do you think the war zone's a good idea? Please say you don't!"

"Francisca," he replies in his most conciliatory voice, "we looked at all the vessels leaving New York, and since *Antonio López* leaves while I'm playing for the President of Americà, we had to find another one. Fortunately we found one that leaves only three days later. It was really our only choice."

Rodón is unappeased. "First of all, you keep saying '*we*'—when we know Amparo had nothing to say about this. And it's not correct to say it was your *only* choice. If you asked Ambassador Riaño, he would have them hold the *Antonio López* for a day and we can all go back together. And return *safely*!"

"I certainly wouldn't ask him to do that, and I think you're just being argumentative to say he will. The next Spanish vessel doesn't leave here until early April. Titín's been away from the children for three months, so waiting another month is out of the question."

Rodón lowers her voice. "I know that's a hardship. But I've talked to Titín about this, and she says she could wait, so don't push this off on her! You're the one who's anxious to get back home. Titín could wait, but you can't! You can't wait to see your amante again! That's it, isn't it?"

Granados promises to ask Riaño about holding *Antonio López*.

Washington, D.C. March 7, 1916

It snowed heavily yesterday and last night in New York; this morning the cab moves slowly through the slush and ice from the Hotel Wellington to Pennsylvania Station. It's still dark as night when Granados boards the train. The morning express steams through New Jersey after picking up passengers in Newark.

To get from New York City to Washington, D.C., requires a four-to-five hour ride, covering roughly two hundred fifty kilometers. The train picks up speed as it crosses the marshlands of northern New Jersey, threading through the smoke and fire of industry. Though he's heard in advance that the jaunt will not be scenic, Granados is surprised at the proliferation of industry–extending farther beyond the city centers than back home in Catalunya. Stations fly past like placards: Elizabeth, Rahway, Metuchen, New Brunswick, followed by a stretch of New Jersey countryside north of Princeton Junction. The air is clearer and Granados sees blue sky for the first time in several days, days when he's been too busy to open up the corners of his mind where the events of recent weeks are stored. As usual, Granados is content to be traveling alone. What better time for reflection? And as usual, the rush of events in recent weeks has kept his head spinning.

After a stretch of New Jersey countryside, the train passes through Trenton, North Philadelphia, Philadelphia, and Wilmington–a mostly unbroken array of smokestacks and redbrick housing for the families of industrial workers and tradesmen. Granados looks out the smoke-streaked window of his coach car. A somber haze hangs over this backside of America's vaunted prosperity, just as it does over Badalona and the mill towns of the Llobregat River, which surround Barcelona.

Granados is still disconsolate over the news that Rubén Darío died on February 6 at his home in León, Nicaragua. Concluding a life lived at full throttle, he slipped away after a long, unsparing illness. Granados regrets never meeting Darío–he was in Puigcerdà when the poet visited Els Quatre Gats–yet he felt a strong sense of kinship with him. Both born in 1867. Both prodigious artists, who wrote their masterpieces in the same year, 1910. When Darío published "Poema del otoño" in the same month as the release of Book One of *Goyescas*, Granados and Clotilde believed it was not mere coincidence: there must be a fateful bond between these two who'd never met.

Darío, the bard of Latin America, often urged artists of the New World to explore the music and art of other worlds, while Granados has now brought the Old World art of Goya to the Americas with his distinctive musical interpretation. They've both had complicated lives, neither adhering to monogamy—though their way of expressing love for more than one woman has differed. Darío went back and forth between Francisca Sanehy and Rosario Murillo for several years, returning to the latter when he went home to die.

But what drew Granados to Darío, more than demographics and genius, was reading his poetry with Clotilde in the garden at Tiana. A decade of poetry there makes the passing of this man especially jarring. Especially the lines she recited on his last day before he left for America:

> I know there are those who ask:
> why do you not still sing
> those same wild songs of yesteryear?
> They do not see the work of just an hour,
> the work of a minute, and the wonders of a year.
> I, now an aging tree, used to moan so sweetly
> from the breezes when I began to grow.
> But the time has passed for youthful smiles:
> so let the hurricane move my heart to song!

The train is south of Wilmington, passing through the Maryland countryside, crossing the Susquehanna River, skirting the gray waters of Chesapeake Bay. The fields are greener, heralding the arrival of spring.

The train cuts through a stretch of Maryland countryside north of Baltimore—brown fields turning to green with the warming effects of the bay—and chugs through the rolling green hills and valleys bordering the nation's capital. Granados straightens the leather band with the medallion of Beethoven on his right wrist and reaches into his jacket pocket to scan the card that Ambassador Riaño sent him. "Embajada de España, 1521 New Hampshire Avenue Northwest." He's been told the White House is at 1600 Pennsylvania Avenue, and wonders if it's close to the embassy. But since he'll be with Riaño, he's not concerned about getting there. One of his teeth is bothering him, and he hopes the pain will go away before he has to play for the President of the United States of America.

The train begins to slow as it passes the tobacco plantations and horse farms in Maryland's Prince George's County and splits rural villages on the northern outskirts of Washington. Granados looks out and sees a much greener landscape. As the train pulls into Union Station, he experiences the first tremor of concern, arising from his complete unfamiliarity with places he's about to visit–Spain's Embassy, the White House, the hotel reserved by Riaño–and from misgivings about his ability to communicate in a city where English is said to be more prevalent than in New York. Yet he understands why Casals believes playing at the White House is important, and consoles himself that Juan Riaño will be by his side, guiding him, introducing him, and translating for him. Granados fidgets with his Beethoven wrist band.

The cabdriver takes him up Massachusetts Avenue and around Mt. Vernon Square, where fruit trees are beginning to blossom across from the Beaux Arts-style Carnegie Library, then west on K Street to Connecticut Avenue, then northwest to Dupont Circle, circling round to New Hampshire and stopping in front of the Ionic-columned, four-story embassy. Riaño greets Granados in the entryway, and after minimal diplomatic courtesy asks him about his plans for returning to Barcelona.

Granados hesitates, surprised by the urgency in Riaño's voice. "Well, I've changed our plans. Because of this concert for the President, we couldn't get the next Spanish boat until next month. And we're not willing to wait that long. It's much too long to wait. So I made reservations on a Dutch liner. We're leaving on the 11th."

Riaño doesn't hold back. "Maestro, I think you must be completely out of your mind to risk sailing on a belligerent vessel when there are Spanish boats making regularly scheduled trips between New York and Barcelona! And, by the way, these Spanish boats have never been attacked by the German submarines. Furthermore, it'll be more expensive for you to go to England then across the English Channel then down through France by rail. If you include the cost of hotels and meals, it'll certainly turn out to be much more expensive to take the route you've chosen. Not less. And–not to alarm you–but by going through England and France, which are at war, you'll run into checkpoints and police watching everywhere. Compare that with taking a Spanish vessel from here and getting off the same boat within a mile of your home in Barcelona."

"I don't know what to say," Granados says with a sinking feeling. "You obviously have more information about these things."

"Maestro, it's my business to know what's going on in the world. Just as you know how to take the colors of Goya's paintings and bring them to life in your music. What you've done with *Goyescas* is nothing short of revolutionary. Surely there's been nothing like it here in the Americas. And if there are any who say 'nay,' I'd suggest they're simply envious of your genius. Sí, mucho genio. But that doesn't make you a genius on how to get home safely. That's why I'd like you to listen to my advice."

"Yes, I'm listening, Don Juan," says Granados. "What would you have me do?"

"I'd have you go back to the travel agency and cancel your reservations on the Dutch boat, and rebook passage on *Antonio López*. You should be able to get a credit."

Granados fights back. "Claro, but surely you understand I have two reasons for going back home through London. The most important is getting home sooner. The second is finding more venues for my opera. That means New York, Chicago, California, Buenos Aires and–the only one left in Europe, London. From what I was paid by the Metropolitan, I can barely pay my way back home. But now I have a contract to go to Buenos Aires, and I want to talk to people in London."

Riaño smiles. "I do understand that. And I don't blame you, not at all. But there's no certainty of getting a venue in London. Look, maestro, I've talked to Señor Zaragoza of the Compañía Transatlántica in New York and he'll hold *Antonio López* so you can take it after you return from here. The vessel will leave the day after tomorrow–so you don't have to go through the war zone. I can have it delayed–unless you tell me you're not interested."

"I didn't say I'm not interested," Granados replies. "Not at all. I've listened to what you've said. I need to think about it and I'll let you know tomorrow–after my concert for the president."

"You'll be coming here for tomorrow's luncheon, right?"

"Of course. I'll be here by noon."

"Excellent! Now you'll need to get over to the White House to rehearse. My driver will take you, so they won't stop you at the gate."

"But you'll be going with me, won't you?"

Riaño claps his hand on Granados' shoulder. "As a matter of fact, I won't be. You see, these events at the White House are done on a rotation, so all of the diplomatic corps gets to spend the same number of evenings with the President. But tonight isn't my turn."

Granados is on the verge of panic. He shakes his head in disbelief. "But I assumed you'd be there! You're the ambassador of my country. I need you there to introduce me, to translate if they don't speak French or Castilian. Oh–this is quite a shock!"

"I'm sorry," Riaño says. "I should have told you before you came."

"No, no. I would have come anyway. It's too important. But tonight will be very difficult without your being there."

Riaño shakes his head. "It can't be changed. I'm not in control of the President's protocol. But the ambassador of Chile will be there, and the minister from Salvador. You might look for them. Now, I've made a reservation for you at the Willard Hotel. I'll have your luggage sent there, except what you need for rehearsal this afternoon. Is there anything else I can help you with, maestro?"

Granados points to his jaw. "Yes. I have a toothache that won't go away and I'd like to see a dentist. Could you help me with that?"

Relieved to be asked for something he can control, Riaño picks up the phone and quickly arranges for Granados to see his dentist, Dr. Edward Boe, whose office is at 14th Street and C, close to the White House.

Granados climbs into Riaño's town car that has been waiting for him on 14th Street. He has a temporary filling on the molar farthest back in his lower right jaw, and Dr. Boe's printed list of prohibited foods–duck, pork, salmon, cheese, patés, mustard, pepper, and vinegar–along with tobacco and alcohol. More importantly, the area around the molar has been numbed with novocain.

"A la Casa Blanca, Señor Granados?" asks Riaño's chauffeur.

"Sí, por favor."

The town car stops at the gate and is quickly waved onto the long, curving driveway across the north lawn of the White House to the portico. A member of the President's staff welcomes Granados and guides him to the East Room, where Julia Culp is practicing with her Dutch accompanist. Granados apologizes for arriving late. After his description of visiting the dentist in a jumble of languages, they choose their only common one, French.

Julia Culp is a tall, handsome contralto of thirty-six, whose relatively short range, medium-size voice and extraordinary control of tone and dynamics are best suited to a career of recitals and concerts. She's often referred to as "the Dutch Nightingale." Culp left the Netherlands to advance her studies in Berlin, where she debuted in 1901. Since then she's performed in Europe with Edvard Grieg, Richard Strauss, Camille Saint-Saens, and Ferruccio Busoni, and sung in England under the batons of Sir Henry Wood and Sir Thomas Beecham. Two years ago, she brought her finely controlled voice to the Americas, touring both continents each year and singing with many notable artists, including Caruso. President Wilson's daughter Margaret–an aspiring soprano–is especially fond of

Culp, and has booked her for two White House "Musicales" this season, with Granados and later with the Australian pianist and composer Percy Grainger.

"Miss Wilson's quite excited about your coming," Culp says.

"I'm flattered," replies Granados. "I wonder where she heard my music."

"Maestro Granados, since I arrived last month, I've heard about nothing but 'the opera by the Spanish composer.' Even Caruso is excited about your opera, *Goyesque*. That's high praise from an Italian tenor!"

"Ah, Caruso. You know him?"

Culp laughs. "We sang together in South America, but I wouldn't admit to knowing him. Who could ever know the great–and shameless–Caruso? At any rate, I'm not surprised to see you here. Miss Wilson's quite keen on staying abreast of everything in the world of music."

Granados smiles. "I suppose it would have been discourteous if I'd declined the invitation."

Culp laughs. "If you had, it would have been quite a novelty!"

"You mean, this is truly a command performance."

"Quite so," says Culp, "but it's also grand for one's career, is it not?"

Granados hesitates. "Oui, but in my case I've had to change my plans for returning home. So instead of going back the way I came, I'm going on a Dutch boat. Through London."

"Oh? Which boat?" asks Culp.

"Holland America. *Rotterdam*."

Culp's words are encouraging. "The Holland America Line is the finest in the world, and *Rotterdam* is queen of the fleet. A splendid vessel–I've taken it several times. You'll not regret that change."

"I should ask you to talk to the people who think I've made a big, big mistake going through the war zone."

"War zone? I wouldn't call it that, maestro. The war is on the continent–in the trenches. Yes, there are submarines, but I'm told the British Navy has solved that problem. You have nothing to worry about. You'll have a fine voyage back on *Rotterdam*–and if you can, do stay a few days in London. And I'd suggest you talk to the people at Covent Garden. I don't sing much opera, but I did Elgar's oratorio *Dream of Gerontius* with Sir Henry Wood. Sir Henry's a splendid man! You must talk to him. Also Sir Thomas Beecham. After such a triumph here in America, they should be very interested in seeing you!"

Sir Henry. Sir Thomas. Good idea going to London. More venues for Goyescas. *Buenos Aires then London then everywhere!*

The piano in the East Room is the "gold piano" described by Casals when he played for President Theodore Roosevelt twelve years ago. A gift from Steinway & Sons of New York, it has a gilded case supported by golden eagles with wings spread, that constitute its three legs. Along the sides are clusters of gilded foliage framing the shields of the original thirteen united American states, and on the inside of the cover is a painting that depicts the nine Muses. Since arriving at the White House, the piano has been played by, among others, Josef Hoffman, Ferruccio Busoni, Sergei Rachmaninoff, and Jan Paderewski–who was here two weeks ago. And tonight it will be Granados' turn.

After checking into the Hotel Willard and resting for an hour, Granados returns to the White House in formal attire shortly before eight o'clock. This time he's greeted by Margaret Wilson, who takes him to a small parlor.

"I understand you've met Miss Culp. And, I trust, had some time to practice," she says in French. She's a tall, fair woman of thirty with a narrow fine-boned face resembling her father's. After several years of vocal training, she enjoys singing and sings well enough for small groups–though with marginal aspirations for a concert career. It was her initiative that revived the "East Room Musicales" of the Roosevelt presidency, after a hiatus under President Taft. Tonight she's wearing a long white satin gown draped in tulle, with a crown of red roses on her curly brown hair.

"It's quite an unusual piano," says Granados.

Margaret laughs. "Yes, quite unique! One of our guest pianists complained that all the glare from the gold made it quite impossible for her to read her music." She leans toward Granados. "And a little secret between us: it's a devil to keep in tune. Did you notice?"

Granados relaxes. "I'm so glad you mentioned that. I wouldn't want to offend anyone."

"That's the price you pay for having perfect pitch. Not me."

He laughs. "Yes, it's *one* of them."

"Well, I brought you here so you could meet my father. He asked to see you personally before the concert." She gestures to a closed door at the end of a short corridor. "There's a meeting now, but he'll be out shortly."

"That's very kind, Mademoiselle Wilson."

"You wouldn't suspect it–with everything else he has on his mind–but my father's quite devoted to music. He recognizes how important it is in human progress. Did you know he played the violin as a boy? Sang in the Princeton

Glee Club–a choral group. And in graduate school helped organize a chapel choir. He still loves to sing. But I should warn you," she says lightly, "when we sing the national anthem tonight, you'll probably hear his voice–he loves holding the high note three measures from the end, and the only way he can hit that note is to sing it falsetto. I warn you, because he did it one night standing next to the German ambassador's wife, and if we had a photo of her expression, we could probably use it to bargain for an end to the war." It's obvious Margaret is amused by and devoted to her father.

The door at the end of the short corridor opens and Granados sees two men walking toward him. He recognizes President Wilson from the many photos in newspapers and magazines. Margaret steps forward and introduces him to her father. The President extends a dry bony hand to him and introduces a tall slender man with keen gray eyes, long hair that has fallen over his forehead, and a long, drooping moustache. "Maestro Granados, this is Senator Stone–one of my most distinguished colleagues."

Senator William Stone of Missouri is the chairman of the Senate Foreign Relations Committee. He's spent the last half hour in what both will later describe to the press as "a very frank talk," with Stone seeking and receiving a firm commitment from the president to keep the United States of America out of what Stone calls "the disastrous war in Europe." As a leader of the so-called "isolationist" bloc in the Senate, Stone views this idealistic president with suspicion. After Stone thanks Wilson for making time available for him and takes leave, the president leads his daughter and Granados into the Oval Office.

"Welcome to the White House, maestro. Ben-ven-ee-doze."

"Thank you, Señor Presidente."

"I understand that you and I don't have a common language, so I've asked Margaret to translate. What we do have in common is music, right?"

Granados nods.

"Father, I've told the maestro of your devotion to music," says Margaret.

Wilson beams. "You did?" He turns to Granados. "Then you know how I love to sing."

"Yes, Señor Presidente."

Wilson frowns. "And she told you, no doubt, that I reach for that high note in our national anthem. That I don't always hit it just right."

Granados smiles. "Yes, she told me. But reaching that note is difficult even for Enrico Caruso–he told me himself."

Wilson finds this hilarious. He turns to his daughter. "See, I'm not such a wretched tenor after all! But while I have you here, maestro, would you mind if I asked you a question or two. Having to do with the war."

Wants my opinion of the war?

"No, I wouldn't mind."

The President leans forward, making contact with the intense blue eyes behind wire-rimmed glasses. "Well, your country has stayed out of the nasty war in Europe. A wise choice. And my country has also remained neutral, though our friends in England and France want us to join their side. We don't think they should have gotten into this mess in the first place, and it's not our job to get them out of it. Still, if the United States could help bring about peace in Europe, that would be very desirable. I'm not sure it can be done, but as long as we're neutral perhaps both sides would let us be the peacemakers. Does that seem reasonable?"

"Señor Presidente, you should know that I abhor war, and as an artist I try to stay as far away from politics as I can. My opinion is that art and politics don't mix. But of course I agree, it's a horrible war."

"It's a complicated situation here, maestro. We have people who say we should go to the aid of the French and British, that America's vital interests are intertwined with theirs. And there's some truth in that. On the other hand, Senator Stone and others represent states in the middle of our country where there are many Germans who came here and became American citizens. Naturally they don't want a war against their kinfolk. It would be like a civil war, brother against brother. And my country learned how costly that can be. I grew up in the South, and saw how destructive civil war can be. So it's not an easy question, is it?"

"No, Señor Presidente. It's not easy."

"Tell me if you will maestro, what do people in your country think of the war in Europe? Is there sympathy with the French and the British? Or with the Germans and Austrians?"

"As I said, Mr. President, I wouldn't be the best judge of that. You might ask that question of our ambassador, Señor Riaño."

"Ah, Riaño! Splendid ambassador! Stellar man! You know he really had his work cut out for him when he came here after our war against each other. I have the utmost respect for Ambassador Riaño. But I'm asking you, maestro, especially because you are not involved in politics. I'm interested in what average people in Spain think about the war. Can you help me?"

"As long as there are no reporters listening, yes," says Granados, his eyes twinkling.

Wilson tilts his head back and laughs. "Yes, we certainly see eye to eye on that!"

"Well, to answer your question, I'd like to say that in my region–Catalunya–many people thought the policies of the central government in Madrid were mistaken, including those that led to war with the United States."

"Catalunya? Ah, you're saying there are strong regional differences within your country."

"That's correct. And many people in my part of España believe we'd be better off as an independent country. I don't happen to agree. But that's not your answer. There's good reason for Spaniards to be suspicious of the French, after they came in and took away our freedom. Not so long ago. And the British were their allies in that. But there's no love for the Germans either. Both sides are wrong. And we'd celebrate the end of the war. It may sound selfish, but many artists have become victims of the war. That's a tragedy because art is universal, it crosses all borders. I love the music of Wagner and Saint-Saens and Mozart and Chopin, and it doesn't matter what country they were born in. Does that make sense?"

Wilson smiles. "Yes, it surely does. Thank you!"

In the White House tonight, the state drawing rooms, corridors and the East Room are resplendent with cut flowers. Two large vases standing on pedestals, which have been here since before Casals' performance in 1904, were made in the French village of Sèvres by a firm that was founded by King Louis XV and Madame de Pompadour in the 1750s. Their design, pink and white with gilded trim, is named "Mahón"–after a Catalan town on the island of Menorca that was captured by the French in what was considered among the greatest triumphs of the Seven Years' War. Tonight the Mahón vases made in Sèvres are filled with American Beauty roses–deep red, pink, white, peach, coral, magenta, and lavender.

Three-hundred-and-thirty-nine guests are received by President Wilson and Edith, his wife of two months, in the Green Room shortly before nine o'clock. Among the guests are ambassadors and ministers representing eight nations, including Britain and France; the secretary of State, Robert Lansing, and four other Cabinet members; several generals of the U.S. Army and a like number of admirals; a dozen U.S. senators and congressmen; prominent Washingtonians and industrialists.

Granados opens the program with the sixth of his transcriptions of Scarlatti sonatas, *Danza–Valenciana*, his favorite encore piece, and *Allegro de Concierto*. The audience responds with warm but certainly not delirious applause. Culp sings four short songs by Schubert, including the beloved "Ave Maria," and receives a hearty ovation. Granados returns to play Chopin's "Nocturne in C# minor," and "El Pelele," which elicits the most enthusiastic applause. Culp concludes the program with an old Dutch song, an old French song, and two vocals by the American organist and composer James H. Rogers. There are no encores.

After the concert, a buffet is served in the state dining room. The audience forms in small circles: generals and their wives here, admirals and their wives over there, diplomats and their wives clustered by language group, industrialists encircling members of Congress. President and Mrs. Wilson leave shortly after the "Musicale," and Julia Culp sets up her own reception line at the entrance to the dining room. Margaret Wilson is in the far corner of the room with the minister of Siam. Granados nibbles from a plate of food and sips from a champagne glass. Earlier, he chatted with Minister and Señora Zaldivar from Salvador and shook hands with the ambassador of Chile. He wonders what might be gained by remaining here with a room full of strangers, and decides to go back to the hotel.

Late the next morning, after a fitful night of agonizing over plans to return home, Granados checks out of the Willard Hotel and takes a cab to the Spanish Embassy for the luncheon in his honor. Riaño gives him a warm abraçada.

"Was your room satisfactory?" asks Riaño.

"Yes, very comfortable."

"Well, the Willard's been around for a long time. Quite a history! When Lincoln came to be inaugurated as our President, they were so afraid he'd be assassinated that he was smuggled into the Willard. He stayed there for two weeks until he took the oath and moved into the White House."

But Lincoln was assassinated!

"He should have stayed at the hotel," says Granados.

"Oh? Yes, I know what you mean." Riaños laughs. They walk into the ambassador's office and sit at a large table covered with azulejos–tiles from Órgiva, near the Riaño family vineyard and olive groves. Granados is anxious to tell the ambassador of his decision. With a voice conveying his resolve, he says, "I've been thinking all night about what you said yesterday, Don

Juan, and I agree with you absolutely. I'm most grateful for your advice. I've talked to my wife and both of us are determined to follow it. I will go to the travel office first thing in the morning and change the reservations back to the Spanish boat."

Riaño replies with a broad smile, "That's wonderful news, maestro! I'm so glad, so relieved you've made that decision. I've delayed the departure of *Antonio López* until tomorrow, in the late afternoon, so you and your wife will have no difficulty boarding it on time."

"Well, I'm relieved too. It means we'll be back home by the 18th or 19th. That and the coming of spring are enough to cheer me greatly. And once more, thank you for your advice!"

Gracias a Dios! One less thing to keep me awake!

"At your service," says Riaño.

"By the way, are there reviews of last night's concert?"

"Yes, there's a long article in the *Washington Post*." Riaño goes to his desk and retrieves the newspaper. "Here it is–and to translate it roughly, most of it's about how the ladies were dressed and coiffed. And about the flower displays."

Granados frowns. "What about the music?"

"Let's see. Ah, here it is." He translates into Castilian. "It says, 'Madame Julia Culp, soprano, and Mr. Enrique Granados, pianist, were the artists of the evening, giving a program that was selected and arranged by Miss Margaret Wilson. Mr. Granados played several of his own compositions and selections from Chopin and Scarlatti, and Madame Culp was heard in a varied program of songs, opening with a group of Schubert. She sang later old Dutch and old French songs and concluded with two of James H. Rogers–"Wind Song" and "The Star." A buffet supper was served.'" Riaño puts the newspaper back on his desk. "That's the only reference to the music."

"That's the review of the concert? Just that, in such a long article?"

"You have to understand, maestro, this is not New York or London or Paris."

"I do understand," says Granados. "It was a social event, with a bit of music added!"

Granados returns to New York on the afternoon train, arriving at Penn Station around nine-thirty. It's snowing again while the cab heads up Seventh Avenue, splashing and sliding through slush and puddles to the Hotel Wellington. By the time he reaches his room, Granados is exhausted. Francisca Rodón is with Amparo, waiting for him.

"I'm here to convince you to come back home with us," says Rodón, planting herself in front of him. "And I won't take 'no' for an answer!"

Granados looks over at Amparo, who's nodding her head. She tells him she's begun to pack and will be ready to leave on *Antonio López* tomorrow.

"We're in agreement, Doña Francisca," Granados says. "I had a long talk with the Ambassador Riaño in Washington, and I'm absolutely persuaded to change the reservations back to the Spanish boat. Even though everyone says *Rotterdam* is the best way to go to Europe. I'm going to change our reservations, so you don't have to waste any more time trying to convince me."

In the morning, Granados enters the travel office of Thomas Cook & Sons just after it opens for the day. Arthur Bromley looks up, surprised to see him at the front desk. "Maestro Granados, good to see you again. To what do we owe the pleasure of your visit?"

Granados tells Bromley he wants to exchange his reservations on *Rotterdam* for passage on *Antonio López*.

"Oh my! The *López* left yesterday. Yes, March 8 was it's sailing date. Unless for some reason it was delayed."

"It was delayed," says Granados. "Ambassador Riaño was able to hold it until this afternoon. I'm here to reserve a First Class cabin for myself and my wife. We'd like to leave today!"

Bromley shakes his head. "Well, before we get too far, I should check availability on the *López*–if indeed it's not going to leave until this afternoon. Come over to my desk." Bromley picks up the phone and is told by the Compañía Transatlántica Española that there are still cabins available in First Class. He instructs the company's agent to hold one of them in the name of Granados. Turning around, Bromley affirms that it's still possible for Granados to take *Antonio López* this afternoon. "Of course, you'll forfeit your passage on *Rotterdam*, he says.

Granados is aroused. "No, that cannot be! When I changed plans to take *Rotterdam*, you gave me credit for the earlier reservations. I just want to change back to the original plan. Why do you want me to forfeit what I paid you?"

"I'm very sorry, Maestro Granados. Surely you remember my telling you that your passage on *Rotterdam* is not refundable. I was very clear. Now, I can make you reservations for the *López*, but you'll not be able to recover what you paid me for *Rotterdam*. I'm very sorry."

"But that's more than two hundred dollars! I can't afford to lose that!"

Bromley shrugs. "I wish there were something else I could do. What I can do is arrange for two passages on *López* with First Class accommodations. Would you like me to do that?"

Granados ponders the choice.

More than two hundred dollars. Too much. Can't afford it. Passage to London paid for. Why pay twice? And London could mean another venue.

He looks up and asks, "You're sure I can't get a refund on what I paid for *Rotterdam?*"

"Yes, I am very sure, maestro," replies Bromley. "It's my job to be sure about such matters."

Granados stands up. "All right then, we'll go on *Rotterdam*." He turns to leave.

Bromley steps around his desk to shake hands. "I apologize for the misunderstanding. I'm sure you'll enjoy *Rotterdam*. It's one of the finest in the world."

Back in the hotel, Granados tells Amparo about his visit to the travel office. She's confused. "You mean, you didn't want to lose the two hundred dollars? You were being frugal? You?"

He nods.

Amparo steps forward and puts her arms around him. "Oh, I'm so pleased—you were being frugal! Don't worry, we'll have a fine time in London! A few more days and we'll be back home."

Granados sends a telegram to Riaño to explain his decision, and thanks him for being so gracious and helpful. He concludes, "Once more, I'm most grateful. I say farewell now. Believe me I am yours, very truly."

With travel arrangements resolved, there are two more days in New York, time to say farewell to the friends who've done so much for Granados and Amparo in the past three months.

At lunch on Thursday, March 9, while Francisca Rodón and Paquita Madriguera are boarding *Antonio López*, Henry and Lucie Schelling give Amparo a cashmere cardigan sweater with brass buttons, "for those cool days on deck," and a pearl necklace. Choked with tears, she embraces them. Granados receives a coat and cap of tightly curled wool from the Astrakhan region of Russia, "to keep warm on the voyage to England," and a large velvet sack with one thousand dollars in gold coins, a gift from Schelling, Casals, Paderewski, and Kreisler. Granados swears he'll keep the gold forever–"so I'll never feel poor again." Schelling makes the practical suggestion that it be converted to paper money at the bank before sailing, but Granados is adamant. He clutches the velvet sack full of gold. "No, Henri, I will keep this the rest of my life–forever!"

When Granados visits Malvina Hoffman to say farewell the next day, he learns that Mildred Bliss and her maid will also be boarding *Rotterdam* tomorrow. Granados is delighted.

"And where will you be staying in London?" asks Malvina.

"Oh, I have a friend from Barcelona–Ismael Smith–he lives there now. I asked him to make a hotel reservation, but he hasn't told me which one."

"Ismael Smith–the sculptor? I knew him in Paris. He was crazy about Rodin's work. Yes, Smith, curious name for a Spaniard. About the time I was helping Rodin move his sculpture and equipment, I ran into Smith. Poor man! He'd lost everything when the war broke out. He told me he was going to Russia, which I thought was a singularly bad idea at that time. Never saw him again."

"Well, he's in London."

"Say 'hello' and wish him good luck."

Before lunch, Granados and Amparo write a letter to their children, saying they're leaving for home. To Amparo's affectionate note, Granados adds a request that they give his greetings to Dr. Pi i Sunyer, Gabriel Miró, and Solita's fiancé Rossend Carrasco. He also sends a note to Schelling, in which he thanks him and asks him to pass along his gratitude to everyone Granados hasn't been able to thank personally. And he writes to his old colleague Amadeu Vives, with whom he worked in founding the Orfeó Català twenty-five years ago:

> At last I've seen the realization of my dreams. Per fi! It's true that my hair is turning white, and yet one could say that I am just beginning my work. I am filled with confidence and enthusiasm to work more and more. I am a Spaniard. Alas, no other Spaniard has begun any earlier. I am a survivor of the

> sterile battle to which the ignorance and indifference of our country subjects us. I am dreaming of Paris, and I have a world of ideas.

There's been more snow overnight and the last of the tiny flakes are blowing across Central Park as Casals leads the way on the path around the reservoir. "You'll be going back tomorrow. I envy you. I'd rather be back in Catalunya than anywhere. Oh, I have a nice life here. Very comfortable. But it's not really my own life!"

Granados chuckles. "Pau, your life is your music."

Casals frowns. "Yes, but at Sant Salvador I can have everything. Music, peace of mind, comfort, family."

"Everything except an audience."

Casals sighs. "Yes, that's right. The audiences are all far away. And even farther away as long as this war goes on! I hoped it would be over by now, but everything I read says it's getting worse. This battle in France–a place called Loos, where the British attacked the Germans and in three weeks, forty thousand casualties–forty thousand! Pointless casualties–the line hasn't moved in more than a year and still they throw young men at each other, the generals all so eager for war, no interest in peace. Horrible, dreadful, what madness!"

"Gràcies a Déu! España is neutral. And also Americà."

Casals shakes his head. "Yes, Americà's still neutral, but who knows for how long? Meanwhile the American army's chasing around México to catch Pancho Villa. Just shows, you put men in uniform and give them guns, they go out and shoot people."

"Who's Pancho Villa? I've just seen his name in headlines."

"Probably one of our cousins," says Casals. "Who knows? Francisco Villa is a Mexican general who ended up on the wrong side of a political fight. When the United States threw its support to the other side, Villa retaliated. In fact, in this morning's paper there's a report that the American army will send a huge force into México to punish Villa for killing several Americans. This country seems to prefer fighting Mexicans or Indians."

"Or Spaniards."

"Sí, senyor. If they have to fight, they'd rather it's with people who are hopelessly outmatched–shooting arrows at them–rather than with the Germans. But one of these days the Germans are going to sink another ship, like

Lusitania, and when that happens the Americans may have to get into the war in Europe, whether they like it or not."

"Que terrible!"

Casals slows down as they reach 5th Avenue. "Anyway, you'll be going back tomorrow. I'll miss you! This has been splendid having you here. I don't expect to be back home 'til next summer. Hope you'll come in September and stay a long, long while."

Granados catches up with Casals and puts his arm around his shoulders. "It's been more than splendid having *you* here! I could never have rehearsed the orchestra without you. Just wanted to run and hide! Especially without knowing English."

"But you've gotten along fine, haven't you?"

"Yes, thanks to you and all the people who converse with me in French." Granados laughs. "When I went to see President Wilson in the big oval office, his daughter was there to translate. He speaks a little German but nothing else."

"And what did you talk about with President?"

"Oh, not much. He talked about wanting to keep Amèrica out of the war. His interest in being the peacemaker. He mentioned the war with España, which I pointed out was the fault of the government in Madrid. But of course I added that I'm an artist, and believe art and politics should never be mixed. And, let's see–yes, his daughter said the President likes to sing, and with the national anthem he reaches for the high note near the end and shifts into falsetto. Sure enough, when they sang it before my concert he reached for the note, and sure enough it was falsetto. And he was, as she predicted, flat."

Casals laughs. "Shows art and politics don't mix. Now tell me, 'Ric, you're going to Buenos Aires with *Goyescas* in May, and looking for other venues. But surely you won't stop with *Goyescas*."

"Of course not! It's fine music–could have been even better with a decent libretto. But I'm already working on a sequel to the piano suite, and a series of songs with verse by Mestres. I'll complete the Symphony in E Minor, and of course the cello concerto–dedicated to you! As for operas, the next time I'll start with a decent libretto. There are so many great stories which can be staged. Gabriel Miró and I are planning an opera–*Jerusalén*–he's a marvelous writer! And there are great epics–of Comte Arnau and El Cid, the war against the French, Emperor Augustus in Tarragona, Guifré el Pelós, Colom's discovery of the new world, our Santa Eulàlia. And the amazing life of La Duquesa de Alba–the mystery of her death–so much intrigue! And I'll finish the last two parts of *Dante*."

"That sounds wonderful! It's a lifetime of work, but you can do it. As you did with the art of Goya. Why not?"

Granados holds up his hands. "But, Pau, I must remember how I wrote the *Goyescas* piano suite."

Casals shakes his head. "You mean, that summer in Tiana?"

"That was the key to unlocking the butterflies."

"You'd have me believe she was more than a fine and charming lady, with a villa away from the city, more than a lover?"

"Yes! She was my collaborator."

Casals frowns. "But you've certainly written wonderful music sitting all alone."

"Not like *Goyescas*."

"You're right. Not like *it*." Casals nods, striding purposefully. He's never had a muse, never thought of collaborating on a work of art. Surely not with a woman. Not with Suggia, not with Susan. Their role has been to distract him from time to time from his true love, his cello. To Casals, the woman in Tiana is just another of Granados' fantasies. He remains skeptical, but shrugs it off, reluctant to offend. "I understand. You mean, you're hoping for more music like *Goyescas*."

"Not hoping. Planning on it."

Casals claps him on the shoulder. "Meravellós! As for me, I'll tour the Amèricas while they're having a war in Europe, and then go back home, establish a permanent symphony orchestra in Barcelona. To play nothing but Catalan music." He turns to Granados, smiling. "You see, you're not the only dreamer."

Granados is surprised, and elated at the possibility of Casals moving back home. "Oh, that's a wonderful idea! Let me know if you need a pianist."

"Fat chance! You'll be taking your operas all over the world. And I'll be waiting for you to come home and tell me of *your* adventures!"

It's midnight, and Amparo has fallen asleep in their suite at the Wellington. Granados finds the room key on the coffee table, buried in gifts purchased for their children, and slips out quietly, walks down the corridor, and takes an elevator to the lobby. The night clerk shows him to the smoking parlor, where there are telephones. He dials Malvina Hoffman's number–memorized. She answers in a voice revealing she's been awakened.

Granados apologizes for phoning so late. "It's not my habit to do this," he says in a wavering voice.

"My Lord, Enrique, what's the matter? You sound as if it's something dreadful."

He hesitates, but it's too late to turn back. "Malvina, I called to tell you I've had a terrible premonition–that I'll never see my children again."

A pause at her end of the line. "You've had a nightmare?" she asks.

"No, not that. Haven't even been to bed. It's a premonition–came to me so strongly I can't push it away. I'm terrified. Don't know what to do. And Amparo had the same premonition. She took a pill to help her sleep. She was crying over and over: 'I'll never see my children again!'"

Malvina is now fully awake. "That's dreadful! Of course it's your imagination."

"That may be," he replies. "My father died young, so did my brother. Too young. And I'm nearly fifty. I have a nightmare in which I see my children all together back home and someone comes to tell them that I've died. And it's as real as if I were in the room."

"I've never had a premonition," Malvina says, "but I imagine it's horrible. Is there anything I can do?"

"No. I don't think so. I just needed to tell someone."

"Well, that was the right thing to do," she says.

His voice is barely audible. "I'm sorry, I just had to tell someone. And I'd like to ask a favor. If something happens, would you be a friend for my children–as you've been for me?"

"Of course! But that won't be necessary. Enrique, we all have fears, and when we find there's nothing to fear any more, we look back on them and it's amusing how fearful we were. When I was a girl, I was deathly afraid of ghosts. I'd lie in bed and hear noises and was sure it was ghosts coming to get me. Of course they never did. After a while, I'd just fall asleep. I'm sorry you had the premonition, but I'm expecting you back here in New York with your next opera, and I'm expecting you to come here to practice. And I promise I'll keep the Chickering in tune!"

Her voice is reassuring. Suddenly Granados is overcome with weariness. "Thank you, Malvina. I promise, I'll be back."

March 11, 1916

Holland America Line's SS *Rotterdam* is being loaded at the Hoboken Terminal on the New Jersey side of the Hudson River. The temperature has dropped since yesterday's snowfall and the wind is brisk coming down the river. The waiting room is bustling with groups of friends and family members, most of them in high spirits as they give the passengers a rousing sendoff. Among them is Mildred Bliss' family, with whom she's been staying since her husband returned to his post at the American Embassy in Paris. She's traveling with her maid and chaperoning three young American women, whose families gather around them in an ever widening circle.

Nearby are the mother and brother of Tingle Culbertson of Sewickley, Pennsylvania, a town on the Ohio River north of Pittsburgh. Culbertson is tall, handsome, and fair-haired, the second son in an affluent family, who returned to his father's steel products business after graduating from Princeton University five years ago. Now, in search of "something of higher service," he has signed up for the American Field Service, assigned to a French ambulance unit in the combat zone. Also headed there is the young American volunteer, Daniel Sargent.

Granados and Amparo wait for boarding with a group that includes Casals and Susan Metcalfe, Henry and Lucie Schelling, Jan and Helena Paderewski, Fritz and Harriet Kreisler, María Barrientos, and Otto Kahn. Schelling presents a large gift box from Tiffany's, and Granados opens it with bashful pride. It contains a large silver bowl on a pedestal, with the names of everyone present today, as well as Robert Bliss, Clarence Mackay, and two other members of the Metropolitan Opera board.

"It's your 'loving cup,'" says Schelling. "Open the envelope."

Inside the envelope, Granados finds a check for $4,100. He looks at it again, to be sure it's American dollars, not pesetas. He thanks everyone with a Catalan abraçada.

A lot of money! With Buenos Aires and London, farewell to poverty!

After boarding, Granados takes Casals out of the stateroom to the promenade deck. "I'm sorry to be such a bother, Pau, after all you've done for me. Have to tell you something, I've had a kind of–premonition–that I'll never see my children again."

Casals shakes his head. "Déu meu! What are you saying? Premonition? What's a premonition?"

"It's a very strong feeling, a foreboding. I know it sounds melodramatic, but it's not just me—Titín had one too. And I'm telling you because you're our children's godfather."

Casals does his best to reassure him, but when it's time for guests to leave the ship, knows that he hasn't succeeded.

En Route to England

When Granados told Amparo of changing reservations to *Rotterdam*, he described it as a cash-free exchange. A bit of wishful thinking. But now, since he could not have switched back to *Antonio López* without losing what he paid for *Rotterdam*, why not celebrate his triumph in New York with passengers like Mildred Bliss, who embody success and are accustomed to fine hotels, gourmet restaurants and luxurious ocean liners?

SS *Rotterdam* is the fourth vessel to bear that name for the Holland America Line, to carry its passengers and cargo across the Atlantic. Since her launching eight years ago, she's been the company's flagship, acclaimed with pride as "the Queen of the Spotless Fleet," luxurious in every way. Her size, powerful engines, and enormous bilge keels account for a smooth ride in almost any weather, virtually eliminating seasickness. She is longer, faster, newer, sleeker, and plusher than ordinary vessels such as *Antonio López*, and the first ship on the transatlantic run to have a glassed-in promenade deck.

Life on *Rotterdam* for its five hundred First Class passengers is sublime. Oversized rooms, with private baths and brass bedsteads. A grand staircase, finished in wrought iron with polished brass balusters, set within a six-story vestibule. The Palm Court, decorated in period Louis XVI, with stained glass and ceramic tiles depicting scenes of bygone centuries, and light filtering through a cut-glass ceiling. The Social Hall or ballroom, finished in Spanish mahogany, with a Steinway concert grand in its center. A well-stocked library, finished in Italian walnut, also Louis XVI; and upper and lower smoking rooms, connected by a staircase within the main vestibule. The Verandah Café, sheltered on three sides with a full view of the ocean, facing aft. An immense two-story dining saloon, finished in Empire style, with mahogany columns supporting a balcony; orchestral music played during lunch and dinner while French cuisine is served à la carte, with no extra charge. White tie for gentlemen, dinner gowns for ladies. At the head of the dining room, another Steinway concert grand.

For diversion, First Class passengers are enticed by a constant round of lectures, dances, games of bridge and euchre, gymkana deck games, and meetings of the Daughters of the American Revolution, Masons, and clubs devoted to photography and music. They can enjoy the expansive, glassed-in promenade deck under nearly all weather conditions, often entertained by the ship's band.

Mildred Bliss' suite, one level down from the promenade deck, consists of a living room, master bedroom, two bathrooms, and individual chambers for her maid and the three young American women she's escorting to London. At thirty-four, Mildred is only a few years older than the young women, but her marriage to an important American diplomat, and living with him in Brussels, Buenos Aires, and Paris–entertaining politicians and artists mostly of her parents' generation–have moved Mildred into the cohort that dances a few numbers after dinner, then retires. So this evening, after dancing with each man who sat with her at the captain's table–Captain Baron, Clarence Mackay's brother Charles, a Canadian named Hume Cronyn, and Granados–Mildred excuses herself, to the chagrin of an eager cluster of men waiting in the stag line for a whirl with the luminous, chestnut-haired woman in a daring emerald green ball gown by Jeanne Hallée. The young women, and the young men they met the first night at sea, dance on, hoping the band will play forever.

It's the seventh night out from New York, and Mildred is alone in her suite, except for the maid who is fast asleep. In the bathroom, she unfastens her gown and lets it drop to the marble floor. She removes her silk undergarments, tossing them on the gown for the maid. She rubs her face, neck, and arms with lotion, slowly as her skin absorbs it, then unpins her hair, shaking it onto her bare shoulders. A glance in the mirror reveals the effects of too many extravagant meals and too little time walking from place to place, as is her custom in Paris. She reaches down and pulls a brass handle on the drawer of a mahogany dresser, retrieves a sleeveless, low-cut, green dressing gown that she enjoys wearing in the privacy of her suite, and pulls it on, welcoming the soft velvet against her skin, luxuriating in the feel of being just one thin layer of fabric from nudity. In the living room she fills a small glass with tawny port from the cellars of José Maria da Fonseca, then slides onto the divan and opens a book by the American poet Amy Lowell. She reads "The Road to Avignon" as her drowsy eyes flutter:

> The minstrel woos with his silver strings,
> and climbing up to the lady, sings:
> Down the road to Avignon,
> the long, long road to Avignon,
> across the bridge to Avignon,
> one morning in the spring.

Step by step, and he comes to her,
fearful lest she suddenly stir.
Sunshine and silence–

Mildred hears a faint knock at the door, and wonders if it could be the young women returning from the dance. It seems too early for that.

"Is that you Elizabeth?" she calls out.

There's no answer, but after a few moments there's another knock, this one more insistent.

Mildred wraps a woolen shawl over her shoulders, and goes to the door. "Who is it?" she asks without opening it.

"It's me, Enrique. Can I speak to you?" His voice is an urgent whisper.

Images race through her head. She thinks of Granados as a musical genius, a tender soul behind a devilishly handsome face. Since meeting in Paris two years ago, they've enjoyed an easy and mutual affinity, and he's never said or done anything to cause her discomfort. Not even his note that suggested they were "almas amigas"–that simply meant a shared reverence for what he called "the delicacy of his artistic spirit." Yet she's wondered, was that all it meant? Equally harmless were his bubbly delight in hearing her translation of "La maja dolorosa" into French, and their conversation about grieving for dead lovers in which he clung to the abstract, in the aftermath of playing *Tonadillas* for her. Granados had been perfectly circumspect, so she was comfortable sharing her secret: a feverish love affair and the lover's death the year before she met Robert Bliss. Now, as she takes care to cover herself with the shawl, Mildred wonders if he might have misinterpreted her holding him close on the dance floor earlier this evening.

She opens the door. Seeing his eyes, she experiences a new sense of discomfort. "Come in, Enrique. Come in."

"Are you alone, Mildred?" he asks in a wavering voice.

"Yes, yes," she replies, her discomfort rising. "The girls are still at the dance." She takes his arm, draws him gently into the suite and closes the door. "Please come with me," she says.

Granados follows, remaining on his feet as she slides back onto the divan. "I shouldn't be here, it's not proper," he says, "but I was hoping you'd be alone. It's private. Amparo's fast asleep–there's nothing wrong with this, but she wouldn't understand a married man coming to see a married woman in the middle of the night. If you wonder, it's not what it might seem. Nothing you couldn't tell Robert about. Nothing like that."

Mildred smiles, her anxiety allayed.

"Mildred, I came to confess that I'm—I've been having the most terrible premonitions. That I'll never see my children again."

Mildred reaches up and takes his hand. "Sit down, Enrique. Let's talk about this."

Granados sits down on the corner of the divan. "My father and brother both died young. I'm nearly fifty. And I had a premonition just before leaving New York. Tonight it came back—just as I was falling asleep. It's very strong."

"This is entirely irrational," Mildred says firmly. "You know that. Yes you do. You've had this dread of sea travel, so it's natural you'd have a premonition like this—even if you believe you've overcome your fear. And you've been away from your children for so long it's natural you're worried about not seeing them again. But I assure you, it's entirely your imagination."

Granados dissolves into tears. "I can't help it. It's so strong. Like a terrible dragon breathing fire." He lowers his head to his knees and shakes with sobbing.

Mildred realizes she'll not be able to reason with him; his fear is overwhelming. She tries another approach. "Look, if I can't convince you these premonitions are entirely unfounded, at least I can ask you to make me a promise. Robert is coming from Paris and will meet me at the train station in London. I want you to call me the morning after we reach London so we can go together to the ticket office—you and Amparo and Robert and I—and arrange to cross the English Channel on the same boat. Then we'll take the train to Paris and put you and Amparo on the first train for Barcelona. You'll be home in a week. How does that sound?"

Granados is drying his tears with a handkerchief. "Thank you. It's very kind. I apologize for being such a problem."

"Nonsense! You're not a problem, you're a friend of ours and we'll help you get through this." Mildred rises from the divan and goes to a small desk in the corner of the room. On a piece of *Rotterdam* stationery, she writes the phone number of the place where she and her husband will be staying in London, and returns to the divan. "Here's our phone number. Do you have a number for your hotel?"

Granados shakes his head. "I'm sorry, I don't know where we'll be staying. I asked a friend to make reservations, but he hasn't told me which hotel."

Mildred holds the paper with her phone number up in front of his face. "I want you to promise me you'll call this number. And we will get you home safely!" She bends down and kisses him on both cheeks. "Je t'aime, Enrique."

"Yes, I promise," says Granados. "And I love you too."

Chapter Eleven

In the late afternoon of Sunday, March 19, SS *Rotterdam* rounds Lizard Point on the southwestern tip of England and drops anchor off the port of Falmouth. Nearly all of her First Class passengers, who are bound for London and other British cities, gather with their luggage to be led down the gangplank to a tender, the size of a tugboat. The tender plies the short distance between the small harbor and large vessels such as *Rotterdam*, which could be tugged in only with great difficulty. Among the many passengers leaving–all stepping carefully with the asynchronous rocking of ocean liner and tender–are Granados, Amparo, Mildred Bliss, her maid and the three young women she's escorting, as well as the young American volunteers, Tingle Culbertson and Daniel Sargent. From Falmouth Pier they're taken to the train depot for a long ride to London's Paddington Station.

At Paddington, Robert Bliss is on the platform with a large bouquet of roses. Granados and Amparo wait for their luggage cart to emerge, while two carts stacked with luggage for Mildred and her coterie are being loaded into a taxicab that will take them to a friend's home in Kensington. Ismael Smith hasn't appeared.

"I hate to leave you, Enrique," says Robert Bliss, "but from here, we're headed in opposite directions."

"Oh, please! You should go ahead," says Granados. "I'm sure my friend will be here any minute. He's the only one who knows where we're staying, so there's nothing for us to do but wait."

Before leaving, Mildred reminds Granados of his promise. "You have my number, and I expect *you to call me* as soon as you get up in the morning! Robert said he'll take us to the ticket office." She embraces him and follows her husband to the town sedan.

By the time Ismael Smith arrives ten minutes later, the Bliss party is gone. "You must be exhausted," says Smith. "Lo siento—sorry to be late. Should have been here to welcome you."

"Don't worry about it," says Granados. He tips the luggage porter while Smith hails one of the dark blue cabs waiting outside.

"I have a nice room for you at the Savoy Hotel," Smith says in an excited voice. "I chose the Savoy because it's very, very nice. And so close to everything! You'll be able to walk around, just as if you were back home."

Granados asks Smith if he made any appointments to discuss *Goyescas*.

Smith shakes his head and explains he wasn't able to make any calls without knowing which day the *Rotterdam* would arrive. "But I'll call them in the morning," he adds. "If you want to leave on the 24th, you have four days in London for meetings—and time for a bit of sightseeing and shopping." He turns to Amparo. "I don't imagine you'd object, Senyora Granados."

Granados tells him about his promise to Mildred Bliss. "Because of that, Ismael, please make appointments only for the days *after* tomorrow."

"Your wish is my command!" Smith replies with a pixyish laugh.

Granados is awakened in the morning by a maid who's gathering their pile of traveling clothes for cleaning and pressing. He rolls over and goes back to sleep. Shortly before noon, after breakfast in the room, he's dressed and ready to call Mildred Bliss. He looks for the jacket he was wearing the night she gave him her phone number.

Where was it? Ah—the inside pocket right side. Never took it out. Or did I give it to Titín?

"Titín—did I give you Mildred's phone number?" he asks.

She shakes her head. "You did not. You must still have it."

"Then it's still in my dinner jacket. The one—"

"The one we put in the pile of laundry last night?" The pitch of her voice rises. "And the pile is gone. Gone! The maid must have taken it. Did you hear the maid this morning?"

"Yes, and I went back to sleep," he says.

"Mildred's phone number is in the laundry," Amparo says. "You'd better call them right away. So careless! Let's hope we can retrieve it!"

How careless! But no disaster. Made it across ocean twice–crossing channel can't be so bad. Send Blisses telegram when we get home.

Mildred and Robert Bliss wait until Monday evening before starting their search for Granados, who still hasn't called. They look through the phone directory, imagining that he might be in a hotel with a Spanish name. There are several that evoke places favored by British tourists: Madrid, Sevilla, Granada, Alhambra, Mallorca, Costa del Sol, and Ronda; and others with Spanish surnames: Quijote, Velásquez, Cervantes, and Goya; and still others with Castilian words: La Sierra, Bello Monte, Las Brisas, and El Valle. Mildred calls every one of them on Tuesday morning; none have guests with the surname Granados. She also calls the Spanish Embassy in London; they've had not any contact with anyone by that name.

By Tuesday afternoon, Mildred has exhausted the list of hotels. "What next?" she asks Bliss when he returns from the American Consulate.

Bliss shakes his head. "Well, the phone could ring any minute."

"But it's been two days and it hasn't happened."

Bliss sighs. "You're right. And tomorrow's Wednesday–I'd like to leave on Friday. You and I must decide how best to get across the channel, and I've gathered the information to help us with that choice."

"It was a good idea, wasn't it?" asks Mildred. "Calling the hotels with Spanish names? I suppose we could call every hotel in London."

Bliss smirks. "Yes, dear, it was a good idea. But do you know how many hotels there are in this city? Hundreds! His friend could have booked him anywhere. Or invited Granados to stay with him. Whoever he is. I'm afraid it would take us several days, and by that time he'd probably be back in Barcelona."

"You're right. And I have these girls to escort to Paris."

"Exactly. We have to make plans. Now, the people at our consulate here say there are only two choices left. The submarines have taken their toll. Obviously, the Germans would like to shut down England altogether. Anyhow, one way is from Dover to Calais, the other Folkestone to Dieppe. Folkestone is longer–four hours–and there's no escort ship, but that area's supposed to be free of submarines."

"Well, let's take that one!"

"On the other hand, we've been offered a freighter from Dover with a Royal Navy convoy. That offsets the higher risk. And it would only take two hours."

"Yes. I'd surely be more comfortable with the Royal Navy to protect us," says Mildred. "Wouldn't you?"

Bliss ponders the choice. "Probably so. It's shorter. And protected. And with the longer distance from Folkestone, there's more potential risk. Since nobody's been very good at predicting where the U-boats will be."

"All right," says Mildred. "It's Dover. I'll talk to the girls, and if they agree–I'm sure they will–we'll go down and get our tickets tomorrow. And we'll keep looking for the maestro."

Granados' hopes of finding new venues for *Goyescas* in London are not being realized. He accepts this without deep regret, recognizing there isn't the same kind of momentous opportunity that Schelling orchestrated at l'Ópera de Paris. Might be different if Schelling were here; perhaps not. Sir Henry Wood is in Nottingham for the entire week. As for Sir Thomas Beecham, an assistant says he's in Scotland for a long weekend, but might be back for appointments next Monday or Tuesday. For a moment, Granados ponders staying over–but only for a moment; he doesn't mention it to Amparo. Instead, he leaves his card with Beecham's assistant. Another disappointment is learning that the Royal Opera House at Covent Garden has been closed for the duration of the war. The facility was requisitioned by the Ministry of Works for furniture storage.

In the face of these setbacks, and eager to please, Ismael Smith arranges a brief meeting with Rupert D'Oyly Carte, son of the famed impresario, who's been managing the family enterprises since the death of his father. Richard, the elder D'Oyly Carte, was a booking agent and theatre manager who had the prescience to combine the talents of playwright William Gilbert and composer Arthur Sullivan. Their comic operas were enormously popular with British and American audiences, though virtually unknown on the Continent. Both Gilbert and Sullivan prospered and were knighted. With his share of the earnings, Richard D'Oyly Carte built the Savoy Theatre on the Strand as a venue for Gilbert & Sullivan's works, and so successful was he in this venture that he built the Savoy Hotel next to the theatre. It too became a London landmark and the most profitable of his enterprises.

Smith has convinced Granados that Rupert D'Oyly Carte, scion of the family fortune, might help find a venue for *Goyescas*, unaware that since the death of his father, the son's interests have largely shifted from the opera company to making the Savoy Hotel one of Europe's most prestigious. In addition, he's engaged in a wartime career as a King's Messenger–allowing the Admiralty to exploit his connections in the international hotel business to gather information deemed useful to the British war effort, and to move it via diplomatic pouches to the right place, at the right time.

Granados and Smith have a brief meeting with the forty-ish, inveterate dandy whose haughtiness is legendary even among his peers–the swellest circle of British aristocrats–and the family of his wife, Lady Dorothy Milner Gathorne Hardy, daughter of the fifth Earl of Clarendon. D'Oyly Carte's expression, as a secretary leads Smith and Granados into his office, resembles that of an entomology professor watching common fruit flies at a picnic. "Ah yes, gentlemen, now let me see," he says with a toxic blend of pomp and circumstance. "We're in the music business, aren't we? Which genre is yours, precisely?"

"Maestro Granados is a composer," says Smith, who's become passably fluent in English. "His opera was just presented by the Metropolitan in New York."

"Why then, well done, maestro! And of course you've presented it at La Scala?"

Granados hears the taunt, shakes his head, and looks past the scion. He consoles himself that Schirmer will make an Italian translation of *Goyescas* for La Scala–when it reopens, after the war. Granados notices a large photo behind the desk: D'Oyly Carte aboard a sailboat, dressed in white slacks, blue blazer, ascot, and white captain's hat with its visor pointing toward his priggish mouth.

D'Oyly Carte rolls his eyes. "Of course not, you're not Italian! How crude of me. You're Spanish. Of course they haven't seen it in Milano." The conversation never rises above that level. The only positive result is D'Oyly Carte's offer of a complimentary champagne dinner at the Savoy Grill.

Complete waste of time! Rupert's a pedant–a prig! Can't blame Ismael–tried his best. Foolish of me to expect more.

In their remaining time in London, Smith takes Granados and Amparo on the historic sightseeing route. They shop for gifts at Selfridge's–Amparo's delighted with its restaurant, beauty parlor, and rooms for reading, writing, and resting–like a gentlemen's club, only for women. Smith finds Granados a new treatment for intestinal pain at Boots the Chemist, and a pair of fine shoes in a shop on Regent Street. They dodge around the double-decked buses as they cross Piccadilly Circus, where suffragettes parade with banners reading: "Votes for Women Wanted Everywhere!" They attend a concert devoted to

Chopin's nocturnes and ballades at Aeolian Hall, and introduce themselves to Aeolian's London director who'd heard Schelling play *Goyescas* at Queen's Hall two years ago, and who doles out a British snippet of praise. They lunch at Panini's, where artists are welcome to dine in a special room whose walls are covered with their autographs–Granados recognizes those of Caruso, Puccini, Fernandez Arbós, Mascagni, and Sarasate–and adds his own to the wall. Later, back at his flat, Smith makes an impression in clay for a life-mask of Granados, which he plans to cast in bronze and send to Barcelona.

"What's the difference between a life-mask and–the other kind?" asks Granados.

"The life-mask is cast when you're alive," says Smith.

Later that day, they go to a travel office on Regent Street to buy tickets for the channel crossing. Smith hands Granados a plain brochure for the small steamship SS *Sussex*, which will cross the channel from Folkestone to Dieppe on Friday afternoon March 24. "I think you should take that one," Smith suggests.

"Are there any other choices?" Granados asks.

"Well, there's a small freighter that used to take passengers from Dover to Calais. I'm not sure it's still running. The trip is shorter, but they've had problems with submarines in that area."

"I'd just as soon avoid them!" says Granados.

"Ès clar–of course. Besides, the Folkestone run will cost you less."

"Will Mildred and Robert will be on our boat?" Amparo asks.

Granados shakes his head.

Never found the phone number. No way to call Mildred. She couldn't call me. Who knows? They might be on our boat.

"We'll take the boat from Folkestone," says Granados.

On their last evening in London, they meet Ismael Smith in the sumptuous lobby of the hotel, and amble over to the Savoy Grill. The maitre d' greets them as he would old school chums, and seats them at a table with a view of the Thames. The captain makes a suggestion: "I think you'll want the Dover sole tonight. It's fresh from Billingsgate Market this morning, and poached in chablis. With a tiny bit of dill. A tiny bit. Or you might wish to try the quail. Or our specialty, the Beef Wellington. But of course you can't get sole where you're going. Spain, isn't it?" Granados scans the wine list and selects a bottle of Chateau d'Yquem, the most expensive one listed.

This dinner's all we'll get from D'Oyly Carte—may as well enjoy it!

D'Oyly Carte is in the Grill tonight, stopping at selected tables. Two of them are close by. Granados hears his greeting: "Good evening, Doctor Baldwin," and watches as he's introduced to two women who appear to be the doctor's wife and daughter. Granados hears the word "Sussex" and the phrase "crossing the channel." From the context Granados concludes D'Oyly Carte is wishing them safe passage. At another nearby table, Granados hears him greet a "Doctor Osler," and watches the introduction of a tall young man sitting with him. Granados hears "Oxford"—wondering if the two men are father and son. The Baldwin family seems to know the young man, because there's chatting back and forth between the tables.

D'Oyly Carte stops to shake hands with Smith and Granados, his voice less haughty than in their earlier meeting. In welcoming Amparo, he sounds faintly genuine. Granados and Smith thank him for his generosity, and then there isn't anything else to say. "Bon voyage," says D'Oyly Carte, and moves on to other tables.

Folkestone

The taxi driver picks up Granados and Amparo at the main entrance of the Savoy Hotel and drives down the Strand, past Charing Cross Station. He points to Red Cross crews, wheeling wounded British soldiers from the Western Front out of the terminal, and loading them into a long row of ambulances. As families of the wounded watch anxiously, young women place bunches of flowers on their laps. The taxi driver swings around Trafalgar Square, down The Mall with St. James' Park on the left, and past Buckingham Palace to Victoria Station. At the station, Granados and Amparo follow their baggage cart to Platform Two and board a green coach car of the South Eastern and Chatham Railway for the trip to Folkestone.

Seated next to the window on the right side of the train, Granados looks upriver and sees the Chelsea Bridge as they cross the Thames, then watches London's urban sprawl south of the river slide past for twenty minutes, followed by pink and white flowers of early spring blooming along the roadbed, and the rolling emerald carpet of the English countryside. How splendid it must be back home—at the Sala on Avinguda Tibidabo, and in Clotilde's awakening gardens in Tiana.

Off to his right is a large graveyard, with marble markers shining in the sunlight and cut flowers adorning some of the graves. Can it be Holy Week? No, Amparo said Easter is late this year, on April 23—which occurs only once or twice each century—that means they'll have a full month of Lent after their return. If the graveside flowers aren't for Easter, might they be for soldiers killed in action? On the other side of a tunnel, the fields are even brighter green. The rolling hills are dotted with clusters of small cottages, their white stucco walls gleaming like fish bones on the beach, cross-hatched with dark-stained wooden beams.

The train cruises through the pastoral beauty of Kent. As it passes another village, Granados sees the placard: "Chiselhurst." There are pine trees mixed with flowering fruits and elms on the curvaceous hills, evoking the time he spent in the orchards of Murcia. Granados stretches his fingers.

Haven't played much not since New York. Once twice on Rotterdam. *Mildred and Titín sitting nearby making requests.*

The train clatters through a long tunnel, and now Granados feels the roadbed tilting toward the seacoast. A stream runs under the train. Hedgerows separate the farms—larger in this area, each with a substantial manor house. Sheep graze on the hills; ivy climbs up brick walls and the bridges over the tracks. On horse farms, spring colts wobble uncertainly in corrals. An imposing manor house with four spired turrets stands on a hilltop. In the distance, a small castle gleams in the sun with a heraldic flag waving in the breeze.

So clean and quiet! Like the area near Olot. How different from grime and noise of New York and London.

Between Hildenborough and Tonbridge, the train stops for signals, and to let a troop train carrying more wounded soldiers go through. When Granados opens the coach window to breathe the pastoral air, he hears the trilling of a nightingale in the balmy silence of the English countryside.

Can't be! Just my imagination. No—there again! That grove of trees. A nightingale! How? Time for their return from North Africa? Yes indeed! Glorious spring! Hearing one here means they're back in Tiana.

"Did you hear that?" he asks Amparo.

She looks up. "I hear motor cars and cows. Is that what you mean?"

"I mean a nightingale, Titín."

She laughs. "Oh, but aren't you always hearing them?"

He shakes his head. In a low voice he replies. "It *is* one."

"I'm proud to be married to a man with such a rich imagination," she says with an affectionate smile.

Under way again, the train picks up speed as it rushes between fields already plowed and waiting to be planted, orchards with trees sprouting small leaves and flowers, and pastures where sheep and goats tend their newborn. Five deer leap over a hedgerow and enter a grove of trees. Hamlets are dominated by Anglican churches shaped like small castles, their towers bearing crosses on high. In one hamlet every house has a red-tile roof, as in the villages of rural Catalunya.

Autumn when we left home. Now it's spring. What a splendid day! Sure it's just as splendid back home.

They encounter another train coming up from the seacoast. There's a sound of air being compressed as they pass within inches of each other. Granados sees a man walking his dog on a country lane, a small herd of black and white dairy cows–all with their newborn calves–and a lone sailboat on a lake in the distance.

How safe it seems! A boat–surrounded by hills. Never far from home. Perfectly safe!

The train slows for its final stop in Ashford, with its fields of yellow flowers, like those that adorn the vineyards of Penedès and Sant Sadurní d'Anoia. The train speeds toward Folkestone. The hills are rockier here. He sees a flock of sheep without lambs, and wonders if they've been taken away for slaughter.

Need to think about that–should never eat lamb again. Spring–time of birth and time for lambs to die.

As the train rushes through another village, there's an odd placard: Westenhanger. Sounds German, strange when the other names are so perfectly English. After emerging from another long tunnel, he sees large gardens of white lilies and yellow daffodils. And in the distance the first sight of the gray-blue English Channel. Clouds are forming. The sky's no longer perfectly blue, as it was back in London. The hills are craggier here and windswept; the tree line lower, the vegetation sparse; and the houses stuccoed with slate roofs, as they might be in the area south of Girona.

Granados thinks of what's next, what new venues for *Goyescas*? New York is a fait accompli, but he'd like to have it performed again next year at the Metropolitan. In three months *Goyescas* will be presented at the Teatro Colón. That should lead to other opportunities in South America, perhaps Santiago and Rio. Then Havana and Mexico. And when the war is over, Paris, London, Milano, Vienna, Berlin and St. Petersburg. But *Goyescas* is just the beginning.

Beyond *Goyescas*, the other works to be composed; Casals described them as "a lifetime of work." Back to Tiana–that will stimulate the creative juices. And with added income from *Goyescas*, reducing his time devoted to teaching. More time to spend with Clotilde, more time with Miró on the opera *Jerusalén*.

He chides himself for succumbing to the premonition.

Crossed the Atlantic twice. Three weeks at sea—nothing bad only French and British sailors trying to intimidate. A few days of seasickness. After short trip across the channel my darkest fears and premonitions will rest forever.

He fiddles with his Beethoven wristband.

My good luck charm. Viva Beethoven! You'll get me home.

The train is on the outskirts of Folkestone, a resort area with several stops: Shorncliffe, where most local residents returning from London get off; Folkestone Central, beyond the barracks that date from the Napoleonic Wars, for people headed for the resort hotels and inns; Folkestone Warren, where the trains are shunted off the main line, switched over to a siding to change direction, and hooked up to tank engines that guide them down the hill; and Folkestone Harbour, accessed by trains that descend the steeper grade at much reduced speed. On the lower level, the roadbed extends onto the dog-legged stone pier itself, in the shadow of the passenger and cargo vessels, and two ships of the British Navy.

At the top of the grade, Granados looks out and sees the English Channel glimmering under a clear blue sky, with racing shadows from scattered clouds. Because it's a clear day, he can see the tip of Cap Gris Nez—the closest point on the French Coast. He sees SS *Sussex* for the first time, moored at the end of the pier. Ordinary and undistinguished.

SS *Sussex*

It's a clear and sunny Friday afternoon on the English Channel off Folkestone, uncommon in late March. There are rolling swells and a gentle breeze as the steamer *Sussex* heads down the southeastern coast of England on its thrice weekly run to Dieppe.

The only clouds to mar the expanse of blue sky can be seen north of the Dover Straits, slowly coming down from Le Pas du Calais and heading toward the channel, yet so slowly it's reasonable to expect this short run will be smooth and uneventful, especially as the course of *Sussex* takes her southward and away from the weather. As passengers stroll on Promenade Deck, waiting for the first lunch call and looking out across the placid channel, the war seems far away: a battle being fought at Verdun, where French troops are repulsing a German assault at a dreadful cost; German aeroplanes striking English coastal towns not far from London, killing civilians in Dover and East Kent; bitter memories of unforgivable slaughter at Gallipoli; U-boats sinking ships nearly every day; the unforgettable demise of the SS *Lusitania* only ten months ago; and the doleful conversion of Paris from a "city of lights" to a darkened medical center for the wounded and dying young warriors of Britain and France. For those heading deeper into the war zone–military personnel destined for the front, young American volunteers who'll drive ambulances and staff the triage stations, and Parisians returning to their not-bombed but still threatened city–this run of the unremarkable, even distasteful *Sussex* as it chugs through the flat blue-gray coastal waters is a respite, in sweet contrast to what could lie ahead.

Sussex, a single-screw steamer of 1,350 tons, has experienced a few nautical reincarnations. Built in Glasgow in 1896 for the London Brighton & South Coast Railway Company, she was designed to carry civilian passengers on a run from Newhaven to Dieppe, which with her speed could take less than four hours. Newhaven was closer to London, and Dieppe closer to Paris, so until the war broke out this route was advantageous. Shortly after the commencement of hostilities, however, Newhaven was taken over by the British military. Today's route from Folkestone to Dieppe has replaced the Newhaven to Dieppe run–and its longer period of exposure to submarine attacks on open waters. During the first year of the war, *Sussex* was converted to deliver troops to the continent, then was redeployed as a passenger vessel. At the time of her reconversion last year, she was sold to the French railway company, Chemins de Fer de l'Etat Francais, and as she leaves Folkestone at eleven forty-five this morning, she's flying the French tricolor.

Under French management, *Sussex* conforms to the minimal standards of cross-channel ferries, with tangy odors and flavors of engine exhaust, sweat, fuel oil, garlic, Pernod, stale urine, and vestiges of seasickness. For passengers, the saving grace is that the ordeal lasts only a few hours. The crew of forty-five is mixed–most are French, some Belgian–and except for the bar steward who's making only his third run, most have worked for Chemin de Fer since *Sussex* was returned to passenger service. The steward, who showed up with the purser earlier this week, lacked documentation, but had a personal recommendation from a French admiral in Bordeaux, therefore was hired.

Today a total of three-hundred-eighty-six passengers walk up the gangplank to board *Sussex*, including commercial travelers, French citizens returning to their homes, soldiers of belligerent countries, department store buyers heading for Paris, a pair of Belgian honeymooners, young American volunteers bound for the ambulances and clinics of the Red Cross, academics and bankers, an acting troupe from Italy, wives and other family members of soldiers engaged on the Western

Front, citizens of nonbelligerent countries for whom this is one of the few ways to return home, and the grandson of the Qajar Dynasty's Shah of Persia.

Captain Henri Mouffet stands in the pilot house on the bridge, surveying the waters off his port bow. He's just reread and pondered the unusual orders received from the company, Chemin de Fers, early that morning: to deviate from his normal route. Instead of crossing directly from Folkestone to Cap Gris Nez–visible on this clear day, then traveling down the French Coast to Dieppe, Mouffet's been ordered to stay close to the English coast, then cut over to Dieppe. This requires a much longer run in open waters–similar to the old route from Newhaven–but since the submarine attacks have been largely between Dover and Calais, he assumes this rerouting is intended to reduce chances of encountering U-boats. And his normal route seems more hazardous since the sinking two weeks ago of the French steamer *Louisiane*, torpedoed along the coast between Boulogne and Le Havre. That's the apparent reason for his order to deviate.

At the same time, Mouffet–who's spent years on the channel–is more concerned about the danger for all passenger ships since the Dutch liner *Tubanta* was torpedoed and sunk by a U-boat last week. He wonders–if that passenger ship of a neutral country was destroyed–how could any vessel be safe in these waters? Of course, it's unlikely that a submarine would attack this small and unarmed vessel carrying only civilians and the day's mail. Then why the unusual order to deviate this morning?

Mouffet shrugs; the war is becoming impossibly complex. He's heard reports that the German naval fleet received new instructions last week: in the war zone, to destroy all commercial ships of the enemy without warning; outside the war zone, to attack all armed ships, enemy and neutral, without warning; and under any circumstances to avoid attacking passenger ships. He hopes this won't be too complicated for the U-boat commanders. Soon after learning about the Germans' new instructions, Mouffet heard that the Royal Navy offered an armed escort for cross-channel vessels, an offer that was said to be refused by his company.

That seems to have been the right decision, for no unescorted passenger ships have been bothered in the channel itself; an escort might only invite a submarine attack. The less resemblance to a warship, the better. Mouffet knows that the British Navy's deployment of "Q-ships"–apparently unarmed vessels with hidden gun turrets, which lure U-boats to the surface to destroy them–can backfire if sub commanders shoot first, then ask questions. He'd like to paint "THIS SHIP FOR PASSENGERS ONLY" on the side of his vessel, but perhaps that would be considered a ruse and only provoke an attack. He shakes his head: the war has become too complex.

In addition to pondering the orders to deviate from the normal route across the channel, Mouffet is concerned about the new steward, whom he suspects of pirating champagne from the vessel's stores on the last two runs. How could the passengers have drunk that much? And he wonders if the upright piano, bolted to the floor of the First Class Smoking Room, is in the proper place. There have been complaints, because most music lovers are women and the Smoking Room is limited to men; but aren't most pianists men?

Mouffet is also concerned about important persons and celebrities on board his ship. From a note received yesterday, he knows that one of today's passengers–the American professor James Mark Baldwin–is a personal friend of Monsieur Wilson, the American President; the professor and his family will be at the captain's end of the dining table for lunch. And just before departure, Mouffet was told that the American Consul in Paris, Robert Bliss, and his wife had made other arrangements for crossing the channel.

Captain Mouffet would rather not know which important people and celebrities are crossing on his vessel; it only creates tension. But these passengers expect to be identified and treated with special care–seated at the captain's end of the dining table–and if they aren't, it could cost him his job. There's another source of concern: if their travel plans are known to someone as ordinary as the captain of a cross-channel steamer, who else might be apprised? Would knowledge of that incite the Germans to attack? Mouffet doesn't trust the British. Their soldiers are valiant in battle on the Western Front and he has nothing but admiration for them. But at the top of the Admiralty, there are men like Winston Churchill, whose motives are not above reproach. Would they leak the fact that some American dignitary was on board, to provoke an attack that would draw the United States into the war? How can he trust the British, when there's been so much history?

The captain looks out across the channel and sees no sign of trouble. "I think the Boches are taking the day off," he says to the pilot, using the disparaging term for the Germans–said to have originated with Alsatians whose hatred for their Teutonic neighbors is legendary. Mouffet turns to leave the bridge. "I'll be downstairs for a short nap before lunch."

Samuel Flagg Bemis, a twenty-four-year-old Harvard graduate student from Medford in Massachusetts, is crossing the channel with a Second Class ticket.

It saves him money, and for such a short passage he can forego the meal on board and have dinner in Dieppe. Bemis came to Europe last fall to pursue his doctorate in diplomatic history and international law. After five months in England, interviewing government officials and writing a portion of his PhD dissertation, he's headed for Paris to complete the work for his degree.

An inquisitive nature, and the opportunity to observe some of the machinations behind daily headlines in England, have raised several questions in Bemis' mind, all without answers. What will break the stalemate on the Western Front? What can the Allies do to end the German blockade of the British Isles? What will motivate America to enter the war? During his last week in London, there's been speculation that if any more Americans are killed in torpedo attacks, President Wilson might break diplomatic relations with Germany. One Foreign Ministry official, admittedly not of the highest echelon, told Bemis of conversations about provoking an incident "to get the Yanks to join us," but these days rumors are raw meat for the lions of war, and Bemis gives this one little credence.

The vessel's only piano is in the First Class Smoking Room, aft of the bridge on Promenade Deck. A dozen passengers, all male, sit on faded chintz-covered cushions, placed on mahogany benches that line the walls of the room. Some tamp their pipes or puff on cigarettes, waiting for the lunch call. The steward brings wine or brandy and soda from a small bar tucked behind the piano bench where the pianist sits, flexing his hands. He runs his index fingers down his moustache, then upward where it curves to a pair of points.

"Un vin blanc, Maestro Granados?" asks the waiter.

The pianist replies, "Merci, non," moves the piano bench an inch or two farther from the keyboard, extends his hands from a cuff-linked white shirt and navy blue jacket, and begins to play. If he were at his Pleyel at the academy, he'd begin with scales and arpeggios, then veer into a long passage of improvisation, moved by the sights and sounds around him and by memories rising in revelation, but now he commences with the first movement of Schumann's Sonata in G minor. The piece that won him the Concurs Pujol thirty-three years ago. Followed by his own compositions, emerging one by one. For each, there's an image or vignette from his life…

"Lento Con Éxtasis"–slowly with ecstasy, from the piano suite dedicated to María Oliveró. Despite the ensuing complications, memories of her as a fine student, always excited when she came for her lessons. An excerpt from "La Nit del Mort"–night of death, from an unfinished orchestral score. "Valenciana"–seventh of the Spanish dances, his first popular success. Without which he would never have dared to court and marry Amparo. The allegretto movement from *Valses Poéticos*–composed in Puigcerdà and dedicated to Malats. "The Maja and the Nightingale"–his reason for going to America, for sailing across the sea, after vowing never to take that risk. And finally, the first movement of Chopin's "Nocturne in C# minor," which he heard when he first went to Paris. Granados relaxes and lets his imagination take him to pure improvisation.

On my way home. Going to lunch we'll look out and see the coast of France. London not very rewarding. Diverting yes. Amusing not rewarding. London–extravagant gardens all around palaces and parks. Everyone said flowers earlier more beautiful than ever. Strand is like Gran Via. Early spring means trees flowering along Tibidabo behind academy. Springtime–most romantic of all. Magical years in Tenerife. With Vives in Paris Casals in Playa Salvador Rusiñol in Sitges. Seeing Titín in València–we just met. So many romantic times! Romance–my splendid garden with Clotilde. Unsanctioned love–forbidden strolls down La Rambla hand in hand never celebrated by others. Love darkened by timing fate circumstances. She's known me well loved me well filled my afternoons evenings with joy laughter. Hearing nightingale's song last train station before channel. Their time–and mine–to return to Tiana.

Unseen by Granados, a young man in a tan suit has entered the Smoking Room from Promenade Deck. Standing with hands clasped behind his back, he towers over the steward, who waits for his order. The young man has a broad forehead and high cheekbones, wide full lips and a long tapering jaw. His blue eyes follow the dance of the pianist's fingers with curiosity and wonder as he whispers to the steward. He moves quietly to his left, where he sees the side of the pianist's face, so pale in sharp contrast with the black of his hair and moustache.

The young man is twenty-five-year-old Wilder Penfield of Hudson, Wisconsin, a Princeton graduate and Rhodes Scholar who's studying medicine at Oxford. His father was a homeopathic physician, avid hunter, and music buff with a fine voice, born in Ohio and married to Jennie Jefferson from Hudson. Jennie–attractive, with a strong, romantic spirit–moved with him to Spokane Falls, where her second son, Wilder, was born. When Wilder was eight years old, Jennie lost patience with her husband who spent so much time hunting in the woods that his medical practice was on the verge of collapse. She moved back to Wisconsin with her three children, where they lived with her parents in the antebellum Italianate-style Jefferson home on Third Street. Wilder was an athletic boy who inherited his father's appreciation for music, pleasant baritone voice, and perfect pitch. Since Jennie left his father, Wilder has only seen him once; at thirteen he went west to spend the summer with him. Twelve years ago.

Life among the prosperous families of Hudson was comfortable, devoutly Protestant, and unostentatious. His older brother went to work at grandfather Amos Jefferson's bank, but Jennie had grander plans for Wilder. Inspired by a lecture given in Hudson by a visiting Rhodes Scholar, she was determined that her son would also win a Rhodes. She chose Princeton for him–and persuaded its officials to grant him a scholarship–because more of its graduates were winning Rhodes scholarships than of any other college in the U.S.A.

At Princeton, Penfield was an outsider from the Midwest, who was taunted when he wore a green tweed suit his mother had chosen for him in St. Paul. He quickly adjusted, taking it to a pawnshop on Witherspoon Street and buying a dark suit so he'd fit in with the Eastern prep schoolers. Making the varsity football team, which won the national championship in his junior year, was his ticket to acceptance. In the fall of Penfield's sophomore year, Princeton's president Woodrow Wilson was elected governor of New Jersey. Two years later, Wilson was launched as a candidate for president of the United States. Penfield was one of the early organizers of Student Volunteers for Wilson. After being passed over the on the first round, he was awarded a Rhodes Scholarship.

In the summer of 1914, before leaving for England, Penfield was engaged to Helen Kermott; by the time he arrived at Oxford in January 1915, the war was fully joined. He heard students talk of little else but the war–frequent criticism of America's unwillingness to enter it, and disapproval of President Wilson for remaining neutral. For a while, Penfield, midwestern and conservative, believed this was Europe's war, that America had no business sending her young men to die in Europe's territorial battles.

Yet he's become uncomfortable in his privileged position at Oxford, while young men who would have been his classmates are instead fighting and dying on the Continent. So with an opportunity to alleviate the suffering of the wounded, he signed up to work at the Red Cross hospital in the village of Ris Orangis south of Paris. To get there he has to cross the channel.

The improvisation and Granados' reverie are over. He turns, hearing sounds that were lost: the clamor of seagulls off the port rail when the door is opened, the baritone voice ordering "un vin, s'il vous plait."

"That was magnificent," says Penfield, reaching the piano bench in two graceful strides.

Granados hesitates. Most words in English are still unfamiliar, even after four months in the United States and England. "Thank you. Do you speak French? Francais?"

"Oui, un petit peu," replies the young American, and their conversation is launched. "Whose music is that?"

"It's my music."

"You are Cuban?"

"No. I'm from Barcelona."

"Oh. That's in Spain, n'est-ce pas? You're going home?"

"Yes. We've been in Americà. My opera was presented at the Metropolitan."

"Splendid! What's the name of your opera?"

"It's *Goyescas*. From the art of Goya."

"Goya! I love his paintings. And El Greco's. I prefer those that show human dignity and strength. I'm not very fond of abstract art."

"Have you seen Goyas and El Grecos?" asks Granados.

"Oh yes. There's a museum in New York that has all of the great Spanish artists. It's called The Hispanic Society of America. So your opera was presented by the Metropolitan? I love opera! When I was a schoolboy in Wisconsin, my mother took me–on the train–to see the Metropolitan. It came to St. Paul on its tour around the country."

"Yes? Which opera?"

"It was *La Boheme*. And who was singing the role of Rodolfo? None other than the great Caruso."

"Ah, Caruso. What a coincidence! Caruso was singing *Pagliacci* the very same night as the premiere of my opera. They were performed together."

"Forgive me for asking, maestro, but if you're going back from New York to your home in Barcelona, why did you come through London?"

Granados hesitates. "Well, I intended to return directly, on a Spanish boat. Then there was a change in plans, and we just missed it. So going through London was the fastest way home–because I couldn't refuse to play for the American President."

"President Wilson? You played for him?"

"Yes. At the White House."

"Why, I know the president. He was once president of my college. I was one of the students who helped him get elected."

"Oui? Well, I found him to be a very nice man. He seemed to enjoy music, and–." He looks straight at Penfield. "If you don't mind my asking, why are you going to a war in which your own country's not involved?"

Penfield nods. "As you know, we're neutral. As is your country. But have you wondered, what does neutrality mean? Is it a denial of violence? Or avoidance of it? Now, if this ship were to be attacked, what would our principled neutrality mean? Could you and I remain neutral when our friends and loved ones were endangered? How would we react?"

Granados says, "I'd make sure my wife was put in a lifeboat. That would be most important. As for me, who knows? But I wouldn't stay on the ship. Not after what happened to *Lusitania*."

Penfield nods. "But I didn't answer your question. Why am I going to France? It's just the right thing to do, even though I hate war. We all hate war, my friends and I. There's Culbertson–sitting over there in the blue jacket. I knew him in college. He's going to Paris to drive an ambulance. And the others, the Crocker brothers and Sargent–same story. None of us has to do this. But you know, maestro, sometimes when you make a decision it's not from thinking things all the way through–it's from the heart. That's why we're going to France."

"Yes, a matter of the heart."

"As far as I'm concerned, maestro, it's the same with love, and that's why after I get my degree in medicine I'll go back to my hometown and marry my fiancée, the girl I love–Helen Kermott."

"Oh, you have a girl. How long have you loved her?"

"I've loved her for several years. Seems I've always loved her. You know what I mean, maestro?"

Oberleutnant Herbert Pustkuchen crouches in the jungle of instruments, dials, wiring, and pipes in the control room of the German submarine UB 29. A black jungle that is his command post, smeared with oil and grease and dripping water. This U-boat was launched in the port of Bremen just six weeks ago, and assigned to patrol duty in the English Channel. Pustkuchen was given a copy of the new general orders: in the war zone, destroy all commercial ships of the enemy without warning; outside the war zone, attack all armed ships, combatant and neutral, without warning; and do not attack passenger ships under any circumstances. Those are the written orders and they seem reasonably clear, but the verbal message from his flotilla leader, Commodore Michelsen, is unmistakable: "If it's flying a British or French flag, sink it!" Pustkuchen hopes that if he encounters a vessel flying an enemy's flag, he'll be able to determine if it's carrying freight or passengers. But what if it's carrying both passengers and military supplies? As was *Lusitania*, according to Commodore Michelsen.

Because the British have deployed decoys–visibly unarmed vessels with hidden guns that have lured U-boats to the surface, then raised a white ensign and fired upon them–Pustkuchen can't bring his craft to the surface for better identification. He must determine whether or not it's a passenger ship through the periscope, while running below the surface. And if he errs, there are instructions on what notes to enter in his log, and how to answer questions if there's an official inquiry. Pustkuchen has also been ordered to patrol close to the English coastline, to look for enemy vessels such as minesweepers. His recent arrival in this area means he's not familiar with the routine channel crossings of *Sussex*, now the only regularly scheduled vessel for civilian passengers and mail.

This is why, when Pustkuchen first sights *Sussex* through his periscope near Beachy Head, he's unsure what type of vessel it is. The silhouette doesn't conform to that of ordinary packet steamers: it has two masts and one stack, a bridge resembling that of a warship, and a strange structure on the stern. Moreover, it's sailing down the English coast instead of crossing directly toward one of the French ports; it's painted black all over; and it's flying no flag at all. He wonders if it could be a decoy trying to lure him to the surface. It's time to decide, or else he'll be drawn away from the area he's been ordered to patrol.

It is two forty-five on the *Sussex*. Some First Class passengers are still leaving the dining room, climbing up the stairwell for a stroll on the Promenade Deck or descending to the lounging saloons located on the Lower Deck. Prince Bahram, the son of the shah of Persia, is sitting with a group of Italian actors in the First Class Gentlemen's Saloon, showing them how his new life jacket, purchased at Harrod's in London, can be tied over his silk robes.

Samuel Bemis is standing on the port side of Promenade Deck. He notices bales, rafts and flotsam drifting past and wonders: are they part of some wreckage? Could another ship have been torpedoed? And he wonders why the flag has been taken down from the mast on the stern of *Sussex*.

Captain Mouffet has also noticed that the tricolor flag is no longer flying and asks the first mate to investigate. The first mate is told by the chief steward that he saw the new man–the one who was tending bar–carrying a tricolor bundle into the luggage room during lunch, and reports this back to the captain who's standing in the pilot house. Mouffet is troubled by this report, but not sure it has any significance.

Professor Mark Baldwin, the American psychologist and writer, is sitting with his wife Helen on Promenade Deck near the two lifeboats at the stern of the vessel. He's returning to Paris, his principal residence, where he's now foreign correspondent of the Institute of France–succeeding William James as professor of psychology at the School of Advanced Social Studies. Helen is returning to her volunteer work with the Red Cross, and their daughter, Elizabeth, will once again assist in the laboratory of Val-de-Grace Hospital, preparing antityphoid serum for the French army.

During his tenure at Princeton and Johns Hopkins, Mark Baldwin was regarded as one of the most influential psychologists in the world. He and President Wilson have much in common: both born in the American South, whose early boyhood memories included the demise of the Confederacy; both graduating from the College of New Jersey, before its name was changed to Princeton–perennially the most favored of the Eastern schools for southerners; later, faculty colleagues at Princeton. Baldwin was still tenured faculty when Wilson was named the college's president. And though Baldwin's influence in his field has declined since he was asked to leave Johns Hopkins after discovery of his visit to a "Negro brothel," his friendship with President Wilson has survived the scandal.

Baldwin is smoking a French cigarette; he asked for Galoise at the tobacconist's, but was handed a different brand. At the time he'd been more concerned with the safety of his wife and daughter as he waited in Liverpool for their overdue ship from the United States to steam through the hazardous Irish Sea–where *Lusitania* had been sent to the bottom. Today's crossing, in comparison, is like riding an excursion boat on Chesapeake Bay. "What do you make of this?" Baldwin asks his wife. "Unseasonably warm. Clear skies. Seas as smooth as the Bay of Naples!"

Seagulls are whirling around the stern as *Sussex* approaches a freighter coming up the channel off her port bow. The Baldwins are pointing at the bales, rafts, and a swarm of wreckage they've seen, bobbing up and down in the swells to the sides and aft of where they're sitting.

"Isn't that a lifeboat, dear?" asks Helen.

"Yes it is. There's another one." One of the crew told him before lunch that two ships were sunk nearby the night before; he decided not to pass this on to his wife and daughter. After all, the crewman said *Sussex* is different: a harmless, unarmed passenger vessel. That put Baldwin's anxiety to rest.

Baldwin's family couldn't find seats together for lunch, so he and his wife dined with the first service, and Elizabeth waited with the other young men and women for the second.

"Do you suppose Elizabeth is still with those young men?"

"Yes. They're up there at the rail. Near the bridge. And being well attended, I'd venture." The Baldwins met Wilder Penfield and the other volunteers at the boarding terminal. They're pleased Elizabeth can be with other young Americans going to serve in France.

The professor observes that *Sussex* has turned away from its course along the English coast, and as he pivots at the rail to look westward toward France, he notices a polelike object in motion several hundred meters off the port bow. A submarine? He dismisses the notion, preferring to think the object is another piece of wreckage.

At the periscope of the UB 29, Oberleutnant Pustkuchen has decided to attack this unidentified ship. He's still not sure whether it's purely a passenger vessel or some other type–even a minesweeper–but has no doubt that it belongs to one of his country's enemies. With his bow pointing toward *Sussex*, at a distance of 1,300 meters, he gives the order to fire one torpedo.

On the bridge the pilot lowers his glasses and points to a moving object he believes is a periscope. Mouffet realizes that a freighter, whose name is clearly visible through the binoculars, *Nieuport XIX*, will soon block their view of the submarine. "Find out who that is!" he calls out to the First Mate. "They're cutting too close!" As the freighter lumbers past, the men on the bridge scrutinize the area where they'd seen the submarine's scope. At first the sea is clear, then suddenly the water is roiling with the wake of an approaching torpedo. None of these men have ever seen one, but it can't be anything else. "Full to starboard!" the captain shouts and the pilot begins to turn the ship away. The men on the bridge know the diversion will not be sufficient, that the torpedo will strike, that there'll be a disastrous explosion.

A passenger standing next to Samuel Bemis cries out, "What's that?" Bemis is looking off the port side and sees the swirling wake of something just beneath the surface shooting toward the ship. As he forms the word "torpedo," it crashes into the port bow.

Penfield and two of the volunteers–Tingle Culbertson and George Crocker–are on the Promenade Deck just below and forward of the bridge, leaning against the starboard rail with Elizabeth Baldwin and another ambulance volunteer, Alice Ruiz, watching seagulls swimming in the waves streaming from the bow of their ship. They've been practicing French to prepare for the work ahead and enjoying the comraderie. They've also noticed the wreckage and the lifeboats on the water around them, but their attention is now drawn to a group of seagulls swimming in the water off the starboard bow.

When they were leaving Folkestone, Penfield noticed more ships in the harbor, more than he'd seen three months ago, and wondered if they were delaying passage because of so many recent sinkings, wondered if they'd been warned against crossing. But now, cruising on a bright and smooth channel, he's put aside such concerns. And, after all, hadn't Captain Mouffet told Culbertson before lunch there's absolutely no risk for an unarmed passenger ship making this trip?

The young men and women standing on the forward section of the Promenade Deck are distracted by an airplane flying off the stern at a right angle to their foaming wake. "Is it one of ours?" asks Culbertson.

"Well, it didn't shoot at us–it must be," replies Penfield.

Two more hours–safely in France. Train to Paris another to Barcelona. To l'Estació França–home at last! Children waiting at the station. Walk into sunshine smell our own sea–feel our own breeze–past the park past l'Arc de Trionf and up Ronda de Sant Pere to Girona–one more block then home! Home–with Eduardo Solita Enric Victor Natalia Paquito. Friends–Miró and Pí i Sunyer. Academy with Marshall students. Beloved Clotilde–spirit's magically entwined with mine. In her garden where we recite poetry. Darío–poor Darío! Can't forget his poem so cherished by my beloved:

> *I know there are those who ask:*
> *why do you not still sing*
> *those same wild songs of yesteryear?*
> *They do not see the work of just an hour,*
> *the work of a minute, and the wonders of a year.*
> *I, now an aging tree, used to moan so sweetly*
> *from the breezes when I began to grow.*
> *But the time has passed for youthful smiles:*
> *so let the hurricane move my heart to song!*

Wasn't that a nightingale? The last train stop. Sign of what's to come? Sign that now at last it's my time? Per fi! At last!

The torpedo fired by UB 29 strikes the port side of *Sussex* just forward of the bridge. It's a glancing blow, thanks to the helmsman's sudden turn to starboard, but the explosion is sufficient to rip off a large section of the hull from the bow back to the bridge. It's seen floating past by Samuel Bemis, who's getting up after being knocked off his feet. But since the precise point of entry of the torpedo is just in front of a major bulkhead, the force of the explosion serves to seal the next compartment from flooding, and hundreds of mailbags piled up inside the bulkhead reinforce it, allowing the compartment to resist pressure from the water outside. Were it not for this combination of skill and circumstance, the heart of the vessel would have filled with water, and *Sussex* would be headed for the bottom.

At the instant of contact there's a dull sudden shock, followed momentarily by a deafening explosion. Only men who've been in combat have heard noises comparably loud, and in battle there's a persistent dreadful cacophony made by devices intended to cause sudden violent death. On this ship, cruising across the channel on a clear and almost waveless day, all ears ring after the explosion blows away the ordinary sounds of the ship's engines cranking, steel hull cutting through the water, sharp crying of seagulls, and the passengers' own chatter. For a few moments, there's a breathless silence, then a wave of debris and water striking the remainder of the ship, then pandemonium.

Passengers on the Promenade Deck in front of the bridge are all killed or swept into the channel, where they're unlikely to survive a combination of injury, concussion, and numbing cold water. Inside, the First Class Gentlemen's Saloon on Lower Deck bears the brunt of the explosion, along with the crew's quarters and lavatories and one of the baggage compartments. In the saloon, the son of the shah of Persia and the troupe of Italian actors are killed instantly, along with most of the other men there. A few passengers who tarried during the second lunch shift, and the stewards serving in the First Class Dining Saloon on Main deck, are killed or seriously injured. The First Class Ladies Saloon on Lower Deck is damaged and there are a few injuries, painful but not life-threatening. Three lockers for storage of life jackets in front of the First Class Dining Room are obliterated.

The explosion rocks the entire ship, sending crew and passengers sprawling. The wave of debris causes many injuries, and those killed on board are all victims of crushing steel, concussion, and fire. There is sheer panic for about twenty minutes and a wild scramble for life jackets–which most passengers are unable to put on properly–and a rush to the wooden life boats–which fully loaded will accommodate less than one half of the passengers. The inflatable life rafts can also be employed, and they will float no matter how they land on the water, but it's soon obvious that *Sussex* wasn't carrying sufficient emergency craft for all of its passengers in the event of its sinking.

When loading begins, it's mostly civilized, except for a Belgian doctor and several Belgian nurses whose skills are needed to attend the wounded on board; they push others aside and jump into the first boat. Male passengers and stewardesses help women and children line up for the boats, trying to prevent men from jumping into them. An English nurse refuses to go, saying, "Give my place to a man with a family of children. I am only a single woman." A Greek man of about forty runs up and down the Promenade Deck, screaming hysterically. He just found the bodies of his wife and son, crushed by the twisting of steel at the edge of the explosion.

The forward stairway leading up to the Promenade Deck was in the section now blown away, so passengers and crew on the Main Deck must go all the way back, where they join Second Class passengers crowding into the aft stairway. They are more fortunate than Third Class passengers, whose area is on the Main Deck in front of the bridge; many of them are killed or blown into the water.

Many First and Second Class passengers leap overboard without life jackets, fearful that *Sussex* will go down quickly, or that the submarine will fire another torpedo to finish the job. Many of the jackets stored on the Promenade Deck are rotten; those stored on the lower deck are more reliable. First Class passengers are unaware that there are life jackets in lockers on the Main Deck next to the Second Class Smoking Room and lavatory. Since there's been no emergency drill for such a short run, many with jackets don't know how to put them on. Even those with life jackets properly fitted are likely to die of exposure in the cold water of the channel.

Captain Mouffet, just a few meters from the center of the explosion, is knocked across the bridge. He's bleeding from a small laceration on his forehead where it struck a doorframe, his right shoulder is badly bruised but not dislocated, and his right knee is injured, possibly fractured and unable to support any weight. Mouffet orders the pilot to reverse the engines, and orders the First Mate to get passengers off the ship, loaded into lifeboats and life rafts.

"You want to abandon ship?" asks the mate.

Mouffet scowls. "I will give that order when it's necessary! What I need at once is a report on damage down below. 'Til then I'll stay and wait to see if it starts to go down." Just then the radioman arrives to report that when the main mast collapsed the radio was silenced. "We'll keep trying sir, but I think our best chance is for someone to find us."

"That's not good enough!" roars Mouffet, shaking off the searing pain in his knee. "Set up another antenna and let Boulogne know what happened! You understand?"

Mouffet looks off the port bow where he'd seen the periscope. He braces himself for the sight of another torpedo churning toward his ship. And he notices that the freighter that passed *Sussex* much too close, blocking his view of the area where he'd seen the periscope, is now steaming away to the north-east. That it's leaving his ship in obvious distress can mean only one thing: the freighter's assignment was to prevent *Sussex* taking evasive action. "Poutains de merde! The fucking Boches!"

Samuel Bemis has time to brace himself for the shock. Many of those around him are knocked off their feet and scattered onto the deck. He sees that the bow has been blown off, and feels the rest of the ship beginning to sink forward. The thought of another torpedo being launched by the submarine is chilling. He's morbidly familiar with how fast *Lusitania* went down, how even a minute's hesitation could seal one's fate, so he hurries to the place on the Main Deck where he's seen life jackets. They're gone. Inside the Second Class Gentlemen's Saloon on the Lower Deck, he finds one, rotten and frayed, and ties it on with a piece of rope. Back on the Promenade Deck, one lifeboat is being lowered and another filled with women and children. At this point Bemis is convinced that his greatest chance of safety lies in getting clear of the ship, which he believes is going to sink. He removes his shoes and climbs over the rail near the stern, finding a shelf above the propeller just as a life boat loaded with people comes by. He steps off into the boat, quickly realizing that it's already unstable, and jumps to a nearby life raft–designed for emergencies only–which barely supports his weight. He floats away from *Sussex* with a life boats, rafts, and passengers hanging onto deck chairs, or whatever debris promises to support them.

There is no warning for Mark and Helen Baldwin, who are still standing after the explosion. His first words are, "We're struck. We're going down!" He sets out to retrieve life jackets, and after finding several that are rotting and defective, he returns to guide his wife to a group of women and children waiting for a lifeboat. Helping each other take off their shoes and put on their life jackets. Then he hurries forward to find his daughter, who'd been standing close to where the bow was sheared off. There are piles of wreckage in his path, swarms of distracted and confused passengers and bodies of the dead and wounded. In his path is a young French girl who pleads, "Monsieur, sauvez moi!" Baldwin stops for a moment to help adjust her life jacket and show her where to go for a lifeboat, then continues his search. Elizabeth and her friends are gone. In horror, he retraces his steps and finds his wife just climbing into a lifeboat. As it's being lowered, he looks inside and sees Elizabeth stretched out on a seat in the boat, her head and face covered with blood, lying as if dead. Instinctively, he seizes a rope being used to lower the boat and slides down it to rejoin his wife and child.

Penfield is close to the explosion, with Elizabeth Baldwin, Culbertson, and George Crocker; it fills his ears with a dreadful roar. He's thrown against the bulkhead under the bridge and twirled around several times. He sees people spinning through the air; everything in slow motion. He expects to tumble into the water, thinking that the wreckage of the ship is turning with him—slowly—while he's rising into the air and falling again. Penfield believes it's the end of his life and he's falling into the sea. Instead he lurches into a pile of debris. He resists, thinking: "This cannot be my end. My work in the world has only just begun. This cannot be the end." His mother's vision for him is too strong. Instead of heavenly hosts waiting for him, the message is: this is not the end!

Penfield looks around for Elizabeth Baldwin, distressed to see that she's gone. Through the acrid smoke he finds Crocker, unconscious, with a probable concussion. Penfield drags him back to where the deck is still intact and leaves him there. Judging that the ship may have but a few more minutes afloat, he decides to spend his time with those who can help themselves get off. If they stay on board, and *Sussex* heads for the bottom, they'll surely perish.

After a coolheaded examination of his own left leg, Penfield feels a compound bone fracture in his ankle and a fractured kneecap. Looking over the side he sees a lifeboat capsizing from having been overloaded. He sees an elegantly dressed young woman, wearing her thin yellow blouse over a life jacket, pushing a life raft over the rail with two young men, then hears a splash. On the starboard side of the ship, the last lifeboat is being readied. Women are loaded first, but panicky men jump in as it's being lowered; others slide down ropes into it, landing on top of those already on board. In his last glance over that side, Penfield sees a face just above the surface of the water, deadly white with terror.

In what remains of the First Class Gentlemen's Saloon, a British Army officer who went down to look for survivors finds two Belgian crewmen cutting fingers off the corpses to salvage their rings; he drives them away with a pistol. On deck, the same officer finds Culbertson taking photographs. He reprimands him, and orders him to assist the wounded. Culbertson finds George Crocker, now joined by his brother, Charles, and stays with him until he recovers consciousness.

The First Mate reports that some of the crew have raided the bar and are drinking champagne in the First Class Dining Room. "Get their names!" shouts Captain Mouffet, "and we'll see they pay for it when we get to port!"

Despite his shattered leg, Penfield is providing and directing care, acting as if he were in a military hospital. Making decisions on who will survive without care, who needs care, and who will not survive no matter how much care they might receive. Culbertson lays down on the deck beside Crocker, who seems improved; Penfield is still concerned about the extent of his head injury.

Penfield sits on the deck, resisting the waves of pain from his leg, watching *Sussex* stabilize and remain afloat–not plummeting as he feared, like *Lusitania*. The sun is still shining and the water is lapping the side as quietly as ever. People are murmuring, "she's going to float" and "the wireless has been fixed. Help is on the way." For that reason, Penfield has decided to stay on board, and he's encouraging others to do the same.

When the torpedo strikes, Granados and Amparo are sitting in deck chairs with Gertrude Warren and Blanche Handyside, who's just stood up to catch a better look at the seagulls in the water below. The explosion throws all four of them onto the deck where they remain motionless, bruised, and disoriented as the wave of debris and water reaches them. With sounds of distress and panic rising all around, they signal to each other that they're not injured. Their eyes are burning from the smoke.

Dios mío! Dios mío! The end–we're going to sink! Have to get off! Chaleco salvavidas–life jackets!

Granados remembers seeing a storage locker for life jackets in back of the engine room, and scrambles to retrieve four of them. There's a crowd in front of him with the same idea, and by the time it's his turn most of the jackets have been taken. He grabs four without checking their condition and brings them back to the three women. They've had no instruction in putting them on. Granados recalls a sign on the life jacket locker during their voyage on *Rotterdam*, when passengers were shown what to do in case of an emergency: "Be sure to put the jacket on right side up. Be sure not to put the jacket on backwards. Be sure to tighten the belt." If the jacket's put on upside down, the passenger will turn upside down in the water and drown. And if put it on backwards, it will force the passenger's face under water.

"Come–come! To the lifeboat!" he cries, taking Amparo by the hand. He turns to the American women. "You–come too!" he says in English. As he pulls the strap on his jacket, it breaks. "Useless!" he cries.

Handyside is still struggling with her life jacket. She motions for Granados to go with Amparo. "You go! We'll be there in a minute."

In frustration, Granados flings his life jacket and it sails overboard. Amparo drops hers on the deck as they scurry to a lifeboat being loaded with women and children.

On their way to the lifeboats, they encounter Mario Serra, son of the Catalan painter Enrique Serra, whom they met briefly after lunch. "I'm staying on board," Serra says, "and you should too, senyores. The captain says not to panic. The ship is not sinking. Please stay on board!"

Granados clasps him on the shoulder. "No, Mario, we must get off this ship. Our lives depend on it! Come with us!"

Serra steps back, shaking his head, and Granados leads Amparo to the nearest lifeboat.

"You get in," he says, helping her over the gunwale.

"You come too."

"No. It's not right. I'll wait. There are rafts for men. Don't worry."

As the boat is being lowered from the davit, several men and one member of the crew jump in, despite cries that the boat will be overloaded. Granados grabs another man who's poised to leap from the rail. "No! No!" he cries. The man turns and punches him in the jaw.

Granados falls to the deck. He shakes his head, trying to clear it. Salty taste of blood in his mouth. He sees Penfield sitting on the deck and crawls over to him. "We're going to sink! We must get off!"

Penfield shakes his head. "No, maestro! We're not sinking any more. I'm going to stay. You stay too. Please stay!"

"No–my wife is in one of the boats! I told her I'd be in a raft. She'll be worried. I can't let her be out there alone!"

Penfield snaps back. "Look–she'll be safe in a boat. A ship will come to rescue us–she'll be picked up. We'll all get to shore!"

She's out there alone! Can't abandon her!

"No!" he shouts at Penfield. "I must find a raft."

"Please wait! People will take care of your wife."

Granados shakes his head. "I must take care of her! Au revoir."

Oberleutnant Pustkuchen watches the scene through the periscope of UB 29. He sees that the bow of his target has been blown off, that the hull from the bridge to the stern is still afloat. He also sees lifeboats filled with people. At this distance, he can't see the heads and shoulders of others who are bobbing in the water, some dead, others still alive. He's surprised there were so many passengers on board, and wonders if his suspicions of it being a combat vessel were unfounded. But there's no time for idle speculation–this is an enemy ship, aiding the enemies of his country. Pustkuchen expects the remaining hull will fill with water and sink, but since it's still afloat he considers shooting another torpedo to make sure it goes down. To do that will require time to get into position, and he'd rather be prepared for any enemy warships responding to this one's distress call. He speculates that he might be able to sink a British cruiser, but also reminds himself to be careful–most surface warships these days are armed with depth charges.

Granados finds a group of five men launching a life raft off the port side. "Come with us," says the youngest of the men, who seems to be in charge. He says they'll drop the raft over the side, then jump in the water and climb onto it. Granados says he's not a swimmer. "All right–you go first, and jump *onto* the raft," says the man with a blend of English, French, and hand signals. "Wait a minute, sir. Just a minute! I'll let you know when." He points to Granados' shoes. "You should take your shoes off, sir. Don't worry–it's an easy jump. Only five meters, no more than the height of a room. You can do it. You should roll when you land. To break the fall."

Granados unlaces and kicks off the new shoes he bought in London.

Barely know what he's saying. Jump onto raft. Only five meters. Roll on impact. Can do that. Not afraid. Must get out there and find Titín!

He climbs over the rail and holds on, waiting as the raft is dropped. The young man shouts, "Now! Jump!" Granados lets go of the rail and pushes off. He lands and rolls, wincing in pain as his right shoulder absorbs the impact. His right side is dripping with cold water. The raft is stable. He hears and feels splashing as the five men jump into the water. The young man who gave him the signal fetches two oars from the water and brings them aboard. Three more men and a woman climb over the ship's rail and leap toward the raft. Then two more men. There is shouting on the deck of the ship above him, but down here there's only the sound of splashing.

Granados helps the first man climb aboard, then moves to the center of the raft and watches as each new arrival is helped up by the one who just climbed out. Now they're all aboard, nine men and a woman, all shivering and dripping wet. The raft is bobbing gently in the channel. "Sit down, everybody!" says the young man. He hands one oar to a tall man across the raft and they begin to paddle away from *Sussex*. Granados sees that the lifeboats are about two hundred meters away, too far for him to discern which of them is carrying Amparo.

The sky is clouding over now and the wind is picking up force as it sweeps down from the Strait of Dover, where–unknown to Granados–Mildred and Robert Bliss are on a small freighter crossing from Dover to Calais in a storm with a boatload of English soldiers, protected by an escort ship of the British Royal Navy.

Titín! Titín! Where? Saw her get on the boat saw it being rowed from the ship. She was on second boat.

Two men paddle with oars and the raft approaches a cluster of lifeboats. Another raft floats past, with a woman who's stripped off all of her clothing and is teetering on the bow, her pale skin dripping and shaking. "Where is he? Where is he?" she cries in a desperate voice. A man and a woman reach up and grab her arms. She seems to faint, then collapses and disappears into the raft.

Around him Granados sees a harrowing scene. People in life jackets are floating like fishing bobbers, those who are still alive gasping as they paddle feebly toward the lifeboats and rafts, and the dead ones silent and pale with their faces lapping in the waves. Some, whose jackets are upside down, are floating with heads under water and legs above. Others, whose jackets are backwards, are drowned with just the backs of their heads and shoulders visible. A few survivors are swimming with resolute vigor toward the lifeboats. Others cling to spars, deck chairs, oars, and bits of floating wreckage. From time to time one of the swimmers simply stops moving and disappears without a cry.

Like scenes from Dante–except not with raging fires and smoke. Cold and watery inferno. Far worse!

The raft bearing Granados is now within fifty meters of the closest of the lifeboats. They are heading back toward *Sussex*, which seems stable, no longer threatening to sink and suck them down with her. Hope spreads that the ship will remain afloat, not follow *Lusitania* to the bottom. If rescuers don't arrive before dark, survivors will be better off with the boats clustered, closer to *Sussex*. Of course it's hoped that the rescue ships will soon appear. Some are obsessed with spotting the first dark point of a mast breaking the blurred gray horizon.

The lifeboat carrying Amparo has been on the verge of capsizing ever since it was launched. The fear-crazed rush of men to get on board might have tipped it over while it was being lowered from the davits, as occurred to another boat. However–with the excessive weight of its passengers evenly distributed and floating on a calm sea–so far it's remained upright. But now a wind from the north is beginning to churn the channel's water, and at the moment when Granados sees Amparo, and asks the young man to paddle the raft toward her, two large men stand up in her lifeboat, their intentions unknown. The boat capsizes and all of its occupants are thrown into the water.

Thirty people–half without life jackets–are now struggling to overcome the weight of their wet clothing. The water is cold enough to numb them and sap their strength to remain afloat, and eventually they'll lose consciousness. To avoid this they can try to right the capsized craft and carefully climb back into it. Once back in the boat, their odds of avoiding another capsize will be improved with each person who drowns and fails to return.

Watching in horror, Granados stands up for a better view of the chaos in the water. He hears Amparo cry out and follows the sound with his eyes. He sees her, all alone, treading water. Her gray hair is soaked and darkened, her eyes are wide in panic. Seeing Granados, she raises an arm and smiles, momentarily masking her anxiety, as if merely knowing that he's survived can somehow keep her afloat.

Titín–must help her! Can't leave her! She needs me!

Granados puts his foot on the gunwale of the raft.

"What are you doing? Get down!" shouts the young man, reaching up and grabbing Granados' arm. "Don't jump!"

"That's my wife!" Granados shouts back and wrenches his arm free.

"No! No! You can't swim!"

"It doesn't matter!" He sees a splintered board in the water and leaps toward it. Just before the shock of hitting the water, he hears Amparo's voice, but doesn't comprehend her urgent plea: "No!" she cries. "No, don't jump!"

He comes to the surface flailing and grabs the board. His long hair is a wet blinding mask over his face, and when he takes his right hand off the board to brush it aside he begins to sink. There's barely enough buoyancy in the board to keep him afloat. With his face uncovered he can see Amparo. He's never learned to swim, but knows that kicking his legs under water will push him toward her. He holds the board tightly and kicks. In two minutes of struggling they reach each other. She takes hold of the board. Their eyes meet.

"You fool!" she says. "You can't even swim. Now we're both in trouble."

"I couldn't leave you," he says, spitting water.

"You fool!" she cries again.

"The children need you, Titín."

Amparo shakes her head. "Keep your mouth closed. The water's bad for you."

The north wind is whipping the channel into choppy waves, making it more difficult for anyone in the water to see the lifeboats and rafts, or to be seen by anyone wanting to pick up survivors. In the boat farthest away from where Granados and Amparo are struggling to stay afloat, Blanche Handyside, who saw Amparo's boat capsize and witnessed Granados' leap from the raft, asks the men who are rowing her boat to turn around. "There are two people over there who need our help," she urges, "please help!"

The man looks at her with resignation. "Madame, there are two hundred people out here who need help. Would you have us capsize to help those two?"

Handyside lowers her head. When she looks out to the spot where she'd seen Granados and Amparo, they are gone. As she intensifies her scan, their heads pop back into sight.

Granados holds onto the board with one arm and tightens his other arm around Amparo. Alone, she's a strong enough swimmer to stay afloat or find a boat or raft to hold onto. But with Granados' clumsy efforts and the combined weight of their wet clothes, she's reaching the limit of endurance. Without her to tread water, the board will not keep them afloat. Amparo feels Granados' arm loosening.

"Hold on to me!"

"I'm trying. I'm sorry, Titín. So sorry."

"Don't speak–save your strength."

"Titín, te adoro. I think this is the end." Granados eyes are smarting from the salt. Each time he gasps for breath, he swallows more water and chokes.

He feels his strength being drained away. Each time it's harder to kick his legs. Waves of weariness bear down upon him, at closer intervals, incessantly. His fear of drowning subsides as he prepares to be devoured.

Adiós Titín. Adiós mi querida. Sorry—didn't love you better. Farewell everyone! So close to home—my cruel fate!

Amparo feels his arm released from her waist. She wraps both arms around him and kicks with legs that are numb with cold and fatigue. "Oh God, forgive us! Que nos perdone!

On the day before SS *Sussex* sailed from Folkestone, Mildred and Robert Bliss—after waiting in vain for a phone call from Granados—took a train from London to Dover, where they boarded a small freighter to cross the channel with a Royal Navy escort. "The weather was cold and drizzly and the outlook grim," Mildred later recalled in a letter to Malvina Hoffman. Because of the weather, and reports of submarine activity in the channel, their departure was delayed. In the morning, according to Mildred, "the weather was dirtier than the day before, the storm blowing in gusts of wild wind, and sheets of rain!" It finally broke in late afternoon, allowing the vessel—"with decks crowded cheek by jowl with English soldiers in lifebelts"—to sail from Dover and in less than two hours to cross the channel.

Upon arrival in Calais, the Blisses were horrified by rumors that the steamer *Sussex* was torpedoed and many lives lost. So many questions. Could Granados and Amparo have been on it? Since *Sussex* was the only vessel in regularly scheduled service, how else would they cross over? Could they have crossed safely on its previous run? Or were could they still be in London? "My heart stood still," Mildred wrote Malvina, "and I hardly dared ask whether the ship had been sunk. To my great relief they said, no, the bow had been blown off, but *Sussex* had been able to make port under her own steam."

Still not knowing the fate of Granados, the Blisses caught a train to Paris where they were greeted on the platform by Percy Dodge—one of Robert's colleagues at the embassy. Dodge shook Robert's hand and flung his arms around Mildred, saying in a trembling voice that she—the tall, redhaired wife of an American diplomat—had been reported drowned. "I've been here all day, meeting every train arriving from the coast," he said, "and thank God—here you are!"

Mildred shook her head. "Drowned? Where did those rumors come from?"

"They assumed you were on the ship that was torpedoed. The *Sussex*. Because that was the only way to get across."

Robert placed his hand on the younger man's shoulder. "It's the only regular service but we were able to cross on a freighter with a naval escort."

"Well, that explains it," Dodge said. "I'm so relieved to see you, Mr. Secretary!"

Mildred, pondering the next question, managed to ask: "So the *Sussex* did not sink? Is there any news of casualties?"

"There were some killed in the explosion," Dodge replied. "And some who left the ship were drowned."

Mildred's heart stood still. A dreadful question loomed in her mind, one she hardly dared ask. Her voice was a breathless whisper. "Drowned?" she asked. "Who was drowned?" She braced herself for the answer she dreaded, and in a mystical way knew was forthcoming.

Dodge shook his head. He could only remember there was a Spanish composer and his wife returning from America. Survivors reported the composer tried to save his wife, and they both went down together.

Mildred's knees buckled and Robert caught her as she fell toward the platform. "Oh no!" she cried. "Oh my God, no! His premonitions. If only he called. Oh, the children!"

Robert held her in silence until he felt her grief subsiding. Later, as they collected their baggage and waited for the embassy car to take them home, he asked Dodge for more details.

"The tragedy," the embassy staffer said quietly to Robert, "is that those passengers who survived the explosion and stayed on board were all saved. The *Sussex* was able to reach the port of Boulogne under her own power."

The following day, Robert Bliss arranged for the Granados luggage—sitting unclaimed at the dock in Boulogne—to be shipped to the children at Girona, 20, in Barcelona.

Epilogue

March 24th, 1936

The captain of the charter boat recognizes the middle aged woman from Barcelona, who arranges for him to take her to a certain place in the channel off the French port of Dieppe. She does not come every year, but nearly that often, and each time it is the same ritual. She sits with her bouquet of flowers in the cabin of his launch until he reaches the designated place. When he stops, she walks to the stern, tosses the flowers onto the waves, and bows her head. After a few minutes, she crosses herself and signals for him to return to France.

This is the first time that Clotilde Godó Pelegrí has come to the channel since her father died. He agreed to come with her only once, shortly after the end of the Great War, but when it was time to leave Dieppe she was seized with a terrible fear of the waters that had claimed the life of her maestro and lover, and they returned home. After that, she doubted she'd ever have the courage to return, but every day she prayed to the Virgin of Montserrat. One day she simply knew that she could come, that she must come, and when she arrived in Dieppe she looked down from the terminal and saw this captain and his charter launch. She knew that the Virgin was with her and she would have no more fear.

Today is the twentieth anniversary of the submarine attack on the SS *Sussex*, which resulted in her maestro and his wife—the mother of his six children–being swallowed up by these waters. Witnesses to the tragedy said that it was he, hearing his wife cry for help, who dove in to rescue her. They were last seen in each other's arms, going down together.

Twenty years ago. And longer since Clotilde saw him last, the evening before his departure for New York: a solemn farewell in the garden of her home in Tiana, where he composed his masterpiece, where she still lives with the Pleyel grand piano, inscribed with his signature, the piano on which *Goyescas* was created.

Twenty years have passed, yet the memory of his voice and the sound that came from the Pleyel–but only when his hands played it–still echo in every beat of her heart. Across the years his voice calls to her, and as she casts the bouquet of flowers onto the waves, her eyes fill once more with tears.

Enrique Granados touched a wide variety of people. These are some of the others who survived him…

Dr. Salvador Andreu i Grau (1841–1928). When the famous Doctor Andreu died at age eighty-seven, his business interests were passed on to his surviving sons.

Carmen Miralles de Andreu (1863–1944). At the outbreak of the Spanish Civil War in 1936, Republican forces loyal to the government occupied Barcelona. As members of the alta burguesia–a class generally sympathetic to the Nationalist forces under General Franco–Carmen, her daughters, and their families fled into exile in Italy. Carmen returned to Barcelona in 1940, and died four years later in her residence at the Hotel Majestic, four blocks from the church of La Concepció, where she and Salvador Andreu were married sixty-one years earlier.

Andreu Descendants. The eldest son, Salvador Andreu i Miralles, followed his father into pharmacy; after thirty-seven years battling multiple illnesses, he died in 1921. Carmen Andreu i Miralles married José Maria Munné Vidal in 1911. Francisca ("Paquita") Andreu i Miralles, the family's most talented pianist, did not marry until three years after Granados' death; she continued to play the piano and compose throughout her long life. José and Juan Andreu i Miralles, who also earned degrees in pharmacy, managed the enterprises founded by their father and eventually sold them to a Swiss pharmaceutical company. (Doctor Andreu's little cough pills, brand-named "Joanolas," can still be purchased in Barcelona's pharmacies.) Madronita Andreu i Miralles devoted a lifetime to filmmaking; her first husband was a Colombian named Mauricio Obregón Arjona, whom she married in 1919; after Obregón died, she married a U.S. citizen named Max Klein.

Four generations have descended from Salvador Andreu and Carmen Miralles. Flora Klein, Madronita's daughter and youngest of the grandchildren, recently completed editing her mother's fifty years of filmmaking; her collaborator was Madronita's grandson, Mauricio Villavecchia, who created the musical background for the documentary, "An Instant in a Diverse Life."

Andreu Properties. The heritage of Salvador Andreu and Carmen Miralles was passed on to their descendants, but their residences didn't fare as well. The villa in Sant Gervasi was occupied by military forces loyal to the Republican government in 1936, when most of the family went into exile. After returning, they found the villa in a wretched state of disrepair, and settled elsewhere in Barcelona; the site is now occupied by a high-rise apartment building. Xalet Andreu in Puigcerdà, which in its heyday could accommodate up to forty-five overnight guests, was too large for the surviving family. It was converted to a resort hotel in the early 1940s, and in 2001 converted again into twelve luxury condominiums, within the outer dimensions of the original structure. The Sala Granados on Avinguda Tibidabo remained as a recital hall for events sponsored by the academy until the early 1930s. The building became a residence and still stands, though in deplorable condition.

James Mark Baldwin (1861–1934). A pioneer in the field of social psychology. After his daughter, Elizabeth, was severely wounded on the SS *Sussex*, Baldwin sent a telegram to his old colleague at Princeton, President Woodrow Wilson, urging a stronger position on Germany's submarine warfare. As a result, Wilson sent a sharp note of protest to the Germans, which led to a deterioration of relations between the two nations and, within a year, to declarations of war. (Following the attack on the SS *Sussex*, there were unconfirmed rumors that British and French agents had conspired to provoke the incident in order to draw the United States into the war. Wilson's old friend and colleague, Baldwin, was allegedly the pawn in this scheme. If Baldwin were on board, attacking *Sussex* might trigger United States entry into the war. Samuel Bemis, a fellow passenger on the vessel and later a professor of history, wrote of hearing such rumors at the British Admiralty in early 1916, but there's been no confirmation of this imagined conspiracy.)

Robert Woods Bliss (1875–1962) and Mildred Barnes Bliss (1879–1969). The Blisses came to New York to attend the opening of *Goyescas* at the Met, and donated to the "loving cup" fund presented to Granados when he left New York. Mildred was a passenger on the SS *Rotterdam* from New York to England, during which passage Granados told her of his premonition of death at sea. (In a letter to Malvina Hoffman shortly after the incident, she described her efforts to "save" Granados.) Robert continue to rise in the Foreign Service, achieving the rank of ambassador to Argentina before retiring in 1933. He was called back during World War II to serve as consultant to the secretary of state. The Blisses founded a research library at their palatial Georgetown residence, Dunbarton Oaks, later conveying the property to Harvard University. Organizers of the United Nations held preliminary discussions there. Much later, Mildred Bliss was a guest of President John F. Kennedy at the White House recital by Pablo Casals.

Enrico Caruso (1873–1921). He befriended Granados in New York, when he was rehearsing the role of Canio in *Pagliacci*–performed the same night as the Met opening of *Goyescas*. (A memento of their friendship, a caricature of Granados by Caruso, survives at the Enrico Museum of America in Brooklyn.) Like Granados, Caruso died at age forty-eight in the prime of his career, of complications from an abdominal abscess.

Pablo Casals (1876–1973). A close friend of Granados for thirty years, and godfather of the six Granados children. He became the world's most renowned cellist, performing well into his mid-90s. He played at the White House for President Theodore Roosevelt in 1904, and fifty-seven years later for President John F. Kennedy. Casals left Catalunya near the end of the Spanish Civil War, and except for one brief visit to bury his second wife, he never returned. He played the Catalan "Song of the Birds"–his final piece in every concert–at the United Nations Day in 1971, at age ninety-four. With his third wife, cellist Marta Montañez, he founded the Festival Casals in Puerto Rico. He died there at age ninety-seven.

Clotilde Godó Peligrí (1885–1988). Those close to Granados during the last few months of his life were aware of how important the relationship with Clotilde had become. The three-month separation from her certainly influenced his choices in returning to Barcelona. Many years after his death, she gave Granados' personal diary–which he entrusted to her when he went to New York–to his daughter Natalia, who'd become a friend of hers. A large section was cut out of the diary, presumably relating to Granados' romance with Clotilde; these pages have never been recovered. Several years after Granados' death, Clotilde married again, to a Barcelona physician, but this union ended after one year. Thereafter, she lived alone, virtually in seclusion. She told her grand-niece Elena Godó Oriol, who visited her often in the final two decades, that she hadn't touched the Pleyel since Granados' death. (But in a recent interview, her neighbor across the street said she once heard Clotilde play Granados' "Spanish Dance Number Five"–a difficult piece, surely not playable without some regular practice.) Paquita Madriguera, who became a close friend of hers, recalled that on the anniversary of Granados' death Clotilde would travel to the French coast of the English Channel, and scatter flowers on the waters where he died. For three years (1936–1939), Republican forces occupied her home; she returned after the war. Clotilde survived Granados for seventy-two years, and died at age one hundred and three.

Granados Family. On the evening of March 24, 1916–while the damaged SS *Sussex* was being towed into Boulogne–the Polish-born pianist Artur Rubinstein was giving a concert of Spanish music at El Palau de la Música in Barcelona. The program included "La Maja y el Ruiseñor" from Granados' *Goyescas*. In the audience were the six Granados children. According to Natalia Granados i Gal, many years later, the music critic Rafael Moragas–who organized the private recital of Book One of *Goyescas*–received news of the attack on the *Sussex* during this performance, along with a report that Granados and Amparo were missing. Upset and unable to confirm that they'd been orphaned, Moragas did not tell the children what he'd heard.

The oldest son, Eduardo Granados i Gal, assumed direction of Acadèmia Granados after his father's death. Four difficult years later, he passed the torch to Frank Marshall and went to Madrid to pursue a career as a composer; he died of typhus in 1928. The oldest daughter, María de la Soledad Granados i Gal ("Solita"), married diabetes specialist Dr. Rossend Carrasco i Formiguera and taught elementary piano students at the academy; she died in 1936. Enrique Granados i Gal, who vowed that he'd learn to swim so he wouldn't die by drowning, became the patriarch of a family of champion swimmers. Victor Granados i Gal lived longer than the rest, dying in his mid-nineties after a colorful career that included marrying a member of the Llimona family, leaving Barcelona after her death, and sending his five children to Soviet "youth camps" (which were in fact labor camps), playing cello with the Los Angeles Philharmonic, marrying American movie actress Tallulah Bankhead, selling some of his father's unpublished works to Nathaniel Shilkret, a New York publisher (and leaving others in a Manhattan taxi), starting a restaurant in New York, and finally returning to Barcelona to die in the home of his daughter, one of the children he'd abandoned. Natalia Granados i Gal was more conventional, marrying family friend Dr. Antonio Carreras, with whom she established a collection of her parents' correspondence, memorabilia, artwork–and what remained of Granados' personal diary. When Natalia died in 1987, the collection was inherited by her son, Antoni Carreras i Granados, who published a short biography of his grandfather in the mid-1990s and donated most of the collection to the Museu de la Música for scholarly research. As of this writing, "Toni" Carreras lives in Barcelona, in a tall building overlooking the beach and the Mediterranean. The youngest of Granados' children, Francisco "Paquito" Granados i Gal died in his teens.

Granados' Academy. After Frank Marshall acquired the Acadèmia Granados in 1920, he moved it from Girona, 20, to Rambla de Catalunya, 106–co-located with his own residence. Mostly due to the legal snarl caused by Granados and Amparo dying without leaving wills, he changed the name to Acadèmia Marshall. Under his direction, the academy continued to grow and flourish, and in 2001 celebrated its centenary under the direction of world renowned pianist Alicia de Larrocha, a protegée of Marshall.

Granados' Music. Granados left one hundred forty works, ranging from music for solo piano, chamber music, lyric dramas, solo songs, choral music, operas and orchestral music, arrangements of Bach, Chopin, Schubert, and Scarlatti. Most were unpublished at the time of his death, and many remain so. Some works, neither published nor performed publicly, have disappeared. Granados' music is best known through the piano interpretations of de Larrocha and transcriptions by Andrés Segovia and Miquel Llobet for classical guitar. (Recordings by Segovia, John Williams, Julian Bream and the Romero Family have preserved them in the classical guitar repertory.)

The music of Granados might have become better known if his heirs and librettist Fernando Periquet had come to an agreement on sharing royalties from the opera *Goyescas* and *Tonadillas*. This impasse lasted until the 1930s. Also, Granados and Albéniz lost favor with many Catalans, whose culture and language were suppressed by the Franco government, and who considered both composers to be too closely identified with Castilian Spain. (Exacerbating this was an effort by Franco to appease the Catalans after the war's end by staging *Goyescas* at El Liceu in 1939–preceded and followed by the Spanish National Hymn, during which the audience raised hands in the fascist salute.) Another factor in obscuring the work of Granados was the isolation of the Iberian peninsula from the rest of Europe from the mid-1930s to the late 1970s. A final reason for the relative obscurity of Granados' music is its categorization as "late romantic music," in contrast to the "modern music" of 20th century composers such as Stravinsky, Copland, Shostakovitch, and even Manuel de Falla, a contemporary of Granados.

If Granados was indeed on the verge of a sustained creative outburst, the operas and chamber pieces and orchestral music that he'd begun to compose might have taken him to a greater level of worldwide recognition and critical acclaim. But what might have been remains undefined, as with others–Chopin, Mozart, Schubert, Mendelssohn–who also died young.

To the saga of Granados' lost and forgotten music another chapter was added in November 2003. A visit by Dr. Walter Aaron Clark to the heirs of Nathaniel Schilkret in New York revealed the existence of the entire score for *Cant de les Estrelles*, of which the piano piece had been missing for many years. This score was among those sold by Victor Granados to Schilkret in 1939. As reported by Dr. Clark, *Cant de les Estrelles*–composed at the time of Book One of *Goyescas* and premiered by Granados in March 1911 at El Palau de la Música along with Book One–was sold for $250. The proceeds were quickly spent by Victor Granados, causing a rift with the other surviving children. Also according to Dr. Clark, Schilkret had acquired the score itself, but not the rights to publish or perform it. His efforts to obtain these failed largely because the rest of Granados' heirs were upset with Victor for pocketing the money. Without their unanimous consent, the score was essentially useless. Schilkret left the scores of *Cant* and other works to his daughter. Sometime later, there was a fire where they were stored and many works were lost. Somehow *Cant* survived. Shilkret's daughter passed away but her son, Neil Shell (name changed by him), retained possession of the score and is presumably its sole owner. In order to edit, publish and perform *Cant*, the score would have to be acquired from Neil Shell. At the time of this writing, it's hoped that this newly discovered work may someday be performed again, after nearly a century.*

Malvina Hoffman (1885–1966). American sculptor. During Granados' stay in New York, Schelling introduced him to Malvina, who invited Granados to come to her home on East 36th Street for daily practice. Granados told Malvina that her place was "my home in America." The night before he left New York, Granados phoned her to disclose his premonition of death at sea. Malvina continued to work as a sculptor, and in 1929 exhibited one hundred ten life-size pieces representing the "Living Races of Man" at the Field Museum in Chicago. She also did a bust of Jan Paderewski from sketches made when both were guests of Ernest and Lucie Schelling at Céligny in 1919. In 1942, Victor Granados showed up at Malvina's home, citing her promise to his father that any of the children would be welcome there. Victor stayed for a year and a half before going to Hollywood to seek his fortune. At age eighty-one, Malvina died in the same New York studio-residence on East 35th Street where Granados had practiced.

Archer Milton Huntington (1870–1955). After building the Hispanic Society of America on the former Audubon estate, Huntington added adjacent buildings for the American Geographical Society, the Museum of the American Indian, the American Numismatic Society, and the American Academy of Arts and Letters. With construction of the IRT subway from midtown Manhattan, Huntington envisioned this complex would become a destination to rival Times Square. It never happened. The surrounding neighborhood is primarily residential, affordable enough to attract new immigrants but not moneyed investors. Perceived by most New Yorkers as too remote, Huntington's world-class collection of Spanish art is visited by relatively few of the city's residents and visitors.

Yet his vision of establishing a center for celebrating Hispanic culture was realized. Before he died in 1923, Joaquín Sorella y Bastida finished "The Provinces of Spain," commissioned by Huntington, which fills the walls of the west wing of the Society. Other important exhibits were: "tapestries and Carpets from Palacio del Pardo" (1970) and "America Sculpture by the National Sculpture Society" (1923), the year in which Huntington married a well-regarded American sculptor, Anna Hyatt. Starting in the early 1920s, Ruth Anderson assembled an enormous collection of 14,000 photographs which documented life in provinces of Spain. Huntington also purchased the collection of papers of Juan Riaño y Gayangos, Spanish ambassador to the U.S.A., from Raiño's widow in 1940, the year after his death.

---

* For much of this updated information I thank Dr. Clark, from whose biography on Granados it was obtained, and the pianist Douglas Riva.

In the main gallery of the Society, along with Goya's portrait of La Duquesa de Alba, remain the notes from *Goyescas*, written by Granados on a stone column during his visit in 1916, and the life mask of Granados made by Ismael Smith.

When he died in 1955, Huntington left the Society sufficient money in endowment which allows it to continue to operate half a century later.

Fritz Kreisler (1875–1962). After World War I, Kreisler was for many years a revered and popular performer in the U.S.A. and Europe, despite being considered by music critics to be too sentimental and compared unfavorably with contemporaries Jascha Heifetz, Yehudi Menuhin, and David Oistrakh.

Madriguera Family. Paquita Madriguera (1900–1965) was one of Granados' most talented students. During his stay in New York, she was in the city with her mother, Francisca Rodón, intent on launching her American career. Paquita cut short a promising career in her early twenties to marry an Uruguayan, and after his death she moved back to Barcelona. She later married the renowned guitarist and transcriber of Granados' music, Andrés Segovia. Her brother, Enric Madriguera, lived in the Americas most of his adult life, organizing a Latin orchestra and competing with the better known Xavier Cugat (also born in Catalunya). Their younger sister Mercedes, a toddler when Granados left for New York, became keeper of the family's mementos and spent her last years in Barcelona. She died in her early nineties in 2003.

Frank Marshall (1883–1959). Born of English parents in the Catalan coastal city of Mataró, Marshall was a protégé of Granados and his deputy at the academy. He assumed the directorship of the music school four years after Granados' death. (See also section on Acadèmia Granados, above.)

Gabriel Miró (1879–1930). In his last letter to his children, Granados asked to be remembered to the writer Gabriel Miró and Dr. August Pí i Sunyer, who introduced Miró to Granados. Miró shared Granados' struggle to earn a living and overcome ill health. Before Granados left for New York, they discussed collaboration on a number of projects, including a choral work to be named *Jerusalén*. Had Granados survived, Miró may have become the librettist he was seeking. Miró and Pí i Sunyer stayed overnight with the Granados children after they learned of their parents' death. Miró spent his last years in Madrid, and is best remembered for his novels that satirize the clergy of Spain.

Enric Morera i Viura (1865–1942). Composer, conductor, and music teacher in Barcelona; closely associated with the modernist movement. (In 1901, he broke an agreement signed with Granados and Albéniz for establishing Teatre Líric Catalan as a vehicle for their lyric dramas. This was cited by Albéniz as his primary reason to stop construction on a home he was building in Barcelona, and leave the city forever. Granados was similarly disenchanted, but due to Morera's standing among the Catalan modernists, he was obliged to work with

Morera from time to time in order to have his own music performed.) After bankruptcy in Sitges and an unsuccessful effort to start a new life in Argentina, Morera returned to Barcelona and served as deputy director of the Municipal Musical School from 1911 to 1935, while composing lyric dramas, operas, chamber and choral music, popular music, and band music for the sardana, the Catalan national folk dance. In 1922, his third effort to establish the Catalan Lyric Theatre was unsuccessful. His last composition was finished shortly before his death. Ironically, his stature in Barcelona is greater today than that of Albéniz and Granados. (See also section on Granados' Music, above).

Nin Family. Joaquín Nin y Castellanos (1879–1949) was born in Cuba and returned there in the final decade of his life. His wife, singer Rosa Culmell, left Joaquín in Paris after years of physical and verbal abuse. When she returned to Barcelona with her three children, Granados offered her a job teaching voice at his academy. In 1914, Rosa moved to New York, where she sang the American premiere of *Tonadillas*. The daughter of Joaquín Nin and Rosa Culmell, Anais Nin, was a writer and diarist whose intensely personal journals were celebrated by the literary world in the 1960s. Her younger brother, Joaquín Nin-Culmell (1909–2004), was a pianist soloist, composer, professor of music, and once chairman of the music department at University of California at Berkeley. He died recently in San Francisco.

María Josefa Oliveró y Saderra (1888–1965). After leaving the academy, María spent a brief time at the Benedictine Abbey of Sant Pere de les Puelles in the Barcelona suburb of Sarrià. With her sister, Mercedes, she then embarked on an extensive tour of Europe, during which she learned to speak English. Later, she accompanied her gravely ill sister to the Shrine of Our Lady of Lourdes in France, where Mercedes' bone disease (probably a form of leukemia) was said to be "miraculously" cured. María's father, Luis Oliveró Genescà, attended the memorial service for Granados and Amparo, perhaps an indication he was not fully aware of his daughter's involvement with her maestro and the circumstances of her leaving the academy. During her father's lifetime, María lived with her family in a villa in the Bonanova area, not far from the villa of the Andreus; when her brothers left home, the family moved to a smaller home on Carrer Muntaner, and after her father's death the two sisters lived in a flat on Carrer Bailen, where María died. (The once gravely ill Mercedes lived to be ninety-seven.) Until the early 1930s, family members recalled María playing piano, with Mercedes on violin, though there was apparently no piano where she lived during the last thirty years of her life. María never mentioned to any of her relatives that she once studied with Granados, or was a student at his academy. Nor did any of her descendants know that Granados' *Escenas Románticas* was dedicated to her until they were advised of this by the author in 2002. She left no letters, but there are a few poems, expressing gratitude to God and to her sister, written in the 1940s and 1950s.

Ignace (Jan) Paderewski (1860–1941). Paderewski became best known for his virtuosity as a concert pianist. In addition to circling the globe as a performer, Paderewski composed a wide variety of piano, vocal, and orchestral works. (He and Granados were both guests at the Schellings' villa at Céligny when Archduke Ferdinand was assassinated in June 1914. Paderewski was in New York at the time of the *Goyescas* premiere, and contributed to the "loving cup" given to Granados when he left for home.) After organizing a series of benefit concerts for Polish victims of World War I, Paderewski suspended his concert career and returned to Poland to serve as prime minister and minister of foreign affairs, and represented his country at the Treaty of Versailles. He resumed his concert career in the 1920s and '30s, until the Nazi invasion of Poland. He died during a tour of the United States raising money for Polish relief, and is buried at Arlington National Cemetery.

Wilder Penfield (1891–1976). From the small river town of Hudson, Wisconsin, Penfield became a football star at Princeton, and was awarded a Rhodes Scholarship to study medicine at Oxford. He was on the SS *Sussex* en route to Paris to volunteer his service in a military hospital. He was the last person to try to save Granados, urging him to stay on the ship. Penfield went on to become a leading neuroscientist, establishing a center in Montreal that pioneered new treatment for epilepsy. He remained an opera fan for the rest of his life, and after his retirement wrote two novels.

Fernando Periquet Zuaznabar (1873–1940). Intensely devoted to the art of Goya, Periquet was a journalist and writer of poems, stories, novels, plays, and musical comedies who had no experience writing an operatic libretto until his collaboration on *Goyescas*. In 1917, negotiations with Granados' heirs over legal rights to the opera broke down, and were not resolved for many years. After Granados' death, Periquet wrote several articles about his deceased collaborator, published a play, and wrote a libretto for a light opera. Periquet's interest in Goya didn't die with Granados. He began, but didn't finish, a libretto with a theme that resembled that of *Goyescas*. Shortly before his death, a screenplay written by him was the basis for a film entitled *Goyescas*, which was a forerunner of today's movie "blockbusters," and won an award in the Venice film contest. Periquet was an ardent supporter of Franco during the Civil War. Though in his early sixties, he volunteered for the Nationalist army, and was wounded fighting at Tablada. As a reward, Franco's government appointed him head of the Spanish Customs Service.

Kapitan Herbert Pustkuchen (died 1917). Pustkuchen was commander of UB-29 from the time it was commissioned on January 18, 1916 until

November 2, 1916. Shortly after he turned over command to Lieutenant Erich Platsch, UB-29 was sunk by depth charges from HMS *Landrail* south of Goodwin Sand, resulting in all hands lost. Pustkuchen died when his second command, UC-66, sank in 1917.

Juan Riaño y Gayangos (1865–1939). Riaño's father's family was from Granada, where it owned a vineyard; his mother was a London-bred Spanish aristocrat, and he was schooled in England. Riaño began his career working for Count Morphy, patron of both Casals and Albéniz. He was promoted to the rank of minister to France in 1905 and married an American, Alice Ward, who said she'd be his bride after he was promoted. In 1913, after several assignments, he became the first ambassador to the United States after the Spanish-American War. (Riaño attended the premiere of *Goyescas* at the Met, and tried in vain to persuade Granados not to return home via London, which would take him through the war zone.) After the death of Granados and Amparo, Riaño raised money for their children. He later became the dean of the diplomatic corps in Washington, and was retired by his government in 1926. He and his wife then moved to Newport, Rhode Island. After five years, with funds insufficient to maintain their life style, they sold their home; his wife returned to Washington, and Riaño remained in Newport. In 1938, the year before he died, his request for financial aid was denied by the Spanish government, and Riaño died in near poverty in Middletown, Rhode Island, where he's buried.

Pablo Ruiz Picasso (1881–1973). In Barcelona, Picasso learned Catalan, studied art informally, and joined the ranks of artists and writers who formed the tertulia at Els Quatre Gats. In defiance of his father–who taught traditional painting at the La Llotja art school–he began to sign his art with his mother's family name: Picasso. For the next five years, he divided his time between Barcelona and Paris, after which he spent the rest of his life in France. Throughout his life he evolved rapidly and with ease from one artistic style to another. His Blue Period began while he was in Barcelona, followed by his Pink Period, Cubism, Collage, New Mediterraneanism, Surrealism, and others that blended various styles. Picasso's political beliefs reflected his early experiences with near poverty and his hatred for the damage inflicted on his homeland by the fascists during the Spanish Civil War. His enormous painting, *Guernica*, is considered by many to be the ultimate statement against war and violence.

Ernest Schelling (1876–1939). Granados' close friend during the last four years of his life. Schelling played Book One of *Goyescas* at its London premiere, encouraged Granados to convert it to an operatic version, and introduced Granados to the leaders at the Paris Opera, who accepted the work for its world premiere. After its postponement due to the outbreak of war, Schelling persuaded the Met to produce it and arranged for Archer M. Huntington, founder of the Hispanic Society of America, to subsidize the production. Schelling continued to perform and compose, and years later founded the Young People's Concerts for the New York Philharmonic.

Ismael Smith (1886–1972). A promising young Catalan sculptor and painter who went to Paris, then London, in quest of wider recognition. He lost most of his accumulated work in Paris when the war broke out. Smith made arrangements for Enrique and Amparo Granados during their stay in London, and tried unsuccessfully to introduce Granados to principals of the Royal Opera and Royal Philharmonic. In the 1920s he gave up his artistic career, moved to New York, and devoted the rest of his life to investigating the causes of cancer, and finding a cure for it. He was committed to a mental hospital in 1960, and died there a dozen years later.

SS Sussex. Built in 1896, she was used as a troop carrier early in the war, then returned to passenger and mail service in 1915. Severely damaged by the UB-29's torpedo on March 24, 1916, she remained afloat and was towed to Boulogne. After extensive repairs, she reentered the French mercantile marine and was scrapped in the late 1920s.

Lluisa Vidal (1877–1918). Vidal took piano lessons from Granados and Albéniz, along with her sisters María and Frasquita (who later was the second wife of Pau Casals.) The Vidal family was often invited to the Puigcerdà chalet of Salvador Andreu and Carmen Miralles, along with Enrique Granados. Lluisa Vidal's interest in painting led to studies with Ramón Casas, and a youthful rivalry with Pablo Ruiz Picasso, who at that time was imitating the work of Casas. Along with Granados, she resisted pressure to include "political correctness" in her artistic expression. After returning from studies in Paris, Vidal had her first show at the Sala Parés in 1914; the show closed (as scheduled) on the day of the assassination of Archduke Ferdinand. In additional to painting, Vidal contributed sketches to Casas' magazine, *Pèl & Ploma*, and to the feminist journal *Feminal*, published by her friend Carme Karr. With Karr and others, she was a founder of the Pacifist Feminist Committee of Catalunya. Vidal died in the influenza pandemic of 1918.

Thomas Woodrow Wilson (1856–1924), 18th president of the United States. After three years trying to effect a peace agreement among the warring countries and pledging to keep the U.S.A. out of World War I during his reelection campaign, Germany's insistence on pursuing submarine warfare provoked Wilson to declare war in April 1917. Though he was credited with bringing about the armistice, Wilson's approach–a blend of rigidity and idealism–was a victim of "realpolitik" at the Versailles Peace Conference. His dream of a League of Nations to preserve the peace was defeated by the U.S. Congress. Wilson spent his last months in office incapacitated by a major stroke, and lived his final three years in seclusion.

Glossary of Catalan and Castilian Words

abraçada–common Catalan word for "hug" or "embrace," exchanged by men and women while greeting and taking leave (Castilian word is "abrazo")

acadèmia–Catalan word for "academy," as in "l'Acadèmia Granados"

adéu–Catalan word for "goodbye" ("adiós" in Castilian)

alma–literally, "soul" in Castilian; often used in the expression "mi alma"–"my darling," and used synonymously with "mi amor" ("my love")

alta burguesia–Catalan term for upper middle, or industrialist class

Apel.les–Catalan first name; in Catalan, there is usually a "." with a double "l"–as in "paral.lel"

Avinguda–Catalan word for "Avenue," as in "Avinguda Tibidabo" in Barcelona ("Avenida" in Castilian)

azulejos–brightly colored, ornamental glazed tiles, a legacy of the Moorish occupation, which endured in the southern Spanish region of Andalucía for seven centuries

blau–Catalan word for "blue," as in "Tramvia Blau" ("Blue Trolley Car")

bon profit!–common Catalan term when a meal is served, to wish each other enjoyment ("buen provecho!" in Castilian)

bon sort–common Catalan term to wish someone "good luck" (Castilian term is "buena suerte")

bon dia, bona tarda, bona nit–Catalan for "good morning," "good afternoon," and "good evening" ("buenos días," "buenas tardes," and "buenas noches" in Castilian)

bones familias–refers to the "best families" of Catalan society, the highest level of the alta burguesia

botifarra–Catalan for a spicy sausage loaded with garlic; grilled whole or sliced for use in soups and stews

brindis–Catalan and Castilian word for "toast," as in "drinking a toast"

capricho–literally, Castilian for "fancy" or "caprice"; also the name for Francisco Goya's series of satiric sketches

cant–Catalan for "song" or "lyric poem" ("canción" in Castilian)

carrer–Catalan word for "street," as in "Carrer Fontanella" ("calle" in Castilian)

cava–a sparkling wine made in Catalunya, similar to French champagne, and made essentially with the same process

colegio–Castilian for "secondary school" or "high school" ("col.legi" in Catalan)

Cristópher Colom–Catalan translation for "Christopher Columbus," early explorer of the Americas (also "Cristófor")

d'acord–Catalan expression to indicate agreement, as in "all right" or "OK" ("de acuerdo" in Castilian)

deixeble/a–Catalan words for male and female students who are protegées of a master teacher ("discípulo/a" in Castilian)

Dios mío!–literally, Castilian for "My God!" and used commonly to express surprise and shock ("valga'm Déu!" in Catalan)

dona–Catalan word for "woman," also used to indicate someone's wife ("esposa" in Castilian)

duquesa–Castilian word for "duchess," as in "La Duquesa de Alba," Goya's portrait subject, friend and reported lover (same word in Catalan)

enamorado/a–Castilian word for "someone who's in love" ("enamorat, -ada" in Catalan)

escenas–Catalan and Castilian word for "scene" or "episode," as in Granados' work *Escenas Románticas* ("romantic episodes")

escudella–literally, the Catalan word for a large earthenware soup bowl; also used to describe a dish that includes rice, vegetables, and an assortment of meats–a favorite of composer Isaac Albéniz

España–Castilian for "Spain" ("Espanya" in Catalan)

espectacles–Catalan for "show" or "entertainment event"

estany–Catalan word for "pond" or "small lake"; used to denote the artificial reservoir in Puigcerdà where Dr. Salvador Andreu built his vacation home

estúpido/a–Castilian word for "stupid," often used in playful conversation ("estúpid/estupida" in Catalan)

extraordinari!–Catalan exclamation for "fabulous!" or "excellent!"

eixample–Catalan word for "expansion," as in l'Eixample–the area of urban growth in Barcelona beyond the original city walls

felicitats–Catalan for "congratulations" ("felicitaciones" in Castilian)

festa–Catalan word for "party" or "celebration" ("fiesta" in Castilian)

Guerra Civil–Catalan and Castilian for (the Spanish) civil war, 1936–1939

guàrdia/es–Catalan word for "police officer/s"

homenatge–Catalan word for "homage" or "recognition" ("homenaje" in Castilian)

lleteria–Catalan word for "dairy or ice cream store"

maja/o–Castilian word, originally for the flashy street women and men of Madrid in the time of Goya, later in reference to aristocratic women who dressed in the maja style

marquès/esa–Catalan for "marquis/marchioness," titles bestowed by the monarch, ranking below "duke/duchess" and above "count/countess" (slightly different in Castilian: "marqués/esa," with accent over "e" reversed)

meravellós!–Catalan expression for "marvelous!" or "wonderful!" ("maravilloso!" in Castilian)

mestre/a–Catalan word for "teacher"–in music, a term of respect for conductors, composers, and soloists ("maestro/a" in Castilian)

molt bé!–Catalan term for "fine!" or more emphatically, "terrific!"

molt de gust–Catalan term for "pleased to meet you"

moltes gràcies–Catalan phrase for "many thanks" ("muchas gracias" in Castilian)

moza–Castilian term for "female servant" or "maid"

musa–Catalan and Castilian word for "muse"–most often a person who inspires an artist to his or her greatest creativity

novio/a–Castilian for fiancé/ée ("promès/promesa" in Catalan)

obra mestra–Catalan for "masterpiece" ("obra maestra" in Castilian)

pa–Catalan word for "bread"("pan" in Castilian)

palau–Catalan word for "palace," as in "Palau Mojà," or "Palau de la Música," the orchestra hall opened in 1908 ("palacio" in Castilian)

Passeig–Catalan word for "boulevard," as in "Passeig de Gràcia"

per fi–Catalan expression for "at last" or "finally" ("por fin" in Castilian)

peu de porc–Catalan term for "pig's foot," found in some meat and vegetable stews or braised and served alone–a favorite of Isaac Albéniz

plaça–Catalan word for a central "town square" ("plaza" in Castilian)–every town has at least one

predilecto–Castilian for "favorite" or "preferred" (in Catalan, "favorit")

princesa–Catalan and Castilian word for "princess," also used to denote wealthy young women of the alta burguesia

principal–Catalan word used in Barcelona to designate the largest, most prestigious floor of a multiple family building, usually the first (but not ground) floor–Granados' residence at Carrer Girona, 20 was a "principal"

puro–Catalan and Castilian word for "cigar"

puta–Castilian for "prostitute," and used colloquially as an insult

querido/a–Castilian term for "beloved"

riu–Catalan word for "river," as in "Riu Segre" ("río" in Castilian)

rossinyol–Catalan word for "nightingale" ("ruiseñor" in Castilian)

'Saco–friendly nickname for Isaac; similarly, men with given names Enrique or Enric are often "'Ric," Santiago becomes "'Tiago," Salvador "Badó," and Joaquim or Joaquín "'Quinito." As used by Isaac Albéniz in Chapter 4, a pun is made with the nickname "'Ric," which by adding the superlative ending "-issimo," means "the richest" or "most delightful"

sala–Catalan and Castilian for "room," as in the "Sala de Descans" ("relaxing room" at the El Liceu opera house)

saló–Catalan word for "salon" or "hall," as in "Saló de Cent" in Barcelona's city hall

senyor, senyora, senyoreta–Catalan words for "man," "woman," "young single woman"–also used as respectful title: Senyor Miró, Senyora López, Senyoreta Godó ("señor," "señora," "señorita" in Castilian)

Setmana Tràgica–Catalan term for "Tragic Week," usually referring to the citywide civil disturbance in Barcelona in July, 1909

suquet–Catalan word for a popular stew that includes vegetables and fish or crustaceans

tantísimo–the Castilian superlative for "the very most"

tartanita–Catalan word for "shack" or "shed"–used to describe the structure built for Granados on a country estate in the coastal village of Vilassar del Mar, where, reportedly, he did some work on the opera score for *Goyescas*

teatre–Catalan word for "theatre" ("teatro" in Castilian)

tertulia–Catalan and Castilian word for "a group of persons who gather regularly for discussion." Casals formed a notable tertulia of musicians in Paris; Dr. Salvador Andreu gathered his friends from music and the arts in his Sant Gervasi villa, and at his vacation home in Puigcerdà

tonadilla–a vocal piece, often accompanied by piano, based on some ancient and medieval folk music; adapted in 19th century Spanish music; further adapted by Granados for the early 20th century musical stage

torre–in Catalan and Castilian, literally "tower"–used also to describe a large family residence with a garden

tramvia–Catalan word for an electric-powered "street car," which ran on fixed rails along most of the principal streets of Barcelona

tripa catalan–a popular Catalan stew containing some of the least choice parts of the pig or cow

vi–Catalan word for "wine," as in "vi blanc" (white wine) and "vi negre" (red wine)–"vino" in Castilian

xalet–Catalan word for "chalet," as in the large Swiss-style villas built by Doctor Salvador Andreu and others in vacation spots such as Puigcerdà

*

* * poetic title of a musical composition, used by Robert Schumann and Granados to denote intensity and/or passion, as in Granados' *Escenas románticas*–dedicated to María Oliveró

Acknowledgements and Sources

It is common for writers, politicians, entertainers, and performers to leave behind boxes of written material when they die. Not so for most composers, whose legacy is their music. Especially not so for Enrique Granados, who had little need for letter writing, as he lived most of his life in one city. His being unprepared for death and leaving behind no last will and testament–meant very little paper trail for any future study of his life.

Throughout the investigation of his life and the world he lived in, my effort to gather and assemble all the apparently missing pieces in the puzzle was made possible by a great number of people who were willing to come to my rescue. I've also been blessed by the appearance of people who had the answers to questions I lacked the prescience to ask.

This is, I hope, a complete list of those people, with apologies to anyone I've missed!

There were a few people who understood what I was hoping to accomplish, and stuck with me through several years of ups and downs. **Douglas Riva** was the first of these, who opened his extensive archives of articles, photos, clippings, and letters; who opened doors, made introductions–validating me with his contacts in the music world; who answered scores of questions, suggesting where I might go to find certain missing pieces; who read the first draft of my novel and gave me many comments and editorial suggestions. **Brigitte Frase**, an accomplished writer, editor, and book reviewer, took my early, very rough drafts, and while critiquing my work unfailingly showed me how to make the tough decisions: what to cut and what to keep in the final draft. Writer and editor **Brenda Griffin** and historian **Peter Raudenbush** read the first draft chapter by chapter and gave me the kind of feedback only true friends dare to give. (They also would send emails asking when the next chapter would arrive, which I took as a compliment). With their help, the manuscript improved chapter by chapter. **Walter Clark**–author of *Isaac Albéniz, Portrait of a Romantic* and a forthcoming biography of Granados–was a major source of information about Albéniz, his family, his patrons, and his death. We exchanged information about Granados as our work continued on parallel tracks. I'm grateful to Walter for finding vital statistics on members of Granados' family and especially the military records of Granados' brother, father, and grandfather–all officers in the Spanish Army. And for reading and critiquing my manuscript. **Sally Dixon,** whose background in the arts and cultural life broadened my perspective, read most of the first draft and made many valuable suggestions. She encouraged me to retain several passages that give the reader a sense of "being there" during the time of Granados.

Several others were willing to be early readers of the manuscript. **Pat Barone**, author and editor, had the perseverance and insight to steer me away from a tendency to diffuse the point of view, and prod me to clarify tense and time. **Naomi Karstad**, a soprano of exceptional voice, helped me understand the world of opera and the tensions between singers, players, conductors, and impresarios. **Jack Osander**, author of two recent novels, read the first draft, offering many editorial suggestions, and encouraged me to write in my own voice. **Mònica Pagès**, author of *The Granados-Marshall Academy, One Hundred Years of Piano Teaching in Barcelona*, the most comprehensive chronology of the academy that Granados founded, confirmed that the story of Granados' life and times was rendered authentically. **Mason Riddle**, a writer and fine arts critic, answered many questions relating to painters and painting in the late 19th and early 20th centuries. And **David Walton,** who spent thirty years in maritime business on English Channel, was an invaluable source of information on weather conditions, passenger safety, the smells and sounds of a steamer crossing the channel, geopolitics between combatants and attitudes toward neutrals, where and how the S. S. *Rotterdam* would have disembarked passengers, rail service from Falmouth to London and London to Folkestone, descriptions of the S.S. *Sussex* incident in archives of the National Maritime Museum, German submarine policies, variations in the cross-channel service from 1914–16, and much more. For several weeks, as I wrote the last two chapters, David challenged me to confirm or authenticate every finding and conclusion. If a piece was missing, he helped me find it.

Since Granados had been dead for eighty-two years when I began work on this project, I greatly relied on descendants of the principal characters in the story.

Andreu-Miralles Family. **Eulalia Graells de Reynoso** and **Flora Klein Andreu**, great granddaughter and granddaughter of Salvador Andreu and Carmen Miralles–patrons of Granados–were especially generous in setting up interviews with other family members: Benita Reynoso Andreu, Mercedes Andreu Bofil Vda. de Miquel, Carmen Miquel Andreu de Malagrida, Javier Villavecchia de Delás, Marta Obregón Andreu, and Mauricio Villavecchia Obregón. They shared family history, memories and photographs that were immeasurably valuable in all the scenes set in Sant Gervasi and Puigcerdà. I also received a copy of a CD that included an interview with the patrons' daughter, Paquita Andreu i Miralles, and a recording of her playing a piece that she composed to impress Granados.

Godó Family. **Elena Godó Oriol**, grandniece of Clotilde Godó Pelegrí and her spouse, **Ángel Parés Pujol** provided interviews, correspondence, site visits, photographs, and memorabilia relating to Clotilde Godó and the family history. They also introduced me to the late Adela Godó Vda. de Rojas, cousin of Clotilde, whom I interviewed by phone. Through many conversations and extensive correspondence, they shared with me the story of how *Goyescas* was composed, as related by Clotilde Godó. They also gave me insights into her personal life and provided news articles collected and saved by her over the seventy-two years she survived Granados. They played an audiotape for me in which Clotilde Godó confirmed that *Goyescas* was composed at her home in Tiana, and that she paid for Amparo's passage to New York.

Carreras-Granados Family. In two interviews **Antoni Carreras i Granados**, grandson of Granados, provided information and anecdotes about his mother, Natalia Granados, and her five siblings. His book *Granados*, ("Gent Nostra" Series, Edicions Nou Art Thor, ca. 1994) was an important source of information and contained several photos from the family collection.

Madriguera Family. **Mercedes Madriguera Rodón** provided me copies of articles written by her older sister, Paquita Madriguera Rodón, one of Granados' most celebrated disciples, as well as copies of programs for a concert given by Paquita at age twelve in 1912, with Pablo Casals conducting (including four of Paquita's compositions on this occasion). In addition, Mercedes Madriguera also provided a genealogical chart of her family, and copies of concerts given by her sister in Barcelona, the United States, and Latin America. Mercedes Madriguera died in May 2003 at the age of ninety-two.

Oliveró Family. **Esperanza Oliveró and Lluís Oliveró Capellades** provided important information about their great aunt, María Josefa Oliveró Saderra, the young student of Granados who became infatuated with him and was the dedicatee of *Escenas Románticas*. Her descendants provided family history and recollections of their great aunt during the last thirty years of her life and two poems written by her. They were surprised to learn from me that she studied with Granados and had a piece dedicated to her.

Nin-Culmell Family. **Joaquín Maria Nin-Culmell**, in correspondence and through a phone interview, described his mother, Rosa Culmell, moving the children back to Barcelona where Granados offered her a job teaching voice at his academy, and the family's later move to New York where his mother sang Granados' *Tonadillas* in its American premiere. (He admitted having been only eight years old when Granados visited his home in New York.) Nin-Culmell died in January, 2004 at age ninety-five.

Condé Family. **Dionisio Conde Gali**, great-grandson of Eduardo Condé, Granados' first patron, related in an interview that Granados remained close to the Condé family, and disclosed a close connection between Condé and Salvador Andreu (details such as their building the first two swimming pools in Barcelona).

Penfield Family. **Priscilla Penfield Chester** and **Jefferson Penfield,** daughter and son of Wilder Penfield, and Lewis Jefferson, who wrote a biography of his grandfather, were a vital source of information about the man who was apparently the last in a series of people who tried to save Granados. Others who provided information were Fred Kermott, nephew of Penfield's wife, Helen Kermott, and Dr. William Feindel, a colleague of Penfield's at the Neurology Center of McGill University, Montreal.

In addition to the descendants of principal characters, nine others inspired and assisted me beyond measure. The pianist **Alicia de Larrocha**, the world's greatest interpreter of Granados' music, was the original source of my interest in him. She introduced me to his piano music twenty-five years ago, and through her leadership in l' Acadèmia Granados has remained a source of inspiration. **Magda Oranich i Solagran**, Regidora del Ajuntament de Barcelona and former member of the Catalan Parliament, and her spouse, **Enric Leira i Alwinall,** have been most generous in explaining the history of Barcelona and Catalunya, making important introductions, opening up Granados' former residence at Girona, 20, for an extensive tour, taking me to El Cercle del Liceu, and time and again helping me to become immersed in Catalan culture so I could begin to understand it. **Romà Escalas** and **Judit Bombardó** of Museu de la Música have been unbelievably helpful in the dozen times I've sought information from their archives of Granados and his colleagues, the most extensive collection of letters, notes, clippings, and photos in Barcelona. From discussions with them, I learned of many nuances and bits of information including how his music was regarded during his lifetime, the difficulty of teaching the music of Albéniz and Granados during the Franco years, the museum's collection of instruments, the "loving" cup given to Granados in New York, the marriage of Granados' son Victor and one of the Llimonas, the reasons for Granados' music being relatively unknown. How valuable **Carol Hess**' bio-bibliography on Granados was–I referred to it so often that its binding had to be reinforced with duct tape. This book would not have written without **Charlie Girsch**–author, inventor, and creativity guru who handed me a quotation from Mary Richards, possibly paraphrased: "We have to believe that a creative being lives within ourselves, whether we like it or not, and that we must get out of its way, for it will give us no peace until we do." **Bill Herbst** of Minneapolis provided interpretations of Granados' life based on his methods of determining personal choices, characteristics, and personality. These allowed me to push ahead on my intuition about events that may have occurred but for which there was no paper trail, and invariably that led me to the answer. And thanks to **Cindi Winkle** for printing copies of the first draft and subsequent drafts for my readers, editors, and prospective publishers.

It's important to recognize that in the past six years there have been many others who personally made efforts to respond to my questions, and in several instances came forward without being prompted. These deserve mention here:

Ramón Abad, Instituto Cervantes, New York–for the history of Spanish music in the U.S.A.

Miriam Aguado Tiana, Catalunya–for showing me the way to the home of Elena Godó Oriol, Clotilde Godó's grandniece, whose phone and address were unlisted.

Raimon Alamany i Sesé, Josep Sabatè Amorós, and **Josep Maria Cuinart**, Escola d'Administració Pública de Catalunya–for a tour of the building once occupied by the Granados family and l'Acadèmia Granados at Carrer Girona, 20, Barcelona, as well as documents relating to placing a bronze plaque on the building in 1918

Xavier Albertí–for information on the character and career of the dancer, Tórtola València. (In 2001, Sr. Alberti produced a stage show based on her art, which was performed at El Liceu in Barcelona and Teatro Maestranza in Sevilla.)

Xosé Aviñoa–professor of music history, Universitat Autónoma de BCN in Pedralbes–for comments on the place of Granados in music history, Spain, and Catalunya; Granados' connection to modernisme; and why his work has been relatively unknown.

Frederic Barbera and Ian MacDonald, Lancaster University, England–for information on the friendship between Granados and the writer Gabriel Miró.

María Luisa Beltràn Sàbat–director, Institut Municipal de Serveis Funeraris of Barcelona–about death dates, funerals, and burials of various persons.

Hispanic Society of America, New York–to former director **Ted Beardsley** for his recollections of Archer Huntington, information on the Madrigueras, letter of introduction to Mercedes Madriguera; to **Mitch Codding** and his staff members, **Susan Rosenstein and John O'Neill,** for information on the history of the institute, Archer Huntington, Ismael Smith, Goya's *La Duquesa*, Joaquim Sorolla, Granados' visit in January 1916, the papers of Juan Riaño y Gayangos; and to **Sarah Miró** for information about the work and life of Basque painter Ignacio Zuloaga y Zanora, and Catalan painter Miguel Viladrich Vilá, from Granados' home province of Lleida, whose passion for the dancer Tórtola València resulted in his attempted suicide at her Paris home.

Barbara Berliner, New York Public Library–for assistance in locating the *Clave* article by Paquita Madriguera, and for copies of the *Journal of Commerce* and *Commercial Bulletin* for vessels' departure from New York for London and Spain in March 1916 (including schedules for SS *Rotterdam*, SS *Antonio López*, and SS *Manuel Calvo*).

Sebastià Bosom, Arxiu Històric de Puigcerdà–for information about the town, the pond where Salvador Andreu built his chalet, and biographical information about Andreu.

August Bover i Font–professor, Department of the Catalan Language, Universitat Autónoma de Barcelona and co-editor, *Catalan Review*–for assistance in accessing the archives in various universities in Barcelona, and about regulations by Franco's government on the teaching of Catalan.

Richard Brundage, G. Schirmer, Inc.–for providing copies of contracts with Granados, including royalty agreements, signed in 1913–1916.

Rachel Chrastil, Jon Butler, Danelle Moon, and **Gaddis Smith**, Yale University and Yale Library–for research on the life of Samuel Flagg Bemis.

Francesc Cortès i Mir–professor of 19th and 20th century music, Universitat Autónoma de Barcelona and Escola Superior de Música de Catalunya–for discussion of Granados: his place in the music composed in his epoch, his political orientation, how he squeezed composing in between classes, and the likelihood of him having a piano student as collaborator; Enric Morera's personality and his reasons for going to Argentina.

Joana Crespi–directora, Secció de Música, Biblioteca Nacional de Catalunya–for locating items in the collection relating to Granados and his colleagues.

Hannah Cunliffe, London, England–for research on maritime issues: pianos on board ships, segregation by gender, routes from England to France.

Barbara File, Archives, Metropolitan Museum of Art–for information on paintings at the museum in 1916. (When Granados visited the museum, he was especially interested in seeing the Goyas and Sorollas.)

Enrique García-Herraiz, Madrid–for extensive correspondence on the life and careers of Ismael Smith i Marí; copies of the Ex-Libris bookplate design for Granados.

Carlota Garriga–subdirectora de l'Acadèmia Marshall–for touring the academy's collections, and review of materials relating to Granados, including photos, copies of recital programs in Barcelona, 1906–1914.

David Gast–research associate, Horseless Carriage Foundation, La Mesa, CA–for informatio about Rochet-Schneider motor car purchased by Salvador Andreu in Lyon, France.

Basil Greenhill, Cornwall, England–for perspectives on the question of women being allowed in steamship smoking rooms in 1916.

Beth Ann Guynn, Special Collections, and **Sally McKay**, Getty Research Institute, Los Angeles–especially for the letter from Mildred Bliss to Malvina Hoffman (from the Hoffman Archives).

James B. Hill and Cory Blad, John F. Kennedy Library, Boston–for information and photos of Pablo Casals' recital at the White House, November 13,1961; also, President Kennedy's schedule that day, list of dinner guests (including Mrs. Alice Longworth, daughter of President Theodore Roosevelt, and Mrs. Robert Woods Bliss), the dinner menu, musical program, correspondence between President and Jacqueline Kennedy and Casals, Washington press coverage of the event.

Kathryn Hodson, University of Iowa Libraries–for photos, brochures, and news clippings of Anna Fitziu, who sang the female lead in the Met production of *Goyescas*, along with documents from Records of the Redpath Chautauqua Bureau, Special Collections, University of Iowa Libraries, Iowa City, Iowa.

Bernard Holland, music critic of the *New York Times*–for comments on recordings of Granados' music.

Dell Anne Hollingsworth, Harry Ransom Humanities Research Center, University of Texas, Austin–for information relating to Granados' 1916 recording of his own music on a Welte Mignon "reproducing piano," preserved on a CD *The Composer As Pianist*, along with a negative review of the concert by Granados and Anna Fitziu at Aeolian Hall, New York on February 16, 1916.

Joan Horsley, maritime researcher, London–for reasons behind SS *Rotterdam* not having an escort in British waters, 1916; details of the history of SS *Sussex*, its building and ownership through the years; instructions in how to obtain the complete ship's plans; photos of the vessel before and after the torpedo attack; relative importance of lifeboats, life rafts, and life jackets for survivors; reports on official inquiries on the incident, including testimony by Charles Crocker of the American Field Ambulance Service; and sources of witnesses who confirmed what happened to Granados and his wife in the Channel.

Joseph R. Jones, retired professor of Spanish, University of Kentucky–for commentary and discussion of Granados's music, especially the two-part article in the journal *Dieciocho*, (University of Virginia, Fall 2000 and Spring 2001) entitled "The Collaborations of the Composer Enrique Granados and the Librettist Fernando Periquet y Zuaznábar," describing the gathering of information about Goya and his art, and their revival of an earlier musical form as the basis for the opera *Goyescas*.

Helena Jonquera, Pianos Victor Jonquera–for information on the Pleyel piano that Granados arranged to be sent to Clotilde Godó's home in Tiana, on which he later composed *Goyescas* (The piano is now in Jonquera's warehouse.)

Marvin Krantz, Library of Congress–for the Edith Wilson Papers, and the diary of Ike Hoover, chief butler of President Wilson, who recorded every detail of the president's day on March 7, 1916.

Mark Larrad, Rochdale, Lancashire, England–for information on the importance of Granados' Catalan Lyric Music, and reasons behind its relatively cool reception in Barcelona; also, for information on Granados' half-finished *Dante* for voice and orchestra

Eldora Larson, St. Croix Historical Society–on Wilder Penfield growing up in Hudson, Wisconsin.

Michael Lewis, National Maritime Museum, Greenwich, England–for complete ship's plans and photos of SS *Sussex*, permitting the author to identify where casualties took place after torpedo struck.

Elaine Lilly, University of St. Thomas, St. Paul, and **Joan Roca**, Minnesota State University, Mankato–for getting me started learning Catalan using tapes, CDs, a grammar book, how to access radio broadcasts from Barcelona; and the book for conjugating Catalan verbs.

Dan Linke, Seeley G. Mudd Manuscript Library, Princeton University–for locating most of the documents relating to James Mark Baldwin, a member of the Princeton Class of 1884 and Thomas Woodrow Wilson, Class of 1879, later professor of political science and president of Princeton.

Don Manildi, curator, and **Max Brown**, archive assistant, International Piano Archives, University of Maryland–for files related to the Ernest Schelling Archive (donated by Schelling's widow, Mrs. Helen Scholz).

Aldo H. Mancusi, founder and curator, Enrico Caruso Museum of America, Brooklyn, NY–for information about Caruso's life and career, especially for discovering in the museum's collection the caricature made by Caruso of Granados.

Mac McClure, pianist and former student at l'Acadèmia Marshall–for comments on the music of Granados (from someone who plays it often), Granados' pedal technique, about other composers in Barcelona, and why Granados' music is so little known and played.

Courtney McKenzie, Johan Onnink, and Janis Goller, Holland America Lines, Amsterdam–for information about the Dutch company's service from New York City to Europe in 1915–1916, archive and details about SS *Rotterdam IV*, prices of First Class passage from New York City to England in 1916.

Willis Miller, *Hudson Star-Observer* (Wisconsin)–for information about the town where Wilder Penfield grew up, his parents, and their families.

Brian Sullivan, Harvard University Archives, and **Nick Miller**, intern–for documents relating to the life and career of Robert Woods Bliss, Harvard Class of 1900.

Jason Milton–for analysis of Atlantic shipping routes and estimates on nautical miles from Gibraltar to Buenos Aires, and Gibraltar to New York.

Tom and Marie Milton, Hastings, New York–for assistance in finding Douglas Riva early in this project, and information about the mental health center where Ismael Smith died in Westchester County, New York.

Minnesota Public Radio–for a brief piece on Granados (probably from CD liner notes) along with playing one of his piano compositions on or about March 24, 1998, which launched my investigation.

Lorin Misita, The Ritz-Carlton, New York–for information on the hotel, then on Madison Avenue, where Granados and Casals played a concert January 23, 1916.

Betty Monkman, Office of the White House Curator, The White House, Washington, D.C.–for documents related to the recital by Granados at the White House, March 7, 1916.

Carlos Murias Vila–for extensive information on the dancer Tórtola València, her schedule of appearances, men whom she inspired, anecdotes and events of her life.

Mary Ann Newman, New York and Barcelona–for ideas on how to approach a fictional account of Granados' life in the culture of Catalunya during the early 20th century.

John Pennino, Metropolitan Opera–for review of the archives, photos, and set drawings related to the production of *Goyescas* by the Met in 1916; also information on singers Ida Quaiatti, Enrico Caruso, and the impresario Giulio Gatti-Casazza.

Rebecka Persson, Boston Atheneum–for information on the exhibit "Granados and *Goyescas*," the 1982 commemoration of Granados' 115th birthday.

Juan Romero de Terreros, Embassy of Spain, Washington, D.C.–for information on Juan Riaño de Gayangos, Spanish ambassador to the U.S.A. in 1916.

Christa Schepen, Gemeentearchief Rotterdam, Rotterdam, Netherlands, for passenger list for the voyage of SS *Rotterdam* from New York on March 11, 1916.

Iñigo Semur Correa, a Barcelona contractor–for a complete plan of the Xalet Andreu in Puigcerdà during its 2001 conversion to condominiums.

Rigbie Turner, curator and **Sylvie Merian**, archivist, Pierpont Morgan Library–for surfacing the letter from Granados to Paris critic Georges Jean-Aubry about Granados' work *Liliana*, the fragment of *Follet* with notes in Catalan, the sketchbook notes on *Ovillejos* (an early predecessor to *Goyescas*) and *Tonadillas*, Granados' drawing of "maja dolorosa" with black mantilla, drawings of a maja on a balcony, and a sketch of a maja de paseo (resembling Clotilde Godó in photo).

John S. Weeren, Seeley G. Mudd Manuscript Library, Princeton University–for information on Tingle W. Culbertson, Class of 1911, who survived the torpedoing of SS *Sussex* but was later killed in action during the Meuse-Argonne offensive in 1918.

Susan Ybarra, genealogist, Apple Valley, CA–whose assistance locating the birthplace of Clotilde Godó, Igualada, and her birthdate, May 10, 1885, greatly facilitated my meeting with Elena Godó Oriol, Clotilde's grandniece, in fall of 1999.

In addition to the personal contributions made by all of the above, I was able to find the following documents and archives that illuminated the life of Granados:

Agualarga, "Principios del Siglo," a collection of photographs, Barcelona at the turn of the century, Agualarga Editores, Barcelona (1999)

Ajuntament de Barcelona, *Barcelona Visions*, Barcelona (1999)

Ajuntament of Lleida, *Història Gràfica de Lleida*, Leida, Catalunya (1991)

Alba, Victor, *Catalonia: a Profile*, Praeger, New York (1875)

Albet, Montserrat, *Pau Casals and His Museum*, Fundació Pau Casals, Barcelona

Aldrich, Richard, *Concert Life in New York, 1902–23*, Books for Libraries Press, New York (1971); and "Granados in His Own Music," *The New York Times* (1916)

Alier, Roger, *El Gran Teatro del Liceo*, Editorial F.X. Mata, Barcelona (1991); "L'Ambient Musical a Barcelona," *La Renaixença*, Barcelona (1986)

Alsina, Marc and Pilar Ferrés, *Russet, 100 Anys de Ratafía*, Imprenta Aubert, Olot, La Garrotxa, Catalunya–the history of the Gou-Codina family company, making ratafía for a century

Altman's, *Spring and Summer Fashions Catalog*, 1916, Dover, New York (1995)

Amores, Juan B., *Cuba y España, 1868-1898*, Ediciones Universidad de Navarra, Pamplona (1998)

Andreu Batlló, Javier, "Un Adelantado de la Farmacia el Doctor Don Salvador Andreu", University of Barcelona (1969)–on Andreu's career as pharmacist and pharmaceutical maker

Andrews, Colman, *Catalan Cuisine*, The Harvard Common Press, Boston, (1999)

Armengol, Ferran, *El Tramvia de Montgat a Tiana*, Argentona: l'Aixernador (1994)

Arroyo, María Dolores, *Cayetana de Alba, Maja y Aristócrata*, Ediciones Alderabán, Madrid (1999)

Aviñoa, Xosé, Universitat Autónoma de Barcelona, Pedralbes, "Del Modernisme a la Guerra Civil (1900–1939)," *Història de la Música Catalana, Valenciana i Balear, IV*, (1900–1939), Edicions 62, Barcelona (1999); *Del Modernisme a la Guerra Civil* (1900–1939), Barcelona, Edicions 62, 1999; Morera, Gent Nostra Series, Edicions de Nou Art Thor, Barcelona; *La Música i el Modernisme*, Curial, Barcelona (1985)–describes the development of music in Catalunya during the "modernist" period–an important source of who was composing and performing music in that time; also by Aviñoa and others, *Modernisme i Modernistes*, Ediciones Lunwerg, Barcelona (2002)

Bachs i Galí, Agustí, "Francesc Ferrer i Guàrdia i l'Escola Moderna," from Arxiu Històric de Barcelona

Bañón Verdú, Jorge, "El Ictíneo" (the world's first submarine), *La Història del Arma Submarina Española*, Barcelona (1997)

Bair, Deirdre, *Anais Nin, A Biography*, G.P. Putnam's Sons, New York (1995)

Baker's Biographical Dictionary of Musicians, G. Schirmer, New York (1958)–numerous biographies of musical personalities

Baldock, Robert, *Pau Casals* (translated by Jorge Vigil Rubio), Ediciones Paidós, Barcelona (1992)

Baldwin, James Mark, *Between Two Wars, Vol. 1*, "The Sussex Affair," Chapter XII, publisher unknown. In this portion of an account of his life, Baldwin describes in detail the events leading up to the torpedoing of the SS *Sussex*, the explosion that seriously wounded his daughter, Elizabeth; being rescued and taken to Boulogne; and his telegram to President Wilson protesting the U-boat attack on an unarmed passenger ship.

Ballell, Frederic–scenes of Catalan life spanning the years 1895–1916, by an acclaimed photojournalist

Barbera, Frederic and Ian MacDonald ed., *Epistolario Completo de Gabriel Miró*, Instituto Juan Gil-Albert, Alicante (2001)–includes letter from Miró to German and Eda Bernacer on April 8, 1916, describing how he and Dr. August Pi i Sunyer broke the news to the Granados children of their parents' deaths, and stayed with them at Carrer Girona, 20, through the night

Beardsley, Theodore S., Jr., *The Hispanic Impact Upon the United States*, G. K. Hall, New York (1976)

Beckerman, Michael B., *New Worlds of Dvorák*, W. W. Norton & Company, New York (2003)–new view of Dvorák searching for better understanding in America where he'd composed some of his best works, reinterpretation of his work and life

Beckett, Tom, *Through You I Live Forever* (player piano ads from 1905–1929), Beckett Prod., Dallas, TX (1977)

Beesley, Gracie, Lightoller, and Bride, *The Story of the Titanic As Told By Its Survivors* (ed. by Jack Winocour), Dover, New York (1960)

Bemis, Samuel Flagg, former chairman, Department of History, Yale University. His account of what happened on the SS *Sussex* was titled "Memorial of Samuel Flagg Bemis," addressed to Robert Lansing, Secretary of State of the United States of America (1917). Also, Bemis' unpublished autobiography, written in 1964, and his testimony in the United States claim for damages from Germany in 1928, which included compensation for Bemis, who was injured in the explosion and suffered from exposure while awaiting rescue in the English Channel. Later, as chairman of the History Department at Yale, Bemis wrote *A Diplomatic History of the United States* (Holt, Rinehart and Winston, New York [1936]).

Bennahum, Ninotchka Devora, *Antonia Mercé, "La Argentina,"* Wesleyan University Press, Hanover, N.H. (2000)

de Bernieres, Louis, *Corelli's Mandolin*, Martin Secker & Warburg Ltd., London (1994)–how a small Greek island got caught in the crossfire during World War II

Biancolli, Amy, *Fritz Kreisler–Love's Sorrow, Love's Joy*, Amadeus Press, Portland, OR (1998)

Blackburn, Julia, *Old Man Goya*, Pantehon, New York (2002)

Bliss, Mildred, "The Last Trip of Enrique Granados & his wife" (as told by Mrs. Bliss in a letter to Malvina Hoffman, March 20, 1916), The Getty Center for the History of Art and the Humanities, Los Angeles; personal letter from Granados in June 1914; musical program for recital by Granados and Emilio de Gogorza at Bliss' home in Paris on June 21, 1914, along with guest list, sketch of seating arrangements, and dinner menu (from Bliss Collection, Harvard University Library)

Boladeres Ibern, Guillermo de, *Enrique Granados, Recuerdos de Su Vida y de Su Obra*, Editorial Artes y Letras, Barcelona (1921)

Borja-Villel, Manuel J., *The Art of Ismael Smith*, The Hispanic Society of America, New York (1987)

Briggs, John, *Requiem for a Yellow Brick Brewery*, Little, Brown, New York (1969)

Brody, Elaine, *Paris the Musical Kaleidoscope*, 1870–1925, George Braziller, New York (1987)

Brown, Henry Collins, *Delmonico's: A Story of Old New York*, Valentine's Manual New York (1928)

Burns, Jimmy, *A Literary Companion–Spain*, John Murray Publishers, London (1994)

Bush, Eric Wheeler, *Gallipoli*, St. Martin's Press, New York (1975)

Butlletí de l'Orfeó Catalá, Barcelona (1916)–a collection of memorials to Granados by his musical contemporaries in Barcelona and Madrid; list of contributors to various memorial funds for Granados (1916)

Byron, Joseph and Clay Lancaster, *Photographs of New York Interiors at the Turn of the Century*, Dover, Mineola, NY (1976)

Caja de Ahorros del Mediterraneo, *Azorín y El Fin de Siglo* (1893–1905), València (1998)

del Campo, Ángel, "Granados," in *Temas Españoles*, Publicaciones Españolas No. 473, Madrid (1966)

Carr, Caleb, *The Alienist*, Random House, New York (1994)–based on career of future U.S. President Theodore Roosevelt as New York police commissioner

Carr, Raymond, *Modern Spain, 1875–1980*, Oxford University Press, Oxford, England (1980)

Carreras i Granados, Antoni, *Granados*, Gent Nostra series, Edicions de Nou Art Thor, Barcelona (1988)

Caruso, Enrico, Jr. and Andrew Farkas, *Enrico Caruso My Father and My Family*, Amadeus Press, Portland, OR (1997)

Casals, Pablo, "The Story of My Youth," *Ovation* (October, 1983)

Casas, Penelope, *The Foods and Wines of Spain*, Knopf, New York (1982)

Castillo, Montserrat, *Lola Anglada*, Editorial Meteora, Barcelona (2000)

Català, Victor (Caterina Alberti Paradís), *Solitud*, Editorial Selecta, Barcelona (1996)

Catalan Review–International Journal of Catalan Culture (English and Catalan, quarterly, 1999–2004)

Caulfield, Carlota, "Carmen Tórtola València (1882–1955)," Mills College, CA (2002)

Centers for Disease Control, U.S. Center for Infectious Diseases–general information on Typhoid Fever and Crohn's Disease

Centre Cultural Caixa Catlunya, "Els Anys Fauves, 1904–1908," Barcelona (2000)–exhibit of art from the Fauvist Period

Cercle del Liceu, *La Pintura Modernista del Cercle del Liceu*, Barcelona (2000)

Chase, Gilbert, *The Music of Spain*, W. W. Norton, New York (1941)–for comparison of the music of Albéniz and Granados

Círculo Mercantil, Industrial y Agricola, Bodas de Oro, Igualada (1949)–Golden Anniversary commemoration of the organization that was primarily founded by Juan Godó Llucià, Clotilde Godós father; the booklet describes the concert given by Granados in September 1910, and a subsequent concert that included performances by Clotilde and Paquita Madriguera, and another performance by Madriguera in 1918 (documents provided by Elena Godó Pelegrí)

Ciurans, Enric, *Adrà Gual*, Gent Nostra Series, Edicions de Nou Art Thor, Barcelona

Clark, Walter Aaron, *Isaac Albéniz, Portrait of a Romantic*, Oxford Univeristy Press, New York (1999), *Isaac Albéniz: a Guide to Research*, Garland Publishing, New York (1998); and *Poet of the Piano, Enrique Granados and His World*, publication forthcoming by Oxford Univesity Press, New York (2004); also program notes from 2003 production of *Goyescas* by Central City Opera, Central City, CO (2003)

Clout, Hugh, (ed.), *The Times of London History Atlas*, Times Books, London (1997)

Collet, Henri, *Albéniz et Granados*, Editions d'Aujourd'hui, Paris (1929)

Collins, Theresa M., *Otto Kahn: Art, Money, and Modern Time*, University of North Carolina Press, Raleigh (2002)

Colomer Pujol, Josep M., *María Barrrientos*, Gent Nostra Series, Ed. de Nou Art Thor, Barcelona (1984)

Cooke, Charles, "All About the Gold Piano at the White House," *Washington Star*, August 21, 1966

Cooke, James Francis, (ed.), *Great Men and Famous Musicians on the Art of Music*, Theo. Presser, Philadelphia (1925)

Corredor, José Maria, *Conversations With Casals* (trans. André Mangeot), Dutton, New York (1956)

Cortada, James W., *Two Nations Over Time: Spain and the United States, 1776–1977*, Greenwood Press, Westport, CT (1978)

Crohn's and Colitis Foundation of America, "Questions and Answers About Crohn's Disease," New York (2002)

Crow, John A., *Spain, the Roots and the Flower*, University of California Press, Berkeley (1963)

Cullell, Pere i Andreu Farràs, *L'Oasi Català*, Editorial Planeta, Barcelona (2001)–a description of the financial, social, cultural, and marital interconnections between families of the alta burgesia in Barcelona–includes anthology of political and industrial leaders

Current, Richard Nelson and Marcia Ewing, *Loie Fuller, Goddess of Light*, Northeastern University Press, Boston (1997)

Darío, Rubén (Félix Rubén García Sarmiento), *Poesía*, Editorial Lumen, Barcelona (2000)–translation of "De Otoño" by the author; *Eleven Poems of Rubén Darío*, G.P. Putnam's Sons, New York (1916); Antología, Colleción Espasa Calpe, Madrid (1992); and several other poems from dariana.com

Diari d'Art i Cultura amb Menú Gastronómic, 4 *Gats*–a newsletter of Els Quatre Gats, Barcelona (1999)

Diari de Barcelona (a major daily paper)–read selectively, 1905–1916

Doerries, Reinhard R., *Imperial Challenge* (trans. by Christa D. Shannon), University of North Carolina Press, Chapel Hill (1989)–describes life and diplomatic role of Count von Bernstorff, German ambassador to the United States from 1908 to 1917, including his receiving an honorary degree from Princeton and attendance at a dinner party with Wilder Penfield and Penfield's mother in June, 1913

Doughty, Oswald, *A Victorian Romantic: Dante Gabriel Rossetti*, Oxford University Press, London (1960)

Douglas-Brown, Deborah J., "Nationalism in the Song Sets of Manual de Falla and Enrique Granados," doctoral dissertation, University of Alabama (1993)

Duffey, David, "The D'Oyly Carte Family," from the Gilbert and Sullivan Archive, London, England

Dumont, Henri, *Goya*, The Hyperion Press, New York

Eccles, Sir John and William Feindel, *Wilder Graves Penfield* (1976)

Editorial Boileau, Appendix to the Section DANCES, from "Integral para piano de E. Granados," relating to Granados' "Danza Gitana" and "Danza de Los Ojos Verdes," his penultimate work, written for Antonia Mercé's show at the Maxine Elliot Theater

Ellis, Cuthbert Hamilton, *The London, Brighton & South Coast Railroad* (1839–1922), London (1923)

Enciclopèdia Catalana, *Història de Barcelona, Volum* 6, "La Ciutat Industrial (1893–1897)" and *Volum* 7, "Segle XX," Barcelona (1995)

Encyclopedia Titanica, Passenger Biographies, "Colonel John Jacob Astor IV"

Escola d'Administració Pública de Catalunya, Memòria de Creació i Constitució (1914), Estudi 6, Barcelona (2000)–about the school of public administration that now occupies Carrer Girona, 20

Ewen, David, *Composers Since 1900*, H. W. Wilson Co., New York (1981); *The New Encyclopedia of the Opera*, Hill & Wang (1971); and *The Book of Light European Opera*, Holt, Rinehart & Winston (1962)

Feminal, Carme Karr, Karr, (publisher and editor), various issues from 1901-1916, including articles on La Comtessa de Castellà; pianist Paquita Madriguera; sopranos Gaietana Lluró, María Barrientos, and Conxita Supervia

Fernandez-Cid, Antonio, *Granados*, Samarán Ediciones, Madrid (1956)–biography of Granados; and "El Piano de Enrique Granados," Fundación Juan March (1991)

Fernéndez-Armesto, Felipe, *Barcelona, A Thousand Years of the City's Past*, Sinclair-Stevenson, London (1991)

Fiedler, Johanna, *Molto Agitato, The Mayhem Behind the Music of the Met Opera*, Nan A. Talese/Doubleday, New York (2001)

Fontbona, Francesc, "Francesc Miralles: Del Modernisme al Noucentisme," in *Història de l'Art Català, Vol. VIII*, Edicions 62, Barcelona (1985); *Casas*, Gent Nostra Series, Edicions de Nou Art Thor, Barcelona; and "Picasso and Els Quatre Gats," from a series by María Teresa Ocaña, Bullfinch Press/Little Brown, New York (1995)

Franck, Dan, *Bohemios*, Ollero & Ramos, Madrid (1998)

Friends of France, "The American Ambulance Field Service Membership List," Paris (1916)

Fundació Pau Casals, *Pau Casals, La Música Per Viure*, Barcelona (2001)

Gándara, Francisco, "Reminiscencias de Granados," *Las Novedades*, New York (1916), and interview with Granados for *The New York Times Magazine* (1915)

García-Herraiz, Enrique, "Ismael Smith i Marí" in *Goya, Reviste de Arte*, Madrid (1987)–the most extensive history of his life and death in a sanitarium in White Plains, NY in 1972; *Ismael Smith, Gravador*, Barcelona (1986); "Más Sobre Smith," from *Ex-Libris*, Barcelona (1990–1991)

García-Pérez, J., *Casals*, Gent Nostra Series, Edicions de Nou Art Thor, Barcelona

Garland, Iris, "Modernismo and the Dancer, Tórtola València," Simon Fraser University, Vancouver, BC (2001); "Early Modern Dance in Spain: Tórtola València, Dancer of the Historical Intuition," *Dance Research Journal* (Fall 1992)

Gatti-Casazza, Giulio, *Memories of the Opera*, John Calder, London (1977)

Gay, Peter, *Mozart*, Viking Penguin, New York (1999); and *Schnitzler's Century* (1815–1914), W. W. Norton, New York (2002)

Generalitat de Catalunya, "La Sardana, Història i Actualitat," *Quaderns de Cultura Popula*, Barcelona (2000)

Gernsheim, Alison, *Victorian and Edwardian Fashion, A Photographic Survey*, Dover, Mineola, NY (1963)

Gifra, Pere, "Nineteenth-Century American Travel Writings on the Catalan-Speaking Community," *Catalan Review* (1999)

Glendinning, Nigel, *Goya and His Critics*, Yale University Press, New Haven, CT (1977)

Godó Oriol, Elena, May 1998 letter to the editor of *La Vanguardia*, in which she corrects the article written by Ernest Lluch, asserting that *Goyescas* was written in Vilassar de Mar. Citing her great aunt, Clotilde Godó Pelegrí, Godó Oriol states that the piano suite *Goyescas* was composed on the Pleyel grand piano that Granados purchased on behalf of Juan Godó Llucià, father of Clotilde, in Paris and shipped to Clotilde's home in Tiana. Lluch, in a later article, accepted the correction.

Gómez Amat, Carlos, *Historia de la Música Española* (19th century), Edicions 62, Barcelona (1999)

Goldenberg, William, monograph on Granados' personality and character, presented at the Boston Atheneum, Boston (1982)

Goodwin, Evan, "Little Blue Light–Giacomo Leopardi," *Little Blue Light* (2002)

Granados i Campiña, Enrique, letters: to Joaquín Malats de Pichot (1910), Biblioteca de Catalunya, Secció de Música; to Ernest Schelling (1912), Metropolitan Opera Archives, New York; to Mildred Bliss (June 1914), describing her as an "alma amiga"–roughly translated: "soul mate," Bliss Papers, Harvard University Libraries; and the facsimile of the original "special edition" Number 2, given by Granados to Clotilde Godó Pelegrí in 1911 (copied for the author by Elena Godó Oriol)

Granados' music, CDs recorded by Alicia de Larrocha, Douglas Rivas, several others; CD jacket notes

Granados de Carreras, Natalia, "*Goyescas* and Enrique Granados" (trans. by Norman P. Tucker), Boston Atheneum, Boston (1982)

Gray, Christopher, *Fifth Avenue, 1911, From Start to Finish*, Dover, Mineola, NY (1994)

Grinnell, George Bird, *Audubon Park, the History of the Site of the Hispanic Society of America*, Hispanic Society, New York (1927)

Hamilton-Paterson, James, *Gerontius*, Vintage Press, New York (1990)–journey of Sir Edward Elgar to the Amazon Basin of Brasil in 1923

Harvard University Press, "Harvard College Class of 1900, Report VI 1925"–biographical information on Robert Woods Bliss '00

Hayes, Carlton Joseph Huntley, *The United States and Spain: an Interpretation*, Sheed & Ward, New York (1951)

Heller, Mikhail and Aleksandr M. Nekrich, *Utopia in Power, The History of the Soviet Union from 1917 to the Present*, Summit Books, New York (1986)

Herbst, William, transcript of interpretative session–Enrique Granados, based on Herbst's astrological data and analysis, Minneapolis, MN, (1999)

Hess, Carol, *Enrique Granados, a Bio-Bibliography*, Greenwood Press, New York (1971)

Hijuelos, Oscar, *A Simple Habana Melody*, HarperCollins, New York (2002)–Cuban composer returns to his home town with memories of his one great song

Hill, May Brawley, "The Woman Sculptor, Malvina Hoffman and Her Contemporaries," Berry-Hill Galleries, New York (1984)

Hill, Thomas R., "Ernest Schelling, 1876–1939"–doctoral dissertation, Catholic University of America (1970)

Hillwood Museums and Gardens, monograph on the pottery from Sèvres, France, which was in the East Room of the White House in March 1916

Història de Catalunya, Volume VI (1869–1939), "La Setmana Tràgica"–on the origins of the disturbance, exact location of churches and other religious buildings burned in July 1909, and their proximity to Granados' neighborhood; repercussions of the violence, executions, and final toll of casualties

Història de la Cultura Catalana, "El Modernisme, 1868–1939"–descriptions of founding the Auto Club of Barcelona (1902), first Hispano-Suissa cars made in Barcelona (1904), how the Cercle del Liceu was strictly a men's club, modeled after the British clubs, and how violinist Arturo Toscanini got his first chance to conduct, in Barcelona, when the conductor, Cleofonte Campanini became ill. (Later, with the Chicago Opera, Campanini conducted the American premiere of Granados' *Dante*.)

Historic Archives of the City of New York, "New York Midtown, Block by Block Map"–showing all properties and their owners in 1916-1920

Hoffman, Malvina H., *Heads and Tails*, Bonanza Books, New York (1936), and *Yesterday Is Tomorrow, A Personal History*, Crown Publishers, New York (1965)–both autobiographical (the latter describing Granados coming to practice on her Chickering piano, his premonition, and visit by his son Victor in 1942); and photo book compiled by Hoffman for the American Sculptors Series, W. W. Norton, New York (1948)

Holland, Bernard, "Old Records in High Tech and Low," *The New York Times* (1999)

Homberger, Eric, *The Historical Atlas of New York City*, New York Historical Society (1994)

Hoover, Ike, "White House Diary"–President Wilson's chief usher for many years, including the time of Granados' White House recital, from the Wilson Papers at the Library of Congress, Washington, D.C.

Hughes, Robert, *Barcelona*, Knopf, New York (1992); and *Goya*, Knopf New York(2003)

Hull, Anthony H., *Goya: Man Among Kings*, Hamilton Press, New York (1987)

Huntington, Archer Milton, *The Hispanic Society of America Handbook of Museum and Library Collections*, Hispanic Society of America, New York (1938)

Iglesias, Antonio, *Enrique Granados (Su Obra Para el Piano)*, Editorial Alpuerto, Madrid (1985–1986)

Instituto Nacional de Solidaridad, "Personajes En La Historia de México, Francisco Villa," México (1993)

Jackson, Shirley Fulton, *The United States and Spain, 1898–1918*, Florida State University, Tallahassee (1967)

James, Robert R., *Gallipoli*, MacMillan, New York (1965)

Jardí, Eric, *Història d'Els Quatre Gats*, Editorial Aedos, Barcelona (1972); "La Ciutat de les Bombes: El Terrorisme Anarquistas a Barcelona," Barcelona (1964)

Jeffers, H. Paul, *Diamond Jim Brady: Prince of the Gilded Age*, E-books, New York (2002)

Jiménez Losantos, Federico, "Antonia Merce: 'La Argentina,'" from *Los Nuestros* Series

Journal of Commerce, New York, March 1916–"Marine Intelligence," a listing of all transatlantic steamers arriving and departing at the Port of New York

Kahn, Alfred (related by Pablo Casals), *Joys and Sorrows: Pablo Casals*, Simon & Schuster, NY (1970)

Keegan, John, *The First World War*, Knopf, New York (1999)

Kent, Adam, "The Use of Catalan Folk Materials in the Works of Federico Mompou and Joaquín Nin-Culmell," doctoral dissertation, Julliard School of Music, New York (1999)

King James Bible, Psalms 22, 23.

Kirk, Elise K., *Music at the White House*, University of Illinois Press, Urbana (1986)

Kirk, H. L., *Pablo Casals*, Holt, Rinehart and Winston, New York (1974)–Casals biography. The author drew heavily on chronology of Casals' life, especially scenes when he was with Granados and anecdotes by Casals about his international performing career.

Kolodin, Irving, *Metropolitan Opera*, Knopf, New York (1967)

Kurlansky, Mark, *The Basque History of the World*, Walker, New York (1999)

Landow, George P., "The Dead Woman Talks Back: Christina Rossetti's Ironic Intonation of the Dead Fair Maiden," National University of Singapore

Larrad, Mark, "The Lyric Dramas of Enrique Granados," *Revista de Musicología*, Madrid (1991); "Enrique Granados"–listing for *Grove Dictionary of Music*, New Edition (2002); and "The *Goyescas* of Granados," dissertation, University of Liverpool, England (1988)

Larreta, Antonio, *Volavérunt*, Editorial Planeta, Barcelona (1999)

de Larrocha, Alicia, "Granados, the Composer" (trans. by Joan Kerlow), *Clavier*, New York (1967)

Legation de España en Washington, official papers of the Spanish Embassy during the years of Juan Riaño de Gayangos' service in the United States (1910–1926); resolving a dispute over whether he became U.S. citizen (he did not), response to Riaños request for financial assistance in 1938 (denied), and correspondence following his death in 1939

Le Monde Musical, "Enrique Granados," Paris (1911)–review of his concert at Salle Pleyel (from "Algunas Opiniones de la Prensa Sobre Sus Conciertos," a collection of press reviews in Paris, Madrid, Barcelona)

Littlehales, Lillian, *Pablo Casals*, W. W. Norton, New York (1929,1948)

Link, Arthur, *Woodrow Wilson*, "The Road to the White House"; *WW*, "Confusions and Crises, 1915–1916," Princeton University Press (1964)

Litvak, Lily, *España 1900–Modernismo, Anarquismo y Fin de Siglo*, Edit. Anthropos, Barcelona (1990)

Livermore, Ann, *A Short History of Spanish Music*, Vienna House, New York (1972)

Llongueras, Joan, *Evocaciones y Recuerdos de Mi Primera Vida Musical en Barcelona*, Lib. Dalmau (1944)

Llorens, Jordi, *Obrerisme i Catalanisme* (1875–1931), Editorial Barcanova, Barcelona (1992)

Lluch, Ernest, three articles about Granados in *La Vanguardia* (1998–1999)

London Newspapers, March, 1916–*The Daily Mail, The Evening News, The Morning Post, The Star, The Times*–for events in London while Granados was there, and news of the war, Channel crossings, and torpedo attacks. From the Newspaper Library of The British Library, London

Longland, Jean Rogers, "Granados and the Opera *Goyesca*," The Hispanic Society of America, New York (1966)

Lynch, Don and Ken Marschall, *Titanic, An Illustrated History*, Madison Press Books, Toronto (1992)

MacKenzie, Compton, *Greek Memories*, University Publications of America, New York (1987)

Madriguera Rodón, Paquita, "Enrique Granados," *Clave: Voz de la Juventud Musical Uruguaya* (1961); *Visto y Oído*, Editorial Nova, Buenos Aires (1947); and "Enrique Granados, El Artista y El Hombre Estudiados e Interpretados por La Eximia Pianist"–a presentation to an unnamed Spanish audience sometime in the 1940s. (These documents were provided in Barcelona by her late sister, Mercedes Madriguera Rodón)

Maragall, Joan, *El Comte Arnau*, Edicions 62, Barcelona (1995)

Marco, Tomás, *Spanish Music in the 20th Century*, Harvard University Press (1993)

Márquez Villanueva, Francisco, Harvard University, monograph on relationship between Granados and Gabriel Miró in "Literary Background of Enrique Granados," presented at Boston Atheneum (1982)

McCully, Marilyn, *Els Quatre Gats: Art in Barcelona Around 1900*, Princeton University Press, Princeton (1978)

McDonough, Gary Wray, *Good Families of Barcelona, A Social History of Power in the Industrial Area*, Princeton University Press, Princeton (1986)

McKinley Health Center, University of Illinois at Urbana-Champaign, "Gastroenteritis" (2002)

McMullen, Cliff, "Royal Navy 'Q' Ships," based on information from H. M. LeFleming, *Warships of World War I*, Ian Allan Ltd, London (1967)

Meeks, Carroll L.V., *The Railroad Station, An Architectural History*, Dover, Mineola, NY (1995)

Mendelsohn, Joyce, *Touring the Flatiron Building*, New York Landmarks Conservancy, New York (1998)

Milà, i Vidal, Anna i Gou i Vernet, Assumpta (ed.), *Guia Sumària del Museu Cau Ferrat* (de Santiago Rusiñol), Diputació de Barcelona, Servei de Cultura, Barcelona (1994)

Miller, William H., Jr., *The Fabulous Interiors of the Great Ocean Liners in Historic Photographs; The First Great Ocean Liners in Photographs 1897–1927; Pictorial Encyclopedia of Ocean Liners, 1860–1993; Picture History of the French Line*; Dover, New York

Mills, Dorothy Jane, "The Sceptre: Austrian Food," Patrician Publications (2002)

Miró, Gabriel, *Nuestro Padre San Daniel*, Ediciones Cátedra, Madrid (1988); "Los Huérfanos de Granados," *La Esfera* (1916)

Montero, Mayra, *The Messenger* (trans. by Edith Grossman), HarperCollins, New York (1999)

Montparker, Carol, *A Pianist's Landscape*, Amadeus, Portland, OR (1998)

Moorehead, Alan, *Gallipoli*, Harper, New York (1956)

Musa, Mark, *The Portable Dante*, Penguin Books (1995)

Museu d'Art Modern, *La Pintura Moderniste del Cercle del Liceu*, Barcelona (1994)

Museu de la Música, Institut de Cúltura, Barcelona–thanks to Judit Bombardó, photos were found of Granados and Clotilde Godó Pelegrí (posed by an Ortiz y Cussó piano, with Clotilde dressed in maja-style costume; photos apparently taken by two Barcelona portrait studios, Gran Galería de Barcelona and Antoni y Emilio Napoleon); interpretation of the significance of these photos by Romà Escalas, director of the museum; identification later confirmed by Elena Godó Oriol, Clotilde's grandniece; subsequently it was determined that the "sheet music" on the piano was Goya's *Capricho* Number 27, entitled "Quien Mas Rendido?" ("Who is more affected?"), with Goya bowing low and La Duquesa de Alba turning away.

Museu Nacional d'Art de Catalunya, *Ramón Casas, El Pintor del Modernisme*, Barcelona (2001)

The Musical Observer, New York, February 1916–on promising future for Granados

National Climatic Data Center, National Oceanic and Atmospheric Administration (USA)–daily temperature and precipitation at Central Park, Manhattan, for the period December 1915 to March 1916

National Digestive Diseases Information Clearinghouse, National Institutes of Health, "Crohn's Disease," Bethesda, MD (2002)

National Maritime Museum, United Kingdom, complete ship's plans for the SS *Sussex*–exterior and interior, all decks and dimensions

New Grove, Dictionary of Music–traditional library and online versions

Newspaper accounts of the torpedoing of SS *Sussex*–USA dailies: New York, Washington, St. Paul, MN; England: London dailies, Folkestone weekly; Spain: Madrid and Barcelona dailies

New York City, aerial photo of Midtown Manhattan, copyright 1924 by Arthur S. Tuttle, Chief Engineer

New York Musical Publications (1916)–*The Musical Observer, The Record, The Musical Times*

The New York Evening Journal articles and other materials on Anna Fitziu, American soprano who sang Rosario in *Goyescas* at the Met, from University of Iowa Libraries, Iowa City

The New York Herald, review of Antonia Mercé's dancing Granados' "The Tango of the Green Eyes" at the Maxine Elliot Theater, New York, February 10, 1916

The New York Times, daily from December 1, 1915, to March 31, 1916; June 18, 1999; and article about the "Old King Cole" mural by Maxfield Parrish hanging behind the bar in the Hotel Knickerbocker while Enrico Caruso was living there

Nin, Anais, *Little Birds–Erotica*, Pocket Books, New York (1979); *Linotte–The Early Diary* (1914–1920), Harcourt Brace, New York (1978); and excerpt from her *Diary, Volume V*: 1947–1955, in which she recalls Granados protecting the Nins when they returned to Barcelona, and giving her mother a job at his academy of music

Nouvion, Francois, "Florencio Constantino," monograph on the Bilbao-born opera tenor, from Welcome to Tenorland, http://tenorland.com

Noyes, Dorothy, "Breaking the Social Contract: El Comte Arnau, Violence, and Production in the Catalan Mountains at the Turn of the Century," *Catalan Review*, Volume XIV, Numbers 1–2, North American Catalan Society (2000)

Ocaña, María Teresa, *Picasso and Els 4 Gats: The Early Years in Turn-of-the-Century Barcelona*, Bullfinch/Little Brown, New York (1996); includes "Picasso and Els Quatre Gats," by Francesc Fontbona; "Els Quatre Gats Seen Through the Metamorphosis of the Blue Period," by Claustre Rafart i Planas; "From Els Quatre Gats to Cau Ferrat–the Artistic Links Between Santiage Rusiñol and Picasso (1896–1903)" by Vinyet Panyella; and "The End of the 4 Gats," by Josep Palau i Fabre

Olian, JoAnne (ed.), *Parisian Fashions of the Teens*, Dover, Mineola, NY (2002)

Opera News, Metropolitan Opera, New York–opera history, portraits of artists

d'Ors, Eugeni, *La Ben Plantada*, Edicions 62, Barcelona (1980); *Pablo Picasso En Tres Revisiones*, Editorial El Acantilado, Alicante, Spain (1930)

Orwell, George, *Homage to Catalonia*, Harcourt Brace, New York (1952)

Pagès i Santacana, Mònica, *Acadèmia Granados-Marshall, 100 Anys d'Escola Pianística a Barcelona* (2001)

Pahissa i Jo, Jaume, *Sendas y Cumbres de la Música Española*, Librería Hachette, Buenos Aires

Patchett, Ann, *Bel Canto*, HarperCollins, New York (2001)–in which an opera soprano becomes a hostage of terrorists in Lima, Perú

Payne, Stephen, *Grande Dame: Holland America Line and the S. S. Rotterdam*, published by Holland America

Penfield, Wilder, "Some Personal Experiences in the *Sussex* Disaster," *Princeton Alumni Weekly*, Vol. XVI, No. 29 (1916); *The Torch* (a novel), Little, Brown, Boston (1960), and *No Other Gods*, Little, Brown, Boston (1954)

Pereña, Josep, *Els Darrers Dies de la Vida de Jacint Verdaguer*, Editorial Barcino, Barcelona (1955)–about the last days and death of poet priest Father Jacint Verdaguer

Periódico de l'Anoia, Igualada, November 1988 article by Magí Puig i Gubern about three distinguished pianists born in Igualada and students of Granados: Rosa Artés, Paquita Madriguera, and Clotilde Godó Pelegrí; sources for article included Adela Godó Vda. de Rojas and Mercedes Madriguera Rodón, sister of Paquita. The article confirms that Granados' *Goyescas* was composed on Clotilde's piano in Tiana; the reporter also refers to Clotilde as a person "ben plantada" (translated: "attractive, pleasant, well-proportioned"). It's an echo of Eugeni d'Ors' 1911 novel *La Ben Plantada*, whose heroine is an attractive, dignified woman who stood tall and strong.

Periquet, Fernando, "*Goyescas*: How the Opera Was Conceived," *Opera News* (1916) and "Story of the Opera" in *Goyescas: An Opera in Three Tableaux*, G. Schirmer, New York (1915)

Peterson, H.C., Propaganda for War: *The Campaign for American Neutrality, 1914–17*, Univeristy of Oklahoma Press (1939)

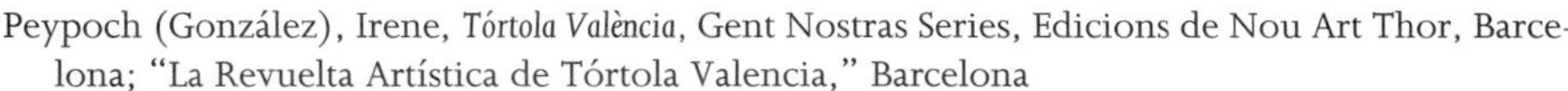

Peypoch (González), Irene, *Tórtola València*, Gent Nostras Series, Edicions de Nou Art Thor, Barcelona; "La Revuelta Artística de Tórtola Valencia," Barcelona

Phillips-Mats, Mary Jane, *Puccini, A Biography*, Northeastern University Press, Boston (2002)

Pound, Reginald, *Sir Henry Wood*, Cassell & Company, London (1969)

Powell, Linton, *A History of Spanish Music*, Indiana University Press (1980)

Preston, Diana, *Lusitania: An Epic Tragedy*, Walker, New York (2001)

Preston, Paul, *Franco, A Biography*, BasicBooks/HarperCollins, New York

Princeton Alumni Weekly (several issues) and Princeton Alumni Records (several entries)–about Wilder Graves Penfield, Class of 1913; James Mark Baldwin, Class of 1884; and Thomas Woodrow Wilson, Class of 1879

Prose, Francine, *The Lives of the Muses*, HarperCollins, New York (2002)

Proust, Marcel, *In Search of Lost Time, Vol. I–Swann's Way* (trans. by Lydia Davis, ed. Christopher Prendergast), Viking Press, New York (2003)

Ramsay, David, *Lusitania: Saga and Myth*, Norton, New York (2001)

Ramos, Vicente, *Gabriel Miró*, Instituto de Estudios Alicantinos, Alicante (1979); and *Vida de Gabriel Miró*, Gráficas Diaz, Alicante (1996)

Registro Civil de Tiana, death certificate of Clotilde Godó Pelegrí on March 21, 1988 (born May 10, 1885 in Igualada), listing cause of death as cardiac insufficiency. It was signed on March 24, the seventy-second anniversary of Granados' death

Registro Mundial, Unión de Productores de España, "Homenaje al Maestro Granados" (the event honoring Granados at El Saló de Cent), Barcelona (February 1911)

República de España, Ministerio de Defensa, Archivo Militar de Segovia–complete military records of Granados' brother, Calixto Granados Campiña; his father, Calixto Granados Armenteros; and his grandfather, Manuel Granados, all officers in the Spanish Army (research findings of Walter Aaron Clark)

Reviews of Granados' concert at El Palau de la Música, March 11, 1916–including world premieres of: *Goyescas* piano suite Book One, "Cant de Les Estrelles," and "Azulejos," the piece started by Albéniz and finished by Granados. *La Vanguardia, El Noticiero, El Diluvio, La Publicidad, El Poble Catalá, Musical Emporium, Diario de Barcelona, Pel i Ploma, Revista Musical Catalana, La Veu de Catalunya, Primavera, l'Avença, Joventut, La Renaixença*

Reviews of Metropolitan Opera premiere of *Goyescas* on January 28th, 1916. *The New York Herald, The New York Times, Novedades* (a Spanish language publication in New York)

Revista Musical Catalana, read selectively, 1905–1917; in April 1916, a list of contributors to the memorial fund for the children of Granados, among whom was "Srs. Godó i Cia."–that is the father of Clotilde Godó Pelegrí

Revista Musical Hispano-Americana, Madrid (1916)–a collection of remembrances of Granados by contemporaries such as Debussy, Saint-Saens, D'Indy, Fauré and several from Spain

Riaño de Gayangos, Juan, *Diary* (from 1890s to 1930s), written in English, describing his early career, appointment to the U.S.A. in 1910, friendship with Archer Huntington, reception for Granados at the Spanish Embassy in Washington, advice to Granados to avoid the "war zone"–which included the British Isles

Richardson, John with Marilyn McCully, *A Life of Picasso, The Early Years, 1881–1906*, Random House, New York (1991)

Riera i Tuébols, Santiago, *Narcís Monturiol*, Generalitat de Catalunya, Barcelona (1986)–biography of the inventor of the submarine

"The Ritz-Carlton, New York"–brochure describing exterior and interior of this luxury hotel; in 1916 located at Madison Avenue and 46th Street, New York, NY

Riva, J. Douglas, "The *Goyescas* for Piano by Enrique Granados," doctoral dissertation, Northwestern University (1985); *The Goyescas for Piano by Enrique Granados: A Critical Edition*, New York University (1982); "Enrique Granados' Sketch Book," "Apuntes Para Mis Obras"–Riva's 1988 discussion of the notebook at the Pierpont Morgan Library in New York

Robinson, Francis, *Caruso: His Life in Pictures*, The Studio Publications, New York (1957)

Roca, Francesc, *Teories de Catalunya*, Editorial Pòrtic, Barcelona (2000)–an extensive analysis of Catalan society

Rodereda, Mercé, *Camellia Street* (trans. by David H. Rosenthal), Graywolf Press, St. Paul, MN (1993)

Rojas, Carlos, *La Barcelona de Picasso*, Plaza & Janes, Barcelona (1981)

Roosevelt, Theodore, *The Rough Riders*, Scribner, New York (1920)

Rosen, Barbara, *Arriaga, The Forgotten Genius*, Basque Studies Program, Reno, NV (1988)

Rosenthal, David H. (ed.), *Modern Catalan Poetry*, New Rivers Press, St. Paul, MN (1979)

Rosenthal, Harold (ed.), *The Royal Opera House, Covent Garden* (1858–1958), London (1958)

Rouché, Jacques, letter to Granados dated June 22, 1914, in which he formally accepts *Goyescas* for early 1915 (reprinted in Antonio Fernandez-Cid's biography of Granados)

Rubinstein, Artur, *My Young Years*, Knopf, New York (1973)

Rudo, Marcy, *Lluisa Vidal, Filla del Modernisme*, Edicions La Campana, Barcelona (1996)

Ruiz Lena, Justo, "Official Exercises of Peral Submarine in the Bay of Cádiz" (1890), Naval Museum of Madrid

Ruiz Tarazona, Andres, *Enrique Granados, El Último Romántico*, Real Musical Editores, Madrid (1975)

Sachs, Harvey, *The Letters of Arturo Toscanini*, Knopf, New York (2002)

Sagardía, Angel, *Albéniz*, Gent Nostra Series, Edicions de Nou Art Thor, Barcelona

Saint-André, Peter, "Enrique Granados," *Monadnock Review* (2000)

St. John, Marshall C., "Pablo Casals Scrapbook" (1996–1997)

San Agustín, Arturo, "La Dansa Despullada" (Tórtola València), *El Periódico*, Barcelona (November 2001)

Santos Torroella, R., *El Pintor Francisco Miralles* (1848–1901)

Saveur, "Finest Train Station Dining By Far" (Gare de Lyon, Paris), The Saveur 100 Issue; "Dinners from Old New York"–article featuring history of Delmonico's restaurant (1867–1923), New York, NY

Schelling, Ernest, letters: to Mildred Bliss, citing the contributors to the "loving cup" presented to Granados before his departure from New York; to Robert and Mildred Bliss, enclosing the letter that Granados left with Schelling, thanking him for everything and asking that he thank all of the friends who'd been so generous while he and Amparo were in New York (from Bliss Collection, Harvard University Library)

Schirmer, Gustave & Sons, music publishers, copyright agreement signed by Rudolph Schirmer and Granados, by which Granados granted publishing rights to Schirmer for his works for a period of two years and Schirmer agreed to pay Granados 6,000 francs annually as advances against royalties; and copyright agreements in 1913–1915 for works that included *Dante*, *Danzas Españolas*, *El Pelele*; and the royalty agreement for the libretto alone with Fernando Periquet four months after Granados' death

Schonberg, Harold C., *The Lives of the Great Composers*, W. W. Norton, New York (1970); *The Great Pianists*, Simon and Schuster, New York (1963)

Scientific American, February 6, 1904, "The New Stage of the Metropolitan Opera House, 1904"

Scott, Michael, *The Great Caruso*, Knopf, New York (1988)–includes details of Caruso's public performances from 1907–1917

de Segarra, Josep Marià, "Memorias," *Història Gràfica de la Catalunya Contemporànea*, Barcelona

Segovia, Andres, *An Autobiography of the Years 1893–1920*, MacMillan, New York (1976)

Shaffer, Peter, *Amadeus*, stage play, Harper & Row, New York (1980)–rivalry between Mozart and Salieri

The Sketch, London, reprinted in *The Theatre*, "Enrico Caruso and the 1906 Earthquake," Museum of the City of San Francisco

Skvorecky, Josef, *Dvorák in Love* (trans. by Paul Wilson), The Hogarth Press, London (1989)–a lighthearted fantasy that takes place during Dvorák's stay in New York

Smith, Peter C., *Heritage of the Sun*, Balfour, London (1974)–about disguised merchant ships (Q ships)

Socias i Palau, Jaume, *Rusiñol*, Gent Nostra Series, Edicions de Nou Art Thor, Barcelona

Solrac, Odelot, *Tórtola València and Her Times*, Vantage Press, New York (1982)

Soules, Mrs. L. Lohmeyer, dissertation for Catholic University (unpublished), "Music at the White House During the Administration of Theodore Roosevelt"

de Soye, Suzanne, *Toi Qui Dansais, La Argentina*, Les Editions La Bruyere, Paris (1993)

SS *Sussex*–press accounts in March and April 1916 in New York, Washington, London, Paris, Madrid, and Barcelona

Stephens, Randy C., RPh, "Migraine Headaches: Facts You Should Know," United States (2001)

StreetSwing.com, listing of performances by Antonia Mercé ("La Argentina"), 1910–1920

Subirá, José, *Enrique Granados: Su Producción Musical se Madrileñismo Su Personalidad Artística*, Zoila Ascasíbar, Madrid (1926)

Szulc, Tad, *Chopin in Paris*, Scribner & Sons, New York (1998)

Taylor, Robin Elizabeth, "Enrique Granados: *Goyescas*," master's thesis, San Jose State University (1976)

Teale, Edwin Way, *Springtime in Britain*, Dodd, Mead, New York (1970)–about the seasonal presence of nightingales in southeastern England

Termes, Josep, *Història de la Cultura Catalana, Vols. IV-VII*, Edicion 62, Barcelona

Thomlinson, Ralph, *Demographic Problems, Controversy Over Population Control*, Second Edition (1975)

Time Out, Barcelona Guide (2001), "Walk 3: the details of *Modernisme*"–describing the many modernist buildings in neighborhood of Granados' residence at Carrer Girona, 20, most of which are still standing

Torres, Marimar, *Catalan Country Kitchen*, Addison Wesley, Sonoma, CA (1992)

Trend, J. B., *Manual de Falla and Spanish Music*, Knopf, New York (1929)

Towne, Ruth Warner, *Senator William J. Stone and the Politics of Compromise*, Kennikat Press, Port Washington, NY (1979)

"The U-boat War 1939–1945"–information on history of submarine warfare in World War I, in particular UB 29, the submarine that attacked the SS *Sussex*; "His Imperial German Majesty's U-boats in WW I," from *Fur Kaiser Und Reich*, Uboat.net/history (2003)

United States of America, 64th Congress, 1st Session, "President Wilson's Remarks Concerning the German Sinking of the Unarmed Channel Steamer *Sussex* on March 24th, 1916"–from archives of Brigham Young University, Salt Lake City, UT del Valle Inclán, Ramón, *Sonata de Primavera y Otras Obras*, Editorial Porrúa, México D.F. (1990)

La Vanguardia, Barcelona–read selectively 1905–1916

La Vanguardia, Barcelona, May 3, 1916–article about memorial service for Granados and Amparo, including list of attendees (among more than three hundred others: Alarma, Marquès de Alella, Andreu Badia, Cabot, Carreras, Conde, Fabra, Godó, Gual, Llobet, Marsans, Marshall, Mas, Mestres, Moragas, Morera, Marquès d'Olèrdola, Oliveró, d'Ors, Pellicer, Pi i Sunyer, Pujol, Rusiñol, Suárez Bravo, Villavecchia)

La Vanguardia, "Cien Años de la Vida del Mundo, La Música Catalana"–centenary issue of the daily paper, Barcelona (1881); in magazine form, devoted to the history of music in Catalunya, including articles on Granados and his colleagues

Van Vechten, Carl, *The Music of Spain*, Knopf, New York (1929)

Vásquez Montalbán, Manuel, *Barcelona* (trans. by Andy Robinson), Verso, London (1992)

Verdaguer i Santaló, Mossen Jacint, *Els Millors Poemes*, Proa Colmna, Barcelona (1998)

Vila San-Juan, Pablo, *Papeles Íntimos de Enrique Granados*, Editado Por Amigos de Granados, Barcelona (1966); "Los Cuatro Pianos de Enrique Granados," *La Vanguardia* (1966)

Villalba, P. Luis, *Enrique Granados: Semblanza y Biografía*, Imprenta Helénica, Madrid

Voltes i Bou, Pere, *Els Godó, Editors i Diputats per Igualada*, Grafiques Anoia, Igualada, Catalunya (1991); see also Cabana, Francesc, *Fabriques I Empresaris de Catalunya*

Washington Post, review of Granados' recital at the White House, "Wilsons Give Musicale: Distinguished Assembly Includes About 300 Guests," March 8, 1916; and *Washington Star*, reporting on President Wilson's meeting with Senator William J. Stone of Missouri, chairman of the Senate Foreign Relations Committee

Watson, Edward B.and Edmund V. Gillon, Jr., *New York, Then and Now* (photography), Dover, Mineola, NY (1976)

Weintraub, Stanley, *Silent Night, the Story of the World War I Christmas Truce*, The Free Press, New York (2001)

Wetmore, Karin E., "The Early Career of James Mark Baldwin, 1881–1893," master's thesis, Indiana State University (1981)

Willard Inter-Continental, "The History of Willard Inter-Continental Washington," Washington D.C. (2003)

Woehl, Arlene B., "Nin-Culmell: España Me Persigue," *Clavier*, January 1987–information on the life and careers of Joaquín Nin-Culmell, youngest child of Joaquín Nin y Castellanos and Rosa Culmell de Nin, and younger brother of Anais Nin

Wolinsky, Theresa and Mother Clara, "Old World Turn of the Century Recipes" and "Old Warsaw Polish Recipes," by Joan Baptista Xuriguera, *Els Verbs Catalans Conjugats*, Editorial Claret, Barcelona (1999)

Ongoing Publications

Newspapers and publications (online): *La Vanguardia*, *El Periódico*, and *Avui*–Barcelona; *El País*–Madrid; *Enciclopèdia Catalana*, Barcelona (for biographies on approximately 250 contemporaries of Granados and descriptions of every village, city, and neighborhood known to been visited by Granados); *Grove Music Online*; *Directori de la Música a Catalunya*; *Butlletí de la North American Catalan Society*, U.S.A.

Libraries, Archives, Museums, and Music Halls Visited by Author

Minnesota: St. Paul Public Library, Minneapolis Public Library, University of Minnesota, Department of Music, Washington County Library; Wisconsin: Hudson and UW River Falls Area Research Center; New York: Hispanic Society of America, New York Public Library, The New-York Historical Society, Pierpont Morgan Library, and Metropolitan Opera Archives; Massachusetts: Harvard University Library–Cambridge; Washington, D.C.: Library of Congress; Maryland: International Piano Archives–College Park; Massachusetts: JFK Library–Boston; England: The British Library London and Folkestone Library; Barcelona: National Library of Catalunya, Arxiu Històric de la Ciutat, Arxiu Municipal Administratiu, Biblioteca de la Universitat Autónoma, Arxiu Fotogràfic; Catalunya: Arxiu de Puigcerdà, Arxiu Municipal, Tiana; Madrid: Museu del Ferrocarril de Vilanova i la Geltrú, Catalunya; Fundación de los Ferrocarriles Españoles (Biblioteca).

New York: Metropolitan Museum of Art and Hispanic Institute of America; Enrico Caruso Museum of America–Brooklyn, NY; England: British Museum, Museum of the History of London, National Maritime Museum; Madrid: El Prado, Reina Sofía and Sorolla museums; Barcelona: Museu de la Música, Museu d'Història de Catalunya, Museu Marítim, Museu Picasso, Museu d'Art Modern, Arxiu Històric de Navegació; Catalunya: Museu Cau Ferrat, Sitges; Vil.la Casals (Museu de Pau Casals), Sant Salvador; Museu de Jacinto Verdaguer, Mossò y Poeta de la Renaixança Catalana, Vallvidrera; Wisconsin: St. Croix County Historical Society.

Barcelona: El Palau de la Música, El Gran Teatre del Liceu, Sala Granados (Tibidabo, 18); Catalunya: Auditori Enric Granados, Lleida; Auditori Pau Casals, Sant Salvador; Teatre Municipal, Puigcerdà; France: Palais Garnier, l'Opéra de Paris; New York: Carnegie Hall and Old Met (39th Street); Washington, D.C.: The White House, East Room

For more information, see www.enriquegranados.com

The Music of Granados

The American pianist Douglas Riva is internationally recognized for his "profound knowledge of Spanish music" (*La Vanguardia*, Barcelona), and the late Catalan composer Xavier Montsalvatge described Riva as "an exceptional pianist." Riva's interpretations of the works of Enrique Granados have earned him a place as one of this composer's leading exponents worldwide. The Madrid daily *El País* describes him "one of the principal apostles of Granados' music." Natalia Granados, the composer's late daughter, used to say, "Mr. Riva knows everything relating to my father, to perfection."

In recognition of Riva's credentials as a Granados interpreter, Naxos Records initiated a series of his recordings of the complete piano works of Granados, the sixth of these released in June 2004. Critics in the U.S.A. and the U.K. have described these recordings as "splendid" and "outstanding" while acclaiming his "superb artistry." Spanish critics writing in *Scherzo* praised Riva's interpretation of Granados' masterpiece *Goyescas* as "belonging to the privileged class of the very best versions." London's *The Guardian* described Volume 3 of the series as "a totally compelling performance [that] demands to be heard."

Riva was the assistant director of the eighteen-volume critical edition of the Complete Works for Piano of Enrique Granados, directed by Alicia de Larrocha and published by Editorial Boileau, Barcelona. An active recitalist, he has performed at the White House and Carnegie Hall, and has recorded numerous programs for television and radio in Spain, Portugal, Holland, the U.S.A. and Brazil.

Douglas Riva started his musical education at the age of nine, studying both piano and flute. At the age of sixteen he was principal flutist of the El Paso (Texas) Symphony Orchestra. Later, devoted exclusively to the piano, he continued his studies at the Juilliard School, New York University, and the Acadèmia Marshall in Barcelona, founded by Granados.

Track List, CD, *Piano Music by Enrique Granados*

Douglas Riva, Piano

1. **Azulejos** (Mosaic Tiles), DLR Vl:3 10:01
   Isaac Albéniz, completed by Granados

Piezas sobre cantos populares españoles, DLR V:2
(Pieces Based on Spanish Folk-Songs)

2. Añoranza (Nostalgia) 2:40
3. Ecos de la parranda (Memories of the Fiesta) 3:54
4. Vascongada (Basque Dance) 3:59

Escenas románticas (Romantic Scenes), DLR V:7 24:27

5. Mazurka 4:24
6. Recitativo 1:46
7. Berceuse (Lullaby) 2:52
8. * 4:38
   * * Lento con éxtasis
9. Allegretto 1:08
10. Allegro appassionato 6:55
11. Epílogo (Epilogue) 2:39
12. **Allegro de concierto** (Concert Allegro), DLR V:8 8:22

Escenas poéticas (Poetic Scenes), DLR V:10

13. Danza de la rosa (Dance of the Rose) 1:39
14. **El pelele** (The Straw Man), DLR 11:5 4:53

Goyescas, DLR 11:4

15. Los requiebros (Flattery) 9:52
16. Quejas o la maja y el ruiseñor 6:19
    (Laments or the Maja and the Nightingale)

Notes for CD, The Fallen Nightingale

Granados' close friend Isaac Albéniz began composing *Azulejos* around the time of his final illness, leaving it incomplete upon his death in 1909. Albéniz' widow, Rosina, asked Granados to complete the work. Although *Azulejos* is frequently attributed to Albéniz, in reality, the work was written by both composers. The title refers to decorative tiles, often arranged in mosaic patterns, which are typical in some regions of Spain. Granados added 89 measures to the 62 composed by Albéniz capturing the warmth and mystery alluded to by the title.

"Añoranza," "Ecos de la parranda" and "Vascongada" from *Piezas sobre cantos populares españoles* were composed *circa* 1895. The collection is nationalistic in inspiration and the individual pieces are notable for their romantic brilliance and technical complexity.

One of Granados' finest works is the lyric and emotionally charged suite *Escenas románticas*, premiered in 1904. *Escenas románticas*, with its combination of elegance and passion, reveals the extent of Granados' influence by composers Robert Schumann and Frederic Chopin. The curious title of the third movement, * * *, derived from Schumann's *Album for the Young*, Op. 68, represents an emotion so intense it cannot be named. Granados added the tempo indication, *Lento con éxtasis*. "Epílogo," which has a tempo indication, *Andante spianato*, copied after Chopin's Op. 22, *Andante spianato et Grande Polonaise Brilliant*, is one of Granados' most emotional works, pouring forth poetic exaltation.

Allegro de concierto is one of Granados' most brilliant and virtuostic compositions. It was composed in 1903 as an entry in a competition organized by the Madrid Conservatory for a piece to be used as an examination work for graduating piano students. There were twenty-four entries. Granados was declared the winner and Manuel de Falla was recognized with an honorable mention.

"Danza de la rosa" from *Escenas poéticas* was probably composed *circa* 1912. It is a delightful miniature which conveys the fragile perfection of a rose blossom.

Granados' masterpiece *Goyescas* is one of the truly great effusions of Romantic pianism and one of the most important Spanish keyboard works. The title *Goyescas*, meaning Goya-esque or Goya-like, is highly unusual in the complex nature of its inspiration. Through the influence of writer Fernando Periquet, Granados became inspired by Spanish painter Francisco Goya (1746-1828). Granados drew inspiration from the painter's depiction of the atmosphere of Madrid and its colorful people. Granados explained his fascination in a 1910 letter: "...I fell in love with the psychology of Goya and his palette... That rosy-whiteness of the cheeks contrasted with lace and jet-black velvet, those jasmine-white hands, the color of mother-of-pearl have dazzled me..."

Goyescas is a suite of six varied pieces which are connected by brilliant pianistic colour, jewel-toned harmonies, violent mood swings, and post-Romantic fervour. *El pelele*, inspired by Goya's painting of the same title, depicts a group of majas tossing a straw man into the air. Although this brilliant composition is not technically part of the suite, Granados himself often performed it along with other pieces from *Goyescas*. "Los requiebros" was inspired by a Goya etching, "Tal para cual." Granados used a melody from Goya's time as the basis for this magnificent set of variations. One of the most poetic pieces of Spanish piano music, "Quejas o la maja y el ruiseñor," dedicated to Granados' wife Amparo, is based on a folk-song from València. Granados transforms the haunting melody through a series of variations, each more highly perfumed than the previous, culminating in a cadenza imitating the song of a nightingale.

This performance follows the critical edition of the *Complete Works for Piano* of Enrique Granados, published by Editorial Boileau, S.A., Barcelona, Spain, Alicia de Larrocha, Director and Douglas Riva, Assistant Director.

Douglas Riva
Madrid, 2004